# Growing Tears

Forever Yours Sequel

Melissa M. Marlow

Poehler Publishing
Coon Rapids, MN 55433

©Melissa M Marlow. All rights reserved

No part of this book may be reproduced, stored in a retrieval system, or transmitted by any means without the written permission of the author.

First published by Poehler Publishing 11/30/2011

Soft Cover
ISBN-10: 0983524521
ISBN-13: 978-0-9835245-2-6
E-book
ISBN-10: 098352453X
ISBN-13: 978-0-9835245-3-3

Printed in the United States of America

This is a work of fiction. Names, characters, businesses, places, events and incidents are either the products of the author's imagination or used in a fictitious manner. Any resemblance to actual persons, living or dead, or actual events is purely coincidental.

Cover Art and Photos within book are provided by A Photo Creation by Melissa

## Table of Contents

*Perfect Wanting* ............................................................. 1
1. Surprise ................................................................. 2
2. Very Real ............................................................... 12
3. It's Time ............................................................... 18
4. You Know That ........................................................... 26
5. Shocking News ........................................................... 35
6. Communications .......................................................... 43
7. James Can Save Me ....................................................... 52
8. Competing ............................................................... 58
9. Frankenstein ............................................................ 67
10. Visitors ............................................................... 76
11. Who Is What ............................................................ 81
12. The Choice ............................................................. 91
13. Dad's Understanding .................................................... 101
14. Unwanted Surprise ...................................................... 107
15. A Shower ............................................................... 118
16. Didn't Think Of That ................................................... 129
17. The Medications ........................................................ 139
18. Self Control ........................................................... 145
19. Oh Poop ................................................................ 154
20. Never A Woman .......................................................... 160
21. Together ............................................................... 168
22. On Their Own ........................................................... 175
23. Not Healthy ............................................................ 182
24. Unbearable ............................................................. 192

| | |
|---|---|
| 25. Not As Planned | 201 |
| 26. The Promise | 209 |
| 27. Jake's Help | 214 |
| 28. What... How... Couldn't Be | 220 |
| 29. Little One | 226 |
| 30. To Suffer | 233 |
| 31. One Finger | 242 |
| 32. Missing You | 252 |
| 33. Going Home | 259 |
| 34. Waiting | 267 |
| 35. The Release | 273 |
| 36. Skinny Dipping | 283 |
| 37. Teasing | 294 |
| 38. Private Talk | 304 |
| 39. Bad Timing | 310 |
| 40. A Little Fun | 319 |
| 41. Who's Feeling | 333 |
| 42. Paybacks | 341 |
| 43. Calling | 351 |
| 44. A Little Practice | 363 |
| 45. Visitors | 371 |
| 46. Exciting | 384 |
| 47. Readings | 395 |
| 48. Sparks | 405 |
| 49. A New Day | 414 |
| 50. The Love Story | 422 |

| | |
|---|---|
| 51. Old Tale | 431 |
| 52. New Feelings | 440 |
| 53. The Passion | 451 |
| 54. Saying Goodbye | 462 |
| 55. End Of Sadness | 469 |
| Characters | 474 |
| Upcoming Sequel – A New Beginning | 475 |
| 1. A little doctoring | 475 |

# Perfect Wanting

    **H**ave you ever wanted something so bad that you would do almost anything to get it, but once you got it... you didn't know what to do with it? Think about this: You find the perfect pair of Jeans. You try them on and they are everything you want them to be. They compliment your body and make you better than you are. They fit every curve of your body. You want to wear them every day because they make you feel so good, but if you wear them every day they will get worn and faded and one day they will give out and be gone.

    That was my biggest fear with my James. That our love would get warn out. I didn't want him to ever be gone. Now that he was in front of me, kissing me, filling my needs, I was afraid that I would not be able to fill his.

    The last couple of nights we got very hot on the phone. What we had seemed real, but was it? It was like a dream, but seemed very real and I did things that would embarrass me if I was really with him that way. Would I be able to satisfy him the ways he needed in real life? I couldn't take my eyes off him. He was real, he was here, and he was mine. All mine, hopefully for the rest of my life.

# 1. Surprise

**W**here do we go from here? I wanted him for the rest of my life and I knew, at least I thought I knew that he wanted me for the rest of his life. I gazed into his eyes that were still so sad. I love him, and I hope that he sees that in mine. I put one of my hands on his face. He was thinner, but felt real. I was still wrapped around him, but couldn't stop looking at him.

Today wasn't Monday, it was Saturday, and he came home to me because I needed him. The kissing resumed; the deepest kiss we could have without being in each other's skin.

"Hey, guys!"

Shit, Brian, why are you interrupting this? I have wanted this so bad; why can't you just leave us alone? James broke the kiss to look up at Brian.

"You might not want to keep her in the water very long."

James looked at me smiling, "Why?"

"Um, she gets really weak, and you wouldn't want her to fall asleep in the water."

His gaze turned to sadness as I watched his face change.

I couldn't take my eyes off of him, even though the sadness was not what I wanted to see, "Brian, James is here now. I will be okay."

My James smiled at me again. I was in heaven.

"No, James. I'm not kidding; we need to get her out of the water."

He took his eyes off of me; no, I didn't want that. Come back to me here.

"Brain, here I will lift her to you."

He was pushing me out of the water. I didn't want to let go of him.

"Sarah, I will be right there. It's okay, let go. I will be right with you. Just get in the boat."

I let go of him, but I did not want to. Brian took my hands and pulled me to the boat sitting on the side of it. He was pulling me in. Mykala wrapped a towel around me, and Danelle put her arm around my shoulder. I didn't take my eyes off of James. He handed a ski to Brian, and then the other one. I went back to pull the rope in. He came up the side of the boat with one swift movement, pulling himself in. He moved to the front with Brian and they were whispering. I didn't want anyone else to have my James; he was mine. Well, at least he was looking at me. I didn't want the girls fussing with me.

## *James:*

I couldn't take my eyes off of her, but I wanted to know why they were being so protective of her. I knew she had gotten weaker. She did look so very thin, but she looked good to me, too. I wanted to touch her and kiss her till there was no tomorrow. I was standing in the front with Brain.

"So, why was she water skiing?" I wasn't looking at him at all.

Brian hesitated before he answered, "She is very persuasive."

I smiled. She did have that way about her.

"You tried to kiss her. So, I guess I am supposed to punch you now?" I was completely smiling at my sweet Sarah. I had no intentions of hitting him. I just wanted to scare him a little.

"I wasn't the only one and I don't know how you do it?"

He caught my attention so I turned toward him, "What do you mean?"

He looked very uneasy, but was trying to find his words, "If I was alone with her I wouldn't..."

I couldn't help remembering touching her face softly and then... "I take a lot of cold showers and she lets me do this."

I was smiling at my sweet Sarah and went to her to hold her. She was so beautiful that I didn't know if I could keep my hands off of her. Danelle and this other girl were wiping her off. Was she really this weak? She didn't feel weak; she had strength to hold on to me. I liked when she was aggressive and I am totally turned on. I shooed them away, so I could put my arms around her.

"Do you want help with the wet suit?" I started to unzip it.

She looked at me like she wanted me to take over taking care of her. Her hands traced my arms. I slowly unzipped the suit to help her out of it. She slipped it off her arms. I was shocked to see her frail body, so thin, and with skin almost translucent. I couldn't believe my eyes. Truly, there was almost nothing left of her little body. I felt terrible that she had gotten this bad in the little time that I had not seen her. At my gasp, she attempted to pull the wetsuit back on, but I wouldn't let her. She could tell by the dismayed look on my face, how shocked I was.

"Sarah, it's okay I am here now"

I helped her take it off the rest of the way. I wrapped the towel around her. Danelle was up by Brian and the other girl. Danelle was a cute girl, but at the moment she had a major frown on her face. She was pissed with me; that's for sure, but that is what I liked about her. She didn't put up with any bull shit. I turned my sweet Sarah away from me and put my arms around her and sat down on the back seat to hold her. I looked at Danelle; she was so angry. I couldn't help but feel I had to say something. She came back by us and helped cover Sarah more. I put my hand on the top of her head. "It's okay now; I will take care of her."

    I looked at my sweet Sarah, and she was just staring at me. I wanted to kiss her more. I touched her face, and she closed her eyes pushing her face to my hand. I wanted to take her away from everything and just make her better.

    Brian drove the boat in to the dock. I looked around, but I could tell the only thing she was thinking about was the shock of me being home. I was so happy to fill the need. I wanted this badly for so many days. I held her closer to me and kissed her cheek. Then I brought her hand with my ring on it to my mouth. She had made me so happy that she wanted to be with me. I kissed every finger looking at her as I did this. She smiled that precious sweet smile that I couldn't resist. I turned her hand over to kiss her palm. She traced her thumb over my face as I did this. She was happy. I loved to see the passion in her eyes. The engine was cut and the boat glided toward the dock.

    I had to push her away to help.

    "No, James."

    I saw the devastation in her eyes making me feel sad and guilty for not coming home sooner.

    "It's okay, Sarah, I'm not leaving you; I'm just helping. You are leaving with me. I will not go without you."

    She seemed to ease a little, but the tears in her eyes were welling up. I had a hard time letting her go. I kissed her forehead and sat her back down. I grabbed for the dock, jumped out, and secured it to the dock. Danelle and Mykala were helping her stand up and step on the seat and then on the side.

    I grabbed her from them, "Do you want to get dressed?"

    She wasn't saying a whole lot. It was making me nervous. Danelle got out and took Sarah to the beach to get her things out.

    I turned on Brian, "She is that bad?"

    He was surprised that I didn't know. He seemed to be searching for the answer, "Let's see. She has been with us about an hour and a half, but she went skiing so you might have about a half hour and she will need to sleep."

    My heart was breaking, "Two hours?"

    "Yeah, that's about all she can do, and then the sleeping, the deep sleeping. No response, nothing, so I would get her to where she is going pretty quickly."

    I felt horrible. I couldn't believe that my dreams were so off and that I had no idea of her condition as it was today. We stay awake longer than that on the phone. They just didn't know my Sarah. She couldn't be that bad.  Danelle was helping her dress as I looked at her.  She wasn't taking her eyes off of me, maybe to make sure I wasn't leaving without her.

Brian spoke to me again, "James, get going.  She will need to rest.  She has the dance tonight and she will need to sleep at least 3 hours or she won't be able to get through the night."

"Then she won't do it."  I was angry.  If she needed to rest then I wasn't going to let her dance.

"James, that is how she got by without you here.  She has a commitment and she will want to do it.  She is very persuasive."

I grinned because he was right; she was *very* persuasive.  I stared at her as I approached her.  I took her bag keeping my eyes locked to hers, "Are you ready?"

She remained in a trance staring into my eyes but she was smiling.  Oh how I loved that smile.  I started walking up the hill with my arm around her.  She seemed so okay.  She was smiling and walking with me.  She even had an upbeat in her step, but she was so thin.  Every rib showed and her hipbones did stick out a little.

I turned to Brian and Danelle, "Thank you.  She will see you tonight."
I turned back to look at my Sarah, and said to her, "She's mine now."
That look of satisfaction on her face melted every inch of me.

I couldn't stop looking at my James.  He was so much my protector and he was here to take care of me now.  I would follow him to the end of the world if that is what he asked me to do right now.  We walked out to his bike.  I panicked as I stared at him.  I was scared to ride.  I was getting tired.

"Can you ride to Tony's with me?"

I knew I couldn't drive, because I was getting tired.  I looked at him and then at my car.

"Sarah, if you can't ride we can take your car."

I loved to ride.  I told myself I can do this.

I tried to smile, "Yeah, I'm fine."

I wasn't really fine.  I needed to sleep, but James was here and I wanted to be with him.

"Do we need to go to the trailer?"

I smiled with guilt on my face, "Nope"

"Don't you need to get your stuff and check in?"  He was worried, but I couldn't have planned this any better.

"I do have to check in, but I brought my stuff to your place yesterday.  I was going to get some real sleep in your room and take a shower for tonight."

The corners of his mouth turned upward with a mischievous look giving him this amazing appeal, "Did you know?"

"Know what?"

"That I was coming home?  I wanted it to be a surprise."

"It was, I didn't know." I wanted him to feel that this was his doing.

He got on the bike, but I was hesitant. I told myself that I could make it to Tony's because I have my James. I could do this. I got on the back and put my arms around his waist, "OH, how I missed this." He pulled my arms tighter turning a little and kissed my lips softly. He let my lips go, but stayed there a minute to search my eyes, "Are you sure you're okay to ride?"

I felt my eyes sparkle as I enjoyed every inch of his face but I had to be realistic, "Just to Tony's okay?"

"Okay." The hesitation came through with his answer, but he focused on the task and started to drive. I was kissing his back and holding him so tight. We turned off the lake drive onto the highway. I moved my hands under his shirt tracing his stomach and his chest, and of course I couldn't stop kissing his back. I knew the sleep was coming on quickly because when I closed my eyes it was getting harder to pry them back open. I moved my hands to his thighs and squeezed them and moved them closer to him. The bike was slowing as he pulled over and stopped.

"Come here little girl. You have got me so hot." He was pulling me in front of him to face him. My legs laid over his, and the kiss came so deep so passionate. He held my face in his hands, but he was standing now, "Are you sure you're okay?"

I wanted to tell him the truth but the desire was building in me. I wanted to feel every inch of him next to me so I just nodded.

He tilted me back to lie across the tank and traced his hands up the front of me. I enjoyed this a little too much because his touch was what I desired. My heart was beating so hard and my chest was heaving to breathe. His mouth came to my chest and he kissed it so lovingly. He was getting worked up and the heat was building. He pulled me to him and wrapped one hand around my waist to my back and pulled me to him to feel him. I gasped when I felt his desire. The kiss was so deep, and I was getting so lost. I needed to sleep right now. I released the kiss and put my face to his chest.

"Sarah, you are not okay?"

I shook my head no. I couldn't even open my eyes to look at him. I wanted to feel him so bad, but the sleep was coming and I couldn't keep going.

He lifted my face, "Sarah?"

I forced my eyes open so I could feel the satisfaction that he was here in front of me, but I was done.

"Shit, they weren't kidding."

My eyes fell heavily as I wrapped my arms around his chest and put my head down on him. I felt him just holding me.

His chest seemed to be hurting, "Okay, baby, it's okay. I will get you to Tony's."

I held on, but felt him holding me in front of him. I couldn't move behind him because I wouldn't be able to hold on.

I felt the bike slow again as we pulled into Tony's. I was able to wake enough to get this much out of it. He stopped and pulled my face up so he could see me, "Sarah?"

I was finally able to open my eyes so I smiled at him, "It's okay, James, I took a nap."

He was breathing so hard, "You scared the crap out of me; what the hell was that?"

"James, I just get tired."

His face was so sad because it hurt him letting him see me like this, but I was going to be better now that he was home. I tried to give some reassurance that I was doing better. He rested his forehead on mine. I heard someone walking out of Tony's, but I didn't have the strength to look.

James moved to look, "So, you must be Jake?"

I let my face fall to James's chest but turned to see Jake, "Jake, this is my James; James, this is my Jake. I mean my doc, Jake."

James pulled my chin up, "Sarah, are you okay to get up?"

I had no strength but I managed to smile at him. He pulled me off the bike, but was still holding me and supporting me with his arms completely wrapped around me. He was moving to Jake, "Nice to finally meet the man who was taking care of all of my Sarah's needs."

He was extending his hand, but I didn't like what he said. I let go of James, "James, be nice. He was and is still taking care of me and you best be nice Mr. or...."

He turned to me and kissed my forehead, "I'm sorry, and you'll what? I don't think you can do anything, not in your condition."

He was still extending his hand to Jake. Jake shook it as James leaned into him, "Sorry man, just a little jealous. I really do appreciate all you have done for..." He turned to kiss my forehead again, "my sweet, Sarah." He took my face in his hands, lifting me to look at him, "Are you okay? I'll go upstairs and take a shower...." He whispered in my ear, "cold shower" and then he was louder again, "So you can have a minute to talk to Jake."

"Yeah, I'm okay."

James kissed my lips soft and light then he grabbed a bag from his bike and ran up the stairs.

I didn't know what to say to Jake, and I needed to sit down. I headed for the steps. Jake was watching me and I could tell by the look on his face that he knew what was coming, "I suppose our dancing is off?"

"No, Jake, the dance is not off. I still want to dance with you." I was moving to sit down on the step, "I just need to sleep first."

"But, he is here."

"Jake, he is very understanding. He knows you held me, and he knows you gave me what I needed. Like he said... he was jealous, but he understands you have been there for me and he respects that."

Jake seemed determined as he walked over to where I was sitting and he bent down kissing me right on the lips, "Sarah, just wait. Don't go up there. Don't be with him, just wait. Please."

"Jake, I am not going up there to be with him. We're supposed to wait till I am 18. I just need to lie down." I was leaning my head on the post at the bottom of the steps.

Jake felt my forehead, "Sarah, you are burning up."

I tried to look up at him, but I was almost completely gone.

"Sarah, you are not okay."
I shook my head no.
He picked me up and started walking up the stairs to James. James came out the door in a towel, "What happened?"
"What were you two doing? She shouldn't be doing anything."
"When I found her she was water skiing."

## *Jake:*

"She promised me she wouldn't do any activities. James, get out of the way. Shit... what the hell. She knew it was absolutely a no... no... for her."

I laid her on the bed; feeling the warmth coming from her body told me she was burning up. I looked at him, "James, I can't give her ibuprofen when she's sleeping; she needs to cool down now. Couldn't you tell she was burning up?"

"Yeah... no... I don't know. I was just happy to..."

I couldn't even look at him. I went to the bathroom and turned on the water. I made it semi warm, but maybe a little cooler. James was carrying her into the bathroom. He walked into the shower with her. He was crying so I couldn't watch.

"James, only keep her in there until she is awake."

He sat down holding her. I had to leave. I stood out of the bathroom just listening for them to need me. He was pleading with her to wake up; the tears in my eyes were coming. I wanted to be there to hold her to make her feel better and I couldn't; it was him that she wanted.

He sounded a little excited, "Sarah, that's it baby come back to me. Sarah, Sarah, open your eyes and look at me now. That's it baby, if you don't I will have to leave. Sarah, Jake needs you to take something. Keep those eyes open or I am leaving. Jake, come get her."

I moved around the corner as soon as he said my name. I picked her up from his arms and carried her back to the bed.

"Jake, it's okay. James is home to take care of me now. You don't have to worry anymore."

"Sarah, stay awake. James said he'll leave again. Don't you dare. Sarah! Fight this; you need to take these."

I was putting them in her mouth and giving her a sip of water, "Sarah you have to swallow or these won't help."

His strong voice came from behind me, "Sarah, I will have to leave."

She opened her eyes again and swallowed them. I laid her back down. She curled into me and I backed away. I couldn't look at him, "James, she will be better in a little bit, but you need to be here to hold her. It helps her fight whatever this crap is. Just..." I grabbed the glass of water and sat it on the sink.

"You love her."

I couldn't believe he was saying or asking me that.

"I know you do. I felt it. I feel what she feels."

"Yeah, and you do some shit that is out there. You could help her." I turned to him. He did look as bad as I felt. "She says you give her your soul. That helps the most."

"She told you?"

"James, I was holding her... in this state once when you did it."

He just stared at me. I don't think he knew what to say.

"James, if you can. Please do that; it helps her the most."

I couldn't stay to watch; I had to leave. I went out and went down to Tony's. I would check in a half hour to see if she was better.

## *James:*

I wanted to know what it looked like when I did that. He saw what I did to my sweet Sarah, but I have never seen it. I hovered over her looking at her. I usually closed my eyes to concentrate on passing through her, but this time I just wanted to watch her. I was thinking very hard on doing this. I was trying very hard to make this happen. I have never been this close to her when I did this. I stared at her harder, and she gasped as her body arched for only a couple seconds, and then she relaxed. Oh shit, that wasn't what I was expecting. Jake saw that? I moved away from her. She moved to curl into me. I was so happy that she was responding now. I touched her face, and she pushed to my hand.

I kissed her hand, "Sarah, I love you."

"James... I love this, but I need you for real."

"Sarah, open your eyes."

Her eyes slowly opened and blinked a couple of times as if she was really seeing me, "James, you seem so real. I love you, but I am so tired right now." Her eyes closed again.

I couldn't handle this. It is tearing me apart. I moved closer to her and lifted her so I could hold her. I kissed her forehead, traced my hands down her arms, and touched the lower part of her back. I had no idea she had gotten this bad. She should have gone in a long time ago. No wonder my... Clarissa sent someone to watch over her. She was amazing to look at so peaceful. I scooted down to be closer to her. I kissed her lips, and she was kissing me back. I released her lips to let her sleep, and I closed my eyes to join her.

I heard a knock on the door. I tried not to move her so she would still sleep. I went to the door opening it to find that it was Jake again. I opened the door for him to pass me and go to her.

He felt her forehead and glanced at me, "Did you do what I asked you to do?"

Shit it didn't help, "Yes, I did, why what's wrong?"

"Come here and feel her. She is getting better again."

I walked over and felt her forehead but my attention was on him. He took her wrist and was watching his watch. I couldn't take my eyes from him, because I knew he was here to help her, but I hated him with a passion. He wanted my Sarah and she cared for him. This was not going to be easy.

"You know she loves you?"

I was happy he knew this, "I kind of hope so."

"When I held her she didn't look at me. She wanted it to be you."

The tears were coming to me. I love her so much. I needed to hear that. I wanted to break down and fall apart.

"We used you to get her to respond to us. We threatened her with you, but it kept her fighting harder. I am afraid she won't fight as hard with you here. She thinks everything is going to be okay, because you being here is going to fix everything."

I closed my eyes; was he telling me she would be better if I left?

"James, all I am saying is you have to keep a close eye on her until Monday. We will find out what it is and get rid of it.

I turned my eyes to her but asked, "It is her appendix then?"

"Well, I am pretty sure it is, but she said you felt the spreading, and that's the part I don't understand. I won't know for sure until I open her up and look what is going on inside."

I moved around the bed and lay down so my face was near her stomach. I glanced up at him, "Do you want to know exactly where it is?"

He was torn. Like he didn't know if he could watch what I was going to do.

He sat down on the other side of Sarah, on the bed, "You can really tell me that?"

"I feel what she feels, but it's more than what she feels. I am tuned into it, so I can pin point it."

I laid my face on her stomach.

Jake pulled her back so she wasn't curled up.

I moved over her a little more and touched her stomach to feel it. I lifted my face, "It's coming from there."

I kept my hand on the spot.

He put his hands were mine were, and I moved away from touching her.

He put both hands on her stomach; his fingertips moved to the spot and felt around, "It has to be her appendix; feel this."

I put my hands where his were, but he pushed my fingers down and I could feel a hard lump.

"See, it's really enlarged." He let go of pushing my fingers into her stomach.

I wanted to know more, "What is all this then?"

I could see his dislike for me but his curiosity made him ask, "What?"

I traced my hand, "It's spreading, and it's worse than it has ever been. I feel it here…" I moved to show him everywhere I felt it, "…all of this area."

"That is the part I don't get."

I could tell he wasn't happy that he didn't understand. I took her hand and put it to my face and kissed it.

"I will let her sleep longer. She is pretty determined to dance tonight. She will wake up in about an hour looking and acting fine. Don't be alarmed by it. Just keep a close eye on her, okay."

"Where are you going?"

"I will be there tonight. I kind of took your place bartending. It's yours when you want it back, but keep a close eye on her."

"Of course, but she shouldn't dance tonight?"

"Well, I guess that's up to you and her, but she will win."

"Why are you so sure?"

"Um... Just a hunch; do you want me to check her before she goes down?"

"Yes, of course."

"I will be back by 4:00 pm. Try to keep her resting until then."

"You got it, and Jake... I may be jealous of your time with her, but I really am thankful. I do love her and would do anything for her."

"I get it."

He turned to walk out. I gazed at my Sarah and curled up to hold her. I rested my face to hers and closed my eyes.

## 2. Very Real

### Sarah:

**I** didn't know if I was dreaming before or if he was really here. I stared at him as I touched his face. I traced my hands down his chest. I pulled myself up a little to look at him more. I whispered in his ear, "James?"

A smile grew on his face.

"James, you're really here?"

He opened his eyes and the glimmer in them was as good as the smile he had on his face, "Come here, I need to feel you."

I was so happy this was real, so I curled into him. I kissed him so softly and he did not refuse me. We laid there kissing endlessly.

"Sarah, you should really be resting."

"You are kidding me!" I wanted to make love to my sweet James, or at least try.

I pulled his shirt up and started kissing every part of his stomach and chest. His hands were entangling in my hair.

He was arching his back, "Damn it, Sarah." He pushed me away. "Do you have any idea of how bad you have been the last two hours?"

"But... I am better now, James." My heart was breaking.

He pushed me away. He must have read the despair in my eyes, because he put his arms around me again and ran his lips, caressingly, over every inch of my face. I wanted to feel him so badly. I couldn't stop touching his body. He pulled me to him, "Sarah, you need to rest; I need to feel you, and I don't know what else to do."

I crawled on top of him as I released his lips, "James, I want you too."

"Jake said you need to rest if you want to dance tonight."

"Shit, I forgot about that." I was bummed.

Jake was right; if I wanted to do the dances tonight I really needed to sleep more. "James, what time is it?"

He was tracing my thighs. I was getting more excited to be with him. He was confused as he answered, "2 pm."

I was more determined, "I do need to rest, but, James, you are really here, not in my dreams, right?"

He sat up wrapping his arms around me. He traced his hands along my side to pull up my shirt. He untied the bathing suit top and pulled it so it loosened enough to pull it over my head. He scooted to the end of the bed and pushed me off, "Wait just a minute." He walked over to the door and locked it.

I grinned agreeing with him, "Good idea."

"Yeah, people feel the need to check on you." He was walking back to me. He only had on boxers.

"James, why are you only partially dressed?"

"I had to take a cold shower with you. Jake said it was the fastest way to get your temp down."

I looked at him guiltily, "So, I get really bad when I am extremely tired."

"Yes, you scared the shit out of me. I thought I was going to lose you forever."

The desire to feel him was burning in me as he walked back to me. He stopped in front of me and pulled my head to rest on his stomach, "Sarah, we can't do that; you know that, right?"

"Why?"

"It would kill me if something happened to you, when we were doing something as beautiful as that."

I kissed his stomach, and he laughed, "Sarah, you are going to make this very hard, aren't you?"

"Yep."

He directed me to crawl up to the pillows. He crawled over me kissing my stomach and then my breast, moving upward to find my lips. He pulled me to my side and kissed me passionately. He traced his hands over my back down to my butt pulling me to feel him, "Sarah..."

"Yes, James."

"Shower."

"No, James, just..." I put my leg over him and wrapped it around him, "Let me feel your happiness, James."

"But the movement could be too much."

I moved to him to feel his heat, "Just be really slow and careful. I will let you know if anything hurts."

"Sarah, no!"

I moved to him more to taunt him by kissing his neck.

He rolled away from me, "Sorry, Sarah. I will be right back." He got up and went to take another cold shower.

I put my tank top back on and felt dirty. I hated that he left me here. I curled up in the blankets and hugged a pillow.

He came out in a towel and looked at me. He came to sit on the bed next to me rubbing my back.

I turned to him, "You okay now?"

He traced his hand along my face, "You need to sleep."

"I need to feel you."

He took my hands and pulled me off the bed. He unbuttoned my shorts and lowered them, watching my face. I just gazed into his eyes. He lowered my suit bottoms and his eyes moved away from mine. As he came up his eyes connected with mine again, but he was tracing his hands along my waist bringing up my shirt and slowly brought it over my head. We only lost eye contact when it went over my head. His eyes locked with mine and he pulled the towel from himself. He just looked at me as he wrapped his arms around me, "You need to rest, so no getting your heart rate up."

I smiled and closed my eyes, "Too late."

He laid me down, "No funny business just touching."

As he crawled on the bed to lay with me, he traced his hand over my stomach, "Sarah, have you been eating at all?"

"James, you know the answer to that."

He laid on his side pulling me to him. We entangled our legs together. We could feel the heat of each other.

His face cringed like he was in pain. "This isn't going to be easy for me."

"I know, James." I put my hands on his chest to feel the beat of his heart. I kissed under his chin.

"You are treading on dangerous ground, little girl."

I laid my head on his shoulder. He traced his hands down my back. It felt so nice and comforting that I went to sleep easily.

"Sarah, what time did you want to get up?" No answer.

He was still here. I was pleased, but when I opened my eyes he was completely dressed, laying on the bed next to me, with his eyes wide open just staring at me. "James, you were supposed to hold me."

The strong line of his jaw didn't look so stern when he smiled, and then he traced his fingers along my cheek.

"I did, until I was going to take advantage of you; then I went and took another shower. I knew you needed to rest." He kissed my nose, "What time did you want to get up?"

"3:30pm, so I can take a shower."

"Well, you might want to hurry; it's almost 4:00 pm."

"Shit, James, I wanted to practice before people started showing up."

I still didn't have any clothes on. I looked at him pleading for him to not look at me so I could get up.

"Sarah, you are still embarrassed to be naked in front of me?"

I grinned and wrapped the blanket around me, "Mysterious, that's all." I went to the bathroom to take a shower.

"Sarah, I am going to run down stairs to get you something to eat; you should have food before you go down."

"Fine."

I heard the door. I hopped in the shower and took a really quick shower. I got out and wrapped a towel around me and walked out to get my bag. Jake was standing in the doorway.

"You make him leave when you take a shower?"

"Jake, out. He just went to get food."

"He actually wanted me to take your temp and pulse before he would allow you to come down."

That did make me feel loved, "Fine, but outside 'til I am dressed."

He stepped back out and closed the door. I grabbed my bag and brought it to the bathroom to change in there. I definitely wanted to wear the skinny jeans, the loose tank top, and of course the boots. I took the towel off my head and was fluffing my hair as I walked to the door to let Jake in. I pulled the door open, "You can come in now."

I walked away from the door after opening it, heading back to the bathroom and sprayed my hair with spritz and toweled it a little more. I walked back out, "Jake, you can come in here."

He was still standing in the doorway, but when I invited him in, he advanced. He glanced out the door and closed it, "Sarah, it's okay if you need to rest. We don't have to do the dance."

"Jake, what are you talking about? You know I feel up to it. I am up and moving and I slept so well."

"Really? You slept with him here?"

"Jake, it's not about that. We haven't been together completely yet."

"You haven't?"

"No, Jake. It's more than that. He is good to me and he loves me. He would hardly touch me, because he knows I am sick."

"You really expect me to believe that?"

"Yes, I do. Weren't you supposed to be taking my temp and checking my pulse?"

"Yeah..."

He came over to me and held up the thermometer, so I opened my mouth. He took my wrist and looked at his watch to count. The thermometer beeped so I looked at him. He took it and looked at it raising his eyebrows.

"What, it wasn't bad was it?"

He was still counting.

I decided he needed to smile, so I rambled out some numbers, "17, 34, 1, 48, 93..."

He gave me a really dirty glare.

"Come on, Jake, I feel good and I will get to dance with you."

"Does he know that?"

"Nope, didn't think it would bother him."

"It will. Sarah, it would bother me."

"I promised you."

"You also promised to not go water skiing today."

I was pleased with myself and felt guilty at the same time, "Jake, I knew I was done for the rest of summer. I wanted to have my last little bit of fun. Sorry about that."

James walked in. He evaluated the scene, "So, doc, how is our little girl?"

I stuck my tongue out at him and walked back in the bathroom. I blew dried my hair a little to get it more fluffy. I put makeup on and brushed my teeth.

"Sarah, you need to come eat."

I walked out. They were sitting at the table together talking quietly. Jake better not say I shouldn't go down.

"What is it?"

"Does it matter? You need to eat."

He got up and moved to me. He had a forkful of mashed potatoes and sour cream and gravy. He had his hand cupped under it. He fed it to me and kissed me.

He walked back to the table looking at Jake, "Sometimes, the only way to get her to eat is to force the issue."

He was walking back to me with another forkful. He fed it to me.

"James, fine... I will eat."

He smiled and walked back to the table. I went and sat down.

"James, I have to go practice. Can I eat more later?"

"You can't go down, right Jake?"

Jake looked at me shaking his head no. I glared at the two of them. I went back in the bathroom and brushed my teeth. I walked out and sat on the bed.

"So, which one of you two decided not to let me go down?"

They both looked at each other and neither one of them could look at me.

"Jake, you know I am done for the rest of the summer; you know I have been working on this all week. And James, you know better than to tell me that I can't do something. That's more of a challenge than anything. I am fine and I am going. If you both feel this strongly about me not going down there, maybe you both should realize I really need to do this and want to do this and you both should be there in case something happens."

Neither of them moved. I looked at the clock. It was 4:40 pm., and I needed to practice. I took a deep breath, pushed myself up and headed to the door.

Jake stood up, "No."

I looked at James; he was trying to explain, "It's for you, it's what's best."

"Jake, you're fired. No more being my doctor." I tried to walk past him.

"No, and you can't fire me. Clarissa is the only one that can do that."

I was getting steamed and desperate. When I was very close to Jake I pleaded, "The dance, Jake."

He didn't take his angry eyes off of me, "James, help here."

I looked at Jake saddened by his choice to not have this last time to dance together.

James was moving to me pulling me to look at him, "Sarah, you have to settle down a little 'til you are better; please just don't go down there."

"James, it's for Tony."

"And yourself, you love to dance."

"Yes, I do and I won't be able to for a long time. Please James, Pleeeaaassseee."

"Go back in the bathroom, while we discuss it."

"I could go down and practice while you discuss it."

He was more stern, "Sarah, bathroom."

I stormed to the bathroom and slammed the door. I was over reacting and I knew it, but I didn't like that they were deciding for me. Maybe they were right and I decided to give in.

I walked out beaten, "Do one of you want to go tell Tony the bad news. You guys are right; I won't go," I sat down on the bed knowing they had won.

Jake stood up, "Sarah, you can go, but if we see any sign of weakness we're pulling the plug."

"What?"

"You can go, but if you get tired you're done."

"Really?"

I walked over to Jake and hugged him and whispered, "Your song first."

I went to James pulling him out the door.

"Sarah, slow down. You'll get warn out."

I stopped at the bottom of the steps, and kissed him hard and quickly.

"Sarah, are you sure you want to wear those pants? I am getting hot and bothered."

"Is that how I won?"

"Maybe."

"So, you won't have to be alone with me."

"What? No."

I kissed him, "Good, later than."

I let go of him and ran through the kitchen.

Tony yelled at me, "Slow down girl, you'll make me worry again."

"Tony, I've got this."

# 3. It's Time

    **I** went to the stage where Kate and Sandi were waiting already. I started the music from last week and went out to dance with them. They remembered the dances well. We went to the next one that we did last weekend and I was pleased that they were keeping up. We were laughing and having a good time. I looked at James behind the bar. He was watching me and I gave him the biggest smile. Jason was already there and was behind the bar also. They were talking and laughing. I was really enjoying dancing. Everyone was here by 5:00 pm and it was a packed house. We did all the dances from last week, and I could see Jake dancing behind the bar. I couldn't help myself, and I had to laugh at him. Kate and Sandy were always a great help. We were dancing and it was getting hot. Danelle was there, but she wasn't dancing and Tommy wasn't there. I tried to coax her out to the dance floor, but she would only come out for a couple of minutes then go and hide. Mykala came over and asked if I was doing better. I smiled and let her know I was doing okay. It was almost time for Jake to come out here.

    I went to the stage and let it die completely down. James looked at me curious to what I was doing. I couldn't help but smile at the love of my life. He will just have to understand.

"Okay, ladies, are you ready?"

They all cheered.

"I can't hear you!"

They screamed louder.

"Do you want the *hottie* from behind the bar to come out here or not?"

Jason grabbed James's arm to stop him from coming to me. I smiled guiltily at him.

"Jake, do you want to satisfy all these hot girls out here?"

He jumped over the bar and came out to the dance floor pointing at me.

I shook my head no, and started the music.

"Here you go, girls."

He started with the routine, but looked back to find me. I moved out to the floor, but behind him and started with the routine. He moved to dance it backwards looking at me. I motioned to get the girls that weren't out dancing, but he moved to me and we had our dance. It was hot and sexy, but it was short because he was supposed to bring business up. He moved around the groups helping them with the steps; he moved to Danelle and spent extra time there. It was great. As the song came closer to the end, I ran to the stage. I let it play all the way through. I was still doing well.

"Okay, ladies, say good bye to the man of your dreams, and if you want more of him he's behind the bar. We're taking a 15 minute break."

There were boos and hisses. Jake ran back to the bar passing James. The look on James's his face was not good.

I went to the bar and pulled him to the kitchen and pinned him against the wall, "What are you thinking, because you don't look happy."?

"You think he's hot."

"No, you're hot to me; he's hot to them."

"You would never do that with me."

"Hell no, you're mine." I felt like I was pleading.

"You like to dance like that?"

I did get some relief from this, "Yeah."

"You are so dancing with me."

"Whatever you want, James."

"You are so hot in those jeans."

I leaned into him and got really close to his mouth, "So, you think I'm hot in these jeans?"

He wrapped his hands around my waist and traced them lower, as he pulled me to him, "Yes, hot."

I kissed his lips and whispered to him, "Got to go, baby."

I ran from him to the stage. The timer had 2 minutes left. I put on a CD that would play 4 songs in a row. James came back out looking for me, but he couldn't see me behind the lights.

I sat down, because I was starting to get a little tired, and I still had a dance to do, not including dancing with my James. I had to cool it for a little bit.

Brian came and found me, "Are you getting tired again?"

I looked at him with surprise, "A little."

"Do you want me to get James or the Doc?"

"NO, No please... Brian, I just need to make it through the next lesson. I just need to cool it for a little bit."

"Do you want me to get you something to drink?"

"Yeah, water would be good."

I was watching Brian as he went to the bar. He went to Jake, but he must have said something. Jake went to Jason and James and said something. He moved away from the bar with a water bottle and made his way around the outside of the room and the back way into me.

He knelt down in front of me, gazing into my eyes, "Thank you."

If I love James this much why do I feel badly when I look at Jake?

"Are you doing okay?"

Brian was walking over, and I looked at him scolding him with my eyes.

"Sarah, be nice. Everyone has to watch you."

"Yeah, I am just saving energy for the next one. I am fine."

"I'm going to get James to bring you up stairs now."

"Jake, NO, please? Just let me get through the next one. It's only an hour... please?"

"Your pleases don't work with me, because this is your life, Sarah."

"Jake, fine." I grabbed his arm, "No, please, just let me get through the next one, and I will go up peacefully."

"You are so stubborn."

"Yeah, I am. Please, please let me stay. I will behave."

"I've heard that before."

I gave him my best determined puppy eyes I could and he melted. This was really cool. I didn't know I had that much power, but it was working.

"Fine, but if anything happens, remember I will feel like it's my fault."

I touched his face, "If anything happens then it's my fault. Go before he figures it out."

James was already wondering what was going on, because he wasn't seeing me on the floor. Jake moved around the back of the room back to the bar. Both James and Jason drilled him with questions. He avoided them by taking orders again. All three of them were busy behind the bar.

When the four songs were almost done, I found another track with four more songs on it. I put it in and let it play. I was enjoying watching everyone having fun. I decided to play the second training a little early. I put it in to have it switch to after these songs ran out.

As they ended I spoke again, "Okay, ready for the next one?"

The cheering started again. I didn't pull Jake up, because this one was the country one and he wasn't big on the idea in the first place.

I called Kate and Sandy out to help me. They were great again. It was a very sexy country dance and they were having a little fun with it. We were laughing and having a good time. When it was done I called for another break. I had done this one so early there would be a whole hour left for dancing. People were ordering a lot again. All three guys were so busy behind the bar, and I was watching my James, but he was too busy to notice me. There were a few older women in the bar hitting on him. I started to laugh. One of them tipped him, but his hand lingered there a little long for me. I was getting a little jealous, but James put up with a lot worse than that from me. Plus he just does it because of the tips; it was my idea in the first place.

He was talking to all these girls and flirting with them. He had the best girl in the place, and he was giving them all attention. I couldn't help myself; I had to say something.

I walked by him, "You're an asshole."

He didn't realize I was talking to him. I saw him wait on another girl and they are flaunting it all in front of him. He better look away. He should be more concerned with Sarah then all these little sluts that want one thing. He did it again. Shit.

I walked right up to him, "You are an asshole. You have the best girl here, and you flirt with these nobodies; you have some nerve."

He looked at me like he was going to hit me.

Jason walked over and grabbed his arm, "James, go find Sarah and dance; we'll take care of this."

He just stared at me, trying to intimidate me, but I wasn't going to back down. She needs to know that he is a jerk for acting this way. I was steamed, and now it was my job to take care of her. Not him. He wasn't even paying attention to what was going on with her. She was good at making everyone think she was okay, but if he loved her as much as... shit... as me then he should be looking and watching her.

Oh that wasn't good; Jake and James having words behind the bar. Shit... what was all that about? Shit... not this. I put a CD in for dancing. This one was good for three songs.

James came and found me on the stage, "Sarah, dance with me please."

I moved to him with a smile on my face, "James, whatever you want."

I felt his anger lessen. He led me to the dance floor. He was a better dancer than he had ever showed me in the past. We danced with our legs in between each other's, with his hands slowly caressing my hips.

I noticed that he would look at Jake, and I would pull his face back to me, "James, do you want to go upstairs?"

"Not yet, baby; I'm really liking this."

He held me behind my lower back. It was very sexy, and I was enjoying this too much. I was getting hot for him. He danced a few songs with me. I was getting more tired, but I wasn't ready to go upstairs unless it was to get hotter with James. He took my face and kissed my lips, so deep I was getting dizzy. His mind wasn't on me really. He kept looking at Jake to see his reaction. Jake was getting angrier behind the bar. This was getting to be too much, and I was getting winded.

James kissed my hands, "You are so mine, later."

I smiled at him, but was relieved he was moving back to the bar. I went back to the stage to play more music. I put in another CD that had 4 songs on it. I was letting them play through, but things were getting heated behind the bar. I didn't know what was going on exactly, but I didn't like what I was seeing. I was out dancing with Kate and Sandy and looked over. James was lingering with the same girl as before. He wasn't paying her attention, but his hand lingered in hers.

Jake looked really pissed. He was saying stuff to James, and I stopped to watch. James was getting steamed.

Oh shit I am done now. I started walking to the kitchen quickly, and I caught a glimpse of Jason trying to get James's attention. I ran faster, but saw him come over the bar before I got to the kitchen. He stopped me in the kitchen by grabbing my arm.

"Sarah?" His voice was desperate.

I didn't know how to talk to him or even look at him.

"James, all of this is just too much. I am 16, and I can't do this anymore."

I just walked away. He cramped over as Jason walked in. I didn't wait to see what was going on; I had to go right now.

## *James:*

I couldn't move; the pain was excruciating, and coming from my stomach, but it wasn't me.

Jason came in, and I pleaded with him, "Jason, stop her. Don't let her go anywhere; something is wrong with Sarah. Don't let..."

He was running out after her.

Jake came in, "What is wrong? Are you okay?"

I looked at him desperately, "It's Sarah... not me."

"Where is she?"

"Jason went to stop her."

"Fuck," He put my arm around his neck and was helping me outside. The pain was getting better as I moved more. It was getting easier, and he let go of me. I went to the stairs; she was sitting there leaning over getting sick.

"Jason, Jason over here." I went to pick her up.

"No, James, it hurts so badly. I can't stand it!"

"I know, baby. Jason, get the truck!"

Jake was talking to me, but I was still pissed at him. "We'll take my truck; it has a back seat."

He ran away from us, and I was trying to lift her again.

"No, James, don't move me."

She looked up at me, and I could see the pain on her face as she begged me, "Make the pain stop, James...make it stop!"

"Jason, Sam's here. Go get him."

Jason stood there gapping at me.

"Jason!!! Get Sam now!"

He ran from us.

"Okay, baby we have to go now. I have to lift you to get you in the truck."

"No, don't move me, James. Make the pain go away, James. Please just make it stop. Shit... this hurts, James."

She was grabbing my shirt begging me. I didn't know how to help her. I had to ignore her pleading. I picked her up as she was gasping in agony. I looked for Jake; he was pulling up to us in his pickup truck. He jumped out and opened the door for me.

She was screaming in agony, "James, please help me. You are supposed to take care of me. James, fuck, this fucking hurts. Shit. Auh. Fuck."

Jake was directing me, "James, give her to me."

I didn't want to let her go. I was supposed to make her better, not him.

"James, give her to me, and get in. I will give her back to you."

I glared at him. I didn't want him to hold my Sarah ever again. Shit this sucks. I handed her to him and got in. He did give her back, and she screamed from the pain again.

"Doc, can you give her something for the pain?"

"No, I don't carry stuff like that. We have to get her to the hospital."

"We have to wait for Jason, and Sam."

They came running out the door. Jake told Jason to drive. I scooted all the way to the other side of the seat, so she could lie out.

Jake was in the middle, but turned backwards to face us, "James, I have to feel the spot. I think it might be her appendix that is infected. If it burst we only have a little bit of time before it could kill her. Let me... please."

I glared at him. I didn't want him to touch her; she was mine, "Jason, go already."

I glared at him with hate, but gave into him, and scooted her down so he could feel the spot. I cringed, knowing this would hurt to move her.

She was screaming again, "NO, it hurts, James, no. Make it stop."

Sam turned to look at us in the back seat, "James, this isn't good."

I couldn't hold back the tears. I held her face close to mine. "Baby, just hold on for me, please, Sarah, please don't do this."

"James, make it stop hurting. Please, James, now."

I couldn't make it stop, because I didn't know how.

Jake was trying to be gentle, by lightly pressing on her stomach.

"James, it still feels the same. We might have more time." He pulled out his phone, "Yes, we need a police escort. We are..." He looked at Jason, "What road are we on?"

"Hwy 57 heading east."

"We are on Hwy 57 going east. We are in my pickup; it's a medical emergency. Yes."

He hung up the phone and looked at me, "The escort is on its way."

I knew he wanted to say something, "James, you can help her. You've done it before."

I closed my eyes, "Sam, you are stronger. You need to help her."

"You know we can't do that. If we do..."

Jake was talking to me again, pleading with me, "James, I have seen you do it. You did it today, and you know how. Just help her."

She was in agony, and she was moaning. I knew I shouldn't do it anymore. Somehow I knew that it wouldn't be good.

"Sam, please. You have to help her."

"James, you didn't give her part of your soul, did you?"

"Yes, I did and you can too, please brother. You are stronger and have more to give."

"James, how many times?"

I had done it so much over the last few weeks that I had lost count, "Sam, a lot. Now please help her."

"James, you know if she doesn't make it, you will die too."

"I know, but Sam you are stronger than I am; if you help her once... it won't... kill you like it could me."

Jake was looking at me funny. I hated that he was looking at me that way, "What?"

"What you did for her could kill you?"

"I have given her so much of me that yes, if she dies I will...too, but I couldn't live without her anyway, so it wasn't a loss for me. Sam, please?"

"I can't do that. I would be connected to her forever and she is yours, brother. I couldn't handle that."

"Damn it, Sam, please."

"NO." He turned away from me.

Jake wouldn't stop staring at me, "James, there is another way."

I looked at him not understanding what he was talking about. How? I didn't have anything left.

She screamed in agony again.

"Jake, what? Anything. I can't allow her to hurt like this."

"James, if you can't give her your soul, then talk to her. She listens to you. Demand it. Say what you have to. Just do it."

He turned away from me. My tears were streaming down my face. I saw the lights from the cop cars. One moved in front of us and the other stayed behind. I was hoping this will help get us there sooner.

"Sam, call Clarissa and Dad; they are still at the hospital. Tell them to meet us in the emergency room."

"Jason."

Fuck, I can't handle this. She was screaming in pain. It hurt so badly, and I could feel how bad it was.

"Jason, call her parents. Tell them she is going to the hospital."

"Sarah, Baby. You have to fight this, Sarah. You have to talk to me. Sarah, talk to me now, or I will leave."

"NO, James. Help me. You are supposed to be here to take care of me." She was pulling at my arms.

"Sarah, baby. You have to fight this or..."

I didn't want to say it. She will feel sad.

"Baby, all those times I gave you my soul..."

The tears were coming and I didn't want to think she wasn't going to make it. I was not ready to die, but if I couldn't have her I didn't want to live either. She was in so much agony.

"Baby, you have to fight. You have my soul almost completely, and if you die so will I."

"No, James, no. Fuck this hurts. Just make it go way. Shit, James, this hurts so bad."

"Jason, how far?"

"Maybe, 15 more minutes. James, I am going as fast as they are letting me go."

Jake was leaning over the seat again. He was feeling her head.

"James, give me her arm."

I lifted it to him and watched him.

"James, talk to her, like.... you know. Get her going, please, James."

He gave her hand back to me; I took it and brought it to my mouth. He turned around. I started to kiss her hand and brought it up so I could trace my mouth down her arm. She touched my face. I tilted her to the side a little kissing her neck and reached her ear.

I breathed into it, "Sarah, I want you to make love to me like in our dreams. I need to feel you around me, the warmth, the rush, the explosion of enjoyment." She was pulling my hand to her breast. I was very uncomfortable with everyone hearing everything.

I was trying to whisper in her ear, "I love you. Do you remember the fog, swirling it with our hands together? Try to think how peaceful it is, how we lie on the rug in front of the fireplace. How perfectly we fit together. Sarah, you have to come to me right now; I need you. She turned to me more grabbing at my shirt. I was kissing her neck, and I touched her stomach tracing my hand over it. She heaved a breath.

Jason was slowing; we were getting close.

"Sarah, do you want me tonight?"

"Yes, James, whatever you want. I am yours, forever."

I started to kiss her ear with so much passion.

"Yes, James, please."

She wasn't screaming anymore. We pulled into the emergency bay where the ambulances park.

Everyone else was out of the truck; but I was still holding my Sarah. Jake came and opened the door.

"James, you have to give her to me."

I didn't want to let her go. "Jake, you are going to have to take her from me. I can't do it. I can't let her go."

"James, she will die in your arms if I don't get her in there right now."

I held her tighter to me. If she dies in my arms then I would die holding her. What way would be better, but to die in the arms of the one you love.

# 4. You Know That

"James, snap out of it, and give her to me now. I can still save her."

I didn't understand what he was saying until I felt her letting me go.

"No, you don't!" I held her tighter and gave her the biggest dose I could muster. She completely arched her back and gasped for air.

"James, NO!"

"Yes, Sarah, you are not getting rid of me that easy. Damn it, Sarah, I can't and won't live without you."

"James, I thought you couldn't do that again."

"Jake, I had to."

I pushed her to him.

"No, James, don't let me go. Help me." She was gasping from the pain, "James, please make the pain stop."

I was moving out right behind her getting out of the truck. Jake was transferring her to a gurney. I ran to her side holding her hand. She looked so scared. I wanted to hold her more. Jake kicked into doctor mode.

"Jason, how long until her mom and dad will get here?"

"At least another half hour, they didn't have a police escort."

"Shit."

He wanted to know that why, "Why?"

He didn't look at me.

"Jake, why?"

"Someone needs to sign the release forms for me to do the surgery."

"I will sign whatever you need."

"It has to be a guardian or parent, James; you can't do it."

She was in agony again and was moaning with pain.

"Jake, can you give her something now?"

"Yeah." He was helping the others push her in. He went to the counter as they brought him a white jacket, and he was barking orders. Everyone was running to do what he was saying. I watched him, and then he walked back over with a shot and shoved it in her arm.

"This will help her, but, James, we have to get her going."

I was relieved to see Clarissa coming in with Dad.

"James, Jake, what is going on?"

I just looked at them desperately. I didn't know how to help my sweet Sarah.

Jake was dealing with them, "We can't do the surgery until someone signs the release forms."

Clarissa moved to the other side of Sarah, but looking at me first and then her, "Sarah, honey?"

My sweet Sarah looked at me so sad and scared, but she wasn't screaming anymore, "Do you feel better?"

She tried to smile at me, "James, it still hurts, but not as bad. You need to fix this. Your dad said you would take care of me, please make it go away."

"Sarah, if I could do that I would have done it a long time ago."

Clarissa was trying again, but she was looking at me, "James, you love her, you want to marry her?"

"Yes, of course I do." I looked at my Sarah. I brought her hand to my face and traced my fingers over her forehead.

"James, go sign the release forms, I will take care of the rest."

I walked over to the counter and signed the forms, but watched what she was doing. Dad walked over to me and put his hand on my shoulder. I couldn't look at him, only because I would have had to take my eyes off of Sarah. Clarissa was trying to talk to her, "Sarah?"

She looked at Clarissa.

"Sarah, baby. Sarah, do you want to marry James?"

I watched as she nodded.

The tears were welling up in my eyes. I couldn't ask her to do that when she was in this awful condition. She is being forced, and not given a choice in life, but yet... she would be all mine. I wouldn't have to let her be away from me anymore.

"Sarah, baby, you have to say it. Do you want to marry James?"

She closed her eyes, and grimaced in pain, "Yes." Her eyes came back to mine, "James, this still hurts."

She was reaching for me and pulling me to her.

Clarissa started directing people, "That's it. I am emancipating her as an adult. You are all witness to this. Carl, you can marry them now. I will take care of the paperwork."

Jake was getting upset. I saw him pacing. I knew he loved her enough to want to stop me.

"I will do it without the release forms; take her back now."

Clarissa moved to him, "Jake, NO." She stopped them, "Jake, you will lose everything. I won't let that happen. Your father would never forgive me."

"But you will let him marry her?"

"They are life partners; it was foreseen."

"I don't believe in all this crap. She is 16, and there is no way she is ready." He turned to me pleading, "James, you know that. You yourself want her to wait to be with her until she was 18. James, don't do it."

"Jake, have compassion for him. He is... He loves Sarah, more than life."

I understood how he felt. I didn't want her this way either, and I felt like we were forcing her. I only wanted her if she loves me and if she chooses it.

I leaned over her with my face less than an inch from hers, "Sarah?"

She was melting me with her eyes that were begging for help. She was still in a lot of pain, and the tears from my eyes were flowing so much that they were dripping on her face.

"Sarah, Jake said he would do the surgery without the papers. I will wait forever, 18, 20, 25, 30 years for you to be ready to marry me, but you have to tell me what you want."

She turned to look at Jake and I could see the sadness in her eyes. Then she turned back to me and her eyes brightened a little, "James, marry me?"

I kissed her soft sweet lips. Dad came to the other side of the bed. He did some talking in the Indian language of his world. I wasn't paying too much attention to him. I couldn't believe she was going to be mine forever. I was kissing her hand.

And now in English, "James, will you cherish her and love her forever, provide for her and share with her your life plan?"

There was so much more than that, "Yes, I will."

My tears were still falling. She lifted her hand to touch my face. I felt like I was losing her right here and right now, even though she was going to be mine.

"Sarah, will you cherish him and love him forever? Provide for him and share with him your life plan?"

The tears were coming to her eyes. I kissed her cheek.

"Yes, I will."

"Then you will share your life now and forever. You are now married."

I kissed her soft sweet lips and she was responding to me. She just filled every dream I had.

"James..."

I painfully broke the kiss, but hesitated to let her go.

"James, later. I am so tired."

Her eyes got so heavy that they didn't open after they closed this time.

I didn't want to ask for Jake's help, but I needed him. I took an unpleasant breath turning to him. He was a complete mess.

"Jake, can you still handle helping her?"

I can't explain his face; pain, sadness, or maybe just disgust. In any other situation I wouldn't have asked him or expected him to help her, but I needed him.

"Yes, take her back. I will be right there."

He walked over to me, exasperated, determined to make his point, "You shouldn't have…"

"Jake, I told you I love her."

"Then don't hold hands with a different girl just to bring up your tips. She deserves more than that."

"You knew she loved me and still you held her. You fell in love with her."

His eyes squinted to a glare and he just stood there not moving.

All I could think of was how I needed him to help her, "Jake, please… I know you do care about her; if you can, please help her now."

His irritation disappeared from him as the realization showed on his face that she was still needed his help. His eyes turned sad and his face worried as he walked away. I stood there watching him hurry down the hall. He stopped before walking in the operating room, nodded to me, and then went in. I collapsed on the closest thing I could find in the waiting room.

On the one hand, I didn't want anyone to talk to me, to look at me, to do anything.

On the other hand, I wanted to know what was going on with Sarah. I felt like my head was in a cloud, totally foggy…Sam…Sam?

He knew what I was thinking, "No James, it will be easier if you don't know."

Clarissa moved to sit with me. Dad was in a wheel chair again moving closer to me.

I dropped my face to my hands feeling I needed to say something, "Thank you."

I didn't want to see their concerned faces. It was getting harder to breathe, almost so much that I was going to go crazy. I stood up trying to ignore everyone looking at me, "I need to be alone. I will be out in the ambulance bay. Come get me if…."

I couldn't finish what I was thinking or what I was going to say. Jason and Sam got up to follow, but I couldn't say anymore so I just walked out. The hard part was as I was walking out I met Sarah's parents.

If they knew what I just did, they would never forgive me. Tucker put his hand on my shoulder, but if he knew it might have been more of a punch in the face.

Sarah's mom had questions, "You are back? Wasn't that supposed to be Monday?"

I couldn't even look at her. It would be devastating for them if they knew I had just married their 16 year old daughter, so I just walked away.

Jason took over, "Yeah, I got this."

I knew I had to speak, "Just don't tell them about the…'

"James, you and Sarah will have to deal with that one. I am not getting in the middle."

I was thankful. He went in with them. I walked around to the ambulance bay and sat on the ground. I was trying to feel what she was going through. I needed to know if she was going to be okay. I was concentrating on her, but I was getting nothing.

My phone buzzed. It startled me, and I looked up at Sam, but he shrugged his shoulders.

I opened it, "*1-, 2-, 3-, Breath.*"

It took my breath away. I only did that with one person. I couldn't believe my eyes. It had only been maybe 15-20 minutes; there was no way she was texting me. I looked at Sam again confused.

"Who was it?"

I couldn't say anything. She wasn't like us. Who could it have been? I just stared at him not knowing how to explain this. He got up and walked over taking my phone and looked at it, "What does that mean?"

I shook my head. He handed it back to me. I closed it and put it away. I put my face in my hands, because it didn't mean anything. I started to concentrate on her again. I needed to feel if she was okay. She must not be feeling anything, and that was a good thing, but I couldn't feel her. I had to ask, "Do you know how she is doing?"

He closed his eyes to concentrate so I let him be. He would tell me if he felt anything. I looked up to the sky maybe to ask for help, and I saw a shooting star. I knew it was an old wives tale, but I have nothing to lose. Please, please give me my Sarah back.

My phone buzzed again. Someone was playing with my emotions. If this is Jake I am going to kill him. I opened it.

"*I love you more than you know.*"

I asked Sam, "Anything yet?"

"James she's okay, but it's just not good. I mean she is doing fine, but what they are doing...it's not good. Who was that?"

I didn't know what to tell him, so I held it up for him to look at it. He walked to me taking the phone. He read it, gave an airy sigh, and asked, "Who is that?"

The tears were welling up in my eyes again. I shrugged my shoulders because I couldn't talk about it.

"James?"

I put my face in my hands, "Sam, those are things I say to her."

"What?"

"I say those things to her." It buzzed again.

"James?"

"I can't look at it Sam; you look at it and I... just don't know."

He opened it, "James, could this be?"

"NO, it can't."

"Who do you think it is?"

"I don't know, but she is the only one I have ever said either of them to. It would have to be someone who has looked at her phone or mine."

"You really think someone would mess with you while she is in there?"

I didn't want to know but I had to ask, "What did the last one say?"

He walked back over to me handing me the phone. I thought I was going to lose it when I read it, *"I love you, James."*

"Shit, I have to..." I got up and went storming in. I walked past everyone in the waiting room, and up to the window. The girl behind the desk glanced up and buzzed me in. Sam was right on my heels. I was walking back to where she was supposed to be. A couple of people tried to stop me, but Sam did a good job diverting them. We made it to where she was. I looked through the window. She was still there. I turned to Sam searching for answers to questions I didn't have to ask.

"James, what are you thinking?"

"I'm not, I just don't understand and I hate that I can't feel her."

I needed to know for sure, so I glanced in the window again. Jake saw me and shook his head no. I turned away. I moved to the wall next to the room and sat on the floor. Sam came and sat by me.

Someone came out a door from the other side. It was Jake, so I stood up with anticipation.

"James?"

I could tell he wasn't happy and maybe he felt almost as bad as I did.

"Shouldn't you still be in there?"

"Yes, but you need to know. It's going to be a little..." He couldn't look at me.

"Jake, what?"

"How long ago did she start getting sick, James?"

"The day I left...a little over 5 weeks ago."

"James, it was her appendix, but it had been leaking this whole time. That is what the spreading was. We have to get rid of all the poison in her body, and James... it spread a lot."

"So, what are you telling me? Is she going to make it?"

"I can't promise anything; it is complicated and very serious."

"Your gut feeling... is she going to be okay?"

"James, we had to cut her more than we thought."

"I don't care about that. I just want her back."

"Well, that is always a risk; the other is..."

"There's more?"

"Yes, James. We are taking everything out and washing it off. It is the only way to get most of it out."

"Everything?"

"Well, in that general area you showed me. We can only do so much, so she is going to be down for a lot longer than I thought, if she..."

"I will take care of her... anything, just make her better."

"I am trying, but James, just be patient. It has been leaking a long time, and there is a lot of it everywhere."

I sat back down, "Jake, just go help her. You can tell me what to do later."

I knew he wanted me to leave the hall. I think he even gestured for Sam to get me out of there. I was thankful when Sam sat down by me. Jake gave up and walked back in the operating room.

I let Sam know what I was thinking, "I thought he was the one messing with me, but he is still in there."

"You don't think it could be her?"

"NO, how?"

"James, you don't know hardly anything about what you can do, do you?"

"What are you talking about?"

"How many times did you give her your soul?"

"I don't know, 15-20 times over the last 5 weeks."

"Holy shit, James, she might be doing it without even knowing it."

"No, she is under."

"Your soul?"

"Is that even a possibility?"

"Yeah."

"Really?"

"I think you should learn more."

"Are you ready for taking over?"

"I thought I was, but after tonight, NO."

"What changed your mind?"

"Tonight, when you asked me to help Sarah, I could have helped her. I could have stopped it from getting worse and even made it a little better, but James, that is not my decision, to save someone or not. If it is their time then I cannot change that."

"I am sorry I asked."

"No, that's not what I am saying. I don't know if I am ready, because telling you *no* was the hardest thing I have had to do in my life. I don't know how strong I would be if I was asked to save people all the time."

"You stood up to me. You could handle anyone." I put my arm around him.

"You're not mad at me?"

"Sam, I shouldn't have asked. I just love her so much."

"I know; sometimes it comes over me that strong, and I want to hold her myself."

"Not you too?"

"I know it's not me. Amelia is mine, but your feelings are so strong; dad even likes to hold her and tell her stories. James?"

"Yeah."

"Do you really think she was ready to marry you?"

"Nope."

"What are you going to do?"

"I have no idea. Why? Do you have some suggestions?"

"Nope. I was just wondering."

"I don't even know how to tell her parents."

"That could be scary."

"You have no idea."

"At least you already bought the ring."

He made me laugh. This waiting was going to drive me nuts.

"James?"

"Yeah."

"Do you realize this is the longest time we have spent together since you turned 13 years old?"

I glanced at him, "I wasn't a very good big brother was I?"

He sighed not answering me and tried to change the subject, "Dad is supposed to come home tomorrow."

"Shit."

"What?"

"I won't be able to help; I have to stay here."

"We're ready. Clarissa is really great."

"Oh, I drove your vehicle."

"What is it?"

"I'm not telling, but when I come back to get my bike, I will bring it to you."

"Fine, and thanks."

"I suppose I should go talk to her mom and dad."

"Are you ready for that?"

"Nope."

"I think under the circumstances, you are allowed to be off the hook for a little bit yet."

"No, Sam, its time."

"But I like it, just you and me."

"Okay, but I will have to talk to them soon."

I put my arm around his shoulder, "Thanks for staying with me."

"Thanks for letting me."

We sat there 'til I was having a hard time keeping my eyes open. Someone was coming out the other door again. It wasn't Jake. It was a nurse, so I stood up. Was she there to tell me something? She knew I wanted info.

She gestured to the cart she was pushing, "I am just getting more supplies. They are not done."

She walked away. I relaxed while Sam was concentrating on how it was going again.

He finally spoke, "James, they are doing a really good job getting it all."

I was relieved. At least it was good news. The nurse came back with a cart full of supplies. I was instantly worried that it was all for my Sarah.

"No, this is not all for her. I got enough to restock." She moved into the room.

I gasped, "She scared the shit out of me."

"James, it should have. She was lying; it IS for her."

"What?"

"Gotcha."

"You suck!"

I was almost laughing, but he almost gave me a heart attack.

My phone buzzed again. "*1-, 2-, 3-, Breath*"

I hated this, "This is freaking me out. Sam, can you hold my phone, and don't tell me if it buzzes anymore."

"Really?"

"Yeah."

I handed it over to him and sat back down.  He sat next to me.

"Sam, how long has she been in there?"

"I think it was about 8:30 pm by the time they took her back, and it's...."

He pulled out my phone and looked at it, "It's 12:30 am."

"She has been in there for four hours?"

"Yeah."

"I should really go talk to everybody."

Someone walked out the other door again.  I stood up.  It was a different nurse this time, and she seemed to want to talk with us.  She walked over to us, "Dr. Phallen asked me to tell you that they are putting things back together.  It will be a while yet."

I took a deep breath, "Sorry kid, I've got to go talk to everyone." I pulled him up, and we walked to the waiting room.

# 5. Shocking News

**W**e got to the doors of the waiting room, pausing for just a minute, so I could gather my thoughts. I knew what I had to do. I am supposed to be more of a man than a boy, as Paula had once said. I scanned the room noticing everybody as I walked to Sarah's mom and dad. Tucker stood up.

"Tucker, please sit, it's going to be a while yet."

He sat back down. Clarissa was pushing dad over to be with them to comfort them if they needed it. Clarissa had a box of tissue and stood behind Paula. I squatted in front of them. They must have a million questions. I looked at both their faces. Where was I going to start?

Paula was starting to cry.

I grabbed a Kleenex from the box Clarissa was holding, "Paula, no it's not bad news. It's not good, but she is doing much better."

As I talked about Sarah the tears were starting to well up in my eyes again, so I bent my head, "Shit, where do you want me to start?"

Paula reached down and lifted my face to look at her, "What happened to her?"

"It was her appendix. It didn't burst, but her getting sick was from it leaking for so long. From what Jake thinks, it probably has been leaking since I left. That was the first time she got sick."

I needed to take a deep breath.

Paula laughed a little, "I thought she was pregnant."

She got my attention with that comment, "NO, it's not...."

I couldn't say it. I looked away, so they couldn't see my desire to be with her. We had been together in so many ways, my dreams and giving her my soul. It may have been real, the feather was real, and I couldn't really talk to them about this.

"Jake came out and told me they had to get all the poison out, so they had to make the cut bigger than he originally thought it would be. The bad part is they had to take her insides out and wash them all before they could put them back in."

I peaked at them to see how they were handling this. I was a mess and the tears were streaking down my face. They weren't doing great either, but it was going okay, so I went further.

"Before I came out they were putting things back. They said it would be a while yet, but I thought you should know she was on the good side now."

Tucker put his hand on my shoulder, "James, thank god you were here. Why are you here?"

Okay we were getting to the harder part, "Sarah asked me to come home on Tuesday. I got some help and finished everything early. I came home today to surprise her. She didn't know until I showed up at the lake, when I caught her water skiing."

Paula was not pleased, "She was water skiing?"

"Only 'til she saw me. I took her back to Tony's, and she was already really weak by then. Jake gave her something and checked on her while she slept."

I could see that they were not happy, but they were doing okay.

"Jake and I decided she was well enough…" I was having a hard time with this. I knew I didn't watch her close enough. I swallowed, "She was at the dance… I didn't keep a good eye on her… she was doing fine… I didn't pick up on the signs, and I had no idea how bad she had gotten…I would never have let her do the dance if I truly knew how…"

I tried to choke back my tears. I had to breathe. I felt like this was my fault.

Paula lifted my chin, "James, she is stubborn. We don't blame you. She does what she wants. We can't tell how bad she is when she doesn't tell the whole truth. Now you know how we feel."

I wiped my tears trying to continue, "But there is more."

Tucker moved to the edge of his seat, "James, what is it?"

Oh shit this is not going to be good. Jason moved to us too. I think everyone was prepared for him to kill me.

"When we got here, they wouldn't take her back unless someone signed the release forms. I signed them."

Paula spoke up, "Yes, thank you, James."

I knew she wasn't going to be thankful after this. I saw Clarissa nodding to let me know I should continue. I didn't know how to tell them this.

"In order for them to accept my signature, we had to…" Shit I can't tell them this. Fuck, I don't want to do this… not without my sweet Sarah by my side.

Tucker put his hand on my shoulder again, "James?"

I directed my attention to him, "My mom is a judge, and she emancipated Sarah as an adult and we got married in the emergency room."

I grimaced, bracing myself for the blow. I was willing to take everything they would throw at me, so I didn't move. I kept my face down, but stayed to take it. They weren't saying anything; they weren't even moving. I didn't know what to do.

Jason walked up behind me; he grabbed my arm to pull me up and away from them.

"Jason, it's okay." I still didn't look at them. I was 'waiting for the firing squad' as Sarah would put it.

"No James. You need to let them absorb this. Come on, we need to go for a walk."

I stood up trying to understand why they weren't lashing out at me. They weren't looking at me or each other. Clarissa had her hand on Paula's shoulder. What were they thinking? What were they going to do? Shit. I should have had a plan, so they would know that I would make this as easy as I could for Sarah. Please say something. Yell at me; hit me, something... anything?

Jason was pulling me, "James, now!"

I let Jason pull me away. We got out the door, and I stopped,

"Jason, I can't leave. If they come out I need to be there. I need to be with her."

"James, they got a lot more information than anyone can handle already, and they need space to process it all. *They* can't leave; that is their baby in there."

"But she's mine now."

"No, she will always be theirs first."

I wasn't pleased about that, but I knew he was right.

"Jason, I will stay away from the waiting room. I need to go back in there."

"James, no. Just cool it for a minute."

"I will come up with a plan, so she can have a normal life until she is 18, but then she is mine."

"James, you are talking hastily, slow down and relax."

I moved around him, "Jason, I am sorry." I walked back in and went straight to the desk. The nurse saw me coming and she let me back immediately. I glanced back at them as I walked in, but they didn't even look at me. I walked straight to the surgery room and peeked in the window. Jake saw me and nodded this time. I was relieved and sat on the floor outside the room.

A nurse passing in the hallway stopped and looked at me. She walked away and came back with a wheel chair, "Here this might be more comfortable and we won't trip over you."

I gave her a thank you smile and got up. I sat in the wheel chair pushing myself back and forward.

The plan... a plan. Okay, first she will stay with me at Clarissa's till she was well enough to go to school. I needed to take care of her school stuff, so when she was ready she could go.

Second, when she was better she would go back to living at home with her mother. That way she would have a normal teenage life. I would try to get to her every day. Making sure she was doing her homework and staying on track.

Third, I will bring her home when she turned 18. Shit, I need to get a house for my sweet Sarah. A home for her...it would have to be special.

Fourth, I will love her for the rest of my life.

I smiled. She was going to be okay, and she was mine forever.

I had my plan, now waiting again. Where is Sam when you need him? I didn't wait very long and he was walking down the hall.

"You needed me?"

I chuckled to myself that he was intuitive as I was. It seemed a little weird. Now I know how Sarah felt, feels. Whatever...

Sam sat with me, and we found another wheel chair for him.

He had a problem with just sitting there and not talking, which is what I wanted. He took my mind off waiting for her.

"I think that went well."

"What?"

"You talking to her parents, but you did leave them a little stunned."

I took my hands and rubbed them over my face, "Yeah, I was kind of looking forward to being yelled at, hit, or something."

"No, I don't think they have moved at all."

"Really?"

"Yeah. I think they're a little numb right now."

I guess that's better than I was hoping for.

"Have you figured anything out?"

"I think so."

"Well?"

"I get her till she is better, and then she can go back to living with her mom and finish school. When she turns 18, I will bring her home, but I do have to get a house in the next year and a half."

"So, what are you going to do? If you want to give her a house you have to make a lot more money than bartending."

"Sarah found a program at the University of Minnesota, and that is what I want to go into. If I can get that worked out, then I will do that."

"Well that's a start, but you better get on it right away. Her parents will do better if you have it set in stone."

The thought of Sarah living with me in a house, our house, was pleasing, "Sam, she's mine."

"Yes, James, she is, but you are going to have to be really strong. She is very young and it is going to be really hard. You do know that?"

"But she is mine. I love her, and Sam, she is so smart; you have no idea."

The other door opened. I turned to see that it was Jake. I stood up, and he didn't look happy, "James, sit."

"If you don't mind I just..."

"James, she is back together. The next 24 hours are critical."

"But you took care of everything. She is going to be okay?"

"James, it was..." He put his hands to his face, as if to rub out the tension there, and said, "Shit, James, it was really serious. I have never seen anything quite like this before. We had her under for a long time and you know... it's just not that good."

"So are you telling me she still might not make it?"

"James, let's just see how she does. She probably won't wake up for a while."

"A while? What are we talking here?"

"I don't know. A day, maybe two, and when she does she is going to be in a lot of pain."

"What?"

"James, we took a lot of things in and out of her abdomen. Her body is going to have to adjust, and it will be very painful."

"You can give her stuff to make her more comfortable, right?"

"Well, we can try to keep her comfortable, but James…it's just not good."

"When can I see her?"

They were coming out with her. She looked so sweet, and peaceful. I started walking to her.

"James, not yet. She has to go to Intensive Care. We need to watch her carefully in a clean room. We have to take precautions to help her the best way we can. I am supervising everything. You will have to wait until we get her settled."

"But…" I started to walk to her.

"NO, James, not yet."

My heart was dropping.

"James, go to the third floor. The waiting room is a lot bigger there. Everyone will be more comfortable there."

"That is where my dad was; I know it well."

"Good, meet me up there. When they have her comfortable I will come for you."

"Jake, I know you love her. Please, please don't keep her from me."

"James, I'm not."

I didn't know how I felt about him being able to be with her and keeping me away, but I had no choice. He was the one that could help her, and I couldn't do anything right now.

"James, go up stairs, and I will come get you soon."

He walked away getting on the same elevator with her.

I was unaware of what came out of my mouth, "I'm not ready for the firing squad again."

Sam grabbed my arm and pulled me down the hall, "Yes, you are. Let's go."

We walked to the waiting room. Tucker and Paula seemed alarmed to see me walk out to them. I couldn't tell if they were angry or just upset. "She is out, and they are bringing her to intensive care on the third floor. Jake will come get us when we can see her, but she won't wake up for a while."

Tucker was a little upset, "A while?"

"Jake said it could be 24 to 48 hours. She needs to rest and he said it was pretty bad, so there might be a lot of pain when she wakes up. Are you up to going upstairs now? I can take you up."

They both got up. They weren't lashing out at me yet. Dad and Clarissa, Jason, and Sam came upstairs with us. We walked out into a large waiting area.

A nurse met us, "James?"

I turned to her with hesitation, "Yeah."

"Come with me please."

My heart leapt. He was going to let me see her. I followed her back, "We are getting her settled, and it will be a little longer. Dr. Phallen wanted us to let you see her, but you will have to stay outside. There is a large window for you to see her."

We stopped in front of a room. She put on a gown and was pushing me in front of the window, "Stay here."

She walked in the room and pulled back the curtain. My heart was falling from my chest. Sarah was lifeless as they moved her around. I put my hands on the window. I felt like I was going to die. I felt a hand on my shoulder. I couldn't look to see who it was.

"James?"

I was finding it hard to breathe again. I couldn't stop the tears as they trailed down my cheeks. I didn't want to take my eyes off of her.

"James, it might be better to go back to the waiting room. It will still be a while."

I knew it was Jake. His voice was piercing me with every word. He was pulling me away. I kept looking as long as I could see her, as he pulled me from her. "James, I will come get you as soon as I can, but they need to get her set up, so we can monitor everything. I will check her vitals when they are done, and then I will come get you, but it will have to be a short stay."

I had nothing to say. I didn't know what to say. He was the one that was going to make all the decisions of when I could see her, so I didn't want to do anything that would prevent me from seeing her.

He was handing me pillows and blankets, "James, take these out to the others. Try to keep everyone comfortable. I would send everyone home, but I don't think anyone would leave."

I shook my head no. His voice was killing me. He held her. He filled her needs more than I could. I hated him as much as I was thankful he was there for her. I closed my eyes to try and shake off this feeling of wanting to kill him. He was pushing me back to the waiting room. I walked out feeling numb not knowing what to do. I laid the pillows and blankets on a couch and went to stand by a window. I closed my eyes, so I could search to feel for her. I would take pain if that was all I could feel. I just needed to feel something, anything, but it was still empty.

I heard Laura, "James, how is Sarah?"

I couldn't look at anyone, "Still sleeping."

I closed my eyes and rested my head on the window.

"James?"

This voice I needed to hear, "She's not in pain, James."

I looked at my little brother, "That I do feel, but Sam I would take the pain to feel her."

I turned back to the window, to wait to feel again.

Tucker had questions, "Feel her? You mean touch her."

He was angry. I had nothing. Sam went to them. I couldn't deal with anything until I could feel something.

"Our family has special gifts."

Dad spoke up, "Tucker, when we care about someone… the way James cares about her… well, he can feel her feelings."

Jason was even trying to help explain, "James gave her part of his soul to help save her."

Shit, Dad didn't know that. So of course he scolded, "James, you know you can't… shouldn't do that. If she doesn't… James, what were you thinking?"

I didn't look at any of them, "Dad I wasn't, and it helped her. I had to."

"Well, what that means to us is that James feels everything. The connection is both good and bad. James, I thought I at least taught you about that. You would have died with her."

"I know, but I would not want to live without her anyway."

I heard Paula, still not looking at them, "James, you feel everything she does?"

I grinned to myself, as I thought about her kisses on my lips, "Yes."

"So what is she feeling?"

I finally looked at everyone, "She hasn't felt a thing since they put her under." I went back to looking out the window. Oh, how I missed her feelings. I would give anything to have her mad at me right now. When she's angry with me I found that exciting, and a challenge to make her happy again. Sarah, please give me something… anything.

Sam walked over to me, "Do you want to see?" He had my phone in his hand.

I looked into his eyes with the question as I opened it, "Sam, is this even possible?"

"Old stories didn't involve cell phones, James, I guess anything is possible."

I looked down at the phone again reading it, *"1-, 2-, 3-, Breathe."*

I closed my eyes, and then I was drawn to get answers from my Dad. He returned the acknowledgement of what I was asking. Was it really her? Shit, this is driving me crazy.

I gave the phone back to Sam, "If it buzzes I want to know right away."

I was thinking really hard. Sarah, give me something else; I need to feel you. Give me something else please, Sarah, I need to feel you.

I saw Sam jump out of the corner of my eye. He pulled out the phone and smiled, "What did you just do?"

"I asked her to give me anything, and that I needed to feel her."

He handed me my phone, so I opened it to read, *"Cayuse"*

My heart was beating hard and fast. I needed answers from Dad. He was beginning to get the whole picture. He wheeled to me, "James?"

"Dad, is it possible for her to communicate with me when she is like this?"

"Maybe, why?"

"I thought someone was messing with me. I have been getting texts from... I think her."

He smiled, "It could be possible."

"How can I get to her? If she is with me, how can I... dad help me. She needs me."

"James, have you ever gone to her?"

"Yes, many times. It's always more real when I am sleeping, but a few times I could touch her when she was awake."

"You are stronger than you know, James."

"Dad, how do I get to her?"

"You just answered your own question."

"I need to sleep?"

"Yes, if she is this weak it might be the only way."

I smiled wondering how I was I going to be able to sleep now. I might be able to be with her.

Sam was pulling me out of the waiting room, "James, there is another little waiting room down this hall. You can sleep there."

I was following him in a hurry. I needed to get to her wherever she was. I walked in the room. It was all chairs.

Sam grabbed a pillow and propped it against a chair, and I sat down with my head back. I closed my eyes and wished for sleep. It wouldn't come because I was too excited.

"James, stop that. Let the sleep take you."

"I am trying. I'm just too excited."

"Don't think about it. Think about being with her and not getting to her."

I started to think about being with her in the house. Her favorite part was tracing the fog with our hands.

# 6. Communications

**S**he was there in front of me, and I reached for her, but couldn't touch her, "Sarah?"

She said nothing. I moved to her, and I was so close to her that I could almost feel her breath. I reached to touch her face, but couldn't, "Sarah?"

I moved around her. If I could feel her, my body would have been tracing hers. As I came back to the front of her, I whispered in her ear, "What do you need, Sarah?"

"Help me."

She was breaking my heart. I whispered to her lips, "Sarah, how can I help you?"

I woke, my phone was buzzing. I was gleaming as I looked at Sam.

Excitement entered his eyes, "You were with her?" He was handing me my phone.

"Yes."

I opened it and read the message, "Feel."

I was gasping for air, "My sweet Sarah."

"What? What did it say, James?"

"When I was with her she asked me to help her. I asked her how."

I held up my phone for him to see it.

"Feel?"

"Sam, I have to get to her."

I knew now what I had to do. At once I stood up and ran past the other waiting room. I could feel everyone watching me, as I approached the nurse's desk, "I need to see her now."

"Sir, you will have to wait until Dr. Phallen says it's okay."

"Get him now."

Jake seemed to appear out of nowhere, "No, James, not yet."

"You don't understand she has been com…"

He pulled me into an empty room.

"James, people won't understand. You need to be more careful."

I pulled my phone out, "She has been trying to communicate with me. I paged through the messages showing them to him, "Look, look. Jake, I need to see her."

"Wait, she has been texting you? How? That's not possible."

"I don't know either, but Sam and Dad told me to sleep. In my dream she begged me to help her; I asked her how, and when I woke this text was on my phone." I handed him my phone with the text message on it.

With a look of disbelief, he read the one word printed on the front. "Feel?"

"Shit, James, this wasn't even 5 minutes ago."

"I know. Jake, I need to see her now. I need to do something."

"Are you sure someone isn't messing with you… someone else who wants her and wants to drive you crazy?"

"It's you and me. I know others have feelings for her, but you and I are the only ones that talk to her on her phone. Look… it doesn't come in with the number it would be coming from."

"Matt talks to her on her phone too."

"But he wouldn't know about this."

"Okay, James. This isn't real."

"Jake, yes it is. I didn't believe it either. Jake, please let me see her."

"Okay, but she isn't doing well. James, it can't be long."

"Anything."

He guided us back out and to intensive care. He handed me a gown and we stepped in the room. He gave me a mask, but I shook my head, "She needs to feel me, Jake."

"Well, at least wash your hands."

I washed them good and hard, but as quickly as possible.

"Fine, but don't take too long." He added, as he turned and walked out.

I approached the bed with trepidation. She looks incredibly weak and defenseless, with plastic tubing weaving in and out of her body. I traced my hand along her face to wipe the hair from it. I picked up her hand and pressed it against my face. I turned it to kiss her palm. The ring was not there. I felt my heart drop. I leaned over, and softly kissed her forehead.

She was so intoxicating for me. I slowly breathed in her essence, "Oh, Sarah, what have you let happen? You should have told someone how miserable you were."

I moved to her ear, "I love you more than you know, little girl."

I brought her hand to my face again to trace her palm along my cheek, "Sarah, try to touch me. I need to feel your touch. Please, baby, give me something, anything."

I continued to touch her with my lips, my hands, and my face.

Jake had returned, "James, it's time to let her rest."

"She is resting."

"No, she's not, you have to see this."

"Wait, where is the ring?"

He walked over to a closet and pulled out an envelope with all her stuff in it. He pulled it out, "Is it real?"

"Yes!"

"That is a very expensive ring."

"It doesn't compare to how much I love her. It would have been more if I could have afforded it."

He handed it to me, "Okay, I have to show you this."

I kissed her hand one last time and followed him.

He brought me to a machine with white paper being dispensed. He was showing me lines depicting her vital signs, which were all over the place.

"James, this was before you came in, and this is while you have been in here."

I was so happy, "She can feel me." I could hardly breathe. I wanted to rush back in there.

"James, this does not mean it's good. She isn't resting and healing. This is not good for her."

I put my hands to my face and rubbed up and down, "This is what she wants; she told me."

"James, she doesn't always do what is best for her; she mostly does what she wants. This wasn't good for her."

"Jake, you know that is what she needs."

"James, we'll take it slow. Give it an hour and you can try again, but if it affects her this way, we'll have to slow it down even more."

He was annoying the heck out of me. On one hand, I disliked him intensely, but on the other hand, there was also respect mixed in. I figured I better handle this with tact.

"Thank you. I know this is hard for you, but I do appreciate it."

I meandered back out to the waiting room and looked at everybody. I decided to try and get more from Sarah. I went to the other waiting room to see if I could sleep. I had to see her. I lay back on the chair and closed my eyes. I wanted to see her so bad. I was pushing for sleep, and it wouldn't come. I tried to take it slow, thinking about the fog and swirling it with our hands. I traced my face along her neck trying to take in her scent.

There she was. I smiled at her, but her expression didn't change. I moved closer, because I wanted to feel her. I was so close that I could put my arms around her. She looked at me with those haunting green eyes, and they were so appealing. I stretched out to touch her, but she was just out of reach, "Sarah, what can I do? I need to feel you and your touch."

I was next to her body and my lips were almost on hers, but I couldn't feel her, "Sarah, please tell me what it is you need."

I felt her move in me; her soul was in me. It didn't pass through like I did, it stayed and lingered. I could hardly breathe, "You need to feel more... what? Talk to me, Sarah; help me. I want to help you."

She moved away from me and was drifting way, "No, Sarah, don't go. Tell me what you want first. Something, don't go yet."

She turned to look at me, "*James, help me more.*"

As soon as she was gone I woke up. I was trembling. She was inside of me. Is this how she felt when I moved through her?

"James?"

Sam was watching me. I couldn't shake the trembling. I stood up and started to pace, "Sam, it's her. She is trying to tell me how to help her."

My phone buzzed. I was shaking so bad that I couldn't make it stop so I handed my phone to Sam, "Please, tell me what it says."

"James, you might want to look at this one."

I took the phone pleased with what it said, "*Mom, dad.*"

I started to pace, "When Jake lets us back in her room, her mom and dad will go in with me."

It was time to talk to them again. We walked back to the other waiting room. Dad's eyes connected with me, but I shook my head at him, heading over to Tucker and Laura, "I know all this is hard to believe, but she is trying to communicate with me. I didn't believe it myself at first. She is still not feeling anything, but she would like to see you next."

Laura started to cry, "How do you know?"

I held up my phone for her to see my last message.

"She is unconscious; she can't be doing that."

"I don't know how she is doing it, but it might be because she has part of my soul. I'm really not sure, but she is trying to communicate with me and she wants to see you."

Tucker was wiping the tears from his eyes.

"I know this is a lot to handle. Shit, she has been communicating with me for a little while now and this is freaking me out."

Paula was getting upset, "When?"

"As soon as Jake will allow us, he said in an hour from when I was back there."

I looked at my watch, "I am hoping in the next 15 minutes. If he doesn't come out we will go back. He seems to give in a little more when I push the issue."

Paula wanted more, "Are you sure you are not just wanting it so badly that you are making this happen? If you have feelings, than what else do you want?"

I went to look out the window again, "If it was what I wanted then it would have been me that she would want to see."

I smiled thinking about how stubborn my Sarah was about things. I was getting lost thinking about the house. How was I going to find that house? I would have to search high and low. Where was it? Up here, down in the cities, where could it be? I had to find our house, our dream. I closed my eyes and thought of her standing in front of me, and my arms wrapped around her... kissing her hand, and her fingers. Taking her hand in mine swirling the fog. I traced my hand over her face and she leaned into it.

"James?" The dream faded.

"James, its time."

I was relieved to see Jake.

He moved closer to me, "Did you see anything more?"

I smiled, "Yes, Sarah would like to see her parents if it would be okay."

He didn't seem to believe me.

I pulled out the phone and flipped it to the last message. He still had a hard time believing me, but with raising my eyebrows I tried to get the point across, "Told you, it's her."

I think he was starting to get it. I wasn't doing this for myself.

He turned to invite them back. I followed to the room. He handed us all gowns, which we put on, and then entered the room. I went to wash my hands again.

He was pulling out masks, "Jake, no. She will want to feel them."

He directed them both to wash their hands. They both moved to the sink, and I went to my sweet Sarah and whispered in her ear, "You asked, and they are here." I kissed her cheek and then her hand. They both moved to the other side.

"Tucker, you might want this side. She wants to feel you both. Kiss her and touch her. She needs to feel your love."

I moved to the large glass window looking down the hall. I wanted to be the one she wanted, but this time it was not my turn. I watched them talk to her, knowing they love her as much as I did. Selfishly, this was killing me. She wants them and not me.

Jake signaled for me, so I went to see what it was that he felt was important. He pointed at the charts, "See, it's not good for her."

I was confused because she needed to feel loved, so she would fight. Why was it doing bad things for her?

Jake spoke up, "Sorry, she needs to rest more."

I walked to the side Tucker was on, "Sarah, more rest. We'll be right here. I love you."

I kissed her forehead, and she moved to my lips, startling me.

"Jake, did you see that?"

"Yes, James, but look what it did to her."

I looked at the chart again and that made the lines go everywhere.

She was getting excited, "See, its good Jake. She wants to come back to us."

"James, she needs to heal, to rest. This really is not good for her."

"Okay, we'll wait longer."

He shook his head no, but said, "That would be better."

We walked down the hall to the waiting room. I went to my place by the window. I wanted to go back to sleep to see her to be with her, but I was tormenting myself.

Sam walked over to me, "James?"

"Yeah?"

"James, this is not good."

"What do you mean?"

"She is saying goodbye to them."

"What?"

"She is slowly letting go of the people she loves; I feel it."

"NO, she's not. She wants to feel them, so she has the desire to come back to us."

"No James, she is saying good bye."

I felt sick to my stomach. I was helping her say goodbye, "Sam, how do I stop her."

"She has um… five more, no six…no five, more people she wants to say good bye to."

"No, she's mine."

"James, do I have to remind you. You will die with her."

"No, Sam." I moved closer to him, to talk quieter to him, "Sam, tell me how to stop her, now."

"James, if it is chosen. I can't stop it."

"So, I am supposed to die?"

"No, you weren't, but she…"

"No, Sam. I don't believe you. Tell me how to stop her."

"One… To start with, don't let her say goodbye to anyone else."

"Okay, no more people to see her."

"That includes you, James. No more going in to see her, not till this changes."

"Oh Sam, I don't know if I can do that."

"James, you asked."

"Okay for now. What else?"

"Go talk to her in your dreams, threaten her, bribe her, or make a deal with her. She needs to show some improvements before you let anyone else in to see her."

"I can try."

"Go."

I walked back in to see Jake.

He was not happy, "James, no more it was too much."

"I know, Sam is stronger than me and he said she is saying good-bye. No more people to see her, not till we see improvements."

His eyes questioned me with surprise.

I sighed, "No, Jake, not even me. I have to go and make the deal with her. She has to start doing better if she wants to see anybody… Okay?"

"Yes, that sounds good to me. I didn't like what it was doing anyway."

"Thanks, Jake."

I went straight through the big waiting room to the little one where I was going to see my sweet, Sarah. I lay back in the chair and closed my eyes. I didn't coax the dream. I just rested till I dosed off. There was no need to hurry if she was trying to leave. The dream came faster than I thought. She was there, but I didn't move to her, keeping my distance. She was moving closer to me. I closed my eyes, and when I opened them again she was so close to me. Those beautiful green eyes were staring into mine.

I could see the dark circle that was around the green, but she was melting every part of me. I wanted to hold her.

"Help me."

I had to turn away from her. Her voice was softer more luring, "James, help me."

My heart was hurting with the wanting to grab her and hold her, but I had to be strong, "No, Sarah, not till you show improvements."

She was moving around me to find my face; I could almost feel the touch of her hand around my waist tracing the top of my pants, "Please, James."

"What do you want me to help you with, Sarah?"

I felt her touch me, and it sent a shock through me. I woke up not able to catch my breath.

My phone buzzed, and I opened it, "Carl"

"Not this time, baby."

I closed my eyes to calm myself. I wasn't budging this time. It didn't take long for the sleep to come. She was there again, but she was pouting.

"You don't want to help me?"

"Oh, yes, baby, I do. I want to so bad, but you have to show me you are going to fight to be stronger."

"How?"

I smiled, "I need to feel your touch, the real touch."

She put out her hand palm up, "Help me."

I moved closer to her to put my hand on hers. I couldn't feel her.

Her eyes were very sad, "Carl now?"

"Sarah, I can't feel you."

I felt one finger trace the palm of my hand. I put out my other hand. She put her hands under mine. I was looking into her eyes. I could feel a finger on each hand tracing mine. My breath was increasing. I was looking at her wanting to grab her and hold her. I tried to entangle our fingers. It was working. I could feel her. I took a step closer, "Sarah, baby, do you feel that?"

"I think so."

"Come on, baby, try really hard."

She extended her fingers and squeezed. I felt it, but I didn't know if she was feeling it.

I took another step closer, staring into her eyes, "Sarah, do you feel this?"

Her eyes brightened, "James, maybe a little, but I am so tired."

"Then sleep, Sarah. I will be here when you wake."

"Carl?"

"Maybe Jake."

"He's not next on my list."

"Your list for what?"

She moved to me and reached up to kiss my lips, I could feel her. I couldn't help myself. I pressed my open lips against her top lip and then her bottom lip. I felt the kiss, and it felt so good. I moved closer to deepen the kiss, and I let her hands go, so I could wrap my arms around her, but she was gone. I woke up in a panic. I got up and rushed out of the small waiting room, past the large waiting room and stopped at the desk, "I need to see Dr. Phallen, now please."

Jake answered his page immediately. He moved quickly to me with a touch of scolding in his voice, "James, you said you wouldn't see her."

"No, we need to look at her stats. Jake, please. I won't go near her."

He walked with me to her room. I looked at her longing for her, remembering how I was kissing her in our dreams, and how sweet it tasted.

"James, what?"

"She came to me in her dreams."

"What?"

"Just look over the last 15 to 20 minutes. Does anything look different?"

He was skimming down the chart. She was stronger here, and here, "but I'm afraid, James, that you're pushing too hard. She just really needs to rest."

"Jake it's not me. I fell asleep and she came to me. She wants me to help her say her goodbyes. I ignored her and walked away, and she was more aggressive. She was trying to feel me. We had a connection, and she felt me."

"James, turn her away and tell her to sleep. She has plenty of time to say goodbye or feel you. She really needs to sleep."

My phone buzzed; I shook my head as I opened it. He moved to look over my shoulder.

"Where are you?"

I heard him gasp. I shook my head, "I can't stay away from her. Tell me if you could?"

"Try texting her back."

"Who would I send it to?"

"Don't send it. Just type it. Tell her to rest."

I typed it, "Sarah, rest. I'll be there shortly."

"You shouldn't make promises like that."

"Jake, if I sleep I will see her. If I don't, she keeps this up."

"Go sleep and convince her to sleep, please. Do whatever you can do to make her rest."

"Jake, you said she was stronger in a couple of spots on that chart thingy."

"James, she needs to rest to heal. Just try to get her to rest, and tell her to quit saying good bye."

"Jake, if she tried to feel me, I promised her that I would let someone else see her."

"Who?"

"She wanted my dad; I promised you."

"I can't. I know she is saying goodbye. I can't say goodbye to her like this."

"Do you want me to send Carl in?"

"James, what if she says her goodbyes to everyone before she is doing better?"

"I am blaming you when she asks then."

"Fine, I don't care. Tell her she will have to wait awhile, because I said so."

"You got it."

I walked out. I knew he was going to go to her. I wanted to be there, but I would kill him if... I just had to leave.

I went to the large waiting room and walked to the window. It was starting to get light out. I glanced around the room at everyone. It seems like they were waiting for anything I could give them, so I gave them the good part, "Jake, said she had a couple of strong moments, but she needs to sleep."

I looked back out the window. My phone buzzed again.

I opened it.

"Please."

She was breaking my heart. I typed in, "Jake, won't let anyone."

I thought for sure he would try, but maybe it was too hard for him.

My phone buzzed again, "Why?"

"Because you need to rest."

I put my phone in my pocket; I couldn't answer it. I wouldn't allow myself to sleep to be with her. She needed rest. I went and sat on the couch. My phone buzzed again. I ignored it. Sam came and sat by me. My phone buzzed again. I took it out of my pocket resisting opening it to see what it said.

"Aren't you going to look?"

I am so miserable, "I can't... she will want to say goodbye to someone else, and I am not going to let her. She needs to sleep to get better."

"James, what if what she needs is you. Go sleep in the other room; go to her. I don't feel that it is bad that you do this."

"Really, Jake wants me to make her rest."

"But if she is determined and doesn't get any response..., James, go sleep. It will be better."

I got up and went to the small waiting room by myself. I closed my eyes and waited to sleep. I opened it to see what she had sent me. "Cayuse."

What did that mean? I closed my eyes again to wait. I found it very hard to let the sleep come. I was going to see her, and I would want to hold her. I think I was fighting it off for that reason.

# 7. James Can Save Me

## Jake:

**I** was evaluating her stats again. It did get better when he said he kissed her. I didn't want her to say good-bye, not yet. I knew she was technically married to him, but I love her... so I marked the chart and went to her. I held her hand and leaned to talk in her ear.

"Sarah, if you are trying to say goodbye to everyone you need to stop. You are going to live."

I kissed her cheek, oh that wasn't enough. I leaned to her ear, "Sarah, may I have one more dance?"

She squeezed my hand. I couldn't believe she responded to me. Oh my god, what do I do now, "Sarah, I will be right back."

I walked over to the chart and marked it. Then I pulled it out to look at it. It hadn't gone nuts like it did before, but she was stronger during that time.

I marked it again and went to her again, "Sarah, I am going to ask you questions. Squeeze my hand once for yes and two for no."

"Are you in any pain?" She squeezed twice. I took a deep breath.

"Sarah, do you love me?" I waited for her to squeeze, but nothing.

"Sarah, are you confused about how you feel about me?" She squeezed my hand once. Shit, now what am I going to do?

"Sarah, do you think you're going to die?"

Nothing. I shook my head, "Sarah, do you know James will die if you do?"

She squeezed twice. Now, I have to use him.

"Sarah, he gave you his soul. He will die with you if you do."

She squeezed my hand twice.

"Sarah, I wasn't asking you. I am telling you."

She squeezed my hand twice.

"Sarah, you need to rest. You need to sleep."

She squeezed my hand twice.

"Sarah, talk to me please."

I put my ear to her mouth.

"James, can save me...doesn't know how."

She was out. I tried to get her to come back to me, but she didn't move. I ran to the chart. I marked it and pulled it up to look at the whole thing. She did okay; she was stronger when she was communicating. Okay, this is way beyond what I knew. She just might live; it was looking a little better for her. She just needs to sleep. What did she mean, *'James could save her but didn't know how'*? Do I tell him this? If it will save her... yes.

I walked over and kissed her cheek, "Sarah, I will tell him. Hang on, baby."

I went to walk out and her vitals went haywire. I ran back to her, "Sarah, knock it off. I said I would tell him."

Everything evened out. She was stubborn even when she was out.

I went to find James. He wasn't in the big waiting area. They all jumped at the sight of me, but I couldn't say anything. I still didn't like the way things looked. I needed to talk to James. He said Sam was stronger so I wanted him to go with me, "Sam, can you show me where James is?"

"You're the doctor you should know."

"Sam, please come with me and show me where he is."

He got up rolling his eyes, "Sure, doc."

We headed down the hall together.

Sam wanted to know why I made him come with me, "So, what is up?"

"It will wait until we are with James." He had no idea that I wanted him there not only because he understood this better than me but also as some protection.

We entered the room; James was sitting with his head in his hands. He already knew I went to her.

"James, I had too; you said for me to talk to her."

He lifted his head, "I know; it's just hard."

"James, do you know what she said to me?"

"She talked to you?"

"Yes, but James, it was about you."

The pain on his face was hard to watch. I knew he loved her more than his own life and the best part was he didn't look like he was going to kill me anymore.

"James, she said you could save her, but you didn't know how."

He shook his head, "What the hell am I supposed to do?"

Sam stood up, "I need to talk to the elders and maybe dad. I will be back."

He walked out and left me alone with James. "I should really go back too... but James, I won't try to talk to her again. I am sorry."

"She talked to you. That is more important than how I feel about it." He put his head back in his hands.

I was confusing her. She was married now to him, and he did love her. I will try to stay as her doctor only.

## *James:*

She was confused about how she felt about him. She loves me. How can that be? We have so much desire to be together for the rest of our lives. She asked me to marry her. What is she confused about? I laid back and closed my eyes.

There she was, but she was so much sadder. I wanted to go to her, but it wasn't right. She looked at me with tears running down her cheeks.

"Sarah?"

"I am sorry, James, I love you. You need to come with me now. We will be together forever if you come with me now."

"Sarah, it's not the right time; we have to grow old together. We have to make little Sarah and James babies. We still have a lifetime to be together."

She was distressed by what I said, "James, what if there are no babies?"

"Will I still have you?"

"Yes."

"Then we'll have Mustang ponies, or puppies, or anything. All I want is to be with you."

She was moving to me, "Do you know what to do now?"

"No, Sarah, what am I supposed to do? Please tell me?"

"Love me."

"But I do, more than you know...more than anything."

"No, James, love me."

"Now? here?"

"Yes, it is you that will heal me inside faster than anything."

"I need to find a private room, Sarah. Can you hold on for a couple more minutes?"

"I am waiting for you."

"Can it be in our dreams or does it have to be real?"

"Our dreams are real, James. Please find me soon. I am really tired."

I woke immediately, and knew what I had to do. I had to find a place to be alone. I sneaked to the empty room Jake had pulled me into earlier. I locked the door. No, this wasn't going to work. I went to find Jake.

"James, we need to let her sleep."

"Jake, she told me how to save her."

"How?"

"You don't want to know." I couldn't look at him. He would not be happy that I had to do it this way. "Jake, if I promise to not touch her or go near her can I sit in her room with her? It would make it easier for me to do this."

"What are you going to do?"

"Jake, honestly, you don't want to know."

"Don't you think you should wait to hear from Sam and the elders?"

"Can I use my phone in here? I will call Sam."

"Yes, but not in the room."

I opened it and called Sam, "Have you talked to them?"

"Yes, it is a possibility, but James it might hurt her."

"She told me what would help her, but do you mean the same thing?"

"You need to make love to her."

"Sarah told me that; are you telling me it will hurt her?"

"It will only feel like it's hurting her; it will actually heal her from the inside out."

"That is what I needed to hear. Thanks Sam." I gave Jake a pleading look, "Jake, this will help."

I could see the hesitation as he asked, "Is it a supernatural kind of thing?"

"Yes, but you don't want to watch."

"Fine, it will save her?"

"Yes, please, Jake. Let me do this."

He walked me to her room. I pulled out the lounge chair, pulled the curtains shut, and stopped to wait for him to leave, "You don't want to watch. I am going to sit in this chair. You might want to shut the machines off."

"James, what are you going to do?"

"You don't want to know, but I have done it before." I was getting excited. I was going to hold my sweet Sarah.

He was looking very upset with me. I think he got the gist of it, "James she needs to rest."

"She will rest better after this."

He walked out with a lot of attitude. I peeked out the curtains and watched him walk until I couldn't see him anymore. I pulled the door shut and locked it.

I sat down in the chair and got comfortable. I wasn't quite asleep, but I was in that dream land because she was there.

She is so beautiful. She is standing there waiting for me. Her back is to me but she spoke, "I thought you weren't coming."

"Sarah, why would you think that?"

"You were taking too long."

She could make me smile. I walked to her, and then I traced my hand down her back. She was standing in the white gown I had bought her. As I moved close to her, I traced my hands down her arms and moved to kiss her neck. She wrapped her hand around my head to pull me closer to her. I traced my hand to her stomach and pulled her to feel my excitement to be with her.

"Auh, James, I need this."

I moved one strap off her shoulder to kiss it ever so lightly and moved up to kissing her neck. I traced the edge of the gown moving to kiss her so luring. She was healthier here in my dreams. I moved to her other shoulder and slipped the strap off of her. I kissed her tenderly. This perfect being was mine, heart, body, and soul.

I traced my hand around her neck and put it under her chin to pull her face to mine. I softly kissed her lips, encouraging her to open her mouth and accept my tongue. She turned in my arms and wrapped her arms and hands around my neck. I leaned down into her as I traced my hands around her waist placing my hands along her back, moving them slightly over her. I was completely melting with every touch. I wanted this to be the most wonderful feeling she had ever had. I swept my hands under her legs to lift her. The kiss was making me want to rush to be in her, but I had to go slow. My desire was so much more controllable when we were in this dream state. I laid her down. She squirmed a little. I released the kiss to see why she squirmed. She was happy; my heart felt like it was beating out of my chest. I gazed into her eyes and my enjoyment was taking over because I could feel her. I could lay with her right now and be totally satisfied not doing anything else. I searched her eyes, not sure if this was the right thing to do. I wanted to give her pleasure, and reminded myself, *slower James*. I traced my hands down her legs to the bottom of the gown and pulled it up as I stroked her lovely soft skin. I loved to look at her to find the desire in her eyes. I lifted one of her legs and used both hands to hold it. I kissed her inner thigh and she closed her eyes. I squeezed it with my hands as I kissed it with passion. I traced the back of my hand along her thigh closer to her. As I traced it over her, the heat coming from her made me want to be in her more. The heat was luring me into her. I turned to her more and put both my hands on her hips. I squeezed them to show her the desire she was giving me. My hands roamed restlessly over her body pushing the gown up further. I stopped just under her breast. I traced my hands over her stomach, and her ribs. I kneaded there to see if this felt good to her. Her emerald eyes held me captive. I needed to be closer to them, to sink into them, they were so incredibly deep. My heart was pounding out of my chest. I traced my hands down to her underpants and grazed my finger just under the edge of the lace. Glancing back up at her, I noticed how she bit her bottom lip as I slide them down and off of her. I went down to kiss her stomach, and traced my face over her to lick, suck, and kissed her till she was arching her back. I slide one arm under her to support her back. I pulled her to my mouth more, and couldn't help myself, but I had to be more aggressive here. I wanted her to feel complete pleasure from everything I could give her. She closed her eyes and was moaning. Her noises were making me hotter. She wrapped her legs around me, but traced her legs against my body. She was moaning more as her breathing was increasing. She was coming, and she was so ready for me. I wanted to be in her, but she needed to feel she had something to come home to.

I continued till she was almost screaming with pleasure, "James, now."

"No, baby, I have more."

I lowered her, but her legs were trembling a little. I traced my hands along her sides bringing the gown up and over her head. I was lowering my body to trace hers, and the heat was so luring. I was concentrating on her pleasure. I cupped her breast and move to her to taunt her. I licked her nipple and cupped the other one. Her hands were entangled in my hair pulling me to her more. I lowered to her again, and she opened her mouth to gasp for air. The moaning was returning with a vengeance. I moved to her again. The heat was too luring, that I pushed to her. I went into her so easily. I pushed as far as I could, and she gasped.

I stopped completely and traced my hand against her face asking her, "Pain?"

"No James, good."

I felt myself wanting to push harder and faster, but if this was for her I had to stay in control to go slow and move around, but she was pushing to me. I would move and she would push to me. I had to concentrate to stay slow with her. I found her lips and they engulfed mine; the touch of her tongue to my lips and then her lips moving to where it touched was too much. I was moving to her faster. Our kiss released so we could breathe. I would move to her and she was pushing to me. She squeezed me as I pushed to her. I moaned. I was supposed to be giving the pleasure, but she did things that made it feel so good for me. I moved to her again, and she squeezed again. I wasn't going to be able to go slow if she kept doing that. I stopped completely inside. She was still pushing to me. I kissed under her chin, her neck. I had to move to her. I pushed harder to her and her hands moved to my back as they clawed into me. It hurt but the desire was so strong. I pushed to her faster and harder. She was moaning with pleasure. I couldn't stop the rush, the release was coming. I felt her warmth around me and I released. She moaned and grabbed to hold me. I pushed a little more. The pleasure was so intense. I kissed her neck and her cheek. I pushed to her more. Oh, this felt so good. I wanted to hold her.

She whispered, "James, I must sleep now; it's too much."

I pushed to her. I wanted more and I didn't want this to be over. I was touching her and she felt me.

"No James, sleep." She was fading.

I was pleading with her to say, and then she was gone.

# 8. Competing

She left me. I felt hurt, sad, and lonely. I wanted to hold her to touch her more. After this I was never leaving her side again. They were going to have to tolerate me being here from now on. I unlocked the door and slid it open. I crawled back in the chair and closed my eyes. Nobody came in. I pushed the chair a little closer to her and closed my eyes. Again, nobody came in. I thought for sure Jake would be running in here the first chance he got. I pushed the chair closer and closed my eyes. Still no one came. I was really brave and moved the chair all the way to her bed and then, of course, I heard someone coming.

I hurried and sat down closing my eyes. I couldn't tell if it was Jake or the nurse, but they were not going to get me up, because I wasn't moving. They were checking her incisions; she didn't like what they were doing. I could tell by the noises my sweet Sarah was making. I wanted to stop them from poking at her; they were hurting her. All I could think was they should let her sleep, because that is what Jake said she needed the most.

She had been happy after I came to her, and she was peacefully sleeping, but now she wasn't. This person stormed out of the room. I peeked up as this person left; it definitely was a female nurse.

There was rushing back to the room, and it was the nurse again, but Jake was with her. I was worried again. I pushed the chair back and stood up. He was barking some orders to her and she rushed out of the room.

He turned on me, "James, what the hell did you do?"

"Why?"

"Because, I put a draining tub in for the poison, but it was supposed to seep out slowly. Now, it is like her body is pushing it out."

"That's a good thing, yes?"

He wasn't pleased, "Yeah, but no."

"Jake, she would sleep if they would quit poking at her."

"Okay, if you are done you can go now."

I looked straight into his eyes, "Jake, I'm not leaving her this time; she is my wife now. I am staying."

He was glaring at me, "I don't want you to get in the way."

"Jake, you want her alone without me here. I promise I won't get in anyone's way. If I do you have my permission to push me around."

He stood up more and walked towards me, "I am not afraid of you, so don't try to intimidate me."

"Jake, I wasn't. I would never be that stupid. If I hurt you or was even mean to you, I know I could lose her. She makes me want to be better than I am; so no, Jake, I am not doing anything like that, but I am not leaving either."

"So, if I... let's say... kissed her right now you wouldn't do anything to me?"

I tried to keep my face neutral, and my temper down. I sat down in the chair, "She's sleeping; how much are you going to do?"

He was trying to make me angry; maybe to get me kicked out. I wasn't going to fall for it. He whispered in her ear and kissed her cheek. I closed my eyes and sat back.

"James, stop that. I'm tired."

I got to my feet astonished that Sarah spoke. Jake... I knew Jake was as surprised as me. I grabbed her hand and kissed it.

"James, please. No more, I am so tired."

I leaned over her, "Sarah, Jake's here; do you want to say hi?"

I knew I had to let her know we weren't alone. I didn't want her talking about what we did in our dreams.

She opened her eyes a little and turned to look at him with the slightest movement. She smiled, "Hi, Jake."

She turned her head to me and tried to roll towards me, "You could have told me, James."

I couldn't help myself, and I laughed a little.

"Shit guys, this hurts. What did you do to me?"

Jake was trying to tuck pillows behind her to help her lay on her side.

"No, don't do that, this hurts too bad."

He started to pull them back out, so I helped her lay back.

"Shit, it feels like someone tore my insides out."

I took advantage of this, "Jake did it." I was gleaming.

"James, there is something else sore too."

"Sarah, I don't think now is a good time for discussing...."

"Then be nice to Jake."

"He's the one who kissed your cheek."

"You let him?"

"He was trying to make me jealous."

She was talking with her eyes closed. The joy I was feeling was over the top.

She smiled slightly, "Did it work?"

"Yes, it drove me crazy."

"Jake, you shouldn't do that, it's hard on my James."

She opened those beautiful eyes landing them on mine. They softened as she smiled and closed her eyes again.

"Jake, pain is bad."

"Okay, okay, Sarah."

He walked away. I stayed and held her hand bringing it to my face to kiss the back of it.

She opened her eyes again, "I must look horrible."

"You are the most beautiful person in the world, Sarah."

She smiled, but grimaced with pain.

"It's okay. He's getting you something."

"James, you saved me. You brought be back. You do know if you would have come with me, then it would have been me and you for eternity."

"Sarah, we will still have eternity."

"I'm not that great."

"Yes, you are and you're mine."

"My, Cayuse."

"Sarah, your ring. I have it."

She had her eyes closed and she grimaced.

"Sarah, pain or memory."

"We're married?"

"Sarah, we had to so I could sign the papers. We can get a divorce and get remarried when you're ready."

"No way, you're mine now." She smiled and then went to a grimace again.

"Sarah, is it the pain?"

"Yes, it's getting really bad, James. Shit, what did they do?"

"They had to take it all out."

"What out?"

"Everything, your appendix was leaking. Jake thinks it was leaking since I left. It was really bad."

"This feels really bad."

I smiled and touched her forehead, "Jake is getting you something."

She squeezed my hand so hard it hurt. I didn't pull away; I just endured it for her. Jake walked in with a shot and went to the other side looking at me very angrily. He was shoving it in her arm. She grimaced again. Her hand tightened; I didn't think she was this strong. It only took a couple of seconds and the grip lessened, her face softened, and then she was sleeping. I looked at him and let go of her hand and sat back down still glaring at him.

He smiled, "It's better for her if she sleeps through the pain."

"Yeah, I guess you're right."

"You know marrying her was wrong, don't you?"

"NO, it wasn't. You just didn't want it to be with me. If it would have been you, you would be perfectly fine with it."

"Yeah, I would be. I could give her everything she wants."

"Except for me."

He wasn't happy. I really didn't mean to hurt him, but he does want her.

"Don't you think you should go talk to everyone?"

"If I leave, are you going to let me come back in?"

"Probably not, shit. Yes, you are what she wants." He looked beaten. I didn't want to hurt him anymore. I know how I would feel if I lost. I got up to head out but stopped at the door just for a moment, "Jake, you... just thank you."

He nodded. I went out to talk to the family.

I walked out to the waiting room. They had helped Dad to the couch where Clarissa was curled up to him with her head in his lap. Dad went to wake Clarissa, "NO, she is still sleeping."

Jason sat up; Kylie was here now. She was sitting behind him holding him. She came to life when he sat up. Looking at Sam, I had to laugh. He was almost as tall as me and he was curled up in a chair. He wasn't moving. Now to Tucker and Laura; neither were sleeping and they weren't holding each other. They were on the same couch, but they were apart. Where was the passion? I squatted down between them, and put a hand on each of their knees.

"She is sleeping now, but she is going to be okay now. She woke up for about five minutes, but was starting to feel the pain so Jake gave her something to help her sleep and ease the pain."

Laura finally looked at me with compassion in her eyes, "How is she, really?"

"As stubborn as ever; she was scolding Jake and me."

Laura chuckled a little.

Tucker had questions too, "James, how bad is it really?"

"Sarah doesn't know yet, so we might want to be careful about what we say in front of her and we should wait to tell her."

I hesitated until he nodded, so I continued, "The incision is big, running almost across her completely from hip to hip, but low like a bikini line. There is another one going up almost half way to her bellybutton."

The tears were coming from his eyes, "Will she be able to have children?"

It was like a light bulb went on in my head. She had asked me if I would be with her without children. Shit, does she already know that? I looked at him confused, but it didn't matter.

"I didn't ask. It's not important because she is still alive."

"James, it is important to her."

I did feel the same way, but if she couldn't I still only wanted her, "Well, we'll just have to ask Jake that then, for her."

It was Laura's turn again, "James, what are you thinking, planning, because she is too young to be married?"

I knew that too, "If it's alright with you, I will take her home to Clarissa's with me. I will have Wilson to help me cook for her, so I can devote all my time to taking care of her."

They were not happy with this and I knew I needed to say more, "But, when she is well enough to do things on her own... she can go back to living at home with you, go to school, and be a teenager. I want her life to be as normal as it can be, and I will wait 'til she is older."

She looked a little more pleased with this.

"We will pay off her car with the money we have been saving for a house."

Tucker spoke up with this, "You two have an account together?"

I smiled at him, "Yes, we were planning for the future after she was 18. We were saving for a house, but we will use that money to pay for her car. I will have another year and a half to save for a house."

"She won't want to come home now."

"You don't know that."

Laura looked at me disapprovingly, "She won't want to be away from you."

I smiled; I did know that, "But, I will make it a priority to see her every day, even if it is only for a half hour. We'll do homework and go on dates."

Tucker laughed, "Yeah, good luck with that one. James, I am moving home in September."

"I will help you, but let's take care of her first."

They weren't getting mad at me. This was going way better than I could ever imagine.

"I am sorry, but I need to go back in there. I will come get you when she wakes up again."

Clarissa had gotten up and walked over to me, "James, honey, you need to eat something. If you are going to do all that and take care of her you have to keep your strength up. Let us take you downstairs to feed you."

I looked at her. I knew she was right, but I couldn't leave. I had a hard time just coming out here, "If you want to get me something that's fine, but I am not leaving. I need to go back in there."

I gave everybody a quick once over, but I knew I couldn't stay out here much longer. I had to get back to Sarah, so I headed back into her room.

I scooted the chair all the way to the bed and sat down. The nurse came in, so I pushed the chair back and stood back from them. I just watched what she was doing.

"Well, if you're going to be in here, come here."

I moved closer to the bed watching her.

"You're not squeamish about stuff are you?"

I shook my head. She was taking the bandage off, "I am changing the drain tube; are you going to be okay?"

"Yeah." I watched. "I haven't really seen it yet."

After taking the bandage off, she washed it. My heart was hurting for Sarah. She wasn't going to be happy about this at all. She liked to look good and this was bad. I kept my eyes on her taking her hand in mine bringing it to my mouth to kiss her. Thank god she was sleeping. There was a sack that the nurse changed out and then she put a new bandage on the incision.

"This is where you are going to help me. We need to turn her to try and get the poison to flow to the drain tub. We need the poison to stop seeping out of the incision."

I put Sarah's hand down and waited for directions.

She smiled while she asked, "So, you're married?"

I nodded watching what she was doing. She moved my hands where she wanted them.

"Isn't she young for that? Here, pull her to you."

I didn't look at the nurse because I was pulling Sarah to me, "Yeah spur of the moment."

"That's good; hold her there." She was tucking a bunch of pillows down behind her to hold her.

She glanced at me, "She's okay now, you can let go."

I took my hands off her. The nurse came to my side of the bed and moved Sarah's hands, so they wouldn't get tangled in the tubes and stuff.

She turned to me, "There, she should be good for a while. Let me know when she needs more pain meds."

I nodded, and she left the room. I traced the hair from her face more and kissed her cheek. I pulled the chair to her bed again, and put my hand through the bars and entangled my fingers with hers. I wanted to know if she moved. I leaned back and closed my eyes.

"James?'

Her voice came piercing to me. I stood up and moved to her.

"What's wrong?"

"Pain, James, please."

She was breaking my fingers again. I pushed the nurse button, but Jake came.

"Like clockwork, she needs more pain meds."

I smiled at him as he moved around the bed.

"Sarah, I am going to give you more meds; you will sleep more."

She didn't acknowledge Jake at all. Her eyes were scared and pleading as I held her there.

"Sarah, Jake is going to help you."

She didn't even smile this time.

"It's okay; this will help you."

She gripped harder when he gave her the shot. She was pulling me to her, so I leaned over.

"James, it hurts."

"I know, baby, just a little bit."

"No, it's burning inside me."

"What do you mean?"

"I feel it moving in me, and it burns, James."

I glanced at Jake. I couldn't tell him what I did, "Jake, can you go get Sam for me?"

"She shouldn't have any more visitors for a while."

"Jake, supernatural thing, please."

I tried to get her to focus on my eyes but she was crimping her face with pain, "James, it burns."

"Jake, please, now."

He left the room, so I traced my hand down her arm. I didn't know that was going to happen, "Sarah, please just hang on."

"You need to get it out of me. The burning is so bad."

"I don't know how. It's not real, Sarah, it was in our dreams."

She opened her eyes and was very angry with me, "James, it's real. Get it out."

"I can't even if it is. How am I supposed to get it out?"

"Shit, James, it is burning so bad."

She was actually relaxing. The pain meds must be working. Her face was relaxing.

"Sarah, are you feeling better?"

She was sleeping.

Sam came whirling into the room.

"What, James? What is it?"

"Sam, you said it may hurt her. What did you mean?"

"Well, if you are as powerful as me, it will burn the poison out."

"You didn't tell me that. The burning is hurting her."

"But it is also healing her."

"She was in a lot of pain."

"But it is healing her."

"Sam, I am hurting her."

"No, James. It just feels like it hurts. It is helping her." He grinned, "It must be working."

I sat back down and entangled my fingers with hers again.

He moved to the other side of the bed, "May I James?"

"What?"

"Feel?"

"No, what? No, Sam."

He did it anyway. He moved his hand under the covers and placed it on her stomach tracing over the incision, "James, it's almost all gone. Give her a little more time."

I shook my head, "You don't listen."

"And you need to learn. If you put it…" He raised his eyebrows and gestured in a way that I couldn't believe, "…on the incision, it will heal quicker."

"Okay, that is just sick."

"James, when you get her home, try it, she will be happier."

I shook my head. I couldn't believe he was suggesting that.

"If you have any more questions, or want to learn more I will be in the waiting room."

I just nodded and sat back in the chair. The next time she woke up I wanted her parents to see her. They really needed to. I closed my eyes to doze.

"James, I told you. You are in our way."
I didn't even hear them come in.
"James, you might want to think about going home and sleeping."
"Have you slept?"
"No."
"DR?" The nurse gave him away, so I smiled.
He wasn't happy with her, and he gave her a look, "Excuse us."
She looked at me and gave me a little wink before she walked out. I moved to stand next to him.
"You slept?" I couldn't help but grin.
"So did you!"
I was still smiling, "Yes, I did."
He turned to me, "Is this how it is going to be with us, competing?"
His eyes looked really familiar, like I almost knew him more than our brief meetings.
"Jake, I'm not competing; I already have her."
Now came the glare. He walked around the bed, "Hold her to you."
I followed his directions. He moved the pillows away. He put his hands to support her, "Okay."
He was looking at me slightly as he took off the bandages, "Have you seen this?"
"Yep."
"Does it bother you?"
"Nope."
He started to push on her stomach.
"Does this bother you?"
"What?"
"Me touching her?"
"Nope."
He started to wash the area clean, "It's slowing; I think we'll leave the bandage off."
"Jake, she was scratching at it. You might want to put one back on."
I didn't want her to see how bad it was. Not yet.
He traced his finger over the incision, "I took my time with it, so there should be very little scaring."
I was getting irritated now. The heat was building in me.
"You are sure this doesn't bother you."
I swallowed, "Nope. Does it bother you?"
"How would this bother me? I'm a doctor."
"I see you're wanting to be with her."
"Nope, can't desire something you never had."
"Are you talking her, or anyone?"
"Never did anything, ever. I would have kissed her if I knew how."

"Well, it's good you didn't know how then. I would have to hit you then." I was getting hotter. I was going to kill him, "Do you think you're better for her?"

He raised his eyebrows with a smirk on his face. He finally quit pushing my buttons to finish putting the new bandage on her.

She was waking a little. I leaned into her ear, "How is the burning?"

She lifted her hand to pull my face closer to hers. I let my cheek touch hers.

"Better."

"Can you stay awake to see your mom and dad? They are so worried."

"Yes, a little."

"I'll go get them."

"NO, James. Don't leave me."

I loved that she wanted me to stay, so I looked at Jake, "Do you mind?"

He walked out with a lot of attitude.

"Sarah, are you really okay now?"

"Yes, James, I am so sorry."

"For what?"

"We were supposed to be together."

"Sarah, we are together from now on, but we're still waiting 'til you're 18."

"James, we're married now."

"But it would be better to wait, and you're not winning this one."

Tucker and Paula walked in. I moved a little. She didn't want to let go of my hand. With my eyes, I tried to let her know that it would be okay.

Paula put her arm around my waist, "James, I am grateful for what you are doing. You must be very strong to wait."

My heart skipped a beat, but I recovered by moving away to get her a chair. I got one for Tucker too. I sat at the foot of the bed and rubbed her feet that were tucked under the covers. I wanted to make sure she knew I was very close to her and that I was never leaving her again..

Paula seemed worried, "James, you should go eat."

Sarah had that petrified look on her face so I couldn't leave her. I smiled at her, "I will wait till she is sleeping if you don't mind."

They hugged her and kissed her. Everything was going to be okay. They didn't discuss the plan to which I was thankful for. I knew that was going to be a challenge with my sweet Sarah. She was so determined to be with me, but she needed to have a normal life, even if we were already married. She was starting to dose off. I suggested they go and sleep awhile, so they could come back rested. It would be better to stay strong. I kissed my Sarah on her forehead and walked out with Tucker and Paula.

# 9. Frankenstein

**M**y days and nights ran together. I woke when she woke and slept when she slept. I had no idea of what day it was. Every time she woke she was a little stronger and stayed awake a little longer. When she started to feel pain, Jake was right there to put her back out. I was grateful, but the more time she was awake the more time he spent in the room with us. I didn't mind as much as long as he wasn't touching her. I was getting more irritated the more he talked to her. He touches her forehead, her hand, and her legs. It was too much for me to be comfortable with. People took turns seeing her when she was awake. I tolerated it only because she was so special, and people cared about her. Not as much as me, but I had to share because I was going to have her to myself soon enough.

While she was sleeping I decided I needed to stretch my legs and moved out to the waiting room. Clarissa and Dad were there. They looked like they had gone home and cleaned up. Dad wasn't using the wheel chair anymore and he looked great. Tucker and Paula looked better too. I went and sat with them. If I knew what they were going to talk to me about I would have avoided the whole thing.

I sat in a chair between them. Clarissa approached me.

"James, Paula is missing work and she needs to get back to the city. She wants Sarah closer to home."

I was agreeing with her.

"I talked to Jake and she is really not fully ready to be off of some of the medication."

"Well, I will stay and bring her home when she is ready."

"We know that, dear, but that won't be for a long time, so I have set it up to bring Jake home with us. He will stay in Will's room and help you."

I could not believe what she was saying. I didn't want him there. She was mine.

Completely irritated I complained, "He can't come home with us."

"James, he is and you will have to be strong enough to deal with it. She needs stuff and you are not able to give her what she needs medically. Paula will go home today and you will take Sarah home on Friday. Paula will be able to come to the house whenever she has time and you will allow her to see Sarah anytime she wants."

I agreed with that part of it, "Of course, anytime."

My sweet Sarah was coming home to be in my bed, and my arms. My emotions were a mixture of excitement and fear, but a little angry about this Jake thing.

"What day is it today?"

They all looked at me, "What, I have been sleeping when she sleeps."

Clarissa eased, "It's Wednesday."

"What time is it?"

"About 5 pm."

If Paula was leaving she should have time with Sara, "You should go wake her. She is doing better. She will want to see you before you go."

She got up and took Tucker with her. He was more torn over the whole thing, and yet very hard to read.

Clarissa directed me to the table where she was setting out food for me to eat. I was so hungry.

"When was the last time you ate, James?"

"I don't know, I think Saturday."

"What, how can you go that long without food?"

I shrugged my shoulders, "I was too busy to eat."

Dad came and sat by me, "You are going to have to do better than this if you are going to take care of her."

"I know, but Wilson will be there to help with the food, right?" I looked up at Clarissa to see if that would be correct.

She reassured me, "Yes."

My dad was firm, "Its time you learn, James."

"I know it is; there is so much, but I thought if I left I would lose everything. So... I didn't want to know about any of it. That way I wouldn't miss it."

"James, my blood still runs through you."

I realized I was going to be special for the rest of my life and I liked the idea of it.

"Sam is still stronger than me."

"Yes, but only because he learns, listens, and uses them."

"So, they will get stronger if I use them?"

"Yes, but you need to learn and stop using them before you know the outcome."

"Yes, father." I had a touch of sarcasm in my voice.

"Sarah is not the only one who is stubborn."

I chuckled, "Can we wait 'til Sarah is better?"

"Yes, because I am going to teach her too. She might have more control over you than I do."

I shook my head. Clarissa ran her hand through my hair. I closed my eyes. She has been so great; I wanted to get to know her, but after Sarah was better.

"I took care of the medical bills."

Unable to believe what she just said, "You didn't have too. I could have worked more and paid them myself."

"I know you could, but it wouldn't be a great start. You have to focus on getting her up and healthy."

"Thanks, mom." She pulled my head back so I could see that I made her happy.

The tears welled in her eyes, "You called me mom."

I stood up and hugged her. Dad came and wrapped his arms around us. There was always love growing up. Dad never held back from hugging us, and I was grateful for that.

"Guys, I need to get back to Sarah."

Paula and Tucker were talking with my sweet Sarah, but she was getting tired.

Tucker addressed me, "Jake gave her more pain meds."

"But she was doing okay?"

"She was getting warn out and the pain was increasing. I think she will sleep a while."

They kissed her and left, but reminding me Tucker would be back Thursday and Friday before we left and Paula would be by the house Friday night.

I was okay with whatever they wanted. When they left I found the chair.

I slept until morning waking a few times, but she was sleeping every time I had woken up. This time was different; she was looking at me. Those eyes melted me every time I saw them.

I smiled as I gazed at her.

"Hi."

"Hi."

"Hold me."

She was going to make this hard. I got up and moved closer to her. I wrapped my arm around her the best I could. She scooted over in the bed.

"Sarah no, I might hurt you."

She smiled, "Just come here and hold me."

"I will hold you as much as you want when we get home tomorrow."

"James, you are my husband. OH?" She put her hand to her mouth to cover it; there was a grin under it. "That sounds funny."

I grinned at her and shook my head, but let her win. I crawled into bed with her and wrapped my arms around her. She nuzzled into my shoulder. I rested my lips on her head.

Jake walked in, "James, you can't wait to get in bed with her?  Get out."

I smiled at her.

"Jake, I asked him to."

"No, Sarah; James, get out."

I started to move away from her.

She held tighter, "You don't have to listen.  I will tell you if anything hurts."

"Sarah, he's the boss."

"No I am.  I think I know when something hurts."

I smiled at her, "Sarah, you don't know how.  You won't tell me just so you get what you want.  He's the doc and he knows what's best for you."

I moved out of her bed, but continued to lean over the bed and held her hands looking at her."

"Sarah, before you go home tomorrow you need to get up and take a shower and use the bathroom.  I need you to be able to do those two things before we leave tomorrow."

"Yeah, I will do it."

"You have lots of people coming to see you today, so you will want to take a shower as soon as you can."

I looked at her happy.  She hadn't had very many visitors.  Jake must have called to let everyone know it was okay.  I wanted her to myself, but it was for her.  She wasn't looking happy though.

"Sarah?"

"No, James.  I don't want people to see me this way.  Please tell them no."

"Sarah, I will help you take a shower.  You will be as beautiful as usual."

"Great."

Jake was removing almost everything, tubing, hanging stuff and disconnecting monitors. "Brian, Danelle, and Tony are really excited to see you."

I looked at James begging him to not let them in.  He just smiled at me and it made me angry.

"Sarah, lay back."

I did what I was told, but huffed a little."

They both laughed a little.

"I am going to take the bandage off, so you can take a shower."

I looked at James.  He moved so quickly to my face cupping my cheeks making me look at him.  I knew it was bad if he was doing this.

"Sarah, it doesn't matter.  It will heal and Jake said there would be little scarring."

I tried to watch Jake, but James was holding my face to look at him.

"It's bad?"

"No, Sarah, it doesn't matter."

Jake was washing it off and then looked at us, "Sarah, it's beautiful if I might say so. I did beautiful work. It's already healing."

I pulled my face away from James. He let go of me, so I could look at Jake. James's face was so strained and Jake's face was happy. I needed to decide this for myself. I closed my eyes not wanting to see either of their faces any longer, "Both of you out."

Jake didn't get it at all, "Auh, if you're taking a shower we both can't leave."

I opened my eyes and glared at Jake, "Out!!!"

"Then don't move until I send in a nurse."

James was shaking his head no, "I am not leaving you."

"James, out please?"

"No, Sarah, what if you need something?"

"I need to see this without your faces looking at me."

Jake was more stubborn, "You cannot get out of bed without someone here. Promise you will stay in bed."

"I haven't been out of bed in a few days. I don't know if I can walk, so I will stay put."

James was more upset by me asking him to leave, "I can't leave you again, not yet." The sadness was overtaking his face.

I lifted his chin to connect with his eyes, "I need to see this without you here to tell me it's okay. Please, James."

The strain of being beaten was written on his face. He moved away from me and moved to the door without taking his eyes off of me.

I tried to stay confident that I wanted this so I gave him a sweet smile and gently said, "Out."

Jake was walking to the door, but didn't look back at me. As he passed James, he grabbed his arm to pull him out with him. I wanted the door closed and the curtains pulled, so I waited to look. The nurse walked in, "You're awake?"

I watched her. "So, I have met your husband. Did you know he doesn't leave... ever?"

I smiled.

"So, you want to take a shower?"

"No, I just didn't want them here when I look at the incision."

"Why? I have never seen anything done this well. Dr. Phallen is amazing and so young. He's got all of the nurses giddy over him."

That did make me laugh silently.

"So, did you look yet?"

"Nope."

"Well, what are you waiting for?"

"Scared."

"Do you want me to get the shower ready while you look?"

I nodded my head.

She went in the bathroom.

I looked down. I am a fricking Frankenstein. No wonder James was trying to keep it from me. Shit, I closed my eyes and the tears streamed out.

I didn't want to live my life with this scar. I wish he would have left with me when we had the chance to be together for eternity without scars or pain. This is so bad that I was finding it difficult to breathe.

The nurse came back out, but I couldn't look at her, "Are you ready for a shower now?"

I shook my head no and pulled the pillow over my face. I just wanted to be alone now.

"I'll come back, but don't do it on your own."

I nodded with my face in the pillow. I knew she left when I heard the door close.

A voice came to my ear, "Sarah, I told you I shouldn't leave."

"I'm the female version of Frankenstein." It was muffled, but he could hear me.

"Sarah, it will look better when it heals; nobody will be able to tell. Besides, Sarah, it just doesn't matter. I still get to have you."

"Why would you want to?"

"Because, I love you and that just doesn't matter."

I heard Jake, "She doesn't think it's good, and it is the best I've ever done."

I couldn't contain my disappointment making the crying turn to full out hysterical sobbing.

I heard James try to make Jake understand how I was feeling, "Jake, can you just…"

"What? Sarah it's beautiful. I stitched inside and out. It will heal so nicely."

I was screeching angrily while blubbering with sobs.

James understood that I needed time to take this all in, "Jake out please, give me a minute."

"She is that upset?"

"Yes, out. Close the curtain and don't let anyone in 'til I come get you."

"James, you have to behave; this is a hospital."

"Out, now."

I heard him leave and then I heard the door close and the key being turned and locked. The curtain was pulled. He was coming to scold me. I held the pillow tighter to my face.

"Sarah," he was kissing my hands.

"S-a-r-a-h."

"No, James, just let me be sad."

He pulled down on the pillow, "Please, Sarah."

I wasn't budging. He crawled into bed with me. He was coaxing me to put the pillow down. He pulled the pillow away from my face, but I kept my hands over my face, "James, I don't want to play. I am not happy looking like Frankenstein."

He started to kiss my lips, so softly, "Oh, god Sarah, I have missed your lips."

I moved my hands to his face to hold him, so I could feel his lips more as they moved so softly to mine. The kissing was working, as I melted with each touch of his lips and the warmth of his breath, as he moved down my neck and under my chin. I tilted my head back for more.

He was more aggressive with his nibbles and kisses, "Sarah, if I keep this up, I will need a shower."

When he lightly touched my stomach it made me flinch, but it was soft and gentle. As his hand roamed his mouth made its way back to my ear breathing into it, "See, we don't even notice it. It just doesn't matter."

I turned to face him to see his eyes, but I got more. I felt tingling in my lips, as his touch explored them until I captured his mouth for a very deep kiss. I taunted and he teased as we both smiled, and I didn't want it to stop.

He slowed, "Sarah, I will need a shower. I haven't touched you in so long."

I grinned with my kisses

"Oh, I like that much better." He rested his forehead on mine, "Are you ready for a shower?"

I couldn't talk, so I just nodded.

"Do you want me to get the nurse or do you want me to help you?"

I just looked at him leaving that for him to decide.

Slowly he slid away from me and off the bed. While he was moving away from me he did pull my legs with him moving me to the edge of the bed. I looked into his eyes, which showed a mixture of being nervous and happiness. We gave into our desires when he cupped my face in his hands leaning to me and I grabbed his shirt pulling him closer to me. Our lips met in a very heated moment causing warmth to fill my heart and body. He moved closer and was more intense. I was getting so wrapped up in him, but this hospital room was not the place for this.

He pulled my hips closer to the edge of the bed and then gripped them, "Sarah, I need to work on this control thing; it's been a while."

"Just look at the scar; that should take care of it."

He looked down with his forehead resting on mine; he moved his hands from my hips to trace the inside of my thighs, "this isn't helping."

"James, shower. I feel really gross right now."

"You smell sweet."

"You're lying."

I could see the mischief growing on his face with that flirty grin, "I really need to get the nurse, Sarah; I am really getting hot."

"James, please just try to behave."

"You're the one who is making me do it."

"I didn't make you do anything."

"Yes, you did. You had to know I still think you are attractive."

"Maybe with clothes on, without them I am Frankenstein."

"Sarah, stop. If I try any harder you're going to have to help ME in the shower."

He helped me slide off the bed to my feet, "How are you doing?"

I shrugged my shoulders and grabbed his arm. He took my hands and was going to lead me to the bathroom. I went to take a step and it really hurt. As the tears came to my eyes from the pain, panic filled my airways.

"Hurts?"

I nodded and held my breath.

"What do you want me to do?"

It hurt so bad that all I could do was look at him. I had no idea what we should do."

"Well, you cured my hotness."

I almost laughed, "Don't make me laugh, James; this fucking hurts."

"Sarah, can you stay there? I'll go get the nurse."

"NO, James, No. Just set me back on the bed."

He picked me up and lifted my legs to the bed, "Better?"

"Yeah, but I don't want to do that again."

"You need a shower. Do you want to cheat, and I will carry you to the bathroom?"

"No, I think we should get the nurse."

"That bad?" He looked like he felt so bad for me.

"Yes, James, that bad."

"Okay, I'll be right back."

He went and unlocked the door and pushed it open, but left the curtains pulled in front of the door.

He came back with the nurse and Jake was on her tail.

"What were you trying to do?"

"Walk to the bathroom."

"Sarah, you don't have to walk. Just stand and turn to sit in this wheel chair that can be wheeled into the Shower."

He looked at James, "See, you need us to take care of her. Stop trying to do things without us."

I didn't like that he was scolding James, "Jake, be nice. He helped me feel better."

"Sarah, you could make it worse by walking."

"Jake, please settle down. We got you as soon as I felt pain."

The nurse was laughing. They helped me stand and then sit. The nurse wheeled me into the bathroom closing the door, "Why do you talk to Dr. Phallen using his first name?"

"He was a friend before being my doctor. Sorry, I will try harder."

"No, we all think it is funny. He is so cute and all the nurses love that you guys do that. He doesn't seem so snooty."

Jake wasn't snooty! I didn't like that so I forced a smile.

"Do you want your husband to help you?'

I liked her better after that offer, "Really?"

"Yes, I will get him. Don't move."

"I will stay here, and it's James."

She walked out saying his name and returned with him in tow and showed him how to use the shower; the head could be used on the wall or you can take it down and use it. She left the bathroom. He stepped in front of me, "You are going to torture me."

I had no intention of teasing him now, "I have a hard time with you seeing me naked; its worse with someone I don't know."

He laughed and slowly untied the gown sliding it off me. Then he helped me with my underpants. This was really weird. He stepped out of the way and turned on the shower. He reached with his hand to pull it down and handed it to me. He closed the curtain, "Sarah, you have to do most of it. If I touch you I am going to go crazy."

"James, think Frankenstein."

"Now, you're making me angry. Hold the shower head away from your back; I am helping you."

I held it out and he came in. He took it from me, and then he tilted my head back soaking it with water. He handed the shower head back to me to hold. He washed my hair, tracing his fingers through it and then rinsing it. He took the bar of soap and put his hands in front of the hose to lather up, "Are you ready, because this is going to be too much for me."

He started with my hands and arms moving up; as he moved to my middle section he closed his eyes.

"James, stop, give me the soap I will do that myself."

He opened his eyes, "We were just getting to the good part."

Always making me feel desired I sighed and scolded, "Out, I will let you know when I am done."

He went out the curtain. This was really weird. I washed everywhere and rinsed. I reached to shut it off.

I heard the nurse, "Need help yet?"

James answered, "Yeah, I forgot. Her mom brought some clean clothes. Can you grab me the bag?"

I heard the door and he pulled back the curtain and started to help me wipe off. He slid the underpants over my feet and up as far as he could without me standing, but when we couldn't get any farther he pulled me up to stand there. He wiped me off more and squatted to help pull them up moving his face very close to my body. I was pleased that he stopped at my stomach long enough to kiss it tenderly. I was in heaven that he was still touching me.

The nurse spoke up again, "Need more help yet?"

"Nope, we're almost ready."

He helped me slip on a gown and tucked it around me. He moved behind me to towel dry my hair. He tilted my head back and toweled it more while leaning over me to touch my lips with his. It was very seductive as he whispered to me, "This is going to be easier when I get you home. I will come in with you and hold you."

I couldn't help myself thinking of it, so I had to ask, "Won't you get hotter?"

"There may be playing involved."

"Who's making it hard? I think you are making it harder on yourself."

He smiled and wheeled me out.

The nurse was sweet, "Oh, you look so much better and just in time; there are people here to see you. I changed your bedding and we'll just get you settled and let them in."

I wasn't ready, so I looked to James for comfort.

His eyes filled with brightness as he gazed into mine. He raised his eyebrows suggesting he would like more, "Sarah, you look great."

"I don't feel great."

"You're not supposed to."

# 10. Visitors

**D**anelle was walking in followed my Brian and Mykala.

I hated that they were here seeing me like this. I turned to plead with James, but his warm eyes settled me while his voice soothed me saying, "It's okay."

I grimaced, but it was with a smile.

Danelle came to the side James was on. She glared at him as she got closer, "You have been a bad boy."

"Why? What did I do?"

"She was supposed to talk to me before doing anything crazy."

He laughed, "We didn't have much time to consult with you. It was a spur of the moment thing."

She slowly sat on the bed being so light I couldn't feel the movement either.

She was still glaring at him, "I don't approve."

He was trying to win her over, "Danelle, you can still supervise until she is 18."

"James!" I didn't like him talking about it in front of people.

Brian moved close, but was holding Mykala's hand. He sat on the bed too, but kept Mykala in front of him. He did take my hand in his.

I looked at James wondering if he was okay with this. I wasn't surprised when he nodded and smiled at me, because he was so good at letting me know he loved me enough to be supportive and comforted by other people.

They told me how upset and worried everyone was. Jake came and sat on the bed behind Danelle, but put his hand on my foot.

I glanced at James again and I could see that this irritated him. I didn't like that he wasn't happy. I tried to get his attention then looking at Danelle and Jake to indicate what I was thinking. James wasn't getting my hint, but blew me away with what came out of his mouth.

"You should come stay with us for a weekend before school starts. Jake, when will Sarah be up for company?"

"James, she needs at least four weeks."

"That's perfect. Your mom and dad would be okay with it if Clarissa and my dad were there?"

"James?" I asked wondering what he was doing.

"It will be a slumber party."

"James, I don't know." Jake didn't seem to approve either.

"Sarah, we'll take it easy, but it would be a little fun before going back to school, and it's good for you to be around friends."

Danelle looked at me excited, "You would like that?"

I had to be happy about it now, "Of course," I tried to smile. I did want her to come and stay, but he was up to something and I didn't know what it was yet. "You! That would be great."

Brian took offence, "What about me?"

I squeezed his hand, "Only if Mykala comes."

I didn't want to leave her out. She was getting attached to him quite nicely. He knew he could come without her.

Jake was going to play along too, "We should invite Matt and all his beach buddies."

I looked at him disapprovingly, but he was smiling trying to play James's game. I was done with the games and I needed to sleep. I leaned back and rested my head. I could feel the tension in the room.

I heard James, "Yeah, we should keep it short. Lots of people want to see her today."

I opened my eyes sleepily to see James handing my phone to Danelle, "Here, put your phone number in it, so we can call you."

She did this and gave it back to him and then she hugged me.

Brian leaned in to hug me too, but whispered in my ear, "I am going to miss time with you."

I closed my eyes and as he let go I said, "Me too."

I opened my eyes to smile at him and noticed Jake was standing now and he was moving around Danelle.

James stood so he was right by Danelle stopping Jakes advancement. I saw James stop Jake with his foot, "Settle."

He looked at Danelle, "We will find activities and you can supervise."

Jake looked at James, "If she is supervising then I am in."

I don't think I was supposed to hear James, but he spoke quietly to Jake, "You are the only one I have to worry about."

I wish Jake wouldn't push my sweet Cayuse, but he grinned with a smirk before turning to walk them out.

I didn't want James to worry. I was in love with him completely, "James?"

He moved to sit on the bed facing me.

I reached for his face, "My sweet Cayuse, you don't have to worry about anyone. You are where I need you to be, home with me."

He lowered the bed so I could lay down more and then crawled in bed with me. I curled up to him.

"Sarah, I love you."

"James, no one could love me the way you do."

"As long as you know that."

I nuzzled in and closed my eyes, "I do, James."

I heard Jake walk in, "James, do you have to do that?"

"Jake, she needs to sleep a little."

"She needs to eat and go to the bathroom, or she isn't going home tomorrow."

"Just give her an hour or so, please Jake."

I nuzzled in more. James was being nice.

"Sarah, Sarah, baby. Tony is here."

I opened my eyes reluctantly. I was still in James's arms, and I looked up at him. I cuddled in more and closed my eyes again. I was too tired for any more.

James moved away a little propping me up.

I opened my eyes and Tony was sitting on the bed looking at me. He touched my face, "Oh, how James must hate me. I didn't feed you enough to keep you strong."

He kissed my cheek. Jake was sitting in the room, but in regular clothes now. I looked out the door and some of the nurses were peeking in the room giggling.

I raised my eyebrows with question, "Jake, you have a few admirers."

He stood up and pulled the curtain closed and then sat back down. James laughed. James was getting the moving table set and maneuvered it over the bed.

"Sarah, James is letting me feed you. Sit up." Tony was pleased to feed me.

"Oh, Tony, wait..." He was moving the bed up more, so I was sitting. I grimaced a little, because the pain was bad again.

Jake stood up and walked out.

Tony was nervous, but James spoke up, "Sarah is it bad?"

"A little."

"Jake said we had to lower the dose 'til you get home. Then he can give you all you need. It's just until you get out of here."

I grimaced again.

James was pulling the table back over.

Tony smiled and started to feed me. It was some kind of soup and it was very good.

"Tony, did you make this?"

"Nope, it was a special delivery."

I smiled as Wilson came to my mind.

He was talking to me as he fed me. I was very uncomfortable because the pain was getting worse. Tony could see it and he asked James, "How much does she have to eat?"

"Jake said the whole thing."

I grimaced. The pain was getting worse by the minute.

"James, it's bad."

"Sarah, 1-, 2-, 3-, breathe, baby. You have to try and deal with it."

Tony was trying to feed me more. "Sarah, I know you can't do the dances, but I am going to keep it up. It's really good for business. Jason will help me and Jake said he would come on Saturdays to help. Please don't be mad at me."

I loved this man. He was worried about upsetting me when it was his livelihood.

"No, Tony, never. I am happy it is working."

He touched my face lightly and tried to keep feeding me.

"James, it's really bad and I am going to be sick."

Tony got up, "I'll go get Jake." He went out.

I couldn't help it. I was going to gag.

"Sarah, swallow. You will tear something if you get sick. Just calm down and breathe through your nose. Stay calm. You can do this. You won't have to eat any more. You did really well. Sarah, look at me."

I opened my eyes, but the churning pain was turning my insides out. I wanted to scream. "James, no... bad."

He pushed the table out of the way, and took both my hands. "Sarah, squeeze my hands and breathe. You have to keep this down. The stitches will tear. Look at my eyes, Sarah."

I looked into his eyes seeing the strength in them.

"Sarah, breathe, you can get through this."

Jake walked in and Tony was behind him. I didn't take my eyes off of James.

"Jake, she needs something; she is in terrible pain."

"She has to have less, James."

"But she is going to get sick."

Jake moved to the other side of the bed and sat down, "Sarah, you can get through this."

I didn't take my eyes off of James, "Bucket."

He was being so strong, "Sarah, keep breathing and swallow. It will pass. Jake, get her something now." He was looking at me with very determined eyes but pleading to Jake, "Jake, please."

Jake got up and walked out.

"Is he getting something?"

"I don't know, baby,"

"James, it hurts. Help me, James. I am... I can't handle..."

Tony walked out. I didn't look, but I heard him. I couldn't take my eyes off of James, "How long will the pains last?"

"I don't know, baby."

Jake walked in and put a shot in my arm. I gagged.

"NO, Sarah, stop that right now. It will tear the incision. It will make it a lot worse. Now stop it. Your stomach isn't used to food, so it will take a little while; just calm down and the pain will go away in a minute."

I swallowed a few more times. James's eyes were steady on mine, "You scared Tony."

"I scared myself. This fucking hurts." The tears were running down my cheeks.

"See, when she is in pain she talks like a sailor." Jake laughed with this.

"Jake, this isn't funny. She is in pain."

"Sarah, knock it off. It isn't half as bad as it was. Toughen up a little."

I glared at him, "Don't be a doc ass."

I went back to look into James's eyes. The pain was getting a little better.

"Jake, go get Tony; she is getting better."

"Don't you feel what she does?"

"Yep."

"So, if she was in a lot of pain...?"

"Yep, and it was bad, but she is more important."

He was still looking in my eyes as I saw a slight smile twitch on his face.

"James, I'm sorry. You need to block me. Please."

"I can't anymore."

The pain was getting even better.

"Why?"

He smiled, "Better?"

I was disgusted, "James, why can't you block me anymore?"

"I gave you my soul one too many times, Sarah."

"James, you shouldn't have."

"Yeah, I know, but I couldn't live without you."

Tony walked in and came to my bed and looked at me, "Sarah, you scared the shit out of me."

I tried to make him feel better, "Better now."

He kissed my forehead, "I will go now, but, Sarah, please call me. I will worry until I see you again."

I touched his face and closed my eyes. I felt James lower the bed. I heard them talking, but I was so tired now.

# 11. Who Is What

**I** woke and looked around. James was in the chair sleeping and Jake was looking out the window.

"Jake?"

He turned to me and moved to the side of my bed, "Sorry about making you go through that, but if we are going to take you home tomorrow I have to show them you are making improvements."

I wasn't as strong as they wanted me to be, "Sorry."

"For what?"

"I can't go home tomorrow?"

"You still have a while, and we'll see how long you can go without pain meds this time. Are you doing okay?"

I nodded, but glanced over to James. I was relieved that he was sleeping.

"You do love him that much?"

"Jake, I do."

"You're breaking my heart."

"Jake, I didn't want to."

He came and sat on my bed looking at me, "Are you sure?"

"Yes, Jake, I am."

"It is really hard for me to see him with you. I just keep thinking…"

"No, Jake, it's not right. I love James, and I will be with him until the end of time."

He leaned in and traced his cheek on mine.

I closed my eyes enjoying his caress, but I had to push him away, "Jake, this will never happen. I love James." I touched his face, and he closed his eyes leaning into my touch. I wanted him to know that I did feel horrible about it, "I'm sorry."

This time I couldn't hold back the tears that were for him. I didn't want him to see I cared this much for him, so I pushed him away again.

He held firm, "but, Sarah." His desperate cry of longing came through.

I couldn't open my eyes, "Please, Jake, I am not worth it. Trust me on this one."

He wrapped his hand around my head to pull my lips to his. He didn't touch them just lingering there for a moment. I didn't want him to kiss me, but my heart was racing with the thought of his lips pressed to mine. Freedom filled me when he moved to kiss my forehead, "Jason and Kylie are next, but I will give you a little bit."

He got up and moved away from me. I saw the glare in Jake's eyes landing on James before he went out the door.

I adored my James. He was so patient when it came to me and my needs. I did love him so much. However, I still had to let go of Jake in my heart. I turned away from James to let Jake go. The tears leaked out and ran down my cheek. I tried to stop the pain in my heart. James didn't deserve this. James was my every desire in life and I wanted to be his.

He was there in an instant crawling in behind me. He wrapped himself around me and whispered in my ear, "I know baby, I know."

He kissed my cheek, but pulled my face to his wiping the tears.

"Oh, James. I am so sorry."

"Sarah, we will be okay. I feel it." He wiped my tears and kissed my lips so softly saying, "I have a confession."

Consuming James's sweet kisses I mouthed to him, "What?"

The kiss stopped, "The last two nights after Jake left you. I was desperate to make sure you loved me more than him. I came to you those nights for my selfishness, not because that is what you needed."

I started to kiss him again and slowed, "I am glad you did. I needed you."

He traced his fingers over my face and looked into my eyes, "You take my breath away, little girl."

I closed my eyes to enjoy my Cayuse holding me. I have needed this for so long. The pain was still there, but I did love my James so much.

"James, you can't even wait to get into bed with her. She hasn't even healed yet."

I opened my eyes locking with James's eyes. That voice was very familiar.

Jason was walking in, but James whispered to me, "Are you okay?"

Taking a deep breath and exhaled my answer, "As long as I have you."

He licked his lips as a flirty grin grew on his face as he rolled away from me out of the bed.

I heard Kylie next, "My turn." She crawled into bed with me very carefully and took my hand in hers. Jason and James backed away talking.

"Sarah, I kind of helped Jake undress you, so you are kind of like a little sister to me. I am sorry I was going to kill you. Jealousy does some pretty bad things."

I was very comfortable with Kylie now. I curled into her resting my head on her shoulder, "I would have done the same thing. Are things going better?"

"I am working on anger management. I love Jason and I don't want to hurt him again."

"Kylie, he is a good man, or he wouldn't have walked away from me."

"What?" She was a little put off.

"Kylie, what I mean is... he has standards that set him apart from creeps. You are lucky to have him."

"Oh, you were worrying me."

"You will never have to worry about me. I love James."

Jake walked in, "You people don't know how to stay out of her bed."

We all laughed, but the stomach hurt and I grimaced.

Kylie moved away a little, "No, Kylie, it's okay. Just don't make me laugh."

She scooted closer again.

"So, Jake tells us that we are having a slumber party in a month."

I still didn't like the idea of it, "Yeah, I guess so."

"We'll have fun. Play cards or something."

She must have known that I wasn't excited about having people around while I was like this.

After visiting with Jason and Kylie for a while the pain was creeping back in. The more uncomfortable I got the more my eyes moved to James. Finally he could tell I was almost to panic time. When James moved to me Kylie moved away. James took my hands in his, and calmed me with his deep dark brown eyes, while he spoke, "I know, baby, Jake, pain."

Jason came and sat on the other side of the bed and kissed my cheek whispering in my ear, "She is trying really hard."

I was happy for them both, but I was scared of the pain that was now throbbing. I squeezed James's hand as the pulse tore at my insides.

Jason stood up and put his arms around Kylie, "We should go, but we will see you in a month." They walked out. I am assuming they couldn't watch.

Jake moved to the bed, "How bad is it?"

I was trying to swallow to handle it, but I was gasping with taking in air, and slowly blowing it out.

James spoke to Jake for me, "Um, Jake, it's pretty bad."

He got up, "Sarah, you're not making it more than four hours. You have to try harder.

I leaned back and closed my eyes. James moved to me and started to lower the bed. I curled up as he sat on the bed and rubbed my back, "Jake, she will try to hold on a little longer, but please let me help her."

"What are you going to do?"

Even though he was talking to Jake, his eyes captured mine with warmth and understanding, "I'm just going to talk her through this; can you give us some alone time?"

He wasn't happy but left the room.

"Okay, Sarah, focus on the house. If I am going to find it I need to know what to look for. Close your eyes. Stay away from me and look around. I will see it too."

I closed my eyes. I was picturing the kitchen.

"That's it... the Kitchen. Now look around. I need to see it."

I was trying to concentrate. I started with the left side where the sink was. There was a dishwasher, but the rest of the wall was covered in cupboards. There was one window above the sink. It was quite large; I could see a barn off to the right, the lane to the left. Straight out there was a fenced in area.

I begged, "James, the pain."

"Keep going, Sarah, its good, but I need more."

I started again, but I moved to the left where there was a door to go to the rest of the house. I kept moving to the left. The rest of the appliances were here, the fridge and stove. There were also cupboards on this wall. At the end of this wall was a large closet; I walked to the end and looked past this area. I had never seen this before.

This time I pleaded, "Shit, James, that's all. I need something."

"No, Sarah, just relax. You are doing really well. Think more."

I tried to get back to it. It wasn't as clear, but there was a table with four chairs. The window on the other side was large and set out from the house. There was a bench to sit on along the window to look over the yard. There was a tire swing hanging from a tree. There were sliding doors to the left. This room was bright like a sunroom would be. And then everything went all black, "James, no more. I need something." I was curling up trying to hold my insides together.

"Okay, I will go get Jake."

I grabbed at him, "NO, just push the button. Don't leave me."

He continued to rub my back and pushed the button. The nurse came in.

"Where is Jake, I mean... Dr. Phallen?"

"He stepped out. Do you need something?"

"Yes, he knew she was in pain. Did he leave orders for pain meds?"

"No, I'll see what we can do."

"James, my phone... his number is on there."

He took my phone and called him, "Where are you?"

"She is in a lot of pain."

"Well, if you're not going to give her something, then get in here and watch her yourself."

"No, I am not kidding. Get your butt back here."

"Yes, now."

The nurse came back in. I'm sorry. We can't get a hold of him. I brought ice packs.

"James, no it hurts."

"Sarah, we need you to lay back."

I felt cold packs being packed around my mid section. I closed my eyes and bit my bottom lip to endure the pain.

I heard the nurse, "Are you okay?"

My James was feeling the pain.

"Yeah, I'm okay. Just help her."

I quit complaining; he knew how bad it was. He took my hand and leaned over the bed kissing it. He glanced up at me with worry wrinkles on his forehead and stress on his face, "Sarah, I am sorry."

I gripped his hand tightly and squeezed every time it pulsed. I wasn't going to complain, because he was feeling everything I was.

Jake walked in with a shot in his hand, "Sarah, this will only take the edge off. Once the pain is a little better you are switching to pills, and they don't work as fast, but if you are going home tomorrow you need to get off of these shots."

As he shoved the needle in my arm he noticed the pain on James's face, "You feel everything?"

"Um... Yeah, and if you are going to make her suffer than you better make damn sure you are here to see her."

"Okay, it's just that..."

"What?"

"This is very addictive, and I had to make sure she really needed it, not just wanted it."

"Well, she is in terrible pain. Fuck"

"Is that her or you?"

"Me, I feel the pain too."

I could hear them arguing, but I was just concentrating on the pain to breathe through it. It was starting to ease. They were still bickering as the pain lessened.

I was tired, "GUYS! Pain better; sleep now."

I didn't hear anything after that.

"Sarah, your dad's here."

I opened my eyes to the most beautiful man in the world. James was sitting on the bed waking me by gently caressing my cheek with the back of his hand. Then I noticed Jake was here sleeping it the windows ceil. The pain wasn't too bad so I wanted to stretch but settled for yawning. I gave James a weak smile, "He stayed?"

"I told him he had to. If he was changing the medication he had to see your pain even if he can't feel it."

"Was I that bad?"

James was not happy, "Yes!"

My Dad finally walked into the room. His hug was needed but the twinge of pain was not. I cringed a little sending my dad into a nervous twitch.

The nurse walked in with new ice packs for me, and noticed Jake sleeping in the window ceil. She smiled and spoke softly, "He's human."

Bighting my lips to hold back a laugh that would hurt me, I let her place the new ice packs around me. After she was done with me she walked over to where Jake was, "Dr. Phallen, we made you a cot in the other room."

He was startled and a little off balance, but he knew that James would be irritated by him leaving. In his attempts to get himself together he glanced at James for approval.

"Fine, but if it gets bad I am coming to get you."

Groggily he followed her, but stopped to look at the chart. He was talking to the nurse telling her to give me more in about an hour, so it wouldn't completely wear off.

Dad sat with me and we talked about how I didn't listen or follow orders, and that I would have to do better than this when I went home. He continued to lecture me on how everyone was trying to take care of me and I undermined them all. I just took it. I did give them all a scare, but they wouldn't have to deal with that anymore. I was going to be with James now, because we were married. I still let him go on and on all while wondering if he thought it was normal for married people to live apart.

It wasn't until he asked James, "So, have you talked to her about your plan?" that I panicked.

"Nope, I thought it would be better to wait till she was better." He was cautious with his reply to my dad.

Trying hard not to sound irritated, I asked with curiosity, "What plan?"

James was diverting my attention, "Sarah, we'll talk about it later. Just enjoy your time with your dad."

We did talk for quite a while. When Jake finally came back in he went straight to the window ceil keeping his attention on what was happing outside of the hospital. Watching him like this made me feel bad; he seemed so sad. I wanted to hug him and tell him he was going to be better without me, but I didn't want to upset my James. I wish James could block my feelings because he knew what I felt. I could see I hurt him again. I went back to talking with dad until Carl and Clarissa came in.

Clarissa was so elegant. Today she was wearing pants that looked like silk yoga pants. She had on a matching t-shirt with a zip up jacket over it. She seemed to glide across the room when she made her way to say hello to my dad, "So, Sarah is doing better."

Jake was bitter, "Only when she is drugged heavily."

She walked over to him and said something to him quietly. I was watching, but I was trying to listen to my dad at the same time.

Everyone seemed to be carrying on a conversation, but my eyes must have stayed shut longer than a blink, because the next thing I knew Dad was hugging me and saying his goodbyes. "I will see you in the morning then."

I didn't want to fall asleep, but I was a little foggy. I really didn't like this feeling, and I wanted it to stop. I grabbed James's hand wanting him to help me to shake this feeling. He moved closer so that he could wrap his arm around me and tucked my head into him with his other. I didn't want this; I wanted to shake off being tired, not for him to comfort me into sleeping.

Carl came to me and put his hands to cup my face, "You didn't come to see me last weekend."

"I wasn't well."

He smiled at me and moved to the Lounge chair. Clarissa went to sit with him, "Well, we need to discuss some family things."

My head was foggy, and the nurse walked in with the meds and a glass of water. Jake stood up and took them from her and gave them to me sitting on the bed in front of me. He took a flash light and shined it in my eyes, "Sarah, how are you feeling?"

"The pain is there, but numb."

"Good, but you're going to feel a little dizzy in the head."

"Yep, I already do." I was losing my balance.

"James, you might want to hold her up while you guys talk. I will go."

Clarissa stopped him before he left the room, "Jake sit, this involves you too."

Jake didn't understand how family business included him, so he was reluctant as he moved back to the window, this time just leaning there, as if to keep his personal feelings in check. James raised the bed and propped me up. What I really wanted to do was go to sleep. I was really foggy and my head was spinning.

"We have something to tell you boys. Sorry, Sarah, you will just have to tolerate this if you can, or you can go to sleep. It doesn't matter if you are awake, because this it is about the boys."

I was going to fight to stay awake no matter how I was feeling. I had to hear what she was going to say. I didn't want her to lecture Jake, and I didn't want her to scold James.

Jake stood up more attentive to what Clarissa wanted to talk about and asked, went back to the window ceil and was more attentive. "So, this is about the plan to take Sarah home?"

Clarissa was acting quit nervous, "No... um..." She sat with Carl, and he took her hand to encourage her.

"Well, James, when we had you, there was a lot of love. We wanted to be together, but as you know he was promised to someone else. I was devastated to hear this, so I left and your father stayed. You were the one that would follow in his footsteps, so I had to leave you with him. I went home to live with my parents. They were very supportive, but without your father I fell into a deep depression. I was weak and wanted him to come get me no matter what the price was. He didn't and I found comfort in another man's arms."

I could see how hearing this reminded him of our time apart, how I had done the same thing as his mother had done and how I hurt him so deeply. His eyes glanced to me making my heart hurt with regret.

Clarissa continued, "Okay, this is where it gets a little complicated. I got pregnant and had a child, so when Carl did finally come for me... well I was torn on what would be best for everyone. If we took this child with us he would not have special talents and would know there was something different. I had to make the second hardest decision in my life and I let him go. He went to be with his real father and I went back to Carl, where we had a glorious 3 more years before his father died. Carl had to take over and I had to leave, but I would only wait long enough for one of you to take over for him, James that is why your father pushed you so hard. It was because he wanted to come back to me sooner than later. The man that I found comfort with got married and his new wife took our son as her own. She loved him so much and helped him grow into a beautiful young man. She spent a lot of time teaching him. He was very smart and she developed that. I am telling you this, because… Jake, you are my son. James, Jake is your brother."

Not understanding the expression on James's face I took his hand in mine pulling it to my face and kissed it.

Jake went to her immediately, "I knew it. Deep down I knew. I didn't fit with her; I always hoped you were my mother. The time we spent coloring at the table, the games, the… Shit."

While Jake was showing that he was extremely pleased with the news James seemed confused or internally injured. I had never noticed how much James looked like his mother. It had always seemed to me that he was the spitting image of his dad, but now when I glance between him and Jake the similarities in them was from her, the narrow shape of their jaws, the broad shoulders that were narrower than Carl's, but similar to each others. Their eyes, though James were a deep brown, and Jakes were a mixture of greens and browns, it was the shape that had the same sadness to them. I shook my head in disbelief as I noticed the shape of their mouths, the slight dimple that echoed the corners of the smile. I shook my head feeling like I was in a dream and I took James's hand in mine entangling my fingers with his. Feeling James's hand in mine I remembered what it had felt like when Jake had comforted me with his. James eyes popped up to meet mine now full of misery, feeling what I had just remembered. I wanted to move closer to him; I truly only loved James, but when Jake had held me I did feel like I was in James's arms. He moved closer making it easier for me to reach him. He leaned closer and closer until he rested his forehead to mine. My head was swimming, my heart raced, and the love in his eyes filled me to the core. At this moment in time he and I only existed. It was us and only us together for the rest of our lives and we both knew, as if this was the completion to the union of two people into one.

Carl scolded, "And as far as for you two, no more sharing souls."

James's eyes closed while he took a deep breath sucking me into his lungs. I clung to him needing him to stay with me here in our own world. Everything would be fine as long as we had each other.

Carl's voice was sterner and directed at me, "Sarah, do you understand that if something happens to you, if you die, James will too?"

We had heard this all before, and we wouldn't have wanted it any other way. I would not live without him either. Butterflies danced in my stomach as a glimmer of satisfaction filled his eyes. We had no idea that what we had done would have this effect on us when we were doing it, but I don't think we would have done it any differently if we had known.

"James! Sarah!"

We both grinned but gave up on our little world to pay attention to them.

"James, when you gave her your soul it helped her?"

James was hesitant on replying, "Y-e-s."

"But when she got worse you gave her more?"

"Of course."

"But then she needed more. It wasn't lasting as long?"

He didn't answer right away, because he was thinking about it, "Yeah, I guess. I didn't pay attention to it."

"How many times like 5 or 6?"

He lowered his head peaking back up at me, "More like 20, 25 in the last five weeks."

"Shit, James. Okay, I need to explain something. Did she share her soul with you?"

He raised his head now to stare into my eyes; pleased that he already knew this but I still answered him, "Yes, while she was in surgery, but it wasn't the same... she stayed."

"Okay, you both have to learn the outcome of your actions and promise me you will learn before you use anymore of what you are capable of."

James looked at me like he was sorry. I didn't get why, not yet.

"James, since she did that, is it worse?"

He looked at me not wanting to answer it, "Yes."

"I thought it might be."

What? What was worse? I looked at him puzzled and I wanted to understand. He moved closer. The desire was in him, every muscle in his body was tense. I was going to find out more.

It was like the medicine and James were intoxicating my brain. The fogginess was taking over and I was having a hard time keeping my heavy lids open and on James. This was too much info and the darkness was taking over.

"Sarah?"

"Yeah, I'm okay."

"Sarah, you have to understand this." Carl had gotten up and moved to the side of the bed.

James backed away, so I reached for him, "NO, you don't. I need you."

He took my hand and moved it to his lips.

"Sarah, the desire to be with James... Has it gotten stronger?" Carl did not sound happy at all.

Thinking about my desire for James made me smile. Of course it has, because I love him, "Of course it has. Every day it grows. I love him more with each day."

"Sarah, every time he shared his soul with you it grew more. Almost like there is no option to the matter. You only want to be with him, almost a need to be with him."

Not knowing if he was telling me or asking me confused me, but I was happy about that, "Yes, of course. I love my Cayuse."

James was almost embarrassed and coward away from me.

"Sarah, when he shared his soul with you it became an obsession to be with him. It goes way beyond what you feel and want to feel."

What attention I could hold on to, moved to Carl, "So, when he did that he was putting a lock on me?"

"In a way, yes."

I was happy he loved me so much he wanted to hold onto me forever. Jake got up and walked out. James left me to follow him. Even though I was confused I could not hang on any longer. I closed my eyes and fell asleep dreaming of how much I loved him.

# 12. The Choice

## James:

"Jake, wait... I really didn't know that is what would happen. I don't know much about it."

He turned on me, "I can't compete with that. This whole thing is crap." He started walking away from me again. I wanted to let him go, but I knew I needed his help with her.

"Jake, please?"

He came back and pulled me into an empty room. He was very angry. "What, what do you want from me? You win. You have the prize. You gave her everything and now all she wants is you. It's done and over."

"Jake, I didn't know all this stuff either. I was walking away from it, and I thought I wouldn't have it if I left. I didn't use it to win her heart. I did it to keep her feeling better, happy for one, and not sick for the other."

"You didn't give her a choice."

"Jake, no matter what I used, she always had a choice. I always give her that option."

"She knows you feel everything; I would have kissed her and she would have kissed me back, but she was afraid of hurting you."

"Because she had a choice, brother."

"We are not brothers."

"We are and I need you just as much as she does, but you have a choice too. I hope you make the choice I want and need you to make." I couldn't argue with him any longer and I couldn't be away from Sarah one more minute, so I walked out. What the hell am I doing? I just begged him to come home with us to help me take care of her. He wanted to be with her, and I just invited him in. Fuck, what am I thinking? I calmed myself before I went in to face them. I said a quick prayer to myself that she chose me on her own. No more powers, I had to behave; she had to choose on her own.

    I walked back in. Clarissa and Dad were both sitting on the bed trying to talk to her. Dad seemed worried, "James, when Sarah gave her soul to you, did it linger?"

"Yes."

"So, the desire in you is unbearable."

They had no idea what I feel for Sarah.

Shaking their heads and saying together in unison, "There is going to be passion in your life."

I chuckled. What do you say to that?

Clarissa was concerned about the situation, "James, I am sorry. He is in love with her."

I already knew that, "Yes, he is."

"I warned him as so many others did."

"He also helped her."

"Yes, he did. Where is he?"

"I don't know. I asked him to come back. I didn't know that I was doing that to her when we did it. I just wanted to help her."

Dad put his hand on my shoulder, "Promise you will learn before doing anything in the future."

How could I refuse that?

"James, there is one more thing you need to know."

I didn't want to know what he was going to tell me. I didn't know if I could handle any more. I went to Sarah and touched her face. She smiled and pushed to my hand.

I really needed to know, "Does she really love me, or is it all I gave her?"

"That's what you need to understand. If she didn't already love you and want to be with you for the rest of your life, you wouldn't have been able to do that."

Relief filled my heart and tears filled my eyes. I have never cried before meeting my Sarah, and she touched me in so many ways. Feeling justified I asked, "Can you please tell Jake that? He thinks she didn't have a choice."

Dad shook his head, "You always have a choice."

"That's where that comes from." Both Clarissa and Dad wondered what I was talking about, so I continued, "Do you know that saying?"

He seemed to be deep in thought, "I had to tell myself that for many years." Dad got up and moved to Clarissa on the other side of the bed. I sat down and looked at my sweet Sarah, "I don't think Jake thinks she's ready to go home, and he's the boss of making sure she is okay medically."

"I'm glad you think so." He was walking back in. He didn't look happy, but he walked to Clarissa, "I have wanted you to be my mother since I was little. It always seemed that we had a connection that I couldn't explain."

She smiled at him and put her hand on his face. It bothered me a little; he didn't know either, but he got to spend time with her. It made me a little sad.

I was torn on asking this question, but I needed to know. "Jake, if you took everything out and put it back in..." I just looked at her. "Can she have children? I have seen five."

"You have seen a future with her?"

"Yes."

"James, she shouldn't."

I touched her face, "Okay, we won't."

Dad put his hand on my shoulder.

Jake tried to explain, "James, it's just that god put us together a certain way and when we take it all apart and try to put it back it doesn't want to fit the same. I tried to be really careful and there is always that chance, but it could cause her pain and we would have to watch very carefully to make sure it would grow."

"No, if it will hurt her....we won't. Can we wait to tell her until she is better? She wanted three." I put my face in my hands. I didn't know how I was going to tell her.

"James, Jake said there was a chance. You should wait until she is ready and then decide."

I didn't think it was a good idea to not tell her this, "It might be easier for her to know in advance, so she won't get her hopes up."

Speaking very clear and direct Clarissa pointed out, "She is very determined when she wants something."

I heard Jake, "Yeah."

We both sighed.

Clarissa and Dad got up, "We will leave for now, but James, remember you need to learn before doing anything else."

I knew they were right, but all I could think about was her.

As soon as they walked out Jake asked, "James, I have a few more questions. She is sleeping; do you mind if I go with them?"

I really didn't care if he stayed or left. I wanted to love her so bad my heart hurt. That soul exchanging wasn't good for her or me. The passion was going to be hard to get around and wait 'til she was 18. I crawled in bed and watched her sleeping. She was so sweet and I loved her so much. I traced my fingers on her cheek to just feel her skin.

A nurse came running in, "Where is Dr. Phallen?"

"He stepped out, why?"

"There is an emergency and they are asking for him."

I got up and grabbed Sarah's phone. I took one long glance at her and ran out of the room. As I passed the desk I directed Sarah's nurse, "If she wakes at all call me. I am downstairs with Jake, I mean Dr. Phallen."

As soon as I got to the elevators I called Jake, "Jake-go to the emergency room. Someone is hurt and they are asking for you."

I walked in the same time as Jake.
"What are you doing down here?"
"Looking for you."
I looked over his shoulder and noticed Danelle sitting in one of the examination rooms. I walked away from Jake into the room, "Danelle, what happened?"
Paul's face was grieved while holding a very pale Laura up, "Can you stay with Danelle? Laura isn't doing well."
"Of course." I sat down next to her and that was when Jake walked in.
He sat down in front of Danelle and examined her arm, "How did you do this?"
She smiled with her reply, "Basketball, I slipped."
I could see the concern for her in his eyes. He spoke softly to her explaining, "I am going to have to reset it."
"Is it painful?"
"Yes a little."
I was irritated, "So truthful."
Jakes reassured her, "I will give you something to numb it."
He scooted the chair across the room and then back.
Danelle needed me to stay with her; I could see it in her eyes as they met mine. I tried to give her a smile, but I don't think it was helping her so I asked, "Do you want me to stay?"
"Yes," she was also nodding.
He was going to give her a shot. She turned her head quickly to me. I cupped her face and held it to my chest.
Jake was fuming with anger. I didn't know what that was about but he needed to hurry up. "Jake just hurry." I mouthed to him, "Sarah."
That seemed to help him get past the irritation of me holding her.
Danelle didn't like the shot; she was still sniffling.
Jake was touching her arm turning it and twisting it. He left the room, so I had to ask, "How bad does it hurt?"
"It just freaked me out; it's not so bad."
"Do I need to bully anyone? I could be one of your resources."
She laughed with a sigh. I was trying to get her mind off of it.
"Do you feel a little weird? You were just here."
"Actually, I do feel weird seeing you without Sarah."
I agreed, "It is weird."
"Can I ask you a question?"
"Danelle, you just did."
"Don't be a jerk."
I rolled my eyes, "What?"
"Why do you want Sarah to wait 'til she is 18?"
Jake walked in as Danelle was asking. I really didn't want to say, but here it goes.
"I want her to know I love her enough to wait until she is completely ready."

"What if she is ready before she is 18?"

Jake's mouth turned up with a smirk. That irritated me beyond anything, but I answered anyway, "I don't know. I'm trying not to think about it."

"I can't believe you're not the jerk I thought you were. I usually read people better than that."

"There you go, brutally honest again. I swear that is what I love about you Danelle."

Jake was ready to take my head off. I could see that he didn't like me this close to her, and he didn't like that I was distracting her. I was starting to have fun with this.

As irritated as he was I thought he was going to blow a gasket. He was glaring at me, as he spoke to Danelle, "They won't make it; he can't stay out of her bed even after surgery."

"James!"

I knew he was trying to get me in trouble or keep her preoccupied. He looked funny at me in a funny way, indicating that he was distracting her.

"Danelle, do you think you will be able to come and stay with us for the weekend?"

"James, you want her to yourself all the time; why did you....ouch." Her attention was diverted to what Jake was doing to her arm.

He was pleased with himself, "It's all back in place; how are you doing?"

"That hurt."

"It would have hurt worse without the Novocain."

"Okay, Mr. Tough guy."

"I still have to put a cast on it. Do you want a specific color?"

"No." She sounded like that was childish.

I noticed his eyes stared into hers for the longest time before deciding what color, "Blue it is."

I could see more confusion on her face as she turned back to me. I really didn't want to point out that he was noticing her eyes. I was getting a few feelings from Jake and they were filled with thoughts of how her eyes made him feel safe, or calm. I could feel his heart race as he put the cast on her arm, but glanced up at her eyes quite a bit. Did he like her? Is that even a possibility? She was so young, and he was... I felt my eyes bulge as the realization came to me. Her little heart was doing the ratty tat tat every time he glanced up at her, and his just seem to speed up more and more. I didn't want to give away what I was feeling or seeing or maybe even both, but I could feel a grin growing on my face and there was no way to stop it. She could be the person to make Jake forget my Sarah.

Danelle brought me back to reality, "James, back to my question. Why did you invite a bunch of people to stay?"

"One, she likes to run. She is going to go stir crazy just being stuck in bed. Two, I need to distract her or she will talk me into something she shouldn't do. She is good at that as you know well."

Jake had to put his comments in, "Yeah, she will."

I really didn't like that he knew my Sarah that well. I didn't mean to glare at him but he was pleased to irritate me. He chuckled but kept going, "Ask her what she did to me at the race track."

I wanted more info, "Jake?"

"We went to her work to give them a note so that she wouldn't lose her job for not being able to work, but then she took me to a race track. They knew her there and let her drive on the track. She took the corners driving sideways. She is a little wild."

I don't think Jake liked that this information pleased me. I found it exciting that she liked driving fast. She keeps getting better. I will have to have her do that with me.

Jake explained further, "She made me drive crazy."

That did not make me happy, "She let you drive her car?"

"She lets a lot of people drive her car, James."

He was giving me the shut up stare with raised eyebrows. He didn't want me to reveal that he liked my Sarah. This was getting better and better. Giving into him I continued, "Okay, back to my reasons, three, I thought it would be good for her to see people having fun. She is obsessed with that."

"That's why she made me drive. She said I was too serious."

They spent way too much time together. I didn't like him again.

Danelle smiled funny, "She isn't going to like it. She only has one thing on her mind."

"Okay, back to being brutally honest; what is that?"

"Making you as happy as she is."

I was gleaming, "Danelle, do me a favor and tell her I am happy just being with her... without *that*."

"No, you're not. All guys want *that*."

When someone opens a door you have to take advantage of it. I couldn't help myself, "So, Jake, *that* is what you want?"

The look he gave me could have put me in a grave today. His glared sent daggers right through me while he replied,

"No, actually, I've been too busy for *that*. Danelle, do you want to know something before everyone else finds out?"

Jake was changing the subject and Danelle was excited to get the dirt before everyone else. "Sure."

"James and I are brothers."

She did not believe us, "You are not."

Both Jake and I enjoyed her reaction. I confirmed what Jake said, "Yep, we actually just found that out."

"You guys are picking on me."

Jake was persistent, "No, it's true."

Her eyes squinted still not believing us, "Does Sarah know?"

"Yep, she was there when Clarissa..."

Jake put his two cents in, "MOM"

I finished my sentence, "...told us."

She looked back and forth between us, "You guys are full of shit."

Jake was almost done, "Do you want to come upstairs and ask Sarah for yourself?"

"Yeah, but my mom and dad..."

Jake patted the last part, stood up, and left the room on a mission. He came back in with a wheel chair, "Here... sit. James, hold her hand like you're concerned."

I followed him holding Danelle's hand. Jake stopped at the counter, "I am taking her down for an x-ray."

"Dr. Phallen, we can do that for you."

"No, this is a friend of the family. I will take her myself."

He started pushing her down the hallway. As soon as we passed the corner he stopped and grabbed her hand to pull her out of the wheel chair and we ran to the elevators. When we got in the elevators, we all started to laugh. I watched both of them, and they were looking at each other laughing. Even though I felt like a third wheel it was the most fun I have had without my Sarah with me in a long time. We got out and walked briskly by the counter. He let go of her hand as we passed the nurse's station. I was bummed; that was very hopeful. We walked into Sarah's room, and as we did Sarah turned to see the three of us walk in together.

"Danelle!"

She smiled, and I couldn't help but smile too. She was happy.

"What are you doing here?"

Danelle held up her arm, as she walked to the bed.

"What did you do?"

"Basketball, I slipped."

"Where are your mom and dad?"

"Down stairs, and they don't know I am up here, but I have a question for you."

"What?"

"I think these two are giving me crap."

"They probably are."

"I think so. Are they brothers?"

"Danelle, they are full of it."

I couldn't believe what she was saying, "Sarah! Tell her." I was walking towards her to scold her, "That isn't even nice."

Jake was pleading too, "Come on, Sarah. Why are you doing that? After all the pain meds I gave you."

She smiled guiltily, "Gotcha."

Danelle was confused, "What?"

"Danelle, I am giving them a hard time for leaving me alone. They are brothers."

I moved to her wanting to crawl over top of her and scold her, but knew that was a bad idea. I moved up the bed and took her face in my hands to kiss her. Oh shit, this tastes so sweet, "You are so bad, little girl."

She was smiling with our kiss, "Don't leave me again."

Danelle was getting irritated, "No more than a year, and James, I warned you about the mushy stuff."

I stopped kissing her, but only so I could lean more to her ear and whispered, "He likes her."

"I know, shhhh, but they don't realize it yet."

We both smiled at each other.

"Okay, okay." I moved away from kissing her. Sarah grabbed my face and pulled me for more. I couldn't refuse, and I was so happy right now and she tasted so sweet.

I heard Jake, "See, no more than 6 months."

I couldn't help but chuckle as I let Sarah go.

She was looking at me puzzled, "6 months, 1 year, James, what are they talking about?"

Oops, she might get mad with this. I was going to be very careful, but Jake still thought it was funny.

"When you two will do *it*."

Oh shit, she is mad.

"James, why do you have to discuss this with everyone?"

"Sarah, I don't mean too, but I am proud to wait with you."

"Well, I don't give it a month of living together anyway." She was looking at me seductively.

"That will work because we're not..." Oh shit, the plan, not yet. She gave me a sad look.

"Danelle, I hope your arm is better in a month. Jake, can you please take her downstairs? I need to talk to my husband."

I was moving away from her. I followed them to the door and pulled it shut after they were out. I locked it and closed the curtains. I turned to look at her. I couldn't tell if she was sad or angry. I didn't move just standing there waiting; I knew the firing squad was coming.

"You don't want me to live with you?"

"Of course I do, but you need to be a teenager and do normal teenage things."

"James, this is not normal."

"You got me there." I didn't know what to say.

She lay back down and turned away from me. Now, what am I supposed to do? I sat in the chair. I hated being away from her, but I needed to feel her. It just gets so foggy when I am hot for her. I needed the distance to focus on what she was feeling right now. If I would get too close to her I might kiss her, and once I start kissing her... I'm so lost.

Why was he pushing me away? We finally can be together and it's legit. I am married to him. I didn't want to leave my mother, but we have to be together now. That's how it works. I don't have to hide to be with him anymore. It is our duty to each other now, to be together.

He crawled in behind me.

I huffed, "What took you so long?"

"I needed to feel your feelings. When I touch you they get foggy."

"Do you get it now?"

"Yes, No... Sarah, it's just..., I promised your mom and dad."

"How can you promise that without talking to me first?"

"Sarah, you weren't there to tell them. I had to make it okay for them. They love you and don't want you to get hurt."

"If you push me away, I will get hurt. Do you feel that?"

"Sarah, it's not like I'm going anywhere. We will see each other every day, even if it is for only a couple of minutes."

"But if I live with you we could be together every night. We don't have to do it. I can wait. I just don't want to be away from you."

He traced his face against my neck taking in my scent, "Sarah, I love everything about you, and I wouldn't be able to be in your bed and not want to make love to you. We wouldn't make it a day."

I turned to him, "Really?"

I couldn't hold back the tears. He was melting, and he was looking at me like he could take me right now. If I knew it wouldn't hurt I would beg him to. He closed his eyes and took in my scent again. He wasn't touching me at all but the tightness of his muscles told me this was hard for him. He was right; this desire thing is going to be hard.

"Sarah, when dad was telling us about the sharing of souls... I was wondering; how bad is it for you?"

"I hurt James, but if I didn't I would be pulling your clothes off and begging you, demanding you to take me right now."

"Mine is extremely bad too, and I need a shower right now."

I turned to him and unbuttoned his pants, "You could show me how to help you." I was tracing my finger along his boxers.

He closed his eyes, "Sarah, don't tease me. You will drive me crazy."

"James, I am your wife. Let me help you." I moved my hand to touch him, and his moan told me he liked me touching him.

His hand wrapped around mine but his eyes dug deep into me, "Sarah, I can't. I will want more and that wouldn't be good."

He moved away from me. He turned me down flat. I was hurt. I closed my eyes and hoped for sleep. It wasn't coming, and I was ashamed.

I curled up which was hard to do and it hurt.

"Sarah, what are you doing?"

I didn't reply. How could I tell him he hurt me. I was trying to hold the tears in and it was making it painful? I tried to calm myself and hold it back but I felt my stomach clinch as I held in a sob. He didn't try to make me feel better. He went into the bathroom when I didn't reply.

When he finally came out he made his way to me, "Sarah, why do you feel hurt when I am trying to be good? You know I love you." He was moving to lie next to me. His body was so relaxed now. His face came to my neck to breathe me in, but started to kiss me there. He was tender and luring.

"Why do you seduce me if you are going to walk away?"

He was nibbling on my ear, so I turned my face to him, "NO James. It hurts when you walk away."

He started to trace my lips with his, "I want..." Then a soft kiss to my lips, "You to..." He cupped my lips so lightly licking my lips as he traced over them. I was a goner. "Be so..." The kiss was getting more aggressive, his hand moved to my breast tracing his thumb against my nipple, "Ready for..." It was deep and strong in his kiss. "Me, you will open to me." The kiss was very deep and hard. We kissed for so long that he engulfed my every thought.

"James, you said I was ready for you. You didn't mean it?"

"Yes, and no, Sarah, but you should wait longer. You are just 16."

"Okay and you are 19."

He had a persuasive grin on his face, "Sarah, make a pact with me, no matter what to wait 'til you're 18."

I could not agree to that, "No, we were going to leave it to chance, and now we're married."

"So what is the rush?"

"I want to feel you like in our dreams."

"Sarah, do you think our dreams are real?"

"Yes."

"They're not, Sarah, but we both want it so bad that we make it real."

"NO James, they are real and you won't hurt me anymore, except for now."

He held my face to his, "I don't think they are. When you wanted me to help you with the healing from the inside, there was no scar, and you were healthier."

"Healthier?"

"Yeah, you weren't so skinny. Don't get me wrong, I love the way you look, but it's too perfect."

"So you're saying it won't be perfect?"

"I think you think it's going to be better than it really is."

"How can you being in me be less perfect?"

"In the dream, I can control myself. I can take my time and not loose control. Real life, I don't know if I can control myself. I might push too hard or too far and it might not feel as good as it does in the dream."

"James, your chest, every curve of every muscle that is touching me feels wonderful. When you touch me anywhere, it makes me quiver and it drives me crazy to have more. How can any of that not be perfect?"

"Because, if we wait; it will be better."

"How? Why won't you be with me?"

"I'm scared that I won't be as good as you imagine."

I pulled his arms around me, "I love you, James."

## 13. Dad's Understanding

"James."

"I'm right here, Jake is coming. He already knows."

Jake walked into the room, but I was already in agony. The pain was too much, dying would be easier.

"Sarah, don't think things like that."

"What was she thinking, James?"

"That dying would be easier."

He walked over and grabbed a shot, "Sarah, this is only enough to get you by until the pills work."

I didn't care; I was trembling from the pain.

James was rubbing my back lightly, but he was irritating me more than helping, "James, stop."

I was holding my breath to bear the pain. I moved my hand to my forehead to handle the strain in my face.

I heard Jake, "Sarah, you did so well. You made it almost 6 hours."

"I don't give a shit; this *fucking* hurts."

He tried to touch my shoulder, "Sarah?"

"Don't touch me, don't talk."

The edge was coming off, but it was still really bad.

"James, I don't know if we should take her home today. The car ride alone will be painful for her."

I didn't hear James say anything. I wanted to go home and be with him, but this was too much pain.

The nurse came in and walked over, so I could see her, "Sarah, I have ice packs. Can I put them around you?"

I was in so much pain that I just pleaded with my eyes. The tears trickled out. The ice packs were a welcomed numbness. I closed my eyes and tried to relax. I think it was not only the pain of the incision, but also of how tense my body was in handling the pain.

As soon as Jake saw some relief he came over with the pills and a glass of water, so I took them.

I heard the nurse, "Anything else Dr. Phallen?"

"No, that will be all, Stacy."

I heard her giggle as she walked out.

"Jake?"

I wasn't facing James, but he would understand my question.

"Yeah." He knelt down, so I could see his face.

"How come you never took the time to have a girlfriend?"

He smiled, "Because they all act like that."

"Like what?"

"Stupid and giddy."

"Why me then?"

I heard James stand up.

"Because you had James, so you didn't look at me that way. It was humbling to hang out with you and have fun without you laughing and giggling with everything I said. You acted more mature."

I heard James laugh and sit back down.

"Jake, I'm sorry. You're special and you will find someone as special as you are."

He gave me that sweet smile that made him look his age. He traced the back of his hand along my face.

I closed my eyes, "If you haven't already."

"What do you mean by that?"

"You'll see. It's right under your nose."

"Sarah, what are you thinking?"

"Jake, drugs are working; I'm not thinking."

I heard James laugh again. Without seeing his face I didn't know if he was getting it, but I did hear him move away from me.

"Do you know what she is talking about?"

He must have been asking James because he answered, "Nope." But I heard the laugh in his voice.

I was just setting the looking mode. Hum, that worked out well.

"James, what do you think about bringing her home?"

"Jake, you're the doctor. I trust you will make the right decision and we will do whatever you say. I trust you."

I couldn't help myself; I needed to give my opinion, "If it helps, I don't want to be here anymore."

I heard them both laugh, "I will go get everything ready. Sarah, when we leave we are going to drug you pretty heavily and bring a cooler of ice, Okay?"

"You're the boss."

I heard him leave and I heard my James get up and walk towards me. He slowly came around the bed, "You're feeling better."

I opened my eyes and he was squatting, so I could see his face. I reached out to touch it. He leaned into my hand.

"Sarah, you had me worried there for a minute."

"James, you know you have my heart."

"Yes, but when you do stuff like that it drives me crazy."

"James?"

"Yes."

"You might have to fight me off, but I will wait."

"Wait?"

"If you want me to wait until I'm 18, then we will wait."

"Oh." He sounded disappointed.

"You like when I push the issue?"

There was that sinful, adorable grin, "Yeah."

I confirmed aggressively, "You will still have to fight me off."

He laughed. "No, Sarah, you will have to fight me off."

"Do I still have to live at home though? I just want to be with you."

"Sarah, you are still in high school. Yes, you do."

I closed my eyes. I didn't have fighting in me today, "We'll talk about it later."

"So, you can argue with me better."

"Yep."

He laughed again.

"How is my little girl today?" Dad sounded downright chipper today.

But I was still in pain and couldn't turn to look at him.

James stood up, "She did really good last night and slept six hours in a row, but she is in a little pain right now. The drugs haven't had time to fully kick in yet." James was pulling a chair in front of me, "So, if you want her to see you, you will have to sit here. She's not moving."

I heard him walking to me. He sat down and took my hand, "You're in pain?"

"Yep, it's getting better though. Jake said he will make sure to give me enough when we get home, so I don't have a lapse in the pain meds like I do here."

He touched my face as only a dad could do, "I don't like to see you like this."

"Dad, you know me. I like to have excitement."

He laughed. I didn't, because I knew it would hurt.

"Yeah, well maybe now you will settle down a little."

"I'm married now; I have to settle down."

He cringed.

"Dad, stop that. I was giving you a hard time."

"Did James tell you the plan?"

"Yeah, he was trying to hide it, but it slipped out."

"Are you okay with that?"

"No, but are you guys giving me a choice?"

Both James and Dad answered at the same time, "NO."

Dad glanced at James for a brief moment then he said to me, "I do know one thing."

"What's that?"

"He loves you, and wants you to be happy."

"Yes, he does."

"You are too young to be married though." That scolding tone came out in his voice again.

"Dad, James saved me. It's not like we ran to Vegas."

He chuckled, "Are those drugs working? You're kind of funny this morning."

"I'm not foggy yet."

"What?"

"They make me a little dizzy. James, I need to move."

He came over to the side Dad was on and helped me roll over to my back. He lifted me more, so I wouldn't use any stomach muscles, "Do you want to sit up more?

"Yes."

He raised the bed for me, but watched for my expression. He tucked the ice packs around me again, "You okay?"

"I found the fog."

He leaned over me, "You're feeling the drugs?"

"Yep, and they are really kicking me in the head." I closed my eyes and tried to shake them off.

He leaned me back and lowered the bed a little more.

"That okay?"

"Yeah."

Dad was concerned, "How much is he giving her?"

"The pain is really bad, so quite a bit."

"So, James, do you feel it too…when she is in pain?"

James attention was on me with that gorgeous grin but tried explaining it as I focused my eyes on his, "Yes, I do, but it's a little different. I feel it in her, so it's not so bad for me…accept if she is calling for me or begging me to help her. She sometimes pushes it at me."

"I do?"

His eyes widened when he confirmed it, "Yes, you do."

"I'm sorry."

He laughed, "It's still not as bad as what you feel."

Dad seemed to be confused by our connection, "Does Jake give you pain meds too then?"

"No, it wouldn't help. Mine are not real."

Dad was trying to understand, "You two are that connected?"

We both answered, "Yes."

"I am not going to get used to this; it's weird."

I could see a glimmer of happiness as he replied to my dad, "The funny thing about it is I didn't know that I was doing it."

"What do you mean?"

"When she was getting sick she would call to me, and I would give her my soul to help her deal with it."

"Okay, how does that work?"

"It's like, I don't know how to explain it, but I could move through her. She did better after I did that. I just concentrate really hard about making her better and it just happens."

"But, it's not good for either of you."

"Nope, but I didn't know that at the time. The more she needed it the more I did it. It seemed to help her fight it off. Sarah, how many days did you go without getting sick?"

"I got up to 10 days in a row."

"That's why I did it. I thought it was making her better. It really helped her body fight the infection until it was so bad that nothing worked. I gave my soul to her three times that night alone."

I really didn't believe it, "You did?"

"You were really bad, and I wasn't going to lose you. It was the only thing I could do."

"I didn't know that."

"I even asked Sam to do it. He is so much stronger than me, so he could have focused it all on one area."

"Okay, this is way over my head. James, the connection between you and Sarah…" James's attention came back to me with satisfaction. "…Is because you did this so many times. Wouldn't Sam be connected with her then?"

James was shaking his head, "Yes, he would have and he knew he wouldn't be able to handle the desire for her and refused to help me. I didn't care what the price was; I just didn't want her to die."

"You would have died with her, right?"

"Yep."

"And he still refused?"

"Tucker, he had to. He is supposed to be Chief and if he would have connected with her, he could have died too."

"Okay, well that's a little scary."

"That night was very scary." I could see a hint of disgust with himself. "Tucker, I almost let her die."

"Why? What do you mean?"

"I would have gone with her and I was holding her. For a brief moment it felt like this was the best way to go holding her in my arms."

The fogginess was really thick making is hard for me to stay focused, but I really think he seriously thought about giving into death just so we could be together for eternity. This made me want to kiss him so badly right now.

He gave me a stern look, "Not now, Sarah." But I saw the corners of his mouth turn up.

Dad was edgy, "What?"

"She loves me and wanted to kiss me, but she is really foggy."

"You can hear her?"

"Sometimes it's stronger than others, but mostly I sense her feelings."

"Thank you for not letting her die; I have a feeling you will take very good care of her."

"Now that we are connected, after she is better she probably won't even get sick anymore."

"Really?"

"Yeah, we don't get sick."

"At all?"

"Nope."

"Then how do you die?"

"When it is my time, I will approach it and walk to it."

"When will you know?"

"I still have to learn that."

"Oh."

"Tucker, I thought by leaving I was leaving all that behind. I didn't know I would still have it. So, I have a lot to learn."

I was enjoying this. It was like being told a fairy tale, and the fogginess was making it enchanting.

James seemed concerned, "Are you feeling okay?"

"You feel me, so you know."

"Shit, I'll be right back."

"What?"

"I need to get Jake."

He left the room and dad came to sit on the bed with me. I glanced up seeing a halo around my father's head.

"Do you feel okay?"

"Just dreamy, Dad."

Jake came back in with James and came to my bed. He flashed the light in my eyes, but I had to close them. He held them open and grabbed my wrist, "Maybe I'll give her less next time; she needs to sleep now."

I could tell he didn't like how I looked and then he was floating to James as I felt dad kiss me and my bed went lower. I felt so dreamy.

# 14. Unwanted Surprise

### James:

"How did you ever convince them it was okay for her to leave in this state?"

"James, those people are from a hick town and don't realize that this is bad. They would have listened to anything I said."

I had to laugh. They all did think he was the best thing they had ever seen. We were on our way home. Sarah was sleeping in the back seat. We had her packed down with ice packs and she was out cold. I was a little uncomfortable with Jake, but if we were brothers we had to try to along.

"So what was she like?"

"Who?"

"Clarissa?"

"You mean mom?"

"Jake, she left us and I didn't know she was alive till about 2 months ago, so I am having a harder time with it. Please, let me call her what I need to."

"Fine, but she was great. I would go to work with my Dad and she would play with me. She played tag, board games, and she even colored with me. She talked to me like a real person not like a child. She asked me how I felt all the time and we discussed things."

"Your dad?"

"Yeah, he has been working for Clarissa since I was born."

"Wilson is your dad?"

"Yeah," he laughed. "Why?"

"I love your dad. He is a great man."

"Yeah, he is, but you heard her. She only loved your dad. My dad couldn't let go of her, so he took care of her."

"Please, don't do that with Sarah."

"What?"

"You love her, and want to take care of her, but Jake you deserve to have someone who loves you back."

He smiled, "Yeah, you're probably right. She is going to be hard to get over."

"Jake, I really appreciate you taking care of her now with me."

"I know, but it's hard."

"I'm sorry."

He seemed okay with this for now.

All of a sudden I felt her.

"Jake, you have to pull over. Shit."

"What?"

"She is dreaming. You have.... Oh shit. Pull over."

He was moving to the side of the road.

"What, James...?"

I opened the door and got out, "Jake, wake her up now."

"Why, what is going on?"

I pleaded with Jake to wake her because she was going to have her way with me, "Jake, wake her NOW! Please."

I turned away from him and leaned with my back to the truck bending over. Oh, my god, little girl, you are going to drive me crazy. I could hear him trying to wake her. Oh shit, she has to quit dreaming. I couldn't stop it, and she wanted more. Shit, "Jake, wake her *now*!"

"James, what is going on now?"

"Slap her, shake her, do anything you need to do to wake her up right now!"

Oh, shit. This isn't good. I have to break this connection. I closed my eyes. *Sarah, stop. Jake is in the room. Sarah, please no, Jake is watching.* She was still taunting me kissing under my chin, my neck, tracing her hands down my chest. Her kisses began to move south, and to my amazement her thoughts didn't involve clothes. I had to try again. I cupped her face pulling her up to get her attention. I needed to be very direct, *"Sarah, you have to stop. Jake is in the room with us."* That grin was sinful and she wasn't going to listen to what I was telling her. She wasn't going to stop until she was satisfied. Her mouth followed her hands licking and sucking her way down again. I was in complete pleasure. If I would have been alone, I would have really enjoyed this, but oh shit.

I pulled myself out of the dream and turned to the truck gripping the side of the truck bed and begged Jake this time, "Jake, please wake her now."

He yelled at me, "I am trying, but she isn't budging. What is going on?"

I had to focus on her if I was going to get her to stop. Shit, we're not going to make it until she's 18 if she does this to me in her sleep. Fuck!

That was it, I was completely hers. I leaned my face to the side of the truck, "Jake any luck?" It came out muffled. I started to concentrate on her, giving her pleasure because she wasn't going to stop until she was happy. I closed my eyes and thought about giving her what she wanted. I needed to make her feel special, loved. I took control of making love to her, starting with kissing every inch of her until she melted into my arms. It was a little weird; I thought we were standing and the next thing I knew we were sitting at the house as she sank to engulf me. My mind wondered to the real world thinking *how was I going to explain this one?* I begged once more, "Jake, how about now?"

"NO!"

Shit, here it goes. I held her firm yet tenderly as we moved together. The intense desire was filling me as our bodies rolled together. She wasn't satisfied pulling and pushing to get closer, deeper; she wanted more. I needed to do better to make her happy. I gave into to her completely. Caressing her body, gliding my hands everywhere, I needed to give her everything I had, and that is when she finally began to feel satisfaction. Her gasps between my consumption of her mouth released small high pitch moans of 'yeses'. I knew I was getting her to where she wanted to be. The closer she got to complete release the more I paid attention to what made her escalate. I did what pleased her most over and over until she pushed to me hard and wrapped her arms so tightly around me. I was completely relieved that she was feeling good now. I thought deeply of moving my hands to her neck to kiss and linger there and then to her lips. She had to be happy, or I would endure more.

I felt her, "James, I'm tired now. I must sleep."

OH, shit! Just like that she let me go. I fell to my knees. Fuck, Sarah.

Jake was coming around the Truck, "She won't wake up. What happened?"

"Jake, can you hand me my bag?"

He grabbed it out of the back and set it next to me.

"Jake, get in the truck. I will be right back."

He was hesitant to leave me kneeling on the ground, but he moved slowly back to the driver's side of the truck but kept his eyes on me.

I got up and looked for a good place to change clothes. I held the bag in front of me and walked a little ways finding a place where I could have some privacy. I am going to have to talk to her about this. No more dreaming, especially if I am at school or working; that would be really bad. I walked back to the truck and threw my bag in the back and got in. I glanced over the seat at her and she was smiling. I shook my head and as I turned back forward I noticed Jake staring at me. I knew he wanted to ask me questions. I stopped him before he could ask, "Jake, you don't want to know. Let's just go home."

He pulled out and I leaned back and closed my eyes. I can't believe she did that to me. I was feeling really good, but really embarrassed.

We drove in silence until we were north of the cities. He couldn't stand it anymore. I looked over the back of the seat and she was still smiling.

Jake huffed out, "Are you going to tell me what happened?"

"Jake, honestly, you don't want to know."

"Honestly, I do."

"Jake, the way you feel about her, you won't like it."

"But I need to know."

Trying to think of the best way to explain it, knowing this would hurt him, but then again maybe he will see the connection.

"Jake, she was dreaming." I tried to give him a suggestive gesture.

"And you feel her dreams?"

"Yeah." I raised my eyebrows.

"And she was dreaming of..."

"About????" I tilted my head and rolled my eyes. I really didn't want to say it. I was waiting for him to get it.

"James! She was dreaming about being with you?"

I cringed, "Yeah."

"She can do that to you?"

"I feel what she feels."

"Oh shit, does she do that often?"

"No, not really, but we might want to give her less drugs."

"Okay." He was surprised and laughing at the same time.

"I usually can tell her no, but I think the drugs didn't help me with that."

"You can tell her no."

"Yes, most of the time. Like when you stayed with her, when she was lonely for me. I had to tell her '*no*' a lot. I was studying and working really hard to come home early."

"James, I am so sorry."

"Jake, you helped her. I didn't like it, but I had to let it go because it was what she needed, and I am grateful for that."

"I would be angry."

"I was, but I love her enough that I had to let her have you."

"I didn't kiss her."

"You did when we were at Tony's"

He stared straight forward not knowing what to say, but I knew how he felt through Sarah.

"I only kissed her because I didn't want her to be with you. I thought you two were going to do it. I was trying to stop her."

"We kind of have, it's just not real yet."

"What do you mean?"

"We have our dreams and sometimes they are very real. Like when I wanted you to wake her up. She was dreaming and it was real for me. I couldn't stop her."

"So, is it real for her?"

Not knowing for sure it still made me happy, "Kind of."

"So, why haven't you done it for real?"

"Truthfully?"

He smiled, "Yeah."

"I am afraid I won't be as good. In dream land everything is perfect. Reality, it's not going to be that good."

"What do you mean?"

"It's easier to be perfect; it's a dream. Real, the desire is too strong and I might not be able to control myself and I might hurt her."

He grinned with satisfaction, "You are afraid you won't be good."

I laughed, "That too."

"Wow, so why 18?"

"She will be an adult."

"Is that it?"

"Yeah, she is so young. I feel like I would be stealing candy from a baby."

He laughed, "That analogy is just wrong."

"That's how I feel about being with her before then."

"Have you been with anyone?"

"Yep, actually, a lot of girls. She knows about it. I was searching and when she came in my life, no one else was good enough."

"How long has it been?"

"Eight months."

"Isn't that hard?"

"It would be, but I have our dreams to help me get through, and a lot of cold showers."

We were pulling into Clarissa's. Jake pulled all the way around the back. Wilson was waiting for us as we pulled in. Jake jumped out and hugged his dad. They talked a little and then Wilson hugged him again. Jake told him Clarissa told us about Jake and I being brothers. I could tell he was worried about this. I got out, but glanced back at Sarah in the back seat. She was still completely out.

I walked over to them.

"Well, hello James. How is Sarah?"

I was happy to see him, "Jake saved her life."

"I heard you did a lot too."

"Not what he can do."

He was very proud of his son, "I made her favorite. Will she want to eat?"

"I don't know if we can wake her." Then a thought came to mind, "How are we going to get her in the house?"

The three of us turned looking at the truck. It felt weird but Jake huffed out, "I don't know; I didn't think about that."

Wilson took off to the gate, "Wait, I have an idea."

Jake and I were both puzzled but laughed at the thought of this.

Jake made a comment, "We probably should have thought about it before now."

Wilson came running out with a pool air mattress. We both laughed even harder as Jake replied, "Yes that will work."

We both put the seats down in the front. I laid the air mattress across them. We had a blanket under her so we took the four corners of the blanket and lifted her to the mattress.

"Wilson, this is a great idea. Jake, your side or mine?"

"You're closer to the gate, so I will come through the truck; just take it slow."

I slid the air mattress to me and Jake followed it through the truck. Wilson grabbed it until Jake could get out. Jake took a hold of it. We were walking in and Sarah started to wake up a little.

"Sarah, don't move."

Wilson moved to her side and took her hand.

"Sarah, you can't move. Stay still until they get you inside."

Her eyes did open for a second as she made a connection with Wilson. He gave a warming pat on her hand; he did care about her. Wilson let go of her hand to open the doors. We kept going till we got in my room and down the steps to lay it on the bed.

"Just a second, Sarah."

We grabbed the blanket and lifted it so Wilson could pull out the air mattress.

"Sarah, I made your favorite."

Her eyes were heavy and struggled to open, but for Wilson she did smile.

He made his way out of the room with the air mattress, but was only gone a few minutes when he came running back in and sat down trying to feed her.

"Dad, I don't know how hungry she is going to be."

He was sure of himself, "She will eat for me." He was feeding her, and she was just taking it in. About 4 spoonfuls before she shook her head no. She swallowed and held out her hand to stop him, "I'm sorry, no more. Not yet."

He was saddened by her refusal.

"Wilson, it is great. I will eat more later."

Wilson turned his concern to Jake, "A box came; you should get set up. James, come with me please."

I got up to follow him while Jake went to the box. The box was huge; what could he be planning?

I followed Wilson to the kitchen. He opened the fridge, "Here is the salad, some soup, there is Jell-O, and homemade pudding. I also made some applesauce. She likes food that is good for her."

I was completely astonished and nodded.

"Clarissa said you need lots of ice." He moved away from me gesturing for me to follow him out the door.

When he stopped he moved his hands displaying a large metal box, "Ice machine. This should be plenty, yes?"

I smiled shaking my head. Everything that woman did truly amaze me.

Wilson was moving back to the house, "We should see if Jake needs anything, because I will have to go soon."

"You do?"

"I still have a wife of my own, and she loves me. But when I fuss about others she isn't happy. I will pay for this."

I felt so bad; he didn't have to do all this.

He raised his eyebrows and grinned, "If you know what I mean?"

I held back a laugh knowing he was going to get lucky. What a dirty old man.

"We better get you out of here."

We hurried back into my room. Jake was putting stuff into a sack, "Dad, is there room in the fridge for this?"

"No, what is that for?"

"This is for emergencies."

"Would upstairs be okay?"

"James, do you have a key?"

"Yes, actually, I think I do."

Wilson came over to show me the correct one, but then he walked over to Jake, "She told me this can be your home too. He held out keys for Jake.

He had tears in his eyes, but looked away from him, "Does mom know I know?"

"No, and if you don't mind, can we not tell her? I promised many years ago that we would never tell you no matter how bad I wanted to. Clarissa was very good to us and our family, but your mother would be sad. She loves you deeply."

He glanced up at his father, "Our little secret."

"Do you need anything else?"

"I don't think so. James, did you need anything?"

"Nope," I was preoccupied with Sarah.

"Oh, by the way, James; Jake said you might need some things for her, so I bought a few things."

He was excited to show me and moved to the lounge chair. He had them all laid out; Jake came with us over to the lounge to see what he had gotten.

"See, Jake, all buttoned down in front. She will be able to change easily. I went with men's shirts, so they would be long enough. There are a few shorts, but I was buying lingerie for someone who was not my wife. I didn't know what to get."

"Dad, this is great. We can change her later."

I corrected him, "I will change her later."

"James, that's what I meant."

Sarah decided she didn't want to be left out. "I will change myself."

I walked back to her, "Like you are strong enough to do anything, little girl. You are feeling pain now."

"No, James, those drugs really made me crazy in my mind."

Wilson decided this was a good time to leave, "I have to go make my wife happy." He was cheery as he headed out.

I leaned over Sarah, "He is going to get lucky."

She seemed a little foggy, but she did manage a smile.

"That reminds me, little girl, I have a bone to pick with you."

"Ice first, James."

"Oh, right, the pain. I will be right back."

I ran out to the ice machine. What was I going to use? There were large bags hanging beside the machine. I started to fill them. They were like heavy-duty zip locks.

Jake came and helped me, "Is she in pain?"

"Yes, but she didn't like the drug you gave her. She said it made her crazy."

"James, I gave her a lot for the ride. We will use a lot less and see how she will handle that."

"Okay, but she is going to be a challenge."

I think he already realized that. We walked in with the bags of ice. Jake stopped in the kitchen to get a glass of water. I walked into my room and she was sitting up looking at me.

"James, I'm going to get sick."

I dropped the bag of Ice and ran to her, "No you don't; you have to keep it down. Look at me, Sarah, focus on me. Ready? 1-, 2-, 3-, Breathe."

She took a deep breath with me. Our eyes stayed locked on each other, as I tried to help her concentrate on holding it down. "Sarah, you can do this just don't think about it. Look at me and breathe. That's it, baby."

She closed her eyes and got wobbly.

I held her up.

"James, pain."

"I know, Sarah, we got ice and Jake is..."

"Right here. Is it bad?"

Trying to keep Sarah calm I gave her a glimpse of a smile, but nodded for Jake. It didn't take him long to bring her a pill and had her take a sip of water. I helped her lay back down looking deep into those beautiful eyes that were holding a touch of fear.

Jake moved away from us, but I could hear him doing something in the corner. It wasn't until he was walking back over that he commented, "This is for emergencies."

He walked over and gave her a shot in her arm, "The good stuff, no sickness, no fog, and no dizziness. She will like this better."

Jake put the bag of ice he brought in on her and then went to get the one I dropped. He brought it over and laid it on the other side.

My Sarah's eyes still had fear in them, so I had to try to make her stay calm, "Sarah, it will be okay now. Jake gave you the good stuff."

"James, I heard. Thank you." She finally closed her eyes.

Jake was moving to the box, "James, I need to put this stuff in the fridge; I'll go upstairs."

"Jake, do you think we should have the food up there and that down here; just in case?"

He agreed with me, "I will keep a small amount down here, okay?"

That did make me feel better. I noticed she was relaxing now into the pillow like a purring cat. "Sarah, how are you?"

"Oh, yeah. This is so much better." She lifted her arms over her head stretching.

Jake grabbed at her arms and pushed them down, "Sarah, you don't want to do that yet."

I had to scold him, "How much did you give her?"

"Only half a dose, James." He was smiling holding it up for me to see.

I chuckled a little, "The good stuff?"

"Yep, told you she would like that better."

"It's not going to make her dream is it?"

"It doesn't make her sleepy. However, the pill I gave her will. Sorry, no guarantees."

I shook my head. I knew there was the possibility of her dreaming again.

"Okay, I am going to run this upstairs. Which one is it?" He was holding up his keys. I grabbed the right one and handed them back to him

Sarah was feeling really good and giving me that enticing look. I moved to lie down beside her. How was I going to scold her when the memory of earlier and her eyes were driving me crazy?

"Sarah, you were a bad girl in the truck."

She raised her eyebrows and gave me a mischievous look with cute little dimples dancing in her cheeks, "How was I bad?"

I tried to stay stern, "You were dreaming."

Her mischievousness turned to remorse.

"Yeah, Jake was in the truck and you were aggressive. I told you no and I told you Jake was in the truck with me, but you wouldn't listen. He had to pull over so he wouldn't have to watch what you were doing to me."

She was horrified, "James, I am so sorry. I don't remember doing it."

"I didn't think you would. Jake was trying to wake you, and I had to stand on the side of the truck while you took me, but you weren't happy with a little; you wanted it all and you wouldn't stop. I had to please you before you would stop."

It surprised me that she had tears in her eyes, "Jake knows?"

"Yeah, and he had lots of questions. I had to change clothes. I came before I could give you pleasure enough to let me go."

"Oh, shit that's not good."

"Sarah, you have to try and behave. You had control over me and I couldn't stop you."

"I will suffer from the pain, no more drugs."

"NO! Sarah, I would never ask you to do that. I just need you to not think about it."

She closed her eyes pained, "Not even." I felt her mouth slowly tracing my neck.

"Sarah, that… I can handle. But no more, you know…"

"James, if we're not going to do that 'til I am 18, then I have to have the dreams."

"Well, can we at least do that when we are alone in our room, so I can at least enjoy what you are doing to me?"

She smiled and almost chuckled, but I could see the pain on her face. I scooted closer to her and traced my finger over her face. She closed her eyes and enjoyed the touch.

I glanced at Jake when I heard him walk back in, "You might want to knock before entering this room."

"Why, is she dreaming again?"

I traced my hand along her face, "No, but you never know when it will happen with her."

"James, I'm still awake. I'm sorry you saw that, Jake."

I heard him laughing, "You are a horn dog."

She opened her eyes and looked at me stricken.

"Sarah, I had to explain. He just doesn't understand the desire that is there now that we were bad and shared souls."

She was still gazing at me with regret, but I felt her... "I am and I want you now."

This girl was a dream come true, but... "No, Sarah."

She whispered to me pleading, "I feel really good right now."

I couldn't believe she was hinting at this, "NO."

She finally gave up and closed her eyes.

Jake was standing there watching us.

I didn't want him to see her like this, "I think she needs more sleep. I will stay until she is out. Help yourself to checking out your room."

He blinked a couple times before grinning, "Wow, that sounds weird."

"The remotes are on top of the TV stand. I will be out shortly."

I was thankful when he walked out of the room.

I leaned over my sweet little girl, "Sarah, I will be right back."

She grabbed for me, "NO, where are you going?"

I kissed those sweet lips and mouthed to her, "Cold shower, little girl."

I think she was actually pleased that she could do that to me. I moved to the bathroom, but I left the door open because I wanted to be able to hear her if she needed me.

Hurrying and keeping it completely cold, it didn't take me long to get done. I had had my fill of excitement today, and I didn't want to get out of control; at least not now, not with her in my bed, and in bad shape.

I came out and she turned her head my way.

"How are you doing?"

"I am so good right now."

I put boxers on, but brought the towel with me. I didn't know what she was capable of. I laid it by the bed and crawled to her. I stared at her face, "Sarah, I love you."

She was dreamy again, "I need to sleep, James. I feel so good I could sleep really well now, and I think the food will stay down."

"Good, you're home and you have to eat to stay strong."

I leaned in to touch her lips with mine. I just wanted to feel them. They were so sweet and so soft. I pressed to them softly. She moved her hands to my face, to hold me and kiss me more luring.

"Sarah, no. You need to sleep."

"Then refuse me." She closed her eyes, and I felt her lower to me.

"Sarah, no."

"Refuse me." She lowered to me and I could feel it. I wanted to move to her. I stayed put. I knew this was coming. I just knew the way she looks and calls to me. I kissed her more aggressively.

She whispered to me, "Softer, James. I'm getting a little dreamy."

Getting lost in her I closed my eyes, and she traced her hands down my chest. I opened my eyes and her hands were still on my face. Oh, this was going to be cool. I closed my eyes; I felt her move to me. I felt myself move to her. I wanted her so bad and actually be able to enjoy her.

"Sarah, we shouldn't be..." I opened my eyes and she was enjoying this. I felt myself push to her more. I was still kissing her, and she was holding my face. I wasn't near her body, but I could feel her over me. I closed my eyes and rolled her over. I moved slowly to her. She was enjoying the movements; her noises were getting me going even more. She was tingling; I was giving her complete pleasure. "James, the contractions hurt."

I stopped and opened my eyes, "It hurts? Then we stop."
"No, I am so almost there."
"But it hurts?"
"Just a little more."
I could feel her move to me."
"Sarah, don't come to me. Let me do the work." I closed my eyes. Holding her hips still, so she couldn't move to me. I pushed to her slowly and the tingling started again. I could feel her. Her body wanted to come to mine, but I held her still and moved to her more. The moaning was getting to me.

She heaved a breath, "Yes. James."

I felt her rush and the heat triggered it in me. I was coming. I pushed harder to her, and again. I could have kept going, but she was happy. I opened my eyes and slowly traced her lips, "How was that?"

"Perfect." She was smiling.

I knew I wasn't going to make it long with her in my bed. I kept telling myself 18, 18, 18. I laid my face next to hers, "Sarah?"

"Um, yes, James?"

"We are both horn dogs."

She laughed silently, "I can sleep now."

"I will wait for you to sleep." I went back to tracing her face with my finger. It wasn't long. I turned over to clean myself up. If I was a mess was she? I felt like I was being a pervert, but I checked her. I had to clean her up. She did have pleasure from me. No wonder she thought it was real. She doesn't know that she produces moisture from the pleasure. I should tell her that. I put her back together and kissed her cheek. I moved away from her and got dressed in the same clothes I had changed to in the car. Really didn't want Jake to know we couldn't wait to be together any longer.

I went to the living room. Jake was watching ESPN. I sat down.
"You satisfied her again."
"What..., why would you say that?"
He looked at me with searching eyes.
I tried to hold back a smile.
"That's how I can tell. You get this dumb look on your face."
"Oh."
The subject was dropped, and we watched the TV in silence.

# 15. A Shower

I went and checked on her every hour, because she was sleeping so much. I at least had Jake to talk to and a TV to entertain me.

"James, I think I should go buy a baby monitor; then we can hear her if she wakes up."

"That sounds really good, but you have to shut if off when I am in there with her."

He knew exactly why I wouldn't want him to hear. "James, she is still not well."

"I know, but she drives me crazy."

"You really aren't waiting until she's 18 if you are doing it magically."

He made me feel bad.

We both went in to check on her at 11pm, and she was stirring. He got a pill and a glass of water. We woke her enough to take the pill, but she lay back down almost immediately.

Jake was shaking his head with concern while rubbing his chin, "I really don't want to leave her and go to bed."

"Jake, I will be here the whole time."

"Are you going to sleep in the bed?"

"Why?"

"I was just wondering."

"Nope, too tempting. I thought maybe the lounge."

"Oh, why?"

"I am afraid I will curl into her and hurt her."

He huffed with agreement, "That is what I was afraid of if you slept in the bed."

I knew that wasn't the only thing he was worried about. He left and I closed the door. I put lounge pants on and a muscle shirt and sat down on the lounge. This was not going to be comfortable, but my new home for a while. I closed my eyes.

"James?"

I opened my eyes. Did she call me?

"James?"

I ran to her bed side, "What, Sarah?"

Oh shit the pain.

I yelled, "JAKE!" I took her hands in mine moving over her so that she could lock eyes with mine, "Sarah, stay calm."

"I am calm; this f-ing... hurts."

"Jake!!!"

"I'm here, what?"

I gasped trying to contain the pain in my gut, "Pain, hers. It's worse again. Oh shit... yeah... Jake, it's bad."

"I am only giving her the other half; James, she is doing well."

"Fine... anything." She was moaning with pain, so I moved closer to her. I wanted to help her with the pain.

"Don't touch me."

"I'm not... Sarah?"

I saw the sadness in her eyes when they opened for just a second. I wondered if this had anything to do with what we had done earlier so I had to ask, "Sarah is it from?"

I gulped when her eyes opened again full of sadness and fear. That's it. I was not going to give into her anymore. She will take my refusal.

Jake gave her the shot, "Check the ice."

I held it up for him to see they were both melted, "We should get more."

"I'll get the first bag." He left without hesitation, so I pulled out a book and started to read it to her.

"What are you doing?"

"Close your eyes and picture it. It will help 'til the medicine has time to work."

"You close your eyes and picture it. This hurts, James."

"Do you have a better idea?"

"Fine!"

I had to hold back a grin, as her bottom lip came out just a bit.

I was able to get a few pages in before Jake returned. He put the ice pack on her and finally I saw a little relaxation in her face. It was still hard for me to watch him with my Sarah. He had a pill explaining what the plan was, "I am giving her both this time. We'll see if that is better."

I didn't want to see how things went. I didn't want my Sarah to suffer. "No, I think we should set the alarm and feed it to her, so it doesn't wear off like this."

"That was my plan to begin with, but she did well last night."

"So, how often do you plan on giving her the meds?"

"Let's make it three and a half hours."

I set the alarm and Jake fed her the pill. She wasn't resting yet. Her body was so tense, and I could still feel her pain. I didn't like that she was hurting, so I traced my finger tip across the worried lines in her forehead and asked, "More reading?"

The shot was giving her some relief already; she was melting into the bed. I gave Jake a smile of thanks.

He returned it saying, "I am going back to bed. I will take the next shift."

"Okay."

I crawled very carefully on the bed and propped myself up to read to her. She didn't curl up to me and I was thankful. I resumed our adventure into this story but was easily distracted by sleep.

I hadn't moved an inch when I woke to the alarm. I grinned as I realized she was in my bed; I didn't hurt her, and I behaved. I crawled out of the bed and went to get Jake. I knocked on the door, but he had left the door open and he was already getting up.

I was grateful for his help, "Thanks."

He went to the kitchen and walked into the room with me. We both moved to the bed.

I crawled over it carefully to sit next to her, "Sarah?"

She didn't want to wake up very badly.

"Sarah, come on baby, you don't want the pain to get bad again; you need another pill."

"James, I'm tired."

"You can go right back to sleep. Just take the pill."

I propped her up a little, and Jake fed her the pill and some water. She really wasn't even awake, but she did well. I laid her back down and put my head down.

"Did you sleep?"

"Yeah, you would be proud of us. I fell asleep in her bed and nothing happened."

"Well, that is good. Do you want me to stay, or can I go back to bed?"

I grabbed the alarm and reset it for another three and half hours for the next one.

"Make it four hours next time. Let's figure it out."

I changed it to set it for four hours, "Yeah, go back to bed. I will take more of a nap later. I leaned back and closed my eyes. This time I scooted down more to rest better.

I only dozed off and on. I finally got up about 10 am. She was still sleeping. We still had a couple of hours before having to give her medicine. I went out and filled another bag of ice and brought it in to replace the bag that was almost melted. I went to the lounge and sat down to watch her.

Jake knocked, but walked in. I glared at him.

"What? I knocked."

"You were supposed to knock and wait."

"She is sleeping. I knew she would be."

"But that is when she dreams."

"Oh, yeah. I forget about that. How is our little girl?"

I laughed, "Sleeping."

"I was going to run up and get the baby monitor; do you want anything?"

I shook my head no, "Wait, yes. Get some more books."

"Books… what kind of books?"

"Anything… novels. Something I can read to her when she is awake. It distracts her instead of me personally distracting her."

"Oh, the control thing."

"I've got to try. I think that is why she was in so much pain. You are right and we have to stop."

He was pleased with this, "You love her that much."

"Jake, whatever is best for her I am willing to do it."

"I am going to go. What kind of books?"

"Anything."

He got all bright eyed, "I have a book in mind."

"Well, get more than one."

"Okay."

I jumped in the shower, and took an honest to god real one. I didn't have to freeze this time. I didn't think she would want one today. She hasn't done anything and we keep ice on her so she doesn't sweat. If she did I would just take another one. It felt good to wash in warm water. I probably took longer than normal. I walked out in my towel.

"Hi."

I looked over at her, "You're awake?"

"Not really, still sleepy."

"Will you try to eat for me?"

"No, I'm not hungry."

"Well, you're going to try a little anyway. We need to keep your strength up."

"I don't want to feel sick."

"Sarah! We'll take it slow."

"You look good."

"Um, Sarah, I think we shouldn't do that for a while. I am afraid that is why you were in so much pain. It was worse after both times."

"James."

She was so luring, "Sarah honey, no. Let's just see how the pain is for a while to see if it is better when we don't do that. Let me get dressed and I will get some food."

"J-a-m-e-s." She was melting me with her voice, "I want to touch you."

"Sarah, please let me behave."

"Where is Jake?"

"Why?"

"Because he isn't here, and you could come lay with me."

"Sarah, I did all night."

"You slept with me? In the same bed? James!"

"Be nice. It was nice."

That glisten in her eyes and the grin on her face made me move to the bathroom to get dressed.

"James, why aren't you dressing out here?"

"So, I am not temped. Now behave, little girl."

I leaned against the wall taking a few deep breaths. I should have taken a cold shower. I put my boxers on, my jeans, and a t-shirt. I walked out and looked at her and couldn't help myself from moving to her.

"James, no kissing; I need to brush my teeth."

That made it easy on me, "Before or after you eat?"

"Since I will only be able to stand once I should try to eat first."

I didn't quite make it to her and I turned to go to the kitchen for food. I left the door open, so I could hear her. I warmed up about a fourth of a cup of soup. I also got some apple sauce. I put it on a tray. Drink, what should she drink? To my relief Wilson thought of that also and there were sport drinks in the fridge so I grabbed one and a straw. I walked in with the tray. She was still laying there looking at me with those beautiful green eyes.

I sat down beside her and set the tray on the night stand. "Let's get you up a little."

I pulled her to me. Her face was at my neck as I held her. She started to nibble.

"Sarah, please, you need to eat."

I was pulling pillows from everywhere to prop her up. Her frail arms wrapped around my waist, and she was tracing her hands on my back. She was going to make this really hard. I tried to ignore her touch and how good it felt. I leaned her back to the pillows.

"Food first."

She thought she had won and grinned. I was thinking if I could feed her it would be time for the pill and she would sleep again. I am glad she can't feel me unless I tried for the connection.

She knew immediately who made the soup, "This is Wilson's?"

"Yes, of course it is. He also made you homemade apple sauce."

"Why is he so nice?"

"I think that is his nature. Do you remember him trying to feed you yesterday?"

"Not really, maybe. Did I get sick?"

"You almost did." I fed her another spoonful. "How is your stomach?"

"So far, okay."

I kept feeding her 'til it was gone. I was pleased that she wasn't looking green at all and asked again now that she was done, "How are you feeling?"

She leaned her head back and closed her eyes, "Okay."

"Let's try the apple sauce."

She didn't seem sure about trying it, but I gave her one spoonful to give it a try. She smiled so I continued and she did well. She finished it and leaned back again.

"Still doing okay?"

"Yeah. The pain is starting to come back, but just a wee little bit."

"Wee... little?" She did have a way of making me laugh.

"Ready for brushing?"

"Yes, I hate this feeling."

"I am going to attempt to carry your heavy body to the bathroom."

"I gained weight?"

"No, I was joking. There is not an ounce of fat on you."

With the biggest grin on her face she seemed pleased with this, so I had to scold her a little, "Sarah, it's good to have 20% body fat. Do you know that?"

"Yes, but I like to keep mine down to less than 15%.

"But that is not healthy."

"Um, when you look at me, you seem to like it."

I couldn't deny what she was saying. The thing about that is, I like to look at her no matter what size she was. Her eyes were what got to me. Oh and the smile... and the biting her bottom lip... okay everything.

I pulled the covers back. Her legs where so soft looking. I had to tell myself *no James just teeth*. I leaned over to pick her up. She wrapped her arms around my neck and nuzzled into my shoulder.

"Do you think I can walk yet?"

"I don't know, but we're not going to try 'til Jake is around."

I walked her to the bathroom and carefully put her legs down and moved to hold her up. I wrapped my arms around her carefully under her arms. She grabbed the toothbrush and toothpaste.

She put the paste on herself and turned on the water. As she brushed I watched her in the mirror. She was so cute all messed up from sleeping so long.

"I look horrible." It came out muffled with the toothbrush in her mouth.

"Sarah, stop. I don't like to hear that."

"James, it's okay. I look a little scary. I need to clean myself up."

I closed my eyes and traced my nose along her neck, "Do you want a shower?"

"Yes."

I traced my hand down to her stomach to pull her into me.

"James... no... no. Not there... it will hurt."

I moved my hand back up to her neck and held it there. I started to kiss her neck. Why is the thought of a shower with my Sarah such a turn on?

"Sarah, are you almost done? I am driving myself crazy."

"Yes James, but if this is bad how are you going to give me a shower?"

"I will find a way, if that is what you want."

I opened my eyes to look at her in the mirror. Those green eyes were glimmering with happiness.

"James, I think I have to go to the bathroom, bet you two didn't think of that one."

"No, or at least I didn't."

Her eyes seemed to search my face for a reaction. I didn't have one other than being turned on which did make her ease. I helped her turn to me. I lifted her and moved her in front of the toilet.

## Sarah:

This has got to me the most embarrassing thing ever. He was puzzled of how we were going to do this. I giggled watching him look me up and down and then around me at the toilet and finally gave up asking, "How are we going to do this?"

He was so easy to read, but the situation was not easy to figure out, "Your guess is as good as mine."

"Um, your shirt is long. I could help you take off the underpants; I mean you're going to take a shower anyway. Right?"

"I would love that."

"I will help you sit down and I will leave 'til you are done."

"This is really embarrassing."

"Sarah, I wanted to take care of you, and if you have to go to the bathroom, then we have to do what we have to do. Can you stand?"

"I don't know, because you won't let me."

"Well, we're going to try right now." He let go of me really carefully. There was no pain. "I think I can do this."

He reached down to help lower my underpants to the floor. He came back to my face, "I am a creep."

"Why?"

"I am getting totally turned on, and you're helpless."

I couldn't help but laugh a little, "James, don't make me laugh."

He helped me sit down and smiled at me, "Are you okay?"

"Yes, but you need to go now."

He went out quickly, "James, close the door please."

"But I won't know when you're done."

"James, please."

He closed the door. I sat there and nothing happened. I was nervous about him being right out the door. I waited some more. I concentrated on letting it flow; nothing. Shit... why can't I go? I needed to go so bad. Oh... there it is, shit, this hurts. The stomach muscle definitely didn't like this, "Oh Shit."

James was worried, "What?"

"Um... kind of hurt."

"Are you done?"

"Nope and quit talking to me."

He laughed.

I must have gone for almost 2 minutes. The pain was increasing, but it felt so good to go. I really must have had to go.

"Sarah, how are you doing?"

"Stop talking to me."

"Did you have to poop or something?"

"James, please, and no. It was really hard to go. Stop talking to me."

I wiped and felt really stupid now.

"James, I'm done."

He came back in and lifted me to him too fast. The pain shot through me and I gasped, "James, careful"

"Sarah, that took so long I was worried we were doing something we weren't suppose to."

I gave him *that* look, "We always do stuff that were not supposed to."

He was already unbuttoning my shirt.

"James, I didn't mean that we could do that."

He gave me a patronizing look, "Shower. I want to get it done before Jake comes back."

"Where did he go?"

"To the store."

"For what? Clarissa thinks of everything."

"She didn't think of this."

"What?"

"A baby monitor."

Was I pregnant from the dreams?

He seemed confused by my expression, "Sarah?"

"Is there something you need to tell me, James?"

"What are you talking about?"

"A baby monitor?"

"No, Sarah, no. We actually have to be together for that to happen."

"But I am a mess when… in the dreams."

"Sarah, when you feel the rush. That actually produces fluids, like a guy would cum."

I was completely horrified.

"Sarah, it makes it easier for me, the guy to feel good in you."

"So, what is the baby monitor for?"

"When you are sleeping we can have it on in the living room and hear you."

"What if I start to dream?"

"I already told Jake that when I am with you it is off, and if I am out in the living room I will know you are dreaming and I will unplug it."

He was still unbuttoning my shirt all the way down. He slid it off me and put his arms around me walking into the shower.

"Aren't you going to get undressed?"

"Nope couldn't handle it."

I appreciated that he knew his limits. He set me down, so I was standing and turned the water on. He was blocking it with his body until he could feel the temperature. I covered my scar with my hands. He turned to me when it was perfect, "Sarah, no. Don't do that. It doesn't matter."

He wrapped his arms around me to move me closer to the shower. He helped me wash my hair first. I was standing on my own when he did this. When he tilted my head back to rinse it he came in for a deep kiss. His mouth on mine was mesmerizing. I could have jumped his bones right then if I could have moved without pain. He took the soap and was washing every curve of my body running his hand delicately and slowly over areas he wanted to spend more time on. When he moved back up my body to look me in the eyes again he spoke into my lips, "Oh god, please help me to have strength." His lips pressed to mine hard and deep. My heart was pounding out of my chest with every slight movement of his hand and the maneuvering of his fingers.

"James, can you please get me a shaver, I would like to shave my arm pits."

He laughed, "Don't move." He went out and grabbed one and came back to grab the soap.

"James, this is one of those things, I would like to do on my own. Turn around."

"Sarah, I can help you."

"James, please. I don't like the European look."

He chuckled a little as he turned around.

I quickly shaved my arm pits. I rinsed them the best I could, "Okay James, I'm done."

He turned back to holding me again. He put my head under the water rinsing my hair again. When I closed my eyes he came in for the seductive kiss that took us even deeper into need. The water was tracing down our faces and our bodies were tensely touching in every way possible while he was still clothed.

"James?"

"Oh, shit, Sarah." He was moving to each of my lips, and I was getting lost. I was almost forgetting that I was not stable. I pulled up his shirt, so he helped pull it off. He put his chest to mine with a sound that made me want to touch him more. His chest was moving in and out so fast. The next thing I knew he had lifted me to the wall pressing to me, just with his chest, and his hand moved to my face. He pulled away from me just enough to stare into my eyes, because he was losing control. His kiss came harder, and it felt so good. He wanted me now. He knew it, I knew it, and I liked it until I felt sharp pains in my gut.

I begged, "James, turn the water to cold."

He stopped abruptly. His eyes met with mine again while his chest was still heaving, but he seemed not able to move.

I pleaded, "James, the pain would be unbearable."

I could see it in his face that this was too much for him. Did we go past that point of stopping?

"James?"

Slowly his mouth grew to a grin, "Just trying to get control, baby. I can't move yet." He closed his eyes, "Shit."

"I'm sorry, James, I'm sorry. Don't get mad."

He opened his eyes again with a stricken look on his face, "Sarah, this is not mad, this is... I want you so bad it hurts."

"Turn the water to cold James, if it will help you."

"No Sarah, the cold will make you tense up and that might hurt you. I just need a minute."

I felt like I needed to say something, "James?"

He put his fingers to my lips, "Shhhh, I find your voice luring. Just... shit, are you okay?"

"I think so."

"You think... are you in pain? Oh, my god, Sarah, I totally forgot. You have me so... just are you okay?"

He was checking everywhere to see if I was hurt; like he could see it anyway. I pulled his face back to mine. I knew he would understand that I was okay once he looked into my eyes.

He turned off the water and grabbed a couple of towels. He wrapped one around my body and the other around my hair. He lifted me and walked out to the room laying me on the bed.

"Sarah, I am so sorry…I swear, I will do better next time. I will be more careful."

He ran back to the dresser and grabbed some lounge shorts and a button up shirt. He came running back to me.

"James, you should change first. You'll get everything wet." I took this as an opportunity to check out my husband. I wanted to admire every inch of him, as my eyes trailed his body from his arms, to his chest, and then down. Wow, his body was so amazing. The muscles were more cut than I remembered. He was thinner, leaner. I watched him as he was trying to pull off the wet jeans. I tried to not laugh holding my hands over my mouth and stomach, but choked out, "Having problems?"

He went into the bathroom and grabbed another towel wiping himself off. He was completely naked in front of me. I needed to look away but couldn't. He slipped on boxers and then another pair of jeans, but left them unzipped and unbuttoned. He grabbed another t-shirt and pulled it over his head on the way back to me. He sat down in front of me. He looked at me for a long time.

He slipped the shorts under the towel lifting me by scooping me up with his hand under my back. He looked at me again and took a deep breath. He slipped the shirt on one arm and pulled it around me to go over the other arm. He started to button me up. He slipped his hands under the shirt to grab the towel and he slipped it out from under my shirt. The way he was looking at me and not saying a word, I didn't know if it was safe yet for me to talk to him yet.

"What are you thinking, Sarah?"

"I didn't know if I could talk to you yet."

I was completely relieved when he cupped my face and came in for a soft slow kiss. He moved his hands to the towel on my head and started to towel dry my hair.

"James, when am I supposed to take the next pill?"

He glanced at the clock, "Well, we decided to wait a little longer this time. So now would be a good time."

"Good."

"Are you in pain? Kind of not feeling you right now."

He could make me smile, but, "Yeah, the pain is coming back, but it's not bad yet."

He put his hand on my cheek, and then let go. He helped me by lifting me to scoot down more, and tucking the pillows around me, "I will go get you the pill. You still have your sport drink here."

He got up and walked out of the room. I closed my eyes. The desire was killing me right now. I hated that the pain was coming back. The tears started to trace down my cheeks. I wanted the waiting to be with my husband over.

I heard him from the other room, "No Sarah, you agreed to 18. Don't be sad; it will be that much better. I love you."

I heard the other door, "James."

He didn't reply. Was Jake back? I was feeling more pain. I was concentrating on breathing through it. James came walking back in, "Here, baby."

I put it in my mouth, and he helped me sip from the drink. He had a bag of ice with him, "Can I put this on it?"

I really needed the ice this time, so my only reply could be a nod.

"Do you want me to read to you?"

"What are you reading?"

"I have no idea; it was here in my room. Clarissa must have gotten it." He crawled into the bed on the other side propping himself up. I curled into his leg wrapping my hands around him, so that he couldn't leave me without me knowing. I closed my eyes and listened to him as he read. Slowly the dizziness was coming back, and I was letting it take me away to the dream world.

## 16. Didn't Think Of That

### James:

**I** heard Jake walking in. Sarah's breath was heavy and her body was relaxed. Seeing if she was sleeping I spoke softly, "Sweetie?" She didn't reply, so I thought it was my opportunity to get up. I tried to move from the bed without disturbing her, but that was a little hard.

She moaned. "No, James."

"Shhhh, I'm still here. I held her hand, but I was moving from the bed. Jake walked in holding the baby monitor up. I nodded. He came over and was setting it up.

"She ate?"

I nodded and put my fingers to my lips to quiet him.

He whispered, "Did she get her pill?"

I nodded again giving him a stern look to shut him up.

"Did she just fall asleep?"

Then she was talking, "James."

"No, not yet."

I moved closer to the bed and grabbed the book. I was disgusted, because now I was going to have to read this awful book again. I think he was enjoying that he woke her. I read for maybe another half hour and she was definitely sleeping. I moved from the bed easily this time without a stir from her.

I walked out to the couch and fell to it.

"You are exhausted?"

I rolled my eyes. He didn't help me with that by waking her again. I huffed out, "I made the mistake of giving her a shower. I really need to work on the desire thing. I almost lost control with her."

"James, you know that wouldn't be good."

"Oh yeah, she also went to the bathroom."

"A bowl movement or just urinated."

I had to laugh, "Technical, I am going to have a hard time with that. She just urinated." I laughed even more when I said it.

"Did she say how that went?"

"She said it hurt."

He was really odd. He was just talking about it like it was a normal conversation as he asked another question, "How did it hurt?"

"I don't know; I didn't ask. It was really weird having to help her sit on the toilet and then picking her up off of it."

This time he seemed more human because he laughed, "I didn't think about that."

"Yeah, well, I didn't either."

"Hey, I got us something too."

"What?"

He got up and ran around the couch. He came back with a bag, "Wii, and about 20 games. I bought everything they had. I didn't know what you would like."

"Did you get some books?"

"Yes. I found the perfect books for you and Sarah to read together."

"What are they about?"

"A love story; where they wait until she is 18."

Full of sarcasm, "Great, she'll love that."

"Actually, girls love these books, and there are four in the series."

"Maybe she will like those better than what I am reading to her."

"What are you reading?"

"Didn't bother to look, but it is really boring, so boring that I don't even listen to myself read it."

"Maybe that is why she falls asleep to it."

"Yeah, maybe."

"Do you want to play something?"

"Sure, what do you want to play?"

"It doesn't matter. I never played much."

"I have never played."

We looked through the games and I handed him a driving one. He smiled, "that is what I would pick. I don't know how this works."

We spent an hour putting it together with the TV. I sat down to play, because we still had time before she woke up again. He turned on the TV and we played.

Sarah's mom called and apologized for not coming over Friday, but she was on her way now. I gave her directions, but my stomach tensed and twisted into knots.

"Jake, Sarah's mom is on her way."

"Okay."

"We have to clean up."

"Why? Nothing is messy."

"She has to know I will take good care of her."

"James. You helped her go to the bathroom. How many guys would do that?"

I did laugh lightly, but got up and walked into my room. I had left my wet clothes on the floor and hers in the bathroom, so I grabbed them all and put them in the washer. I walked back in the room and grabbed the dishes from before and brought them to the sink and washed them. I went in the room one more time to check it out. Everything looked organized. I put a pillow and blanket on the lounge, so she could see I wasn't sleeping with her daughter. I just didn't feel right about it, not yet. I heard the door and then Jake answering it, but the voice wasn't hers. Wilson brought down food. I went out to eat; I haven't eaten in a while. We were engulfing food when Paula showed up. I went to open the door and hugged her. My heart raced as I thought 'my mother in law'. Oh... this was weird.

She seemed as nervous as I was. I walked her to my room, but she noticed, "Doc."

"Oh, hi."

I wanted him to be more professional when she was here. I gestured for him to get up. He stood up and apologized for eating. Wilson shook her hand and introduced himself.

"Sarah is a delight."

I was behind her shaking my head no. Sarah wouldn't have met Wilson if we were only here when Paula knew about it. I made him uneasy and he stopped speaking abruptly. I don't think she caught on. We were entering the room and she did look around and then back to me.

"This is really nice, James."

I was embarrassed, "Yeah, Clarissa did a really good job picking everything out."

"Your mom did all this?"

"Yeah, everything was like this when I got here."

"You're sleeping there?"

"Yeah, I don't want to hurt her."

I don't know if she believed me, but she didn't push the issue and gave me a small smile. As she walked over to the bed, I grabbed a chair for her and put it next to the bed. I check the ice pack and it was getting melted. I took it off of Sarah, and explained that it helped with the pain

I went to the other side of the bed and lay across it. I couldn't reach Sarah with her mom there, "Sarah, Sarah sweetie your mom is here."

"James, let me sleep."

"Sarah."

I didn't want Sarah to start dreaming; I also wanted her to know her mom was here, "Sarah, your mom is here. She would like to see you and talked to you. Open your eyes, baby."

She started to blink.

Trying to keep Sarah calm I tried again, "Your mom is right there."

She turned to her mom with dreamy eyes. She seemed a little out of it.

"I'll go get more ice, and leave you two to talk."

I grabbed the bag and walked into the living room. Jake and Wilson were sitting close to the monitor. I gave them a scowling smirk.

"Sarah, how are things going?"

Is what I heard before I shut the monitor off.

"Hey, we were listening to that."

I raised my eyebrows in disbelief, "They can have privacy; leave it alone."

I walked out to get ice; Jake came out grabbing another bag to help. I couldn't help but feel uneasy.

"James, what are you so nervous about?"

"If she will approve."

"What does it matter…you're married now."

He didn't seem to get it, "Jake, she is 16, and they have to feel like I violated her."

"James, you did. In your dreams, but you did."

Not what I needed to hear, "Jake, I already feel bad enough and you're not helping me."

"I'm sorry, but you're just really funny looking when you're nervous."

I grabbed my bag of ice and walked away from him all the way to the room. I walked over to them. Sarah was still having a hard time keeping her eyes open.

Paula had worry lines across her forehead, "Does she sleep all the time?"

"Mostly." Not knowing what to say I reached to put the ice by her stomach. We never put it right on her because of the pressure, "She usually wakes when it gets to be the time for the medicine for the pain. Um, which should be in about a half hour, but I try to feed her before I give her the pill."

"So, she is eating?"

"Very little, but I try to give her a little every four hours. That is how often she is taking the pills."

"So, how does Jake feel she is doing?"

I was grateful to hear him answer, "She is actually doing okay. The pain is really bad, so were just letting her sleep through most of it. We got her at four hours and I will probably leave it at that for a few days. Tuesday, I am thinking we will try to back it off maybe a half hour and see how she does."

"So she is in a lot of pain?"

"I went pee, Jake."

Jake and I glanced at each other and held back the laughter. Her mom didn't think it was funny.

Jake pulled himself together enough to say, "I heard that; how was it?"

"Jake, it hurt"

"What do you mean it hurt? Did it burn, or did the muscles in your stomach hurt?"

"The muscles."

"Sarah, that's okay. That was the first time since the surgery. It will get easier."

I was watching Sarah's mom. She was trying to read us.

"Sarah, your mom is here."

She opened her eyes really happily, "Mom, you're here."

I liked that she was happy, but she was still a little out of it and sounding like she was heavily drugged.

"We'll let you visit. I will get food ready."

Her mom was concerned, "One question. Is she walking yet?"

She could probably see that we were both uneasy about the question. I was thankful that Jake took over again, "No, James helped her."

"So, you brought her to the bathroom?"

I didn't know if this was going to be good or bad. The knot in my stomach did a flip as I thought about how I was going to answer her, but Sarah spoke up, "Mom, he left the room while I went."

Jake was angry, "James, we can't leave her alone."

"Jake, she wanted privacy to go to the bathroom."

"Jake, I didn't move. I stayed there 'til he came and got me."

I noticed her mom was watching us argue, and I wasn't comfortable at all with this subject so I changed it, "I'll go get food. Sarah, you'll try and eat for your mom?"

"Yes, James."

I walked out pulling Jake with me. We argued into the kitchen while I was preparing Sarah's food. I got a very small bowl of the salad that she liked and a small bowl of Jell-O. I put it on the tray and grabbed another sports drink.

"Jake, where did your dad go?"

"He went to clean the pool. I was thinking I would go swimming today."

"Whatever you want."

"You know once the incision is healed that swimming would be the best way to exercise her stomach muscles."

"Great, how long will that be?"

There was a touch of sympathy, "Not for a while."

I walked back into the room, and her mom was talking to her as I put the tray on the night stand. Sarah's mom held up the book, "Mobby Dick?"

"It was here and Sarah falls asleep better if I help her get her mind off the pain that is usually coming back before the medicine starts to work."

She eased, "I like that. I was afraid you guys would get her here and not pay attention to her. A guy thing; you understand?"

"NO! She is too important to me. I love her, and I will take really good care of her."

She raised her eyebrows and glanced around the room, "Well, it looks good so far."

Sarah's eyes settled on me with adoration. I did love my Sarah more than life itself, but now that she was here, she's mine... all mine.

Not taking my eyes from my sweet Sarah, I spoke to her mother, "I'll let you feed her; if she starts to gage call for me. I can usually talk her out of it. It helps if you feed her really slowly."

I moved to Sarah wanting to help her to sit up a little.

"Paula, wait. Can you get up a second, because I need to sit her up a little?"

I pulled Sarah to me and tucked a bunch of pillows behind her. I lifted her from her butt to scoot her up and lowered her back to them. I tucked the ice around her and covered her back up, "Doing okay?"

With foggy eyes, "Yes."

I kissed her forehead and moved the chair back for Paula. She sat down, and I excused myself from the room, "Remember slowly. Call me if she gags."

"James!"

I turned to look, "Sarah, slow and swallow. Eat or I will get mad."

I walked out leaving the door open. Jake had turned the monitor back on. I frowned and shut if off again.

Wilson came back before going home and brought us dinner. Sarah's mom was still in there. I thought she would leave after I gave the pill to her, but what was she doing staying in there for so long? Wilson brought enough for her also. He said it was just in case. I gave him a huge hug showing my appreciation. He was the best person in my life right now next to Sarah, of course.

I went in to check on them. Sarah was sleeping, but her mom was still reading to her.

"James, did you want me to mark where you left off or where I read to."

I don't care for reading, but Sarah liked it, "Um, you can mark it where you left off. It's for her not me. I'm not much of a reader."

That made her happy.

"Is she sleeping?"

"Yeah, I think she has been for a while. I just didn't want to leave."

I knew how she felt, because I felt the same way.

"If you would like, you could come eat with us, taking our time of course and Sarah...." I was counting in my head, "She should be getting up in an hour and a half, and we could try to feed her again. That is, if you would like to stay?"

"Really, you don't mind?"

"Not at all. It's nice having help. I will try to take her to the bathroom though. She hasn't gone since this morning."

The way her face changed it scared me. It was like she disapproved of me or something as she spoke, "James, she also said you helped her in the shower."

Shit how was I going to answer that, "Yep." Well that was inventive.

"Sarah said you wore your clothes in the shower?"

I really didn't know how to answer that, "Yeah, I didn't know what I was doing, but that is what she wanted."

Boy that sounded like I give into her a lot. Was I even answering her questions okay? I gave her a half smile.

She got up and started walking to me...or the door, "James, it's okay. You are doing your best and this is a lot to handle."

She put her hand on my cheek and kissed the other one, "Breathe, boy, I am not checking on you. I just miss her."

I put my head down with relief. She patted my back and went to the living room.

"I'll be right there. I want to lay her down, so she is more comfortable."

I went to her, lifted her, and pulled out the pillows while letting my eyes wonder over my sweet Sarah's face.

I lowered her and she whispered, "James, I love you."

I laughed, "Sarah, no dreaming... your mom is here. Please, Sarah, no dreaming."

"Stop me."

"Sarah, this is not a game. Your mom is here and you will not do that to me. Stop it. No dreaming or I will have Jake take you to the bathroom next time."

She opened her eyes. The green was vivid and bright with ideas. I melted on the spot, but I had to be firm. *James be firm*, "Sarah."

She relaxed into the pillow, her eyes closed, but that smile seduced me on the spot. I wanted to feel those soft luscious lips next to mine. *No, I have to be firm about this*, "Sarah, your mom is still here. No dreaming, please."

The medicine must be working. Her wicked smile was weakening although she managed to lick her lips. My stomach clenched at this one last temptation for me and she replied, "Okay, James, later. "

"No, Sarah, not later. No more dreaming at all."

She stuck out her bottom lip. It didn't matter if she melted me with the pout, I had to stay strong. I kissed her pouty lip, got up, and walked out to the living room turning on the monitor.

Paula laughed, "I was wondering what that was for."

We sat at the small table by the door. Dinner went really well. It was just the three of us, but Paula was enjoying the food. I heard Sarah move and ran to the room and to her.

"Sarah?"

She was uncomfortable and I didn't know why.

"Sarah."

She was still sleeping, so I tucked her back in and went back out.

Paula was concerned, "Was she okay?"

"Um yeah, she doesn't look comfortable Jake, but she was still sleeping."

He got up and went in there right away. I could hear him moving around, but he didn't say anything. He knew we could hear him. He came back out, "Her vitals are fine and she is sleeping, James."

I let it go, but it bothered me. I kept thinking about it... when we were done we all just sat there. Paula wanted to ask questions, so we did answer the best we could. We told her how we got Sarah in the house and she laughed at that. Jake told her about how long we can expect her to be off of her feet, when the incision should heal by, and how we were going to take her in the pool to help her build her strength back up. The pool was heated we could use it well into October if we needed to.

It was time to get Sarah up and feed her. I excused myself and went to the kitchen. I got the soup out again and I did a half a cup; we would try more this time. I got pudding next and then I practically ran in the room and sat down next to her on the bed, "Sarah, it's time to get up and eat."

"You told me no." Her eyes weren't even open.

Realizing what she was thinking about I grabbed the monitor unplugging it quickly. I heard static from the other room. Shit, they know I unplugged it. They both came running in and I just sat there innocent as I could be, "I must have hit it when I put the tray down."

I widened my eyes at Jake to give him a hint of what she was thinking about. A smirk grew on his face as he headed back out of the room. I was hoping he was turning it off.

I leaned into her ear, "Sarah, we will talk about it later. Your mom is still here."

She opened her eyes with fear in them.

"It's okay, she didn't hear much. Just not now, we'll talk about it later."

My reassurance was enough to relax her allowing her to close her eyes again.

"Oh, no you don't. It's time to wake up."

I pulled back the covers, as her mom walked over to us. I pulled her to me and tucked the pillows behind her again and pulled her up to sit more.

"James, quit fussing. I just want to sleep."

"Sarah, your mom is here and it's time for you to eat again. Do you have to use the bathroom yet?"

My asking her if she had to go must have triggered the feeling. She opened her eyes in a panic, "Oh, shit James, yes."

Picking her up I headed for the bathroom. This must have seemed ridiculous, but I want her to see that I will take care of whatever Sarah's needs are. I spoke quickly as I passed her, "I will come get you when she is ready." I kicked the door shut setting Sarah down on her feet in front of the toilet. I pulled down her shorts and then lowered her to the seat. I avoided eye contact with my Sarah. I didn't know how she was feeling yet. I went out and closed the door. As I turned around her mom was still standing there watching me. I was completely embarrassed.

She was smirking, "I bet that is a little weird?"

I couldn't help myself and rolled my eyes, "You have no idea."

"James, I'm done."

I waited for Paula to approve and she waved me away. I went in and closed the door. I helped Sarah to stand. I squatted down to pull up the shorts, while her hands moved to the top of my head running her fingers through my hair. She was wanting me right here and right now and she wasn't feeling much pain at all. This is not good at all, "Sarah, honey, don't think about it. Your mother is right outside the door." I moved up to her, "You are going to be the death of me."

She reached up and started to kiss me. I was trying to distract her, "Teeth, do you want to brush your teeth?"

She smiled with evil in her eyes, "NO." She reached up and sucked my lips.

"No!"

She glared at me.

I raised my eyebrows at her, "Your mom is standing on the other side of this door. Stop teasing me."

She was good at persuading me. The tears even welled up in her eyes. I caved with that saddened face. I couldn't help myself. I took her face in my hands and kissed her deeply. My mind wandered, as I tried to please her, *this would be a very good time for a cold shower.* I was kissing her swiftly to make her happy. I gave her what she wanted until she had enough and released me. Almost falling forward as she pulled away I knew she was satisfied that she won.

I just shook my head, "Why do you do that to me?"

"Because you let me."

"It's going to stop right now."

"Really?"

"Yes, to bed with you." I lifted her and hit the door, "Paula could you please open the door."

She pushed the door open and I brought Sarah back to bed propping her up so she could eat. I could tell she thought I was playing, but I had a new determination to say no to her. However, when she gives me those evil eyes like she is now, I knew she had something else planned to torture me.

"Sarah, stop that." Avoiding her eyes I grabbed the bags of ice and pulled them from the bed. I put the chair by the bed and gestured for Paula to take a seat. She moved into it.

"Remember if she gags call me. She did that with the soup before, just to warn you."

Sarah was gazing at me with sadness on her face and spoke to me with that luring voice, "Where are you going?"

Keeping my attention away from Sarah I spoke towards her mother with a grin on my face, "This is your mom's time. I will be in the living room."

I reached down and plugged the monitor back in, "I'll leave it off so you can talk."

I went out and fell on the couch.

Jake evaluated my collapsed stance, "This is hard for you?"

"You have no idea."

"James, don't stress about it. You are doing your best."

Condescendingly I pointed out, "Jake, she is winning. I give into her whenever she wants and I can't help it."

"What do you mean?"

"This is going to be gross, but I took her to the bathroom. Her mom was standing by the door. Everything was going fine. I waited outside until she was done, but when I went back in she was coming on to me. If she is in pain, why is she so...?"

"Horny?"

"Yeah."

"Drugs do amazing things."

"Jake, does the drug in the shot do that?"

"No."

"Then why don't we use that one; if her mother wouldn't have been on the other side of that door… shit."

"Really?"

"Jake, she was pure evil. She wanted to be caught with me."

"You're married."

"It would hurt her. Jake, isn't there anything else we can use? I don't want to get turned on; I want her to wait and heal."

He just smiled at me.

"Jake, please, I feel like a pervert and she is purposely turning me on. I couldn't leave the bathroom until I kissed her enough for her to be happy. If I let her she would have done it right in front of her mom."

"There is your answer, James, if you let her."

"I am a guy. It is so hard to turn her down. Those eyes get me every time."

"I definitely did not have it as bad as you do. Just tell her no."

"Fine, you get to take care of her for a while. I can't tell her no."

"Yes, you can."

# 17. The Medications

**W**e stayed in the living room until it was time for the pill. "Jake, can we try something else for tomorrow…something less foggy?"

He just laughed at me, "James, she is still in a lot of pain. Give it a couple more days."

I went in and Paula was reading to her.

When I saw my sweet Sarah's face I smiled, "It's time for your pill."

"James, I don't want it yet. Can we wait a while?"

"How is the pain?"

"I really don't have much."

"I'll go get more ice and ask Jake. If you want to try longer without it I think we should give it a try, but you have to tell me when it starts to hurt. It takes a good half hour for the pain meds to help you with the pain."

"I will stay awhile if you don't mind, James?"

"I don't mind at all."

Sarah was giving me a pouting look.

I had to be pleasant but firm, "I know you want to spend more time with your mother, Sarah."

Then she glared at me. I had to walk out so I wouldn't melt to her persuasion. I went to get ice. I passed Jake on the way, "Jake, she just did it again."

"What?"

"She asked if she could wait to take the pain meds, and her mom offered to stay awhile and she was pouting at me. I agreed with her mother and she glared at me."

He started to laugh out loud, "Okay, okay James, we can try something else tomorrow."

"Will you quit laughing; it's not funny."

"Yes, it is. I get to go in next; I can't wait to see this."

"She is all yours, but you have to promise me to not give into her. That would drive me crazy even if it is only the drugs."

"I couldn't even if I wanted to, now."

I was confused. What did he mean by that?

"James, I know you now; you love her and you are my brother. I just wouldn't do that, and I can turn her down."

"Can we leave the monitor on?"

"Yes, just to prove to you I can turn her down."

"Okay, but you are going to regret it."

After about an hour Paula came out.

I sat up, "Oh, shit, the ice."

"Yes, she is in pain, and I think it is getting bad."

Jake jumped up, "It's my turn." He walked to the fridge and took a shot out and warmed it with his hands.

That wasn't even fair of him, "Cheater."

Laughing, "Later, we'll check it out."

I grabbed the pill and followed Jake into the room; the shot didn't work that long. When I walked in her eyes met mine; pleading for help. Oh... shit... those eyes were begging. I walked the pill over to the stand and sat it down.

Paula kissed her on the forehead, "I am coming back tomorrow, if that is okay, James?"

I couldn't take my eyes off of Sarah, but I nodded, "Of course, anytime." I knew it would be good to have someone else to distract her. Even though Sarah's face was strained from pain she was able to give me that evil glare again.

I really didn't want to cave to her so I offered, "I'll walk you out." I followed her out of the room.

## Sarah:

"Sarah, how bad is the pain?"

"Jake, I am fine. I don't want it."

"Really, your mom was concerned."

"No, Jake! I will be fine for a while. I am actually awake for once and it's kind of nice. Why did James walk her out?"

"Because he is worried about making sure that they are okay with you being here."

"Is there something wrong with me?"

"Why would you say something like that?"

I couldn't answer him, but I wanted James to come hold me, "Do I have to take the pill?"

"Are you being honest with me about the pain?"

"It hurts a little."

"Yes, then you have to take the pill, but I am thinking about changing your medicine."

"Why?"

"Um, it might have to do with being... so horny."

"What?"

"Sarah, you were starting to dream about James when we were eating dinner with your mom."

I couldn't help but smile. I wanted James to make me happy, to feel good together. He liked when I dreamt about him.

"You know he is trying really hard to behave, and you're not making it easy on him."

Knowing that my James loved me so much that he couldn't refuse me filled my heart, but Jake... I smiled even more, "If I came on to you, you wouldn't refuse me."

"Yes I would, Sarah. It's different now. You are married."

"But you would still hold me."

"No, I can't do that ever again."

"Why not?"

"He is my brother, and you are married to him...do you want more reasons?"

"No, Sorry." I thought for sure that he would at least hold me.

"Sarah, let's try a different medication this time."

"Okay."

He got up and walked out. He took the pill with him. He came back with something different. He handed it to me and I took it.

"This might not work as well, so you have to tell us right away if the pain gets worse."

I just nodded, "Can you get James for me?"

"Sarah, you really need to rest."

He pulled me to him and moved the pillows and laid me down.

I wondered, "Is this hard for you?"

"What?"

"To take care of me like this?"

"Yeah, a little."

"Are you going to read to me like James does?"

"Okay."

He grabbed the book and opened it to the page where my mom left off. This book was so boring. I tried to get into it, but I wasn't. I needed to roll over or something. I was really uncomfortable and that wasn't including the pain that was starting to irritate my insides.

"Do you need something?"

"Yeah, I need to roll over."

He stopped reading and stood up, "You need more ice too."

"Please help me first. I don't like this feeling."

He pushed me to my side and tucked pillows behind me. He leaned over to my face, "Is this okay?"

I turned to face him a little. He just stared at me and slowly moved away.

"Yes, Jake, its fine, but I could use some ice."

"It's starting to hurt again?"

I saw my James walk in with two bags of ice. I smiled and closed my eyes. He crawled over the bed and tucked them in.

"Here Jake, give me the book; I will read to her."

I was in heaven. This is what I wanted. He propped himself up to read to me.

"James, I gave her a different pain killer. It might not work the same, so if she starts to feel a lot of pain... call me."

"Jake the monitor, will you please shut it off."

"James, no."

"I will be okay."

"James?"

"It's okay, Jake. I'm fine now."

I was filled with satisfaction that my James knew that I needed him, and was okay. He was going to be great shortly. I heard Jake leave the room. I wrapped my arm around his leg. After reading a little while I saw a grin dancing at the edge of his mouth. My teasing him with trailing my fingers over his arm, rubbing my leg against his was working. He finally scooted down to me.

"Sarah, honey. Please stop. It makes the pain worse."

I opened my eyes, but I couldn't stop my mind from wandering to his abs.

"Sarah, stop it now. Just try to go to sleep."

I decided I was going to be a good girl if he was going to stay with me to read. I felt him scoot down some more. His face was at my level. He was reading, and I was watching his face as he read. He peeked at me and scooted closer. I grinned a little and just listened to his words. I didn't move at all. He kept sneaking little glances at me between paragraphs. I just stared at him, wondering how this came to be. He was all mine. I reached up to move my hand over his face and traced my finger down his nose to his lips. They were still moving to the words on the pages until I was between his lips. His tongue came out to meet my finger to pull it in and he sucked and kissed it for a minute. I pulled my finger away. He went back to reading. I traced my fingers along his jaw to admire that strong face. I was completely in love with this man. I let my hand roam down his neck. He stopped reading; his eyes searched my face until our eyes met. He was so beautiful. He went back to reading. I lightly ran my hand down his chest, down to his abs, and further to put my hand under his shirt to touch the skin that encased his abs. He closed his eyes and tilted his head back for a moment. He liked when I touched him. I really liked it when he touched me too, but he went back to reading. I stroked my fingers over the contours of his abs. I could feel them move as I drifted over them. I did find that fascinating. I moved my hand to his chest. He tensed more and stopped to face me. I didn't change my expression; I just gave him the deer in the headlight stare. He didn't even crack a smile this time. He took his hand and let it graze down my arm to find my hand and pulled it back out, but held it as he read. He would kiss a knuckle or a fingertip of mine to keep me happy. I went back to his lips with my fingers. He stopped to suck my finger again. I pulled it out and took his hand to my mouth. He gaped at me as I opened it and kissed the palm of his hand, and his eyes closed. His chest was heaving like mine.

He turned to me, "Fuck this. "

He cupped my face and came in to kiss me passionately. My body tensed with delight. Oh, how I loved to kiss him. He was licking and nibbling my lips seductively, as he traced his hand to the middle of my back.

We heard Jake yell from the living room, "You two okay in there?"

The kissing continued. My body was trembling and Jake walked in, "James no!!!"

He stopped kissing me, "Jake OUT!"

"No, James."

He had a moment to be distracted from my playfulness to notice my body trembling, "Sarah, the pain?"

I closed my eyes, "Yes."

"Fuck! Jake, help her." He moved away from me angrily, "Sarah, you have to tell me."

Jake came to me with the shot, "James, she is trembling."

"I can't feel her when, *fuck*, Sarah, damn it. Why didn't you tell me?"

Jake yelled at James, "James!!! Go... you're not helping."

He didn't leave; I could hear him pacing.

I gripped the pillow under my head to endure the pain. My other hand was gripping the blankets in front of me. The trembling was making it hurt worse, and I was holding my breath to keep my whimpers contained.

Jake put the whole shot in, "James, these pills are not going to work; we have to stay with the other ones."

He walked out, and I heard him coming back with the bottle.

James was pleading with Jake, "Jake when you yelled, that was the first kiss; we didn't do anything."

"I know... I didn't turn the monitor off, but she waited too long. Just look at her."

"Fuck, I am an idiot."

"Shut up, I did...this...I didn't...want...stop...shit this hurts...wanted to be stronger.

He came back to me and grabbed my hand, "Sarah, don't ever not tell me about the pain."

Jake kept his hand on my shoulder. I couldn't open my eyes yet. The trembling wasn't going away.

"Sarah, I need you to take the pill; can you try?"

"Yes."

James put it in my mouth and then the straw. I swallowed it.

I don't know how long they stood there watching me, or how long the pain actually lasted but when I became less tense I apologized, "James, I'm sorry." I opened my eyes for a quick second so I could see him, but I closed them again. I couldn't handle seeing his eyes full of tears. I scared him again. I felt so bad, so I put his hand in mine and kissed it.

"Jake, this is all we were doing, at least until I couldn't handle it and kissed her lips, but I..."

"Shhh, James, it's not your fault. I waited too long." I actually got it out in one breath. It was getting better. "James… tired now."

It seemed that the more the trembling calmed the more tired I was getting. I couldn't hang on anymore, and I let the sleep take me.

## *James:*

"James, you need to settle down."

"I can't; I let her hurt."

"Let's go out and watch ESPN, or play a game or something… anything. You need to settle down."

"No, I am going to stay this time." I walked over to the lounge and turned it to face her. "Jake, I'm sorry. I just didn't do what was best for her."

"James, you are being hard on yourself. She doesn't always do what is best for her. She does what she wants and we are all subjects to her wants and desires, James. You love her and want to give her everything. That is normal. Just relax and say no sometimes."

I chuckled a little, "I still need to stay awhile. I will be out in a little bit."

He left me to wallow in my depression from letting her distract me from the pain she was enduring.

# 18. Self Control

    Jake and I decided to make her take the pills every four hours to keep her comfortable. Paula came over and we had her feed Sarah all three meals. I would go back to taking care of her on Monday. I stayed and laid on the lounge to watch them and when she needed something I ran to get it. I took her to the bathroom a few times. Sarah was not taunting me in any way, but I think she could tell that I felt horrible for the pain I had put her through. Every time I thought she was going to try to get me going my heart would race with anticipation, but her face would turn to concern and she would let it go.
    When her mother left I read to her, but I sat on the chair rather than on the bed. She didn't last long. I was happy she didn't push teasing me. I really couldn't handle the thought of hurting her in any way.

    Monday came as a repeat of Sunday; only Jake was the one feeding her instead of her mother. I was still the one that took her to the bathroom; that was something I didn't want Jake doing. I continued to read to her from the chair. The only thing different was today when she slept I ventured out to the living room. I played a few games with Jake, but I wasn't as talkative. I'm sure he sensed my depression.

    Tuesday, it started the same. Going in and feeding her the pills, taking her to the bathroom, putting ice on her, and then reading to her from the book. Jake came in to feed her and talk with her. I moved to the lounge to watch them interact. I was completely miserable and I just wanted to make her better, so I could have her. She wanted a shower, but I agreed to give her one on Wednesday. I had to keep my distance. I didn't want to hurt her. Otherwise, things went well the rest of the day. When it was completely into the night I wandered back out to the living room. Jake was still up playing video games, so I sat down.

"James, you want to play with me?"

"No." I wanted to hold her... to kiss her. She was in my home, and I needed to be with her. I was in misery.

"James, it wasn't your fault."

"But I can't let that happen again."

"James, how are you going to give her a shower?"

"I don't know; the desire has been building for three days, and I am going to go crazy."

"Think about her mother being on the other side of the door."

"Yeah. Because that worked so well for me before."

"How about our mother on the other side of the door?"

"Yeah, because she understands the passion of wanting to be together?"

"Well, think of someone who will stop you."

"How about the pain?"

"That would work for me. Does it for you?"

"Sometimes, but when she gets me going I forget."

"Just keep telling yourself that."

"Sorry, Jake, I need to sleep."

I got up and went to bed, of course, on the lounge. We were still getting up every four hours to feed Sarah her medication. It would be early morning the next time she would be awake. I closed my eyes to wait.

"James."

When I heard her I got up and went to her; I wasn't sleeping very well these days. She had a little time before she could take the meds, and I was so excited to go to her and have a little time with her.

"James, can you hold me? Would that be okay?"

I moved into bed with her and pulled her to my chest. I was still worried about how she was going to tempt me, but she didn't. I read to her while I held her, and she did not tease in any way. I was happy about that. I fed her another pill, but continued to hold and read to her. I must have dosed off with her in my arms because the next thing I knew it was time for her to get up and eat again. I felt better than I had in days. I kissed her head and she hugged me more. I wanted to do this from now on. Maybe she would understand that we could have more of this if she behaves.

First we started with breakfast. She wanted to talk, but I wanted her to eat so she got no encouragement from me. I was happy just being with her. Next, I took her to the bathroom with an interlude for going, but continued with brushing her teeth. I held her gently around her waist while she did her little morning ritual. However, I found that I was fascinated just watching her. When she was ready to move to the next task at hand she turned to me reaching up to wrap her arms around my neck. No little smirk, no evil glare, just a simple smile from her. I was standing right next to her and I missed her something terrible, like she wasn't her playful self, but I was able to control myself better than I have in a long time. I lifted her and walked to the shower. I caressed her cheek with mine before I let her go. The slightest touch was so satisfying. I rested my forehead to hers, just so we could continue touching while I reached down to unbutton her night shirt.

## Sarah:

As he was unbuttoning my shirt I ran my hands up and down his biceps. These arms were going to be wrapped around my naked body soon, but not soon enough. My pulse raced as my heart pounded against my chest. I knew I could not tease or taunt him, but just to feel him next to me would be so satisfying. I saw a glimpse of a grin so he must be thinking the same thing as I am. I reached as far as I could trying to pull his shirt up, so that we could get it off of him.

"What do you think you're doing, little girl?"

"James, I need to touch you, feel you, anything or the desire is going to break me into pieces."

For some reason he wasn't agreeing with me. He was shaking his head no, "But... Sarah?"

I pulled away just so that I could press my cheek to his. I needed his caresses, "No, James, please." I ran my nose just under his ear, "Just don't think about it and don't kiss me. I get lost in your kisses. As long as you don't kiss me we will be fine."

He laughed a little so I continued. I needed him next to me and if he was going to give in to me I had to take advantage of it. I decided teasing was out of the question, because I didn't want to build any desire, I already had enough. My hands trembled, and my breath quickened as I unbuttoned his pants and unzipped them.

It happened so fast. His hands grabbed mine to stop me from undressing him. Those deep brown eyes were as sad as a lonely puppy, but with a possibility of losing control.

I was so determined to get my fill. I shook my head, "James, think of something else."

"Like what?"
"Anything."

We were fully undressed and he was beautiful. I took a step to the shower.

"Sarah, you shouldn't be doing that."
"It's been a week. I should be able to do a little by now, shouldn't I?"
"We should ask Jake."
"It only hurts a little."
"Well, that helps with the desire, it hurts."

I laughed. He was following me in, but kept his arms out from me to keep me from falling in pain. I reached to turn the water on and turned to him. He moved to hold me. Oh how I needed this. Okay I have to think of a distraction, "James, I have my classes scheduled for college, but I still need to make sure everything is in order."

"We'll go online and find out what you need, and schedule a time to go get them and check with your school to see if we can have you start with classes online for the first two weeks before you go home."

It was working, "See, we can do this."

"Okay more, getting hotter."

"Okay, now for you. Have you thought about school?"

"Nope, distracted." He lowered his face to kiss me.

I pulled away.

"James, try. If you are going to trust me to be this close and not attack you, you have to try. Now... school for you. You are interested in Forestry, right?"

He shook his head no but replied, "Yeah."

"Did you know there are a few choices? I didn't know what you wanted, but if you go to the UofM they have a wide variety."

"You looked on the internet for me?"

"Yeah, while I was getting my stuff done. I have to confess I wanted to keep you close to me."

He smiled, "Okay, we'll look at it today."

"All the classes are here in the cities, but the field work is up north not far from the reservation."

"Really?"

"I thought that would be perfect, because you could see your family when you were up there, and if the elders saw that you were taking care of the land they would be happy."

"It doesn't matter; I'm not going to be Chief."

"I hope not, because now your mine, but they will be happy you still care, and they will be more supportive of Sam."

His hands traveled up my back, and he swallowed hard, "You just get better and better."

We were touching and washing each other as our conversation continued. We could handle this.

"That reminds me of something Jake told me."

My heart dropped. What did I tell Jake that James didn't know... shit?

"Your face just went scared."

"Yeah,"

"Why?"

"What would Jake have told you that you don't already know?"

He was pleased that he caught me off guard and there wasn't anything that I would want Jake to know that I hadn't already shared with James. A grin grew across his face; he was enjoying my panic.

"James, please."

"You took him to a race track and scared the shit out of him."

"Oh that." That was no big deal. I was relieved. "I think I did that to loosen him up. He was so stiff and business uptight when I first met him."

"You should go to the living room and see him now. He's quite comfortable there. You wouldn't think of him as a doctor if you saw him this way. He reminds me of Sam more than any of us."

I smiled while touching his face, "So, things are going okay?"

"Yeah, it's weird though."

"Back to the driving; what about him being scared?"

"Nothing about that, but can you use the track whenever you want to?"

"Yeah, but I only go out there when I need to forget why I am miserable."

"I don't like to hear that."

"I have you now. If I need to feel better, I can seduce you."

He shook his head, "I want to go to the track."

"Really?"

"Yes. I drove motor cross when I was young and I miss it. I have the need for speed."

"We can go when I am better."

He was more determined, "Yes, but we're taking the bike."

"You'll wear your helmet?"

"Of course, I may be crazy, but I'm not stupid."

I tipped back under the water to wet my hair. He came to kiss my neck so fast.

"James, we were doing good, stop that."

"I can't help myself."

I wrapped my hands and arms around him. "If we do anything it has to be in our minds."

He moved away from me, "No Sarah, I'm just playing."

"I feel something else and that doesn't feel like playing."

He pulled away and smiled, "What can I say, you feel really good to me."

"Hand me the shampoo, James."

He did and I put some in my hands and washed my hair. I put more in my hands and washed his while he kissed my body.

"James, you're going to get too worked up."

"Good, I have been so depressed not touching you."

I reminded him, "Rinse, James, rinse."

I moved under the water tilting my head back and he came in to kiss my lips while water ran over our faces. I let him kiss me, which was wrong, because I knew I would get lost in him. I needed to feel his mouth on mine, and I was lost. Lost in the way his mouth led me to some other place and time, a place where we could dream of being together. His body was tensing as our bodies grazed together while our mouths hungrily consumed each other.

I was getting so lost that I had to stop myself and him, "James, I'm done."

We switch spots under the water. I was so caught up in him from the kissing I continued while he rinsed his hair. I kissed his chest and ran my hands over the side of him. He moved out from under the shower and wrapped his arms around me kissing me.

He reached back to shut it off. He stopped and looked at me, "Done?"

I grinned at him, "Yes."

He grabbed towels and wrapped one around me and one around him. He grabbed another and draped it over my head. He picked me up and juggled me in his arms while trying to open the door. He walked with me to the dresser and looked out the door, "Jake, shut off the monitor, please."

"James, no. Don't do anything stupid."

"Please?" as he looked at me with a great big smile.

"If you don't you won't like what you're going to hear."

We stood there staring at each other knowing we were going to let the desire win. He grabbed clothes for me and a pair of boxers for himself. He handed them to me and lifted me to walk me to the bed.

He sat me down hesitating, "How are you doing?"

I was eager to continue the playing, "Really good, James."

He helped me lower to lay down grabbing my feet and put them on his abs. He grabbed the sleeping shorts and put it on my legs one foot at a time. He was pushing them up, but messaged my legs as he pushed them up. He got to my thighs and kissed there, tracing his face along them. It tickled so I laughed. He lifted my butt and slipped them over me. His hand drifted over me, "A little protection."

"JAMES!!!!"

"Jake, I am warning you... shut it off."

I didn't want Jake to hear us. I shook my head no.

Eyes full of twinkling lights and face full of determination he reminded me, "Then it's his own fault." He yelled again, "Jake, shut it off."

"No, remember what you told me. Remember how miserable you were when you hurt her before. You wanted to be stopped, JAMES!"

He didn't want to be with me? He must have seen the strain in my eyes because he moved over me hovering, "Sarah, it's not like that. I just don't want to hurt you."

I didn't say anything; I just stared at him with wonder. He came in for a kiss. A long sensual kiss that made me feel so dreamy. He was opening my towel, and stopped to take me in. His chest was heaving while his eyes searched for anything I could give him. Even though he was supporting all his weight with his arms he lowered his body to graze mine. I gasped with the pleasure of his taunt releasing the air with his name on my tongue, "James." He pulled away from me, but that wasn't what I wanted. I gripped, maybe even dug my fingers into his biceps pulling him back to me, but instead he pushed all the way up pulling me with him to sit up. He slipped the shirt over one arm and then the other. He left it open. I was totally taken by him. He helped me scoot to the middle of the bed and turn me so my head was on the pillows, "How do you feel."

"James, NO MORE!"

We both laughed because of Jake's comment.

"Jake, I was moving her to the middle of the bed."

"JAMES, DON'T DO IT."

I watched James and laughed silently. He moved away from me and unplugged the monitor. We could hear the static all the way from the other room. He came to the door and knocked, "James, I am coming in."

"Jake, Sarah is not dressed yet, so stay out."

"James, you don't want to hurt her."

"I won't, go play a game or something."

He was getting frustrated with Jake. He crawled on the bed to me and lay down next to me on his side. I traced my hand over his chest. He grabbed the book, "Come here, little girl."

He was helping me move to him, as he rolled to his back. He was still in his towel, but I lay next to him with every inch of my body touching his. His arm supported me to hold me next to him and he started to read. I wasn't expecting this, but I laid my head on his chest, put my leg over his, and traced my hand over his chest. I was completely covered, but I was lying next to my James

Jake was coming in, "James, you have to stop."

Jake had his hand over his eyes. Our attention went to watching Jake as he moved closer to us. He still had his hand over his eyes and he was going to get hurt that way.

"Jake, it's okay you can look, but you can leave too."

Jake dropped his hand and walked to the bed glaring at us, "You two have to behave."

We both smiled innocently, "Jake, were just going to read."

He glared at James, "If I have to come in here and give her another shot, I am not going to be happy. It hasn't even been a week, Sarah." He emphasized my name.

"We'll be good. Do you want to listen to the story?"

"Hey, wait I have something better." He ran out of the room and came back with a book. "You will like this one better." He held it up, "Have you read any of these books, Sarah?"

I shook my head no. He wasn't getting the hint we wanted to play. He handed it to James and took the other one. "This is a love story, but they wait."

"Wait for what, Jake." I was being explicit.

"Sarah, to have sex, but you will like it. It's wild and has to do with supernatural things like James."

"Okay, we'll read this. Can you excuse us now?"

He looked at us realizing my shirt wasn't buttoned and James was still in a towel."

"Read... no more of that. It might hurt you, and then I will have to deal with him hating himself. Don't taunt him, Sarah, please for him and me. He has been a pain in my butt lately."

"Jake, I will behave."

"Jake, will you get a pill since you are in here killing the mood."

He smiled; he was pleased with himself, "Yeah, be right back, but no funny business."

I held up two fingers, "Scouts honor."

He went out to get the pill. I crossed my fingers and glancing up at James.

He shook his head, "You are a very bad little girl."

"Don't you mean good?" I raised my eyebrows.

He smiled and opened the book to start reading. I listened as Jake walked back in with the pill handing it to me.

I took a sip of the sports drink and swallowed it, "I hate taking these; I get so foggy."

James traced his hand over my head, "Just a little bit longer, baby." He went back to reading to me out loud. I was paying attention; this had to be better than the other book. I wasn't really a good reader, but I paid attention.

Jake was still standing there with a look of longing on his face. He interrupted, "Sarah, can James come out to play when you fall asleep?"

James stopped to laugh, "Yes, I can and I will. I am happy now."

"Did you already *'Please her'?* as you would put it?"

I was not happy with James, "You make me sound like that is all I want?"

"NO, and no we are not doing that, Jake. I just need to hold her. I miss it too."

Jake smiled, "Fine." He walked over and plugged the monitor back in, "but if anything gets too hot I will be listening."

"Jake, off, I mean it."

He shook his head no as he walked to the door, "I will be listening. Don't do anything that these virgin ears couldn't handle." He closed the door.

"Why did he close the door if he's going to listen on the monitor?"

He yelled, "BECAUSE!"

I laughed. James went back to reading to me. I nuzzled into him. With Jake listening, I was able to control myself better. I just laid my hand on his abs. I listened and paid attention to his words. I kissed him where my lips laid. He ran his fingers through my hair. I was losing track of the words because the fogginess was coming back, "James, you'll have to go back a few pages next time; my head is foggy and I won't remember it."

He kissed my head, "Anything you want, my sweetness."

He continued until I was sleeping.

*James:*

I read until I was sure she was sleeping. Having Jake listening helped me stay in control of my desire. I didn't want to hurt him, and he did love her too. Maybe not in the same way as before, but he still had feelings for her; and he was my brother. I slid from the bed and got dressed and went out to play games with him.

"So, you behaved?"

"Yes, it helped that you were listening."

"I didn't think you could, so I turned it off, but if it helps I will leave it on from now on."

I just shook my head.

"Did she like that book better?"

"Yes, she was actually listening. She asked me to go back and read pages over because her head was getting foggy, and she didn't want to miss anything."

"So, what do you feel like playing?"

"Maybe pool."

"I don't have that one."

"You haven't seen this yet. Come here."

He got up to follow me. He walked in and looked around the room. There was a game room off to the left of the living room. He walked around with eyes popping out of his skull, "If I would have known about this I wouldn't have gotten the video games."

I laughed and we played darts and pool. We wasted time as we waited for her time to be awake. I heard rustling from the monitor. I dropped everything to go back to her.

"James, she is just moving."

"Sorry, I have to..."

I ran to the room and could see she was uncomfortable. I rolled her to her back and touched her face. I felt her dreaming about us, so I lay down next to her. I watched her and felt her movement as she touched my chest running her hands downward.

"Sarah, baby, no. Just wait. Shhhhhh. No more, please."

I closed my eyes and felt her trace her lips over my chest. It did feel good, but I could not endure this laying next to her; I would want more, "No Sarah." I leaned to whisper in her ear, "Sleep, Sarah. Heal. I will be waiting. No Sarah."

It worked. Her dream was moving to something else, something calm and relaxing. My body eased as she released me from her dream. In adoration of my baby I traced the back of my hand along her face gently as she drifted further away.

I took a deep cleansing breath, and then headed back out to the living room.

"That I did hear; good for you, James."

If felt good to make him happy for once. This time we sat and played video games. Wilson came over and brought us another meal. I wouldn't have eaten at all if it weren't for Wilson.

## 19. Oh Poop

**S**he woke later than usual and we didn't wake her for her pill, so I was worried about the pain. As soon as I heard her move, I told Jake to get food ready, but I ran to be by her side.

"Sarah, how is the pain?"

"Not too bad. More like an ache than actual knives shooting through me."

Smiling I replied, "Sarah, you must have felt really good. You slept almost six hours."

"Really?" She was trying to push herself up.

"Wait, Jake is coming and you're not…"

I moved to her to start to button her up, and I heard Jake.

"You left her exposed. You shouldn't do that with me around."

"Jake stop, enough of that talk."

He was laughing. I lay next to her while Jake fed her. She did well, but we gave her another pill because the pain was increasing. I could actually feel the tension in her body.

When he was done, he walked out, "I will be listening."

I rolled my eyes, so she could see my disgust. She cuddled into me. I started the chapter over and read to her. She nuzzled in and laid her hand on my chest. I loved to feel her next to me. I traced my fingers through her hair, as she listened to me read. She curled into me more.

"Sarah, you are moving a lot; are you in pain?"

"No, only when I move."

"Well, stop moving. I will set the alarm for six more hours, but no longer than that. I will have to wake you."

"Yes, James, read on."

I started to read further. The warmth of her body heated my side, making the heat rise in me, but it was a good day and I didn't hurt her. I was getting tired, and scooted down by her more. I tried to keep reading, and I was really getting into this story. It was about the beginning of having feelings developing between two people; it brought back the memories of being with her before she knew the attraction was there. I knew I would have to read this chapter again, so she could get caught up. I put the book down and curled into her more kissing her head and tracing my hands down her face and her arm. I loved my little girl so much, but she was still a little girl no matter how we felt about each other. She was mine though. I rested my face an inch from hers to watch her breathe until I couldn't keep my eyes open any more.

## Sarah:

I woke in James's arms and felt wonderful, so I nuzzled into him more and traced my lips over his. He was kissing me back, and I reached for him for more of a deep kiss. He moved to me and wrapped his arms around me, "Shower."

"Yes, James."

"No. Just me, and a cold one." He rolled away from me.

I grabbed his arm, "James, can't you just…?"

When his eyes came back to meet mine they were filled with so much desire I let go of him instantly. Taking advantage of my release he went to the bathroom to take care of that desire. I absolutely hate when he has to walk away from me. My heart ached, so I closed my eyes, and tried not to imagine him in the shower.

I must have dozed off, because when I woke he was in my arms again kissing me so tenderly and sweetly. He rolled me back, "How is the pain?"

I thought about it, but it wasn't too bad, "Why, how much longer before another pill?"

"If we are waiting for the six hours; you have time to wait. You're awake, so we could play a little." He was a new man without desire built up.

His hand came to my face to caress and luring me into play; slowly and softly kissing me. He let his touch fall to my chest to take in my excitement as he felt it heave. I was in heaven with his touch. He moved his hand and let the kiss go, "We should read. I turned it back a few chapters. I read pretty far not knowing when you fell asleep."

"James, I like the kissing."

He came to me again kissing me, but moved his body away from mine.

"Where are you going?"

"You need to eat and I need to stop."

I kissed him smiling, "Are you sure I can't have more of this?"

He continued to kiss me; I was trying to move to him, but it hurt when I used my feet to push to him. I stopped and cringed.

"See, more time, Sarah. It's okay. I will wait."

"No, James, use your mind."

"You know that is not good for us, and it is better than I can do. Please, time to eat."

He moved away from me and out the door. He didn't take long to get food. He came with the salad I love and a very small sandwich. He held it up for me to take a bite, "See, you don't have to mash it and tear it to shreds; its bite size just for you."

"Wilson?"

"Of course, we wouldn't be eating either if it wasn't for him."

I took the sandwich and ate it all. I was really hungry. When I was done my stomach didn't feel great, "Oh, that might have been too much, James."

"No, you don't, Sarah. Lay back and let it settle. He got up and moved to the other side of the bed grabbing the book to read to me. I cuddled in and listened.

Thursday went really well. I was getting time awake every six hours to mingle with the two of them. I ate four times today, and I got up with help sitting up and being pulled to my feet, but I got to walk from one side of the bed to the other. A really good day and I get to sleep with James next to me now. I just have to behave. He doesn't let it go too far at all; I tried to pout to get my way, but he has so much more control than me. I loved him more for that. He continued to read to me for at least an hour before pill time.

Friday came early. I couldn't sleep any longer, and I needed to go to the bathroom. James looked so sweet sleeping next to me. I didn't want to wake him; he would get up and want to feed me. I rolled out of bed and got on my knees. I knew I couldn't stand on my own let alone make it up the three steps. I leaned over the bed, I had to.

"James?"

His arm came to wrap around me, but I wasn't there.

He panicked and sat up, "Sarah?"

I reached for him from the side of the bed. He moved to me and picked me up, "What were you doing?"

"Trying to get myself to the bathroom, but I couldn't."

"Sarah, please don't do stuff like this; you scare the shit out of me."

"I would just like to be able to go to the bathroom on my own, James, that's all."

"Not yet, sweetie."

I was sad; I didn't want him to have to do everything for me. He carried me to the bathroom, "Okay, you want to do stuff on your own, so pull your shorts down and sit down. If you can do that I will let you do it on your own."

I reached down and slid them down without bending. Now I had to sit. I kept my eyes on him waiting for a funny glance or something, "I feel really stupid."

"Think about the first time I had to take you, and then the time your mom was standing outside the door."

He was almost laughing to himself. I wasn't finding humor in it. I bent my knees to lower myself and nope the pain was too much, and the tears started welling.

"See, Sarah, not yet"

He helped me sit down, kissed the top of my head, and walked out closing the door. I had to go poop, but the stomach was hurting from trying to sit. I tried to relax and the pain was excruciating. The tears traced down my cheeks. I would have been happier to stay in the hospital longer, so a nurse could have helped me. This was going to be another low point in my life.

Finally finishing I wiped and flushed.

"You done?"

"James, give me a minute."

"Sarah, you're not okay."

"James, stay out or I will not behave later."

"Fine."

I heard him yell for Jake. I could hear them talking.

"Sarah, are you done?"

"Just a minute, I am a girl and I am allowed to take as much time as I want in the bathroom."

Of course now Jake was outside the door too, "Sarah, did you have a bowl movement?"

Oh, how humiliating.

"Sarah?"

"What, Jake? Just give me a minute."

I could hear them talking. I heard James say he wasn't going to leave. Jake was trying to say something. I didn't want either of them there.

"Can you both just go in the other room for about two hours and I will stay here for a while."

I heard the arguing. The pain really wasn't easing.

Jake was speaking to me, "Sarah, you have to let me come in."

"No!"

"Then James has to."

"NO!!"

"Sarah, we're both going to be in there in two seconds if you don't let one of us in."

"Stop... no! Please?" I tried to sound angry, but the pain was almost too much and I was crying.

I heard more arguing.

"Sarah, at least tell me if it was a bowl movement. I knew that was going to be painful."

"It would have been nice to know that beforehand."

He was laughing, "Are you done?"

"Yes, but just give me a minute."

"Sarah, James is coming in; I'll get a shot."

Why did they feel like they could humiliate me any time they felt the need? I didn't want James or Jake in here after pooping. I reached back flushing the toilet. At least it would have a fresher scent. James walked in with the most pitiful face I had ever seen, "I can feel your pain.

"I am a girl, and I do like to be in the bathroom by myself."

He shook his head in disbelief, "Why didn't you just tell me? You are in so much pain."

"This is very embarrassing."

"Sarah, you don't have to be embarrassed with me, and your pain was so extreme." He lifted me and helped pull up my shorts, "Did you want to walk?"

"Nope, it hurts to stand."

He picked me up and carried me back to bed laying me down. It was all painful now and I cringed.

"I'll get some ice, and Jake will be right here."

Jake was already walking in the room, "Next time will you at least tell us. I could have given this to you before, so it wouldn't hurt as bad."

With a sniffle I scolded Jake, "Thanks for telling me that now."

"So now, you have to explain the pain. I need to know if everything is working."

He pulled up my shirt just to the belly button and pushed down the shorts below the cut.

James was walking in, "Jake, what are you doing?"

"Finding out where the pain was."

He was tracing his hand above the incision, "Here Sarah, was there pain here?"

"Still hurts there."

He ran his hand under the incision, "How about here?"

"Excruciating!"

"Now or just when you went?"

"Excruciating while I was going. Sever pain now."

"How about as it came out? Did it hurt here or in your back?"

"Jake, it all hurt. The next time I will pay attention. I wasn't expecting that this time. I didn't take notes."

He laughed.

"What?"

"Sarah, I just want to make sure I lined everything up right."

"What?"

"Sarah, I took everything out. I washed every piece of your insides off. They are not going to be happy to be messed with for a while."

"So, what do you mean you lined everything up right?"

"Sarah, there is a lot in there and god put it together, and when we take it out, it's a little hard to put it back in the way he designed it. I only left out a few pieces."

I was so scared, "What did you leave out?"

"Sarah, I'm kidding. We only took out the appendix, but there is a lot in there and if you saw what we pulled out and look at how small you are you would wonder how that all was in there."

"So, is it lined up right or not?"

"Well, I think so, and no I am not kidding. We'll have to take every step slowly to make sure everything is working."

He was holding my hand and James was sitting next to me on the bed. I squeezed his hand, "You knew about the fitting things back in?"

"Yeah, look how tiny you are. Jake was a little concerned if you would have been bigger it would have fit better."

"So, if everything is shoved back in, can I have babies?"

I was asking Jake and he wasn't saying anything. I turned to James with the fear in my eyes. I wasn't ready now, but I would want one with James eventually.

After I turned to James for answers Jake finally answered me, "Sarah, you definitely can get pregnant."

"So, what does that mean?"

"It means that if you don't want to get pregnant you will still have to use precautions."

"So, I can have a baby?"

"That's not what I am saying. You can get pregnant, but we don't know if you can carry it yet."

I started to gasp for air. I pulled down my shirt not looking at either one of them and then pulled my shorts up. I curled up towards James and started to cry. I heard Jake leave. James was rubbing my back not saying a word. He just let me be sad. I cried myself to sleep.

## 20. Never A Woman

When I woke up I didn't want to live anymore. What kind of future would I have if I couldn't have children with James? Yes, I could have a great career. I could have a man that I loved with all of my heart, but why go through all those years of living if I couldn't have a child of my own. James was so good with his little sister. We talked about it and he wanted five; I don't know if I could even carry one. He needed to find someone who could give him a child. I would have to let him go. Maybe if he was the Chief he... no he wouldn't take that away from Sam. He would just have to find someone to love that he could have children with. I took the ring off and let the tears fall again. I wasn't even a woman yet and now I felt like I would never be one.

I rolled back over and tried to go back to sleep. Maybe if I tried hard enough God would come get me now. I prayed to leave earth; it would be so much easier.

"Sarah, before you go back to sleep you need food and your pill." It was Jake.

He came over and tried to set the tray on the end table. He leaned over me and pulled me up and tucked pillows behind me. He handed me the pill, then a sport drink, "Take the pill, Sarah, the pain won't kill you. You will just be miserable."

"I am already miserable. Where's James?"

"He knows what you are thinking and its breaking his heart, and he can't see you right now. He is afraid he will do something that wouldn't be good for either of you. By the way, put the damn ring back on. He felt that too."

"No, Jake, he needs to find someone else."

"Sarah, I didn't say you couldn't have children; I said I didn't know if you could carry one. When you decide you are ready, we will take all the precautionary steps to help you carry it. That's all."

"But I shouldn't."

"That's not what I am saying. I am saying you have to be careful. Who knows, by then maybe your hips will turn out and you will have tons of room for a baby."

"Jake, will you make up your mind; you're confusing me."

He sat on the bed with me. He wiped my tears and slid the ring back on my finger.

"For better or worse, Sarah. This was a grown up decision, and you need to start acting like one... He did say something that you should hear."

"What's that?"

"Please don't push me away."

I started to really cry. I put my hands over my face, "Jake, can you leave, please?"

"Sarah, you have to eat."

I shook my head no; I just need to be alone for a while. He got up and walked out. I took the ring off and put it in the top drawer and reached for the monitor. I almost fell out of bed reaching for it. I yanked it out of the wall. I wanted privacy. I could hear them arguing in the other room. I pulled each of my legs to my chest one by one. I couldn't do it with the muscles that were still really weak. The medicine wasn't kicking in either. I needed to get my mind off of everything. If I could have, I would have run away to home. Deep down I knew James wanted babies, almost as much as I did. He deserved better.

I heard him yell, "THERE IS NOTHING BETTER!"

I heard Jake wrestle with him. I put my face to my knees and cried. I fell to my side still curled up and grabbed the book. I needed to escape. I started to read where I remembered from; until I closed my eyes and couldn't open them again.

When I woke again I was still miserable. I have to push the man I love away, and I didn't know how. I kept my eyes closed and tried to reason with him in my head. He felt what I felt; if I could feel this was right, how I felt, maybe he would. I opened my eyes to try and move, but the pain was still there. I was probably crying too much and used the muscles in a strenuous way. When I looked around the room it was filled with bouquets of roses everywhere. I tried to push myself up, and the bed was filled with rose petals. The room was lit with candles that were burnt down half way.

I felt his face at my neck, "Sarah, there is nothing better, and I deserve the best."

He was kissing my shoulder and breathing in my ear. I lifted my hand to touch his face on my neck. The ring was back on my hand and I shook my head, but couldn't help but smile.

"What have you done?"

"Sarah, I will give you the world if you ask me, but please don't push me away like this."

He turned me in his arms, so I could see his face. He was worn out; he looked like I felt, the look of wanting to die rather than be apart.

"I love you more than I could ever show you, and you are more important to me than breathing. I can't and won't live without you."

He laid me down tracing his fingers over my cheek.

"Tell me what would make you feel better. I know that this is right, and that it is forever, no matter if there are little ones in our lives or not."

He had me convinced until he brought up the little ones. My heart was breaking for him. He could see the torment in my eyes that I wanted that for him.

"Sarah, please tell me what you want, anything?"

"We can't do that."

"I will use my mind if it will make your heart better; the hole in it is growing, and we need to stop it because it is tearing mine to little pieces."

"What I want or what I need?"

"Both… all of it… just tell me, Sarah, you are driving me crazy, and not in a good way."

"James, can you just hold me?"

"That is all you want?"

"No, that is what I need. My day has been a little rough."

"You are my wife; you are in my bed, in my arms, so I think it is a great day."

"Well, let's look at it from my viewpoint: it hurts to poop, found out I shouldn't have babies, the pain in my stomach is killing me and my heart hurts because if you stay…"

"Shhhh. No ifs ands or buts, Sarah. You said you would never push me away."

"James, this isn't pushing; I was letting you go so you can have a full and happy life."

"My life will only be full and happy if you are in it."

"James, I need pain meds; the pain is getting worse. I think it's from crying."

He cringed, "So you're not going to punish yourself anymore?"

"No. It's almost kicking the air out of me."

He moved away from me carefully and quickly left the room. I heard him talking with Jake. He was very aggressive about it, "Jake, she could use a shot."

Jake came in the room so fast I would say he was listening on the other side of the door. He sat down on the bed next to me with a sad look on his face, "How bad is it?"

I was to the point of screaming. He put his hand to my face; "I am sorry I upset you."

I gave him a slight smile, "Pain?"

He was giving me the shot, "No, Sarah, I…"

"Shhh."

"Did you get to see the whole room yet?"

"Yeah, I think so."

He wrapped his arms around me to lift me to see, "Here, you need to see the whole room."

He was pointing in every direction. There must have been over 40 bouquets of roses placed around the room.

"You do know he loves you so much, and he has been miserable all day. You have been torturing him with your thoughts."

"Jake, remember when you first met me and you said you didn't see what the big deal with me was that everybody warned you about?"

He grinned, "Yeah"

"I don't get it either."

"Sarah, I get it now."

"I don't. I don't want to lose James, but I love him so much, and he deserves a whole woman, not a little girl that will never be a woman. This whole thing about inviting people here... Matt, and the girls from school. It gets all bundled and confusing in my head."

"You are thinking too much. Number one, you are more a woman than you know. Second, we don't have to invite Matt."

"Matt's not the problem. It's the girls from school. They used to be mean to me, and now they don't know I exist. I like it that way. I am okay with being nobody."

"You worry too much."

"It's better than thinking about something I have no control over."

That made him laugh, "That is why you are different. You look at things differently. It's not like you're superior, but real."

"Jake, it still makes me sad."

"Why would you want him to find someone else?"

"Because I know in his heart he wants children, and he is so good with his little sister. She is 10."

"I have a sister?"

This is how selfish I was. I had forgotten that fact, "Oh, forgot about that. Yes, you do."

"Is it Tamara?"

He knew her name, "You met her?"

"A couple of times, and she always tries to make me happy."

I couldn't help but laugh. She liked to do that to people.

"Jake I have always wondered; does it work?"

He started to think about it and smiled, "You know I think it did, but I thought she was playing."

"She has talents too, Jake."

I could see the memory linger as he thought about her.

"Jake, where is James? It doesn't take this long to get a pill."

"He has another surprise for you."

"I wish he wouldn't do all this. I don't want him to waste his money this way."

"Humor him. He is trying to show you how much he loves you. Like that rock on your hand."

I held it up, "What about it?"

"That ring alone is worth quite a bit. Truthfully, it's got to be worth thousands."

I started to choke while Jake was patting my back.

"Sarah, are you okay?"

"I knew it was too much. Shit, I don't want to wear it; what if I lose it?"

"It's big enough that you will notice if it's not on your hand."

"I hope he isn't spending more money; we won't have any left in the account for the house."

"You two had an account together before getting married?"

"He had me open one. I put as much as I could in it to save, and he put some money in there from what his mother gave him."

"She paid for my college."

"How is it that she has all this money?"

"Well, most of it came from her parents. They were rich and when they passed she inherited it all, plus she is a judge and makes quite a bit on her own."

I didn't want to be rude but, "Jake, I need James."

"I will go see what is taking him so long. Are you okay?"

"Better, thank you."

He kissed my forehead and walked out. I heard them talking.

James finally came in. The stress on his face seemed to be getting worse. The deep purple under his eyes was starting to sink in. He still was trying to be supportive, "Did you have a nice talk?"

"I wanted you."

He smiled, "Then don't push me away. First, here is your pill and…" he was handing me the drink, "A Sip."

I grimaced at him.

"Now Sarah, close your eyes and…" he laid me back and helped me roll to my side.

"Now no peaking."

"James, you don't have to do that or any of this."

"I know; I want to."

"James, you shouldn't do all this. I just wanted you to hold me. That is what makes me feel the best."

His eyes were gleaming in the candlelight. He put his hand over my eyes to keep them closed for me.

I heard him moving around. He lifted my arm and slid something soft and fluffy between them. I kept my eyes closed, "James, you got me a puppy."

"You're not funny. Keep your eyes closed."

I waited as I felt him lay something over me, light and soft. I felt him move in behind me and wrap himself around me. I heard him with a piece of paper in front of my face. "You can open your eyes."

I opened my eyes slowly while his mouth came to my neck tracing his lips against my skin. He was nibbling at my ear. "Sarah…"

He was breathing in my ear and the goose bumps started. I was trying to focus on the paper.

"James, what is this? Is this something about my car?"

"Sarah, I knew you would worry about it, and you would push yourself to go back to work too soon. This way you can wait 'til you're ready."

"But what does this mean, paid in full?"

"It's paid for, no more payment, no worrying; just take your time to heal."

"James, you really have to stop doing this."

"Sarah, I am allowed. I am your husband, and you are my wife."

The tears started to well up so fast that they leaked out before I could stop them.

"I love to hear, my husband. I still can't believe it."

He was tracing his face along my neck again to take in my scent. I found this very pleasing to my heart."

"Sarah, you haven't said anything about the other stuff."

I put down the paper; I had a huge soft fluffy bed pillow to lie against. I hugged it.

"That is for when we can't be together. You can hug and hold it when I come to you in your dreams."

"But James, I don't want to be away from you."

He grabbed what he had laid over the top of me and wiped my face with it.

"Sheets?"

"But feel, Sarah, its silk. The way you feel to me."

I leaned back into him and tipped my face up to his. He traced his lips over mine. I was trying to move to him, but he wouldn't let me.

"Let's give it a try, Sarah, here."

He was pushing me back to the pillow, and helped me wrap my arm around it. He lifted my leg slightly to drape over it. He whispered softly in my ear, "I want to make love to you."

I felt his mouth trace down the front of me.

"No, James, it has to be real."

"Not yet baby, heal first. Enjoy what I can give you now."

I felt his mouth on my stomach, licking and sucking, taunting me. Then his mouth was on my neck whispering in my ear, "I love the way you feel in my arms."

"James, I need you for real. It's not good to use our minds, remember?"

"Then we shall read."

He grabbed the book and started to read to me. I listened contently feeling his breath at my ear. I was kissing his arm that was wrapped around me, and he nuzzled into my neck more as he read. I closed my eyes and let the fog come over me. He felt so good around me; I tried to shake it off, but I couldn't keep my eyes open.

*James:*

I traced my hands over her frail body. I never wanted to let go. I was racking my brain on how was I going to make sure she never pushed me away again without deepening our connection. My chest was still pounding from being next to her. How was I ever going to let her leave to live with her parents? I can barely handle being in a separate room from her. I couldn't stop myself; my heart has hurt all day. I just needed to have her in my arms. I curled into her more and closed my eyes.

I was in the dream with her, but it was a little different. She was distant and not in our house. She was sad and alone. I couldn't have this. I was trying to get to her to not leave her alone. The closer I got to her the more she drifted away. I called to her, "Sarah!"
She turned and came to my arms. I didn't like that she was in a dream but alone, "Why are you alone?"
"I'm still sad, James."
"But we will be together forever."
"You will make me leave."
"No, I won't."
"Yes, to live with my parents."
"But that is so you can be a regular teenager. It's only temporary."
"James."
"Yes, my love."
"What is our anniversary?"
"July 16th. You are hard to read like this."
"I am sad without you."
"But we are not apart."
She touched my heart when her eyes gazed deeply into my eyes, "Yes, we are."
"What do you mean?"
"We aren't one yet."
"Sarah, it's too early for that. You are sick and we need to wait."
She was drifting away from me. I hated that her sadness was pulling her away from me. I couldn't let her go, "Sarah, please don't go?"
"I am waiting, that's all."
She continued to drift away from me.

I woke in misery. I held tighter to my Sarah. I didn't want her to feel this way. I started to kiss her ear and whispered, "Sarah, we are one. Trust me, I just can't tell you yet."
I heard her, "What?"
My heart sank; she heard me. I thought she was sleeping.
I swallowed, "I love you enough for us to be as one."
"What can't you tell me?"
"I can't explain how I feel to make you understand we are one."
"I love you, my sweet, Cayuse."
Wow, that was so close. If she knew what I had done without her… I was off the hook for now.
"Do you remember your dream?"
"No, why?"
"When is our anniversary?"
I could see the curves of her mouth turn up with a grin, "July 16th."

I was confused. What did that have to do with anything, and why when she was sad was that date important? I need to get Sam here. I need to learn so maybe I could understand things. Is it really her in my dreams, or was it my mind that produced her like that because of how she feels.

I moved away from her, "James no, not yet."
I moved back and pulled out the book and started to read. She held my arm around her. I loved that she wanted me to hold her after the day we had.

## 21. Together

### James:

    **I** slowly moved away from her while she slept. I went out and Jake was sleeping on the couch. I leaned over the couch, "Hey."
    He opened his eyes almost jumping to his feet.
    "No, Jake, just relax. Today was a really rough day, and I am still miserable. She was dreaming or maybe in my dream..."
    "James, I really don't want to hear about the dreams you two have."
    He didn't understand what I was getting at. I shook my head, "It was different. She was lonely and distant. I need to learn more. I don't know if I am creating my dreams or if I am visiting hers. I need to know if it's my feelings or hers."
    "So, what do you want to do?"
    "I really want Sam here."
    "Does he know all this?"
    "A lot more than me, and he loves video games."
    "I could have a partner rather than waiting around doing nothing."
    "Yeah, that is what I was thinking."
    "I will go get him. It's only two and half hours away. I could be gone for a six hour span."
    "You would do that?"
    "Of course; it's all about helping her, right?"
    "Well, it would help me too." I was relieved that didn't change his mind.

"I will wait until she wakes up. I will give her a full shot and a pill. She should be out for the full six hours. That's enough time to get up there and back."

I picked up my phone to call Sam, but dad answered. I explained everything, and he was more than willing to let Sam come and teach me, if that is what Sam wanted to do. He had a lot to learn for himself. Sam came to the phone and was really happy I was asking for his help. I advised him Jake would pick him up.

"James, I don't even know him."

"Sam, he's your brother."

"So, it's weird."

"He is pretty amazing; you might learn something from him too."

"Fine, but I am only doing it for Sarah, so you don't hurt her anymore."

"I will call when he is on his way."

Jake was standing here hearing my conversation. I felt bad so I tried to explain, "He's nervous."

"And you think I'm not."

"He is still a kid, so don't let him get by with shit."

"Great."

We sat and talked about Sam's quirks until I heard Sarah on the monitor. I moved to get to her and he teased, "The wife is calling."

I gave him a disapproving look, but ran to her. I didn't want anything to happen that would make her any sadder.

"Hey, you didn't sleep long."

"You left me."

"I'm sorry, do you want a shower?"

Her eyes brightened up.

We didn't get to play last night, but I knew I could tease him into play in the bathroom. He carried me to the bathroom; I pulled down my shorts until they fell.

He could tell this was urgent, "Bathroom first?"

"Yep," he helped me sit. I hated this part of going to the bathroom; it made me feel really stupid.

"No pooping this time?"

"Gross no James." I must have turned three shade of red.

Reluctantly, he left the room, and I was able to go.

"James, I am ready."

I started to unbutton my shirt as he walked in. He lifted me to my feet, but his eyes drifted downward to the unbuttoned shirt.

"You shouldn't have done that."

"Why James, I thought we were taking a shower?"

He shook his head to get the thought out of his mind. I let my shirt fall to the ground. Feeling self-conscious about my body, I peeked up at him through my eye lashes waiting for something from him. My stomach was fluttering, while my heart pounded. I needed him to want me.

He gave me exactly what I needed when he said, "Shit girl, you are not helping me here."

That was all I needed to continue. I started to lift his shirt.

"No, you get in there; I know you can walk a little."

I pleaded, "Aren't you coming with me?"

"I can't right now. I need to cool off."

Carefully I moved to the shower. I glanced back at him as I stepped in, having every intention of getting him to join me. I tipped my head back letting the water rush over me. I blinked a few times to clear the water, but I found him braced against the shower door to stop his self from coming in. I leaned my head back again, letting more water rush over me. When my eyes reconnected with his I noticed they had grown dark and determined. His jaw was locked with tension, but his tongue came out to moisten his lips. His body pulsed, exposing the tautness of his muscles. I did want a reaction from him, but he was on the verge of losing control. His stance was almost scary.

"James, I'm okay, you can wait in the other room."

"Um, yeah," but he didn't move. I washed with soap everywhere and turned to rinse off.

"James, you're making me paranoid."

"You're so beautiful."

I shook my head not believing his reaction. I moved my hand to cover my scar. I didn't feel beautiful at all. I was leaning back to wet my hair again. I washed it with shampoo, lathering it and moved back to the water to rinse it. I only used one hand. I was very self-conscious about the scar.

"Are you done?"

"Almost."

He was coming in taking his shirt off.

"James, what are you doing?"

He took my hands entangling our fingers together and moved them above my head to the wall. His face was inches from mine, so I nudged his face with my nose watching his expression to see if his desire had gone too far. I kissed him close to his lips; he moved into it, capturing my mouth. Slowly he let go of my hands and moved them to my neck holding my chin up to him and moved closer, so our chests were touching. My heart was pounding like a jackrabbit, but I didn't want him to think I was afraid.

He spoke softly to me, "We have to set guidelines, so I know when it's okay to be with you." He kept his lips grazing mine, and his body was tense, but his touch was tender.

I moved to undue his pants, to push them off of him. They didn't budge, being wet and all. We both laughed, but he was comforting me, "That works."

I shut off the water and kissed his cheek, "Out."

"What?"

"You're all wet."

"So are you."

"But you have clothes on."

He tried to pout, but he wasn't good at it, "James, towel please."

He lifted me, and walked out of the shower, but still kissing me. As he set me down he wrapped the towel around me. He kissed my forehead and walked out. I took a deep breath to handle the adrenaline that was now pumping through my veins. If it weren't for the pain it would cause, I would have pleaded with him to be together. I went to the sink and brushed my teeth, closing my eyes to feel the heat and opening my eyes to shake it off. He walked back in with only boxers on; his hands went straight for my hips and his mouth to my ear. My breath was knocked out of me again. I was instantly gasping for air because of his touch. I hurried and rinsed my mouth and turned to him. What could we possibly be able to do that wouldn't cause pain. I wanted to forget the ache from standing, but it was persistent. His eyes were deep and passionate; I could see the wanting in his eyes, and every muscle was flexing in his arms. He lifted me to the counter top, and the pain shot through my inners, "Nope, James, it hurts."

He lowered me; I could see the wheels turning in his head trying to think of how we could just touch one another. He was moving pulling me with him. He sat down on the toilet and pulled me around for me to sit on his lap. It would consist of bending my knees and using stomach muscles. I tried to move close enough to do this, but I was just about passing out from pain; well, I could see that this was not going to be in the works, "Nope, can't do that either, sorry."

He closed his eyes with frustration and agony.

I could see the pain he was in, "James no, please don't get mad; I'm sorry. I want to; I really do want to," feeling horrible about not being able to be with my husband I lowered my head in defeat.

He stood up and gave me the saddest puppy eyes. I was melting in his arms, "No Sarah, I shouldn't have let myself get carried away. You are doing nothing wrong, and I was asking too much."

"James, take me to bed."

He swept me off of my feet caring me to the bed, but never took his eyes off of my face. I wanted to look away. I was ashamed of the disappointment I was giving him. He carefully laid me down and tucked a pillow under my head, as he knelt beside the bed sitting back on his feet.

I reached to touch that strong, determined, wonderful face that I loved so much.

He took my hand in his and brought it to his mouth kissing my palm then moving and tracing his mouth up my arm to move closer to me. He edged closer and closer lingering on my neck for a second and moving to my lips. The pain was gone for the moment, and I felt the need to feel him again. I wanted more, but I could not move for fear of sharp pains that were inevitable. As he kissed me softly I could feel his body tensing again. His kiss slowed as he sat back on his feet. I kept my eyes on him to read his mind, or his face, anything to tell me what he was thinking. He traced his hand down the front of me softly saying, "So perfect, so beautiful, Sarah."

I let my hand and arm drift over my scarred stomach, so he wouldn't look at it.

He moved off of his feet to be closer to the bed, "No Sarah, you are beautiful." He lifted my hand off of the scar and entangled his fingers with mine. His other hand skimmed over my stomach, obviously turned on. He started to kiss me there, his lips and tongue moving very seductively. I wrapped my fingers of my free hand in his hair, and then he let go of my other hand which I also put in his hair. He licked and sucked at my stomach, and I moaned from the desire to feel him in me, higher than it has ever been before. My stomach contracted and the pain shot through me. I lifted my head to look at him; he must have taken it as pleasure because he came deeper, wanting to entice me beyond control. He moved his mouth to the scar and licked across it, while moving his hand between my legs gently tracing my liquid warmth, "Sarah, you are so ready for me, and it will hurt."

I could hardly breathe from the excitement; my chest was moving a mile a minute, "Yes."

"Yes, it would hurt you, or yes you want me to try?"

I closed my eyes; I want him to try. If I didn't know the pain would be excruciating I would have moved to him already. I just laid there, because I couldn't figure out how to answer him.

He moved away from me standing up, my eyes flying up to meet his. I know I wanted to beg him not to leave me like this, but I had to let him go before we went too far to stop. He lightly knelt on the bed grabbing the long pillow he had just gotten me and pulled it to my side, "I have an idea, but if you are feeling any pain at all, you have to tell me."

I just nodded only because I couldn't talk; he had me so hot for him. He helped me roll to the pillow draping my top arm over it and then lifted my leg to drape over it. He crawled in behind me tracing his hand down my side.

I smiled; it tickled.

He moved his mouth to my neck and whispered, "Any pain you better tell me, or I am not touching you for six months."

I nodded.

He spoke softly to me, "I am not moving to be in you. I am just going to touch you; is that alright?"

I nodded.

He kissed my cheek and started to suck on my neck as he was bringing his body closer to mine. I felt him touching me. I bit my bottom lip; the desire was so intense. I wanted him to push to me to be with me, but he slowly traced himself against me instead. I closed my eyes and the fear was gone. His touch was erotic and his body tense. His hand wrapped around my waist and lay softly on the scar. I'm sure he was making sure I wasn't cringing from pain. This was not painful; this was absolute heaven. He got as close as he could be continuing to rub himself against me, "Oh my god little girl, you are going to be the death of me." His mouth was on my shoulder, with his aroused body sliding against mine. I moved the arm that was under me to hold him in my hand helping him with his strokes against me. I heard him moan; he liked this. His movements were getting faster, and I was squeezing him to help him feel like he was in me. He was touching the spot that drove me crazy and my stomach contracted.

I gasped a little.

He whispered, "The pleasure hurts you?"

"Just the contraction when I want to push to you."

"Just relax, don't push to me. Let me give you pleasure, please."

The tingling was moving from my toes, and I was moaning with every movement. He held my stomach to try and help me to not contract it, "Sarah?"

I was enjoying this so much and the rush came, I whimpered. The stomach contracted and I couldn't stop it.

He held my stomach to try to stop me, "Sarah, no just enjoy it." He continued rubbing his erection against me, moaning, until a burst of liquid pooled in my hand. I could feel him shrinking, and I wanted us to be together so I pushed him into me, tilting my head back with pure pleasure. The warmth inside me told me this was it; we were one now.

"Sarah, no." He seemed to be agonizing that this was bad. It felt good, warm, and satisfying. He pressed his face against my cheek whispering, "You shouldn't have done that."

"Uhm..." I liked how this felt. He was in me, his arms held me tight, and his breath warming my face made this the best moment in my life.

We stayed together quietly trying to calm ourselves, but I felt James's body convulse into mine. I stayed completely still, not wanting the pain to come.

"Sarah?"

He didn't sound too good, "Yeah."

"The warmth of you..." His body tensed as he slowly pushed deeper inside of me. "...it's too..." He sounded like he was trying to stay in control, but his body seemed to be getting more bulky.

I couldn't say anything. I liked that he was losing himself in the way this felt. His grip tightened around my stomach as he pushed and pulled himself from me. He was in complete pleasure, "Oh, Sarah, it's so..." He was moaning growing bigger and harder with every movement. I let him continue until there was pain with every push.

It was like a jab to my inners that had to stop, "James, out."

He pulled away from me and I felt bad that I was leaving him needy. I took his erection in my hand once more to rub against me until he could be relieved. It wasn't working as well, but only because his body was so tense and he was afraid to move. I think I scared him, "I'm okay, just..."

His gasping kisses came to my neck his breath panting. His body was shaking against mine, but he was still stroking himself against me while he pleaded, "Sarah... Did I hurt you? We shouldn't..." I could feel him agonizing over this as his arms held me tighter. His mouth pressed against my skin until his rush came again. His noise of pleasure by my ear made me so happy. His movement slowed while he apologized over and over again. I loved him and now he was mine. My feminine parts were aching from the unresolved wanting. His mouth came to my shoulder and my neck kissing me over and over until he reached my ear, "Are you okay?"

I turned my face to him a little, "I think so."

"You shouldn't have done that. I could have hurt you."

"But James, now were married, or at least I feel that way."

He moved back a little, so I could turn to him more. He placed his hand on my face with concern in his eyes. He started to kiss me very passionately, but kept his eyes open looking into mine.

I couldn't keep mine open. This was too much excitement for me so I was trying to nuzzle into his chest and his lips finally let go of mine, "James?"

"Yes, Sarah,"

"I am sorry, very tired."

I felt his arms wrap around me more to hold me. I wanted to kiss him more. I love the kissing, but the sleep was…

## James:

I pulled her as close as I could to me. Her sadness was gone; she was happy to be my wife. I could feel her enjoyment of knowing we were together, if only for a brief moment.

My heart was still pounding from the excitement she made me feel from not being sad anymore. The tears of enjoyment were filling my eyes. I didn't know if it was her or me, but she was now mine for the rest of our lives, and she wanted to be there with or without children; it didn't matter anymore. She now understood it was all about the two of us together. I had the urge to scream it to the world, but that would entail letting her go and I wasn't ready for that. I closed my eyes to let this moment last as long as it could. My heart was still pounding and the pleasure of feeling her next to me warmed every part of me; I was in heaven.

## 22. On Their Own

**E**ven though I was feeling the best feeling I have ever felt, I knew there were things to take care of to be ready for the next step in our lives. I had to get up and get to it. I softly kissed her cheek and a smile appeared on her perfect little face. She was happy and that warmed my heart.

I got dressed and went out to get started with a new plan of action.

I heard Jake speak from the couch, "Is she ready to eat? I have it ready."

I couldn't look at him, "Nope, the shower was too much for her, and she is sleeping." I started to put things away, in an attempt to keep busy.

"James?"

I still couldn't look at him. I knew how he felt, and I really didn't want to hurt him. She was mine, but he was my brother now, and I didn't want to rub it in his face.

"What?" I was trying to be light.

"You weren't supposed to do anything till I got Sam."

I still didn't look at him, "Jake, she isn't pushing me away anymore; she is happy to be my wife again."

He didn't push further and I was relieved.

I had him show me how to give her the shot and how much to give her. I practiced with a water syringe and an orange. I was really nervous, but I wanted to get Sam here as soon as possible. I called Sam to tell him to be ready and I talked with my dad, who advised me that even though we were married we should be more careful. I was thankful he didn't say what to be careful about. I was ready to be alone to take care of my sweet Sarah.

After Jake left I sat down to make a list of things I had to get done.
1. Register for College: take entrance exam: sign up for classes. Try to schedule them around her schedule, which I had to go over with her again, so I could do my best and get my books for school.
2. Get Sarah's set up for school.
3. Learn about my gifts with Sam… have no idea where to start on this.
4. Find a part-time job, bartending close to here or Sarah's.
5. A list of goals for Sarah to get better: walking, running, eating, everything so she is ready for school.
6. Help her dad move home.
7. Find our house, the one from the dream.

I took a deep breath and pulled out the lap top searching for what Sarah said she had found. I turned it on waiting.

"JAMES?"
I almost tipped over the table getting up so fast to run to her, "Sarah, what? Are you okay?"
She was curled up in a ball, as tears were streaming down her face.
"I'll get the shot." I ran out and grabbed it and warmed it with my hands, as I ran back to her.
"Where's Jake?"
I stopped in midstride; she wanted Jake. I didn't know how to take that; it kind of hurt me that she was asking for him.
"I need help."
"Sarah, Jake showed me how; I have it right here.
"James, help me."
"I am trying… just hold on, baby, I just have to…"
Pain and stress was all over her face. I knew that the pain she was enduring was because of what we did together. Guilt besieged me, and my heart did a nosedive. It had a hole in it the size of the Grand Canyon. I couldn't stand to see her like this. She was gripping the bed pillow so hard it was totally scrunched. I put the shot in her arm.
"NO James."
"What? Talk to me baby. You didn't want the shot?"
I picked her up and pulled her to my lap to hold her. Her body was trembling from the pain. It took a lot longer for it to ease, but I could feel it when it started to work. Her grip in my arm wasn't digging in anymore.
She peered up at me, "James, it wasn't from that, please don't stay away from me. I needed you and I feel that better now that we shared that. Please don't stay away from me. I need you."
Every word coming from her mouth was mending the hole a little. I wiped the hair from her face, but the tears of regret were in my eyes.
"James?"
She was so weak now, she had no grip and her head fell to my chest.

"Sarah, pill. Don't fall asleep. I only have one shot for you. Jake won't be back for five hours, you have to take the pill." I picked her up and walked to the kitchen. I couldn't leave her. I set her on the couch wrapped in the sheet and leaned her back. She cringed a little, but I still had to leave her there while I got the pill.

"Sarah, stay with me here... just a couple more seconds." I grabbed a glass of water and the pill. I put it in her mouth and helped her with a sip. I picked her up and sat on the couch holding her.

Those green eyes pierced my soul as a smile grew on her face, "Did you see what you did to me? You need to look at my stomach."

I was scared now; what the hell was she talking about? What else have I done to her? I pulled back the sheet and looked, but didn't see anything, "What, Sarah?"

"I need to sleep now."

I was confused about what she was trying to show me, but I needed to take her to bed. Her eyes were so tired and her body was so relaxed that when I picked her back up to take her to bed she fell limp in my arms.

I laid her carefully down as a smile crossed her delicate face, "James? Did you see what you did to me?"

"No, what are you talking about?"

She closed her eyes in defeat giving in to the sleep. I pulled back the sheet to see what she was talking about. Slowly I raised her shirt not finding anything different. Seeing her so vulnerable and week was just a reminder of what I had let happen to her. Her skin was a pasty pale; her ribs were visible through her skin, even her hips stuck out from her body. I still found her amazing to look at. I traced my hand down to the place that would prevent us from ever having children of our own. Running my hand over the scar it felt weird. I pulled down her bottoms revealing the scar. OH shit! It was completely healed over, and some of the scaring was almost gone. If it was almost healed on the outside I wondered if the insides were healing the same way. Leaning down to her I kissed every inch of where the scar was.

"James, I am so tired." She was complaining but she still wrapped her hands against my head and entangled her fingers in my hair. Her little noises being half asleep and half enjoying what I was doing to her made me want to continue. I found myself enticing her even though I knew I should be moving away from her. She was moaning with pleasure. I wanted to move to her, but was torn from the thought of hurting her. Yep, the thought of hurting her helped and I was able to push myself away from her. I decided on a cold shower. I came out and looked at my beautiful wife. I tucked her back in and went to the other side of the bed to make the list of things she had to be able to do before I could be with her completely. I felt her heart and she loves me more than I could ever imagine.

As I sit here to think of what I need for her to be able to do, I couldn't help notice my heart was still pounding.
1. Go to the bathroom by herself.
2. Walk up and down steps, and that would be a challenge considering my bed, our bed was down three steps.

3. Sit up without sharp pains.
4. Eat more than a cup of food at a time.

Not being able to keep my eyes off her I scooted down so I was facing her. Even though her eyes were shut they were still perfect; the shape, the size, and those eyelashes so long. They were also perfectly spaced apart by this cute little nose that twitched when I barely touched it. I had to chuckle that this didn't wake her at all. I moved a little closer getting an even better look at her. As my eyes trailed her lip I was thinking of what I enjoyed the most about them. Was it the perfect shape of her top lip, the plumpness of her bottom lip, the way her smile caused slight dimples at the edge? I couldn't make up my mind. I took her hand and moved it to my lips and closed my eyes.

I woke to loud noises. I slid carefully away from her and off the bed. I went out to hush them, because she was sleeping peacefully. I walked out and Sam came running to me to give me the biggest hug. He was rambling about how much fun he had with Jake on the ride down. How great the house was and to which vehicle was his. I was trying to hush him, but the excitement was overflowing. I pushed him out the door and encouraged Jake to take him on a tour of the rest of the house. I checked on Sarah, since she should be waking soon. I noticed she was moving, so I went to get the food ready. She needed to eat no matter what this time. I walked in the room with the tray, but as her big green eyes fell on me my heart took off on its own. I was in love with this girl and those eyes penetrated my soul.

*Sarah:*

"Hi."
"Hi."
"I hope you're hungry." I really didn't want to move at all, so I just watched him. He sat down the tray and then his eyes found mine again, but he was smiling with a funny grin.
"What are you smiling about?"
Then his eyes glimmered, he moved to me, and then he kissed me softly, "You're feeling happy again."
"Yes, I am."
"You need to eat."
He was lifting me to him and tucking pillows behind me, and I nudged his neck with my nose.
"Sarah, Food!"
"What do I get for eating?"
"I'm not playing this game with you. You will eat and that is the end of it." He kissed me quickly and sat down to feed me.
"Can I at least try to feed myself and maybe you could read to me?"
He looked at me distrustfully.

I was irritated, "What is the problem?"

"You don't like when I feed you?"

"I love when you read to me."

He moved the tray in front of me and lay down next to me to read. He waited for me to take a first bite. Once he was reading I slowly ate trying to consume as much time with him as possible. I smiled with every slow morsel.

He finally noticed, "What are you smiling about?"

"Just you."

"What about me?"

I took another bite and smiled.

"What, Sarah?"

I started to giggle and took another bite.

He sat up and turned to me more directly, "What?"

I was smiling even more and took another bite. I was winning and he was really cute when he was irritated.

"Sarah, what? What are you so happy about?"

I took another bite and shook my head no, "Time to eat." I was grinning, "Read please."

He glared at me, "Are you going to tell me what you are grinning about?"

"Nope." I took another bite. He lay back down. Shoot, he really wasn't supposed to do that. He was trying to keep his eye on me and read to me at the same time. I took another bite and was holding back a total grin; I still had his attention. I put my hand over my mouth to stop the laughter. He sat up and grabbed the tray and put it on the night table reaching over me to do this, so I quickly swallowed in case he wanted to kiss me. He put his hand under my butt and pulled me down to lay down. Oh yeah, he was going to give it to me. He was completely hovering over me, "You are going to tell me what is so funny right now."

I liked this game. I had all his attention and I liked it. I pressed my lips together and shook my head no.

"I am going to torture you till you tell me."

I shook my head no again.

He nuzzled my neck.

I tried to sound firm like he was when he told me I had to eat, "NO, no, no, time to eat."

He nuzzled my ear.

"James, food."

He traced his mouth under my chin.

"James, stop."

He moved to my mouth, teasing me with his lips, "Tell me."

I kissed him really quick on the lips, "Nope. I need food, James. Now stop it. I'm not playing." I was trying to have a straight face, but I could not hold the grin in.

"You are totally playing with me."

I started to laugh, "James, don't make me laugh, it hurts."

He started to kiss me; I loved when he kissed me. I was more than willing to return the kiss.

He finally slowed, "Why do you have to always win?"

"That's simple, you let me."

"You are evil."

"Really? You think I am evil?"

He traced his hand on my face, "Oh, yes you are, you make me want to do things with you that are just not possible at this time."

"Store that thought for later. I have to go to the bathroom like right now." I gave him a quaint smile.

He moved away from me chuckling to himself, "Okay Sarah, come on."

He pulled me up and took me to the bathroom. I was still really embarrassed by this. When we went back to the bed he checked the food. I had eaten most of it.

His eyebrows shot up with a questioning gesture, "You were hungry?"

I was and I almost finished it, but I wanted more time with him, "Will you please read some more to me, and maybe get Jake to give me a shot. The pain is starting to be achy again."

"You asked for Jake earlier, and I was wondering why?"

"Because that is why he is here, isn't it?"

"Yeah... But..."

"James, he's the doctor; you are my..." I couldn't look at him and say what I wanted to say. I put my head down, "My lover, my friend, my everything."

He lifted my chin softly to look in my eyes, "I am so in love with you, little girl." He stared at me far too long, which made me a little uncomfortable, even a little nervous. He leaned in to kiss my forehead then moved away from me, "I will go get Jake, but I would rather you wanted me." He stopped at the door glancing back at me with eyes that glimmered and a smile that drove me crazy with lust, melting every ounce of my being.

I waited for Jake, but the pain was worse than I had let on. I was closing my eyes to concentrate on James's face to get me through the pain. I heard a bunch of commotion in the other room.

Jake was walking in, "I heard you need a shot, but Sarah we really have to cut back on these. If I don't they are going to think I am shooting up."

I don't know if he was trying to be funny or if he was serious, but I was holding my breath to keep from feeling the pain. He must have got my non response, because he sat down on the bed next to me, "You are in a lot of pain?"

I nodded, giving him the biggest pleading eyes I could come up with.

"James doesn't know?"

I shrugged my shoulders.

"But doesn't he feel everything you feel?"

The tears started to come to my eyes, and James walked in, "Sarah, you have to tell me when it is this bad. Especially when..." He wouldn't finish his sentence while Jake was there.

Sam walked in, "I heard I am supposed to check out your scar."

I didn't want anyone checking out anything when I felt like this.

Jake didn't wait for me to beg; he gave me the shot right away, but spoke to James, "We need another pill for her."

I shook my head no at James. I hated what those pills did to me and I wanted more time with James.

"What, Sarah... the shot doesn't last very long and you can't have it all the time."

James walked away from me but came back quickly.

Jake moved away and grabbed Sam by the arm, "Sam, you can look at it later when there is less pain. We need to give her some space."

James moved to me, "You know I don't feel your pain when I am full of desire for you, so you have to tell me."

I just nodded. I didn't tell him because I didn't want him to stay away from me.

He put the pill in my mouth and helped me with the water. I searched his eyes to see if he was going to stay away from me again.

"Sarah, I hate seeing you hurt." He lifted me, so he could move in beside me and hold me. He pulled out the book and started to read.

"James..."

He stopped reading and waited to hear what I had to say.

"I don't want you to stay away from me; I need you."

"Sarah, I am not staying away from you. We just shouldn't do that until you...are better."

I nuzzled into him and was ready to listen to his words as he read.

## 23. Not Healthy

*James:*

Sam and I sat at the table to go over some things I already knew, sort of. Sam scolded, "You shouldn't share souls."

"Right, because it connects us, so that if one dies than so shall the other."

"Yes, and the connection is so strong that desire builds and the desire to be together is unbearable, so much that it is not livable to be apart. It will make you crave to share it more and more, and the need will increase."

"What about the sharing of dreams?"

"Dreams are fine, but are you touching each other when you are awake?"

I looked at Jake; he really shouldn't be hearing this, "Yes."

"I mean when you're not together?"

I raised my eyebrows, "Yes." I was ashamed.

"James, you have already gone way further than you should have."

"So what do I do to fix it?"

"Just don't do *that* anymore."

"You mean when she goes home and I talk to her on the phone I can't …" I didn't want to say what I was really thinking so I settled with, "…kiss her?"

"James, can regular people do that?"

"Well no, but when she is so lonely and she needs to feel I care about her, how do I make her feel that without it?"

"James, that is what I am talking about. You two have done so much more than we know about, but from the stories the desire can also drive you crazy."

"Yeah, already there."

"Well the first step is admitting you have a problem." He waited for my reaction, and we all started to laugh.

"How was she able to text me when she was out?"

"You are so connected you communicate on a whole new level than we even know about. Talking and seeing her in your dreams, sharing dreams, being together in your dreams is okay. It the sharing the desires when you are awake that you should not be doing, James."

"But that is how it started, just holding her in her dreams. Then I tried it when I was on the phone with her and it worked."

"No more of that."

"What else can I do?"

"Well, you know how you can feel Sarah? You can feel others too, but you would have to concentrate, probably harder than you have to with Sarah, because she is clouding that part of you now."

"So I can actually feel anyone I choose?"

"Yes, and other things too. Remember the animals, how they trusted me. It was because I was feeling them and channeling their feelings."

"How is that different than what I am doing with Sarah?"

"Because you don't stop at that."

"What do you mean?"

Sam shook his head disapproving, "Because you don't just feel, you reach out and touch. You need to allow your senses to feel, but you must restrain from acting on them. It's like feeling the change in the atmosphere. I sense it by paying attention and focusing on it. You have been focusing everything, all you have on her."

Jake huffed, "No wonder I didn't have a chance." just loud enough for us to hear him.

I didn't like that he was hurt from this whole thing, "I really didn't know I was making her…Sorry, Jake, but I do love her."

"I figured that out, but James she would have…"

"No, please, I really can't even think about that."

"Sorry, James, this is all too much. I am going to go out."

"Jake, I really would like for you to hear this, because what I was doing I really didn't know that it was that bad for her or me."

He sat back down.

I really didn't feel like I was learning anything new and Sam wasn't in the mood. We only talked for an hour or so, and then Jake and Sam were going swimming. I went back to the Internet to try to figure things out about going to school and getting Sarah set up. Paula would be coming tomorrow to spend the day with Sarah; I should be able to get more done too.

I found the program at the U and scheduled an appointment to take the entrance exam. Jake would have to take care of her for a while Wednesday morning. Sam would be here too. I made a note to myself to look up her school schedule for college. Technically, we only have about two weeks, so I had to hurry up and get this done.

Jake and Sam came in and were being loud again. I hushed them, and we sat down to play video games. We were so into playing that I didn't notice my Sarah was stirring.

Jake got up and started walking to the bedroom, "James!"

Surprised I got up, "Oh, Yeah. I'm coming."

I followed him to the room; she really wasn't moving anymore.

"Jake, she really needs to sleep till morning, so she has more energy to see her mom tomorrow."

"She is coming again?"

"Paula is her mom, and she is worried about her."

"Fine, but I feel like we have to be official while she is here."

"No, you and Sam can go swimming; use the water toys, whatever you want. I will stay to get some things done, and her mom can feed her and take care of her. It wouldn't kill you anyway. You're the doctor; you have to be used to this."

The weirdest grin came to his face, "I like this break. I am having fun. Did I tell you that is what she was trying to do for me? She always wanted to teach me how to have fun."

That was my Sarah, it was about everybody else being happy. "I will wake her enough to give her a pill, but you said no shot, right?"

"We are keeping her so sedated I feel bad. She needs to start walking more."

I didn't want her to be in any pain, "But it hurts her."

"You can't keep her like this forever, James. If you agreed to let her live at home, she will have to go anyway when school starts."

I felt like a knife was jabbed into my gut. I didn't want to let her go anymore. I liked sleeping and cuddling with her. I didn't know if I could sleep without her here anymore.

I heard Sam from the other room, "James that is the desire talking. I told you it makes it worse."

I was devastated. I caused this pain myself.

Jake went and got the pill for me and more water. I lay down with Sarah and asked Jake to keep it down, maybe close the door.

"Sarah, sweetie."

"Uhm."

"Can you wake up enough for another pill?"

"No."

"You can go right back to sleep. I just need you to wake enough to take it."

Not opening her eyes she complained, "I don't want to take the pill."

"Sarah, your mom is coming tomorrow, and you need as much rest as possible, so you can visit with her."

"Makes me foggy, no James. I want the shot."

"Sarah, we have to cut back on those. They are very addictive."

"I'm addicted, shot."

"No baby."

She finally opened her eyes to me. How was I going to say no to those?

They actually were getting darker as she replied to me, "You've been working on saying no to me."

"Pill?"

"Can we wait?"

"No, because you will get too bad and need a shot then."

So on top of the deep green luring eyes now she put her bottom lip out; I couldn't help but try to kiss her to get my way this time. I started with the lip.

"James?"

I went in for a deeper kiss; she just tasted so sweet to me, "Yeah?"

She was returning my kiss. I moved closer to put my arms around her lightly placing my hand on her waist. She just did it for me, and all I wanted was to make her give into me and my temperature was rising. I had to let go, "Pill, Sarah."

"More kissing."

"Only if you take the pill."

She opened her mouth. I reached over her and placed it on her tongue and had her take a sip of water. She swallowed it and then complained, "I don't like being foggy, James."

I wanted to make her forget about taking the pill. I moved to kiss her more tracing my lips on hers to get her to respond to me.

"James, help me here."

I stopped, "Help you with what?"

"I don't like the pain meds. I sleep all the time and I want to spend more time with you."

"You will have a life time of me."

"No, you're sending me home."

"Only temporary; I will see you every day and the weekends you're mine."

"Really, do mom and dad know that?"

"No, but were married, so I think they will agree with anything as long as they get you during the week, while you are still going to school."

She was trying to roll to me. I pulled the bed pillow behind her, so she wouldn't have to work so hard at it. She could lay to me without trying; I was facing her and couldn't help myself from moving closer to feel her next to me. She touched my chest and I pulled off my shirt. I loved when she touched me. Her head lay on my shoulder, and I looked down at her as she traced her hand over me. I closed my eyes to enjoy her, "Did you want me to read to you?"

She nuzzled in more; her lips brushed on my neck, "No."

I took a deep breath. Her hand moved from me, so I looked to see what she was doing, "Sarah?"

She was unbuttoning her shirt, "I will sleep better if I feel you."

"No, Sarah. The pain is too intense."

"Not that, James. You're right; the pain was really bad and time will make that possible. I just want to feel you next to me, so I can sleep better."

I helped her and moved so that our bodies were touching and closed my eyes. She was right; I could sleep very well like this.

She was very content with anytime we spent together, as long as I was very attentive, even just reading. Paula was going to be here both Saturday and Sunday to spend time with Sarah. I had plans to get as much done as possible with her here. We switched the medicine Saturday morning to see if she could handle it. It had been two weeks since the surgery and she should be improving and trying harder to be ready for school in two weeks. By six on Saturday she was pretty miserable; Jake had to give her a shot and the heavy medicine. Her mom stayed to help calm her till she was sleeping. Jake gave her the good stuff through eight am on Sunday. Sarah's mom showed up at 10 am and Sarah was slow to wake, but her mom was patient. After Jake came and reassured her that we were not harming her, that we were trying to get her off this stuff that makes her sleep, he went up with Sam to the main house. I gave her the regular pain killers, but I gave them to her every three hours. They didn't put her to sleep. She had a hard time with it. Her mom tried to feed her and calm her with reading, but the pain was pretty bad by the time her mom left at 8:00pm. We ended up giving her another shot. Jake decided to give her the good pill every other time we give her pain killers. I lay with her and read, as we waited for the shot to take care of the pain.

*Sarah:*

This was not fun; they were changing my meds on a regular bases now. I was getting irritated with them both. I didn't like the one that made me foggy, and the other ones just didn't work at all, and no more shots unless I was really bad. Jake wants me to start to exercise. Great...that's all I need, more pain and less meds.

James kissed me good morning and traced his hand down my back, "Time to work."

"Great." I was trying to sound excited for this, but it was really pissing me off.

"We'll take a shower when you're done."

I couldn't get my mind off the pain that was coming, "Yeah, sounds good."

"You don't sound happy. You get to be out of bed today."

I was feeling hateful, and stared at him with an empty look.

"Are you scared?"

"I could just wait for you in your bed for the rest of my life."

"No, you have to have a life of your own or you will be very bored and hate me every time I leave you. Sarah, please give it an honest try." His eyes were searching my face to see if I was going to behave. He didn't sense anything so he continued, "Do you want me to help you?"

It's not that I wanted his help; I just didn't want him to leave me, ever!

"Fine, I will stay with you."

"I didn't say anything."

James had that guilty grin on his face. He was avoiding my glare as Jake came in, "Are you ready to work out Sarah?"

Still being disgruntle and crabby he firmly said, "No."

"Sarah, grow up; you have to start sometime and you are wearing him out."

My eyes flew to James, and he shook his head no and smiled. Assessing James more closely I noticed there were dark circles under his eyes. I was wearing on him, like the jeans. I had new determination to do better, because he needed a break.

Jake started as soon as I showed him that I was ready, "You can walk a little, but with pain?"

Shaking my head, "No. I do not have pain every time. It's getting better."

"That's a better attitude."

"Yeah, Great."

"Okay, we are going to start with sitting up."

"What, that does hurt."

"Let's give it a try." I was already propped up with pillows. He pulled my legs over the side of the bed and helped to lift me to a sitting position. James expression changed.

"James, I'm okay. Maybe you should wait in the living room and relax."

"No, it's okay. I'll stay."

"James." I tried to make it seem like I wanted him to go.

Jake's attention was on James but spoke to me, "Sarah how does this feel?" He was letting go.

"The pain is a little sharp like a really bad cramp."

James was disappointed and irritated. You could hear it in his voice as he talked to Jake, "Lay her back down."

"James, please. I need to try." I knew by the look on his face that he felt how bad it hurt. I tried to be more pleased about this.

He finally got up and walked out.

Jake was honestly concerned, "So how bad is it?"

"Truthfully, worse than a bad cramp."

"Does it hurt this bad when you stand?"

"No. It's more the sitting, tilt. I don't know how to explain it."

He pushed me back so I wasn't slouching, "Does that help or make it worse?"

"Better."

"Then sit up straighter when you are sitting,"

I tried to keep a positive attitude by plastering a smile on my face, but I think my nose wrinkled with every little shot of pain. He helped me scoot to the edge of the bed by wrapping his arms around me and pulling. He stopped at the edge, "Now, we're going to stand up."

"We're or me?"

He grinned, "You're going to stand up." He put his hands out for me to brace myself on, "I will only help a little."

I took a deep breath, and tried to stand. I almost made it, but the pain was sharp, and he ended up grabbing me so I wouldn't fall.

We heard James from the living room, "Jake!!!"

"James, try to ignore it. She has to try to get better at it."

We could hear him pacing and Sam trying to distract him.

I wanted to hurry up and get this over with, "Something else, standing up hurts a little too much."

"Okay, should we just walk a little?"

"I know I can do that."

"Well, let's see how much you can do. You have two weeks until you have to go to school. That will be a lot of walking, standing, and sitting."

"Walking it is then."

He wrapped his arms around my waist to lift me, "Sarah, we have to get your weight. I think you're losing more and if you don't get some fat on your bones, I will have to take you back to the hospital."

That made me fearful. I didn't want to go back to the hospital and I really didn't want to know if I had lost more weight.

"Come on. How about the stairs; they are very little and there are only three. Let's give it a try."

There he was with the *we* again. Why can't he just say me? I was the one in pain here. And I was the one that had to do all the trying.

He had my hands in his and he was standing on the landing, but decided to move more behind me with one arm wrapped around my waist and the other holding my hand. I moved one foot to the first step. As my foot made it to the step I felt relieved. That didn't hurt at all. I gave Jake a great big smile, "That isn't bad"

"You're not to the hard part yet; push yourself up to it."

He had to point that out didn't he? It was a little painful. I swallowed hard and glanced at Jake for approval.

He was grinning, "You did it."

We heard James again, "Yeah, but she could pass out from the pain."

"James, block me. Please, you're not helping."

I quickly moved to the next step with the other leg; if this was going to be painful than I wanted to get it over as quickly as possible. To my surprise this didn't seem to hurt half as bad. I was excited as I glance up at Jake for approval. He did give me a smile but I don't think he got that it wasn't as bad. Obviously, it wasn't as bad; James didn't feel anything. I yelled for him, "James how was that?"

"What?"

I giggled a little. I shouldn't have done that because *laughing* did hurt. Of course James bellowed out after feeling my pain, "What are you doing to her?"

I grumped out loud, "I just laughed, James."

Jake stood there shaking his head, "Okay, one more with the bad side."

I didn't want to do this side again. This was the side that stabbed a sharp pain in my gut. I begged, "I can take it one step at a time with my good side."

He was giving me a disapproving look.

"Fine, your way." I lifted my foot for the bad side and tried to push to the step. The pain was even sharper. I gasped a little and Jake helped a little more than last time. I felt the tears coming. That one really hurt.

James was getting angry, "Jake, damn it, she needs more time."

"Sarah, you need to breathe. Come on breathe; you're tensing and that will make it worse."

I was trying to breathe, but that last one was a killer.

"Now we are going to walk."

I shook my head no. I couldn't do anymore; this was bad. I asked, "More?"

"Yes, more. Try it; to the bathroom, on the scale, and then back."

Hesitantly I took a little step, it wasn't so bad. I took another step and then another. By the time I made it to the bathroom Jake had his arm around my waist supporting my weight. I think he could tell how much it hurt from the wrestling we heard coming from the living room. Sam was holding James back from interrupting our session. The walking wasn't great but wasn't excruciating as the standing and the steps, but more than I had remembered. I stood in front of the scale staring at it. I really didn't want to know how bad it was.

"Sarah, you can use the easy side."

"Jake I don't want to know."

"I have to know. I have to know that you are getting better. Get it over with."

I used the easy side and he helped me to step on it. He made sure I had my balance and then let go. He looked at it, "Okay, got it."

"How bad is it?"

"Let's just say, it's not good, Sarah. You have lost another 12 lbs. You have to do better with eating."

"So I'm just over 100 lbs?"

He just nodded, but didn't scold me, "That should be enough for today, Sarah. Do you want me to carry you back?"

"NO, I am going to walk."

He put his arm around me to help me back to bed. I was really feeling it now. Every step was a torture.

James was getting upset now, "Jake, she is in extreme pain, stop this."

I could hear him, but couldn't say anything. I was concentrating on getting back to the bed. We got to the steps, "Okay, I'm ready."

"You really want to do this?"

"Yep, if I am already in pain what's a little more?"

He smiled, "Okay." He moved in front of me but stayed really close and let me come down to him step by step. That wasn't bad at all. He helped me to lie down, and then he pulled the pillow to me rolling me to the side, "Sarah, honestly do you need a shot?"

I just nodded.

He walked away, but didn't get out the door before James was walking in holding it, "Jake, that was fucking too much."

"James, we have to talk right now."

"Shot first and the pill." He was holding his gut, but only because he really felt everything I did. Jake came back and gave me the shot. James was in front of me tracing his hand over my face, not letting his eyes leave me. He fed the pill to me and helped me with a sip of water.

"James, outside now!" Jake was pissed.

I was worried James would kill him for being so demanding.

"Jake, I'll be out when she is sleeping."

"Sam, will you please come in here and help Sarah? James, I am not going to say it again, NOW!"

Even though Jake's voice was demanding, James didn't move. The worry lines on his face were showing as he held my eyes with his.

I hand to make sure he knew it was okay, "James, I'm okay. Just hurry back, please."

He kissed my forehead and walked out with Jake. They didn't stop in the living room; they went all the way outside. I don't think Jake wanted me to hear what he was going to say to James.

Sam sat on the bed so I could see him, "I have a really disgusting question?"

With Sam I really didn't know what to expect, "What is that?"

"Did James put his…" He was gesturing to his private parts with the goofiest grin.

I could not even begin to go along with this, "Sam, none of your business."

"Sarah. I told him if he put some of his…" his eyebrows went up with a hint of seriousness, "…it could help heal it."

"What are you talking about?"

"Our body fluids heal. It helped you in the hospital and it might help with the scaring."

Everything he was saying was so true and I was excited he knew about it, "Sam, you should see it." I realized what I was admitting, but I wanted him to see, "It was only a little, once, but he didn't tell me that. It just kind of happened that way."

He smiled at me, "You two shouldn't be doing that till you are better, and remember I saw it and it's not for two…" He stopped mid-sentence and cocked his head to the side. His eyes were searching as if he was seeing deep in my soul, "Sarah?"

"What?"

Sam was glaring at me, "Did you guys…use…the. …Feather?"

"We tried but I fell asleep." I shrugged him off. That was no big deal; we are married now.

He smiled a funny smile, "How bad is the pain?"

"Getting better now; the shot works really fast. I hate the pill, because it makes me foggy, so if you lose me in the next 20 minutes that's why."

He was really grinning at me almost to the point that I was suspicious of him, "Sarah, do you need anything?"

"Food, I think I lost more weight. Jake said I was a little over 100 lbs, and James is going to be upset."

"I will talk to Wilson. He should be able to figure a way to get you more calories. I bet that is what Jake's problem is."

"It's not James's fault. They keep giving me these stupid pills that make me....dreamy, foggy, and sleep all the time." I blinked and tried to shake it off. It was well on its way to working.

"Sarah, are you okay?"

"NO, it's these stupid pills."

He took my hand and patted it till James came back in. I tried to focus on James, but he seemed to look worse than I felt.

"Sam, I got it."

Sam moved away as James moved in, "Sam, do me a favor and turn off the monitor. I need to talk to her privately."

He was looking into my eyes the whole time. He laid down facing me taking my hands to his mouth. The next thing I knew the tears were streaming down his face, "I am so sorry Sarah, I am not taking good care of you. I promise I will do better. I love you more than you know."

I wiped his tears, "Foggy, James."

I tried to shake it off, but when I closed my eyes I couldn't open them again. I felt his breath on my face. I wanted him to kiss me, but couldn't even move to ask for one.

## 24. Unbearable

**W**hen I woke he was still here with me, but he was sleeping. I reached for his face and almost shocked him awake. He was startled with his eyes wide open looking at me alarmed and confused. I gave him an 'I'm okay grin'. I could feel his heart pounding in his chest, but his body settled when he asked, "You are better, aren't you?"

"Yes, James. I love you."

Relieved that I wasn't waking him for anything serious he closed his eyes.

"James?"

The weird thing is he was so relaxed that he went back to sleep almost immediately not responding to me at all. I moved closer. I need to be stronger, eat, and take a shower, "James?" he still wasn't moving. I had to wake him up. I had to be stronger so he could rest, but he was resting now I should let him be. I just couldn't help myself; I traced my hands over him. He was so beautiful to me. I kissed his chest and my lip traveled over him, then up under his chin.

This woke him up, "Girl, you are going to be the death of me."

I giggled in his ear, "Sleep, James, I'm just playing."

He snuggled in more, but I wanted to play. I pushed him back and tried to lean over him. I traced my leg along his. It hurt a little, but when I got it high enough, he grabbed it with his hand and pulled it up further and ran his hand over my thigh and rolled back to me a little more. I kissed his lips. He was a little responsive, but his tiredness was keeping him from giving me more attention.

"James, honey, I really need to go to the bathroom and eat."

He seemed a little stunned when his eyes popped opened to look at me.

I nudged his cheek, "You will take a nap later with me."

He dragged himself up slowly pulling me up with him, "Do you want to walk to the bathroom?"

After the pain earlier I really didn't want to but said, "Sure, I can try."

He wasn't really awake, but he put his arm around my waist. I used the easy leg first. It wasn't bad at all, so I decided to stick with that side; I didn't want to feel the pain yet. I took the next two steps fairly easily. He walked with me to the bathroom and helped me sit down, so I could go.

Before he left I asked, "Can we wash the bedding? I have been in bed for two weeks."

He stretched, yawned, and nodded as he walked out. I went to the bathroom and pushed to stand up on my own. It was very painful, but I made it. I was brushing my teeth when he walked back with a scolding, surprised look. "Are you being a tough girl today?" He moved closer to me.

I turned to him and wrapped my arms around him, "James, you're tired."

He was shaking his head, "I am fine; you need to get better."

I reached up to his face cupping it in my hands, "James, I am wearing on you."

He didn't like that I said that, and his face was full of concern, "No, Sarah."

"Yes, James. You are so tired." I traced my fingers under his eyes.

He closed them and pulled me to him hugging me gently, "I feel like I made everything for you worse, that's all."

"No, my Cayuse. You kept me fighting to wait for you and to feel better. It's my turn to try harder."

He kissed my head while he held me.

I pushed him away, "Did you get the bedding in?"

He nodded.

"Then out, I am taking a shower."

"You don't want my help?"

I gave him a seductive look, "James, I will want to be with you and Jake was pretty mad at me for losing more weight. I think I need to eat more, and you will distract me from that."

He was so beat, "I will get you food while you shower; yell if you need me."

I kissed his cheek so lightly, but he moved to kiss my lips. I pulled away, "If you're not careful I will pull you in with me, out."

He smiled and let go backing his way out of the bathroom.

I took a shower quickly. Without him here, there was no reason to linger. It felt good to wash up. I got out and wiped off. I wrapped the towel around me and walked to the room. The door was open and I reached to close it, so I could get dressed. I went through the drawers. I put on sleeping shorts and a cute little camisole. He had a robe hanging on the outside of the bathroom door, so I put it over what I was wearing. I wasn't going to make it back to the bed, and the bedding was gone anyway so I walked to the lounge. I really didn't know how I was going to get to it, so I stood there looking at it.

James came in with a tray while evaluating me and what I was doing, "What are you doing, little girl?"

I glanced back, "I was trying to think of a way to sit down here, but I am not having any luck." I wanted to be playful, "Got any ideas?"

He chuckled a little, "Yeah; let me help you." Setting the tray down on the table and then moving close to me, he wrapped his arms around me to help. I nudged his face with my nose as he was lowering me to the lounge. That was all it took from me, and he pulled me back to him and started to kiss me so deeply. Well, then you could only guess what I had to do. I wrapped my arms around his neck pulling myself closer to him; I was pressing my lips to him. Now we were in trouble; we were both distracted by the feel of one another, and he was lowering me to the lounge only to hover over me. He quit kissing me long enough to slowly untie the robe. A glint of a smile came to his face, as he lowered his body to graze mine. His body was hard and ready. I knew he wanted me, and I definitely liked the way he felt. It was making my body hungry for him, but the thought of the pain seeped in. I traced my hand down his chest holding him there. I wanted him closer, but I couldn't have him closer. The idea of one pain did not outweigh the other in my head. He shook his head to try to get it out of his mind, and slowly moved away from me.

I grabbed his shirt, "James?"

"You need to eat, Sarah."

"James, I need to feel you too."

"But you need food worse than you need me."

"NO, I need you worse than I need food."

I could tell that made my James happy, but he tried to be stern, "Food first."

I let him go. He went to lift my legs to lay over the lounge, but traced them as he moved back up to me to grab the tray beside me.

"If you want me to eat, you have to quit touching me; sort of hot now."

That did make him laugh a little, as he put the tray in front of me. A kiss on the nose is what I got, as he got up moving away from me, "I will be right back."

I took advantage of the time alone, so I started to check out my meal. I knew they wanted to put weight back on me, so the cottage cheese was covered with syrupy pineapples; the potato was covered in butter, sour cream, and cheese. I was thankful that they left my steak normal. I ate as fast as I could handle, because I wanted my play time with James, and I knew he was tired. He was walking back in, but went to the bed first grabbing the book. He came to the other side of the lounge, and sat down putting his feet up. He started to read to me while I was eating. I was giggling at some of the parts in the book.

He stopped and looked at me, "You like this book?"

"Yeah, don't you?"

He tried to be serious and disapproving, but his mouth turned to a grin, "Yeah."

When I was done eating, I sat up all proud of myself gesturing for him to notice.

"You ate it all?"

"I was hungry."

"You need to work out more. You haven't eaten like that in a while. That was a total of three cups of food." He was moving the tray back to the table.

Now we could get to something more important, "Play time?"

He shook his head no. I gave him a pout. I ate all my food so why wasn't he going to give into me.

Trying to make up excuses he expressed, "Sheets aren't done yet."

At least he gave me a good excuse. He took my hand and brought it to his mouth for a slight kiss, and then continued to read to me. His words were getting a little slurred showing just how tired he was.

"James, honey, you should check the sheets, and get me the lesser pain med before you fall asleep."

He shook his head to get rid of the tiredness filling him. He got up and went to check the dryer. Sam came in with him to put them on the bed. I tried to drag my legs off of the lounge to the floor. It hurt a little. I wrapped the robe around me more and tried it again. I was pushing myself from the back of the lounge to stand up. That hurt a lot worse. I did need the pain meds. These weaker ones didn't get rid of the pain; they only took the edge off.

Jake walked in, "Sarah, you are making progress. Do you want to try more?"

"Not if I am not going to get the good stuff."

He didn't look pleased.

I felt like I wanted to try but later, "Jake, how about we do more like after I eat next but before I take the heavy duty pill, so I can sleep through the pain."

He smiled, "That is a deal. About 5:00 pm then?"

I agreed and was walking to the top of the steps watching them put the silky sheets on the bed. James fluffed the comforter over the whole bed, but turned down one edge for a place for me. He was on the opposite side when his eyes met mine.

"Nap time, guys, out."

Sam and Jake both turned to me wondering what was going on with James. I shrugged my shoulders, while James was making his way to me. He picked me up carrying me to the other side of the bed. I noticed the guys went out closing the door behind them. He set me down slowly untied the robe, slid it off of me carefully, and then laid it down at the foot of the bed. His attention moved back to me, as he wrapped his arms around me, and lowered me to the bed. He lifted my legs and tucked them under the covers, "How does that feel?"

To get the full effect of the sheets I glided my hands and feet against them, "Dreamy." I grinned at him, and he returned the smile. "James, I have an idea."

"NO, we're not doing that."

"James, give me a chance to talk."

He did not want to give me a chance to tempt him. I was propped up with pillows behind my back, so I was kind of sitting up. I pulled the sheet over my legs and patted my legs, "I wasn't thinking that; please take off your shirt and come lay over my lap."

He walked to the other side of the bed taking his shirt off on his way. He was crawling into bed with me, but watching his jeans rub against his abs made my eyes bulge with anticipation.

"Here, lay across my lap." He did what I told him. I pulled a pillow to the other side of my legs, so he could rest his head. I started to rub his back.

He was tense at the beginning, but relaxed fairly quickly. He mumbled, "I am supposed to be taking care of you."

"Oh, my Cayuse, you are. I am getting to touch you."

I could see the grin as he turned his face toward me, but still resting it on the pillow. I was rubbing and felt a million knots in his back. I worked on those first. I was a little uncomfortable with the pain, but it wasn't too bad. He moved his hand under the covers and under my thigh. When I worked on a really bad knot he would grab tighter. His noises were telling me he was feeling it, and it was helping to relax him. The thought of pain kept me from leaning to him to kiss him. I did this till I started to drift off, tilting my head back. I would start and stop as I was dozing. He rolled over, took my hands in his, and brought them to his face to kiss them.

I didn't want to stop touching him, "I'm sorry, getting tired."

He reached up and touched my face adoringly, "Sleep it is." He moved from me, but was pulling me down so I could lie down. He was moving all the pillows to the side of me and rolled me to them.

"No, James, I want to see you when I wake up."

"My turn Sarah just rest."

He moved away from me, and took off his jeans, but crawled in to lie by me. He grazed his hands under the camisole and rubbed my back, but did more tracing then rubbing. He let me roll to my back, so I could see him. He was touching my front very lightly with his fingertips, "Sarah, sleep."

I looked at him, as I caressed his face. He closed his eyes, and I felt him rub up against me.

"James, no. We're not supposed to do that, and you are so tired."

"Will it make you feel better?"

"No."

"You are lying."

I felt the pressure of him again as if he was slowly pressing further in, and it felt hot with aspiration. He traced his hand down under my shorts and touched me in my most vulnerable spot. Having the feeling of him in me and his fingers touching me that way, made me close my eyes to enjoy the moment.

"See, you like it."

"What?"

I felt him slowly push into me again, "You are moist, and you want this."

I gasped from the intense pleasure he was causing me. He pulled me to him to look in my eyes. He entangled our legs, "I would touch you for real, but your pain... I can't watch it anymore." His gaze kept me mesmerized; I could see the immense desire in his. I felt him dive deeper again, but the movement was so slow my body wanted to move to him. We were sharing our breath, our heartbeats, and our desire for one another. My breathing was coming faster as the pleasure escalated, and I was getting so confused in what was real and what wasn't. He moved closer to me so that every inch of our bodies were touching, and he started to kiss me, but I was getting so lost. I tried to keep my eyes connected with his, but he was taking me to a place that was full of everything you could ever want.

"No, Sarah, look at me. It's more real."

Trying to stay with him, I opened my eyes in time for his to close a little as he kissed me deeper. They opened back up gazing deeper into mine with determination, as I felt him plunge into me, rubbing against every heated nerve I had within me. His breath matched his plunges.

I was feeling the tingling, "James." I could hardly breathe.

"I know, Sarah, are you okay?"

I was too busy moaning to answer him, so I nodded. I knew I was going to pay for this later, but it was so good now. I held my breath each time he would drive deeper finally letting something escape my mouth, "Oh"

"Yes, Sarah! Yes, it's so..."

As his pelvis jerked against me, I felt a surge that caused ecstasy to rupture from me. His body shivered, and my body trembled sending a cooling sensation to every nerve ending.

"Oh, James, I want this to be real. It's so good."

"I know baby, soon." His mouth was delivering wonderful little kisses all over my face.

"Not when I'm 18?"

His kisses began to linger, as a smile crept to his face, "I don't know if I could wait that long, with having it this way; it's cheating anyway."

I moved to close my eyes wrapping my arms around him to pull myself closer to him, thinking it will help me with the trembling that was so intense. He wrapped himself around me tracing his hands up and down my back, "Wait, Sarah, I have to..." He was reaching down between us and took what he did and smeared it all over my stomach, "I know gross, but it worked before."

When he was done, our eyes met and we both laughed lightly until our mouths met to continue entangling ourselves in each other.

I mouthed, "So much for clean sheets and a shower."

With this we both enjoyed an airy laugh but continued to kiss until we fell asleep together.

I woke glancing at the clock. It was about 4:00 pm, and James was still sleeping. I eased myself from him, and scooted off the bed feet first. I pushed myself up to a standing position. I was so proud of myself that I wanted to wake him, but I couldn't do it. Since it didn't hurt that bad to get up that way, I was ready to take on the steps. I walked up the steps but decided to make it as easy as possible; so with my good side I took it step by step. After getting through the hard part, I made my way to the bathroom to get cleaned up best I could. I was examining my scar which was almost all gone now. I could not believe my eyes that it was even better than I could ever imagine. I touched it and pressed on it, but the pain was still there. I guess you can't have everything, but I was happy that it was hardly noticeable. In my excitement walking back out I almost wanted to run to him to thank him for that, but running was not possible yet. I walked slowly to the bed, and carefully down the steps. I leaned over the bed lowering myself with my arms. Now that I knew that's what hurt less, I could handle it better. I moved to lay on my side curling back into James's arms. I couldn't keep my hands from touching him. First I traced my hand over his back, but then I started to rub at the knots again. They weren't as bad as last time, but that was probably because he was completely relaxed.

I heard him breath, "Little girl, you are going to be the death of me."

I reached up and kissed under his chin. He stretched a little and opened his eyes, "I am so in love with you."

I was still excited to show him the scar, "Do you want to see what you did to me?"

His face went completely pale, "No Sarah, please tell me I didn't hurt you more?"

"No James, just the opposite." I laid back and pulled up the camisole and pushed down on the shorts a little.

He moved to sit up more, still sleepy, but noticed right away. He traced his hand over it and smiled, "How does it feel though?"

"James, we can't have everything." I was still happy about it.

He leaned over it and kissed it softly tracing his mouth back and forth over it, "Sarah, if we do that a couple more times, you won't even see it."

I laughed a little.

"I am serious."

"No, it tickles."

He moved over top of me crawling back up to me. He kissed me softly but eagerly and spoke to my mouth, "You need food."

He filled me with happiness to my inner core. He pulled me up and tucked a bunch of pillows behind me, "I will get you something."

As James moved away from me I couldn't help but think that I was very lucky to have this man in my life; he was amazing to me.

When he was walking back in, he had the tray with him, "Wilson made something special for you tonight."

Why was it special tonight? I thought he made all the food, "Doesn't he make most of the food?"

"Well… yeah, we haven't had much time to help out in that department."

Knowing that it was me that took up all his time, I had to tease, "I don't take up that much of your time, do I?"

He didn't answer my question, but he did tell me what I was eating, "It's Chicken Alfredo Lasagna and garlic toast with a Caesar Salad."

"And I am supposed to eat all that?"

"Sarah, these are sized portions."

I smiled as he walked over to me and put the tray in front of me. He touched my face adoringly, "I have been really bad."

"What do you mean?"

"We can only visit each other in our dreams, no more the way we did today."

"You cannot cut me off cold turkey like that. I don't want to stop unless..."

He sat down and started to feed me. I took the fork wanting to feed myself.

He smiled, "Unless what?"

"Unless we are really together."

He got a guilty smile, "Sarah, do you understand why I wanted to wait for you to be 18?"

"No, especially now that we're married."

"It makes me feel like I'm taking advantage of you, and I think..." He was looking at me through the tops of his eyelashes, "We should try to quit for a while. Only 'til..."

Why did he have to make me angry, "Until when James? What are you trying to accomplish?"

"Until we are in the house of our dreams, because I am trying to make it more special."

I was confused. I wanted to be with him. With what we have already done, it was like we were together anyway and now... no more for who knows how long. I was finding it harder to eat. "Why are you doing this again?" I swallowed and couldn't look at him; I felt weird.

"Sarah, you're misunderstanding me. I am not doing anything to you. We are discussing it. If that doesn't work for you, then we will figure something else out that *will* work."

My stomach was turning, so I was done eating. I set down the fork feeling like I was going to throw up. "Get this off."

"No, Sarah, we're just discussing it. It's not what you are thinking. You need to eat."

"Nope, need to throw up now. Move it or I do it right here."

He grabbed it and sat it down. I was already moving to the other side of the bed. I pushed myself up, but grabbed my stomach because the pain was excruciating.

"Sarah, you're hurting yourself."

I turned to him glaring, "Then get me a fucking bucket."

He grabbed the waste basket and dumped it on the floor, as he brought it to me. After having that special moment today how could he make me feel this badly? I glared at him severely.

"Sarah, stop it. I was just talking to you about it. Please don't do this; it will make it worse." He was trying to talk me out of getting sick to my stomach. I didn't want to get sick either, so I kept swallowing to try and stop it from coming back up.

"Sarah, please we really need to talk about things and, honestly, I am making everything worse for you."

Leaning over, I was able to get one word out, "How?"

He knelt down in front of me and put his mouth to my stomach holding his lips against me, and letting his hands wrap around me. He couldn't look at me but still tried to explain, "When I come to you; when you are awake; I am making the desire in both of us grow to the point where it could drive us crazy, and I don't want to do that to you."

"Oh, like now!"

Finally his eyes came up to meet mine, "Yes, like now. I am so sorry, Sarah. I am driving you crazy. If I bring you home like this, full of desire, it will be really bad, and you will be miserable with being apart."

Anger was leaving me as the sadness seeped in, "Aren't you going to be miserable being apart?"

Agony unfolded from his face, as he moved to stand in front of me cupping my face with his hands, "I am going to feel like my world is coming to an end. I could spend 24 hours a day holding you and touching you, but that is not reality."

My body trembled, as he traced his mouth on mine. I took a deep breath trying to control my emotions as asked, "Why does it feel like you're pushing me away?"

I could see he did not agree with me, "You have got to be kidding me; I could never do that. You know I can't live without you."

I put my arms around him wrapping my hands in his hair pulling myself to him, "Maybe we need to rethink about me not going to live at home."

His lips pressed to mine hard, as he lifted me to him, "I don't want to let you go," came from his lips, as his mouth captured mine.

Our tongues entangled, but I had to plea my case, "I don't want to go."

He lifted me into his arms and sat down on the bed holding me. He was forgetting that the pain of sitting was still a problem for me, but I tried to not care, because I wanted more kissing.

When his kisses stopped he pressed his cheek to mine in agony, "I would love for you to stay. We'll talk to your parents."

That made me happy which I showed with kisses all over his face.

He pulled away from me determined, "But, you have to finish eating." He picked me up carrying me back to bed where he put the tray in front of me, "Please eat; Wilson will be sad if I bring this out like this."

I scolded him, "Then don't freak me out."

His eyes squinted as he watched me, "Your mom said you wouldn't want to go home."

"What?"

"She knows, Sarah."

This concerned me, but she was right, "She knows me better than I do."

"Eat, please. Then Jake wants to have you try some more exercise." Not that I won that argument, but I was determined to stay with James from now on.

## 25. Not As Planned

Jake came in, "Are you ready?"

"Nope, are you ready?"

"What... for putting up with you being a baby?"

"Yep."

He disapproved of my truthfulness and laughed, "James, out."

James was surprised, "I will behave."

Grabbing his shoulders, looking deep in his eyes, I pleaded, "James, out. I will try harder."

He gave me a playful pout, "So you can push me out, but I can't push you out?"

"That is way different than what you were going to do. This is only for maybe an hour."

He was irritated, "Fine!" He stomped all the way out of the room.

Jake moved closer to me, "I haven't checked your incision in a while; do you mind?"

I lay back pulling up my shirt with a guilty grin on my face, but only because he was going to wonder when he saw it. He seemed nervous and pulled up a chair, but then moved it away, and then finally sitting on the bed full of hesitation. The way his face was strained, I knew he wanted to say something.

"What?"

He shook his head before continuing, "Nothing. Okay, let's take a look at it." He pulled down the shorts a little. It was the brightness in his eyes that told me he was pleased with it, "You are healing really fast." I felt his fingers as they traced across the scar, "I do beautiful work. Sarah, have you looked at this? It's hardly scaring at all."

I was holding back a smirk, "Yes, you do beautiful work, Jake." I didn't have the heart to tell him the extra stuff that James did.

He could tell I was holding back, but he didn't let it get in the way. So serious now, "I am going to push a little; let me know where it hurts the most."

I braced myself remembering the last time he did this, "Wait!"

"What?" He was startled.

"Remember the last time you said that?"

I could see a sparkle in his eyes while he held back laughter, "It's not going to be that bad; the infection is not there anymore."

I huffed and braced myself, grabbing the blankets in my hands to endure the pain, "Just be careful, Jake, it still is really tender, and sore."

He was pushing on the opposite side of where the appendix had been, "How's this?"

"Yeah... it hurts a little; no... more like an ache."

He moved to the middle pressing just slightly. He didn't say anything, but his eyes were asking the question for him.

I nodded quickly, "Yep that still hurts."

Then he moved to the side where the appendix had been, pressing gently. His jaw clenched and he bit his bottom lip. It was like he was expecting it to hurt.

I gasped, "Oh, yeah. It's still a 10."

"Can you handle just a little more? I have to feel for..." He was pushing around and the pain was getting worse. It seemed that he was deep in thought as he moved his fingers around feeling for something.

We heard James yell from the other room, "What the hell are you doing?"

Jake was irritated and distracted. He yelled back, "James, stop!"

James came storming in, "What are you doing?"

Jake ignored James and continued to feel around searching for something. He was moving his fingers pushing against my lower stomach. The pain was too much, so I grabbed Jake's hand and my stomach at the same time, gasping for air.

James pleaded, "Jake, that is hurting her; you have to stop."

"James, out; you're distracting me and I am checking to see if everything is moving okay." He continued to move his fingers around and watched my face with concern, "You have only gone once?"

Not only was I worried now, but I was also embarrassed again, "Yeah?"

Finally he quit pushing at my insides. He got up and went to the box and came back with another bottle of pills, "We are adding this to your diet. One every time you eat."

"What is it?"

"Um..." Torn over telling me in front of James or not, his attention went back and forth between us until it finally landed on me, "Sarah, you need to be going to the bathroom more often, and I am surprised you are not having more pain. This will help to soften it, so you can go easier."

"Great, Jake, I just love talking about pooping."

Jake laughed out loud, but James was worried and held my face to look in my eyes, "You are in a lot of pain."

You could see the pain reflected on his face, so I tried to reassure him, "But, James, it's okay. I need to try harder to get better."

"No, you are done for the day. I feel it Sarah, and the pain is..." He was shaking his head no.

Jake was getting irritated, "Sam!!! Can you please get him out of here?"

Sam came running in and grabbed James pulling him away from me. James finally let go of my hands, as Sam got between us and guided him to the door. He was scolding James as they went out of the room, "James, you know it's just the desire that is making this so difficult; go walk it off."

That is when the scene changed and James was really angry, "Sam, get out of my way."

Sam stopped him with his body while he held the door frame to keep James out, "Did you talk to Sarah about it, James? She needs to understand that what you two have been doing is bad. She needs to know how it is affecting you both."

I think I understood what Sam was saying, but I had to make it okay for James to leave, "James, it's okay."

He finally glanced at me, but only for a second. He was very angry as he scolded Sam, "Just shut up! You say too much."

"Not if you talked to her. Go walk it off, James."

Sam pushed James harder but blustered to me, "Sarah did you listen to him at all? You can't do anything while you are awake. The desire will keep building and it will only get worse. It becomes more of an obsession."

His body was pressing against James's body trying to keep him from coming to me, but when he finished James couldn't look at me. He grunted with a loud growl and stormed away.

My heart was aching because it was finally clear. I glanced up at Jake, "Am I driving him crazy?"

Jake actually looked gentle, not so stern, "You're not... but what you two are doing is. Did he talk to you about not doing that anymore?"

"I thought it was an excuse to push me away, so that I would move home. I guess I didn't believe that it could really do that to us."

"The last thing he wants is to push you away. Talking to you about it was very hard for him. You should try harder and don't push him. He is trying to do what is best for you."

I felt awful. All I could think of was how I was going to try very hard to not argue with my sweet Cayuse. I loved him and I was wrong for enticing him.


"Sarah back to work here. You need to be strong enough to go to school."

I was in a daze. I just wanted James to come back. I used all my thoughts focusing on James. *Please come back. Please, James!!!*

"Sarah, hey, you need to work on this."

My mind was not going to be on working hard now. I was too worried about James and how sad it made me that I had hurt him more. I finally gave into to Jake, but I wasn't really happy about it. I wanted James!

Jake leaned in front of me, trying to get my attention. He explained, "I am going to lift one leg and you are going to hold it for as long as you can."

When he let go of my leg in the air, I gasped from the excruciating pain

James came running in. No one was going to stop him this time, "What are you doing to her?"

I didn't want to upset him, but I didn't want him to leave either, "James, just come and hold my hand, so I can try harder."

He was moving to me, but Jake had lifted my other leg and was letting go. This was my good side, so I thought I would be able to do better, but the jab to my inners almost made me throw up right there. I gasped again as I dropped it.

James almost dove to me holding my hand, staring into my eyes, but scolding Jake, "Jake, this is too much. You don't understand how much this is hurting her."

"Yes I do. We've got to get her moving, exercising her muscles. You're going to do this again, Sarah."

He lifted my leg and then let it go. I think James would have grabbed my leg if I wasn't holding his hand so tightly. Oh shit, did this ever hurt. I couldn't hold it at all. He lifted the other leg and let it go, "Sarah, try really hard this time and hold it."

I squeezed James's hand as I tried, but I couldn't hold it at all. The pain was like a knife digging in my gut, shooting arrows of torture through my body. I gave up, and the tears were streaming down my face.

James wanted to take all my pain away. I could see it in his face. I wanted him to know it was okay, so I assured him, "Its fine."

"No! It's not. Jake, she is done."

"Actually, James, I need to walk. It helps stretch it out. Just help me up."

"James, no. Make her do it herself."

I didn't know how I was going to do this. The pain was so intense at this moment that I couldn't move if I tried.

James totally ignored Jake, picking me up, "Not this time, maybe next."

"You are babying her. She is not going to get better if you don't push her."

No matter how much pain I was in, I had to try. I placed my hand on the back of his neck, "Put me down, James, I can do this."

James was letting me down, but certainly didn't like it, "Jake, will you get her a pill please and a shot?"

"NO, James, it's okay. No shot. You can read to me to help me get through it. I have to do better."

He touched my face gently, but snarling at Jake, "I said get a shot for her"

Jake wasn't happy either, but he didn't comment as he walked out.

James set me down so that I could walk to stretch my gut out a little. Fixing my eyes on his and wrapping my arms around his neck, I apologized to my sweet Cayuse, "I am so sorry. The next time you want to talk to me, I will listen to you and not overreact. We can talk about everything again, and I will try harder to understand. I love you so much and I haven't been fair."

"You don't have to be; you are not well."

I leaned my face against his and held on to him, "James, this is really bad and I need to try and walk. Can you get me to the top of the steps?"

In one swoop I was at the top. I tried to take a few steps, but had to bend over to handle the pain. As I stood back up I saw Jake.

He handed James the pill and a glass of water but stared intensely at me, "It's really that bad?"

I tried to straighten up and my knees gave out. James must have been close enough, because I woke up in his arms and Jake was giving me the shot.

"Jake, you said no more shots."

He grimaced, "You weren't honest about your pain."

"But you were pushing so I was trying hard, Jake, that's all."

"We are going to do the exercises in the pool. It will make it easier so you can do more."

I didn't know how James would take that, and with my confusion I glanced back and forth between them. James avoided my glance and moved me back to the bed. He laid me down and gave me the pill and some water.

He grabbed the book and crawled next to me, but this time he rolled to me and put his hand on my stomach. I had to hold the book, but he read.

The next time I woke I think it was in the middle of the night, but James still brought me food. This time it was more cottage cheese with pears, and another piece of the lasagna. I really liked the lasagna. I had to brush my teeth and made it there on my own. James had dozed off while I ate. I ambled slowly to the living room and no one was awake. I crept back and crawled into bed with him and cuddled to sleep.

I woke and this time James wasn't there. I was trying to get up and go to the bathroom. I was determined to do it on my own, plus I had to poop and that was just too embarrassing for me to have the guys have to lift me from the toilet. I managed the trip to the sink and brushed my teeth, and somehow, carefully, agonizingly, sat on the toilet.

When I came out Jake was standing there, "Are you ready for today? You seem to be doing okay."

I grimaced with a grin, "Yeah, I guess."

"You are going to eat a really light meal, and then we are going into the pool. James went to get you a one piece. He didn't want me touching you with a bikini on." He was laughing to himself. Deep down I was thankful.

"Sarah, why don't you sit in the living room and watch TV with us, while you have breakfast. Hopefully, James will be back in time for us to start to work."

"Could you get me the robe?"

"No." He looked at me up and down, not in the way James does, but he turned away to walk out and said, "You are doing good enough to get it yourself."

I was already irritated by this. I walked back to the bed slowly making it down the steps. I put the robe on but leaned down to rest against the bed. I didn't know how I was going to be able to do school in two weeks. I had to push harder. Jake walked back in and saw me hunched over. In a gentler tone of voice, he asked, "Hey, are you okay?"

I turned my head trying to look over my shoulder at him, "Yep, Just taking a breather."

"But you didn't do anything yet."

"Yep, you're right. I'll be right out."

He turned and walked out. I was in agony, not only from pooping, but also from managing the steps. Leaning against the bed, I reached up for a pillow and tried to roll to my side pulling it to me to wait for the pain to lessen.

"Sarah?"

Jake was walking back in and around to the front of me, "Hey, are you okay?"

"Yep, just..."

"Yeah, I know you said that before, but you're just not looking good at all."

"Just hurts a little bit this morning."

"From yesterday, or did you two...?"

"Jake, no. After my lecture yesterday, I plan on behaving for a long time."

"Then what, Sarah, you're kind of green?"

"Jake, I am fine. I just need a couple of minutes to let the pain pass."

"The pain? You are in pain?"

I rolled my eyes, "Why else would I be laying here?"

He walked completely over to me and squatted down so I could see his face, "Sarah, where does it hurt?"

"Same as usual."

"Did you do something, other than yesterday, to irritate it?"

"I went to the bathroom by myself. Let's see: Sitting, standing, which are the hardest things for me to do."

"Did you have a bowl movement?"

God did I hate that I had to tell him these things. I couldn't even talk to him about it, so I just nodded.

"Sarah, we need to go back in for some scans. Make sure everything has room and that it's not tangled in there."

I looked at him horrified, "If you think that you are cutting me open again you can just forget it. I would rather die than feel that again."

"I am not kidding. If something isn't right we need to take care of it now."

The fear of being cut open again brought tears to my eyes.

"Sarah, I'm not saying there is a problem, but we need to make sure. You should have been making better progress by now."

"But I thought, maybe, it was because James was babying me too much."

"By the looks of it, maybe not."

I closed my eyes and the tears dripped out, "Jake, I can't do that again. I have school in two weeks. I'll get up, we'll do the pool, and I will work really hard."

"I think we are going to take you to my hospital."

"No, James is tired. I am wearing on him. Jake, NO!"

"He is going to take his entrance exam tomorrow; we'll go then. Sam can help me with getting you there."

"He's going to be mad."

"We won't tell him unless we need to do something else."

I didn't want to agree, but it seemed that I didn't have a choice.

"Sarah, if I help you, can you at least try to eat?"

"Not if it's going to make me poop."

He laughed but was trying to be serious, "Sarah, at 103 lbs you are going to start to lose muscle tissue if you don't. Have you known anyone who was anorexic?"

"No, not really."

"Let me see if I can explain. They quit eating and after you lose all your body fat, your muscle tissue starts to go. Sarah, you are at that point. You don't have to do the exercises in the pool today, and I am putting in an IV to get you some more nutrients, but can you try to eat?"

"I have no problem with eating."

He helped me up, and carried me to the top of the steps setting me down to walk.

I cautiously padded to the living room in a slouched position, and Sam stood up, "Should you look like that when you walk?"

Immediately I thought to myself, *God, what an insulting thing to say.* Instead of replying, I just gave him a dirty look.

"Sam." Jake was going to fill him in.

I stopped him quickly, "Jake, tomorrow."

He questioned me with raised eyebrows. They both helped me sit, but in a position that was more like lying on the couch. Jake brought me a bowl of cereal and some orange juice.

I ate it all and studied Jake, "I think I need the good pill. Is there anything else we can try? It makes me foggy."

He took the tray but handed me a pill and then said, "Yeah, I will get something else tomorrow."

I gave him a stern look to shut him up about tomorrow. He scooped me up in his arms to carry me back to the room.

I tried to explain what I was thinking, "If Sam decides to listen he will know, but I don't want James to know, so clear your head of it now."

"Know what?" Sam was walking in.

"Sam, I told you no more of that."

"James has been bugging me all morning to check on you."

"Can you block him?"

"Yes."

"If you will, we can tell you; if you can't, then Sam... I can't tell you till tomorrow."

"Wait; let me show him you are okay first."

He touched my arm. I wasn't in pain right now, "Sarah, he could feel your pain a while ago."

"Tell him we're working on sitting and standing."

He touched me again to show James that everything was okay. He moved to sit next to me waiting for an explanation.

"Can you block him? Are you sure?"

"I am stronger than him; you know that."

Jake sat down on the bed to explain to him, "Sam, we're going to take her back in and do some scans tomorrow. I want to make sure everything is all right in there."

"Okay, so why can't James know about that?"

"He will worry and he has to register for school tomorrow. He has other things he has to take care of instead of me all the time."

Sam shook his head disapproving, "You're doing it again."

Shit, the fogginess was coming back. I shook my head, "What?"

"You aren't giving him a choice. I think you should tell him, and Sarah, no more sharing souls; no more wide-awake dreaming, because the insatiable desire becomes too much for both of you."

I was embarrassed, "I promise."

My head was foggy, and I closed my eyes not able to open them again.

## 26. The Promise

**I** woke to James gently touching my face; I knew his touch very well. It was a soft, adoring touch with a hint of desire behind it. I opened my eyes to see his beautiful, strong face studying me. I felt secure in his arms and couldn't keep myself from smiling.

"Sarah, what is going on?"

I was puzzled, and it showed in my expression. I understood when he moved my arm, so I could see the IV. Jake must have put it in while I was sleeping.

I shrugged it off the best I could, "More nutrition, my sweet Cayuse."

His hand went back to tracing my face. His touch was so soft and it was as perfect as the skin on his body. I didn't see how there could be anything more perfect. He was the man, THE MAN, I was completely in love with, and he was in love with me. I took a deep breath to absorb how much I adored him.

"Sarah."

"Yes?"

"There is more."

I closed my eyes; I couldn't keep anything from him, "Yes, there is." I opened my eyes to gaze deep into his. The deep color under his eyes saddened me almost to the point of not wanting to tell him, "Did you get an ugly suit for me to go in the pool with?"

He wasn't happy with my reply, "Yes, and you are avoiding my question."

"No, just taking my time. I don't want you to worry or get upset, and... you are so tired and worn."

"S-a-r-a-h?" He was getting angry.

"See, you are already getting upset and being with me has already been so hard on you."

He tried to calm himself, "But you are mine, so I am happy. Just tell me what it is; you are making me insane here."

"When I got up this morning I had determination to work really hard today, so I took myself to the bathroom. I did it on my own." I was very proud of myself and hoped that it would make him happier. His face was not happy, more like sad he wasn't here to help me.

"James, I did it on my own. That was supposed to make you happy."

Even with a small smile I could tell he was waiting for me to tell him the rest.

"Jake, was ready to push me, so he didn't get me the robe. I tried to get back to the bed, but the pain was really bad. By the time I got there I couldn't stand anymore so I lay down."

"Okay, IV?"

"James, I should be better; I am still losing weight, and I am weak, so… he thought maybe if I had some extra nutrition it might help."

"That's it?"

I was so torn about telling him about tomorrow. I didn't know how to tell him.

"James, what time do you take your test?"

"Why?"

"Please, James?"

"Early, 8:00 am. I thought that would be the best time for you. You are better early in the day, and if those two loafs have to take care of you I just thought it would be better."

"No, that is really good. Have you studied for it?"

"Sarah, you are avoiding something."

"No, what I am thinking… since I am going to sleep most of the day…"

He completely cut me off, "Why are you sleeping most of the day?"

"Too much pain and Jake said I could have the strong stuff every time along with the pill, because the pill makes me foggy and tired, hence the sleeping most of the day."

"The pain is worse?" His face dropped sadly in a worried frown.

I touched his cheek softly tracing it, "James, you need to study while I sleep. Promise me, and I will tell you something else, but you have to promise you will study and take the test."

"I am not promising you anything, little girl, until you tell me."

"Okay." I closed my eyes and was trying to let the sleep take over.

"Sarah?"

"You won't promise, so I need to sleep, James." I slowly opened my pleading eyes to see his sweet face.

He started to move away from me, "If you're not going to tell me, I will just ask Jake and Sam."

"James!"

He stopped, thinking I was going to give in.

"James, I have warned them, and they will not tell you. *And* they will not feel it either. You are getting too good for your own good."

He glowered and slowly came back to me, "Why?"

"James, I won't feel it either. You have to promise me."

"You are a pain in my butt, Sarah."

I was grinning now. He was being stubborn, not saying anything, and I closed my eyes again. I concentrated on him studying and taking the test tomorrow.

"You are getting really good at diverting your thoughts."

I grinned even more, "Do you promise?"

"How can I promise, if I don't know what to study?"

"Don't try that with me. They have a study guide online. I saw it when I was checking it out."

"Why do you have to be so thorough?"

I smiled mischievously, "I have to be to keep up with you. Your special talents make me try harder to be better."

Disapproving, he shook his head.

"Jake said he would help you if you want."

"Fine."

"What time is it?"

"Noon."

"Please get me another pill; I can't stand the pain anymore."

"You will tell me when I come back!"

I smiled at him; oh he just looks so good to me. I wanted to attack him with kisses. He got as far as the first step before I could try to stop him, "Hey, you are forgetting something."

He stopped abruptly his eyes flashing, "What?"

"I really need to feel those lips, please."

He leaned down to me and softly kissed me long and tenderly; it felt like a lifetime, but I was in heaven. He finally stopped and moved away from me. When he came back he had a cup of something and the pill.

"Jake said you have to try and eat something."

He helped me with the water for the pill and fed me cottage cheese with pineapples. It was my favorite snack. I washed it down with water and settled back on the bed. He was crawling back to lay in front of me intently staring up into my face. I've put it off as long as I could; I knew it was my time to tell him.

"I don't remember you promising me?"

"Shit, girl, tell me."

"Promise me."

He looked beaten, "Fine, but I am not happy about this. You are winning this fight."

"No fight, James. Just a little promise, but you have to say it."

"I promise. I promise to study, and I promise to take the test tomorrow, but if I am not happy with what you are going to tell me... I might break the promise."

"Then you don't need to know." I closed my eyes and waited for the sleep to engulf me.

I felt the trace of his lips along my cheek and a whisper to my face, "You are so stubborn, little girl."

I grinned with delight.

"I promise I will get it done."

I opened my eyes. He was so close to me I was melting. I would have given in to him if he would have tried this earlier.

"I am going to the hospital tomorrow for more scans. Jake doesn't like that I am not getting better and he wants to make sure everything is working properly."

The relief on his face was welcoming, "Sarah, you thought I would be mad?"

I nodded.

"No baby. I want you to get better, and your pain is so bad that when you feel it, I almost pass out from what I feel. I wanted this almost a week ago, but I didn't want to scare you. What time are you going?"

I shrugged my shoulders.

"I think I should call your mom. She will worry."

"Wait till we know."

"If it was me, I would want to know."

"I trust you will do what's right; I am foggy right now"

He kissed me softly again and pulled the book out to read to me until the oblivion took over.

## *James:*

I promised to study and take the entrance exam tomorrow. I hated leaving her, but I had to get this done. I couldn't have my wife live in a basement for the rest of her life. I decided that I should work on this now that she was fast asleep. I walked out; Jake and Sam were sitting on the couch. They got really quiet when I came out.

"Guys settle, she told me about tomorrow."

Jake jumped up and came to me to explain, "James, she should be better. I just want to make sure nothing is wrong. Her pain was so bad this morning, and I just want to check things out."

I didn't want him to panic, "Jake, I wanted to ask you to do this last week, but I was afraid it would upset her."

"Why didn't you say something?"

"I don't know. What time are you thinking of taking her?"

"I called; I can get her in at 11:00 am."

"Where?"

"At my old hospital."

"I will need directions. I promised I would still take the entrance exam."

"And you're going?"

"I promised. She also said you would help me study."

"Yeah."

I walked over to the computer and pulled it up. We found the study guide and it seemed easy enough. Jake was helping me look at everything, and then we hit the books. We only took breaks when she woke up. I was able to feed her two more times today. She was so out of it.

I finally gave up studying when Jake was falling asleep at the table with me. I nudged him to go to bed. Sam was sleeping on the couch. I went in to sleep with my wife. I smiled with satisfaction in the word '*My Wife*'. I crawled in bed to cuddle with her. I loved the way she felt, even though she was too thin. I wrapped my arms around her and she snuggled in and put her head on my shoulder.

"James!"
I wasn't really awake, "Yes."
"I have to go to the bathroom, like right now."
I jumped up and stumbled to grab her. I forgot she was connected to an IV. I stopped and moved back to grab it. She actually grabbed it and I carried her to the bathroom. I got her sitting and moved from the room. I went to grab a little cottage cheese and some pears to put in it. She had to eat at least a little every time she was up. I put the cup on the night table and went back to the bathroom and knocked.
"Sarah, are you done?"
She was opening the door.
"You got up on your own?"
She was holding her stomach; I could tell it was painful, but she smiled at me. I picked her up and turned her so she could grab the IV. I walked her back to bed setting her down and moved next to her. I gave her another pill and started to feed her. I could barely keep my eyes open as I struggled to feed her. When she was done I gave her more water to wash it down. I looked at the clock it was 2:30am; I still could sleep for four more hours. It did seem like she was still tired so I asked, "How are you doing?"
Even though those deep green eyes took me to another world, they seemed to be dreamy as she stared at me grinning. I crawled back into bed pulling her into my arms. She nuzzled into me kissing my neck with those amazing lips. The temperature of my body went up about ten degrees. "You are going to be the death of me."
She liked that she could drive me crazy and her kisses became alluring and increasingly seductive. I pulled her closer to me and tilted my head back to enjoy her aggressiveness but knew I had to refuse her, "Sarah, I am so tired, baby, and I have to be awake for this test tomorrow. I can't do this."
She stopped and looked up at me; I avoided those eyes, because they were my downfall. I didn't want to discourage her completely so I glanced down. The heat in me went up immediately, "Oh Sarah, you shouldn't do this to me."
"I love you, James."
I nuzzled down to her to kiss her. I was too tired to be aggressive with her, but the kissing was so soft and sweet; she tasted so scrumptious to me. We fell asleep kissing.

## 27. Jake's Help

### Sarah:

**W**hen I woke he was gone. I panicked; I wanted to wish him good luck. I was so bummed out and sad. The bathroom door opened and he came out with all his attention directed towards me, "I was hoping you would wake up before I had to leave." He was coming to me and I was so excited to see him that I was speechless. He crawled across the bed to kiss me good morning. It was soft and sweet, but stopped abruptly, "Hey, I have a little time; can I help you eat?"

I must have looked like a lost puppy dog, because I still didn't say anything; I just nodded.

He was out of the room and back with food before I moved an inch. "Sarah, your color is so much better; you're kind of pink today." He fed me oatmeal, not my favorite, but it was quick and not bad. He helped me to the bathroom and I got to brush my teeth. When I was back in bed, he tucked me in and fed me a pill.

"Jake's going to wake you at 10:30 am; I will meet you at the hospital. Jake gave me directions."

He gave me a quick grin but then came back to kiss me again.

I was desperate, "Wait?"

He looked at me straight in the eyes almost waiting for me to beg him to stay.

"I wanted to wish you luck."

He smiled a devilish grin, "I don't need luck, baby; I've got you." He kissed me again quickly, "Do you want Sam or Jake to read to you?"
"Nope, I'll just sleep."
"I hate leaving you."
"Go, wait… Are you taking the bike?"
"Sarah, it's still up north."
I was happy with that.
"You don't like the bike?"
"I love the bike just not you on it."
He smiled and shook his head, "I have to go."
"You're right; this would drive me crazy."
He kissed my forehead, "Are you sure you don't want me to get Jake or Sam?"
"No, it's not the same. Just do well and I'll be waiting for you."
He smiled and quickly went out the door. His leaving almost left me feeling lost and sad, even though I knew it would only be a few hours. I pulled out the book and started to read. It didn't take long till the words were fuzzy. I laid it down when I couldn't see them anymore.

"Sarah."
"Sarah." Jake started to shake me slightly.
"Sarah?"
I opened my eyes.
"It's time to get up."
"Can I take a shower?"
"Quickly?"
"Yes."
"Yeah, that's fine. I need to take the IVs out."
"Good. It makes me feel like I'm sick."
"Sarah, you are sick."
"Not."
He raised his eyebrows at me.
"I just thought of something, Jake. What am I going to wear?"
"Last weekend your mom brought your clothes."
"Where are they?"
Jake was taking the needle out.
"Ouch, Jake, that hurts!"
"You're whining."
"Clothes…?"
He started to walk around the room, "Maybe he doesn't want you dressed."
"You're funny. Check the closet and dresser."
He walked to the closet holding up my shoes, "Tennis…"
"Yep, mine."
He ran to the dresser and started opening the drawers. He got to the drawer with all lingerie in it and turned to me with a funny glint in his eyes.
"Jake, not that drawer and don't ask. You don't want to know."
"Yeah, I can figure that one out on my own."

I was embarrassed again. He got to the bottom drawers. "I think this is your stuff. Let me help you to the shower; can you walk a little?"

"I think so; just help me get up the stairs."

He was already walking to me. He helped me sit up a little and pulled me to my feet. He picked me up but not as easily as James.

"You definitely feel heavier than 100 lbs."

I laughed, "That's not nice, and don't make me laugh."

He set me down gently with his arms extended around me. The pain wasn't too bad. I moved slowly to the bathroom.

"Did you need me to help you sit?"

I glared at him. I did need him too, but opted to say no, "I've got it."

"Sarah, if you are going to die from pain, James will feel it.

"I will take a shower first; then if I need help I will ask."

He agreed and got me two towels. He must have the same habit as me. He shrugged when my eyebrows scrunched, "James told me two."

Of course James told him. How else would he know that about me? He moved out the door closing it. I took a shower really quick and got out; I supported my weight on the back of the toilet and the sink to lower myself to the toilet. It wasn't too bad and no poop today, so nothing to aggravate it. I supported myself to stand, brushed my teeth and walked out. Jake was leaning on the wall outside the bathroom, "You okay?"

"Yep; it helped not to poop."

He shook his head chuckling, "You can get dressed by yourself?"

I was instantly scared, "I don't know."

He eyed me as I walked to the dresser. I picked out underwear and contemplated his expression. We both didn't want him to help me, but to bend over... I didn't know if I could get up again.

"Sarah, I am a doctor. I can do this."

He grabbed the underwear and squatted down to let me step into them. He pushed them up to the bottom of the towel, "Your turn."

I reached down to pull them up the rest of the way. I started to look through some stuff. I found cut off sweat shorts. I held them up. He laughed.

"Jake, I don't want anything tight over my stomach."

He grinned grabbing them and helped me step into them. Just like the underwear, it worked pretty slick. He lifted first and then I finished the job.

"Jake, I think I can do the rest myself."

He smiled moving really close to me and whispered in my ear, "If he didn't have that connection from what he did, you would have kissed me." With that said, he turned on his heels and left. I was thankful for that. This was really hard for him to help me, but I wasn't going to have Sam do it. I wasn't ready to battle the hormones of a 15 year old. I looked through the drawers and found a cute camisole and a comfy t-shirt. I liked the way they felt, and besides, I didn't want to struggle with a bra. I slowly walked out to the living room.

"You're ready?"

"Yeah, but I forgot my phone. Can you grab it off the night stand?"

Sam ran back to the room and came out with it in his hand, "Sarah, I think you have a message."

I took it and opened it, *"1-, 2-, 3-, Breath."* I couldn't help but smile. Sam looked over my shoulder. He started to laugh.

"What?"

"That was the first text you sent him while you were under."

"I sent him a text when I was under?"

"You sent him a lot of texts when you were under."

"Really?"

"Sarah, you don't remember?"

"No."

Jake was getting irritated, "We have to go now. We'll have lots of paper work to do once we get there."

I headed to the door. Sam came up behind me and picked me up with no problem. Jake was irritated again, but this time it was because Sam found it so easy to lift me. He was a lot like my James.

Sam shrugged without a care, "James will feel her pain, and I don't want to deal with him if he gets angry."

Jake was not impressed but Sam made me laugh.

"Sam, no laughing, it hurts."

Jake had the back seat of his truck turned into a comfy bed. It was really cushiony. I scooted back and there were a dozen pillows propped to make it more comfortable, "What is under here?"

"It's an air mattress."

"You are kidding."

"No. I thought the drive to the hospital might cause you some discomfort."

I was happy that they thought of everything.

When we got to the hospital, Jake parked in the *Reserved for Doctors* area. He told Sam to help me get out of the car, and he ran in retrieving a wheel chair.

Sam was struggling to help me get out. The pain was starting to kick in. When Jake came back out with the wheelchair, my eyes flew to his, as I moaned in agony, and soundlessly begged for pain killers. He seemed to know what I was thinking.

"No Sarah, I can't."

It was hard for him to tell me *no* this time, but I was hurting pretty badly, "Please, it's getting bad."

He wasn't happy about it but he opened his glove box, "Only half, Sarah, we might need the rest to get you home."

I was thankful that he was helping me with the pain.

"Sarah, you are getting to be a junkie. You are going to go through withdrawals."

"It's better than pain."

"No, I promise you this. It's not."

I wasn't smiling anymore. Jake was guiding me to sit. I glanced up at him, "You are nuts if you think I am sitting."

"You are." He was lowering me to the wheel chair. As I sat the sharp pain shot through me and I gasped. He stopped waiting for the pain to subside, "How did you ever go to the bathroom if it hurts this bad to sit?"

"I tried to breathe through my nose a lot."

He found that hard to believe and headed in to fill out paper work. Sam was wheeling me in following Jake closely. He went over a few bumps that caused more pain. I didn't know if I wanted to laugh or cry because every bump Sam would apologies, but he didn't avoid them either.

We went in through a back door for doctors; Jake pointed where Sam should bring me. Jake followed shortly after us with a clip board filling things out as he walked to us. He took over pushing me as we went into the scanning room. He helped me to the table lifting me and carefully lying me down on the table, "You have to be really still. Can you handle that?"

"Yes, if I am lying down."

Grabbing a blanket he covered me up and started to do the scans. We went from room to room doing different scans. Finally, he brought me to a waiting area and left me there with Sam.

"Have you heard from James yet?"

"No, but I thought he would be here by now."

I was getting worried and I wanted him here. Just as I thought about it, he was walking towards us with the biggest grin. I knew it went well.

"Yes, Sarah, it's all taken care of. I even have classes and books."

Feeling very proud of my man, I held out my hand for him. As he took my hand in his, he turned it palm up where he laid a long hungry kiss on it, but then asked, "What does he think?"

"I don't know. I think he is looking at the results now."

James was going to sit next to me, but he didn't even see Sam sitting there. I pulled him to stop him, "Hey, you're going to sit on Sam."

James grabbed his brother's hand and pulled him into a huge hug, "Thanks, little brother." He glanced back at me while he put Sam in a headlock, "So, who helped you get dressed?"

It wasn't something he should worry about, but Sam replied, "It wasn't me."

James let go of Sam and gave me a concerned look.

"James, he was very careful to not touch me or get close. Don't let your imagination run wild."

Playfully he replied, "I am allowed to be protective."

We only waited a short while before Jake walked out, but he didn't seem happy, to say the least. I would say it was a combination of being completely miserable and totally pissed. He walked past us without stopping but spoke to us, "We're checking her in, and then I will explain."

James stood up immediately. Jake just put up his hand to stop him. I was losing my ability to breathe. The fear absolutely overwhelmed me. I looked down, so they couldn't see my despair. James squatted in front of me, "Hey, don't get upset. We don't know the whole thing yet. Just…"

I didn't want this, and I didn't want to go through anything else. I was petrified as my tear filled eyes found James's face.

"I know, baby. I don't know what to say or do here, Sarah."

I was about to hyperventilate when Jake spoke up, "Sarah, knock it off. You wanted to be an adult, so act like one. Breathe through your nose, and I will tell you the rest once we get you upstairs."

How could he be so cold and heartless? This wasn't the Jake that I was getting to know.

## 28. *What,... How... Couldn't Be*

**H**e couldn't even look at me, so I knew it was bad. I did a lot of swallowing trying to stay calm. We got to a room and a couple of nurses came in to help me get changed and into the bed. They were ogling over Jake. It did ease the tension, because I had to laugh to myself. I nudged James so he would notice, and he let Sam in on the joke. When everyone left the room he closed the sliding door and then the curtain and looked at us. We all had silly grins.

"What?"

I couldn't help myself, "They ogle over you here, too."

He disapproved of my observation, "Okay, here it is in a nut shell. We have to open you back up. Somehow, the intestines got twisted into a couple of knots, and we need to get them untwisted. That is why the pain is so bad, Sarah. You must sleep wildly or something because there are actually three knots."

I looked at him confused.

"Yes, it can happen. You're not weird."

James was deep in thought, "I should call your mom."

Jake added, "I called mom. She and your dad are on their way."

Not believing that this was all happening, "This is serious?"

"Well, I am opening you up again. Sarah, are you getting sleepy yet?"

I shook my head to get rid of the overwhelming shock of having to sleep right now, "A little."

James had questions, "Are you doing it right now? I should call her mom."

"No, but I had to put her out."

I heard that and I was confused, so I asked, "Why?"

"I need to talk to James privately, and you don't need to hear or see this. How are you doing?"

"If there is something else, I want to know. Jake, make it stop."

He came to me and lowered the bed, "Sarah, you don't have to worry. Just sleep for now."

He reached up and turned something on.

I looked at him confused, "Jake no. I don't……..want…."

## James:

"Why are you putting her to sleep if you're not going to do it now?"

Ignoring my question Jake checked Sarah's eyes. Finally he turned back to me fuming. He could have killed me with the way he was glaring at me. Sam was slowly moving in between us.

Jake touched Sarah's arm shaking her a little, "Sarah, how are you doing?"

She was out, and Jake came at me, pinning me to the wall with his arm on my neck, "I thought you were waiting till she was 18?"

I just looked at him stunned. What was he talking about? "Jake, we are."

"She was sick and in pain and you just had to do it."

I was still staring into his eyes not understanding his actions. I was holding him back, and Sam was trying to pull him off, but with the anger he had, he was still coming at me.

"Jake, what are you talking about?"

"James, she is pregnant."

I quit pushing him away and his fist came very close to my face, but he couldn't bring himself to hit me. I wish he would have. I didn't have any excuse to explain how this happened and I looked at Sam for answers, "Is that even possible?"

Jake moved away from me confused by my questioning Sam. I collapsed sitting on the floor putting my hands over my face.

"James, what do you mean?"

"From the dreams, the thoughts of…" I couldn't even bring myself to say it. He wasn't responding, so I looked up at him, "Sam, is it possible?"

Both of our attention went to Jake while he backed away from me completely miserable. I didn't want to believe that I could do this to her so I was hoping that it was because of the dreams and not… I needed to know, "Sam, is it possible?"

He sat down in front of me and talked very softly, "James, did you use the feather?"

"No, not like that." I glanced up at him determined, "I know where you are going with this, but that would have hurt her. No"

"It's not possible with the dreams, James!"

I started to trace back over the last two weeks looking for how it could be possible. I could hardly breathe as I saw Jake put his hands to his face.

"James, are you trying to tell me you two didn't at all?"

I was still searching. I could only think of one possibility.

"Jake, how far along is the pregnancy?"

"I don't know. It's not really even a fetus yet."

"What does that mean?"

"It's not even a baby yet. Okay." He was glaring at me again. "Did you or didn't you?"

My mind was going crazy. I could not believe this.

"How, James? Did you or didn't you?"

I just shook my head; it would have looked like a no to everyone else, but I was really shaking it in disbelief, "You said she couldn't."

"YOU DID? James, I said she *shouldn't*, not till later. Wait till she was older. She might be able to carry it, but now, no. It could kill her, James. Why, she was so sick. How could you? She had to be in extreme pain and you didn't see it?"

"Jake, it wasn't like that. It just wasn't like that at all. It…. She… Shit. If it could kill her get rid of it. You said it wasn't even a baby yet. Get rid of it."

"No, I have to hear that from her."

"Jake, please I can't live without her. Get rid of it."

"Well, you should have thought about that before you did it."

"Jake it wasn't like that. You don't understand."

"I understand you couldn't keep it in your pants long enough for her to get better. You had to have hurt her."

"NO, Jake. It wasn't like that."

"You need to explain it to me than."

"NO, but I wouldn't have done that; it would have hurt her too bad. You have to believe me. Sam!"

He glanced at me.

"Do you feel what I thought?"

"Yeah, but James, I don't want to know that."

"Shit, little brother, help me out here."

"No, James it was wrong no matter if you were just… James you knew you shouldn't have."

"She did it before I knew it was happening."

Jake was advancing on me, "She did what?"

I couldn't face him even though he was in front of me, "How long till she wakes up?"

"I turned it off as soon as she was almost out…maybe another half hour."

"I need to explain it so she understands the importance of getting rid of it."

"James, what if she won't agree to it? It could kill them both."

I couldn't breathe. I was going to lose her. She wanted this, so she wouldn't have to go home. She would want this because she knew I wanted to have babies with her. She didn't want to have a baby for any other reason, at least not now. Would it be enough to make her want to keep it? I couldn't hold it in anymore; I started to cry and I pleaded with Jake, "Please, just take it out of her. I don't care if I ever have kids. I just want her."

"Well, you already had her. Now you pay the price, BROTHER."

"Jake, you don't understand. It wasn't like that. She gets me going and we weren't together, Jake, not like that. We were just…Fuck Jake. We were just playing; I was trying to make her happy. She was already pleased and her noises made me come. After I did… she knew I wasn't… you know… and she pushed me into her. It didn't hurt her because I wasn't….. But I had already… you know, and that is the only possible way."

"That is the only way; you are sure?"

"Yes, unless it could happen within the dreams. I didn't think they were real. Sam, there is no possible way it was from the dreams?"

"No, not possible, or I would be a dad a few times already."

I confirmed it then, "Jake *that* is the only possible time."

He couldn't even look at me. I felt like I lost his friendship, forever. He loved my Sarah, and this hurt him. I knew he knew it was going to happen sooner or later, but he liked the idea that I loved her enough to wait. He at least respected me because of that. Now that was gone. I hurt him on a whole new level, and I may lose my soul mate because of our stupidity. I couldn't move. I sat there and stared across the room, speechless.

"James."

I didn't want to see the pain on his face. All I could do was shake my head in disbelief.

"You need to make her understand, if she tries to do this. If she doesn't make it, most likely the baby won't either. But there is a possibility they could both make it."

The tears were streaming down my face, "Jake, please get rid of it. I will tell her later. I will let her hate me forever if you just do this. You may even win her heart if I told her I made the decision. Please don't let her keep it, not if it could kill her."

"James, you would let her go to keep her alive?"

"Yes, Jake, I know you would love her the way she needs to be loved. I just don't want her to die."

"Would you die with her?"

"I forgot about that. It doesn't matter, because I still don't want her to die no matter what it does to me. I would rather see her with you than let that happen."

He walked over to me and sat down on the floor not saying anything for a while. I was completely devastated on how I could let this happen to my sweet little Sarah.

After a little while Jake put his hand on my shoulder, "I would never fill her heart, James."

The tears were spilling like buckets out of my eyes, "Jake, please get rid of it."

"I can't do that. It has to be her decision."

I put my head in my hands. Sam came and sat by me on the other side.

Jake started to laugh, "If a nurse walked in and saw the three of us sitting here on the floor all crying, she would probably think Sarah is dead."

All three of us started to chuckle. I wiped my face with my sleeve, "Jake, I am so sorry."

"I don't know how to reply to that. You are married to her."

"But I feel how you feel about her. I am trying to be careful not to hurt you."

"I know, but James…" He couldn't finish his thought.

I let it go for a while, but I had to know where his thoughts were taking him,

"Jake, what were you thinking?"

"I just don't understand the desire to be together, that's all."

Sam spoke up in my defense, "Jake, haven't you ever done it?"

I choked as Sam asked Jake this question.

"No."

"Have you ever wanted to kiss someone so badly that it hurt?"

He didn't say anything. I knew it was with my Sarah; it was the time he held her when she needed me. I let him ponder the moment. I felt his desire. It was tearing me up because I could feel it. After really getting a good dose of how he felt I pleaded, "Jake, don't think about it anymore. I see and feel it."

Sam turned to us with surprise, "He held Sarah?"

Jake turned his face toward Sarah, but didn't say anything.

I scolded Sam, "Sam, sometimes it's best to not say anything."

Jake finally answered Sam, "I have never even kissed anyone." He looked down again. Sam was staring at the two of us. He was shocked, "Jake, you are in love with her?"

"Not anymore. I can't; she is married…" Jakes tear filled eyes met mine, "To my brother."

He was breaking my heart. He would have been better for her. She would have made it to 18 easily with Jake. "You did kiss her, but it wasn't out of passion."

He smiled, "No, it wasn't out of passion. It was to make her doubt her feelings for you."

I knew this, because he had already confessed this to me, but Sam understood now.

"So, does everyone fall in love with her or what?"

We all started to chuckle. I couldn't help myself, "I hope not, or she will drive me crazy."

She was starting to move. We all got up. Jake went to the other side of the bed and raised it, so she could sit up a little.

"Shit Jake, am I done already?"

"Nope, you needed a nap."

She was slowly opening her eyes. Oh, how I loved those green eyes. She was dreamy and the sparkles in them were bright. She was confused when her eyes evaluated my face first and then Jakes and Sam's. "You guys look like shit. What happened?"

We all started to laugh. I sat down on the bed. I just stared at her. How was I going to explain this? I decided to go for a diversion, "Jake, should she eat?"

"Um, no, actually, if I am doing the surgery on the intestines tonight she really shouldn't eat."

I gave her a reassuring grin, "How are you feeling?"

She closed her eyes grabbing my arm that was by her side, "Can you just hold me, or give me a dose of the good stuff?"

"No, Sarah. No more. We need to talk."

She opened her soft, flirty eyes and they glistened alluringly.

"Sarah, no. Don't even think about it."

She was stretching and smiled with her eyes closed. I felt her trace her hand down my chest, but nobody could see what she was thinking. I scolded her, "Sarah, no!" She opened her eyes again, "James, I feel so good right now. Just a…" Her thought brushed her breath against my neck.

I had to stay strong, "Sarah, Jake and Sam are here with us, and we need to talk about something really important about you."

Her eyes opened and then searched the room to see if I was lying to her, but they fell back on me, "Am I dying or something? You guys look terrible."

"Sarah, I am serious. I need for you to listen to me right now."

The seriousness came to her face, "You are sad, James; is it that bad?"

"It depends on how you look at it. I am going to try and not show any emotion, because it has to be your decision."

She was going to take it serious, "Jake and Sam have to leave."

"Not this time, Sarah. Jake has to hear it from your lips, or he won't believe me."

## 29. *Little One*

*Sarah:*

**M**y eyes moved to each one of them to see if this bothered all of them, and I knew this was not good news by the way they're faces hung. Bringing my attention back to James I locked onto his eyes, searching for his emotions, but he was maintaining a very neutral face, so I finally asked, "What is it?"

He swallowed deeply, and then he quickly glanced back at Jake, then Sam, and finally turning back to me. I noticed that each of them nodded as he looked at them.

There was something totally wrong here, "Is this why you knocked me out Jake?"

He just nodded avoid my gaze.

James took my face in his hands and traced his fingers along my cheek. I hated when he did this, because it meant that he was trying to make everything okay for me. "Sarah…" He dropped his gaze from me, "…shit, I can't do this."

If James was this upset, what was wrong with me? I looked at Jake for answers, but he wouldn't look at me either. I turned to Sam, and he put his face down immediately.

My heart was racing as my mind wandered all over the possibilities of how short my time was going to be. If James couldn't tell me it had to be bad. I had to know right now, "James? What?"

He glanced at me, and his eyes were full of tears. It was worse than I had originally thought if he was crying. I was starting to panic. I was trying to push him out of the way. I was not staying here if I was going to die. Not here. Not now. "James, take me home, now."

"NO!" He was grabbing my arms.

Jake came to help him hold me in the bed, "Sarah, knock it off. You will make this worse for James. Just be patient; he will get to it."

I stopped struggling, my eyes flying to Jake. The tears were coming to my eyes, as I glanced back at James again. The tears were spilling over as he held my gaze. He finally broke down and sobbed out, "Sarah, you are pregnant."

I stared at him. I don't know if it was the shock or if it really wasn't that bad, but I wasn't as upset as the rest of them. I searched their faces again one by one and I examined their behavior and it wasn't a happy one, especially my James. He wanted a baby and he wasn't jumping up and down with excitement. What was he thinking and how? I was so confused, "How?"

He smiled a little and leaned into whisper in my ear, "When you pushed me in."

I looked at him horrified, "...but you didn't. You were out before you even got..."

He leaned into me again, "I already came when you pushed me in; some must have gotten in."

I knew that he had to be upset because this would hurt Jake. I had to take the blame, "I'm sorry, James. This is my fault; I shouldn't have pushed you that way."

"No baby, don't think that way. I don't care about any of that."

"Then why are you upset?" I grinned at him, "You will be happy now."

"No not now, Sarah."

"Why?"

"If you try to keep it..."

"If...? You already know the answer to that. I know we won't have much time to be together alone, but you see three."

"NO, Sarah, Jake said you shouldn't."

"Why?"

Jake came to the bed, "I told you, you shouldn't because your body isn't ready for one. The pain with this appendix thing could cause you more pain and it may be extreme. Honestly, Sarah, it could kill you if you try to do this now. I said maybe later."

Getting a little more serious I had to set this right for James, "Pros and Cons, right?"

He smiled at me shaking his head no.

"Yes, James. If I have this, I don't have to go home. Pro...If I have this, I am giving you a child. Pro...If I have this, it was made from love. Pro."

He wasn't agreeing with me, "If you have this, it will screw up your schooling. Con... If you have this, it will be a struggle to get on our feet alone. Con...If you have this your pain could be unbearable. Con."

"If you have this," Jake spoke up, "You may not be able to carry to full term and it could die. Con." He continued, "If you have this, Sarah, it could kill you."

That got my attention, but I was confused, "Why would it kill me?"

"Sarah, you have to have surgery to straighten out your intestines. Don't you think you should be completely healed before doing anything like carrying a child?"

"But, I did this. I have to take responsibility for my actions and I am willing to do that. Why are you so upset, James? This should be making you happy. Damn it, James."

"Sarah, if you can't carry it you could die, and if you die most likely it will die too, and seeing that we are so connected I will die with you."

I stared at him but trying to understand all of the options, "If I die, could the baby make it?" Of course my question was for Jake.

He looked down, "Less than 10% chance it will make it, but James will go with you, so who would take care of it if you're both gone?"

Knowing what these two wanted I wanted Sam to tell me the truth. He knew how to use his powers more than James, "Sam, come here. You tell me. You tell me the truth, NOW!"

James nodded and Sam walked over to me.

"Sam, you tell me now. Please. I need to know."

Jake and James both turned to Sam. I didn't want them to influence him, "Jake, James, shut up. He will tell me the truth. He is very strong, and he sees things. He knows the outcome and he will answer me. Sam, does the vision change? What do you see?"

Sam touched my arm and stood there for a while, long enough that James grabbed him, because he was going to fall over. Jake ran around the bed grabbing a chair and helped James set Sam down.

"Sam!" Jake was trying to get him to comprehend what was going on.

Sam opened his eyes, tears welling up. He didn't say a word but shook his head no.

"Sam, no what?"

"Sarah, no one makes it."

The tears started to spill over as he turned to James, "I'm sorry, I should have told you when you were asking Jake to…"

James put his hand over Sam's mouth, "It's okay, little brother. It has to be her choice."

"James, if none of us are going to make it, get rid of it. I thought you would be mad at me if I did."

"No, Sarah. I only want you. I don't care if we ever have children. I just want you."

"Good, because I'm, really, am not ready for that."

He smiled and hugged me so tight, but commanded Jake, "Jake, get it out of her."

"No, Jake. Can you find someone else to do it?"

"Why?"

Uncertain of how this would affect Jake I explained, "It's too much to ask Jake to do this. It's not fair to him." Knowing that I was right I turned to Jake, "Can you find someone else to do it, either today or tomorrow?"

"I scheduled the other surgery for 6:00 pm. We should really do it before then, or we will have to wait a couple weeks and that just wouldn't be good. I will make a few phone calls, but I have the DNC pill right here that will make your body reject it." He held it up in a tube.

James questioned him, "You were ready to give into me?"

"Yes, but I couldn't do it without her consent. I'm sorry, James."

Realizing that is why Jake put me out. I was not happy about this, "Jake, you put me out so you could talk to James about this, before me?"

"More like kill him for putting you through that pain." He smiled at me, "Sarah, if I can't find anybody. I am doing it by 4:30pm. Okay?"

"Honestly try, Jake. It would just be weird."

"Not only for you, Sarah."

He gave me the pill and went out to make some phone calls.

James was concerned with telling my parents, "Sarah, I have to call your mom and at least tell her about the surgery at 6:00pm."

"I don't know if I can keep myself held together to see her before. Can you wait till 5:00pm, so I can be under by the time she gets here?"

"We can do whatever you want."

"Isn't that how we got into this trouble in the first place?"

"Are you telling me to not listen to you?"

I laughed, "James, I am so sorry."

"No, I shouldn't have…" he closed his eyes, "You just make my blood boil."

"I am disgusted; get a room." Sam was giving us crap.

I gave him a disapproving glare.

Jake walked back in about 3:30pm, "Sarah, I found someone. She will be here at 4:00 pm."

"She?"

"Dr. Justin. The doctor you had been seeing. I thought you might be more comfortable with her."

I nodded; not sure if I was ready for this but I was having cramps already and they were getting worse. I grabbed my tummy holding it and took long deep breaths.

"Cramping?"

"Yeah."

"Auh, forgot to tell you about that."

"Jake, cramping makes the pain in my gut 10 times worse."

He held up a shot, "I know that too, but Sarah, when you come home this time no more shots. I did look up some other medications, and I have two different ones on order to be at the house by the time you go home."

"When will that be?"

"Sorry to tell you this, but Friday at the earliest."

"That's kind of fast."

"You will feel a ton better once we get you untwisted."

"And un-pregnant?"

"If you're cramping, it's already gone. Now it's just getting the remains out."

"What?"

"Sarah, we will have to scrape your cervix and suck out the remains."

My heart just about fell out of my chest, and I was back to gasping. I reached for James because I was really scared, "Jake, you could have told me that before."

"Would you have changed your mind?"

"I don't know, but I don't like the sound of that."

He put a full shot in my arm and pulled out another one and put it in my IV, "Sarah, you won't really feel a thing, just the good stuff."

"Can I stay with her?"

"Nope, and I am not either, but Dr. Justin can do it in this room. So we don't have to move her until it's time for Intestine Surgery."

Dr. Justin walked in about 4:00pm. The machine was already in the room. She stopped in front of Jake, "If you left her on the pill, this might not have happened."

He looked down. I had forgotten about that.

James gazed down at me, "You wanted to be with me that bad?"

I whispered, "After you came back, yes."

He hugged me and kissed my forehead.

She looked at him, "Sarah is a little too young for you, don't you think?"

He was devastated.

I spoke up, "Dr. Justin, this is my husband now, James."

She looked at him with a question in her eyes, but he ignored what she had said and kissed my hand. "I don't want to leave you."

"It's okay. You left it up to me, right?"

He gave me a small smile and walked out with Sam.

Dr. Jenkins started to get ready, "So you got married?"

I nodded.

"You're kind of in a mess. I heard about the appendix. The scarring looks amazing. Sorry they have to open you back up."

I shrugged my shoulders, "At least the pain will go away."

She smiled, "You will have to wait the full six weeks to let your cervix completely heal; then and only then you may start the pill, but then you will still have to wait a month after starting them for it to actually work. So... just to make things clear, you are looking at least two and a half months before you can have sex."

"He wanted to wait till I was 18. I enticed him. It wasn't his fault."

"It takes two, Sarah. He wouldn't have let you if he didn't want to."

I wanted him to want to be with me. It made me feel loved.

"That wasn't supposed to make you happy, Sarah. Does your mom know about this?"

"Marriage, yes. Pregnancy no, but I am an emancipated adult."

"Your husband already signed the papers, Sarah."

She was ready to get started, "You will feel pressure and with everything else, I don't know how painful this is going to be. Did Dr. Phallen give you pain medication?"

I pointed to the IV, "Yep."

Not only did it sound disgusting, the pressure was unbearable. I gritted my teeth and took the pain. When she was done, I felt sick to my stomach. She brought a bed pan and I threw up mostly fluids. She turned me to my side, "You are going to bleed for at least a week, Sarah, maybe two. Come see me in two, please."

I glanced up at her nodding. I was feeling nasty now. I had never experienced anything like that. I would never do that again, and I would discourage anyone else from doing it.

James came in right away, to where I could see him. He sat down in a chair, so I could see his face, "Are you okay?"

I closed my eyes and let the tears run. It hurt to blubber so I tried to hold it in, but the tears continued to run from my eyes. He took my hand and kissed it. I pulled away from him. I wrapped my arms and hands around a pillow. He traced his hand over my face and I pulled away from him, "James, just don't." I couldn't even look at him. I was the most horrible person in the world; how could I have been so selfish?

Jake touched my arm, "Sarah, you should let him help you."

"Jake, don't fucking touch me."

He pulled away from me.

I laid there and continued to let the tears run from my eyes.

"Sarah?"

"James, when I am well enough I want to go home."

"Of course. Jake said Friday."

I glared at him, "To my moms." I closed my eyes and couldn't look at him. I knew I hurt him, but this was too much for me to handle right now. I am only 16.

I heard James get up, "What's wrong with her?" He was upset and taking it out on Jake.

"James, it's not a pleasant procedure and her hormones are going crazy right now, so the emotions are going to be messed up for a while. Be patient, James, she'll come around."

I wanted to change the way they were thinking, because it wasn't going to work out. I was not being irrational with how I am feeling. How would they feel if their insides were taken out, then sucked out, and then untwisted? I needed to get my point across, "Jake, what happens if I don't have the surgery?"

"You'll continue to back up and get septic, shutting down your kidneys, liver and eventually dying in agony."

"No surgery. I am not having it done."

"Sarah!" I heard James cry to me, and I knew he was struggling with Jake to come to me.

"No, James. Let her have her space. She'll get better."

I heard them move a chair; I pushed the button. Someone else had to know I didn't want the surgery. Jake knew and moved to me, taking it away as I heard a nurse walk in, "Thank you; I've got this. James, I shut it off, so if you need the nurse, turn it on here then push the button."

He was angry, "Sarah, surgery is not an option. You will have it." I heard him leave the room with heavy steps.

I knew James was sitting in a chair behind me. I was getting sleepy. I didn't want to fall asleep, so I pulled the IV from my arm. The machine gave me away. Jake came running back in.

"Why are you being so stubborn? Stop it now, Sarah."

He pulled my arm out and put it in another spot. He turned something up and I couldn't move any more. I was completely numb.

"James, she won't move anymore, but she can still hear you."

I saw Jake move away. I could see James's shadow moving to me. I closed my eyes. I felt his mouth on my cheek. The tears spilled out. He traced his mouth through the tears, "Sarah, please let me love you. I can't and won't live without you."

I opened my eyes to look at James, but it hurt more to see his sadness. I closed my eyes again. He moved his hand to wipe the hair from my face. I grabbed his hand to stop him. I opened my eyes to see him again. I realized I let them suck the love we made out of me like it didn't mean anything.

"NO SARA, don't feel like that. You are making me so sad. You saved my life; what about that?"

I couldn't hold it in and I started to cry. It hurt so I grabbed my stomach where the pain was coming from and put my other arm over my face.

He kissed my forehead, "Sarah, please think about it this way. Sam said you wouldn't make it through having it. You would have died, Sarah. I would have died, and the creation we made would have died, Sarah. Please let me love you."

His touch was comforting, but this was too much. I didn't push him away. He held my hand and traced his face against mine as I cried more. "I love you more than you know, little girl." He traced my face with his till I slept.

# 30. To Suffer

**W**hen I woke up confusion set in as soon as I saw James. As I scanned the room I saw my mom on the other side of the room. Clarissa and Carl were there too. They were sitting in the big cushion chair. Sam was leaning against the wall across from me. Jake had his back to me looking over everything. They all seemed to get up and move to me, but I wasn't ready to deal with anyone. I closed my eyes to block out the thought of all of them here. I could hear them, but I tried to ignore what they were saying.

Next thing I knew Jake was touching me. I opened my eyes and glared directly at him, "Don't!"

I closed my eyes again when Jake pulled away. I felt James take my hand in his pulling it to his lips. I didn't want to pull away, but yet I didn't want him to touch me either. I opened my eyes to plead with him, "James, please don't."

Not waiting to see the hurt look on his face, I closed my eyes. I didn't want to make a scene, but I wanted to be left alone to feel bad and hopefully fall back to sleep. Thinking that if I could fall back to sleep maybe I could avoid as much pain as possible. I felt my mom take my hand. This felt really, really good. I wanted her to know I needed this, so I opened my eyes and gave her a little smile before closing my eyes again.

There were so many people in my room, but when James got up to walk out I knew it was him.

Mom stood up and leaned over me, "I'll be right back."

I could hear her stop him, "James, this might me too much for you to handle. I know you are young, but you married her, and you need to get your butt back over there and deal with it."

"It's not what you are thinking." He walked out anyway.

I heard someone else get up, so I opened my eyes to see who it was. Clarissa followed James out the door while Carl came to me. He took my hand and I couldn't stop the tears from welling up in my eyes. I knew he knew what I had done, and I only hoped he wasn't disappointed in me. I also didn't want him to tell my mother about the baby.

He kissed my hand lightly, "How is my girl?"

I shook my head no not wanting to answer him. I was miserable inside and out.

"Hey, you were there at my bedside when I was in need. It's my turn to sit with you."

I did like that he was using that as an excuse rather than feeling bad for me.

"I brought you something. I will need it back when you are better, because someone special bought it for me."

He lifted his hand and let the necklace fall to dangle from his finger, "I thought you could use it right now."

Even though he made me happy, I started to cry. I was holding it back which made it painful.

"No, don't do that. You will make me sad."

I tried to put a smile on my face, but the tears gave way.

He put it in my hand and wrapped my fingers around it, "Do you remember what you said?"

I think this was too much for him. He leaned down and kissed my forehead, "I will be back. I need to check on James."

It was too much for me also, so I closed my eyes and let the tears flow.

My mom was being really good about not asking questions and just being here. She held my hand and just tried to comfort me, "Did James bring your book?"

Why was she thinking about the damn book when I am lying here miserable?

"I was getting hooked. I thought maybe I could read to you."

I shook my head no and finally spoke, "Didn't think I was staying."

"Sarah, honey, are you doing okay at Clarissa's? Are the boys taking care of you?"

I didn't want her to think James wasn't trying. He really was and I tried to get it out, "Yes, mom, they have been very good about putting me first."

I wasn't ready to tell her I wanted to come home soon. I knew it would be soon enough. School would be starting and with the sadness I was feeling I didn't want to be grown up anymore. James walked back in with Carl and Clarissa. He had my book and a CD player. I was confused about the CD player.

He held up the CD player, "For later." Then he held up the book, "For now," he handed it to my mom and asked her, "How late can you stay?"

She looked at her watch, "I should be going; I still have to work in the morning."

She gazed down at me. I didn't want her to leave yet. My eyes were pleading with her. She could see my agitation, "I will be back tomorrow."

While James walked her out, Clarissa came to me taking my hand, "Do you want to talk about things? I can kick everyone out."

I pulled her hand to my face and rolled to her shaking my head no.

"You need your mother?"

That was all I wanted right now, so I nodded.

"She doesn't know?"

I couldn't tell my mother what I did, and I shook my head no.

"This would be a lot for any one person to handle. Can I help you with anything?"

I shook my head no again.

"Is James taking good care of you?"

Too many questions were making me feel torn up inside making the tears stream down my face, but I nodded once again. I was so afraid to talk, afraid that I would start to bawl if I said a word. I was holding everything in.

"You do love him?"

I loved James more than life. I nodded profusely.

"Is it just too much to handle?"

Yes, she was getting it, again I nodded.

"Obviously you don't want to hear how great you are doing, because it doesn't feel great."

Relieved that she was getting it without me saying anything, I squeezed her hand.

"Would you mind if I stayed awhile to read with you?"

That would be perfect. If it wasn't going to be my mother at least she was a mother. I tried to smile at her.

"Where would you like me to start?"

I swallowed and tried to talk, "Beginning. I love the whole thing."

James walked back in. He stopped dead in his tracks looking at me, but spoke to everyone else, "Okay, everybody out to the waiting room." He was moving the large chair to the side of my bed for his mother, so she could be comfortable. He lowered the bed, so Clarissa could see me without having to look up at me. I could tell he wanted to touch my face, my hand, or something, but he only smiled at me and then walked out. I knew he still felt what I felt and this was what I wanted and needed, '*to be mothered*'.

Jake walked in, but directed his attention to the machines that I was hooked up to. He took his time writing a few things down on the chart, but he never made the attempt to check on me directly. Again, I was thankful. The best part was when he walked over to Clarissa and kissed her head before he walked out. She closed her eyes for a moment, and then she looked at me with a question in her eyes. I smiled waiting to hear if she could put her thoughts into words. I knew it wasn't about me.

"Do my boys get along?"

I swallowed hard then took a deep breath to answer her, "Yes, most of the time, except when it's about me. James babies me, and Jake pushes too hard."

Her expression relaxed, relieved with my response.

Pondering the thought of confessing about my time with Jake was digging at my gut. If there was any problem with them getting along it was my fault, "Clarissa."

"Yes, dear."

"When Jake came and stayed with me, I found comfort in his arms. I didn't mean to or want to. I just missed James so much, and I was so week that I welcomed it. It seemed to help me fight until James…"

Clarissa patted my hand with understanding, "Sarah, you also helped him. You showed him that there is more to life than work. He will care for you for the rest of his life; that is what he grew up seeing, but he will also find love. Wilson loves his wife and his wife adores and loves him. Jake will find the love of his life, but he will never be far from you."

Felling horrible about my behavior, it was hard to smile this time. It was the thought of him having someone special to love and be happy with, that made it possible for me to feel any relief at all.

"Sarah, however, you and James have not been careful."

I had to take full responsibility for that, "It was totally my fault. He is always so careful with me and so tender. I pushed the issue and took advantage of him."

"I told you the passion in those men is just…" She took a deep breath thinking about it, which made a smile grow on her face. I had to giggle a little; I wasn't the only one that was a complete mess over my man. It was the way she drifted off thinking about Carl that made me a little leery. I realized now that I was scared to be with James, but it was only because I could never go through *that* again.

Clarissa went back to reading my story of first and true love. I felt connected to these characters. It was that deep, forbidden, longing for love that I had for James. I remembered how we started out with play fighting and the intensity in wanting to spend time together grew until I could only think of him and how he was my best friend in the whole world.

The next time I woke it was very dark in the room. James's hand was entangled with mine. Sitting on the chair with his face lying on the bed facing me, it was as if he was watching for the slightest movement. Still with hesitation, I scanned his face to see if there was any hint of him being awake. I was delighted with the sight of his beautiful brown skin, his strong jaw, and that beautiful mouth. What I was not happy about was that his cheeks were getting thin, and the dark rings under his eyes were growing to a deep purple. I knew that it was me wearing on him. I traced his hand with my thumb, and he still didn't move. I was worried that he couldn't be comfortable like this. He needed to go home and rest, not be here worrying about me. It made me really sad. I wiggled my hand free very carefully. I rolled to him a little and couldn't help myself. I touched his face, tracing the hollow of his cheeks and the circles under his eyes. It was making me weepy and the tears helplessly welled up. He opened his eyes, and I rolled away from him. I didn't want him to see my dejection, "Sarah, please."

I reached back and felt for his hand, but only took one finger to hold. I felt him move to lay on the bed with me, keeping an open space between us. I heard him whisper, "Thank you."

The tears were spilling out. I didn't know how to make him understand how I was feeling, but if he really listened to his feelings he should understand.

I heard him whisper again, "I know, baby, I am just so sorry."

It made my heart hurt more, and I was trying to hold back the crying again. I laid there trying to let the sleep come and noticed the CD player was going. Some of my favorite songs were playing; it did seem to help me forget where I was and how I was feeling. The sleep wasn't coming. I said it as quietly as I could, "James."

He didn't respond and I didn't want to wake him. I closed my eyes and let the music take me away. Each song brought me back to different scenes of my life, like my favorite memory of dancing with James in the pole barn. It was a good memory to fall asleep to, and I drifted off to remember the whole night. The glances we took at each other, while no one knew our little secret. How exhilarating that was and how simple life was then. What was the urgency to be together? That was such a great place to be at 16; why couldn't I just enjoy that time and let it last longer. To go back to that would be torture for my new husband, but if he wanted me bad enough we would have to slow everything down. I couldn't help but let it move to the horrible feeling that I had a few hours ago.

The next time I woke up he was still in bed with me, but I heard someone walking in. Jake entered carrying an IV bag replacement. At least they weren't going to force me to eat. That was a good thing. I didn't feel like eating. James now had my hand entangled with his again. I listened. I didn't want anyone to know I was awake yet.

"James, I need to check her. You have to move."

"Jake, please, this is all she will give me." He squeezed my hand to show him.

"Don't let go, just slide out so I can roll her back. Did you help her roll over?"

"No, she won't let me touch her at all."

"James, she is better. She did it on her own."

I thought about that. I did do it on my own; I felt better, I was stronger, and the pain wasn't as bad. Jake was walking to the side of the bed where I could see him. James had moved away but still had my hand in his.

"Sarah, I know you're awake. Do you want me to roll you back or do you want to do it yourself?"

I opened my eyes; shit James feels me. I pulled my hand free and rolled to my back glaring at Jake only. I raised my eyebrows and gestured

James direction to indicate I wanted him to leave. I heard James, "Sarah, I am not leaving."

I just stared at Jake so he also tried with James, "James, please."

"No, Sarah, I am not leaving." He pushed the chair back to the corner and sat down. I could see him out of the corner of my eye; he had his hands over his face. He was miserable; I had to wonder if it was because he was feeling how horrible I was feeling.

Jake was lifting the back of the bed, so I would be sitting up a little as he pulled back the covers. He didn't expose me; he just pulled up the robe that the hospital makes you wear. "It looks good, Sarah, not half as bad as the last time"

I didn't care if it looked better or not, the scar of this time around was in my heart. I scowled at him to show my disapproval. He lowered the robe thing and put his hands to my stomach. I closed my eyes to take the pain. He pushed on the normally good side and it was painful, so I grimaced.

"Hurts a little?"

That was obvious. Next he moved to the middle and pushed around, which was more painful. I held my breath and grimaced even more.

"That's worse?"

I looked at him with daggers and closed my eyes again. He moved to push on the bad side. Oh shit that hurt; I pushed his hands to stop.

"Is it that bad?"

Leaning back I kept my eyes closed and nodded. Now I felt the pain.

"Here, I will turn up the pain med."

I grabbed his hand to stop him, shaking my head no.

"You don't want any pain medication?"

I shook my head no.

"Sarah, you have to talk to me or I don't understand what you are thinking. Why won't you talk to us?"

My eyes were brimming with tears. I was holding my breath to keep myself from completely having a nervous breakdown. I pulled with every effort I could to bring my knees to me. I couldn't move them. I was using the blanket to wipe the tears that were completely spilling over; I still couldn't get one word out.

I heard James, "She can't."

"You feel everything?"

"Yeah,"

"So why won't she talk to us at least?"

"I think she is trying to hold it in. The pain in her heart is too much."

I started to cry more, because he was right. I pulled the pillow to cover my face; I just wanted them to leave.

"Why doesn't she want the pain medication?"

I could hear him sniffling, "She thinks she should suffer for what she thinks she did."

I was relieved, but I didn't want to be comforted. I just wanted to be miserable by myself.

"Well, that's just stupid, Sarah; knock it off."

I flicked him off with both hands.

"See, there is the feisty Sarah that I know. Sorry, I'm not letting you suffer, because you want to hurt yourself. Putting that pillow over your face isn't going to work either. You will pass out before you suffocate and you will drop it."

I flicked him off again.

"Oh, I think you are going to be fine. Now if you would at least tell me to fuck off, maybe I would leave you alone."

I heard Clarissa, "Okay, boys, enough. I think Sarah would like to be alone. Both of you, yes you too, James, out."

I heard her address James more one on one, "James, please lie down and try to sleep while we are here. I will come get you if she will see you."

I was moving the pillow back behind my head so she wouldn't think I was being childish, which I really was. I smiled at her. She touched my face and I grabbed her hand and held it there as the tears ran down my face.

"You should really take the pain meds, Sarah. It isn't good for you to suffer."

I shook my head no.

"Okay, but if you want some, let me know. Would you like me to read again?"

I nodded.

She read so long Jake had walked in and out three times. He never addressed me, but the pain was easing. I think he was giving it to me without my permission. If the truth were told I was thankful.

James finally walked in after hours of being apart. He came to the other side of the bed. Carl was walking in too followed by Sam. James seemed distant, like he couldn't or wouldn't look at me. After a little bit, James finally reached for me putting one finger out. I touched it with one finger, tip to tip. He took that as a sign that I was getting better and he grabbed my finger bringing it to his mouth. I pulled away. He was hurt, but he wasn't going to push further.

Clarissa stood up, "Sarah, honey, we're going downstairs to eat something." She was touching my face. I grabbed her hand holding it to my face. I didn't want her to leave.

Carl moved to take her hand from mine, touched my face, and reassured me, "We won't be gone very long." He let go and guided them out of the room. I rolled away from James and watched them leave me.

James was lowering the bed. I couldn't look at him again. I didn't want to see his sadness. He was leaning over the bed resting his elbows on it, "Sarah?"

The pain in my heart was coming back.

"Sarah, can you at least look at me?"

I shook my head no. It would get worse.

He lay his head down on the bed, "Can you give me anything here?"

I rolled to him a little, but his face would be right there in front of me. I told him, "Don't look at me."

He turned his face away from me. I rolled over towards him and ran my fingers through his hair. I did love him so much, so why did I feel like I had to push him away? Oh yeah, I killed our baby.

He was breathing really deep with quiet gasps of sadness escaping his chest. . I traced my fingers around his face and played with the hair next to his face. I could tell he was closing his eyes just to enjoy my touch even though we were both full of sadness. I touched the hollows in his cheeks. I traced the dark circles under his eyes and whispered, "You're tired."

He didn't say anything. I think he was afraid I would push him away more if he did anything.

I knew I was right, that he was feeling me, when he asked, "Would you?"

"Yes."

He was reading my thoughts which kept him at a distance. That was one of the benefits of him feeling everything I did and it helped with what I needed.

I heard someone walk back in. I pulled away from him and rolled over.

James wasn't happy and scolded Jake, "Damn it, Jake."

"Sorry, I have to get her vitals."

I heard James get up and pace.

Jake came over to me asking, "Are you talking yet?"

I didn't look at him; I just shook my head no.

"I have to check your stomach again; roll to your back."

I rolled back and closed my eyes for the pain. He put his hands on my stomach but under the robe. He started with the best side. He pushed harder and moved around and I grimaced.

"Less painful?"

I nodded without opening my eyes. He moved to the middle and really pushed around. I grabbed his arm to stop him, as I gasped for air.

"Still painful?"

I opened my eyes to give him a dirty look.

"Really painful?"

I nodded.

He moved to the bad side and was gentler, "Sarah, I have to really feel here; this was where the bad twist was. I am going to push kind of hard here." He started to really push on my stomach. I sat up more, and almost screamed, "JAKE!"

"Stop, Jake!"

My eyes flew to James. His eyes were strained with pain because he felt it too. I closed my eyes and leaned back.

"She speaks."

I couldn't muster any energy, and couldn't respond. I heard him doing something with my IVs, so I forced myself to open my eyes. I knew he was giving me pain killers, so I grabbed his hand shaking my head no.

"If you won't talk to me, I am doing what I think is best. Do you have something to say?"

I leaned back again and closed my eyes shaking my head no. He won the battle.

"Sarah, you are going home tomorrow. You will have to talk to us then, so we can take care of you."

I didn't move.

## 31. One Finger

**I** must have gone to sleep, because when I opened my eyes my mom was here handing a bag to James, "I don't know if I found all of them, but there might be some more in the bag at your house."

He gave me the biggest grin, but he left the room.

The CD was playing lightly in the background and she was coming to sit with me. They had the bed still low, so someone sitting with me could see me. I was happy that she was here again.

"So, they tell me you won't talk."

I shook my head no, "Just a lot of pain." I closed my eyes to get it out.

She didn't realize I was talking about my heart.

"James wants to help you; why won't you let him?"

I just shook my head no.

"Did you two fight about something?"

I shook my head no more prominently.

"Do you want to go back to Clarissa's when you leave the hospital?"

I nodded and then shrugged my shoulders. I didn't know how to talk to her. She didn't understand the whole picture, but Clarissa walked back in and smiled as she talked to my mother. I was panicking a little.

"Sarah..." She held my hand, "Just needs her mother right now. She's not thinking about going home yet." She looked at me, "Am I right, dear?"

That was it exactly, so I nodded again. My mom smiled with the thought that I wanted and needed her. She stood up and came in to hug me. I started to tear up and looked at Clarissa for help. I didn't want to cry. It hurt in my heart too much.

"Um, you might want to read to her. She likes that best."

I tried to put a smile on my face, but the tears were running down my cheeks. Clarissa handed me a Kleenex to wipe them dry, as I sniffled a little.

My mom sat back down. The crease in her forehead told me she was worried about me. She took my hand in hers, asking, "You are very sad, Sarah. Is there something else that is upsetting you?"

I wanted to tell her; I wanted to blurt it all out. Not being able to hold back the sadness that was engulfing me from the core, I broke down with a sob. This feeling was horrible, and I wanted to push her away. Not only was this painful to my heart, but the crying caused internal pain to my stomach.

Clarissa moved quickly to hand my mother the book, "Um Paula, the pain is worse when she cries. If you would please read to her, I'm sure that would help her the most. You could take over where I left off. Is that okay, Sarah?"

Wanting to end the crying, I nodded and tried to put a smile on my face.

Mom frowned again; she was not happy that Clarissa knew more about her own daughter, how I was feeling, and how to make me happy, but she started to read anyway.

The boys stayed out, but Jake did come in and checked everything. He only stopped once to examine me.

"Sarah, sorry I have to check it."

I was finally feeling a little better, so I shook my head no.

Of course he didn't listen. He was raising the bed and tilting it back. I glared with disapproval and mom noticed I was unhappy.

Clarissa didn't tolerate my objection, "Sarah, he is doing what he is supposed to."

My mom looked at her slightly confused.

When Jake got the bed where he wanted, he grabbed a jar of something, "This is for the scar to help keep it moist, so it won't get irritated."

He put gloves on, so I had to wonder what he was up to. In the back of my mind I wondered if that was... so unspeakable... I couldn't even say it to myself, but I had a sneaky suspicion it was from James. When Jake's hand was close to putting it on me, I searched his face to see if he would confirm or deny that it was. He wasn't going to say anything, so I stopped his hand with mine.

He was all smug and doctor like, "Are you telling me no? Because unless you talk to me, I am doing what I think is best." He didn't even smirk.

I let go and looked at my mom worried that she was going to start to ask more questions.

She was really confused and said, "Sarah, if this is something you don't want then say something. You have never held your tongue like this. Why won't you say anything?"

I closed my eyes and struggled to get it out, "Can't." I was holding the tears back again. This sucked. I hated every feeling I was having, but didn't know how to change it. I just would be happier to not deal with this at all, to not exist at all.

James walked in, "That's not possible Sarah. I can't and won't live without you. You know that."

I gave him an inquiring glance about the stuff that Jake was putting on me. I wanted to know if it was from him or not.

The smile on his face made him look guilty, as he came to stand by my mother. His voice came out joyful as he spoke to my mother, "Old Indian remedy for scars."

Well that answered my question. Deep down I knew it anyway, and I had to stop them. I wanted to be scarred to punish myself for what I had done. Pushing Jakes hand away, I tried to stop him, but it was already on. I was wiping it off with the robe.

James was so sure of himself as he spoke to Jake, "Maybe more when she is sleeping?" Then he looked directly into my eyes, "Unless you talk to us, Sarah."

My mom spoke up, "It's obvious she doesn't want it, why would you insist on this?"

James put his arm around her. He was so good getting out of trouble with my parents; it was quite irritating. I heard him say, "We're just trying to get her to tell us no, or just talk to us. It really is just an old recipe that might help diminish the scaring." He was so proud of himself; honestly, I really wanted to wipe that smile off his face.

I was glaring at him, and crossed my arms in defiance. James had moved to Clarissa where Jake was already filling her in on what they were doing. Her hand clasped to her mouth trying to contain... I think she was laughing.

That was it. I was not going to deal with them or this, so I closed my eyes in defeat. Ganging up on the sick person, that is real mature, but I really can't fight it.

Jake moved his hands under the robe again starting with the good side. The pain was still there; it was no better than before. I gasped a little for air.

"Pain? Sarah, tell me how much and where it is."

I took his hand and moved it down showing him where the pain was. He pushed again causing more pain than I needed to feel.

He moved his hands to the middle, but he was doing a mixture of moving his fingers, pushing, and squeezing different areas. It did make me gag. He grabbed a bucket and put the bed up a little, "Did it hurt?"

I nodded taking the bucket.

He glanced up at my mom and James, "This is so cool when you know what to feel for. She is so thin you can feel everything." He was happy with this, but I sure wasn't. I wanted to jab at his inners until it hurt him. He moved his hands lower than the scar and pushed around. I knew that was for the other thing. He pushed more, and I felt a rush coming from within me down there. My eyes flashed to his alarmed at what I was feeling right now. He knew something wasn't sitting right with me and pushed the nurse button while telling the rest of them to leave the room.

Two Nurses came running in. Everyone was leaving except James. I wasn't comfortable with him here while I was making a mess in the bed.

"James, you have to leave now. It's for her comfort, not yours." He looked at me to see if I was okay with it. I did want him to leave. I didn't even look at him.

Jake was talking to the nurses. He moved his hand to the bad side and pushed around.

The pain was excruciating. I closed my eyes and gasped for air again.

"Is it still really bad?"

I nodded with my eyes closed.

"Sarah?"

I didn't want to open my eyes. I just wanted the pain to go away.

"Sarah, look at me now. I know you don't want to talk to me, but do you want to understand?"

That did make me open my eyes. I wanted to know what was going on.

"Your body is clotting and what you felt was me pushing out a large clump of it. You did feel it?"

I nodded.

"They are going to clean you up, but we will need to continue that pushing to get rid of a lot of it."

I just leaned back and nodded. He was directing them on what to do, so I tried to block it all out. He leaned over me and whispered in my ear, "They will help you clean up; when they are done I will let everyone back in. Can you please say one word to me if you are okay with that? Please?"

"Yes."

There was comfort in the squeeze of his hand before he moved away from me. The nurses helped me from the bed and to the bathroom to wash up. I noticed the bed and it looked horrible; the blood was everywhere. My mom would have freaked out if she would have seen that. They helped me with something that looked like a huge diaper.

The one nurse could tell I was repulsed with this thing, so she tried to explain, "No tampons, not for a while. You will have to make it through this bleeding completely not using them. You will have to wait till your next period before using them. Do you understand this?"

I nodded, but I felt like I was going to pass out. They practically carried me to the bed. It was completely remade. I laid back and closed my eyes. They lowered the bed, so I could be more comfortable again. I rolled to my side and held my stomach. I listened to the nurses talk about Jake. They were saying that he would never spend this much time with any other patient, let alone talk to them directly. I put what they were saying to my mind bank, and tried to breathe out my nose.

James was the first one in the room. He approached the bed, so I could see his face, "Jake told me it was bad. Are you okay?"

I wasn't okay, but I nodded anyway.

"Can you give me anything? Please, Sarah?"

I stuck one finger out, and he touched it with his finger tip. He laughed a little. He squatted down beside the bed and kissed the tip of my finger. He wasn't supposed to do that, so I pulled it away.

His brown eyes warmed me as he said, "It's all you would give me; I had to try. I love you."

His face showed signs of being tired and worn out. I took my one finger and traced under his eyes where the darkness had filled in.

He closed his eyes, "Yes, I am tired." He opened his eyes to look at me again, "Why won't you talk to me?"

The tears started to fill my eyes, and I closed them.

"I'm sorry... Don't think about anything... It's okay... I have something special for you, but I will wait till everyone is gone."

I shook my head no.

"Will you say yes if I didn't spend any money on it?"

My James... so sweet, so loving, and my forever. I didn't want him to spend any more money on me and I didn't really feel like I deserved anything from anyone.

"Is that a yes?"

I pointed my finger at him to let him know that I was okay with that. He touched it with the tip of his finger."

Everyone was coming back in the room. James was lowering the bed. I didn't want to see anyone except for James. He pushed a button I was unfamiliar with, and I started to feel dreamy within seconds. Not foggy, just sleepy and wonderful. I didn't want to feel this way, so I shook my head no protesting what he was giving me.

Warming me with his eyes he replied, "It's for the pain, Sarah; you are not suffering. I am sorry, but I can't watch it."

Mom sat down, "Are you okay?"

I was feeling really good now, except for my heart, so I nodded. She held up the book and I agreed. Clarissa offered to take everyone down to eat; my mom opted to stay with me. Clarissa offered to get her something, but my mom said she would be fine. I was very happy she was here to mother me again. She started to read, so I closed my eyes to enjoy my story.

I felt someone kiss my forehead which startled me. My mom was leaning over me, "Sarah, sweetie, James is going to call me in the morning if you are still here. Saturday I can spend the whole day if you would like?"

That would make me happy.

James walked her out. Clarissa and Carl moved to my side. Sam was at the end of the bed, "Sarah, you're not mad at me for telling my mom and dad, are you?"

I looked at them shaking my head no. I reached for Clarissa and she took my hand smiling at me, "I'm not going to pretend like everything is okay, but Sarah, it was the right choice if you think so or not."

I found that hard to believe even knowing the outcome. It just broke my heart, and I couldn't talk without having a nervous breakdown. My gaze lingered on Clarissa wondering how I was going to make a request. Trying to prepare myself to ask, I closed my eyes and breathed through my nose, "I don't want to go home until I can go to the bathroom by myself."

Carl had tears in his eyes. I didn't know if it was because the tears were streaming down my face now, or he could feel my sadness. The pain I swear seeps in through my mouth making it so I could hardly breathe. I was completely sniffling now. He wiped my tears, "We will make sure the boys know, but you can stay upstairs with us if you want. We will be here for the week."

I was relieved after hearing this. I turned my eyes to Clarissa asking for her approval. She did grin as she let me know it was okay, "Yes, we will talk to James."

I felt better about going home to Clarissa's.

"Would you like a nurse to come home with you?"

They had already done so much for me, that I didn't want anything extra, "Only bathroom, alone."

"That is an easy enough request."

James walked back in with the bag my mom brought.

Clarissa assured me that they would be ready for me to come home, "It's late, and we're going to go home and sleep a little. If you are coming home tomorrow, we have a lot to get ready."

They were going to leave me alone again. I was still worried about being able to go to the bathroom on my own. Clarissa sensed that I was panicking. She did reassure me, "I know, dear, just being ready for anything, and we will talk to them."

When everyone left the room, I closed my eyes to rest. It wasn't until Jake walked back in that I opened my eyes again. At least he wasn't trying to irritate me. "Sorry, Sarah, we need to message your stomach again." He started to lower me back not waiting for my approval. Avoiding the pressing he went directly below the scar and started to message there. The pleasure of the release of the clot was immediate. Jake was confused when I gasped asking, "Is it painful?"

It felt wonderful and weird at the same time, so I shook my head no. He pushed the button and a nurse came in. She was there to take me to the bathroom to change this thing that I considered to be a diaper.

Jake was a lot more sympathetic when it was just the two of us. He gave me that sweet look of worry that I remembered from the doctor's office when he came with me. He finally asked, "Still not talking?"

I shook my head no. In all reality, I didn't want to feel this way. I loved James more than life, but I think it was too much for me. Just from him asking the tears were coming to my eyes, again.

"I hate seeing you like this. Remember what happened the last time you were this sad?" He was waiting for my reply but then gave into his warning, "Don't make me crawl in bed with you. James would kill me."

That did make me feel a little better. In fact I had to smile.

He saw the improvement, "At least you didn't flip me off."

I was feeling better, maybe even a little playful. I lifted my hand flipping him off. He laughed and walked out, so the nurses could get me cleaned up.

The nurse was raising the back up, so I was sitting more. She moved my feet to the side and lowered it closer to the floor, "I heard you want to be able to go to the bathroom by yourself."

That was my main concern for going home.

"I put the pad out for you; if you need help I am right here, and I will be with you the whole time."

I scooted to the edge of the bed. The pain was sharper to stand, so she put out her arm for me to support my weight against. I slowly walked to the bathroom. The pain was knifelike with every step.

"Do you need help?"

I gave up, nodding. She helped me remove the pad, which to me was a diaper. She helped me to sit down, and I was able to go. I wiped and she helped me stand. When I glanced back at the toilet I noticed there was still so much blood. Worried, my eyes flew to hers.

Trying to calm me she said, "It is normal after something like that." She helped me get a new diaper on. I walked back to the bed, and she helped me to sit. I curled up on the bed, and she lowered it a little, which allowed me to lie down, "I will let them know how you did."

James came in walking directly to the IV stand pushing the button again. I tried to get him to stop by shaking my head no.

"Sarah, I feel the pain. You do not deserve to suffer."

I didn't want comfort. I felt like I had to pay for what I had done. Next thing I knew James was crawling in bed with me. I moved over as far as I could so he wouldn't be touching me.

"Here roll back, so you can see this."

I tried to roll back, but I would be touching him. He scooted over, so I had more room to not touch him.

"Sarah, do you remember this?"

He had my book of poems from him. I was not happy that he had this and I gave him a disapproving glance, as I pulled it to my chest.

"You're mad?"

Even though he wrote the poems, I felt like this was my private happiness that he gave me. I traced my hand over its cover, remembering how sad I had been without him here, and how those poems helped me get through my time away from him. The tears were filling my eyes.

"I hope you don't mind, but I put what we could find in it, ones you hadn't added yet. I don't know if we found them all. Did you carry them with you?"

I opened the book and slowly turned the pages. As I glanced at each page the tears welled in my eyes so much that they spilled over the edge, glided down my cheeks, and dripped on the pages. I tried to wipe them up as soon as they fell, but when I got to day five I had to stop. I handed the book back to James and rolled away from him.

Keeping the space open around me, he moved as close as he could get and whispered in my ear, "I know this one well. It's from my heart. *Sarah, in my dreams you are there, a kiss, a touch, a stare. Your skin is so soft and smooth, the touch so sensitive too. I long for you when we're apart; the pain is in my heart. I will return for you my love, and in your arms I shall fall; you are my dream after all.*"

As he recited my poem I started to cry more. I curled up as much as I could while holding my stomach, because the crying was making it more painful. He reached over me and gave me another dose of pain meds. I grabbed his arm to stop him from pushing the button.

"No, Sarah! I will not let you have any more pain."

He put his hand on my stomach to help stop it from moving, but was very careful not to touch me anywhere else. He whispered into my ear, "I love you, little girl."

That didn't help; that made me cry harder.

I pulled the pillow in front of my face to muffle the sobbing. My sweet loving, James, oh how I love him, but my sadness was hurting him. Knowing I could not live without him, I had to at least try, so I moved my fingers to his and intertwined them. As the pain subsided, I was able to fall sleep.

When I woke I could tell it was very early, the sun was peaking at me as it was rising up over the world. James was nuzzled into me. He felt so good, but I didn't deserve to feel good right now. I felt him move away from me, but his mouth was still at my ear. He breathed, "Please, Sarah."

All I could think of was, NO, it hurt too much. He moved further away and went to pull his hand away, but I held on to that.

He whispered, "Are you sure?"

I nodded.

"Sarah, I will take anything."

After it was silent for a while he spoke again, "Sarah, I have to ask you one more question and I need you to answer me." He waited for me to respond. I couldn't move.

"Did that hurt you bad enough to not love me anymore?"

I turned to look at him frowning. His eyes were closed and tears were dripping from his eyes. I touched his tear and my mind was confused; how he could even ask such a question. I did love him more than life itself; it was just this hole in my heart; it was so deep and empty. I didn't want to live anymore. I wanted to beg him to wait longer, but I didn't know how to ask and I didn't know how long it would take. It hurts to breathe right now. If I tried to talk, the air would engulf my pain and wipe out any improvements I have made. I turned away from him, but I pulled his hand to my mouth.

"Sarah, I am so sorry."

He pulled away from me getting up; my heart was now being shredded to little itty-bitty pieces. He was leaving me, because I couldn't explain. He walked to the window. "Baby, I'm not leaving. I feel you and I can't breathe."

He opened the window taking in a deep breath, "I don't know how to help you."

"James!" It took everything I had to say his name. I couldn't breathe. The sadness engulfed the air from my lungs.

"Oh, Sarah, it's worse when you talk." He was wiping the tears from his eyes. I couldn't handle the pain in my heart and in my chest. I closed my eyes, to try to get through this torture in myself, as the tears were falling I nodded.

James threw himself down on his knees next to the bed, "Sarah, you don't have to say a word; I didn't realize that was why, but please, Sarah, don't hate me."

I shook my head no.

"I will take anything, anything you can give me. I can't live without you."

I put my hand out with my finger pointing out to him. He touched it with the point of his finger. He put his head down on the bed next to my stomach. I rested my hand on his head and cried back to sleep.

Jake was trying to wake me, but I kept my eyes closed and shook my head no.

"Yes, Sarah. I am not going to make you talk to me. James explained what it does to you, but you have to get up, so I can message the stomach again. You need to go to the bathroom, and you have to eat."

I didn't want to do anything. He was pushing me back; I tried to stop him so I could search for James. I wanted to make sure he was okay.

"He is not in here, Sarah."

I didn't understand why James wasn't here with me after understanding how sad I felt. Jake ignored my need for James to be here. He started push at the bottom of my stomach. I closed my eyes. It felt good that he was pushing that out of me. I cringed a little, but I felt like he was getting rid of some of the sadness as each gush went out of me.

He stopped, "Sarah, are you okay?"

My eyes felt groggily as I tried to open them to nod at Jake.

"That feels good to you?"

I nodded again.

"Do you want me to do it more?"

Not knowing if I wanted to feel better or not I shrugged my shoulders.

He sat down, "Can you tell me?"

I shook my head no.

He started to message my stomach again but advised the nurse that he would let her know when I needed help getting cleaned up. I really didn't like how messy this made me.

After the nurse left I watched Jake as he messaged my stomach more. It was hard to control my pleasure as each gush released a little more of the pain that was coming from within me. I sank more into my pillow relaxing with each rotation on my stomach.

He chuckled with a grin on his face, "This feels good?"

I nodded, but his gaze moved over me to the door where James was standing and watching. Pleased that he was back I smiled with satisfaction that I had the man I loved, and some of my sadness was going away. He started to walk to me not saying anything. Then a cramp interrupted this really good and relaxing feeling that I was finally able to have without feeling completely miserable. I cringed in pain.

"Jake, what is it?"

"Where does it hurt, Sarah?"

I pushed his hand down further to the right side. He continued to message. I grabbed the blankets at my side and gripped firmly to handle the pain. It wasn't budging. He stood up to message the area better, moving his hands in a circular motion until it released. I was instantly relieved, as I felt the gush. I opened my eyes slightly looking at each of them, but that seemed to make me tired making my eye lids heavy.

"Sarah, no don't fall asleep. You need to get cleaned up and eat."

I shook my head not being able to keep my eyes open, so I closed them but said, "Not now, better." I released my grip and was letting the sleep take over.

"She speaks."

I held up my hand very slowly flicking him off. He just laughed at me. I pointed my finger out for James. He touched it with his, but his eagerness came through; he took my whole hand and was trying to bring it to his mouth.

I pulled it away, "Not yet."

The sleep was coming, but I could hear them.

"Jake, what was that about?"

"Her body is starting to heal and what just happened was that the clotting was released. I guess it feels good for her to get rid of it."

"I felt it, you know."

"What?"

"It's like it was getting rid of some of the bad feelings."

I had to let him know, "Yes, James."

I rolled to my side and curled up to sleep.

## 32. Missing You

I woke with the room full of people again. My mom was there.
Jake was the first one to notice that I was up, "You're awake?"
I nodded.
"Okay, everybody out to the waiting room; I will get everybody when she is ready."

I was panicking. I wasn't ready to go home. I haven't gone to the bathroom by myself. Clarissa said she would talk to them. *Tell them that I didn't want to go home until I could go to the bathroom myself. Everybody was walking out, but I didn't understand why she didn't stop this from happening. I wasn't supposed to be getting ready to go home. No one had to leave the room yet, because I wasn't ready to go home. Why isn't Clarissa stopping all of this from happening?*

I wasn't ready for all this and Jake was persistent on getting me going, "Sarah, the nurse is going to help you. She will come get me when you are cleaned up."

Everything was happening so fast. The nurse came over, lowered the bed, pulled my legs to the side, and held her arm out for me to try and stand. I wasn't ready for this because it would mean that I would have to go home soon.

She held out her arm, "You want to try this yourself, right?"

Now I was irritated, but I nodded and pulled myself up. The pain was a little better until I took the first step. Even though the pain was still there I was able to walk to the bathroom. She had some things folded on a small table for me, "Your mom brought you some stuff. We thought you should try to go with a regular pad today, so you will have to remember to get up a lot more."

Since I was up and moving it was only normal for me to want to clean up. I had to take a deep breath and swallow hard before I could get out, "Shower?"

She smiled at me, "Of course, if you're up to it."

I nodded. I was hoping to wash away more of this disgusting feeling. She started the water for me and pulled the shower head down. I shook my head no, so she put it back up. She directed me where everything was and looked at me as if to ask if I wanted to do it on my own.

I nodded.

"You want to be by yourself, don't you?"

I nodded again.

"I'm not supposed to leave you. I will turn around and you pull the curtain when you're in, okay?"

I nodded.

She did what she said she would do. I got undressed and the diaper was gross. I rolled it up and threw it away and got in the shower; the pain was slightly bearable. I didn't have the urge to scream with every step.

I stood under the water for so long she asked, "Are you doing okay?"

I knew she had to hear me. I took a deep breath through my nose, so that I could reply, "Yes."

I washed my hair, rinsed it, and let the water flow over my face. I took soap and washed everywhere, trying to get the disgusting stuff that had dried from earlier. Then the cramping started. I braced myself against the wall, with my hands holding me up. I started to gasp.

She pulled the curtain back a little, "Are you all right?"

I could hardly open my eyes to look at her. I didn't want this to turn into something gross.

"It would be better if you don't fight it and let it pass. It's okay. I will clean it up; just let it go."

I shook my head no.

"Are you done with the shower?"

I nodded.

She shut the water off and put a towel around me and helped me walk out and sit down on the toilet. She was very respectful, and she walked out closing the door a little. The pain was horrible. Now the shower didn't seem like such a great idea. I just couldn't stand the smell anymore. Blood has a really weird smell to it almost like too much iron in the water or something. I felt what seemed to be a big clot pass from me. I pushed myself to get up and put the stuff on she had folded for me in the bathroom. As I maneuvered out the door I gestured back to the toilet. I was a little worried about leaving it there for anyone to see. Some of this stuff really disgusted me.

"No, Sarah, we didn't want you to get rid of it. Dr. Phallen will want to look at it to make sure your body is doing what it is supposed to be doing."

I shook my head no; it just seemed gross.

"Don't worry about it. I'm sure he isn't going to be weird about it. He is pretty professional about things like this."

She was helping me back to bed, and I could see the question in her eye, "How do you know him so well? He treats you special. I don't think he has slept more than a couple of hours since you got here."

I closed my eyes and tried to get it out, "Brother-in-law."

"Oh, that would be weird."

I nodded.

"Did you want to go home today?"

I shook my head no.

"Okay, I will let your mother in law know. She asked me to check with you."

I smiled knowing Clarissa *was* taking care of it. I lay down and curled up. She tucked me in and grabbed a couple more pillows tucking one in front of me, "It might help. I will let Dr. Phallen know you are good now." She walked out.

Both Jake and James walked in. James grabbed a towel and walked over to me, as Jake came right to me to feel my stomach. I stopped him from pushing on it. It would be a lot messier with only a pad on and not the diaper.

"Sarah, I need to check the intestines. Please let me do this."

I rolled to my back.

James was towel drying my hair a little, "Is this okay?"

I nodded.

His lovely mouth was close enough for me to touch. I wanted to kiss it so bad, but that wasn't going to happen. It leads to very bad things, things that are terrible and painful. I closed my eyes to try and forget how perfect he was.

*Oh shit.* Whatever Jake was doing hurt so bad. Kissing and desire is what got me in this heartfelt pain that engulfed every bit of life from me.

I grabbed his hand to make him stop.

"Sarah, stop. I have to do this."

James took my hand trying to hold it, but I pulled away and grabbed the blankets in my hand.

"Is it really bad?"

I nodded.

Jake stopped, "Sarah, the next step is to get you to eat. You have to get some weight on you."

I gave him a desperate look. He pushed the button on the IV drip to give me more pain killers. All I could do was shake my head no.

"Sorry, I can't let you suffer like you want. I will go get the others. Clarissa has lunch right from my Dad. You are kind of in for a special treat, but it is a very light meal."

I grimaced with half a smile.

"My dad wouldn't be pleased with that reaction."

I glared at him.

"I do believe you are feeling better."

I shook my head no. James stopped toweling my hair and nuzzled my neck. Jake went to get everyone. I hated that they were all here for me. I really wanted to be miserable by myself.

I could see James's mind searching my feelings. His eyes softened as he scolded, "Sorry, that isn't going to happen. A lot of people care about you, so stop punishing yourself and try to be pleasant."

I furrowed my brow to tell him I didn't like the way he talked to me.

He leaned to me but not touching me at all, "I will behave if you let me..." He moved his face as if he was tracing mine.

I looked down.

"May I?"

I shook my head no.

He moved his mouth close to my ear, "Please, I miss you."

I shook my head no and the tears streamed down my face as he pulled away from me.

His eyes searched deep within me for an answer, "Why Sarah?"

I shook my head no, and of course I started to sob.

"I'm sorry. I shouldn't push. I just miss you so much. I will wait and I will take whatever you can give me."

I pointed two fingers at him.

He chuckled, "We're making improvements." He put his two fingers against mine smiling. He moved away so others could come closer. He made his way to the window ceil and opened the window, "Your pain makes it hard for me to breathe." He leaned back his head resting it against the wall. I only wish I wouldn't do this to him. I love him so much.

To my surprise, Wilson was the one delivering my special food. He brought chicken, broccoli and cheese soup. The best part was he was feeding it to me. My mom wasn't pleased.

"You'll never come home if you keep getting babied like this."

Wilson looked at her embarrassed but reassuring her, "Only special occasions, Miss Paula." He was smiling at me. I put up my hand to stop him when I was done.

"You don't want anymore? You only ate half."

I shook my head no.

He pulled out his salad, "How about your favorite?" He was so excited; I couldn't turn him down. He fed me a forkful. It went down okay. I ate another forkful and shook my head no.

"You don't want anymore?"

I shook my head no.

He got another forkful, "I'm not stopping until you say when." He feed me another forkful but not looking at me; he was talking to everyone else; it seemed like everyone was talking to him distracting him from me, so I couldn't stop him. I put my hand up to stop him.

He finally turned to me, "Do you have something you want to tell me, dear?"

I gave him a disapproving look.

Clarrisa stepped in to my relief, "Okay, that is enough pushing her. Nice plan, boys. Wilson, she isn't ready to talk; leave her be."

It felt weird that everyone was here in my room and making sure I was getting better. I didn't feel this special. I heard James move, so I opened my eyes. I didn't want him to leave, but he moved closer, pushing the button for pain meds. I shook my head no.

He grinned while soothing me, "I feel what you feel. That is enough suffering for today."

It wasn't good for him to say that out loud. I didn't want to see every one's concern, and I didn't know how to explain that I deserve to suffer for what I have done.

James leaned down to whisper in my ear, "You didn't have a real choice; don't think that way."

Insecurity barged its way in again making me feel horrible. I had to be close to running out of tears because this was a regular thing for me now. They filled my eyes so quickly that they spilled out before I could wipe them.

His eyes filled with sympathy, "Sorry everybody, she needs a nap."

My mom spoke up, "Can I stay to read?"

I wanted her to stay, and I didn't want to talk about anything with James, so I nodded. I knew she would leave me alone and just read. James was going to move away from me, but I wanted him to know I needed him here. I put up one finger up to him. He was hesitant about taking it, almost like he couldn't just have that. Finally he took it wrapping his hand around it with a grip and kissed the tip of it. I didn't want to pull away because my mom would wonder why I would do that to him, so I let him. When he let go he made his way back to the window ceil turning his head so that he could take in the fresh air.

"Paula, is it all right if I stay?"

"Of course, James. Are you doing okay?"

I felt the distance between us as he replied, "Yeah, I am doing okay." He was hurting, and it was my fault.

He was not happy with my thoughts, "No, Sarah, I just feel what you do; that is all."

As mom read to me, I was able to relax into another world; I didn't have to think about any of my life and the way it was right now. I had wanted excitement, and I had wanted to do things fast; well, sometimes you get what you wish for. I tried to put it out of my mind again and listen to the story. We were getting to a really cute part in the book. I think James and I both knew it. James moved to a chair next to the bed putting his head down next to me, but looking away from me. He traced his finger along my leg but on top of the covers. I watched him while my mom continued to read to me not noticing our interaction. I traced my fingers through his hair. He was so sweet to me. I bet if he knew it was going to be like this, he would have kept looking for someone else. He turned his face to me still laying it down, but shook his head no. He knew what I was feeling, thinking, or whatever it was; he knew what was going through my mind. I traced under his eyes with my finger; he was beginning to look like how I felt. He closed his eyes and I did the same.

I woke to Jake touching my face. I opened my eyes and pulled away from him.

He gave me that comforting look, "I knew what would help you the last time you felt like this."

This was not making me feel better. I shook my head no.

He smiled and looked down causing my eyes to follow. I noticed James was curled up on the bed nothing touching me except for his hand on my stomach. The tears started to well up in my eyes realizing that he loved the baby that was no longer there. I picked up his hand and removed it from me and rolled away from him.

He was waking up, "Sarah, that is not true. Stop that."

Jake looked at me and then at him.

James was upset but tried to explain, "She thinks I wanted her to keep it."

Jake pulled up a chair, "Sarah, James asked me to take it without telling you."

My eyes darted to him with surprise.

"You heard me right, Sarah. He didn't want it if he couldn't have you. He doesn't want any children if it means it would be without you."

James was moving away from me back to the window ceil. I found this all so confusing.

"He wants to help you so bad. He would even let me love you if it would help."

"Jake!" James was not happy about that comment.

I don't think James agreed to that and neither did I. I love James and only him. I closed my eyes. I just can't do this. It's too much to handle right now.

"Jake, don't push her. It's too hard for her. I am so sorry, Sarah. I should have given you more time like Jason wanted to do. I see that now. I haven't been fair to you."

I was shaking my head no, and the crying was in full blown mode, now. I didn't want James to feel this way. I love him! I grabbed my stomach again to try and hold it still.

"There... that is why I was holding your stomach, Sarah. I feel the pain and want to take it from you. That was all. Damn it, Sarah. Quit thinking about this. It was bad that we let it happen; it was bad we had to get rid of it, but it would have been worse to keep it. It is not your fault any more than it was mine or Jake's. Quit taking all this pain on yourself..." He moved back to me and sat on the bed behind me reaching for my stomach, "Please let me help you."

I touched his hand and laid there not being able to say a word.

"James, come get me when I can let people come in. I will give you two a little time, and for god's sake, James, will you please get out of her bed."

I couldn't help myself; I laughed a little. He smiled at me and walked out. James laid down, not moving any closer, but kept his hand on my stomach to help me with the pain.

I was breathing heavy and through my nose to muster up enough gumption to say something. I could only get a whisper out, "I love you, James."

"Then let me love you back, PLEASE!"

I couldn't get any more out. It was hard enough to do that. I just wrapped my fingers around his. He moved closer to me.

"James."

"See. You are pushing me away."

I couldn't get anything else out. I pleaded with my mind hoping he would feel me. Just wait, James, please, just... I need more time, please.

"Okay, baby. I just miss you."

## 33. *Going Home*

**I** made it through the rest of the day without anyone mentioning going home. I still needed help going to the bathroom, but I was able to do most of it myself by the end of the day. My mom left about 10:00 pm; Carl, Clarissa, and Sam left about 11:00 pm.

Jake came in at 11:10 pm and messaged my stomach again. There was no gush at all. I was waiting for some relief, but nothing happened.
"Sarah, is anything coming out?"
I shook my head no.
He smiled, "It may be all gone. How does it feel when I do this?
I swallowed, "Okay."
They both grinned at me, "Talking now?"
I shook my head no.
"Well then... I am checking the other stuff."
I grabbed Jake's hand, and really shook my head no.
"Oh, yes, Sarah. I haven't checked it almost all day. If you are going home tomorrow..."
I shook my head no again.
"Yes, Sarah, so if you want to go to the bathroom by yourself, you have to try harder. I can't keep you here anymore, even if I wanted to. Your vitals are good and you're doing so much better, so I have to discharge you."
I shook my head no.
"Yes, and this time I am very ready. I have anything and everything we could think of that you may need."
I was beaten.

"You can get up and go now before you sleep. Do you want me to get the nurse?"

I shook my head no and looked at him totally pissed off at him. He was getting cocky. He lowered the bed, so I could put my feet down and reach the floor. He put out his hand for me. Avoiding his help, I slid my feet to the side and pushed myself up. The standing on my own took my breath away.

"Jake, you're pushing her too hard." James wasn't happy about Jake pushing me.

"No, James, she is doing this on her own."

I walked to the bathroom on my own and closed the door. I was gasping for air leaning against the door.

"Sarah? Are you okay?" It was James; he knew how bad it hurt.

I locked the door.

"Sarah, you aren't supposed to do that. What if something happens to you?" I heard Jake through the door. He wasn't happy with me. I heard him walking out talking to James, "I will get the key."

I heard James move, his voice was just outside the bathroom, "Sarah?"

I turned to lean my face on the door. I unlocked it, "James, just a little privacy, please."

"Okay, baby. Let me know if you need a nurse."

Feeling relieved that he was okay with someone else helping me, I went to the bathroom. There wasn't a quart of blood anymore. It was easing a little. I washed my face and brushed my teeth. When I was done I opened the door; he stumbled towards me from leaning against it with his face. When he balanced himself his face was right next to mine, but he froze in that spot. He didn't move at all and just waited for some reaction from me. I wish I could give him something but not yet. The only thing I could give him was an apologetically glance.

"Sarah, anything right now... I just need something. Please."

I turned to him, longing for him, but I couldn't give him what he wanted. I leaned my face just slightly to touch his. My heart was pounding. I think his was too, because his chest was heaving with every breath. He leaned into the touch more, and Jake walked in jingling the keys.

"Damn it, Jake, you have lousy timing." My James pushed himself away from me irritated.

That is when I made my move around him leaving him standing there alone. I cringed with sitting down on the bed and gasped as I pulled my legs up to the bed. I pulled the covers over me and tried to curl up best I could with the back up the way it was. James was still standing in that spot pondering the touch.

Jake continued to walk in. As he passed James I could hear him, "Sorry, I didn't think that was even a possibility."

James didn't say anything and he didn't sound like he moved at all. Jake, however, moved to me, "Sorry, Sarah, I have to feel your stomach again."

I rolled over to my back as he lowered the bed to help me lay back. He was pushing against my stomach, but was trying to talk to me while he was doing it, "Sarah, your mom is coming up tomorrow. Are you going to tell her you want to go home with her, or are you coming back home with James?"

My eyes darted to James, waiting for him to say something. I wanted to be with him, but I was behaving so badly that I wouldn't blame him if he wanted a break.

He turned to move to the side of the bed, "You know where I want you."

I was hoping that he would still want me.

"So you are coming home with us?"

I kept my eyes locked on James to make sure this was what he wanted. Feeling relieved as I watched James smile. However, I cringed when the pain shot through me.

"Sarah, right there?" Jake was pushing more.

No, I am just cringing because it feels good. I nodded letting him know that, yeah, it hurt there.

"We'll do one more scan before you go home, okay?"

Jake gave me a pat on the arm with a grin on his face, but turned away from me putting on a rubber glove. I wasn't paying attention to what he was doing. All my attention went back to James. I loved my James so much. Jake was smearing stuff on the cut again. I grabbed his arm and shook my head no.

He smiled, "Have you looked at it?"

I just shook my head no as I closed my eyes. I put my hand over it.

"Fine, but by the time you get home you won't be able to see either one. I almost wish I could market the stuff. How does that sound to you, James?"

I heard him laughing and I opened my eyes to see him grinning at me. He raised his eyebrows, "That would be one hell of a job."

I shook my head no in disbelief that he would even think about it. Jake reached up and gave me a dose of pain meds. I was disgruntled that he wasn't respecting my wants at all.

"Does this pain killer make you foggy?"

I shook my no.

"Sarah, this is non-narcotic. You can have as much as you need with no addiction." Proud of himself he continued, "I have a case at the house."

I shook my head no.

"Hey, you two behave. I have to sleep for a couple of hours. I think I am on 36 hours of being awake. James, stay out of her bed." He walked out.

James just stood there. I took a deep breath through my nose, "Have you slept?"

A weary smile crossed his face, "A little."

I moved over in the bed. He came and lay down beside me. He did give me my space and didn't touch me.

He whispered to me, "Before, thank you. I really needed that."

I didn't want to encourage more. I needed more time, but I was happy it made him feel better. He traced one finger down my back slowly, "Is there any chance of…"

I rolled back a little to glance at his face, "I need more time, James, Please?" I didn't turn away from him this time. I need him to be okay with waiting for me.

With complete understanding he touched my nose, "Anything you want, Sarah, but... please let me love you."

I nodded and rolled back over to curl up with a pillow. I did feel better with him here.

I woke feeling a little better than the day before. James was in the window ceil. I didn't understand why he was there instead of next to me.

He noticed me right away, "Your mom is on her way up. Sam is teaching me how to feel others."

I liked that he was not only focusing on me.

He didn't look pleased, "Your pain is too much sometimes, and it hurts so bad that I had to learn to feel others. I'm sorry."

I shook my head no.

"What, Sarah?"

I closed my eyes; this was going to hurt again. I took a deep breath, "Good."

He shook his head no as he moved kneeling next to the bed pleading, "I only want to feel you."

I wanted to feel him too just not in a way that would be harmful. I thought about touching his face.

Closing his eyes in complete satisfaction his words glided out, "That is what I miss, but Sarah, no. No more of that."

Leaning over me he put his face close to mine. I could feel his breath, "It has to be real from now on. Play fair, Sarah, and we will take it really slow this time. I want you to be happy here." And he touched my chest where my heart is. My heart was pounding so hard.

He seemed to be evaluating me but then he grinned, "Here she comes and she is worried about you. Do you have to go to the bathroom?"

It was like just being asked triggered that feeling and yes I had to go again. I nodded, so he quickly moved away from me lowering the bed to make it easier to reach the floor.

"Sarah, your mom wants to know you are okay. Can you talk to her, or is it still too much?"

I nodded.

He laughed, "That wasn't a yes or no question."

I found it a little funny that I didn't answer him the way he wanted me to.

"Sarah, you're up?"

Even though I didn't want to take my eyes off of this amazing man I turned to her and nodded. I pushed myself up and slowly walked to the bathroom closing the door. I heard mom talking to James.

"Should she be doing that on her own?"

"She wants to do it on her own, and Jake said as long as she wants to, it's good."

"So when are you bringing her home?" It was silent. Three weeks, James. I start school in three weeks. Tell her three weeks.

"I want to make sure she is okay first. If I bring her home no one will be able to take care of her. She would be alone."

"Yeah, I didn't think of that."

"How about we plan on the Sunday before regular school starts, and see how it goes."

"Of course. That is very responsible of you. Are you sure she will come home?"

"I think she will. I just don't want to leave her alone right now, if you don't mind."

"James, you don't have to be careful with me. I understand you two decided quickly on the marriage thing, but now you two have obligations to each other, and I want to help you two to make it work."

"Thank you."

"You do realize this is going to be work?"

"I know." I could hear the tone of his voice and it wasn't sounding excited anymore.

My heart sank a little. I finished with washing my face and brushing my teeth. I walked out a little less happy. I could see the worry on his face as I walked back out to the bed.

However my mom was happy to see me, "So what is the plan today?"

"Jake was hoping to schedule a scan this morning."

It was weird, because he walked in at that exact moment with a wheel chair. "Sarah, guess what time it is?" He was all happy.

I didn't want to do anything else so I shook my head no, "Sleep?" I got it out without struggling.

"Yes, it is, and I am ready to put up with anything you can throw at me today, Sarah."

I flipped him off.

My mom didn't like that, "Sarah, why would you do that?"

He was laughing, "It's okay. I was pushing her earlier and this was her way to tell me she wasn't pleased."

"That still isn't right, Sarah."

James was holding the gown around me, as I got up and moved to the wheel chair. Mom went to the waiting room. What I did notice was that Carl and Clarissa were nowhere to be seen. Why wouldn't they be here?

James took my hand, "They are getting ready for you."

He was doing it again, answering my questions without me saying a word.

I had two different scans and then they brought me back to a waiting area. James and I were on opposite sides of the room. He was being good about letting me have my space. There was nothing to do, and I couldn't close my eyes to take a nap. I was worried about what he was thinking. Of course he knew what was going through my mind, and he smiled and softly said, "I was thinking that you might let me hold your hand."

I wish I wasn't so confused over how I felt. Yes... No... and either way it would be too much for me, so I gave him a slight smile.

He was making his way to me, "I like that, your smile... I miss that."

He took my hand and turned it palm up, tracing it with his finger.

You would never guess that someone stroking the palm of your hand could be so intimate. I found myself leaning into him. My heart was acting on its own and pounded in my chest. He was good at making me feel special. He leaned in more bringing his face next to mine. I could feel his breath brush against it with warmth. I gripped the arm rests to stop my hands from trembling. With his warm breath came a plea, "Sarah?" How one word can fill you full of need confused me but I wanted, no I needed, his touch at this moment. He pulled back, just enough to gaze into my eyes. The deep brown penetrated into my soul warming me to my inner core. I wanted his lips to touch mine. I wanted him to pull me into his arms. Just when I thought I could handle his touch, we were rudely interrupted.

"You two ready to go back upstairs?"

James closed his eyes, "Damn it Jake, you have the worst timing."

I smiled with relief. I love James, but I don't want to do start anything that would lead us back to this again.

I heard Jake say something to James, but I couldn't make it out. I was being wheeled to the elevator.

"Sarah, everything looks fine. You are going home."

I still had mixed feelings about this. I was nervous and I wanted to spend more time with my mom. We got back upstairs and Jake informed my mom. She seemed as disappointed as I was. She helped me get dressed in my sweat shorts and t-shirt I had on when I was admitted. She showed me she had packed a little more clothes for me. I was happy about this. No more sexy lounge wear, which would certainly complicate matters. James slowly re-emerged from the hallway.

"Jake said we had to wait for the paperwork so we have time to kill. Sarah, why don't you lay back down for a while?" He handed my mom the book. I could see that she was more than happy to read to me.

James interrupted her before she even started to read, "Oh, a few people are coming to my mom's next weekend to see Sarah; will you be there?"

"I forgot. I have to help Tuck pack things up at the cabin. He is coming home. There is just not enough business up north."

"Yeah, he was starving half the time."

"That is really hard to hear, James."

"I just meant it would be good for him to come home. Won't you want to see Sarah this week sometime then?"

"I was thinking maybe Friday before I head out of town."

Trying to make both my mother and me happy he agreed, "That sounds good."

Mom opened the book, her eyes on me, "Do you want me to read to you?"

I nodded, "Yes"

She really smiled at me, "You are talking today."

The corners of my mouth lifted, "I'm trying."

With some relief she laughed a little and started to read.

We were getting to a good part of the book again, where they were admitting their affection for each other. I loved this part. I was smiling with my eyes closed. James was sitting on a chair on one side of the bed, and my mom was sitting, reading, on the other side. He gently ran his finger under my arm. Wanting more I moved my hand to the bed. He was tracing my arm down to my hand, and then each finger. Feeling secure in my love for him I opened my eyes to see this beautiful man. His eyes were watching what he was doing, while a smile lingered on his face. I had liked the intimacy of him tracing the palm of my hand so I turned my hand over so he could do that again. It was like a rush when he touched it. My pulse quickened, my body was shaking, and my stomach did a flip, which did cause a twinge of pain. His grin was full of concern, but he knew how to calm me. He laid his face in my hand and closed his eyes. The shaking was being calmed by the weight of his face and I was able to close my eyes again. My mom, oblivious to our connection, kept reading so long I dosed off a little.

"Are you ready to go sign some papers, James?"
That woke me abruptly, the thought of going home.
Jake was walking in with a grin on his face. "I can't wait to sleep in a real bed." His smile was as wide as the room we were in.
My mom seemed as shocked as I was.
"No, Paula, you can rest for a while. I need James to go sign papers. Then we'll come back and get Sarah. You two can have alone time."
She was as happy as I was that we were getting some alone time. I missed her, but I really didn't want to go home and be alone all the time. After they left she was going to ask me questions; I just knew it. I was only hoping they would be easy ones.

"So can you tell me how it is really going?"
That seemed easy enough. I shrugged my shoulders, "Okay."
I could tell she was struggling with trying to be upbeat, "So, you're married now. How is that going?"
I was thinking to myself, good till now, but I couldn't say that, "I've been in pain most of the time."
"I came to the house; do you remember that?"
"Some of it. The drugs made everything foggy."
Still trying to be positive she continued, "James is thinking when you start school you will come live at home. How do you feel about that?"
I didn't know how I felt. I wanted to come home, but I also didn't want to be away from James, so I just shrugged my shoulders."
"Sarah, are you on birth control?"
That did surprise me in a way that made me choking up. The tears were coming, so I closed my eyes.
"Not yet, mom... I still have pain."
"Oh, so that's not a problem yet?"
I couldn't open my eyes, but I shook my head no.
"Really, the way you two are, I wouldn't have expected that."
I didn't know what to say. I wanted to tell her, but I just couldn't talk about it yet.

"You know he is more a man than a boy, Sarah, and it will come soon enough. You are still young and you really need to be careful, so you can finish school."

Not being able to talk about it, I just nodded.

Jake and James walked back in. I could feel James's eyes on me. Maybe wondering where the sadness was coming from. He helped me up and into a wheel chair. I didn't want to leave my mom yet.

The sadness in her eyes showed as she said to me, "I really am not ready to let you grow up yet."

James must have thought I was feeling sad for leaving my mom because he let it go without probing for more.

I tried to give her a smile to reassure her that it would be okay, even though I wondered myself if everything was going to be okay.

We all walked down together. James went to get my mom's car, and Jake went to get the truck. James pulled up first. He helped me stand up; I hugged my mom, and kissed her.

She stopped for a minute, "I miss you and can't wait for you to come home."

I felt horrible, as I watched her get in her car and drive away. Jake pulled up. James helped me to the front seat, tucking in pillows beside me and tipping it back all the way. He ran around and got in the back seat but moved as close to me as he could, resting his chin on the back of my seat. I turned my face so that we were less than an inch apart. We shared our breath, our stare, and our love as we waited for Jake to get in. I was happy that he still wanted me after all I have put him through; finally satisfaction filled my heart and I smiled with happiness.

"GOD, I love your smile, Sarah."

Jake got back in after James, and then we were on our way home. I closed my eyes for the ride, but I could feel his breath against my cheek the whole way. The butterflies were dancing in my stomach as we drove. My head was a little dizzy, and I would grimace off and on over the bumps. Jake apologized with every jolt. It was James's breath on my face that filled me with comfort and love.

## 34. Waiting

**W**e pulled up to the front of the house. Jake and James got out and came around to get me. They helped me in while Clarissa and Carl were waiting for me. They had the lounge set up for me in the living area that looked over the lake. Directing a surprised glance at James he smiled slightly.

Leaning into me he quietly whispered, "It is what you wanted." He carefully backed away but his smile remained on his face.

As I got settled in, James laid my poem book and the book we were reading next to me. He plugged in the CD player and pulled it close to me, so I could turn it on. Wilson came with food, but he let me feed myself. I was getting tired, but Jake put another IV in and hooked up vitamins and fluids.

He seemed pleased with himself when he was done, "We're not going to let you get worse this time." He made sure everything was working and informed me, "Someone else is going to look after you for a while. I am going to bed for about 10 hours in a real bed. Don't wake me unless you have to."

I was ready for a nap myself. Everyone left me, but James. He stood there looking at the lake and then down at me, "Does this work for you?"

I nodded and closed my eyes.

He sat down beside me on the lounge, "May I... if I behave?"

My eyelids were so heavy that they remained closed, but I nodded again.

He touched my hand slightly. I turned it palm up and he traced his fingers there until I fell asleep.

*James:*

    I sat and looked out at the lake as she slept. I didn't know how I was going to leave her side. The pain, the heartache, and the emptiness she was feeling was too much for her and almost too much for me. If I could take it away from her I would in a heartbeat. I gave into time and closed my eyes to rest. I hope she didn't plan on sleeping here for long, because it was very uncomfortable.

    She was starting to whimper in her sleep, like she was in pain. I opened my eyes. I wanted to help her, but how? She was crying in her sleep; my heart was aching for her. I moved closer being very careful to not touch her. I didn't want her to back away from me again, and she was talking in her sleep.

    "JAMES!"

    I thought my heart was coming out of my chest through my throat. I leaned in very carefully to whisper in her ear, "Sarah, my sweet Sarah. It's okay, honey. You are home now, and there will be no more pain."

    She turned her head to me. I could feel my breath bouncing off of her skin. The agony of wanting to touch her, to feel her, was burning in my chest. Would she pull away from me, and could I take that again? I could feel the blood pumping through my whole body, as my heart pounded against my chest. I just had to try. I lightly kissed the corner of her mouth being very careful not to touch her more. She turned her face to me. Was she actually going to let me kiss her? Anxiously, I waited for her to respond. She has peacefulness about her, and no longer looks like her mind is running wild. Do I dare try again only to be rejected once again? I traced my lips on hers, holding back the desire to kiss her long, hard and passionately. She is not pulling away from me. I moved to almost hover, but if she was going to let me kiss her, I wanted to feel her whole lips, to taste her sweetness. I wanted so badly to touch her face to pull her to me. I had to take a few deep breaths to calm myself, because if she was letting me, I didn't want it to end. I didn't want her to push me away. I cautiously pressed against her top lip, and she lifted her mouth to me. I moved to her bottom lip; she was kissing me in return. I could hardly breathe. The kiss deepened and…oh god…she was returning my kisses. I felt the desire building in me. I was so happy the tears were coming to my eyes. She brought out all the emotions I could not store anymore. I loved her so much that this was heaven for me. I kept my clenched hands at my sides determined not to touch her. I just wanted this… her… so bad. I needed this; to feel her still wanting me. I made her hurt so bad that I was afraid I had lost her forever, even though I felt her tell me she loved me. I ran my tongue over her mouth intensifying the kiss. I wanted to feel more of her. She opened her eyes. I stopped kissing her out of fear, as I stared into those beautiful green eyes. A soft and regretful look was on her face. I wanted to stop her from this dejected feeling coming back over her. She licked her top lip and bit her bottom lip. My heart was sinking as I worried that I pushed it too far. My mind was racing with wonder on what she was going to do and it left me not knowing what to do. I looked at her pleading to not turn away from me. She brought her hand to my cheek. The pleasure was so fulfilling, that I leaned into her hand and closed my eyes. It was a mistake to let her eyes go, because that's when she turned away from me. My heart felt like it had stopped, and my stomach twisted in dismay. She wasn't disgusted, but I felt her sadness and the pain in her heart. I moved away from her and leaned back against the lounge. Depression engulfed me, forcing a gasp from my mouth. Not only did the sadness take my breath away, but the pain in my heart was like someone had ripped it to shreds. I lay there trying to calm myself and separate from her feelings, but only because they were so hard to feel. I didn't know if I should apologize for kissing her or thank her. I needed for her to do that for the last three days.

She spoke to me, "I'm sorry, James."

"Don't be sorry, my sweet Sarah; that was the best kiss I have ever felt in my life." I didn't know what to say. I felt her pain engulfing her more knocking the air from my lungs. Knowing I should have refrained from kissing her, because I was causing her pain now as she sniffled. I pleaded, "No, Sarah, I am sorry. I should have waited longer."

What I said must not have been that bad, because she reached back for my hand pulling it to her stomach. I rolled to her and held it firm but not pushing on it. I wanted to yell at her to get over this, to stop feeling this way; she had to let it go, but if I did she would not understand.

"Sarah?"

She didn't reply.

"Would you be more comfortable lying down? I could move." I just wanted her to respond to me. She didn't say a word, but as she took a deep breath she quivered from crying. My heart sank; the sadness was going to be very hard to get rid of. I moved to put the pillow down, so I could lay her down width wise on the lounge. I knelt to the side of her, tipping her down. She wouldn't look at me keeping her face toward the back of the lounge. I wanted to force her to look into my eyes, but she needed more time. I covered her up and whispered in her ear, "I know baby; it's okay."

It wasn't okay; I needed her too, but if I didn't want to lose her forever it had to be okay. I moved away from her and sat on the floor in front of the lounge looking at the lake again, as my heart was finally slowing. When I was capable of getting up I had to go outside to get air just so I could breathe. Her sadness knocked the wind from my lungs and I could hardly breathe around her anymore.

I was heading to the patio door, but as I passed the kitchen I heard Clarissa, "James?"

I still couldn't breathe, but I turned to acknowledge her. I didn't want any lectures. I had a hard time looking at her.

"You are doing amazingly well, James. This would be too much for most men."

I closed my eyes and the tears started to come to my eyes. I was miserable and still couldn't breathe. I gasped to catch the air with my lungs that were almost empty. I felt dad's arm come around me and guide me outside. I sat down in a chair putting my face in my hands trying to fill my lungs with air.

I didn't realize Jake and Sam were in the pool till I heard Jake, "Did you need me to check on her, James?"

I just shook my head, as I felt dad's hand on my shoulder. I heard Clarissa come out, "I know you don't want to eat, James, but have you looked in the mirror lately?"

I looked up at her. Did I look that bad?

She smiled at me, "You need to keep up your strength, or you will not be able to handle this. Please eat."

She had brought out a large platter of food, sandwiches, salads, and fruit. I sat and ate as much as I could, which when I was done seemed like a lot. I sat back in the chair and took another deep breath. I was getting up to go back to my Sarah. Clarissa put her hand on my shoulder.

"You get worse when you are around her; the connection is too deep, James. You need to stay away for a few hours to regenerate your strength. Go down take a shower, a nap, go swimming, do something other than back to her. I will watch and read to her, but you need a break or you will break."

I was determined to go back to her. I went to walk inside, but Dad stood up in front of me, "James, you two pushed too far with what you were doing with your minds, and you need to wait till that wears down a little. Then you will be able to handle things better. How much has Sam told you?"

I didn't feel like I had learned anything more than what I already found out from the mistakes I had already made. I just shrugged my shoulders.

"Do you have more questions?"

I did want to know one thing. I was hesitant, but glanced at him while I asked, "It is bad for us to use our minds to be together."

"Yes."

"But when she dreams, I feel it. It is very real for me. Is that bad?"

Dad seemed to be remembering something from his past as he smiled, but then I heard Jake laughing. He was filling Sam in on what happened in the truck when we were bringing her home that time. Sam started to laugh out loud. I shot them a disgusting look, not liking they were enjoying my discomfort.

Dad was more understanding, "She dreams about being with you, and it fills you with happiness."

He smiled at me, and I tried to not smile back.

"James, that only makes it worse for you. If you were to dream about her, does she feel it?"

"I think so."

"When she is awake, she feels your dreams?"

"I guess I really don't know, but I definitely feel hers even when I don't want to. It really depends on how determined she is."

He chuckled to himself, "You two are going to have to learn control, James. It is bad for the one not dreaming. The desire builds more and pretty soon we won't be able to get the two of you out of the house. You will only want to be together and nothing else will matter."

Well, I can believe that; the desire was almost unbearable now.

"James! Learn control and we will have to teach her control. It took your mother and I five years to learn and then misery for another..."

Lost in thought as his eyes drifted to Clarissa with a face that told me he felt the same way about her as I did about my Sarah, and then he let go a sigh, "...10 years to breathe."

They did the same thing, but they learned the hard way.

Clarissa was smiling as she added, "If you are anything like your father, it is very fulfilling and you only want more and more. How do you think he was able to wait so long for me?"

I really didn't want to hear about their sex life, but I felt better about wanting Sarah all the time. I stood up and stretched, "I'll go take a shower."

Dad stopped me with, "Why don't you go for a swim, James, and have a little fun. It will help to curb the desire. Trust me."

Knowing that I should listen to them and do what they were telling me, but this had to do with my Sarah. She was mine to take care of not anyone else's responsibility.

"James, we will listen for her, and I will check on her."

I noticed they had the baby monitor on the table in front of them. I raised my eyebrows hesitantly.

Clarissa reassured me, "We just want to make sure she didn't need anything. Jake is here if she needs medical attention, so we are listening for her."

Tamara came walking out till she saw me and came running to me, "Where have you been, little girl?"

"Wilson was playing a game on the computer with me. I now have 3 pets I own."

I didn't know what she meant by that but she had something else on her mind rather than explaining it to me she took off down the steps and jumped into the pool with Sam and Jake.

When Wilson emerged from the house he sensed my need for reassurance, "I peaked in on her. She is sleeping."

I didn't know how to say what I was thinking.

He put his hand on my shoulder, "James, she is okay."

Shaking my head no, "It's not that. I just cannot say thank you enough for all that you do."

Putting his hand on my dad's shoulder, "I am sure you are as good of man as your father. You will be okay and I do understand."

My dad put his hand on Wilson's, "Be thankful for him, James, he has taken very good care of my family when I could not."

I thought about Jake and felt remorseful, for this was how it was going to be for him, but he deserved so much more.

Not wanting to deal with anything else I went down to get swimming trunks on.

Even though I was in the pool playing with Tamara I found myself inquiring for information from Clarissa on if Sarah was awake, or in need of something. She shook her head no every time. I was enjoying myself, but my mind wouldn't let go of Sarah. When I finally let my guard down, I saw

Clarissa get up and walk into the house. My eyes flung to dad wanting to know if Sarah needed me, and he nodded but spoke too, "She is awake, James, but let her have female time. Just relax and enjoy the water."

I tried to not think about her, but the distraction was too much. I finally gave up going in to take a shower. I put shorts on and a clean t-shirt. I threw all the clothes that needed cleaning in the washer including the sheets from the bed again. I wanted it to be clean for her when she would decide to come back home here in the apartment and into my arms. I went out and ran up the patio stairs to head in to be with her.

Dad grabbed my hand, "Sit boy. She needs female time. Let your mother be with her awhile."

I sat down in the chair, but my patients wore short. I couldn't sit still as I waited.

"Self-control, boy, self-control; it will be better for her to be more patient."

I was driving myself crazy waiting. I was trying everything to preoccupy my time by shaking my knees, tapping my fingers on the table, taking deep breaths, but still not able to handle the waiting to see her again.

## 35. The Release

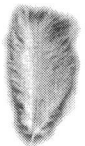

### Sarah:

Clarissa and Wilson came to help me sit up. I looked around for James. I behaved badly, and I wanted to apologize to him. I should have never kissed him. He will think the sadness is gone and it's not.

"Sarah, I sent him away for a while. He needed to rest and build his strength."

The thought of him needing to be away from me to be able rest and build his strength; made me feel sad. I didn't want him to be worn out from dealing with me. Wilson was bringing me a tray of food, and Clarissa was tucking in pillows to make me more comfortable.

I looked at them both, "Bathroom first." I moved to get up. The lounge was closer to the floor than I would have thought, so it was a little harder to stand up. I almost made it, and the pain shot through me yet again.

James came running in with a worried grimace. I didn't want him worn out completely, so I shook my head no. He needed to know I didn't need the help. He stopped and stood there wanting to come to me. Clarissa had grabbed my waist and helped me to stand the rest of the way. I tried to make him see I was okay and waved my hand for him to go back out. Sadness filled his face, but he needed a break from me even though deep in my gut all I wanted was to be near him. Clarissa grabbed my attention, "Are you good now?"

"Yes, thank you."

I walked to the bathroom, and she stayed by my side the whole way.

"I put a basket of supplies by the toilet for you, dear. I was under the impression that you may need a few things for a while. Are you okay doing things on your own?"

I was very thankful for all her help, "Yes."

She stopped at the door with a quizzical look on her face, "You are trying harder aren't you, dear?"

I nodded, "I don't want to be hard on him."

"I understand that, dear, but you are allowed to have your own feelings even if no one else understands. Take your time."

It was actually a lot easier to go to the bathroom in here. The toilet had a separate stall with a door to make it more private. I could support myself by holding onto the walls as I tried to sit. The basket was filled with a wide variety of products. Clarissa thought of everything making me feel overwhelmed. Digging through the basket I found the normal stuff like makeup, toothbrush, toothpaste, Midol, floss, mouth wash, and a different tube. This one I didn't recognize at all, it said KY jelly. I stared at it wondering what this was for. Well, if I know Clarissa, she thought of everything, so she must have something special in mind. I went back to freshening up by brushing my teeth, washing my face, and then I noticed myself in the mirror. I was looking really pale, and my hair was a mess. I took a brush out and went through it. Thankfully, she had thought of everything, and there were pony tail holders and bobby pins. I pulled my hair up and fluffed it. I put a little cover up on and a little powder. Not getting rid of the washed out color in my face, the makeup did seem to camouflage it. I stared in the mirror wondering how James could love me this much to deal with me. I gave up wondering and headed back out. As I opened the door she moved back to me, not helping me, just being there if I needed it.

"You look better. Do you feel better?"

"A little cleaner."

She did laugh with a sigh, "I have been talking to Jake, and he doesn't know if you will be able to handle the College classes for a while, because of all the walking involved, and you will have to do a lot more studying, too. What do you think, dear?"

I was confused. What did I think about having to do it, or how I was going to do it? "I have to be able to do it. I am already set up. I just need my car, so I can get there."

She laughed a little, "I made a phone call, dear. You can still take the classes, but you can do them online if you would like."

I gasped, "How do you do that? If I would have asked they would have turned me down."

"There is nothing like a donation to get what you want."

That guilty feeling was seeping back in. I didn't want them spending money on me like this.

She could tell I felt bad. "It wasn't much, and it will give you a little more time to heal. Oh, I also got you a gift."

She had already done so much. Why did she have to do more? I shook my head no, but only because I shouldn't get anything more than they were already doing.

She grinned, "You will need it if you do the classes online. James helped me set it up, and he did something to it that I don't know how to stop, so you will have to ask him."

I sat back down on the lounge, carefully.

She handed me a bag, "These are your books for your two classes. They sent them over on Friday for me, and here you go."

She was handing me another bag that was more like a back pack. I opened it up and pulled out a new laptop. Glancing up to her I shook my head no. This was too much.

She was more concerned about it being a good one, "It's okay, right?"

I nodded but again speechless. I opened it and turned it on. I was curious to what James did. As it started up a song played. 'Smile' by Uncle Kracker. The tears were coming to my eyes. James knew how to fill my heart in every way.

Clarissa frowned, "It wasn't supposed to do that. I just expect you to do well. James tells me you are very smart and have good grades. It seems that the college was very aware of your intelligence which made it all easier to make happen."

That was it. I couldn't hold my emotions and guilt in. The tears leaked out trickling down my cheeks.

Clarissa was going to try to distract me, "Do you know what you want to do with your life, Sarah?"

I shook my head no.

She seemed okay with that and tried to comfort me, "Well, you do have time to decide."

Noticing that the song on the computer was repeating I glanced at it again.

"Okay, put it away. It's time to eat."

I set it down but left it on to listen to the song over and over. It did make me feel a bit better. Wilson came in carrying a tray and cheerfully put it in front of me, "Doctor's orders for fiber, hope you like it anyway."

He was hopeful. I had to put him at ease, "Everything you do is good."

That was a little long but I got it out. They were surprised at my response. I wanted to please them more, so I started to eat right away.

Wilson was happy, "You seem better today."

I was doing better, but all this special treatment put talking out of reach for a while.

Wilson sat down, "James said you were up to three cups of food each time you ate before you went back to the hospital. I didn't want to push my luck, so there is only two and half cups of food, but the half is your desert, so if you don't eat that it's okay."

I tipped the cup up to me wondering what specialty he made. It was a cheesecake desert. I glanced back up at him with a slight grin, but his cheeks flushed with embarrassment. Shaking my head in bewilderment, I wondered how I could be so lucky as to have this many people who cared about me. I took a deep breath, swallowed, and said, "Thank you…" I closed my eyes with an effort to hold off the heaviness that was working its way in.

My eyes popped open when Wilson touched my face. I immediately wanted to retreat when the fear came over me. That was too much for me. He shouldn't have done that. He pulled away the instant he saw that I was going to lose it completely. I gasped for air but nothing came to my lungs. Concentrating on air, just a little air is all I need, I gasped again and this time I got a little air. Oh my god… this one was hard. I closed my eyes and took another gasping breath. The air was making it in through my internal blockage but with the air along came the tears. He stood up moving away from me in fear.

Clarissa reassured him with a friendly pat on the arm, while James came running back in holding his chest, "What happened?"

Clarissa stopped him, "Just too early for touching. Wilson touched her face, and she is having a hard time with it."

He moved in front of me, "Sarah?"

I was concentrating on breathing.

"Sarah, look at me."

I opened my eyes, and the tears were streaming down my face.

With his warm brown eyes trying to calm me he explained, "Hey, it's okay. He just wanted to make you happy. Come on, breathe. It's not a big deal, Sarah. He cares about you a lot."

I didn't want to feel this way. I felt horrible for scaring Wilson. Taking another deep breath to try to calm down, I stared into the eyes of the man I love, silently begging for some relief.

He knew how to deviate from what was bothering me. He asked, "Did you like the song?"

Feeling a little distracted, I closed my eyes and nodded.

"Did you try the food yet?"

I shook my head no.

"Look how you rate; you have cheese cake."

I opened my eyes and they fell on the most amazing sight. James's deep brown eyes were filled with happiness, as he stared into mine. I felt the air move into my lungs a little easier, but I felt bad when, out of the corner of my eye, I saw Wilson walk out of the room. I swallowed and tried to plead with James, "I'm sorry."

"Hey, it's okay. Just no touch yet, right?"

I nodded.

He leaned into me very carefully whispering, "I don't like anyone else touching you either." Mischief was written on his face.

This eased the pain in my chest.

"I will let Wilson know you didn't mean to hurt his feelings if you are okay now."

I did feel horrible for scaring Wilson.

"Hey, it's okay," he repeated, "Eat please." He got up and went to the kitchen. I saw James hug Wilson.

Clarissa was hesitant, "You don't do that when I touch your face; can you tell why you reacted that way?"

"I don't know." The tears came back to my eyes.

"It's okay; I was just wondering if it's a guy thing or not. You don't have to know."

She wasn't the only one confused by my reaction.

"It's fine, dear; we just need you to eat. Do you want me to read to you?"

I agreed because I needed the escape. She read for a while, and then James came back and took over the reading. Clarissa went back out to the deck.

After Clarissa walked out he giggled to himself but explained, "I didn't want to miss this part coming up. It was where they were sneaking off to be together in her room."

This book was a really good distraction. I tried to eat, but it went slow now. He was reading the part where the desire was building; he would read a sentence and then glance at me with a flirty grin on his face. He read another line or two and did a quick peek at me. While he read I was trying to finish the food, but found his little flirtations a distraction. I took my last bite proud that I had done it. He finished the good part in the book and set it down like he was proud of himself for getting through that part.

Laughing, he asked, "Do you remember that feeling, Sarah?"

I thought about it with a grin on my face. I did remember the wanting to sneak off together with him. As he moved next to me my heart did a little skip and hop. He was careful where he sat keeping very little space between us. Taking my fork he filled it with some cheesecake. With a gleam in his eye he continued, "The last time you had this, it almost got you in trouble."

I frowned at him.

Now avoiding my eyes, he fed me a bite, "I wanted you so bad I almost..." His eyebrows rose just a bit, "Just touching you..."

After rolling my eyes I gave him a stern look, but swallowed the mouthful.

Now he took notice of me, "Not this time though."

I was having very mixed feeling. Keeping watch for my reactions, he fed me another bite. I closed my eyes to enjoy every melting morsel of it. I did this with each bite enjoying the heavenly flavor that danced on my tongue.

Just when he was going to feed me the last bit he hinted, "Do you want to share this bite?"

Playfully, I pushed it to him shaking my head no. Taking the bit in his mouth he moved closer to me. His mouth teased with a taunting gesture to share the cheesecake that was in his mouth. His eyes penetrated deep into my soul searching for the answer. Finally giving up he swallowed and said, "Just checking."

Even though he seemed to give up he continued to linger with just a fraction of space between us. The warmth that radiated from his lips seemed to caress mine without a touch. The fear of what would come if he were to press his lips to mine left me hesitant on wanting him. My heart was racing with anticipation, while nothing bad was happening; there was no sadness, no loss of air, and no deep down regret for what I had done. His eyes moved back and forth between mine searching for a reaction from me.

I froze in place when he touched his lips gently to mine. My mind flooded with thoughts of fear, relief, regret, pleasure, and the one that surprised me the most was the desire to press my lips harder to his. This breakthrough was amazingly fulfilling.

I felt my lip twitch, but James must have felt it too, because a question entered his eyes, as his lips pressed harder to that spot. The way his eyes comforted me kept me from pushing him away.

"Are you ready to let me check your stomach, Sarah? Oh shit. Sorry."

James closed his eyes and that is when I lost the air from my lungs. I gasped while James scolded Jake, "Jake, your timing really, really sucks." James moved away from me to the window holding his chest.

Jake moved to sit on the chair next to the bed, "Sarah you have to breathe. James, can you take the tray to the kitchen?"

James glanced back at Jake with a fiery look in his eyes. I wanted to plead with him to not be angry with Jake. It wasn't his fault that he had bad timing.

James rolled his eyes after a moment, and then took the tray angrily in his grasp, as he headed to the kitchen.

I know James thought Jake did this on purpose, but I truly believed that Jake was oblivious of his uncanny bad timing.

Jake leaned in, "Is he pushing you?"

I held up my fingers to indicate a little.

A grin grew on his face, "Do you want me to talk to him?"

I shook my head no. I swallowed and closed my eyes to get it out, "Trying." I opened them after I got it out to see if he understood.

Satisfied he replied, "Good for you, Sarah. That is good to try, and now it's my turn to try."

I shook my head no, profusely.

The smirk on his face was funny, "Not that."

I didn't understand how he took that.

The mischievous side of him came out, "You shouldn't come on to me like that especially when James is walking back in." Jake was taunting James, which wasn't good after interrupting our private moment.

I flicked him off to show my disapproval. Jake was enjoying this way too much as he broke out laughing out loud.

I was worried that James would lose his temper with Jake, but the only reaction James had was to move to the window that framed the lake like a picture. The song was still playing on the computer, and then it came to the chorus. I could see a smile grow at the corners of his mouth, but Jake started to poke at me without noticing James's change in attitude.

I didn't want him to prod my stomach, so I pushed his hand away to stop him.

"Sarah, stop it. I have to do this. We are not going to let you get worse this time, and there will be no bullying us into getting what you want."

James came back and sat down on the opposite side, cupping my face in his hand, bringing all my attention back to those eyes that sucked me into another world, "Just let him, Sarah. He needs to make sure you are okay."

How could I refuse this man of mine with those eyes that brought comfort, safety, and warmth?

Jake tried to push on my stomach, and it just wasn't working, "Sarah, I am sorry, but you have to lay down more."

I scooted down and he shook his head no, "Can you turn to lie down? I need you flat to really feel the insides."

I sat back up and turned sideways and lay back down. It was a little painful and James put his hand out for me to hold. This time he didn't look at me but said, "Just in case you want to."

I grabbed his hand, as Jake started to push. I squeezed James's hand with the pain. He glanced down at me, "As tiny as you are, I am surprised you have this much strength."

I wanted him to distract me some more, but he went back to staring out the window.

Jake was concerned, "Did that hurt, Sarah?"

I nodded.

"I think it should be getting better and less tender when I push on it."

James spoke for me, "It isn't as bad as it was a couple of days ago."

I wanted to get his attention, so I squeezed his hand.

He glanced down, "Sarah, it isn't."

I frowned at him.

Jake moved to the middle, and I cringed again. It did hurt more than the last spot. Now James's eyes met mine. Jake moved to the bad side. I squeezed James's hand so hard it almost hurt mine; I gasped for air.

"Ouch, Jake, that is bad. Sarah, shit that hurt."

I didn't want to hurt him, so I let go of his hand.

"NO, it's okay. How do you have so much strength in your hands when you are so weak?"

I shrugged my shoulders, but I didn't take his hand again. I was still frowning with disapproval of having to have my stomach poked and probed. Jake moved around a little bit more in the bad spot but didn't push.

"Sarah, it still feels good. Do you have to go to the bathroom?"

I shook my head no.

"Sarah, did you have a bowl movement yet?"

I was so disgusted talking about the pooping, "No."

He grinned, "That is probably what the pain is. Will you please tell me when you have to go? It might be as painful as last time, and I will give you a good dose of pain meds before you go in." He reached up and gave me a dose now. I didn't want it, but he did it anyway and grinned, "You are not suffering: sorry, James's orders."

He was avoiding my glare, but with a grin on his face.

Jake started to message lower, and this was so soothing that I closed my eyes.

Inquisitively Jake asked, "This feels good to you?"

He laughed when I nodded with approval. James's hands replaced Jake's as he took over messaging my stomach. When Jake moved to leave the room I turned to James, but closed my eyes with satisfaction from how good this felt.

"Sarah, this is hard for me."

The fear seeped back in, and I grabbed his arm to stop him.

He removed my hand from his, gently. Pulling my attention to him he assured me, "I want to help you."

Giving into his touch I closed my eyes to enjoy this feeling once again. It didn't last very long before the gush released. I grabbed his hand to stop him, and the fear took over my eyes.

With concern he asked, "What?"

I was pushing him away while trying to sit up.

It wasn't surprise on his face that I saw; it was more like an understanding, "Bathroom?"

I nodded, but I was panicking a little because I didn't want a mess. He moved out of the way quickly while I was trying to get off the lounge. There was pain now. I tried to stand, but he had to help me. I went to the bathroom moving as fast as I could with the sharp pain in my gut.

It was no surprise that I passed a clot, but it was a little bit bigger than any I had seen before. I didn't know if that was normal. With the need to know if it was okay I walked back out wanting to ask Jake. James was laying down on the lounge with his eyes closed. I touched his leg when I got back and he sat up right away, "Are you okay?"

I shrugged my shoulders. I really didn't know if this was normal. It was such a relief that he could feel my needs, "You need Jake?"

I nodded in defeat ashamed of wanting Jake.

"Hey, it's okay. I don't know this stuff. He is here to help, Sarah."

I tried to sit down next to him, but it hurt to sit so I went right to laying down. He turned to me lying on his side. He put his hand on my stomach again, "You like that?"

"Feels good." I closed my eyes.

"Even when that happens?"

I nodded, "Pushes it out." I opened my eyes to find his gaze.

He was happy to be close to me. He rested his head on his hand so he was closer to my face. He was content just staring at me. There went my heart again, racing uncontrollably. He took my hand in his bringing it to his face. He started to kiss it, "Is this okay?"

Oh how I did not want to feel scared anymore, so I nodded.

He kissed every finger, and then my palm.

This closeness was a comfort, but passing the clot was exhausting and I closed my eyes.

"You need a nap?"

For some reason that always took a lot out of me. I nodded agreeing with him.

He leaned over me almost traced his lips against my face warming my cheek with his breath. Even though I was so tired I could feel the blood pumping fiercely though my veins. When he got close to my ear I opened my eyes with a new desire to try. My mouth was near his ear I wanted to make sure he knew how I felt from the deepest part of my heart. I took a deep breath, closed my eyes, and whispered, "I love you."

He pulled away startled but his eyes captured mine for a very long moment. With satisfaction his eyes closed dreamily, "That was the most amazing thing I have ever heard." This time when his eyes opened they sucked me in and warmed me to my core. That flirty grin that I loved so much came to his face as he said, "We should get you comfortable if you need a nap."

I did agree with him, but didn't like that he was moving away from me. Next he pulled me to my feet, which brought our faces nose to nose. All those feeling of wanting rose from within, again. Attempting to be vulnerable he tilted his head down so our lips were so close to touching. Carefully and slowly I lifted my head a little hoping I was letting him know what I wanted. Insightful of my feelings he pressed his lips to mine, not moving, not taunting, and yet kept his eyes locked on mine with wonder. To both of our surprise a tingling sensation came to the surface of my lips as he glided his against mine.

I felt a smile grow on his mouth until we heard someone coming. James turned away from me to see who it was, but we both already knew... Jake.

"Jake, I am going to kill you for your great timing."

Jake broke out laughing, "I think I have a built-in radar to her needing more time."

I bit my bottom lip wondering if he was here because I did need him at this time.

He calmed enough to ask, "Did you pass another clot?"

I nodded while we rearranged ourselves, so I could lie down on the lounge chair.

"Does it still feel good to get rid of it?"

Again I nodded, but I needed to ask him about the size of it. I stared at him with my eyes wide open. He needed to know I had a question.

"What?"

I swallowed, "How big?"

Squinting his eyes slightly, "You want to know how big is normal?"

I nodded but felt like passing out, so I closed my eyes.

"James, she is tired. What did you do to her?"

I opened my eyes to see he was joking with James, however James didn't look pleased. He wouldn't do anything to me if it would hurt me.

Jake explained, "Normal is the size of a gulf ball."

I was frustrated now.

He saw the troubled face I was making, "How big was it?"

I held up my fingers to show more like a baseball size.

This concerned him, "I was giving you stuff to clot, so you wouldn't have to deal with the bleeding, but I am going to have to cut back on that, Okay?"

I nodded.

"I also gave you stool softener to help you go."

I gave him a dirty look.

"Sarah, it won't hurt as bad if it's softer."

Rolling my eyes to show my disgust I scolded, "Hate talking about pooping."

This made them both laughed. We could hear them laughing outside, too. If anyone was in here they would have laughed at our reaction. We all turned to the monitor at the same time to see if it was on. Great, everyone knew about me pooping.

Sam came running in laughing, "Sorry Sarah, I'll shut it off now."

Not happy that everyone knew about my pooping problem I grunted out, "Sleep, out."

He stopped in his tracks and then turned around and left. Jake stood up to leave also, "I am leaving the monitor on, so you sleep, okay?"

I nodded. James came back to sit next to me. I could tell he wanted to touch me, but was thankful that he loved me enough to let me have some space, "Do you want me to read again?"

Satisfaction filled me when I knew he was going to stay with me. H moved to the chair and started to read, putting his feet up on the lounge. I closed my eye and enjoyed the story until I fell asleep.

## 36. Skinny Dipping

**W**hen I woke this time no one was with me. I looked outside and I could see two people on jet-skis. I wondered if it was Jake and Sam. As they came closer, I noticed it was Carl and Wilson. They looked like two kids out there. It brought warmth and joy to my heart and a smile to my face.

I turned to Clarissa, as she walked back in. She brought the sunshine with her wherever she was. She glanced outside and lightly laughed, "Yeah, those are my boys."

Surprised that she stated it that way, I must have given her a look of puzzlement.

That's when she raised her eyebrows and gave me a look that was proud, "At least they get along. By the way, Josie is here. She is Wilson's wife and Jake's mom." She only paused because I wasn't pleased with the way she stated that. Clarissa was Jake's biological mother. With authority on her face she continued, "She would like to meet you. Jake has been spending so much time here taking care of you that she is concerned."

She leaned down and whispered, "She thinks we told Jake."

I opened my eyes more not taking them off of Clarissa.

"Jake is with her on the deck. Would you like to come out?"

I was awestruck by Clarissa; she left me speechless, because I wanted to make her happy, but I really didn't want to meet Josie yet.

"James is taking a nap. Do you want me to wake him?"

I shook my head no.

It made me feel better that he was sleeping, but his voice rang out, "I am awake."

I heard him but didn't see him.

"James, you should sleep downstairs. We can look after her."

He sat up at the foot of the lounge chair.

I giggled. As great as Clarissa is, James was the only person in the world that could draw my attention away from her.

His eyes locked to mine and my heart pounded a few extra beats. Falling deep within his dark warm eyes I saw a sparkle in them. He knew what he did to me just by looking at me. It was like Clarissa wasn't there, because we were so hooked on each other. He spoke softly, "It is just like the first few nights I spent with you. Do you remember hogging the couch and me sleeping on the floor?"

That did make me feel a little bad. There was no reason for him to sleep on the floor when there were so many beds here.

He chuckled, "I didn't want to be that far from you."

This time my heart skipped a beat. I did love my James from the deepest part of my heart. He got up stretching, "I will get your dinner. Do you want to try and eat it on the deck?"

I pointed out the window, "They are having fun."

James looked out the window, while he sat down at the end of the lounge. He enjoyed the site as much as I did.

Clarissa's voice came out pleased, "You are getting a kick out of them?"

I nodded excitedly, as she turned to take in the enjoyment herself. She finally noticed I was paying attention to her, "How about I get your dinner and James can help you to the deck."

If I was going to have to go to the deck to meet Josie, anyway, I guess I could try to eat out there. James came over, as I scooted to the edge of the lounge. I put out my hand to stop James from helping me, "I need to do this."

He stepped back grinning. I pushed myself to try and stand, but he had to grab me before I fell over from the pain, "Hey, you don't have to push so hard. Time will help with that."

He smelt so good, and his arm wrapped around me felt wonderful. He was more concerned if I was okay rather than how we were standing. "Are you okay to walk?"

I was okay to walk, but I wasn't okay being this close to him. My mixed feelings were driving me crazy. I couldn't handle being engulfed with heartache, or the loss of air from my lungs. I nodded and swallowed deeply. The warmth of his body holding mine was making my body have desire, and this scared me.

James's face grew to a smile. He must feel my want and he moved closer to me, so that his mouth was less than an inch from mine, "You smell tasty to me, too."

How could I be this mixed up, and how could he love me this much? All I knew at that very moment was that I was longing for him to kiss me. I still didn't care for James reading my mind, "I didn't say that."

He smiled and nudged my face probing me for more. When I did give in, he moved closer so that he was standing directly in front of me, but he let his arms drop from my waist. All the while my heart was racing again; oh did I want him to try, but... He nudged my face a little more; I think he was testing the waters. This time I did the opposite of what he wanted, but only because my feelings were really mixed and confusing.

I felt the smile on his lips, as they pressed against my skin while saying, "Okay, food."

I quickly looked up at him, "No?" My eyes stayed locked to his.

"What do you want me to do, Sarah? I can't handle being rejected again. I would rather not try then have you pull away from me."

I lowered my face. I felt horrible that I was sending him mix messages, "Food."

He lifted my chin a little with his hand trying to see deep inside me. I had a hard time letting my eyes linger on his. I didn't know if I would pull away. It totally depended on if the sadness swept over me engulfing my breathing. How could he know if I would pull away if I didn't?

"It still hurts you," but he moved his mouth over mine and traced my top lip with his. The breathing was getting a little tight; I didn't know if it was because it felt good or if it was that fear of feeling too much. His eyes were still locked on mine. He was going to move away from me, but I didn't want him to. I cupped his bottom lip with mine and he closed his eyes out of the pleasure of it.

"Are you two coming or not? Shit."

James broke the kiss resting his forehead on mine smiling, "Saved again by Jake's bad timing."

I smiled and turned my head to look at Jake, disappointed. James put his arm around my waist, "He is never going to leave us alone, is he?"

I shook my head trying to walk with him. It was hard enough to walk alone let alone holding his waist. I let go and he reluctantly let go of me, but stayed close behind me in case I needed help. Jake opened the door and Clarissa followed us out with a tray of food. I moved to the table, but sitting on a chair didn't sound good to me at all. It was like everyone could read my mind, because Jake came quickly setting a pillow on the chair, "See if that will work."

Before I sat down, I turned to Josie putting out my hand, "Hello."

She looked at me suspiciously, and she wasn't taking my hand. I was completely confused by her reaction. I turned to Jake with wonder.

Before he had a chance to elaborate she spoke to me, "Jake said you didn't talk."

I wasn't ready for questions. I felt the panic deep from within my gut. Thank goodness for James being close to me. He pulled me close, taking my face in his hand, to bring my attention to him, but he spoke to Josie, "She is trying really hard today." The warmth of his deep brown eyes penetrated my heart easing the pain that was on its way.

He lowered me to the chair which made me face her. I didn't want to do this anymore. It was very uncomfortable. Clarissa came and sat by me grabbing my hand and pulled my attention to her, "Sarah, no. It's okay."

Tears were already filling my eyes, and I was shaking my head no letting her know I couldn't do this anymore. She grabbed my face, "You can do this. Concentrate on eating."

I closed my eyes.

Jake didn't even like the way his mom questioned me, "Mom, please. This is hard for her. She has had two surgeries in the last month."

Thankful that he was sticking up for me, I glanced up at him.

He gave me a reassuring grin, "How is the sitting?"

I shook my head no. James leaned down with his elbows on the back of the chair whispering in my ear, "I will take you out of here right now if that is what you need."

I did want him to take me out of her right now. I only wanted *him* to be next to me. I only wanted to be alone with James. At least I was doing better with trying to be with him.

Clarissa was more direct, "Jake's mom took time to come here and meet you, Sarah, so will you please try?"

I was just starting to feel better and Josie was a little uncomfortable for me. I couldn't do this until Clarissa's eyes locked with mine. I would have thought that James got his eyes from his dad, because they were so much alike, but the softness, the warmth, the comfort was from her. She was so good to me, so if she wanted me to try I would. I just had to concentrate on the food and lifting it to my mouth.

Jake squatted beside me, so that I could see his face as he said, "I'm sorry, you're doing better than I thought you would, otherwise, I wouldn't have allowed this."

If I was doing better than why didn't I feel better?

"How is the sitting?"

I shrugged my shoulders, but gave a small grin saying, "I'll try."

His question moved to James, "It's painful for her?" Why did he even ask me if he wasn't going to believe me anyway?

Josie must have thought we were all nuts. She watched the exchange between Jake and James and then the dispersion of the medication into my IV line.

I shook my head no, but of course they didn't listen.

James picked up the chair I was on and scooted me in. His breath grazed my ear, "I have to go for a couple minutes. I can't watch your pain."

I turned my face toward him for a slight caress. I needed him, but he needed to be away from me. I nodded slightly gesturing that I agreed even though I didn't…

Clarissa said, "If it gets to be too much, James, we will come get you."

Tamara came bouncing out and over to me.

I was very happy to see her, "Tamara, are you playing your game?"

I heard a huff of laughter from Clarissa. She knew what I was up too. I needed to ease the stress that was going on out here between Josie and me.

"You want me to make everybody feel happy?"

I nodded but not before she started waving her hands in the air, twirling them around and then giving a big bow at the end; like that was the end of a major production. She rose asking, "How do you feel?"

I hoped Josie felt happier because I did, "Better."

She smiled and skipped off, and I did notice a smile on Josie's face.

Wilson and Carl walked in the gate. Wilson saw me and seemed worried about something. Seeing that look on his face made me feel bad. They walked up to the deck and Carl asked, "How is my girl?"

I really wish that I could just say what I was thinking. I smiled at Carl to let him know I was okay.

Wilson kissed his wife's cheek avoiding my gaze. I had to apologize for earlier; "I'm sorry."

He shook his head in disbelief, "No, Sarah, it was my fault."

I shook my head no, "You helped me."

That seemed to ease his discomfort with me, "You're trying to talk more?" His eyes moved to meet mine, and they actually were watery. He did care about me.

Jake stepped in, "Sarah, quit trying so hard, or you won't have the energy to eat."

Clarissa handed me a fork, "Sarah, it's three cups of food this time and no desert."

I nodded and started to eat. Way too many emotions, and it was hard to eat. I ate most of it before my stomach began to twist and turn. The feeling that was coming over me sent pure fear to my heart. I was about to panic; this was too much food, and I didn't think it was going to stay down.

My eyes must have been completely horrified, because Jakes reaction reflected my emotional upturn, as he yelled for James, "James, we could use your help."

He came running out of the apartment, up the stairs, and to me before the first gag, but only getting to me in time to see me hold back a heave. Pulling me to face him, he gazed deep into my eyes. It was an instant calm but the turning stomach didn't settle yet. He finally broke into a grin, "Hey."

I gave him a worrisome look. I knew I was going to lose it even if I didn't want to.

He encouraged, "Breathe through your nose; you can do this."

I swallowed.

"Do you want to lie down?"

Thankful for his suggestion I nodded, but I shouldn't have nodded. It sent me spinning, and my stomach took a turn for the worst. I shook my head no knowing that I had to make it to the bathroom.

"Yes, you can. Do you want water?"

I shook my head no.

I heard Wilson, "She doesn't like it."

I closed my eyes nodding my head yes. I did like it, but I tried too hard. The weird part was that with the upset stomach I could feel the emptiness moving into my chest. The hole was getting bigger, and my stomach was turning more; yep, the sadness was taking over my whole being.

"Sarah, no. If you get sick, it could hurt worse. Come on, baby." He picked me up and grabbed the IV stand and me, bringing me inside heading for the lounge where he set me down.

Nope, it was not going to stay down. I pushed him out of my way heading to the bathroom.

"Sarah, no. It will be so painful."

I kept going that way. I went in and leaned over the toilet. I didn't even have to heave. It was already coming up and out. James wrapped his arm around my stomach to hold it; the pain was overwhelming making my knees give out underneath me. James was completely holding me up, as I started to cry.

James yelled.

## *James:*

"JAKE, I need help here."

I was holding her with one arm, but she was sobbing in pain. The wind was getting knocked out of me with every movement that hurt her. I was holding the door frame to hold her and myself up.

He ran in, "Sarah, you're not supposed to do that."

She had completely collapsed in my arms not supporting herself at all.

"Jake, you have to take her. Her pain is knocking the wind from my lungs." I took a deep breath. It was getting harder and harder to breathe. He took her and carried her back to the lounge. I sat down on the bathroom floor.

I heard Jake yell from the other room, "James, how bad is her pain?"

I was gasping for air, "It's bad, Jake."

"Bad enough that she needs a shot?"

I was almost passing out from the pain, "Yes."

I saw him run toward the door and not very long before he came back through. I propped myself against the wall. After he took care of Sarah, he came back to me evaluating how I was doing. He was concerned, "Are you feeling her more?"

I closed my eyes and nodded.

"I thought without doing that stuff it was supposed to get better."

I rolled my eyes. I thought that too.

"Are you two still doing that?"

"Jake, I swear we're not. I don't know why, but I think it is getting worse. When you came and got her I was almost to the point of passing out from the pain, so either hers was worse than what I felt, or I am feeling it more."

He sat down next to me.

"Jake, is there something we could give her to help her with the anxiety. When she gets uncomfortable, like earlier, a wall of sadness comes over her. It knocks the shit out of me. I can't breathe, and I have to move away from her."

"Maybe ask Sam or your dad about that." He stood up pulling me with him, "Are you okay now?"

"If you are asking me if I can breathe again, yeah, as soon as you took her from me and out of the room that got a little better."

"So when you walk out there are you going to feel it again?"

"I don't know... I guess that depends on if she is feeling it."

Jake walked out first but turned around to wait for me.

I walked closer to her and nothing, "How much pain killer did you give her?"

"A whole shot, because you said it was bad."

I shook my head no, "Well I guess she will be out for a while. I should find out more."

Jake chuckled, "My mom is going to think we are all freaks with the way we all hover over Sarah."

I couldn't help but laugh about that myself.

We walked back out and they were all at the table. Jake and I hesitated as we stood there.

Dad felt my need and stood up, "Please excuse me for a minute." He was walking in the house, "Boys." We both followed. I could see that this was going to upset Wilson's wife, my dad ordering Jake around. He stopped just inside the door closing it, "You two look like fools; what is going on?"

How to explain washed over me, "You know how you and Sam told me not to have a connection when me and Sarah when we're awake."

"James, now what did you do?"

"Nothing and it's getting worse. I noticed in the hospital when she was engulfed in sadness it was knocking the air out of me. When she looks like she is going to hyperventilate, I can hardly breathe. Just now when I carried her in she was passing out from the pain, and I almost passed out. I would have if Jake wouldn't have taken her from me."

He leaned on the counter thinking. It was like he was going through things over and over in his head, "Maybe you need more time not using your powers with her before it lessens."

I glanced at him wondering how much time he was talking about.

He was still thinking about it and he walked back out. Jake and I exchanged looks but he said, "Well, that helped," with raised eyebrows.

I laughed, "Yeah, now what do I do?"

He grinned, "Could the desire be worse, because you're not getting it for real?" He glanced at me with a smirk on his face.

I glared at him.

"I just mean, I have interrupted you every time you were close to kissing her. Maybe it will get better if you do kiss her."

I couldn't help but smile at him, "I was able to kiss her last night, Jake, but nice idea."

"Maybe it's because she is letting you back in."

"I felt it in the hospital before she let me kiss or even touch her."

"So you were able to touch her?"

"Very little, and it drives me crazy. I am afraid she will pull away from me."

"So you kissed her but didn't touch her?"

"Well... kind of. I get to touch her hand, oh yeah she lets me message her stomach like you do."

Almost satisfied he asked, "But you are not holding her yet? Not wrapping your arms around her?"

"Thanks for pointing that out; what is your point?"

"I don't know; I thought you could figure that out. I was just helping you think about it. You know, breaking it down, and enjoying that you aren't getting any." His grin grew which lightened his whole face.

I wanted to kill him.

"Welcome to my world, James."

"You don't miss it if you've never had it."

He glared at me.

"Jake, I mean if you have never had sex, how would you know what you are missing?"

"So, it is that good?"

"It can be. Mostly, it's just the rush of it. However, that's it. With Sarah, it's different. I want to make her feel good. Before I could care less what the girl wanted."

"Okay, you sound like a jerk."

"Jake, it's not the same. I wanted to wait till she was 18. I wanted it to be special for her. Most of the time it hurts for the girl the first time, because she isn't ready, and I'll tell you something else... it's not that great if you're not ready either."

"At all or just the first time?"

"First time and you have no control at all. So it really sucks."

"Great, glad to hear that."

"Just make sure it's with someone you really care about, and hopefully, someone who hasn't done it before."

"But you have, and you want Sarah.'

Thinking about touching my Sarah in the most intimate ways, "Every time I am around her and get to touch her, it's like the first time. I get so nervous about making it special for her."

"But she has dreamt about being with you."

I couldn't help but grin. I couldn't stop thinking about the day with the feather, but if I put that aside, "Well, obviously, we have been close enough at times to get her pregnant."

He glared, "I just don't see it."

"That's a relief. We are way off the subject here, and I still don't know what to think."

He laughed at me, "I guess you have to wait longer like your dad said."

"And we have to not upset her. She was doing so well today."

"I think my mom set her off. She wasn't very nice to start it off."

"She is thinking we are all nuts."

"Right now I am thinking we *are* all nuts. I currently don't have a job. I can't remember the last time I didn't have a job."

"You are just doing this because Clarissa asked?"

"You mean our mom."

I looked at him not understanding how he could consider them both his moms.

"James, I know it has been unfair to you to not know her, but I have wanted this since I was little. I think I even asked once if I was adopted."

"Really?"

"Josie is great. She worked with me, so I could be really smart and she home schooled me until College, but she never really felt like my mother. When I came here, Mom would sit on the floor and play with me; she would hug me; she would talk to me like a person."

"I really didn't remember anything about her, so for me I just never had a mom."

I didn't realize it, but we had moved over to the lounge where Sarah was. We were both sitting on chairs facing the lake, talking. Sarah was right; she did turn my world upside down, in more good ways than bad.

I glanced back at her, "Do you think she will sleep through the night?"

"No, I didn't give her stuff to knock her out. It was the shot; it just got rid of the pain."

Then, this isn't right. I turned around completely, "Why is she sleeping then?"

He looked at her and moved to feel her wrist. He took a deep breath. "James, you just scared the shit out of me."

"What?"

"She shouldn't be sleeping."

I moved to her other side, "Sarah, Sarah, baby?"

Jake was patting her hand to wake her, and I was shaking her by pushing on her arm.

"What are you guys doing? I am sleeping."

Relief filled me as I glanced up at Jake. That was the most she had said in a long time without feeling remorse. We glanced at each other, backed away from Sarah, grabbed our chairs, turning them around, and we both sat down watching her.

I whispered, "Jake, when she talks the sadness engulfs her heart, and she is deeply sad."

"You could feel that?"

I was so surprised, "Not when she just spoke." My eyes were wide open staring at her.

"You didn't feel it just now?"

"Nope."

"This is getting weirder. No wonder my mom thinks were freaks."

I chuckled at this, "Yeah."

We both took a deep breath and stared at her until we were certain she was back out. Finally, we turned to watch out over the lake, but did not move from her side.

After we sat there in silence long enough for both of us to get sleepy Jake spoke, "I really thought having your dad and Sam here... well I thought things would get better."

I agreed with him, "I did too."

"They don't really seem to know much more than you and I, and *I* know nothing."

"Sam said it was because we have done stuff that is not covered in the old tales. We went outside the parameters of my abilities."

"Yeah, got that, but it still sucks."

Pulling out my phone I checked the time, "It's 1:00 am."

"Are they still out there?"

I stood up and walked to the window on the other side of the room, "They are skinny dipping."

"What? They are not."

Instant worry filled me, as I realized I didn't know where Sam and Tamara were. I dug out my cell phone and called Sam.

"How is it going with Sarah?"

"She is sleeping; where are you and Tamara?"

"We are stuck in the apartment. Tamara is sleeping, and I was going to carry her upstairs, but... Do you know what our parents are doing?"

"Yeah, that is why I am calling you. I didn't know where you were. So Tamara is sleeping?"

"Yep, but I am board, and I am not going out there."

I laughed, "I'm not going out there, either." I looked at Jake to see if he would.

"Don't look at me. Are they at least at opposite ends of the pool?"

I peeked back out at them, "No they are taking turns..." I turned to Jake, "Jumping off the diving board."

Jake didn't believe me and walked to the window.

I warned him, "I don't think you want to look out..."

He did and turned back to me, "Okay, I have now seen more than I ever wanted to."

"Told you not to look"

I still had Sam on the phone, "What, who looked?"

"Jake had to see for himself, but Sam I wouldn't look if it...."

"Yuk, James, you could have warned me."

"I was trying, but you had to look."

"I am scarred for life."

I was laughing trying to explain to Jake, "Sam had to look too; he says he's scarred for life."

Jake was laughing also.

"Hey Sam, you should probably plan on staying down there tonight with Tamara. If they go up to bed I will come get you and Tamara. Can Jake use your room?"

"Of course, but I will have nightmares after that."

"I will see you in the morning most likely."

"Great, James, what am I going to do now?"

"Watch a movie and try to go to sleep."

"Fine, but I am not going to try and sleep; I will picture that for the rest of my life."

"Night, kid, try to forget it."

"Good night, but I am not happy."

I hung up the phone laughing. I turned back to Jake, "You can have the couch or Sam's room."

"Where are you sleeping?"

"I can't leave her."

"I'll take Sam's room. I wouldn't want to see them come in."

I laughed and started to walk to the lounge glancing down at Sarah. She didn't look comfortable at all, like she was going to get a kink in her neck. I pulled a pillow over and lowered her to the pillow covering her back up. Jake was watching me and shook his head, "You are really in love with her?"

"More than you could ever imagine."

"Good night then."

"Night."

## 37. Teasing

### Sarah:

**I** woke to a beautiful Sunrise; the gold's and purples were peeking through the light fluffy white clouds in the horizon. I woke to the pleasure of my husband beside me so strong yet so peacefully sleeping. I was afraid to move, afraid that I would be reminded of the pain, but the bathroom was calling to me in more ways than one. I pushed myself to the end of the lounge trying to sit up. I had the back of the lounge to pull myself up. I looked at the IV, knowing I needed a pain killer badly if I was going to poop. I pushed the button five times. I toyed with the idea of how to get up without waking my sweet Cayuse. I tried to push myself up, but it was painful. I scooted more to the edge to give it another try. I pushed up and almost made it, but the pain shot through my lower inners. James caught me and helped me up the rest of the way.

"What are you doing, little girl?"

I smiled at him taking a deep breath, "Bathroom."

"Do you want help?" I shook my head and nodded for him to lie back down. He smiled at me and sat back down. I walked to the bathroom, slowly. I must have been in there for a half hour, taking my time to go. It wasn't as bad as I thought it was going to be, or at least till I tried to stand, then the pain shot through me again. I was able to take the pony out of my hair and brush through my mop on the top of my head. I brushed my teeth and washed my face. I wanted a shower so bad, but that would have to wait till the pain was a little better. I walked out heading back to the lounge.

James was now curled into the spot where I had been. I didn't know how I would get back there anyway. I crawled onto the end of the lounge and lay down on my side facing the window. The curtains were pulled most of the way, but I could still see the sunrise through the open part. I laid there and watched it raise the rest of the way. I felt him reaching for where I was. I was on the edge to not be too close to him.

"Hey."

I rolled to my back finding myself underneath him.

His fingertips played with my hair as the idea of touching me danced in his eyes, but he settled for asking, "Are you okay?"

I nodded.

"Oh, back to that."

Even though the pain wasn't that bad it was still there, and his negative tone wasn't helping me. I felt the sadness moving in so, I closed my eyes to evade this feeling.

"Sarah, please don't be sad. I can't breathe when you are sad."

My eyes flashed open not understanding why he couldn't breathe. He took my hand in his and kissed the back of it causing comfort to my uneasiness.

"That's better. Your sadness is so hard for me, I just need you to try and think of something else." He opened his eyes to gaze at me, but his eyes wandered over me to the window saying, "There, look at that. You can't feel sad looking at the sunrise; it's beautiful."

I turned back to the window. He was right; it was beautiful.

I felt his breath at my ear, "Sarah, did you know you are my sunrise?"

I turned my face back to him. He was resting his head on his hand that was propping him up, so he could see me better. He was very careful to not touch me, but he was staring at me. My heart was racing, as it does whenever he is this close to me. I touched the circles under his eyes, "Are you worn out?"

He smiled slightly, "No, just tired."

The way his face twitched with doubt confused me.

He was still being careful with me, "May I?"

I didn't know what he was asking to do. He held up one finger and moved it to my face. I hated that I was being emotional, so I had to control my feelings and let him try. He slowly traced my face starting with my forehead to get rid of the worry lines. I relaxed and enjoyed his touch so soft and light. He moved his finger over my eyes, my nose, my jaw line, and my neck and back up. He stopped at my chin long enough for me to open my eyes. I was pleased that I could make him smile after making him so miserable. His eyes lingered at the sight of mine while he traced my lips leaning closer to me. My chest felt heavy as my heart pounded against my insides.

"Sarah, can we take a nap downstairs today? This is very uncomfortable."

I agreed with him nodding.

His eyes dropped to gaze at my lips with a grin on his face. The light touch of his finger exploring my lips helped to keep me calm. When he got to the middle I kissed his finger. He propped himself up more to see me better with a more serious face. His eyes searched my face, as his finger played with my features. What I love about my James was his attentiveness and tenderness. Next he lowered so that he could caress my cheek with his. I felt the soft stubbles graze my skin but only for a moment because he moved away to see how that went. I could only stare at him. I worried that the sadness that sometimes snuck up on me would creep back in, but this was very sweet and nice. It was very comforting and I liked this. He didn't move away from me but his hand moved down my arm slowly until he could take my hand in his. Pulling my hand up to his face holding it to his cheek and he pressed to it as if he would enjoy my touch. He turned into it and kissed it as if he were kissing my mouth passionately. I reached up with my other hand to caress the other side of his face. He closed his eyes with satisfaction. He felt good, but how good? Was I asking for something I just couldn't do? Not now. I ran my thumb over his lips; my chest was pounding for him. He stopped my movement as his mouth captured my thumb. I was almost past the point of what I could handle. The heat was rising, and I was getting more and more scarred. I was ready to push him away.

"I hear you, baby. Please just a little more." His eyes came back to mine trying to keep me from feeling the deep pain in my heart. Even though my breathing was getting difficult his stare kept me from letting the sadness take over.

"It's okay, Sarah, nothing is going to happen. We're just enjoying each other. We don't have to go further."

I tried to ignore the mixed feeling of wanting more and being too scared to continue. He leaned in to press his lips to mine keeping a deep eye connection. He mouthed to me, "See, it just feels good. No further, Sarah."

He pressed his lips against my top lip, I pressed mine against his bottom lip and it did feel amazing. We were kissing, and he was taking my breath away in a good way. It seemed to be going really well until we heard a door open.

I could feel his smile against my lips as he said, "How much do you want to bet it's Jake?" He moved slowly away from me and laid his head down looking at me. It was over and I didn't freak out. He took my hand and brought it to his mouth kissing it softly. I closed my eyes waiting to find out who was there. I heard the coffee pot being rattled and started. James giggled a little, and I opened my eyes again. He gestured to the kitchen, "Told you."

I laughed with a sigh because it was Jake. James pushed himself up hesitating just a moment, as his eyes evaluated me. He came in for a quick kiss and got up moving to the kitchen. I tried to watch, but they were out of sight.

"Jake, you just have really bad timing."

I heard them both laugh. They were getting along even better. Pleased, I rolled back to my spot where James had taken over. I curled up to a pillow nuzzling into it. I felt so good. We were able to kiss and I didn't lose it. It made me happy. I heard the patio door, and James was crawling back in with me. He wasn't really close, but he was rubbing my back. He leaned in to whisper in my ear, "Let's go downstairs for a while." He ruined it. I shook my head no.

"Why?"

I couldn't talk about it. It would go further, and I was too scared to be with him. The sadness would take over, and I didn't want to feel that way.

He leaned over me again and breathed in my ear and nibbled on it.

I shooed him away.

"Are we back to that?"

I leaned back to him to find his eyes. I didn't want to ruin what I was feeling, but when my eyes met his I saw sadness in them. I touched his face and he leaned into my caress.

"Sarah, don't you understand? It's okay to not do that. We have a lifetime for that. I just really love to kiss you, and it felt so good that I don't want it to stop, and there is no privacy here."

Trying to compromise, "Nap time."

He was pleased with how this was going. He used the back of his hand to touch my cheek again. He closed his eyes and a great big grin came to his face, "That's okay; I was getting to the point of needing a shower anyway."

That was what I was worried about, getting carried away.

He reassured me, "I was the one that wanted to wait till you are 18, Sarah, and waiting for you is worth it."

I touched my fingers to his lips as they grew to a grin. I squeezed his lips pulling them to me. He raised his eyebrows disbelieving that I would do that to him while he tried to speak through the squeezing, "Oh, you want more?"

I nodded aggressively. He took my hand away from squeezing his mouth and started to kiss my fingers and sucking on them. When he was done with my fingers he moved his attention to my face moving closer and closer as if he was giving in to my want, but instead of kissing me he grinned and replied, "Nap time." His idea was short lived because he moved in for more kissing. I turned away playfully looking at him out of the corner of my eye.

"Are you teasing me?"

I giggled

"You are." He got up on his knees trying to figure out what he was going to do to torture me. I turned away closing my eyes pretending to snore.

"You are teasing me. That isn't nice."

I felt light and happy. Carl walked out upstairs and I heard him from above, "You two better stop that before Clarissa comes out, or she will kick you back downstairs. Tamara is too young to see stuff like that."

Pushing James away, I looked up at Carl smiling.

"And you're smiling today. I knew it was going to be a good day."

James started to tickle me.

I scolded, "No, no, no. Please."

He stopped, "Sorry, I didn't think that might hurt you."

I nodded but I wasn't in any pain.

Clarissa must have come out, because her voice carried all the way down to us loud and clear, "Sorry, Sarah, your back downstairs today."

I stopped playing with James, and the fear was moving in.

James tried to comfort me right away, "Sarah, I will sleep on the couch; it's okay."

I turned to him panicking.

"Sarah, don't make it out to be bad." He leaned in to whisper in my ear, "It's okay, Sarah, I will wait till you are 18. That was the plan anyway." He was totally smiling at me, but my fear was moving in and taking over. He moved away from me so that I could have some space, and he went into Tamara's room; he came out in a panic, "Tamara?"

Clarissa was coming down the steps, "If you remember correctly, all of you were spying on us swimming last night, and she stayed downstairs with Sam."

I didn't understand what she meant by *spy*. Jake had walked in to catch the part about the '*spying on us swimming*' part, but quickly turned to walk back out. With how everyone was acting it sent my curiosity to a new level. Let me get all this down: it has to do with the pool, Clarissa and Carl in the pool, and spying. All I could think was they were doing it in the pool last night and everyone saw it.

James gave me a glance while shaking his head, "Remind me when we get their age to not go skinny dipping especially with our kids around."

I giggled for a second, and then it hit me like a ton of bricks. Did he realize what he just said? I was not the only one that was shocked by what James said. It seemed like everything was happening in slow motion as Jake turned to make his way back to me. James regretted saying that immediately as he also made his way to me saying, "Sarah, no don't think about it. I am sorry. I was just caught up in us, their kids, watching them. No, don't think about it."

I could feel the emptiness overpower me into deep sadness, while the tears swelled in my eyes until I couldn't see a thing. My heart sank, and I slumped deeply into the lounge seat. I didn't want anyone to see me in my misery. I buried my face into the pillow. I didn't want this feeling of desolation to come back again. I took a deep breath and James was rubbing my back, "Sarah, I wasn't thinking. I... Shit."

I tried to talk with the pillow over my face, "It's okay, just need a minute." I now felt Jake sit down, and I heard Carl and Clarissa moving closer. I pulled away from James to get him to stop rubbing my back.

I heard Clarissa, "Sarah, you're still back downstairs."

"Mom!" James spoke up, "We can deal with that later."

"You called me mom again. I do like that, but James you need to be more..." She didn't say anything.

I pulled the pillow down to see why she stopped in mid-sentence. My tears were still streaming. But I wanted to know what she was thinking; if I was being immature. If she was getting irritated with me, then I would have to work harder on it. I gasped and sputtered out, "S – s - sorry."

She gave me a reassuring gesture with her eyes, "It's okay, Sarah, you are allowed to feel that way." She gave James a look of reproach.

I turned to him knowing that this was hard on him, and it made me feel bad that my heart was hurting again.

I could tell by the pain on his face, that he could feel my pain, "I don't know what to say, Sarah."

I didn't want him to feel bad, so I put on a smile, closed my eyes, swallowed, and took a deep breath to get my whisper out, "Fine."

"No, I am a total jerk."

I didn't agree, so I shook my head no.

Jake was going to get his input in, "Sarah, it's my turn to inflict pain." He grimaced with the intent on checking my stomach.

James wasn't happy, "I didn't mean to…" He put his head in his hands.

I grabbed for his hand, so he would look at me. I didn't want him to be mad at himself. As he glanced at me, I shook my head no, but he turned away.

I wasn't ready for it, but Jake started to poke at me. I tried to push him away to stop, but he didn't pay attention to me. As I felt the pain, James moved to the window. Carl walked over to him and was talking to him quietly. I wanted to hear what they were saying, so I tried to ignore what Jake was doing, but the pain with the pushing took my breath away. The more pain I felt the more James turned to the window.

Jake leaned into me, "Hey, pay attention here."

I finally gave in to Jake to get this over with.

"Is the pain bad?" He was asking me, but his glance moved to James.

I needed to know if James was okay, but I gasped from the pain. I nodded to Jake about the pain. I saw James grabbed the frame of the window.

I wanted to know what was wrong with James. Why was he over there when he should be here with me? I asked Jake with my eyes but only one word, "James?"

"Hey, you need to pay attention to this. I need to know where the pain…"

I gasped and cringed.

He chuckled, "Oh, there it is."

I gave him a dirty look, "You're trying to hurt me?"

"NO, just getting your attention."

I didn't want to deal with Jake now that there is something is wrong with my James. Carl grabbed James around the waist and was walking him to the door. I glanced up at Jake again feeling the pain in my heart getting worse, as I watched James leave me. Jake wasn't paying attention to anything except pushing on my stomach. He pushed it again and I gasped.

"Right there, Sarah?"

I nodded and covered it with my arm shaking my head no.

"Sarah, stop. You have to let me check it."

I was more determined, "James!"

"No, Sarah. Stop. When he feels your pain, it knocks the air out of him. The connection has gotten stronger. Settle down and let him have space."

I didn't completely understand, "How?"

His eyes met mine, but he quickly moved on, pushing me down, so he could feel my stomach, "Shit Sarah, stop. Pay attention and let me know where the pain is."

I was worried about what was happening to James. I stared at Jake with tears in my eyes.

"He feels that too, so stop and behave for a little bit."

I lay down and turned my face away from him, as the tears started to run down my cheeks. I grimaced as he pushed.

"Sarah, you're not helping me."

I took his hand and moved it to where it hurt the most. I moved it to my chest and then covered my face with my arm.

He pulled his hand away from me, "Okay, just relax for a while. I am going to get you breakfast."

I shook my head no. I hated that such a great morning was so easily turned into nothing but hurt and pain.

I heard Clarissa from the kitchen, "Jake, give it a break. Let everything calm down, and then check her."

I glanced over in case she was looking. She peaked around the corner with a grin that made me feel better. Jake went outside, and as he did that she came to me, "James didn't mean to upset you."

"I know. I was worried."

She touched my face endearingly, "I know, dear."

"I don't want… to feel that… way. Deep down he wants…" And the tears came streaming down. I started to push myself up, "Bathroom."

"Sarah, you don't have anything in your stomach; you are going to tear something."

I still tried to push myself up; of course, she helped me towards the end, and I walked to the bathroom. I was swallowing to keep it down. I went to the bathroom, and I was a mess again. I kept breathing through my nose. I got in the shower to try and wash it all away. I stood there for so long I thought I might have used up all the hot water. I got out, and James was walking in with a bag. I wrapped the towel around me. He avoiding looking at me, and sat the bag down, "I didn't know what you would want to wear. I just threw some things in the bag.

I nodded.

He came to me and put his hands on my hips but held his head down, "I am so sorry."

I lifted his chin and shook my head no. He still couldn't look at me in the eyes. He put his face to mine, and we stood there for a long time.

"Sarah, you need to get dressed."

I tilted my head to him, so my lips were close to his.

"No you need to get dressed. This is not helping me, and it will make it worse for you."

I nudged him with my nose. His hands gripped tighter on my hips, and he gave me what I needed as his lips touched mine. I put my hand on his chest to hold him there to which he whispered, "I know." His eyes closed as he released me to leave.

I was desperate for him, "James?"

He paused a moment, "It's okay, Sarah. I'm sorry." But then he walked out. Not only was I miserable, but I was also tearing him apart wanting him and then pushing him away. His desire was getting worse, while my heart was filled with fear. I took a deep breath and got dressed. I toweled my hair and put on a little makeup. I brushed my teeth and took a long look at myself. I was still a mess, and the tears streamed down again. I went to the toilet and put the seat cover down and sat down. I am too young for this shit. What the hell was I thinking? I love James. I want to be with him for the rest of my life. I am still in high school. I was pregnant, and now I'm not. I had a major leak in my appendix. I have had two surgeries in three weeks. It hurts to breath and my heart feels like it's going to explode from having a hole in it, and the worst part is that I overreact to everything. I have tons of people catering to me, when they should throw me to the street for the way I am behaving.

I heard a knock on the door, "Sarah, are you dressed?"
I took a deep breath, "Yes."
"Can I come in?"
I took another deep breath, "Nope... just fine."
The door opened again. James walked in getting on his knees in front of me. He put his head in my lap, "Please forgive me. We should have gone a lot slower."
I traced my hands through his hair and moved a little. He glanced up at me, "This, sitting is hurting you. Why are you sitting here?"
"Needed space, sorry."
He pleaded, "I can take you home."
I shook my head no. I wasn't ready to be completely alone. Mom works all the time.
This made him sigh with a laugh to it, "No. Not your parent's home; our home."
I was confused.
"Sarah, downstairs is our home until we have a place of our own. I have everything clean and you can have your privacy."
I didn't want him to get the wrong idea, "I like this bathroom."
He didn't understand what I was trying to say.
I gave him a sweet smirk as I tried to explain, "I can go by myself."
This made him chuckle out loud as he stood up. He leaned down wrapping one arm around me to help me up, "I will see if Wilson can design something for the bathroom down stairs so you can go on your own."
That was easier than I thought.
His face got that look to it where I knew he had a desire. The pout in his little grin made me melt and those lips as he whispered to me, "Can I do one thing?"
My heart raced as I waited to see what he wanted to do. He cupped my face with his hands and touched his lips to mine slightly saying, "Can you forgive me?"
I closed my eyes with enjoyment of his tenderness and nodded.
He took my hand and opened the door. Nobody was in the room, so I walked slowly toward the lounge.

He grabbed my hand to redirect me, "Breakfast on the deck. There is more air out there."

I questioned him with my eyes.

He avoided my gaze, "I can't breathe when you are in pain."

Again that hurt deep in my heart, and I grimaced with regret.

He pulled me closer kissing my head, "I'm better now." He opened the patio door and Wilson was serving waffles. Josie was here again, and this time she smiled at me. Jake came over to put a pillow down for sitting on.

I stopped him, "Sorry."

He didn't reply, but he grinned, as he turned to his mother, Josie, and kissed her cheek. Of course I tried to sit carefully to avoid any pain.

Josie turned to me, "I heard you have been doing a little better."

I didn't want to be rude, so I gave her a smile and shrugged my shoulders.

Clarissa spoke up, "She has had a rough morning, but she is trying." She gave me that reassuring smile again. She was putting food on a plate for me. I wanted to try and do stuff for myself so I looked at her, but she ignored my gaze smiling more, "You need to eat and keep it down this time."

I didn't want to disappoint her so I nodded.

Jake and James left me alone with them while they started to carry things down the stairs. I was eating slowly watching them come and go.

Tamara came running out and hugged me, "Do you want me to make everybody happy again?"

I loved when she did this. She did her little thing ending in a twirl. She kissed my cheek and sat down on her mom's lap to eat. It worked for me. I continued to eat watching them move more stuff down. Wilson and James stopped to talk for a minute, and his gaze came to me. He came up and kissed Josie on the forehead, "Special project." Then he went to the garage.

I finished eating and sat there quietly. Clarissa noticed that my plate was empty, "You were hungry."

I was pleased with myself, but I wanted to remove myself from the deck. I realized that I couldn't go down by myself. James noticed that I was uncomfortable the next time he went by so he stopped, "Your bag is still up here. I put your suit in it. Jake could work with you in the pool to help with the stomach."

I didn't want to go in the pool, but it would get me out of sitting here. I got up to walk in, but I stopped by Josie, "Nice to see you again."

I think she was easing with the thought of Jake helping me. I continued to walk in, and grab my bag to see what he had put in it. I pulled out the one piece James had bought for me. I was horrified at how hideous it was, but I went to the bathroom to put it on. This really made me look thin. I wrapped the towel around my waist and walked back out.

James stopped doing what he was doing when he spotted me. He opted to move to me and cringed, "That makes you look really thin." He took my hand, "Are you ready?"

I really didn't want to go in the pool, so I shook my head no.

"Why not?"

I swallowed still recovering from the morning and being uncomfortable, "Still bleeding."

"Oh, am I stupid. I should have figured that out."

I shook my head no and shrugged my shoulders, "No tampons."

"More than I wanted to know, thanks."

I giggled silently. We walked outside, and James helped me to a lounge chair by the pool.

# 38. Private Talk

I sat and watched as long as I could, but I was getting sleepy. Jake had disconnected me from the IV lines. The ports were still in my skin, but I didn't have tubes everywhere extending out. Jake walked over to me giving me a pillow only because he saw I was dozing. I rolled to my side the best I could. James was in the pool leaning on the edge staring at me. I was pleased that he was the last thing I saw before my eyes shut.

    The next thing I knew James was lifting me.
    I didn't want to be babied, "No, let me walk."
    He pulled me tighter.
    I wasn't going to argue with him, because I was tired. He laid me down in the bed touching my cheek lightly, "Sarah, before you sleep...the computer is right here and so are your books for your college classes; I set them in the headboard. So if you wake up and don't want to be bothered you can start reading for your classes." His eyes were bright with excitement, his grin pleasing, but he sat down beside me, "You are so beautiful, Sarah, I just can't get enough of you." He got up, and I thought he was leaving, but he walked to the other side of the bed and crawled in, lying on his side, again staring at me. His body was away from me, but his face was close. I turned my head toward him, so I could see my handsome strong man. I loved the way he showed me that he loved me. He traced his fingers over my face, which helped me relax. He leaned into me whispering, "You are home."
    I did feel at home lying here with him, so I turned to watch him. He moved closer so that he could trace his lips over my face; it was peaceful, and calming to me. The sleep was coming very nicely. I was nervous about

being in his bed, but this, this was nice. He pulled himself closer; I could feel the warmth of his breath gliding along my face. His hand wrapped around my neck, and he started to press his lips against mine to open my mouth with his. He was moving closer, and it was getting too intense, so I put my hand on his arm. He took in a deep breath, I think to calm himself. He reached to message my stomach. He was being careful, but the feeling was so good. It made me forget about the intense kissing.

"Are you ready for me to connect the IV lines?"

I opened my eyes, and James put his head down to rest on my shoulder, "I swear, Jake, you have radar that tells you when to have the worst timing."

He was laughing. I couldn't help but laugh a little myself, biting my bottom lip feeling embarrassed by the delight I was experiencing.

He moved away from me smiling, "I know, it's a good thing." He was rolling his eyes.

I had a hard time holding the laugh back.

"So you think this is funny, too?"

I couldn't stop myself. I held my stomach as the laughter burst out.

Jake was attaching everything again. He gave me a small dose of pain meds, but it was just a little. He asked James, "James, I know you hate leaving her, but I have doctor questions, so could I have a minute alone please?"

He was shocked, "You have never asked for privacy before."

"It's for her, not for me. I think we humiliated her enough before with the whole family there. Please, James, I will come get you when I am done."

He looked at me to see if I would be okay with this, so I nodded to let him know it was. James walked out; I knew he wouldn't go far. I waited to see what Jake wanted.

"Did you go yet?"

Oh, the pooping thing again. I avoided his gaze but nodded.

"How bad was it?"

I swallowed and took a deep breath, "Not too bad."

He was very serious and professional, "How is the clotting?"

My heart was pounding a little, so I closed my eyes, "No clots."

"Is the bleeding worse?"

I shook my head no.

"Is it slowing?"

Okay this was going to take a little more effort. I closed my eyes for this one, "It's worse when I'm up." I opened my eyes to read him.

His face was comforting, "That's normal. James was rubbing your stomach, does that still feel good?"

I nodded.

"You know to not use tampons though, right. The nurses told you."

I nodded.

He looked at me uncomfortably, "I know James is determined to behave, but Sarah...," he was studying my face, "Nothing in you for six weeks."

I smiled at him, "No."

"No you can't wait that long or no you won't let it happen?"

"It won't happen." I was very serious.

He looked at me not giving me any indication of what he was feeling. Then his eyes narrowed, "You should wait longer, so you can go back on the pill."

I agreed with no problem.

"I mean... after the bleeding stops, it will probably be a month before you get your period, and that is when you can start the pill, but you need to take the pill for a whole month before you even think about it, okay?"

I nodded, agreeing with him.

"You are agreeing very easily; do you understand?"

I nodded and pushed out with a deep breath, "No sex!"

He chuckled as his face dropped. He glanced back up at me through the tops of his eyelashes. He looked like a little boy who was trying to get by with something. He was so cute sitting there nervously.

"Is it that good?"

I was surprised by his question. I didn't know how to answer him. I got pregnant without fully being with James; so honestly, shit... the dreams were wonderful. I didn't know how to answer it.

"You're not going to answer me?"

I took a deep breath, "Don't know how."

He grinned shaking his head.

"Dream, amazing... pregnancy is not."

"So when you were together the time you got pregnant, it wasn't pleasing for you?"

I smiled at him, "It wasn't like that."

"You're confusing."

I touched his arm, took a deep breath, and eased into an explanation, "James is slow, soft, and passionate, takes his time, and never pushes me."

"When you got pregnant was that the first time?"

I nodded, "But he was already pleased, soft, so it didn't hurt."

"So you haven't really been together, like mad passionate love for hours."

I smiled and shook my head no, "He's afraid he'll hurt me."

His brows furrowed, which made me wonder what he was thinking.

He noticed the change on my face, "What?"

"Why?"

"I think I am the only virgin here except for Tamara, and I feel stupid."

I touched his face, "Technically, am I still one?"

"That is what I am wondering."

I shrugged my shoulders, "Can I be if I was already pregnant?"

He looked at me and laughed a little, "I suppose not."

"I'm still scared."

"Why?"

I shrugged my shoulders.

He tried to make me feel better, "Because of what you have been through?"

I nodded. The tears started to well up in my eyes.

"You will just have to be careful, that's all."
I didn't know how to reply.
"Thank you." He was being sincere.
"What?" I didn't understand what the thank you was for.
"Honesty."
I really did care about Jake.
"Do you want me to talk to James? Is he pushing too hard now?"
I shrugged my shoulders, "I don't want to hurt him. I love him."
"Yeah and if he loves you, he will understand this was really hard." His face scanned mine, "And I don't think you are over it yet, to be honest."

My tears started to spill over as quickly as they filled my eyes.

He wiped them carefully, "Don't do that. James will get mad at me if I upset you."

I shook my head no.

"You still hurt though?"

I swallowed nodding.

He tried to comfort me, "To feel this way is normal."

I was very confused.

"Yes, Sarah, it's normal. It's almost like miscarrying, or postpartum. It can really play tricks on your mind."

I laughed a little, "You mean I'm not crazy?"

He shook his head no, "Not at all. Time will help. If it gets worse could you please tell me?"

I nodded because now the tears were a relief that I was okay and not completely losing it.

"James says when you are in pain, being your gut or in your heart, it knocks the air from his lungs. The connection is getting worse for him. Is it getting worse for you?"

I shook my head no, but was more confused as to why it was getting stronger for James and not for me.

"Can I check the others?"

I nodded as he pushed slightly on my stomach and moved to the middle and then the bad side, "You're not flinching."

I shook my head no.

"The pain is getting better?"

I nodded.

He wanted more information, "So going to the bathroom has helped?"

I nodded again and this time I gave him a smile.

"Okay, do you want me to get James?"

I shook my head no.

He gave me a funny glare.

"Need sleep."

"Do you want me to keep him out?"

I shook my head no.

"What do you want?"

I shrugged my shoulders. I didn't know how to feel.

"You don't know what you want?"

I gave him a regretful grin.

He laughed, "That is normal too." He tucked me back in, "Take your time." He wiped the tears from my cheeks, "I miss this."

I felt a little panicked.

"Just talking honestly. You aren't giddy around me, and I like that. You love James, so you can be yourself."

I was embarrassed.

"Is there anyone else like you?"

I nodded.

Probing for more information, "Has James met her?"

I nodded, but tried to keep a straight face, "You have to wait like me." He wasn't pleased with me, but I grinned mischievously, "You will figure it out with time. If I tell you, you will look for it or run the other way."

He stood up, "You want me to suffer?"

I shook my head no, pleadingly.

James came walking in, and he was smiling, "Jake, that's enough."

I glared at him because he was spying, and he knew what we were talking about.

"Yes, the connection is stronger, Sarah. Sorry, very little privacy from me. I don't try anymore, and I tried to focus on other people to drown it out, but it didn't help." He looked at me waiting for me to get mad. I was more embarrassed then mad.

Jake was uncomfortable, too, "Okay, well you two need to figure this out."

He left the room, and James moved to sit by me. He put one hand on each side of me and stared directly into my eyes, "So you are nervous to be alone with me?"

I didn't know what to say.

A sinful grin came to his face, "I'll tell you a secret. I am nervous to be with you, too."

Why would he be nervous about being with me?

"Sometimes when we're alone and the desire in me builds, I want to attack you and take you, but I love you and want you to *want* to be with me. It helps me stay in control of my emotions. I want you to want me as bad as I want you." He shook his head, "Did that even make sense?"

I nodded pleased that he understood.

"I understand your fear now, too. I am glad you talked to Jake, but sweetheart, you can tell me these things. I love you. I would rather know than have you push me away."

I smiled reaching for his face.

"And kissing is all I plan on doing for a long time, if you will let me?"

I nodded, I liked the kissing. He took my hand and kissed it softly, "Nap time, can I lay down with you?"

I nodded.

"This is really unfair, because you talked to Jake. You won't talk to me."

"Emotional." Just saying *that;* made the tears fill my eyes.

He got up, walked to the other side of the bed, and laid down, "God, this feels so much better than the lounge. Wilson should have something for the bathroom by the time you get up."

I glanced at him. His eyes were shut, and his hands were behind his head. I rolled to face him, so I could see him better.

"Don't even think of touching me, Sarah, kind of hot right now." He said this without looking at me.

Relieved that he was letting me know that now would be a bad time to touch him I settled for just feeling the warmth radiate from his skin. Satisfied, I closed my eyes.

## 39. Bad Timing

**I** woke up and James was still sleeping. I grabbed one of the school books and laid it down beside me. This wasn't going to work. I tried to sit up, carefully, so that I would not wake James. I pushed to stand up, which was a little easier than when I was on the lounge. I took the steps one at a time. I needed to make it to the bathroom. I closed the door, quietly, to not wake James. To my surprise something weird was set up around the toilet. I moved closer to it, so I could investigate what it was; I saw that it was a frame with a bar on each side of it which would make it easier for me to be able to lift and lower myself. There was also a basket of supplies right next to the toilet, and the garbage had scented bags. I laughed to myself, just because Wilson had come up with a devise for me, and I had everything I needed. After I was done I went out to the living room and looked around. No one was there, so I walked back to the room. I moved back to my side of the bed and went down the steps. I grabbed the books one by one setting them on the computer. I tried to lift it, and the pain was too much.

James woke immediately, "Sarah, no, don't do that."

I stopped letting go of the books and supported myself with my hand on the bed.

"What are you doing?"

"Trying to get this to the living room."

He shook his head, "You're not supposed to lift anything yet." He rolled to the side of the bed trying to shake the sleep away. I walked around the bed stopping in front of him. I cupped his head with my hands, while his face rested on my stomach. He did fill my heart with so much love, "You're still tired."

He glanced up at me, but then he rested his mouth on my stomach. I didn't know what to do with that. I was a little uncomfortable, because he might stir feelings that I am not ready for.

He lay back, "Shit, I am tired." A light moan escaped him, as he moved to get up, "Mom got you a couple things that may help you; here sit down." He helped me to sit propping up pillows behind me. He pulled out a table that fit around the bed and over me. He put the computer on the table and put the books beside me. He walked to the other side of the bed only to lie down again. Now that we completely switched sides, and James was going to rest again, I grabbed one of the books for my class. I read one of the books until I saw James moving a little out of the corner of my eye. I reached over to him, gently running my fingers through his hair. He didn't open his eyes, but a grin did grow on his face. I pushed the table away and scooted down to lay with him. He took my hand and kissed it.

Jake walked in, "Hey, you two, time to get up. Clarissa wants us all upstairs for dinner." Jake's face brightened when he saw that I was awake, "You're up already?"

I held up one finger to let him know I needed a minute.

"No, not another minute, she wants us to come up now."

He came to sit on the bed next to me, disconnecting the IV lines, "Sarah, when you gain, at least, 12 lbs we will take these out, but not until then. You have to be improving a lot more than this. We will step on the scale tonight to check."

I glanced back at James, as Jake helped me move my feet. I didn't want to leave without James.

"Sarah, I will get him up. Let me help you first."

Jake had good intentions, but I was not happy leaving my James here, especially not letting him know that I was going to head out without him. Jake wasn't giving me a choice as he helped me up, "Sarah, bathroom and I will get him up."

Not really needing to use the bathroom again I tried to protest, but Jake wasn't going to take no for an answer. I finally caved and decided that maybe it was a good idea if I was going to spend a lot of time at the main house. When I came out, James was sitting on the side of the bed, and Jake was gone. I didn't have to leave without my sweet James.

There was a gleam in his eyes as they met mine, "I have to take you upstairs for dinner."

He was happy to see me, but the deep purple beneath his eyes told me something else, "Tired?"

"Yeah, but I feel better."

It did make me happy that he was smiling with the most amazing smile in the world. I loved the way his lips slightly thinned when he smiled, and those dimples that sat just outside his smile were breathtaking to me.

"Do you want to change out of the swim suit?"

I nodded.

He got up and pulled out sweat shorts and a t-shirt. Then he got a pair of underwear out and held them up looking at me over the top.

I shook my head no.

"What! I would like to see you in these."
I still shook my head no, but smiling at him.
He laughed a little, "Do you want help or do it by yourself?"
I swallowed and took a deep breath, "Self."
He smiled and laid them down on the other stuff.

When I was ready I walked to the living room, but he wasn't there. I walked out the patio doors, and he was waiting there for me, "That didn't take long."

I shook my head no.

"There are a lot of steps; do you want to try walking them, or do you want me to carry you, or do you want a piggy back?"

I nodded hoping he would understand it was the last one. He turned away from me and squatted. He understood. I climbed on and he brought me up. He let me down when we got to the top. We walked in; James had my hand in his. He kissed it as we went through the door. We heard voices from the kitchen. We walked in, and they were all sitting at the table. There were two chairs for us left open, and one of them had a pillow for me to sit on. He helped me to sit down. Everyone had plates except for me. Josie was at the table, so I knew Wilson was here. He walked in from the other room and back to the kitchen. I heard him speaking as everyone was eating. James was putting food on his plate but kept his chair slightly turned to me.

Wilson was coming in now, "Sorry, Sarah, we are still monitoring how much you eat." He put a plate in front of me, "I measured everything out, so you will have a well-balanced meal."

I just felt stupid, and I hated that I was treated special. James stopped and leaned into me more whispering, "Settle down, we need to make sure you are eating enough to get better. Eat please; try to eat it all; it's only 3 cups of food."

I looked at him, but heard Clarissa, "Sarah, it is okay. It's only temporary. Get the 12 pounds put on, and then you can eat on your own."

I know it didn't make a lot of sense, but she could tell me to jump off a bridge, and I would want to do it for her. She just had this amazing way with me, and I wanted to make her happy. She encouraged me more, "Take your time. We have all night."

I was completely relieved. James was to my left, and he put his right hand under the table to take my left hand. He traced his fingers over mine as we were eating. I noticed how everybody was very comfortable and when I got to Jake, he was uncomfortable. He seemed to be more aware of everyone. He glanced and noticed me watching him. He lowered his eyebrow to acknowledge me. I searched every face around the table and then back to him. After I got back to him, he did the same thing. He took a little more time stopping at each person to take them in. He started to smile, and as he got back to me a grin grew on his face. I felt a shiver go down my spine. It was almost like you could read what everybody was feeling. James noticed, he swallowed carefully, and leaned more to whisper to me, "What's going on?"

Not only was this very confusing, it was downright eerie. As I shrugged my shoulders for James, I caught Clarissa watching me, grinning, almost like she knew what we were feeling. Next I glanced at Carl, but I was relieved that he was paying attention to Clarissa. That was the perfect opportunity to really look him over. The similarity between James and his father was very evident. I couldn't be happier about this, because if James aged like his father, he would be hot for a long time even when we get old.

James chuckled, "Sarah, I feel everything now."

I don't know if I was more embarrassed about checking out his dad or thinking about how hot James was going to stay. When James and I heard Jake burst out laughing we turned to glare at him, but he wasn't the only one enjoying my thoughts. I could see smiles on Clarissa's, Carl's, Sam's, and Tamara's faces. Why was Clarissa smiling? She was like me, normal, wasn't she? But yet I could feel that they all enjoyed that I thought Carl was hot and James was going to be, too. James pulled me into him, "Sarah, do you feel that?"

Not really knowing what I was feeling, other than thinking that I married a guy that was going to stay hot for years, I shrugged my shoulders.

"Do you feel them?"

I shook my head no.

"Sarah, I feel it. You know what they are feeling!"

I shrugged my shoulders again. He was paying more attention to me, while I ignored what I was feeling just trying to finish eating. When we were done I moved to the kitchen and grabbed a towel to help Wilson.

"Oh no, you don't; I won't have it."

I hated that I was being such a burden, "I want to help."

He shook his head at me and pushed me to sit down. James came out and grabbed a towel to help him. Wilson was surprised when James went out to help him, but even more surprised that Jake joined the two of them. The three of them worked together to clean everything up. Josie had her hand on her chest and warmth in her eyes; you could almost see the happiness.

After everything was done, we moved outside to a large fire pit. Jake, James, and Sam all got it ready. Wilson and Carl were sitting close to each other. Josie and Clarissa sat on the outsides of them. Tamara was roasting marshmallows. Sam was texting on his phone. I knew who he was texting. I inquired within my mind, *"Amelia?"*

Sam was surprised, as his eyes came up to meet mine with misery sweeping over his face, and he nodded thinking, *"I need to go home."*

I quickly looked around to see if anyone else felt that. I could see a slight smile on Clarissa's face, as she stared at him adoringly. I glanced up at Jake, who didn't seem to get that vibe from Sam. I quickly turned to evaluate James's face. He showed no signs of knowing what just happened. He must have taken it that I needed him. His arms wrapped around me with strength and comfort. I let it go and snuggled into James's body resting my head on his chest and closed my eyes to enjoy the moment.

## James:

I loved that she was comfortable to be in my arms. I didn't like when she was upset, and this was so good. I didn't touch her for fear she would move away from me.

Tamara was finally settling down and moved to sit with Jake. I tried to let him know that I appreciated that he was nice to her. Tamara was very happy as she said, "He's nice to me, James."

It was going to be weird no matter what; Jake was our brother. She curled up in his lap. He traced his fingers through her hair, as he watched his Dad and my Dad talking. I noticed Sarah's breathing was getting deeper hinting that she was sleeping. Quickly glancing at Jake, I indicated that I needed help getting up with her.

His attention was back to me almost like he felt what I was wanting, "Is she sleeping?"

I nodded.

Tamara was still moving a little. Jake was going to get up, but I shook my head no, "Wait till she is sleeping."

Dad got up and came to take Tamara from his arms. He was walking back to the house to put her down, and Jake came to help me, but he put his hand out instead of taking Sarah from me. I was able to stand holding her. I didn't like that I had to depend on his help still, but I did take it. I held my grin in, as I glanced at Clarissa, "Good night for skinny dipping?"

She smiled at me almost embarrassed.

Sam stood up, "I am out of here."

I nudged him, "Hey, stay with us. We'll play pool or something after we get Sarah to bed."

That was something for him to be excited about. I knew he was missing Amelia. Sam took off toward the house, while I followed with Sarah in my arms. She nuzzled into me more putting her face at my neck. I loved when she showed me affection. I wanted to hold her forever like this. She was calm and had no pain in her heart. Sam was holding the gate as I walked through. Jake was on my heels not saying a word. I could handle this on my own.

"James, I have to hook up the IV again."

God that was weird; did he feel what I was thinking? Sam continued to open doors for me to go through. I got to the room and laid her down and tucked her in. Moving out of Jake's way he hooked her back up in a few seconds. This was going to be a trying night. She was so confused about her feelings, and yet she loved me so deeply I found it trying on my nerves. I didn't want her to be sad anymore, and I wanted her to let me love and touch her. I stood there not wanting to leave, as Jake headed to the door only stopping to ask, "Are you coming?"

I nodded, "Yeah, be there in a minute."

"James, she's sleeping."

I stared at my baby sleeping there, "I know I will be right out." I traced my hand on her cheek. She nuzzled into my touch. I leaned over her to kiss her forehead, but when she felt my lips she moved her face up to mine. She still had her eyes closed, but I touched my lips to hers. My heart was racing; she was letting me touch her lips, so sweet and so soft. I traced hers with mine watching her. She pressed her lips against my top lip. I could hardly breathe, but I pressed my mouth against her moving my lips between hers as softly as I could. I leaned over her more moving my hand to the other side of her. She moved her lips against mine again. I moved to her whole mouth. She moved her hand to my chest. She didn't want more, but she liked the kissing. I reached for her stomach; I wanted to please her, and she liked that before. She tilted her head back when I started to rub her stomach. She licked and bit her bottom lip, but she was rolling away from me. I lay down next to her carefully, but continued to rub her stomach. The noise she was making was amazingly satisfying. I rubbed her stomach more, and she hugged the pillow next to her. I whispered in her ear. "I love you." And that did not begin to fully explain how I felt about her.

    She turned her face towards me. I kissed the corner of her mouth. Her hand came to touch my cheek, almost to lure me in, as she leaned back to me. My body was touching hers. I closed my eyes to enjoy this slight touch of her next to me. I had to breathe, but I thought it might alert her. I tried to do it very slowly. Her mouth was searching for mine. I rubbed her stomach more, as her hand grabbed mine pushing it to her harder. It felt good to her. I touched her lips again, but she opened her mouth to mine. I kissed her more, licking, taunting, and kissing them. I was getting caught up in her, and I was already incredibly aroused. I knew I had to stop; I had to refuse to give into the passion. She was letting me get closer than I have been in a long time. I pushed to her stomach harder, and she gasped, but I felt no pain within her. Her hand guided mine where she wanted me to be, and I let her lead me in what she wanted. My heart was racing causing pounding thuds that echoed in my ears. She was really enjoying this, and the darkness wasn't sweeping over her. I traced her jaw with my mouth and under her chin. She was getting aroused with me, and I could feel her passion. I really knew I needed to move away from her, but she was really enjoying this, and it was far better than I could remember. To touch her was like heaven to me. Her mouth came back to mine.

    "Are you coming?" Jake was walking back in determined to end my time with her. I raised my head to glance at him. He shook his head no. I kissed her again to show him that she was responding to me, and then I glanced at him, but he wasn't leaving. He shook his head no. I didn't want to listen to him. She was responding, and I needed this so badly.

    "Damn it, Jake, get out." I regretted opening my mouth the instant I did it. She opened her eyes, which locked on mine for a split second, long enough to see a slight smile cross her face and then a touch of fear, before rolling away from me. My heart sank. She was done instantly. I put my head down to rest it against her back, "Jake, I will be there in a minute."

    She was done and I felt it. I closed my eyes to compose myself, so that I could get up. I knew he was still standing there almost demanding that I get up now. "Jake, I said in a minute."

    "James, now." He was really beginning to piss me off.

"OUT!"

He turned and walked out. I leaned over my sweet Sarah to whisper to her, "Are you okay?"

I knew she was. The darkness wasn't there in her heart.

She grinned, "Yes, sleep now."

I kissed her cheek, but I was feeling so good now. I got up and went to take a cold shower. I was so aroused by her that I had to cool off. It took a little longer than I thought, because when I went to the living room Jake was steaming.

"James, don't you think it's too early for any of that?"

I rolled my eyes disgusted, "Jake, I wouldn't have..."

"You were aroused by her?"

"That doesn't mean anything would happen. She just liked it, and I couldn't stop with making her feel good."

"Yeah, that's what got you two in trouble last time."

I stared at him realizing that he was right; I was pleasing her. I wanted to make her feel good and nothing else mattered, "You're right. I will be more careful."

"Damn right you will be more careful. We're talking at least 14 weeks of being careful, and if you are doing what I thought you were doing... that is not being careful."

I laughed, "Fourteen weeks, how about eighteen months."

Surprised by my answer, Jake stopped his rant instantly.

"Jake, I know it's going to be hard, but this was too much for her, and I wouldn't want to put her through this again."

"Then why were you doing that?"

What the hell was he talking about?

He was really pissed at me, "You were touching her."

"No, I was rubbing her stomach, Jake. She is like a little puppy that needs its tummy rubbed. It makes her feel good."

"You weren't..."

"No, but you are right; I was getting hot for her, but the cold showers work. I just waited and took what she would give me."

"I don't like it. You should be more careful."

"She gives me very little, Jake. I had to take what she would give me."

"No, James, you need to control yourself better."

Actually, I had him and his bad timing to control me, "You have impeccable timing."

His anger subsided into laughter, "You want to know what is weird?"

I couldn't wait to hear this.

"I could feel that you were getting too hot to handle it."

"What?"

"I felt that you were ready to push further, and that's why I thought you did."

"What do you mean you felt it?"

"She does too, James. At dinner she was noticing it, and I could feel her notice it. We could read everyone's minds especially each other's. I don't know how to explain it, but I knew what she was thinking.

I was really confused now, "Jake, you are not part of my family, and you are having feelings?"

"I don't know, I guess. I really never paid attention to it."

"Have you felt anything before you met Sarah?"

He stood there thinking about it, "Maybe, that's why I hate the nurses. I always felt like they were thinking things, sexy things, about me. It was a huge turn off."

I couldn't help but laugh. I got him off the subject of me and Sarah, so I was happy now.

We went to the game room to play pool and darts. It was late before I went back to bed. I crawled into bed with my wife and smiled to myself with satisfaction, as I laid down putting my hands behind my head. I wore sleeping trousers to protect myself from her and wanting to be with her. I took one last glance at her. To my surprise she was watching me intently. I rolled to my side, "Did I wake you?"

She smiled at me and shook her head no. I saw those beautiful green eyes penetrating mine. I instantly wanted to pull her to me, to roll under the sheets with her and kiss her until tomorrow. I turned away from her and closed my eyes, "Can you still sleep?"

I didn't hear her, so I had to turn to her. Her feelings weren't telling me anything either. I gave in and rolled to her taking her in. I was relieved that this was what she wanted. I rolled to my back and closed my eyes. I reached for her hand and pulled it to my mouth and kissed the back if it. I prayed for sleep to come swiftly, because I really wanted her tonight, and I knew it was wrong to have these feelings, at least right now. I felt her touch on my arm so light and tender.

I cringed, "Sarah, honey. I am really hot for you, so you need to not touch me, please."

She gripped harder almost digging in. I opened my eyes and turned to her, "What's wrong?"

She had fear in her eyes. I must be turned on, because I didn't feel the pain. She curled up more.

"What do you want me to do?" The pain was growing, so my desire must be subsiding. "I will go get Jake."

She shook her head no. She rolled to her back and pulled my hand to her stomach.

"Please, Sarah, tell me."

She closed her eyes and moved my hand over her stomach.

"You need my help?"

She nodded. Her breathing was hard. I started to rub her stomach watching her face. The grimace on it and the pain I was feeling from her was eye opening for me. She was gripping the blankets in her hands. I moved to sit up to message with both hands watching her. The tears were starting to drip out the sides of her eyes.

I had to yell, "JAKE, are you still awake?"

He came running in, "What did you do?"

Defending myself I shouted, "Nothing, she is in pain!"

She moaned and then relaxed. She opened her eyes, "Sorry, hurt badly. Better now."

Jake directed her with determination, "You need to go to the bathroom now, but Sarah, did it release?"

He helped her up; she was nodding, and I ran to open the bathroom door. He was talking to her, "Sarah, I really need to look at it. I know you don't like that but just this time."

After she entered the bathroom all I could do was stare at Jake with a question on my face.

"I gave her medicine to help it clot, but they were getting too big and painful, so I cut back. She said she had no more clotting, but that is what must have happened. That's why having her stomach massaged feels so good to her. It helps to loosen it… to get rid of it."

I took a deep breath. I was relieved that it wasn't something worse.

She came out, and I took her in my arms to help her back to bed. I tucked her back in, and she closed her eyes immediately. I moved back to the bathroom.

Jake peaked out, "Do you get squeamish?"

Trying to not make him feel stupid, I just shook my head.

"Do you want to see what was causing the pain?"

I changed my mind. Maybe I do get squeamish. It didn't matter that I was shaking my head no. He pulled me in and looked down, "See James that is why she was in so much pain until it released."

I glanced down and it was huge, the size of a softball. I looked away right away, "That came from her?"

"Changes your mind about being with her, doesn't it?"

I glared at him, even though I agreed with him on this.

"I won't give her any clotting medicine any more, but she will bleed more without it."

"With all this bleeding, won't she become anemic?"

This time I surprised him, "Yeah."

"She needs more red meat."

Now he was hesitant.

I grinned, "I do know a little. Do you think she needs blood?"

"Not yet… and if we can keep her eating, then probably not. That and rest, James, will help the most. See you in the morning."

I nodded and crawled back into bed. I had a hard time falling asleep; I was worried about her now more than ever.

# 40. A Little Fun

## Sarah:

**I** laid here with my eyes closed wondering what day it was. I think Wednesday, but it could have been Tuesday or Thursday for all I knew. I slept more than I was awake.

James was still sleeping, and I didn't want to wake him. I grabbed my book and highlighter and started to go through it. I traced the back end of the marker down James's arm; he didn't move. I read through another page before glancing over at him again. This time I took the marker and traced his ear. He moved his hand to swish it away. I covered my mouth to handle the giggle. Waiting till he fell deep into sleep again I read through another page. Now, how was I going to pick on him? I grabbed a Kleenex from the headboard and dangled it to touch his nose. He rubbed his face. I quickly went back to reading ignoring him. I could tell he opened his eyes, but I tried to look like I was very much into my book. He didn't say anything, and he closed his eyes turning away from me. I read through two pages this time to make sure he went back to sleep fully. I dangled the Kleenex right next to his ear. He went to grab it, but I pulled back quickly and started to read another page, as he rolled over to face me. He evaluated me with a distrusting glare, so I looked down and smiled politely. He closed his eyes, and I read two more pages. I took a deep breath and dangled the Kleenex along his face. He grabbed me instantly pulling me down to lay beside him.

"So you like to tease in the morning, do you?"

I giggled, but between the fast movement and the giggling I wrapped my hand against my mid-section to hold it. He let go just as quickly as he grabbed me. I was still smiling, but he was worried, "I hurt you?"

I wrinkled my nose at him. He came in pressing his lips to mine and took my breath away kissing me quickly and passionately. I touched his chest to remind him to take it easy. His kiss slowed until he pulled away from me. I licked my lips and bit my lower one. I didn't want to push him away, but he moved so quickly it startled me. I was waiting for him to respond. Just seeing the tenderness in his eyes filled my heart.

"I love you, Sarah." He kissed my nose, and rolled away from me jogging to the bathroom. I thought to myself that he was aroused with that little bit of teasing, but the shower never started. I heard the toilet flush and the water turn on in the sink. I put my book aside and pushed to get up. The sound of water made me have to go. I had a little pain as I stood, but made it up the stairs on my own, but I did have to hold my stomach. He must have felt the pain, because he opened the door looking at me with fear in his eyes, "Are you okay?"

Really needing to go right now I nodded and blurted out, "Bathroom, water." Trying not to do the potty dance I moved to go around him. He leaned into me skimming my arm as I went by, he whispering, "Oh my god, little girl, I am so in love with you."

I stopped at the door and lovingly gazed at him. Taking a step towards him I wrapped my arms around his neck and tried to hug him with all the tubes wrapping and twisting around us.

"Hey, you said bathroom."

I was happy, as he wrapped one arm around my waist pulling me closer so that we got lost in the ocean of each other's eyes. Everything he gave me distracted me from life. He let go, helping me untangle a little, and moved away from me chuckling.

I took care of everything I wanted to do and was ready to walk out, but hesitated as I spotted the scale. Wanting to gain weight, wanting to get better; I took a deep breath and got on it... 106. Did I gain 3 lbs? I came out feeling excited and pleased with myself. I couldn't wait to tell James that I was getting better. He was lying back on the bed with his arm over his eyes till he heard me. He sat up quickly, "Well?"

I gave him a disapproving glance.

"You stepped on the scale?"

I hated that he felt everything. It was so hard to keep anything from him. Now I didn't feel so excited to share with him. I wanted him to suffer a little for eavesdropping on my feelings. I slowly made it back to the bed carrying my tubes with me. He rolled over to his side to keep his eyes on me waiting for an answer, "Are you going to tell me?"

He was going to pay for snooping, so I shook my head no.

"You lost more? There isn't anything left to lose."

I smiled and went down the steps slowly watching him. He was moving to help me, "Wait... don't come back to bed; we need breakfast." He got up and grabbed the tube and started to guide me to the living room. He was pushing, and I grabbed the door to stop him in protest.

"Sarah?"

I turned around eyeing him.

"What?" He wasn't happy with me, but he was trying to stay in control to not show his disappointment.

Placing my hand on his chest, I took a deep breath in order to get this out, "Gained."

His face changed expressions as I watched. First he smiled; then he got a really serious look, and finally a distrustful look, "How much?"

I held up three fingers.

He shook his head, "Not good enough. Let's have breakfast."

Jake was sitting at the table, "Hey, I was just told to come get you up. My dad has a huge breakfast for you, crapes or something."

James was not going to ruin this for me. I gained weight, and that was good. I gave Jake the biggest grin, while holding up three fingers.

"Three what?"

James took over, "She thinks she gained 3 lbs." He said this with a disbelieving tone in his voice, and I think I even saw his eyes roll a little, so I gave him the biggest frown I could come up with.

Jake's attention came to me inquiring, "What did you weigh?"

I took a deep breath, as James pulled me in front of him holding my hips, and we walked to him. I was able to get it out fine, "106 lbs."

He shook his head, "That's only 2 lbs."

Jake seemed to agree with James that it wasn't good enough. I shrugged my shoulders still smiling.

"Make that 12 more, and I will take you off the IVs."

He did have to bring up the IVs crushing my good mood. Why were they both trying to ruin my good day?

"Sarah, come here so we can disconnect you for now."

I couldn't help but let the smile stay on my face. I didn't lose any weight, so that was good, no matter how they felt about it. I walked to the table as James pulled out a chair for me, but I hesitated with the thought of sitting on the chair again, so I moved slowly. James was helping me to sit, but pulled me back to my feet, "Just a minute. I will get you a pillow." Just grabbing one from the couch it wasn't long before I was comfortably getting the IV lines disconnected from the ports.

"Sorry, Sarah. You will have to deal with this a little longer. We will only hook you up during nap times and bed time to make it more convenient for you; but only as long as you continue to eat and make some progress to gaining weight."

I wondered, "What about school?"

"Well, you've got two and half weeks to gain 12 lbs; let's see if my dad can help with that."

I wasn't happy, but I didn't have much of a choice.


When we got upstairs James let me down. It was a lot easier to get up the stairs if James carried me. After we all made our way into the kitchen

Jake stopped by his dad while I moved around the table hugging Clarissa from behind her.

"Oh, sweetheart, how was your first night downstairs?"

I kissed her cheek, as a grin grew on her face. She took my hand to bring me around to evaluate me from head to toe.

I was very happy this morning, "Really good."

She was pleased with me, that I could see it on her face, "You are trying harder again today?"

I was eager to please her more than James, Jake, or myself.

"Wilson, do you have Sarah's plate?"

He walked over and set it in front of me. It was a small crepe with strawberries and whipped cream on top. I also had two sausage links. No one else had sausage. I searched around the table making sure I wasn't just imagining it and glanced back at her.

"I think you need more protein, dear; now eat."

I ate the whole plateful, and she was beaming as I ate. Now I was overly full and could tell my stomach didn't like it much, because it was gurgling.

Clarissa's eyes darted to me when she heard it, "Maybe that was too much food."

I put my hand to my stomach and nodded.

"Wilson, we're back down to three and half cups next time."

I gave her a dejected expression.

"Yes, I was bad and we upped your intake to four cups. We won't push so hard next time.

I tried to forget that they gave me too much, so I blurted out, "I gained."

Clarissa raised her eyebrows with a question on her face, "Sarah, 2 lbs is not enough."

How did she know that? We didn't tell her. When I turned to James wondering if he told her I was surprised to see his mouth was hanging open. Jake had stopped eating too, to stare at her.

She just continued to talk not paying attention to our reaction, "Well, Wilson has lunch and dinner figured out; what are you thinking you would do today?"

I stumbled for an answer, "Study."

That seemed to please her, but she reminded me, "School doesn't start till next week. You should take it easy. "

"I like to be ready."

I almost laughed when she turned to James asking, "And you?"

He acted like she had scolded him, hanging his head low, "Yeah, I will open the books too, MOM."

We started to laugh together. I thought I was doing ok until the food started turning in my stomach and working its way up. It didn't want to stay down. I grabbed my stomach feeling horribly ill.

"Hey, stop that Sarah. You may want to lie down and let the food settle." She was scolding a little, but it wasn't so bad when she continued, "We're going boating today; did you want to come with?"

I nodded, but Jake did not approve, "Not yet. More rest for Sarah before she should be on the lake. Sorry."

Now I was pouting, and even though the feeling in my stomach was rumbling the distraction kept things from surfacing.

Clarissa smiled, "Maybe next time. You need to go down and rest your stomach."

James helped me down stairs gently setting me down at the bottom of the steps. I walked in on my own into the apartment.

I sat carefully on the couch; Sam followed in, "Jake, are you coming with us?"

He turned to me as if to ask for my permission, so of course I nodded encouragingly. There was no reason to make everyone else miss out just because I couldn't go.

He turned to James, "And you?"

James didn't flinch, or look at me when he answered Jake. "Nope, I am staying here."

He had to stay with me if Jake was going. James went in the room and came out with my books and computer. He set up the table and moved it in front of me. I glanced up at him to see if he was pouting like me for not being able to go, but he walked away and got his books moving to the table.

Jake came over and hooked me back up. After he was changed and ready to go, he stopped before heading out the door. He glanced back and forth between us, "Are you sure you don't want me to stay?"

I shook my head no. I liked spending time alone with James as long as we didn't get carried away. I was relieved to hear James reply, "No, we'll behave. We won't have you here to interrupt us."

I couldn't stop myself from a giggle.

Jake rolled his eyes in disgust, "Sam, let's go."

Sam was quiet but moved to the door. He hesitated at the door and then turned back to say something. I don't think he could say what he wanted to because he shook his head grinning and then walked out.

Avoiding getting caught up in James I started reading right away. Turning on the computer while I was busy had been a pleasant reminder of how much I loved James. The song *Smile* came on as the computer sat ready for use. It did make me smile each and every time I heard it.

"Do you like that?"

All my attention went to this man that I loved so deeply. Words could not even touch the surface of what I felt for him. I gestured that I approved but quickly went back to reading. I went through two chapters before I let myself check on James. He was still busy so I took a notebook out and started back at chapter one and took notes. When I finished chapter one I tore out a piece of paper and crumpled it up into a ball.

I peeked over at James and he looked miserably engulfed in the book. I tossed it towards him but didn't even get close. I tore out another piece crumpling it and tried again. This time I got a little further.

"Sarah, you're going to hurt yourself. Stop it."

He was actually scolding me. He was in for it now. I tore out another piece and crumpled it, but this time when I glanced over he was gone. I searched in every direction for him, but I couldn't see him, "James?"

It was silent, so I pouted. I closed the computer and put it on the table, and pushed the lot away from me. To the best of my ability, I strained my neck to see if I could find him, but still no James. If he wasn't playful this was going to be a very long boring day. I decided to give up and lie down to sulk.

It didn't take long before I felt him tickle my feet. I pulled them up a little and it hurt, but I was happy he was giving me attention. I threw the last crumpled piece down at him, as he popped up by my feet.

He came crawling up the couch over top of me, "You are feisty today."

I shook my head no.

"You are board?"

I nodded.

"I have something to tell you."

I felt uneasiness move into my chest. He was hovering over me and Jake wasn't here to break it up. Shit, what did I do?

"We need to shave your legs."

That wasn't what I was expecting at all. I was totally embarrassed and covered my face.

"Hey, you have been sick. I will help you."

I shook my head no.

"I won't look; it's okay. Sarah, look at me."

I kept my hands over my face.

He nudged under them with his nose, "Come on, Sarah, if we can talk about pooping, we can shave your legs. That's not even half as bad." He tried to kiss me, so I bit him.

He moved away from me, "You bit me."

I smiled, "Not hard."

He laughed and moved away from me, "Okay, but later you are letting me help you."

I shook my head no.

He picked me up, "Okay, we are doing it now. Then we will watch a movie."

I couldn't believe him. We got to the bathroom, and he set me down, carefully, on the toilet, "Is this okay?"

I glanced up at him stunned that he was going to do this. He went to the basket and pulled out a can of shaving cream for the female gender. I shook my head at him and held both sides to help keep myself upright. I was a little uncomfortable from sitting and moving around.

He noticed, "Do we need to hurry?"

I nodded.

He sat at my feet and pulled one foot to rest on his thigh. He had a cup of water, the shaver, and a wet washcloth. He glanced up at me, "I don't know how to do this."

I smiled at him, but I was bracing myself from the pain and got out, "Your idea."

"Okay, hurry, right?" He sprayed some stuff on my leg, and then a little more. He had a very serious and concentrated smirk on his face, "This doesn't look like much."

I shrugged my shoulders. I usually didn't use this stuff. I watched, as he started to rub it on. It lathered, and lathered, and lathered even more. He was laughing, "Okay, less next time."

I nodded.

He took the shaver and went really carefully up the back of my calf and then checked with me, "That okay?"

I nodded approvingly, but I still could not believe he was doing this. He continued till the whole leg was done. He took the washcloth and wiped my leg clean. He carefully put it down taking the other one to rest on him. He used a little less this time. He was really getting into this, as I watched him concentrating on what he was doing. He finished that leg and wiped it with the washcloth. He put my foot back on the ground and then looked up at me satisfied, "You're all fixed up." I think he was checking his work because he was running his hands up and down my calves. He seemed to be handling this better than I could. He got up on his knees putting both hands on my thighs gazing at me, "Sarah, you are going to think I am weird."

He's not weird; he was amazing. I didn't understand what he was talking about, "Why?"

He grinned sinfully as a glimmer of light danced in his eyes finally sharing why he was weird, "I am totally turned on right now."

Feeling completely guilty for putting him through that, I ran my hands through his hair.

"No, don't be sad. We're supposed to be able to talk about everything."

Complete wondering how I can even believe that he was real I cracked a slight smile.

"I just wanted you to know, that I am crazy about every inch of you. It's a good thing."

Not wanting to burst his bubble, but yet I did not want to get wrapped up in him I had to remind him of what would come, "Pain."

A huge grin came over his face, "Yeah, I know. That's why we're going to get you back to the couch; I will clean this up after that."

He stood up helping me up. I stopped him at the door.

"You clean up. I'm okay."

Not wanting to let go he was hesitant, "You want to do it by yourself?"

I nodded as I trudged to the living room. He wanted to play and I was antsy so I changed my direction heading to the fridge. I somehow knew he would have a can of whipped topping. There were two in the fridge. I grabbed one and made it to the couch tucking it away for future use. When he came out he put a movie in and came to sit on the floor in front of me.

He carefully pulled my legs over his shoulders, "Is this okay?"

"Yes." But I was pouting. I felt bad that I made him hot and bothered and I couldn't do anything to help him.

About an hour into the movie he started to trace his hands over my calves, almost messaging them. I leaned my head back and closed my eyes to enjoy his touch. As he did this I became more and more relaxed to the point of dozing off. He woke me up when the movie was over, but only so he could put in another one. He moved back to me and noticed I was tired. He wiped the hair from my forehead, "Were you sleeping?"

Not wanting him to know that I was I shook my head no.

"You are a terrible liar."

Not waiting for my response he turned putting my legs over his shoulder again, "Is this comfortable?"

I stroked my fingers through his hair. He tilted his head back rubbing my calves, "You like this?"

I was happy, "I like being with you."

He pulled my leg up and kissed it then moved to get up. I pushed him back down, "No, James, nap."

He turned more to me, "Do you want to go to bed?"

"Nope."

He smiled and turned back around sitting to watch another movie. He continued to rub and message my calves tracing his hand over them until I was almost sleeping again. It wasn't until my foot jerked away that I realized he had traced his finger along the bottom of my foot. That was my most ticklish spot so I scolded him for waking me, "James!"

"You're ticklish."

"No!"

He waited a short while and he did it again.

This time I had to move my foot to the ground to scratch it, "James!" I pulled his head back, "Not fair."

He was totally smiling and maybe laughing a little, "Okay, Okay. I'll behave."

I pushed his head forward. He waited until I was almost asleep again, and he did it another time.

This was what I was waiting for. I pulled back his head and sprayed whipped topping down his nose.

"You did not just do that."

I still had my finger on it in case he came at me. He wiped it off turning around. He would attack me now so I had to stop him. I sprayed his face again.

"You are in for it, little girl."

I shook my head, "Not fair. No, James."

"You sprayed me with whipped cream, and I don't play fair?"

I smiled, but grabbing my stomach, "Ouch, James, Ouch."

He was pulling me down to him, so he could hover better.

"You are so faking; I can feel your pain, Sarah."

"No, James, NO. OUCH!"

Jake walked in and heard me saying ouch. He was coming to rescue me. I could feel him; he was going to punch James's lights out.

James held up his arm and looked at Jake, "Don't even think about it. She started it, and she is really not in any pain."

I pleaded to Jake, "Help! Not fighting fair."

James wiped his face on my shirt. I tried to push him away. I was having little sharp pains from moving my stomach so much.

Jake leaned on the back of the couch, "You both stayed here, so she could rest."

James and I had the same thought. He grabbed for the can of whipped topping the same time I lifted it and we sprayed Jake with it together. He stood there not saying a word. I squirted some on my finger and stuck it in his mouth, laughing carefully at him. James put his face into my chest, wiping more of it on me. When he lifted his face from my body I held up the can for James. He opened his mouth like a baby birdie and I shot some into his mouth. He crawled towards me and kissed my mouth as messy as he could make it. When he released me we both laughed and I kissed his cheek to share the mess.

We were laughing together but we both turned to Jake.

He was not happy at all. "This is irresponsible, childish, and completely violating the taking it easy rule for Sarah!" He seemed a little more upset than he needed to be. I wish he would relax more and have some fun, do something unexpected.

I don't know who was more surprised by Jakes reaction. As he was scolding us he did something that neither of us could believe. He was licking his fingers that were wiping the Whipped Topping from his face. James and I both busted out laughing and that was when he took a more playful tone, "You two are going to so get it when you least expect it."

I held the can up and sprayed it at him again. He got quite the look on his face and then a flash of something, "Wait, Sam was right behind me."

He ran to the fridge, "I wondered why these were in here." He grabbed one and ran to the door. James took the one I had, did one squirt at me, and ran to the door. Sam walked in and they both doused him in whipped cream. He stood there and took it. They sprayed him from head to toe. When they both stopped he just stood there.

He wiped his face with his hands, which didn't help a whole lot, "Mom is going to kill you both."

We all started to laugh, except for Sam; he just walked out.

Jake's face showed that he was done having fun for now, "I'm taking a shower. Mom wants us upstairs for lunch."

I was pushing myself up to go get changed. I slowly walked to the room with James on my heels. I stopped at the dresser to get a few things as he put his arms around me.

"James, no."

He pulled me closer tracing his hand down my neck and whispered in my ear, "Sarah, take a shower with me."

I wanted to but fear kept me focused so I shook my head no. That is how we get into trouble every time. "No, Clarissa wants us upstairs now."

He bent down to wrap his arms around me carefully and kissed me lightly, "I would be good you know."

I nodded turning to him, "Too good... I wouldn't behave."

The smile grew on his face as his eyes closed. He let go of me only to place his hands on his heart as he walked backwards into the bathroom. He was still in a playful mood.

After wiping my face clean I got changed and started on my way without them. I wasn't going to get into trouble with Clarissa for taking too long. I slowly went up one step at a time. The pain wasn't too bad. Sitting was defiantly worse.

When I walked into the kitchen by myself, I noticed the stern look on her face, "You started it?"

I don't understand my need for being completely honest with her, but I nodded.

"Did you get Jake?"

I couldn't help myself and I grinned while nodding

She smiled, "How bad?"

"He's taking a shower."

She started to laugh and so did Carl. Carl stood up to help me find a seat with a cushion. He kissed my forehead, "You are the one recovering, and you bring joy to their lives."

Surprised with their reactions I tried to explain, "Needed to laugh… good for stomach muscles."

Wilson brought me a separate plate again, and we started to eat. Mine was an omelet with steak and fresh tomatoes dices on top, and two slices of toast heavily buttered.

Sam was the first one to the table. Carl and Clarissa were holding back the laughter, because you could tell he wasn't happy.

"Sam."

He was very angry as he turned to glare in my direction. I patted a chair next to me. I wanted to make him feel better. He made his way to me and plopped down on the chair next to me with a disgruntled expression on his face. Wilson walked in and put a can of whipped topping in front of him. Carl, Clarissa, and Wilson all started to laugh. I put my arm around him the best I could; I didn't even crack a smile. I felt so bad for him.

Tamara walked in, "I get to play next time. Sam tasted good."

That did it for me; I had to laugh, but only because she was so cute in the way that she said it. I glanced back at Sam, "Think of something better."

Clarissa scolded me, "Sarah, don't encourage him."

Full of conviction I held firm, "He has to."

The other two walked in together. James came to me and kissed my forehead. He was so much like his dad. "You got up here by yourself."

I was proud of myself but explained, "Very slowly."

Satisfied he sat down to eat.

I noticed everything Sam wanted, Jake and James got for him. They were trying to make it up to him. He was abusing it, letting them wait on him hand and foot, but they didn't seem to mind.

I was getting tired, since I didn't get much of a nap. Clarissa noticed first, but it was like she was reading me as she asked, "Do you need a nap?"

These feelings were odd. I glanced at Jake to see if he felt it too. His brows were furrowed as he watched her. I knew instantly that he wondered if she could read our feeling also. That was it; I wanted to be alone with her so I could as her what was going on. James was watching me, but I only noticed after searching every ones faces at the table and they landed on his.

He knew what I was feeling and was urgent to get me out of there, "I will take you down if you are ready."

"Yes, please."

He stood and helped me up, "Wilson, I'll be back in a minute to help you."

"No, James; that is why I am here."

"No, Wilson. I will help."

Everything seemed to work like a well-oiled machine. Sam and Jake got up to help Wilson, and I saw Carl take Clarissa's hand. She turned to him smiling and nodding. Tamara got up and went to the kitchen asking Wilson if they could play the animal game on the computer. Wilson, of course, glanced at Carl and Clarissa for approval. They were happy for the distraction so they could sneak off up the stairs as James was giving me a piggy back out the door. When I took one last glance at them, Clarissa knew I was watching. She winked and mouthed, "Passion."

I knew I would have a life time of being happy with my James. I kissed his neck. He turned to try and see my face, "What is that about, little girl?"

I smiled and put my head down on his shoulder, as we went out and down the steps. He walked into the apartment and set me down. I was headed slowly to the room. He was following me. I crawled into bed and curled up to the large pillow. He moved to lie in front of me gazing into my eyes, "You didn't say what the kiss on my neck was for; can you tell me?"

I grinned playfully, "Carl and Clarissa still sneak off to have sex."

He cringed, "You know that isn't something I want to think about."

"James, when we're their age we will still be in love; we will still want sex, and we will still sneak off to be together."

His mouth dropped open, and he just stared at me.

He didn't understand that I needed to know that, "What?"

"That is the most you have said since..." His eyes dropped away from mine. He didn't want to bring it up, but he was really pleased. He was playing with my fingers, as they draped over the pillow. I didn't know how to explain how bad it was, so I just watched him. He took my fingers and sucked and kissed each one at a time, "Take a shower with me, Sarah."

I shook my head no.

He glanced at me from the top of his eyelashes, "I will behave, please. I just need to touch you."

I shook my head no.

"Why?"

Cringing I asked, "Honestly?"

He nodded with a small smile lingering on his lips.

I held up one finger, "Still bleeding... kind of gross."

Warmth, compassion, and complete understanding filled his eyes.

I held up two fingers, "I'm scared I will want to feel you."

Desire twinkled in his eyes.

I held up three fingers, "Afraid of the pain of the contractions when excited."

That deflated all of his hope, but he did chuckle quietly.

I held up four fingers, "Never, ever, want to have to do that again...sucked the life from me." I felt the heaviness move in. It had been a few days since I thought of it, and it didn't take long for the sadness to seep in. I closed my eyes. Now I remembered why it was hard for me to talk.

"No, Sarah. Don't let it in." He was grabbing his chest gasping for air. His pain made me forget almost immediately about my sadness. He rolled to his back taking a deep breath, "Sarah, the connection gets stronger every day."

I pulled the pillow down and touched his chest. He closed his eyes pleased with the touch. I traced his chest to calm him more. He put his hands behind his head and tipped it back. I moved to his abs.

Excited he asked, "I need to feel your touch; do you mind?" He sat up taking his shirt off and laid back down closing his eyes. I traced his body slowly. His muscles tensed with my touch, individually moving. He had lost a lot of weight which I really hadn't notice until now. I watched my fingers move in unison with every hill and valley his body contained while I asked, "Does your mom have feelings?"

He turned his head with wonder, "No, why?"

I traced lower, "She sometimes knows what I am thinking."

He grabbed my hand to stop me from tracing him and turned his face to me, "What do you mean?"

"I can sometimes tell she is listening to my thoughts."

He was very firm, "That is not possible. Do you feel her listening to you?"

"Kind of. It's like we have a connection. Jake feels it too."

He propped himself up resting his head on his hand evaluating me, "Do you know what they are thinking?"

"No, more like if she is unhappy with my reaction... it's like a disapproval, or today when I came up without you and I admitted I started the whipped topping fight, she asked if we got Jake and when I told her yes, the warmth she gave me was very soothing."

"So you think she has feelings because you do?"

I thought about that for a minute, "Oh, sometimes."

"You feel Jake?"

"Yeah, Jake and your mom... I guess."

With a look of worry he seemed unhappy.

"What, James?"

"You feel Jake and not me?"

I understood the face now, "I feel you, but that is all desire. I can't look at you the way I do at them. You are everything that I want to feel."

That seemed to ease the tension that was coming from him.

"I don't feel anything from you, so my thoughts run wild when I look at you."

That made him grin sinfully, but he changed the subject, "We will have to ask her, but you feel things?"

"I guess; I didn't realize that."

He lay back down and pulled my hand back to trace him.

Resuming my strokes over his chest I let him know what I was thinking, "I feel this."

His body was tightening, as I moved over his chest and his abs. When I traced along the top of his pant the smile came back to his face but he scolded, "Girl, what are you doing?"

"I could feel this."

"Don't even go there, little girl. That is how we get in trouble."

I thought about lowering to him. He sat up instantly, "No more of that, and thanks, now I need a shower."

I pulled him back to lie down, "James, you could show me how to please you, just until we could…"

The desire was showing on his face as he regretfully said, "Sarah, I don't think I could handle it."

I unbuttoned his pants and unzipped them, "If you can't, the shower is right there."

"No, I mean I will want you even more and I might…" he closed his eyes liking that I was making a move on him.

I traced my fingers along the edge of his boxers. He relaxed a little and closed his eyes. I wanted to please my man, "Let me do this." I moved closer and traced lower.

His whole body tensed, "Sarah, behave."

Leaning down I whispered, "I think you like this."

With no response from him I moved myself closer to him. I whispered in his ear, "Promise you won't push me."

He opened his eyes, "Of course not."

Soothing him with my stare, I crawled my fingers to touch him. He took a deep breath and stopped me. He pulled me away from him. He rolled to me tracing his hand down my side and nudged my cheek with his nose, "Sarah, I will want more."

I didn't want him to push me further than I could handle but I needed to make my husband feel like my husband. I was tormented on what to do.

"Sarah?"

I let my eyes drift to his. What was he going to say to make this better?

"You want to please me?"

I nodded.

Watching me carefully he took my hand pulling it to his chest dragging my fingers over him, "This is how you please me." He traced his hand down my side again, "This is how you please me." He leaned in and traced my lips with his, "Sweetheart, this is how you please me."

I kissed his lips.

"Auh, and yes, this is how you please me. I love you, Sarah, more than you know." He rolled me to my back hovering over me, "And you need to sleep, so close your eyes." I felt him move away from me.

Worrying I opened my eyes, "James?"

He tried to ease my worry so he smiled, but he admitted, "I need a shower, be right back."

I closed my eyes knowing I caused him misery again.

He whispered. "And my pleasure, stop that."

And yet I felt horrible. I did love James and I wanted to be the woman that made him happy in every way. I just wish that I could make the sadness go away completely.

## 41. Who's Feeling

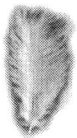

**I** woke to Jake taking out the lines to the IV ports. I glanced up at him groggily.

"Dinner time, and then games."

Wanting to know where James was I gave him a questionable expression.

"Sarah, you need to take it easy."

I raised my eyebrows.

"Sarah, you promise you are going to wait the fourteen weeks."

Oh, he was talking about being with James. Not a problem there so I nodded.

Even though he was a little reluctant he continued, "I don't think I need to remind you what happens when you... well you know..."

I was surprised with this lecture. I wonder if James talked to him.

Changing the subject he went right to the other thing I was wondering about, "I have feelings too, but I only feel you and Clarissa, sometimes my Dad, but never Carl, James, or Sam."

I was confused but also encouraged and tried to give him a thought... a feeling, 'you do feel me; I wasn't imagining it'.

He shook his head with a grin on his face saying, "I feel like you were wondering if you were imagining it or something like that. It's not clear."

That made me smile. He could feel me, but James must have said..., "Did you talk to James?"

"Yes, he told me what you said about it. He wanted to know why we had a connection."

"Why do we?"

Pleased with the connection he humbly said, "I have no idea, but I really think it has to do with Clarissa. James doesn't want to ask. I think he is afraid of what he will find out."

I had to stick by my man, "Then we don't ask."

He shook his head no, "I want to know. It would explain a lot of what I went through at school."

I frowned at him, "Try asking her with your mind. See if she answers you."

He got a great big grin on his face, "I like the way you think."

Still wanting James I inquired, "Where is he?"

Jake gave me a huge smile, "He is helping my Dad with dinner. He has been in a really good mood since you laid down for a nap."

I felt flushed when I thought about it.

"You know he loves you, and he will wait, but you need to not push his buttons."

I was totally embarrassed now, "You guys talk about us."

"Not completely, but I read between the lines. It's the dumb look he gets on his face."

Surprised with his answer my eyes opened wider.

"It's dinner time; let's get these off." He started to disconnect me. I moved to sit up and get to the edge of the bed. He put out his arm for me, so I pulled myself up using his arm.

"Do you need to go to the bathroom before we go up?"

I nodded.

"I will wait in the living room."

I went and had another bowl movement; it hurt a lot more, but I was able to suffer through it. I didn't want to be connected to the IV again. Not yet. I made myself presentable and went out to go upstairs. Jake was standing by the door waiting for me.

Attempting to do the stairs on my own caused me pain with each and every step.

Jake stopped, "You are in pain?"

Trying not to grimace, "Not too bad, but it's better than before."

He moved to catch up to me. James came out the patio door with worry on his face, "Why are you doing that on your own?"

Pleased with myself I boasted, "Because I can."

He walked back in; he couldn't breathe when I felt pain. I did forget about that. I got to the top and walked in through the kitchen. He was cutting and frying away. I knew what he was making, "Fajitas?"

He grinned and grabbed a pepper before moving to me wrapping his arm around me, feeding me a piece, and then he kissed me so passionately I was embarrassed.

"James that is enough Tamara is in the room." It was Clarissa scolding him for being too aggressively amorous in their presence.

He moved to trace my face with his whispering in my ear, "I am so in love with you." He pulled me around and directed me to the table.

Wilson brought me a plate; mine was still being portioned out. I couldn't help but notice that I had a lot of filling for one tortilla.

"We didn't want to give you fillers; you need real food, so yours is rather bulky, but we figured you would only eat one."

That was fine with me. It just seemed to be a lot of food.

James brought over the skillet with filling in it, and Wilson brought over the warmed soft shells. Jake grabbed a pan of Mexican rice. I didn't have any on my plate. My mouth dropped open in astonishment.

Jake smiled at me and gave me a spoonful while everyone gaped at him, "It won't kill her to have a little filler."

Everyone smiled including me. I cut mine in little pieces and used guacamole, sour cream, and lettuce.

James sat down to my right, but was facing me more. He would talk only to me whispering in my ear, "I love that you are talking to me." He moved his hand to my knee his eyes lingered on mine. He was getting obsessive in front of everybody. He leaned in more to my ear, "I loved it when you touched me."

Warmth filled my face, and then I looked around the table to see if anyone knew what James had said. Carl was laughing to himself, and Clarissa was getting irritated.

I leaned to him, "James, you need to settle down. Everyone is getting kind of..." I gestured to the rest of the table. After evaluating everyone, James scooted his chair around to face the table more; he glanced up, and he apologized, but his grin was sinful.

After dinner we moved to the living room. Clarissa wanted family time. Josie showed up again, and she was going to play games with us. Wilson brightened up when she walked in. He catered to everything she said or did. I paid attention to Clarissa to see if I could feel anymore. I didn't know if I was feeling her or if it was just the satisfied look on her face to see him so happy and gloating over his wife.

We were going to play Pictionary. Great; I wasn't feeling that comfortable talking yet. Well, maybe, I would give it a try. It was the adults against us. We were playing for a while and I was trying to watch Clarissa. The only time they would struggle was when she was drawing; with any luck, Carl was the only one who could guess what Clarissa was drawing.

When it was our turn we would do really well, but we had two superpowers on our side. So Sam and James did most of the guessing. The game seemed rigged, because there was a lot of mind reading going on. We were laughing and having a good time. When it was Jake's or my turn we had better luck with guessing each others. I kept urging him to try with Clarissa, but he kept putting it off. I didn't understand why. It would be completely concealed if he asked with his mind. I was getting tired of waiting.

I still had my suspicion she could feel things. I looked at her, "That's not fair; you can almost read their minds."

Jake and James stopped on a dime. James put his arms around me like I said something wrong.

She raised her eyebrows as her eyes fell hard on me, "I am very good at my job, Sarah; I can read most people. How do you think I got so far in my career?" The stiffness was coming over her in a very stern way.

Jake nudged me as if to tell me to shut up.

Clarissa and I exchanged grins because she knew that we all knew. I got the distinct feeling to drop the subject, while James whispered in my ear, "You're pushing her buttons, Sarah, behave."

Wanting re-enforcements from Jake I turned to him and gestured for him to give her a feeling, but he wouldn't even look at me. In my mind I had to ask. 'Jake did you feel that?' He didn't turn to me; he just nodded. James let go of me moving forward on the edge of the couch to get a better sight of Jake. Sam elbowed me in the calf; he was sitting between my legs on the floor.

Clarissa addressed me again, "Sarah, think about it this way. Have you ever noticed someone telling you something, but you can see the uneasiness in their face? You know that they are not telling you everything."

Happy that she was explaining things I glared at James as I answered her, "Yes."

I could feel the warmth from her as she gave me an approving smile, "That's all it is. You can tell what people are thinking by their reactions to questions. In my court I see reactions to questions and I am able to decide for myself. If the person gets off and I have that instinct that tells me that something isn't right... well... let's just say they are watched very carefully."

I wanted more, "Can you show me how to do that?"

She was actually finding it pleasing that I was so interested in her, but I did notice Carl lean back and put his arm around her. It was like a reminder that other people were in the room. She put her hand on his knee to show him she was in control of the situation.

"Sarah, if you are serious about learning, I would love to share this with you."

We shared something very personal, and while almost everyone here could feel us it still seemed more private and personal, like a connection that no one else could be part of.

James moved his arms around me again and whispered in my ear, "Sarah, can you please drop the subject. Wilson is getting nervous."

My attention darted to Wilson. He was very tense. The last thing I would ever want to do is upset Wilson, and I felt bad if anything I said or did would hurt his feelings.

Clarissa noticed this too and she chuckled leaning forward, "And that is your weakness, child."

I leaned back to James. It almost felt like an attack on her part. She leaned back to be held by Carl.

It was my turn to talk, but I didn't know what to say. Trying to change the subject with uncertainty I asked quietly, "Game? Turn?"

I noticed Josie and she was a little uncomfortable, but she was able to express her opinion, "Well I guess you are doing better. You are talking more."

Feeling stronger I replied, "Yes, getting better every day."

We went on with the game. Tamara moved from the adult side and curled up on James's lap. She crawled to me and whispered in my ear, "You want me to make everyone feel better?"

Privately, I encouraged her to change the mood. She closed her eyes and put her face to James's chest. He was laughing. She raised her face looking at James, "Better now?"

Shaking his head in disbelief; he knew what she had done.

We went back to playing the game as if nothing had happened. I still watched but tried not to. The adults won. I put a damper on our side. They were all afraid to read each other's minds. When we were finished, the adults moved to the kitchen and started to play cards. Jake grabbed my arm stopping me, "Sarah, wrong time, wrong place. Josie means a lot to me."

I was feeling badly, "Wasn't thinking, sorry."

James put his arms around me from the back facing Jake, "Do you two want to fill me in more?"

I turned a little in his arms and kissed his cheek, "Later, I'm too tired right now."

We went downstairs and Sam followed. Jake and Sam went to play pool, but Jake offered to hook me back up. I shook my head no.

James tried to remind me that I was tired, "You were tired, Sarah?"

I wasn't ready to go to bed. I shook my head in protest.

His eyes sparked with interest, "Do you want to play, little girl? I could use some kissing myself."

If I wasn't so scared, that look would have won me over, but I shook my head no.

"How about a movie?"

That I could handle.

He put in a movie and grabbed a blanket and pulled me to sit with him. I curled up in his arms, while he covered us in the warm blanket. We could hear Jake and Sam playing in the other room. James took my hand. He kissed my pointer finger, "What were you doing upstairs?"

"Nothing."

He kissed my middle finger sucking on it more, "It seemed like you were up to something."

"Nope."

He took my ring finger and licked it to the point and put it in his mouth to suck on it, "Sarah, you were pushing her buttons."

"No, just curious."

He took my pinky finger and bit the tip softly and then brought it into his mouth completely playing with my finger with his tongue and slowly pulled it out, "You made Wilson uncomfortable." He turned my hand over and kissed my palm softly, seductively.

"I didn't mean to."

He moved to my wrist kissing it with his whole mouth.

He was distracting me, "James movie."

He smiled; I could see it from the corner of my eye.

"So these feelings, what does it feel like, exactly?" He kissed the inside of my forearm tracing his mouth upward.

"Not clear, James…warmth, distrust, anger."

He kissed my shoulder nibbling there, "Did you feel Clarissa's anger?"

"Nope."

He kissed my neck soft and sweetly, tracing it with his mouth. I swallowed. My heart was pounding, and my breathing was getting harder. He moved to my ear, "What did you feel when you moved back to me?" He licked my ear.

"James, tingling."

He breathed deeply in my ear, "Yes, now tingling, but what did you feel from Clarissa?"

I could hardly breathe, while I gasped, "Fear."

He stopped for a minute and he resumed tracing my face with his nose, "She wasn't fearful; are you sure?"

I turned my face to him trying to breathe. I traced my forehead along his jaw, as he turned to kiss my forehead.

"James, tingling is…"

He kissed my cheek. I felt his hand move to my stomach. I was leaning more to him.

"What did you think she was feeling, Sarah?"

I grabbed his thighs squeezing them.

"Hey calm down, sweetie, we're just playing." He kissed the corner of my mouth.

"James, room now, please?"

"No, Sarah, we're just playing."

I turned my face up to him. He kissed my mouth softly and slowly let go, "Clarissa's feeling?" He traced his mouth along my face.

I gripped his legs tighter, "She was intrigued, but determined." I could hardly breathe. His other hand moved to my stomach and he was rubbing and tracing it slowly and tenderly. I felt like I was being suffocated while yet needy. The tingling was rising from my stomach. I never felt wanting like this. It was so intense.

He came in for a very deep kiss, as deep as we could with me turning to him. He was licking and sucking my lips. He wrapped his arms more tightly around me to calm me down, but continued to nibble my ear and kiss my neck.

I begged, "James, room please."

"No, Sarah, we can't go there. Here we are supervised; just enjoy how good this feels." He pulled me to him; I could feel his excitement. I was incredibly aroused too, and immediately my stomach contracted, and the pain shot through me. I sat up and wrapped my arms around my stomach, just in time for Jake and Sam to walk in.

"What are you two up to?"

James sat up and turned us to face the TV more, but whispered in my ear, "Are you okay?"

I nodded, but glanced up at Jake.

James was very calm, "Watching a movie. What are you two doing?"

Jake evaluated us, "You two were making out."

James laughed, "And you still have great timing." James tried to wrap his arm around me, but I grabbed his arm to stop him. It still hurt, not sharply, but I was afraid to let him touch me. I was still trying to calm my breathing. James scooted back but leaned forward to whisper, "Sarah, if you lean back I won't touch you, please just concentrate on breathing." I leaned back and he relaxed to the back of the couch supporting my weight. He covered me back up, and I dug my fingers into his legs. The pain was deep, not sharp. I took a deep breath trying to calm myself.

Jake glared, "You are in pain?"

I managed a slight grin trying to hide the feelings I was having.

"James, she is in pain."

"Jake, shhh, she is trying to get through it on her own."

"You are making her suffer. Sarah, I am hooking you back up, and you can have a pain killer."

I refused. I didn't want to have the pain killer. I took another deep breath.

Jake was becoming more upset the longer he stood there staring at us, "What were you doing that caused pain?"

I must have turned at least two shades of red.

Jake was scolding, "I thought you two could control yourselves; after going through what you did, especially you, Sarah. Do you want that to happen again?"

That did it to me. Between the memory and the pain, tears welled up in my eyes. I was shaking my head no, as James strong arms tensed around me.

"Jake, shut up. Thanks a lot for the reminder." James was defending me in a way.

"It's not like that, and no, we weren't going to do that. I know it would hurt her. That's why we stayed out here, so we would have supervision."

He kissed my cheek, "How are you doing?"

I closed my eyes and tried to relax.

"James, give me her arm." He pulled my arm out. I still had a fist. Jake hooked me back up and gave me a good dose of pain meds.

"I can't leave you two alone for one minute. I told you both not for 14 weeks; can it really be that hard?"

"Yeah," but that didn't come from James or me; it came from Sam.

It was kind of funny that it was from him. We all turned to him.

He seemed to be off in another world. I had to say something, "Sam? Are you thinking about Amelia?"

He smiled, "Yeah."

"How many times have you two been together?"

He got a great big grin, "A couple, but not after her dad found out. Well, let's just say it may be a year before we can be alone again. Remember that time at the lake, Sarah?"

"Yeah, you were awfully cozy."

"That was the second time."

"With all those people around?"

"No, that day on our way back. We parked and well you know… We're supposed to be together and sometimes we just get carried away."

I smothered a giggle, but it hurt anyway.

"I am the only virgin here." Jake was disgusted.

"Jake, it will be more special if it's the right person."

I bit my lip with regret for opening my mouth after the glare he gave me.

"But you know what I want."

James tensed, "What are you saying?"

"James, no, but I want someone like her."

Sam was laughing, "You know who is just like Sarah?"

Both James and I almost shouted, "NO!!"

Sam was startled into silence.

James spoke up, "He needs to figure it out on his own, Sam, or he will think we're nuts."

Full of frustration Jake huffed, "Sam knows this person too?"

Sam grinned smugly proud of the fact that he was *in* on the secret.

It was almost comical watching Jake roll his eyes aggravated, "You're not going to tell me?"

We all shook our heads, and he stormed to his bedroom not happy with us at all.

James asked Sam if he was staying on the couch while he picked me up. After Sam confirmed that he was comfortable staying on the couch James took me to bed. He pulled the bed pillow between us and leaned over it so that he could gaze at me. His eyebrows went up with a suggestive look, "You think *you* got hot?"

I loved the way he looks at me. I nodded profusely.

"I think your noises aroused me more than the touching."

His face changed; his eyes changed from the sparkle of excitement to a concerned sad puppy look, his mouth changed from a flirty grin to a tense jaw before he asked, "Does the pleasure hurt you?"

"It makes me tighten my stomach, and that hurts."

"So even if we snuck and did it with our minds it might hurt you?"

I nodded.

"Damn it. I want you so bad it hurts."

Now that I really let myself get lost in his eyes I saw the pain, "James?"

That flirty grin came back to compliment his face, "Hmmm."

I reached up to touch his face, "Let me help you, touch you."

"Nope, I will wait. It'll be better that way." He rolled to his back and closed his eyes, but entangled his fingers with mine.

I didn't want this to be over, but was relieved that he understood me. I closed my eyes to sleep.

# 42. Paybacks

**I** woke to another glorious day. I stretched my arms over my head and a sharp pain shot through my inners. James sat up immediately gasping for air, "Sarah, are you okay?"

"James, I'm fine. Go back to sleep."

He practically fell back.

I went to the bathroom and everything went okay. I took a shower with the tubes still connected. I didn't want to wake Jake. I was having private time with no one to hover over me. I toweled my hair, put a little makeup on, and brushed my teeth. Now for getting dressed. It was getting a little cooler out, but I really wasn't going anywhere. I walked to the closet to see my options. My pants were all hanging up. I found the oldest pair I owned which would be the largest pair I owned. I pulled them out and put them over my arm. I dug through the shirts. I pulled out a tank top and fingered through my sweatshirts. I found a zip up one. I walked back to the dresser. How was I going to get dressed with these tubes still connected? I dug through the drawer and pulled out underwear, a cute lacy pair. James has good taste in woman's underwear. Mom definitely did not send these. I struggled to get the underwear on having my towel fall to the floor. I then tried to put on my jeans leaning against the dresser. I slowly got them on, while tipping and staggering. They were really loose now. I needed a belt, but I didn't mind the bagginess. I turned to try and figure out how to get the tank top on.

I felt James behind me, with his face at my neck and his hands tracing my arms, "Do you need some help?"

What else could I do but smile? "How long have you been awake?"

"Long enough to watch you dress; it was actually comical."

I pushed my butt back to push him away, "You let me struggle."

He laughed while tracing his hands to the front of my waist, running his finger along the edge of my jeans, "A little big?"

We both heard the door handle; Jake was coming in. James turned me to his body moving his back to the door, "Jake, you have got to learn to knock."

"James, knock it off. You're supposed to be waiting."

"Jake, I was helping her get dressed."

I looked up into his eyes pleading, "James, tubes?"

"Jake, that's why she's not dressed yet. Can you please unhook her?"

I stretched my arm out behind James's back looking over his shoulder. James's mouth was at my shoulder. I watched Jake as he unhooked me. His eyes locked on mine questioning me, so I smiled at him to let him know I was okay.

"You were getting dressed?"

I nodded.

"Of course she was, Jake, out now!"

He moved to close the door, "I will expect you two in 3 minutes, or I am coming back in."

"Jake, get out." James was getting impatient.

Jake closed the door.

"Okay, you can help with my shirt."

James didn't move, "I like this you know." His bare chest was against mine. His face was still down and he was not letting go.

"James?"

"No, I just need a minute."

I nudged his face with my nose, so he would look at me. His eyes moved to mine, and I could see they were filled with desire, so it was not a surprise to feel him backing me to the wall by the bathroom. Entrapping me against the wall as his body surrounded mine, my heart beat uncontrollably. Slowly moving closer he leaned his chest against mine, closing his eyes, and put his lips to my face.

I whispered to him, "James, no…the pain…"

He opened his eyes to look in mine, "I had forgotten how good you feel next to me." His breathing was rugged now.

As a reminder Jake yelled from the other room, "You've got 2 minutes now!"

Even though James was teasing his eyes were determined, "Do you know what you do to me little girl?" He inched away from me just far enough to be able to trace his fingers down the front of me, as he watched my breathing catch from his touch.

Feeling the wanting build in me I not only reminded myself but I also reminded James, "James, my Cayuse, please no. The pain I felt last night is too much."

His eyes glistened and his grin turned mischievous as he spoke in a calm voice, "Just enjoying the scenery."

I pulled his attention back to my face, "James, you should have let me touch you."

The hunger was revealed when he licked his lips, "This is better than that."

"James, please no."

He shook his head no and pulled me to the dresser taking my tank top in his hand. He stepped back a little and helped to put it over my head pulling it down while tracing my body with his hands. He swept me into his arms pressing his lips against mine hard and determined. The embrace was so intense that he was knocking the air from my lungs. I tried to gasp for air but he took that as wanting more. Tilting his head slightly his mouth engulfed mine. Losing my mind I dove in without any more resistance.

Jake walked back in, "I hope she's dressed because your time is up."

We stopped kissing.

I could see the frustration in James's face, "Damn it, Jake, no privacy at all."

We both turned to look at him. He had his hand over his eyes. We both started to laugh.

"Is it safe?" Came from his lips, but he kept his eyes covered.

James took Jake by the waist throwing him over his shoulder carrying him to the living room, trying to dump him on the couch, "You, brother, have to learn how to knock."

Jake was pulling James with him over the couch, "You need to learn self-control."

I walked out after them, but kept going through the room and out the door. I couldn't watch. I walked slowly up the stairs. I heard something crash when I was about half way up.

Carl walked out the patio door, "Sarah?"

"They are wrestling. I didn't stay to see if it was going to get bad."

Carl started coming down the stairs glancing at me as he passed, "Is it bad?"

"I think they are playing, but there might be a little anger on James's part. I couldn't stay to watch." I kept going; as I got to the top of the steps Clarissa came out. I went to her and hugged her.

"Are they really angry with each other?"

"Nope, I think... hope they're just playing."

She smiled at me.

I pulled away from her a little, "Clarissa, I am sorry about last night, but do you feel things?"

She was looking down the steps but turned to me right away, "You are very direct."

It was better to be direct than play stupid mind games.

She was more concerned about what was going on downstairs, "We'll discuss that further when the time is right."

That got my attention, but she turned to me with a grin, "Time for you to eat. You are dressed today, and you look very pretty."

Explaining the attempt at looking normal, "I needed to feel human with people coming tomorrow."

She grabbed my arm and changed the subject completely, "Sarah, are you two being careful? Jake said 14 weeks."

I knew she and Carl understood, but I was still embarrassed. She put her arm around me and tucked my head to her chest, "I know the passion." She took a deep sigh before continuing, "I think it will be good for you to stay at home with your parents for a while."

Even though the air was escaping my lungs and the black hole was moving in, I was able to stand my ground, "No."

She pulled my face up to look at her, "I am not going to be careful with you, Sarah; you are more grown up than your age. Think about this... you are married too young, you have lost a child..."

Trying to contain the pain, I blinked making the tears spill over the bottom of my eyes drenching my lashes.

"...And you still need to finish school."

I nodded, "When?"

"Just as James planned. When you have to go back to high school, you will stay with your parents. It will give James time to grow, learn, and of course earn some money. He wants to get a house for you, and his plan was when you were 18 he would have one for you. So you have to love him, to let him go enough, so he can provide for you the way he wants."

I forced a smile, "I will do it then and...Clarissa...?"

She hugged me in tighter, "Yes, child."

"Do you think I would make a good Judge?"

She chuckled a little, "Or doctor, that might help your life with James too. Understanding things will be easy for you to help them."

I looked up at her with a question in my eye.

"Not now, dear, you don't have to make any decisions yet."

She guided me in the house. I was relieved she was being so comforting, especially after the disobedient way I acted last night. She helped me to sit.

Tamara came and hugged me, and then sat on my lap playing with my hair, "You are very pretty."

I smiled, "So are you, Tamara."

She rolled her eyes, "Well I know that, but you don't know you are pretty. I wanted you to know that."

I glanced at Clarissa.

"Tamara, okay; that is enough. Come here and eat." She went to her mother. Clarissa hugged her tightly and kissed her little face.

Wilson came with my plate, "Do you think Carl needs help?"

I shook my head, "No, he shouldn't, but they are taking longer than I thought they would need."

His face was full of fear, as he took off out the door.

I lowered my face shamefully as I asked, "He is worried that Jake will get hurt." I had already hurt him.

"Sarah, look at me. You have already figured out who would be perfect for one of my boys. I think maybe you have an idea for another."

I saw her eyebrows go up, as if to suggest that she knew what I was thinking and she gave me an approving look. Why didn't she do these things when everyone else was around? They are thinking I am crazy. She does know things. How is that possible?

"Sarah."

I glanced back at her.

She gave me that stern motherly smile, "Don't think about it. I said later when you are ready."

I stared at her while asking, "When?"

"I will let you know; until then quit pushing the issue and eat."

I looked back, as the boys walked in. James had a bruised face by his eye and Jake had a fat lip. Carl had Jake by the neck, and Wilson had his arm around James's shoulder. I stood up and went to the fridge and got ice. Wilson and Carl set them both in chairs but facing me in the kitchen. Carl spoke up, "Don't you two think you have something to say to her?"

I wasn't paying attention to either one of them; I was grabbing ice. I put two bags in separate towels and walked back over to them. I put the ice packs on where they were injured. I looked at James; he wasn't looking at me, "James!"

Carl spoke up, "Oh, I did that when I pulled James off. I thought he was hurting Jake."

I looked up at Carl. I turned to give my attention to Jake. If James did this I was not going to be happy. I started to wipe Jake's mouth.

Wilson spoke up as I looked at him, "I accidentally hit him when I was grabbing him."

I smiled and lifted both their chins, "You two didn't hurt each other?"

They were both smiling and shaking their heads no. I smiled and looked at the men, "Then why do they need to apologies to me?"

They were chuckling a little and said at the same time, "We broke the couch."

And with my sternest voice, "Then you need to apologies to your Mother." I stood up very angry, "...And no more wrestling in the house."

They were both just giggling. I was angry with both of them, "Hey, it's not funny. Your mom worked hard to make it nice for you."

James grabbed me and pulled me to his lap, "You should see your face right now."

"No James, I am not happy with either of you."

"Sarah, it's fake. We didn't break the couch and this..." He was wiping off the redness with a cloth. I grabbed Jake's face. He pulled a cotton ball out of his lip and wiped off the fake blood. I stood up and pushed both their heads away from me. I grabbed my plate and walked over to sit by Clarissa.

James and Jake were laughing, as they turned their chairs around to the table grabbing food to eat. I didn't look at either one of them. I was very mad now.

Carl tried to ease my bad temper, "Sarah, it was just a joke."

I glared at him. Those two hurting each other is not funny.

Clarissa just sat there with a smile on her face.

Wilson tried next, "Sarah, come on it was a little funny."

I really scowled at him, "You could have upset Clarissa with the broken couch thing...not funny."

I looked at her for re-enforcement and her face straightened, "You're right, I would have been mad." But she started to laugh.

Sam walked in laughing. He was listening to the whole thing from the door.

"And you, little brother, I am mad at you too. You were supposed to get them, not me."

James teased, "So you like to pick on others but you don't like to be picked on."

I stood up after my last bite and glared at him, "Mine didn't involve hurting anyone."

"We didn't hurt anyone either. Sarah, come on. Don't be so mad."

I was determined to walk out. I left the table and put my plate in the kitchen. James came running after me and Jake went to the door, "Sarah, it was just a joke."

"James, it wasn't funny." God I hated when he looked at me that way. I was going to soften, and then I remembered I was mad, "No, James. Finish eating. I need time alone." I pushed him out of the way and got to the door where Jake was blocking my exit. I looked at his lip and then at his eyes. Oh he was so cute. Danelle and he will make a really cute couple. I shot daggers at him with my eyes.

He grinned.

I was still angry, "Do you want me to do that for real?"

He moved out of my way. They all started to laugh, as soon as I left the room.

I heard James, as I tried to go down the stairs, "You know we are in trouble now."

"Why, she will get over it."

"No, she will come up with something better."

"No, she won't."

"I will bet you on it."

And then I heard Clarissa, "You two better make it up to her before she does come up with something better, because she will, trust me on this."

It got really quiet. She already knew what I was thinking. Nothing solid but the wheels were in motion.

James came down first. I was at the table reading my textbook. He pulled up a chair really close to me. I frowned at him, "What?"

He moved closer, "Are you really that mad?"

I peeked at him over my book, "I thought you two hurt each other. Yes, I am that mad." I went back to reading.

He touched my thigh, so I slowly moved my eyes to icily stare at him, "No, and move away Mr., because I am trying to study."

He moved away and grabbed his books, opened them, and then sat down next to me. He would glance at me with this pitifully cute grin.

"James, knock it off, or go in the other room."

He started to read his book, but he really wasn't. He was slyly trying to look at me, his eyes not staying on the page.

"James, I mean it."

He pushed the book away from him, and sat there staring at me. Jake walked in looking at James and me. He pulled up a chair on the other side of me.

"James, did she forgive us yet."

I didn't look up, "NO!"

He moved his chair closer, "What are you reading?"

I lifted my face to glare at him, "Back away, Jake. I am not happy with you either."

He moved his chair further from me. They were gesturing with their eyes, but I couldn't see what they were doing.

"Guys, I am going to get madder if you don't get lost."

James grabbed my computer and opened it. Jake turned it on and they both leaned back in their chairs. The song 'Smile' came on and I shook my head no, "Boys, I will go back upstairs if you don't knock it off. "

They both got up. I tried to watch what they were doing. They were in the fridge. They were not going to get me again. That would just be wrong. They were engulfed in what they were planning. I got up quickly and moved into Jake's room, not closing the door. I heard them coming back to the table to an empty table.

I heard Jake say, "She did not go back upstairs."

I could hear them searching all over even the game room. Under things, which I couldn't figure out, because there was no way I could crawl under something without feeling pain. They both took off out the door, so I came out and sat back down. It would buy me a little time for studying.

I read through another chapter with highlighting, and they still weren't back. I heard my phone ringing from the bedroom. James came running back in; he only stopped when he saw me. He fell to his knees grabbing his, "Don't ever do that again."

I grinned but continued reading my book.

Jake came running in and almost tripped over James and noticed I was sitting there, "Where have you been?"

I raised my eyebrows at them. James lay down on the floor relieved I didn't go anywhere.

Jake, however, wasn't used to my running away from things, and he was really angry, approaching the chair where I was sitting, "That was ridiculous, totally wrong!"

Not believing that he could say what I did was wrong after what they did to me, "Really?"

He moved away from me a little, "Okay, what we did was wrong, but look at poor James over there. He can't even get off the floor. "

I peeked over the table at him and smiled. He was still holding his chest. "He feels me; he knew I was safe."

James was shaking his head no, "I freaked out, because I didn't feel anything."

I reminded him, "Your trick was not funny, either."

Jake was more upset, "You're sick, and if you took off, shit Sarah. This was way worse."

I was satisfied, "Don't play mean games on me."

Jake picked me up and hugged me. James watched from the floor with no expression. "Where did you go?" He pushed me away from him to look me over for anything wrong with me.

I finally caved confessing, "I stepped in your room. I swear I didn't snoop, but just inside the door till you mean boys left."

I gestured to James, because Jake was still holding me.

He set me down, "Fine, but if you do that ever again, I will take you over my knee and, Sarah, I am not kidding. It was bad enough for me, but James... you could have killed him." He was moving to the door and then out shutting it behind him.

I walked over to James standing above him. I looked down. There was no way I was making it down there, "You didn't feel me at all?"

He put his hands on my ankles shaking his head no. I closed my eyes and traced my hand down his chest with my mind.

"Sarah, stop that."

"But you still feel me and you said it was worse; you couldn't block it anymore."

"I can't."

"But you didn't feel I was safe. I thought for sure you would figure it out. I can't walk that fast."

He chuckled and he was bending my knees until I fell to them. I slowly sat down on him. He took my hand and brought it to his chest. His heart was beating so fast.

I felt bad, "I'm sorry. I wasn't trying to scare you. I was just angry."

He sat up, wrapping his arms around me, staring into my eyes. They were glossed over. I touched his face to help ease his worry. He propped his knees up to support me and grabbed my face and started to kiss me, very hard, very passionately, "Don't..." he kissed me more, "Ever..." He pressed his lips to my bottom lip, "Do..." he moved to my top lip, "That..." He kissed me so deep I was being lured in for more.

I wrapped my arms around his neck.

"Again..." His lips were soft, full of desire, with the determination to make me know that he needed me.

We must have stayed there for 10 minutes kissing.

Jake walked back in, "Hey it's good you two are making up, but remember to not get carried away."

We stopped kissing, and I hugged him, and he wrapped his arms around me.

"By the way, how did you get down like that, Sarah? Aren't you in pain?"

I smiled at James, "Don't feel anything."

James eyes went large.

I whispered to him, "Yeah, except for that."

The most beautiful smile came to his face, but he put out his hand for Jake to take to help him stand up. Jake pulled and James lifted me as he got up, but he didn't let go. He looked at Jake, "I am taking her over my knee now, so if you hear screaming don't come in." He started walking to the room. I put my head on his shoulder and tucked my hands in.

"No, James. Wait till she is better."

He was moving around us to stand in front of the bedroom door. James looked at him; I couldn't see the expression on their faces.

Jake was more determined, "James, no."

"Jake, get out of my way. I am really mad right now, and I am going to let her have it."

"That is why you are holding her so tight. Come on, James, you will regret it later, because it will hurt her."

"Guys, let's not talk about Sarah like she isn't here." I lifted my head and looked James in the eyes, "James," I leaned into his ear and whispered, "I would love to make love to you right now, but it would hurt."

He slowly let me down staring into my eyes, "Sarah, you are not getting off that easy. I am really angry with you."

Carefully I moved away from him and Jake followed me. I moved to the couch while Jake sat on the arm of the couch to watch me.

Feeling smothered I stated, "I'm not going anywhere."

He smiled wearily, "You are driving him crazy."

That made me feel badly for making it hard for James. I couldn't smile anymore, and then I was reminded how crazy I was making him when we heard the shower. I had to find a way to preoccupy my time, so I wouldn't think about it. I looked at the TV and got up moving to the table to work on notes from the second chapter. I turned on the computer and scanned my class. The first two lessons were listed. I was excited I could get started right away. I was engrossed in the schoolwork. When James came out, he grabbed his book and came to sit at the table with me. He didn't look at me at all. I got through both lessons in one sitting. I opened the other book and went online checking the other class. That one had the first four lessons posted. I huffed a little.

James asked, "What?"

"I thought I was ahead and now I have more to get done."

I don't know why but that made him grin.

"I wanted to get it all done before tomorrow."

Jake was sitting watching TV, but he got up and walked over to look at what I was doing. He laughed and looked at his watch, "Break time you two; mom will want us upstairs for lunch."

I watched him as he moved to the door. He stopped to wait for us, "Both of you, let's go."

I really wanted a minute with James, "Jake, we'll be right there."

"NO. Both of you, right now."

I shook my head no giving Jake my pleading eyes.

His response wasn't what I wanted. First he tilted his head as if trying to read me and then shook it no. He needed to give us a moment, so I nodded. He went out but left the door open. I stood up and walked behind James. I put my hands on his shoulders, "James?"

He touched my hands with his, "Yeah, I'm coming."

I traced my hands down his chest to feel his heart; it was still racing, "James, your heart is still pounding."

He pushed the chair out and pulled me around the chair to be in front of him. He pulled me so I was sitting on his lap facing him. He put his head on my chest and took my hands to kiss them, "Don't ever do that to me again. Please."

I felt horrible that I caused him stress, "No, James, I won't."

His nose traced my chin adoringly until his lips brushed against my neck. His breath was warm and alluring.

"James, don't get me going. It will hurt."

He was muffled as his tried to talk while kissing me, "I can't live without you."

"You don't have to get me going to show me that."

"I want to make you want me as bad as I want you."

I pushed his head away from me, "James, I love everything about you. I want to be with you always. You don't have to get me going for me to want to be with you all the time."

He smiled and picked me up. I thought we were headed to the bedroom, and I was scared that I pushed him too far this time. But… he walked out the door and up the stairs to the main house. He did fill my heart with so much love, that I couldn't wipe the smile on my face the whole time we were heading up. He set me down when we got to the top of the stairs, and we walked in for lunch holding hands.

We sat down at the table and Jake looked at us, "You two took long enough."

We both smiled. I realized it didn't hurt nearly as much to sit when I was thinking about how much my James loved me.

## 43. Calling

After lunch I went back to getting my homework done. I really wanted to have it all done before everyone got here. James was working on his too. We stayed dedicated to it until dinner time. We went back up to have dinner. I was brought my special plate, and they told me it was four cups again. It was getting to be a lot of food. I ate everything, and Jake wanted to do my checkup after dinner. I got him to agree to make it a little later due to eating too much. James and I sat down to watch movies, and Jake and Sam went to play pool again. Today we sat beside each other not cuddling too much. We were being very careful today. Jake would walk in and check on us once in a while, but we would both look at him and then he didn't linger for long. I was falling asleep and leaned into James. His whole body was very tense.

I peeked up at him trying to keep my eyes open, "You're tense."
"You turn me on."
I was confused, "but I didn't touch you."
Guiltily he replied, "You don't have to."
Gladdened, I smiled and curled into him closing my eyes.

I woke enough to tell it was Jake carrying me to bed. I groggily opened my eyes, "James?"
Jake was smirking, "He needed a shower." I heard the water running, as Jake was setting me down by the dresser. He was opening drawers, "What do you sleep in?"
I shrugged my shoulders. I didn't feel like changing.
"You can't sleep in Jeans, Sarah; help me out here."
I leaned over and pulled shorts out of the drawer.

He grinned, "I don't think that will help him."

I really didn't have much to pick from, so I shrugged again.

"Come on, Sarah, don't you have anything repulsive?"

Now he was irritating me, "James bought all of this. I didn't."

He almost gasped, "He buys you this stuff?" He pulled out a camisole and then another one, and another one. "Didn't he buy regular ugly stuff?"

I shook my head no.

"Are regular shorts and t-shirt okay?"

I was so sleepy I didn't care, so I opened a different drawer and pulled out a t-shirt and shorts. I waited for his approval holding them up. He agreed that those would be okay, so I pointed to the door.

He walked out and I shut the door. I took off my bra under my shirt leaving the tank top on, and lowered the Jeans. I stepped into the shorts and threw the t-shirt over the tank top. I opened the door and walked to the bed. Jake back came in following me to the bed with the IV. He was hooking me back up when James came out in a towel. Jake was hurrying, "James, it will just be a minute."

James stood across the room as I lay down. Jake started probing at my stomach; I only cringed a little here and there depending on where he was touching. He was trying to get my attention, but I was entranced with staring at James, admiring the muscles in his chest, the ripples of his abs, the bulkiness of his arms, the strong sturdy face, and the deep color of his skin. I smiled at the man who was in love with me. He stood patiently waiting for Jake to finish.

Jake tried again, "Sarah, pay attention. I need to know where the pain is and how bad it is."

I couldn't take my eyes off James.

"Hey, Sarah, look at me now!"

I turned to him, as he pushed a little harder than needed.

I grimaced, "Yeah, Jake, it hurts there." I gave him a dirty look.

"Now I have your attention."

I was embarrassed. He moved around and leaned in a little, "Are you still going?"

I hated talking about going to the bathroom, but I nodded.

"Do you need to go now?"

I shook my head no.

"You might have to after this." He pushed and poked and moved around nudging my inners one way and then the next.

"Ouch, Jake, not so rough."

He smiled, "Give me your hands, Sarah."

I moved them to where he had his. He moved my fingers under his and pushed around. There was a lump in my lower left side. I looked at him with fear, "Is it a tumor?"

James started to walk over; the look on his face was unmistakable. He didn't want or need another problem with me. His heart sank along with his face.

Jake gave me a reassuring smile and put up his hand to keep James away, "No, Sarah, it's not." He leaned into me, "That is your intestines; you will have to go again soon, but it's hard so you'll need a stool softener. Then it won't be so painful for you."

I was embarrassed again, "Jake, are we talking about pooping? I don't like talking about that; it's like embarrassing and private."

A smile grew on James face as he backed up to the dresser relaxing again.

Jake chuckled to himself, "Sarah, you are so thin I can feel everything. It's really cool."

I gave him a disgruntled look.

He pushed again in the middle but really low. James moved forward again. Jake glanced back at James and then at me, "Sarah, do you feel that?"

I nodded, but it hurt a little, so I cringed again.

"That is your uterus and it's shrinking to normal size. It's good." He turned to James, "It's good."

James eased a little but didn't go back to resting on the dresser. He gave me that amazing smile, but I wanted him to come to me, so I reached for him. He put up one finger, and then moved it to his lips to shhhh me.

I turned my attention back to Jake waiting for the next part. He stood up and looked between James and me, "You both understand 14 weeks, right? No mind games, no nothing." He was really cute, as he was scolding us, in a reminding way. We both nodded, but James had that quirky little smirk of a smile. Jake got up and started for the door, but stopped in front of James, "You can bunk with me. I don't mind. It would be easier."

James's smile grew on his face, as he eyes stayed on me, "No, Jake, I will be fine."

"Okay, but think pain James. Think *her* pain."

James glared at him. "Yeah, that works."

Jake walked out leaving the door open. James closed it. While grabbing boxers the door opened.

James scolded, "Jake, I am getting dressed."

He closed the door again. He took off the towel and put on boxers and lounge pants. I took off my t-shirt and covered up with the comforter, as he crawled in bed with me. He pulled back the covers kneeling next to me, "Can I feel where he was touching you?"

I was confused why James wanted to feel my intestines, but nodded. It was weird that James was happy about this. Moving his hands to my stomach he asked, "Will you show me what he was feeling."

I pushed his fingers to where Jake's had been, "I think it's there."

He pushed around and shrugged his shoulders, "I don't like that he knows more about your body than I do."

I didn't know how to make him feel better about that. He pushed more and moved closer, "I don't know what I am feeling for."

I smiled and then cringed, "Pain there, James."

He lightened his push and moved more softly and then moved back and forth, "Is that it?"

I shrugged my shoulders.

"Show me the other thing he showed you."

I shook my head no, "No, James, that has to do with pooping, and that is just disgusting."

He laughed at me but let it go. He laid down perpendicular to me with his face near my stomach. We heard the door open and we both looked up. He started to laugh. "Persistent little bugger, isn't he."

I laughed too, as he traced his hand over my stomach, not seductively but caring and loving, "Are you still in pain?"

I ran my fingers through his hair, "James, that pain is going away; it's the sadness of what I did hurts more."

He kissed my stomach, "Sarah, everything is going to be okay; the future has not changed. I still feel three." He turned his head resting his face on my stomach.

The tears came to my eyes.

"No, don't get upset. I just wanted to let you know, that it will work out."

I laughed quietly, "I just like the part where we're still together."

He smiled and moved up to lie down with me but rolling to his back, "By the way, it's a lot later in life."

We both rolled to each other for our goodnights, and James kissed me softly, but then he rolled away from me lying on his back again.

I curled up to him, "Is this okay?"

He kissed my head and wrapped his arm around me, "Yes, of course it is."

I closed my eyes and reminded myself to not dream as bad as I wanted to share that with him. I knew the pain would be too unbearable, but the sleep did come and warmed my heart.

As I woke Friday morning my heart was pumping again quite hard. I was curled up to the pillow, but my fingers were entangled with his. I peeked over the pillow, and he was laying there with his eyes open staring at the ceiling. I smiled at him, "What's with the pillow?"

He grinned, "Yeah, it was safer to have something between us."

This made me a little sad.

"No, Sarah, it's getting easier." He propped himself up resting his head in his hand to look at me, "I can't help it if I get turned on by looking at you. It's a good thing, baby. We just have to go a lot slower. Don't want to do that again."

I was happy about that, so I smiled at him.

"We've got a big day, with lots of people coming."

"Lots, James... who is all coming?"

"Jason and Kylie."

I was okay with them being here.

"Will and Katherine, they haven't been here yet

I cringed at the sound of her name.

"You don't want them to come?"

I didn't know how to explain it correctly, but..., "You were right; I have a hard time looking at Katherine. She hurt you."

He gave me a breathy laugh, "You really have a weird way of looking at things."

I tried to smile, but I think it came out as a lame grin. He didn't sound happy about this one, "Brian." He paused waiting to see my reaction.

"Danelle?" I was hoping with Brian coming so would Danelle, since she was my only girlfriend and she was more of an adult then people James's age.

This made him happy, "Yes, she is coming."

I was giddy, "When?"

He shook his head no, "Later."

"Who else?"

"Matt has a few people coming."

My smile dissolved, and I started to fidget.

"Sarah, he makes you nervous."

Not wanting him to see the way they treat me, "He doesn't, but the people he is bringing do."

"Do you want me to uninvite him? I would gladly do this."

I shook my head no, "Did he say who he was bringing with him?"

"One other guy... didn't pay attention to his name, and like a group of girls, ones who claimed they were your friends."

"Yeah, so they can come and laugh at me."

He was confused, "You are really uncomfortable with them?"

I regretfully nodded, as I stared into his eyes.

"Do you really think they will laugh at you after coming here?"

This thought did please me.

James confirmed what I was thinking, "Yeah, baby, you are mine."

He knew how to comfort me. None of them matter really, "You are all that matters to me, James; you do know that, don't you?"

Happiness filled his eyes, as he touched my cheek with the tip of his fingers.

Reality came over me, "Where is everyone staying?"

He started to laugh, "Clarissa got a girl's tent and a guy's tent for everyone still in high school."

"We are not leaving Danelle with those trolls."

That made him chuckle, "No, I was thinking she could stay in here with you."

"James, no. This is where you belong. I can't sleep without you anymore."

Of course he liked that, "I was hoping you felt that way, but she would be safer in here, and I kind of had to promise Laura that she would be staying with you. She even talked to Clarissa. I will be close, maybe just over on the lounge."

He was so good to me.

"Do you realize that most of your friends are guys?"

I traced my hand along his concerned face, "This must be hard for you." I was being playful with him.

He didn't take that the way I wanted him to. He laid back in frustration, "You are not going to tease me with that, are you?"

I pushed myself up and tried to crawl over him to sit on him. I couldn't accomplish it without feeling a few shots of pain run through me. He tried to stop me, but he wasn't trying very hard, so I was kind of successful. I traced my fingers down his chest. He pushed himself to sit up with me facing him. I stopped him with my hand on his heart, "Do you think any little boy could compete with this?"

He smiled wrapping his arms around me "No, I guess not." He wasn't convinced.

I held up my finger with the rock on it, "You are kind of stuck with me for life, James."

A great big grin came over his face, "Damn right, you are my wife."

"Yeah, that's better."

He hugged me lightly and Jake walked in, "I told you two none of that; stop it right now. James, we have to go help with putting up the tents, and Sarah, go upstairs for breakfast."

Anger rose in James immediately, "Jake, damn it, get out."

"No! I'm keeping you safe. Come on, get up."

James lifted me off of him easily; moving me to the side of him. He rolled out of bed glancing back at me, "You heard the man; we have to get going."

I was happy he wasn't going to kill him, but I also didn't want this to end.

Jake came over and disconnected me from the IV lines.

I stopped him, "Jake, can we take this out?"

He glared at me, "Go get on the scale. Your goal for getting rid of these was 117 lbs, but I really want 120 lbs. If you are between those, I will take them out."

I got up and started for the bathroom.

"Oh, I have to see it. I don't trust you."

"What?"

"Sarah, you are very good at getting your way. I have to see it."

I was pouting, but James was laughing, "Sarah, he knows you way too well."

I stumbled to the bathroom and hesitated stepping on it. They both gave me my space as I contemplated moving my foot to it, which would decide my IV fate. I decided to say a little prayer, so I raised my face to ask for help from the man above, "Please help me out here. I want to gain weight. I want to be better. Please God, please, help me out."

They both peaked in the bathroom. I glanced over at the two of them. Jake walked in first, moving to the other side of me, as James walked in. He took my hand to help me step up to it. I closed my eyes with hope while I whispered, "Please, please, please, please."

"No, Sarah, not yet."

I had to see for myself. It was only 109 lbs, "Shit."

James was totally smiling, "You gained four more pounds."

I rolled my eyes with disgust, "How much do you think I would have to eat today to get these out?"

Jake was irritated with my disappointment, "More than your body will let you. Get over it; they are not coming out this weekend."

I had been defeated.

They helped me upstairs to the kitchen. I sat with Clarissa, as the boys went out to help Carl. These were the biggest tents I had ever seen.

They even had warming stoves in them, in case it was a cool weekend, but I didn't think that was going to happen. I was fidgeting all through breakfast, and Clarissa noticed I was nervous, "Sarah, you did want this, didn't you?"

"No, it was James's idea, not mine."

"Oh, really, he made it sound like you wanted this."

"No, I am perfectly happy with not seeing anyone. I have your family now, and that is all that matters to me."

"But James said you wanted it to be as normal as possible."

Frowning at her I set the story straight, "Tell me how this is normal in any way?"

She chuckled, "Well, you will have to try. Maybe he is making sure you want to be with him."

"Why would he even wonder that?"

"Because you are 16, and his desires block your needs. He can't feel your needs of being a 16 year old girl, but he is trying."

I grinned, "Well, I definitely wouldn't want any girl my age to go through that."

"Maybe you should talk to girls your age. Too many young people are having sex, and they don't realize the outcome until it's too late."

What an embarrassing conversation this was becoming. I wanted to explain that I wanted to make him happy which sounded childish now, and that my desires were so strong for him, but I think that is what she was trying to explain to me. Instead of trying to explain myself I took a deep breath and sat quietly.

Clarissa took a deep breath and sighed also, "See, the passion is just sooo..."

I was relieved that she remembered how intense it was. I wanted to go find James and ask him to make love to me right now. I was getting hot just thinking about him.

"Sarah, go take a shower, maybe a cold one. You need to have more control than that."

Alarmed, my eyes flew open to hers.

She grinned with delight, "Jake said 14 weeks, and you really need to wait till you are on the pill, darling."

I was completely embarrassed now. She knew what I was feeling, so she hugged me, "It is harder for them to control their feeling than it is for us. You need to try harder."

I just nodded.

James walked back in, "Ready for a shower?"

Okay that was really weird since Clarissa just told me to take a shower. His face was filled with life. I had to shake off this feeling now so I nodded with the intentions of a cold shower.

He walked me back down stairs and to the bathroom, "We need to shave your legs, so you are looking your best."

Not knowing if he was into feeling my want or if he was just trying to make me feel better about myself. I shook my head with disbelief. He got everything ready and helped me to sit down. This time he had me sit on the counter. He pulled my leg up and rested my foot on his chest. I could feel his heart racing against the bottom of my foot. I couldn't help but stare at him. He shaved my leg very carefully and wiped it with the washcloth. He lowered it slowly with just a glance at me, and lifted the other one to his chest. He shook his head, as I watched him. After shaving that one he wiped it off and then hesitated. It was only a moment and, then he caved into his desires, running his hand up and down my thigh, watching his hand glide over it.

I was getting dizzy from wanting him so badly.

When he peeked at me through his lashes he confessed, "Sarah, your body is calling for me."

My heart was pounding making the sound echo in my ears, "What?"

"When you were upstairs, I felt your body calling for mine. I am having a really hard time right now."

He glanced up to my eyes and gazed deeply into them.

"James, no, I'm so sorry. I can't... the pain would be..."

"I know; it's just so hard when the heat from you is pulling me in." His voice was mixed between excitement and regret. The excitement won as he lifted my shirt, "You want to feel me; I can feel you."

"Oh, I do, James, but no... the pain would be too much." The pain worried me but the reality of it was I needed to *feel* him.

Knowing I wasn't protesting too hard he moved closer slowly tracing his lips over my chest while cupping my breast in his warm caring hand. It felt so wonderful to feel his lips moving against my skin. My mind went blank as I closed my eyes tilting my head back to enjoy his touch. The tingling was starting and I knew what was coming next.

His mouth whispered against my skin, "Sarah, you have about 3 seconds...."

I grabbed for my stomach, but the reality of it was I only had 2 seconds. I was reminded what would happen if I became too excited. I begged, "James..." He pulled me in his arms with every intention to ease the pain.

We heard a knock on the door, "Guys, knock it off. Clarissa told me to remind you that this isn't a good idea."

I could hardly breathe from the pain. Even though James was holding me, supporting me, I felt like I might pass out from this knifelike stab in my gut.

"Jake, nothing is going to happen. Get out."

We heard him, "Sarah, are you okay? Clarissa said..."

I gasped, "Jake, I'm fine." I cringed with pain.

James was carrying me to the shower. He turned it on but only the cold, "Sorry, sweetheart, we have to stop the desire to get the pain to stop." He pulled me in. The cold was shocking and relieving at the same time. The trembling was calming down. He held me wiping my face. I could see the anguish in his eyes, "I cause you pain."

I kissed him, "And pleasure, James, pleasure is so good. The pain almost felt good because..." I took a deep breath, "I wanted to feel you."

His eyes were filled with sorrow, "Sarah, your body was calling for me. You have to not think of me that way. I was losing control."

I giggled a little, as I wrapped my arms around him.

"No, Sarah, it's not a good thing."

"My body was calling for you?"

He laughed, "Yeah,"

I was holding back a grin, "That could be a problem."

He chuckled, "You think?"

"James, you will have to wear big baggy clothes then, because I love the way you look."

He agreed but only with his own desires, "You think you have it bad."

He traced his hand along my face, "How are you? Did the pain stop yet?"

The only thing I could do was nod, while getting lost in those deep brown eyes. He glanced away to turn the water to warm, but his eyes came back to mine full of desire, "I can't help you to finish with taking your clothes off. Can you do it yourself?"

He moved away from me slowly, as I reluctantly nodded. He grabbed a towel, but didn't undress in the bathroom; he walked out dripping.

*James:*

I closed the door and leaned my body on the wall holding my hands against it. My body was aching for her, and I had almost lost control. She needed to move home just so I wouldn't hurt her. I didn't want to let her go, but she was everything to me... my everything.

"James, what did you do?" There was a lot of anger in his voice.

Obviously, I didn't do anything, because I was still completely dressed. Oh, the wet clothes were the giveaway that something was happening. Regretfully, I turned to him knowing there was no excuse for what I was doing, I knew it would cause her pain, and I couldn't stop myself.

His eyebrows rose, "You are all wet."

Angry with myself, I took it out on him, "Very observant of you."

He was moving closer to me nose flaring and eyes fierce.

Knowing he was about to lose it I tried to calm him, "Jake, I don't want to do this. I was stupid."

"What the hell are you thinking? You know what it would do to her. Are you really that stupid?"

He needs to understand that the desire was greater than anyone of us, "It was more than that, *she* was calling for me."

"You are full of it."

"No, Jake, her body was calling to me. This connection is getting to me. I was drawn to come to her. I tried to control myself, but the heat coming from her was too much."

"Don't feed me that bullshit. You are just horny."

I didn't know how to explain it. I put my hands over my face, "Jake, can you please let me change before she gets done? It would be best if I wasn't in here when she gets out."

He glowered at me but walked out to let me change. I left the room before she was done. I hurried when I heard the shower stop. I went to sit at the table, "Is there more to get done?" I was asking Jake, so I could get out of the apartment. It was not going to be good to be alone with her.

"Yeah, you took off too fast. We have a lot to get done. Do you want to go now?"

"No, when she is ready you should check on her."

"Me, I'm not the one who…"

"Hey, I just can't do it right now. The heat of her is extending out here. I need to stay away from her right now."

"You really weren't kidding?"

I shook my head as my eyes found his. I was feeling guilty for having this desire, but I could still feel her wanting me to come back to her.

"James?"

Shit, she was calling for me. I pleaded with Jake, "If I go back in there…" I looked out the window. He got up and walked to the door.

"What do you need, Sarah?"

"James."

"Not right now. Can I get you something?"

"No, I guess I'm fine."

I watched him waiting for him to tell me I could go back to her. I needed to be with her, her body was telling me that it needed to be touched. I had to stay away so I got up and went to walk out the door.

"James, did you tell her?"

I turned to him, "Yeah, I did. I was hoping she would feel it enough to stop it. We agreed to wear big baggy clothes."

"That explains the sweats."

I smiled at him and turned to walk out. Sarah walked into the living room. She didn't keep her end of the bargain. She had on Jeans again and a tank top that accented every inch of her body. Shit… she looked delicious; I stopped walking out and started to move back to her. She was still calling to me. I looked at those beautiful green eyes staring at me. That sincere smile was angled in my direction.

"Do I look okay?"

She really didn't realize how beautiful she was. I wanted to hold her and to tell her she was the most beautiful thing in the world.

Jake stopped me, "Sarah, you look great. Don't you need to rest before people come?"

"Nope, I'm too anxious. James?"

I was speechless looking at her. Jake's face appeared in front of me, "James, do you think maybe a cold shower for you? Sarah can come with me and help."

I looked at him begging for him to let me go to her.

He shook his head no, "James, pain. Think pain, James. Knock it off." I stared into his eyes. He was helping.

"Sarah, honey, you look amazing. Can you go help Jake? I need to take care of something." I tried to give her a serious determined look.

No matter how careful I was, she was going to be disappointed. I could see the question on her face, as she moved toward the door. I was thankful Jake stayed between us, but as she passed him, I could not refuse the calling. I grabbed her hand and pulled her to me. I wrapped my arms around her not wanting to let her go.

Jake was angry, "James, let her go."

That soft tender skin, those green piercing eyes, that adorable little look captured me. Holding her tightly to me with one arm left my other hand free to touch her face, "You didn't wear sweats."

She wanted this; her body wanted this, but her face told me something all-together different. She pleaded with me, "Girls from school are coming. I wanted to look good, James; please don't be mad at me."

She really had no clue what her body was doing to me, "I'm not mad; I am just really turned on right now."

Her hands firmly gripped my arms; her face was serious, "James, pain."

It was like she shut it off right then and there. I didn't have the urge to attack her. I was confused that is was over so quickly. It was simply gone and I was okay now. Just like that she stopped it. Her thinking of the pain shut it off. I turned to look at Jake, but he was still ready to come between us. I glanced back at her relieved, "Sarah, I need to talk to Jake for a minute; do you mind heading out on your own? He won't be but a minute."

Her body relaxed in my arms and her fingertips touched my cheek. Taking a deep breath of air, almost taking in every essence I possessed, she coaxed me to let her go. It felt good that the deep obsession wasn't there for me anymore. After she left, I quickly turned to Jake, "Jake, I am okay now. It was like she shut it off. It is completely gone."

"Did you notice when it happened?"

"Yeah, when she thought about the pain. She said the word and the obsession was gone."

His face crumbled with confusion, "I think you should still take a shower."

I was so happy, "No, Jake, she let me go. Her body isn't calling to me anymore."

"Collect yourself and then come out."

I really didn't need any time to collect myself now. The obsession was gone, and I felt so much more in control of my hormones. I shook my head, knowing that I really need to work on this control thing, especially if her body is going to call out to me that way.

## Sarah:

I was waiting for Jake. I wasn't going anywhere till I knew what that was about. He walked out closing the door, "Sarah, I thought you were heading down."

I was plotting how to get it out of him, "I didn't want to walk alone, and I want to know what that was about."

"He told me he told you... that your body was calling for him, and it was driving him crazy."

I cringed, "Yeah, but I didn't think he actually meant it was really calling to him."

"He was very serious. He wasn't in control at all, Sarah. Did you feel it?"

"I only wanted him when…" I glanced at Jake. I didn't want to discuss this with him.

"Sarah, you need to understand the feeling, so you can stop it from happening."

I took a deep breath, "He said he felt me when I was upstairs talking to Clarissa, and I was thinking about…" I cringed.

His patience was running thin, and the anger was building.

I wanted to be careful on explaining this, "I was thinking I wanted to be with him."

"It doesn't bother you to think of James that way in front of Clarissa, does it?"

"No, she understands the passion."

His eyes got wide, "Okay." He shook his head, "And it stopped when you thought of the pain."

"Really?"

"That is what he said."

I didn't quite understand how it could just stop, because I still wanted him to hold me.

"Sarah, if you start to think about him at all, please help him try to be good and think about the pain."

I tried to hold back my grin, "I will try."

"No, promise me. He was out of control. I almost punched him for what he wanted to do."

"Jake, we are married."

"So, do you want to go through that again?"

I stopped. I didn't even have to think about that, "No, never, Jake. That was the worst thing I could ever imagine."

Of course that made him smile, "That is what I want you to think of whenever he is around. At least for the next 13 weeks."

I was excited; one week was done.

"Sarah!"

I tried to play it off that I wasn't thinking that, "What?"

"You are doing it again. Try to only think of the pain for a while."

My mind wandered to the image of James, but when I diverted it with the pain I was able to agree, "I will."

"I am serious; you are not being fair to him, and when you dress like this it doesn't help."

Was he telling me I looked good? "I look that good?"

His face turned a little pink, but he tried to hold himself strong, "Yes."

I couldn't really tell him, but he made my day.

## 44. A Little Practice

I went down to help, but they didn't let me do anything. The girl's tent was bigger than the boy's tent. There were 12 cots in the girl's tent, and 5 cots in the boys. I got to walk through both. There was a third and fourth tent with full size double air mattresses. I walked over to James and wrapped my arms around him from the back, "Who are the extra two tents for? Are we camping out?"

He turned in my arms, "Nope, you get to have the luxury of staying in the house."

I thought it sounded like fun, so I pouted.

"Bathroom, IV's, that kind of stuff, Sarah. One is for Jason and Kylie; the other is for Will and Katherine. Clarissa didn't want to kick Jake out of his room, so she talked to Will. He said it was still better than what he had at home."

When it was time for lunch, Wilson brought out sandwiches and a salad...my favorite salad. I couldn't help but grin at him. He did know how to soften me up.

"I take it Sarah is not mad at me anymore?"

I hugged him around his neck, so hard I hurt myself. I grabbed my stomach and he panicked, "Jake, she's hurt."

"No, I'm fine. It was just a little too much stretching."

The shock on his face was priceless, and he became very nervous, as he helped me to sit on a bench by the fire pit. It was really cool, and it swayed. There were about 12 deep wooden chairs and two benches.

"Wilson, is Josie coming over too, and are you both staying?"

His forehead creased with confusion, "No, this is your weekend."

"Wilson, you are important to me. Can you please invite Josie and stay overnight?"

He glanced at Carl waiting for a reply, but Carl turned to me pleased with my thought process, "Yes, Wilson, we would love for you to stay. You can have Sam's room."

Sam was walking to get a sandwich, "Where will I stay?"

Carl looked at him, "In the boy's tent."

"That's not fair."

I knew how to make this a better thought for him, "Yeah, but it's close to the girl's tent and you are a flirt."

Grinning from ear to ear, "Oh, yeah, that sounds good, Wilson. I would love to share my room with you."

Wilson and I exchanged smiles. I raised my eyebrows, "How can you say no. Please ask Josie if she will come." I waved for him to come closer to me. James noticed and paid attention to me, but I spoke to Wilson, "I promise I will behave."

He leaned down and kissed my cheek, "You were just curious, but I thank you. I do appreciate it. I will call her."

Carl looked at everybody and then at me and came to sit by me. He took my hand bringing it to his lap, "You love my James."

I turned to him, because I didn't understand where this was going, "Yes."

"You are having feelings?"

I was curious now and nodded. Carl seemed pleased with himself, so he continued, "We didn't think it would happen. You didn't have the child."

I didn't know how to feel, so I stared into his eyes. My feelings were a mixture of not being able to breathe, the dark cloud moving in, and excitement all at the same time. He was talking to me about it. I choked out, "So it is normal."

He seemed pleased with this as the grin on his face grew.

"So are you talking to me about it?"

Being a little more serious he asked, "Do you hear or just feel?"

Not knowing the difference asked, "Hear?"

"Can you hear what people are thinking, Sarah?"

"No." I glanced at him puzzled.

"So, you feel?"

"It's fuzzy, it's more like an instinct. Like when we were playing games the other night and Wilson was getting uncomfortable. I could feel he was anxious."

"Oh, well that isn't much."

Wondering how much more I could have, "Not much?"

"That is why you are curious. It's not clear."

"No, it's not, and I don't get anything from you or Sam. James on the other hand..., sometime yes, and sometimes no."

"I want to try something. I am going to think of a color and you guess what it is."

I shrugged my shoulders, "Okay, um..." I gazed and studied his face, "Blue, green, or maybe black."

He was laughing, "No, fuchsia."

"See nothing."

He yelled to James, "James, think of a color."

I glanced at James and smiled, "Hazel green, it's the color of my eyes."

"Did you feel it, or did you hear him say it."

"I just know that; I didn't feel anything."

Carl yelled to Sam, but only because he wasn't that close to us, "Think of a color, Sam."

I shrugged my shoulders and stared at Sam, "Brown, deep brown. Wait no Yellow."

Sam laughed out loud, "Sarah, no, Black."

This wasn't helping me at all, but Carl yelled to Jake next. "Jake, think of your favorite color will you please."

This time I concentrated on Jakes face, "The color of whose eyes?"

It was almost comical the way Jake was almost startled with my question, as much as James seemed concerned with it.

I turned back to Carl when he asked, "Did you hear him or feel him."

"I don't know. It was like it was coming from my head."

He looked at me suspiciously, and that made me a little paranoid, "What?"

James and Jake were walking over to us, and they were both starring at me.

"We'll do more tests when there are more people to read."

Still wanting to know whose eyes Jake was thinking about, I glared at him with a thought directed at him, *"whose eyes were you thinking of?"* Even though he was evading my question by pretending not to feel me, I knew he did by the smirk on his face. Happiness filled me, because I had a sneaking feeling he was thinking about a girl's eyes.

James came and sat down beside me, "Dad, what is it?"

"We were just playing a little game, James. Hey think of your favorite number."

Carl was waiting for my answer. He was making it so easy on me, because it was James. I always feel what he wants me to feel. I was sure of it, "That is easy, 19."

James was choking on his spit but swallowed hard, "I never told you that."

I shrugged my shoulders, "That is how old you were when you met me."

Carl was enjoying this, "How about you, Jake?"

Studying Jakes face once again but there was nothing. I turned back to Carl, "I got nothing."

Jake was uneasy as he explained, "That's because I couldn't think of one."

It was my turn to prove a point that Jake had feelings too, "Jake what color am I thinking of?"

"Brown, James's eyes."

Of course he was right. I loved James's eyes.

This surprised Carl, "You too?" He smiled and shook his head, as he glanced over at James who was dumbfounded. Intrigued Carl asked Jake, "What color am I thinking of."

"Nothing."

Carl got a deep thoughtful look on his face, "James think of... let's see, think of a number between 20 and 40." He turned to Jake, "Can you guess that?"

Jake's eyes squinted as he stared at James, "32."

James shook his head no, but I knew what he was thinking, so I spoke up, "42."

James turned to me, "That's not a number between 20 and 40."

I grinned and scolded, "Then why were you thinking that?"

He sat down staring again at me.

Carl was intrigued, "Jake, you feel things too, but it's selective."

A look of embarrassment filled Jake's cheeks with pink, as he nodded but pointed to me.

Absorbed in Jake he inquired, "Anyone else besides Sarah?"

Jake explained more, "Yeah, when I think about it, there were lots of people, but I didn't know it at the time."

"Anyone else here?"

Full of pride he pointed out, Yeah, my dad, mom, and Clarissa," he raised his eyebrows, "my mom that is. That's about it."

Carl was pleased, "You have your mother's gift."

You could see the uncertainty of this in his face, as his forehead creased, "Gift?"

"You can't hear them talking, but you can feel what people are thinking. When did you notice this?"

He glanced over at me, "It was Sarah who noticed and started to ask me questions with her feelings."

Carl turned back to me, "You noticed?"

"No, I felt his feelings, because he was feeling the same thing I was."

"And you feel James?"

I was pleased with myself, "I can't hear him, but I just *know*. It's like my own thoughts."

"When there are more people around, I am going to want to do this more. I'm going to test a theory."

I couldn't help myself, "So are you going to tell me what's going on, or am I going to keep guessing?"

He smiled at me and touched my cheek gently with his fingertips.

It was like I instantly understood what he was thinking. I gaped at him and shivered. The heaviness moved into my chest making it hard for me to breathe. I gasped, "It's from the baby?"

Warmth filled his eyes and concern crossed his face, "You felt that?"

I nodded, but the tears were coming from my eyes immediately. James wrapped his arms around me.

Carl was trying to calm me down, "Sarah, we didn't think this would happen. You didn't even carry it for long. It was only a few days that you had it in you. Can you imagine what would have happened if you carried it full term?"

I couldn't handle what I was hearing. I killed something that was amazingly beautiful. I stood up, and I need to run away from this. I didn't want to know anymore. I killed it.

James's arms wrapped around me, and he whispered in my ear, "Sarah, it would have killed us both." He kissed my cheek and was leading me to the house.

Jake yelled after us, "No, James, she has to eat, or I have to hook her back up."

James stopped and turned me to look at him. I was devastated to learn I killed something that was so special. He pulled my face so that his eyes could penetrate mine, "Sarah, you can handle this. It wouldn't have lived anyway, and it would have taken us with it. Please, please don't feel like this. We will have another one someday."

Searching his eyes for comfort, I was left with not being able to tell him how bad this made me feel.

Clarissa was walking from the house, "Carl, did you tell her?"

I was surprised with her question, so I turned to her. She put her arms out for me to come to her. I ran to her burying my face in her chest. She held me tightly while she scolded Carl, "Carl, I told you she wasn't ready. Why didn't you wait like I asked?"

James came over and wrapped his arms around both of us, "This is one of those things that I probably should have known about. Don't you think?"

"If you knew, she would have known sooner. I was trying to protect her from this. I wanted her to wait until you decided to have another child, James. Sarah, look at me." I lifted my face to her, "Sarah, stop this. Things cannot change. You are allowed to feel sad, but what you do to yourself for punishment is not acceptable. It wouldn't have made it. You have to be strong now and come eat. Remember… I will not treat you like a baby."

James was angry with her, and he tried to pull me to him. I clung to her.

"Mom, that is harsh."

"You are no better, boy. You should have waited to be with her. Your desire is going to hurt her worse than anything else. Get some control; talk to your father if you need to. Learn there are ways to block what she does to you. Now go and sit; she will eat now."

She pulled me to the bench, and Carl moved over so that I was sitting between them. James did not sit; he was intensely pacing back and forth looking at me each time as he turned.

"Sarah, look at you, you have messed up your beautiful face." Clarissa dipped a napkin in a glass of water and wiped my face. She whispered to me softly, "If you are old enough to have sex, you are old enough to handle this. Be strong, child, and you will be okay; the pain will ease with time."

I didn't want to hear it, but she was helping.

She huffed with a stern tone aimed at James, "You don't do good things for yourself either. Sit down and eat."

He avoided her look continuing to pace. His mind was going wild. I didn't understand anything that was rushing through his mind. Clarissa was more forceful in her directions, "NOW!"

He didn't acknowledge her but took a sandwich, sat down, and ate quietly.

Clarissa's fury turned to Jake, "So, you too?"

He nodded, but was silent. He didn't want to talk about it. He felt what I was feeling, and he could tell James felt it too.

After eating and sitting quietly for the rest of our lunch, things seemed to calm down. I was feeling better, not so depressed. Clarissa got up and started for the house, but stopped one last time to get her opinion out, "No more baby talk and Sarah... you need to toughen up. Your mother will be here in a couple of hours, and we don't want her to think we are not taking care of you."

I did want to please her, so I agreed with a small nod. James took her spot next to me.

Carl stood up, "No, you don't, boy; we have things to discuss, and we're not ready for everyone yet. Come with me." I wanted to go with James. I needed him right now, but Jake gave me a look, while shaking his head no. He also gave me a feeling, *"Sarah he needs to calm down... stay here."*

I did stay there even though he got up to follow them, to help. They were carrying out pillows and sleeping bags; James handed me a different book, "That is the next one. Let me know if it is good." He kept walking.

Jake was following him and stopped to hand me a pillow and blanket, "I didn't know if you needed a nap."

I was thankful for the thought. I curled up in one of the big chairs and started to read. I didn't get far before I was sleeping.

James was carrying me back to the house before I knew it.

"No, James, I don't want to sleep."

He breathed a small kiss on my cheek while whispering, "Just a little nap. Your mom is going to be here in an hour, and you were sleeping anyway."

I closed my eyes and gave into him and sleep.

I woke to James tracing my face. I was connected to the IV lines again. I rubbed my arm in protest.

"Hey, that is enough of that." James was trying to get me to stop rubbing at them.

"Sarah, your mom is here upstairs with Clarissa. Can you come up?"

Squeezing my eyes tighter in protest I asked, "I have one request."

I could hear the huff of his laugh, "And what is that?"

I puckered my lips waiting to feel those lips.

I could feel the smile with his kiss. Slowly I opened my eyes to see his warm eyes watching me, while he taunted me with little nibbles. I was pleased that he kissed me this way. I licked my lips to show I enjoyed his touch. He came back for more. When he finally forced himself away, he spoke softly to me, "You are going to be the death of me."

"Do you have to say that?"

He was confused by my dislike of that saying.

"I don't like that phrase. I would never want to have you die on me."

Shaking his head and pulling me from the bed, "Come on, Sarah, your mom is here. She is going to be excited that you look so good."

Still bemused from sleep, I stumbled a little; of course, my Cayuse, caught me.

I glanced up to catch the concern on his face, "You didn't sleep enough."

"I'll be fine. When is Danelle getting here?"

"I'm not sure, but I thought we would give your mom the tour of where everyone was staying, so she can report it to Laura."

I smiled and muddled out of the room and towards the door. James had my IV in one hand and his other hand guiding me as he followed. I slowly went up the steps and through the patio doors. I saw her at the table with Clarissa who was drawing with Tamara. Tamara came running and took my hand pulling me to the table, "Sarah, your mommy is here. She's here, Sarah. Aren't you happy?"

Of course I was happy and seeing her here at the table filled me with happiness to my core. I made my way across the room to where she was standing waiting to take me into her arms with the biggest hug. It lasted a lot longer than needed, because I didn't want to let go. I missed her, and she was alone. I hated that fact.

"I miss you, mom."

She pushed me away, still holding my shoulders and studied me. "You are in regular clothes. You are doing much better this time?"

Jake came in, sat at the table, and asked my mom if she had any questions. I held up my arm, "Jake, can we please get this out?"

That seemed to worry my mother.

Jake stood up and walked over to me to disconnect me, "Sarah, we went over this, this morning. No, not until you gain 10 more pounds."

I rolled my eyes.

"So you are doing better?"

Obviously, I wasn't doing good enough to get rid of the stupid IV. I rolled my eyes in disgust.

My mother was scolding, "You are being difficult."

Guiltily I grinned, and James brought her a cup of coffee and sat on the other side of her. I had to defend myself, "No, I am not. I can't do anything without Jake or James controlling what I am doing. I can't even get dressed until Jake disconnects me."

She got a look on her face… like wondering how I got dressed already.

Jake was stumbling to get it out, "We just hooked her back up for nap time."

My mom got a kick out of Jake's floundering, "Jake, I am sure you are doing a fine job." And then she turned to glace at me as she continued, "Sarah can be difficult sometimes."

Clarissa smiled and talked to her directly, "She is only hard on the boys. It keeps them in line. She doesn't put up with their crap."

I think my mom liked that idea.

Clarissa had dinner served while she was there. She liked that they made sure I was eating a certain amount of food. She was very observant of how they acted around me. James gave mom a tour of sleeping arrangements for everyone that was coming, but assured her Danelle would be with me. She seemed happy that he wasn't dominating my life by having to have me all to himself all of the time. They discussed me moving home for school. I didn't say much. I wasn't happy about being away from James, and instead of expressing my dislike, I kept my mouth shut. My mind was racing in a lot of directions worrying about moving home, being away from James, and the girls from school coming here. Clarissa and James seemed to notice because they kept touching me lightly to bring me back to present time here with my mother. As I let myself get overwhelmed with everything running through my mind my heart started pumping faster and faster while the hole was opening and growing in my chest. The more they worked out the plans of me going home the more quiet I became; it was easier for me to try to control this overwhelming urge to freak out. When James handed me a glass of juice I glanced up at him with desperation. I didn't want to feel this way, and it was getting harder and harder to control. He could see the glaze coming over my eyes. Thankfully, he reassured my mom they would talk more about the plans next week and tried to change the subject. It was almost 6:30pm when she got up to leave. We walked her out and James held me the whole way; he knew the depression was setting back in. As we got to her car my car was pulling in. I gave my mom the biggest hug ever and she got in and drove off.

# 45. Visitors

**B**rian and Danelle were getting out of my car. I ran to Danelle hugging her.

"Sarah, you look so much better. The last time I saw you, you were green."

Even thought I was so happy she was here, the darkness was still there, and I was afraid to talk. I clung tightly to her not wanting to let go. James took her bag. James nudged me to look at Brian. Glancing in his direction, I noticed he seemed to be pretty uncomfortable. I walked over to him and gave him the biggest hug, but he didn't really hug me back.

I pushed him away to see his face, "Brian?"

A grin did come to his face, but his attention moved to James while he whispered to me, "You're married."

So the marriage thing was what would stop him from hitting on me.

He leaned down further to me and whispered in my ear, "I didn't know you had it this bad."

James and I both grinned. I loved that James felt everything I did, because he knew what Brian said. I nodded for James to talk for me. I still wasn't talking a whole bunch trying to holding back the tears. "Brian, we have a treat for you. Sarah's friend from school invited a shit load of girls to come to play and stay the weekend. Matt said they were very friendly."

Brian grinned guiltily; however, I wasn't happy with a shit load of girls, so I turned on James without a smile on my face. He knew I wasn't happy again. He pleaded with me, "Sarah, behave. We want Brian to be comfortable and have fun, right? He is your friend."

I did want Brian to have fun, but thinking about the girls that were coming on top of the baby thing this afternoon, talking was completely out for the moment.

James had his arm around Danelle's shoulder, "I will be expecting supervision from you this weekend."

Jake was walking out to help us carry things in. Danelle hugged James's waist, "If she says you haven't been taking care of her, I am going to make this weekend very miserable for you." She looked up to his face to see how that was going for him.

Jake started to laugh out loud, but then he noticed that I wasn't doing well. He tried to change the subject, "So how was the drive down in her car?"

Brian was all smiles, "Great, I love this car."

James turned to him, "Well, if Sarah needs a new one maybe…"

I glared at him disapprovingly; I didn't need a new car; I love my car.

James held back a laugh, "Okay, we'll discuss it later."

Brian's eyes were bright with hope.

I was making Jake nervous with how I was feeling, but he wanted to move things along, "Hey, Brian, you're here first, so you get first dibs on what bed you want. I'll bring you down."

Jake was helping Brian grab his bag. I could tell these two were going to be on their best behavior. James grabbed Danelle's bags; of course, she had more than one, being a girl and all. I took Danelle by the arm and started to walk in. She stopped at the site of the pool, "You have this all the time?"

James spoke for me, "She doesn't use it a whole lot, yet."

Danelle seemed concerned as her eyes moved back and forth between James and me. He tried to smile to show her everything was okay, but she grabbed my arm, "What's this for?" She was pointing to the IV paraphernalia.

I took a deep breath to try and reply but knew I had no hope for talking yet. I glanced to James for help, so he moved up putting his arm around the other side of her, "She needs that till she gains some weight."

She turned to me. She wanted to hear it from me not him. I smiled at her, but the tears were coming which made her uncomfortable, so she looked away. James was directing her in the apartment and led her to our room. James was sitting her bag on the dresser, "We thought you would be more comfortable in here with Sarah, if you don't mind."

"Sounds good to me; a real bed… it has been a long time since I slept in a real bed."

I noticed James had a small blow up mattress on the floor on my side of the bed at the top of the steps. I glanced at it and then at him.

He whispered, "I didn't want to be far from you." He slowly moved around me lightly tracing his hand along my waist and whispering in my ear, "Are you okay?"

My eyes fell to his as they filled with water.

"Sarah, try harder. She is already worried because you are not talking. She doesn't understand. Please, everything will be okay."

I turned to Danelle directing her to the bed, "Go for it."

She ran and jumped on the bed, "I am going to like this, Sarah."

I moved slowly to the bed and lay down next to her.

She sat up alarmed, "Do you two have sex in this bed?"

I couldn't help but laugh.

James pointed out, "Danelle, why do you have to be so direct?"

She was very determined to know this, "Well...?."

James was trying to not answer her, "Do you really think Sarah is up for anything like that?"

Her eyes squinted as her eyes moved back and forth between us again, however, they settled on me in a disapproving way, "You do some big things without discussing it with me."

I had to agree with her, but James helped us get off the subject, "Do you want to go check out where everyone else is staying?"

She was eager, getting up right away to go check it out, but as I sat up slowly James came to me quickly helping me stand.

I scolded, "Let me do it myself."

He put on a fake smile glancing over my shoulder, "She might worry if you cringe, Sarah. Please let me help you."

I gave in glancing at her.

Danelle wasn't happy about the way I was moving, "You are still in pain?"

James explained, "She went in for a second surgery a little over a week ago, and she is doing great, all things considered; she does have some residual pain from that."

She came in front of me, "You had a second surgery?"

I rolled my eyes, "Yes."

"Her intestines were all knotted up. She couldn't go to the bathroom."

Irritated with James talking about pooping again I was able to find my voice easily, "Let's not discuss my pooping, James."

He laughed and so did Danelle. We were walking out of the apartment and James knelt to give me a piggyback.

Danelle scolded, "No, not already, I just got here."

James laughed, "Danelle it's a long walk, and I am just helping her so she doesn't get worn out before everyone gets here."

She looked at him and then at me, "You get tired out that easily?"

I shrugged, "Sometimes."

Danelle knew there was something not quite right, "She speaks again."

James put his hands on her shoulders to guide her down to the fire pit. I nuzzled into his neck and kissed him. He took one of his hands and traced my face holding it to his neck, "It will be okay, baby. Just try to have fun."

We heard another car pull in. James set me down, "Sarah, give her the tour, will you?"

I took her arm and started to walk down to the tents. I walked her into the girl's tent, "Girls."

She looked at me, "How many girls are coming?"

I shrugged my shoulders.

"You have this many girlfriends?"

"Nope, they are pretending, so they can spend the weekend with Matt."

"Sarah, you're not talking very much."

I tried to smile at her while choking out, "Stupid, emotional, bad lately." If I wasn't careful a couple tears could leak out.

The worry showed on her face, "Are you happy here?"

I was more than happy here just not so happy with what I did, "Moving home, two weeks." That did it. My tears spilled, leaving a trail as they ran down my cheeks. I wiped them quickly.

"You don't want to talk about it?"

I shook my head no.

"Good, because I don't like to see you cry."

I chuckled a little pulling her to the boy's tent. Jake came running out and ran right into Danelle, "Sorry, how is your arm?"

She held up the cast, "Still attached."

He laughed continuing on his way up to help James with whoever was here, but yelled back at her, "I want to look at it later."

I noticed her blushing. I had a feeling things were stirring already between them. I walked her into the boy's tent where Brian was sprawled out over the large bed, "Jake said I got first dibs."

I grinned at him and sat down next to him on the bed carefully. He grabbed me pulling me back to lay with him, but I gasped with the pain.

"Sarah?"

I was able to squeak out why I gasped, "Still painful."

He let go right away, "I'm sorry."

Danelle explained, "Brian they had to do a second surgery. James said it was a little over a week ago."

He was impressed, "Can I see the scar?"

I shook my head no, holding my stomach.

"Come on, Sarah, I'm not trying anything… you're married."

I really didn't want to show off any scars, "Not comfortable yet."

The grimace on his face was funny as he said, "Is it that bad?"

I shook my head no, "Jake does beautiful work." I couldn't say anything about James making it heal, but those few words knocked the air out of me, and the tears started to fill my eyes. I turned to Danelle for help.

She did what I needed her to, because she was telling Brian what to do, "You should go help Jake and James."

He glanced between her and myself, "Sarah, are you unhappy here?"

I shook my head no, but the tears started to flow more.

Danelle tried to help me out, "Brain, don't."

I was wiping them from my face.

His concern was mixed with a touch of anger, as his mouth went to a thin line, "Why are you crying then?"

Regretting the tears and loving that he cared I got out, "Happy."

He hugged me as we heard the boys coming down talking to other people, "If James catches you in bed with me, I will die this weekend."

He was right, so I tried to get up, but the pain shot through my inners. Danelle grabbed my hand and helped me to stand the rest of the way.

Brian jumped up in shock, as he watched me hold my stomach, grimacing.

I knew I had to try and ease his worry, "Still a little pain."

I grabbed Danelle's arm and pulled her out with Brian following. Will and Katherine, Jason and Kylie were coming down. Jake and James were carrying everything for all of them.

Will hugged me deeply and whispered in my ear, "Sorry, Sarah,"

I lost it, and I thought I was doing well. The tears really started to stream. James dropped everything and picked me up carrying me away from everybody down to the dock, "Sarah, everyone is going to think you are unhappy with me, please, darling, don't cry."

I nuzzled into his chest, "Sorry."

He set me down on the bench, so I was facing the lake. He squatted in front of me waiting for me to calm down.

I wiped my tears, "I was doing okay till Will said sorry; I assume he knows?"

James was soothing me, "Sarah, of course he knows; he is my brother, but I will talk to him. The subject will not come up again."

Danelle was walking down the dock, "There are going to be rules if I am staying."

We both started to laugh.

Jake came running down behind Danelle, asking, "Is she okay?" Jake put his arm around Danelle's shoulder, "You, girlfriend, are going to help me make them behave this weekend, okay?"

She looked up at him determined, "They are going to have rules." They both walked in front of me, while James moved to sit down next to me.

Danelle crossed her arms and looked at us, "James, no mushy stuff; you already agreed to it."

I turned to him disapprovingly.

His expression told me I should have known this, "It was the only way she would come."

I could only shake my head in disbelief, especially since I really needed him by my side all the time. But Danelle continued, "No making out. It still grosses me out."

Jake was laughing, enjoying all of this, "She is going to make this a really easy weekend for me."

She was stern, "No flirting in front of me."

I raised my eyebrows at her, "Hey, I'm married"

"I am only 15, so I am not ready to hear that stuff."

Realization hit me, as I realized she had a birthday and I missed it, "You're 15?"

"Yep, my birthday was yesterday."

I turned to James horrified that I didn't get her anything.

He knew what I was feeling, so he assured me, "I will get Wilson on it right away."

Jake stole her attention, "You're 15?"

She was still in her scolding mood, "Yes, and I don't want to hear any of this mushy stuff these two start up."

Jake put his arm around her looking at James and me, "Can I keep her?"

I was trying to hold back a smile, and I tried to put everything out of my mind. I didn't even look at James. He was laughing and kissed the side of my head.

Danelle wasn't pleased, "See, that is just not happing. James, you promised to behave, so please no kissing."

James pleaded with her, "I just kissed her head; I can't even do that?"

"No, it's my time this weekend."

James got up and crawled at her, "You want me to kiss your head?" He picked her up and she was yelling at him to put her down.

Jake wasn't enjoying this part of the argument, "You already have your dream girl, James, and put her down."

I grabbed Jake's hand and pulled him to sit with me. He turned to me worried, "He is going to hurt her."

I shook my head and comforted him pulling his arm to hold him tight, "James is gentle; he feels her. It's okay, Jake."

He still wasn't pleased, and his attention stayed on James and Danelle. I was enjoying his dislike of James touching her. Then he was going to lose it, "Would he like it if I kissed you?"

James stopped right away and set her down, "Jake, you wouldn't do that."

He glared at my James. I turned Jake's face to mine and whispered, "A little protective, aren't you?"

His attitude changed instantly, after James set her down, and he spoke very pleasantly to Danelle, "We have our work cut out for us this weekend. These two are inseparable."

She was firm as she looked at him, "I am game if you are?"

He didn't look at her, but I did and never really noticed until that moment her eyes were the brightest blue. My heart started to race because the only thing I could think of now was that it was the color in his mind earlier. Of course, I forgot that Jake and I had some sort of connection, so when I smiled at her and looked at him, he read my thoughts. He gave me a disapproving glare as he shook his head no. I couldn't wipe the smile from my face now that I knew. I shrugged my shoulders and took Danelle by the arm and started to walk with her up to the house. Katherine came and gave me a half hug; however, Kylie gave me a huge hug. Danelle did not look pleased; In fact, she was glaring at her.

She gave Danelle a slight grin and explained, "James talked to us and just letting you know, we don't party anymore. We get along better without that."

Danelle turned on James, "You have a big mouth."

Knowing he could not win in Danelle's eyes, he justified himself, "Just wanting to make you and Sarah happy."

He turned and gave Jake a grin to rub it in, which did irritate Jake. He was angry now.

Jason still had Kylie's hand in his, but wrapped the other arm around me. He whispered in my ear, "We are going to talk later." He kissed my forehead, and I looked at him funny. He just grinned in an odd kind of way. Just then we heard another car pull in.

Matt was a lot louder than the rest of them. I was excited to see Matt, but panic struck me quickly, realizing that girls from school were also here. I turned to James worried. He came to me right away and took my hand turning me to him, "Sarah, you can do this without crying, right?"

I didn't know if I could. They have never been very nice to me.

"Do you want to come out with us, or do you want to wait here?"

I shrugged my shoulders. I was having very mixed feelings.

"Come with me then." He squatted and I grabbed hold, as he lifted me up on his back.

I glanced back at Kylie, "Kylie, will you please make yourself at home?"

Clarissa was coming down; I gestured for her to take care of Danelle. I knew she would take care of my best friend and if she really did see into my mind then she knew I thought Danelle was perfect for Jake.

A large smile came to her face as she nodded to me, "You are getting the hang of it."

I was very sure of my feelings now, giving her a smile back.

"Selective, very good Sarah, very good indeed. I will make her comfortable."

I nuzzled into James's neck and Jake came with to help. There were two cars full of people.

Matt got out and his eyes came to me right away. I did like his smile, and his eyes were actually sparkling as he gazed into mine, "So, this is why you fell off the earth and didn't call me back."

I was confused, because I didn't know he called me. James spoke up, "That was my fault; she needed her rest."

I kissed his neck. Matt looked around, as the girls got out of the car. Alissa was in the front seat, and I smiled at her as she got out of the car. There was Tammy, Laura, Samantha, and Jamie all in his car.

I gave Matt a disgusted, disapproving look.

He chuckled with my evaluation, "James said a lot of variety."

I shook my head not agreeing with that at all. James walked over to Matt and shook his hand. He turned around and said, "Here, help Sarah down, please."

Matt dropped everything and grabbed me helping me to slide off of James's back. He faced James as if to ask a question.

James laughed, "Yes, you can hug her, Matt. I will not kill you."

It didn't take Matt a second to move to me and hugged me so tight it hurt.

James did scold a little, "Hey, I know it's been awhile but take it easy; you're going to hurt her."

James caught me as Matt let go. Matt freaked out a little, "You are still in pain, Sarah?"

I shrugged and nodded at the same time. James explained, "She had a second surgery about a week ago. She just has to take it easy, and we have to be careful around her."

Matt was touching my stomach, "Are you okay now?"

Jake moved over to where we were. James put up his arm to stop him. James asked Matt, "So, do you want to do some introductions?"

Matt studied me, concern for my recovery showing on his face, "Oh yeah, Sarah, you know Blaire."

I waved a little. Then he introduced all the girls. Jake was overwhelmed with the choices, but he could feel them ogling. I could feel his disgust with the way their minds were going nuts over him.

I had to laugh when he rolled his eyes.

"See, that is what I mean."

I tried to calm him, "Just have fun with it."

Blaire had 5 more girls in his car, Brianna, Karlie, Chloe, Mandy, and Alison. I smiled at all of them, but I felt self-conscious. James wrapped his arms around me and kissed my cheek but spoke to everyone, "Well, I hope you don't mind camping. We have tents set up for everyone."

Matt was concerned with this, "You can stay in a tent?"

James shook his head no. Matt took my arm looking at the IV stuff and then at James, "And this, James, what is this for?"

"She has to have that till she puts more weight on. Only at night, Matt, and she is doing better." James wanted to make sure I was comfortable, so he kissed my cheek. He let go of me and started to grab bags with Jake.

## James:

I was worried about my baby. She was not comfortable with all of this. I needed to help her, but I also needed to help everyone else. "Matt which bag is yours?"

He shook his head turning to me, "James, I can get it."

I wanted her to know I was okay with all of this, so I smiled at her but said, "No, you can take my Sarah down. Just be careful, okay?"

He was happy with this, but she gave me that confusing little smirk like I was up to something. I had to make her see I was okay with it. I ran back to her and helped to lift her to his back. I kissed her cheek, "Sarah, it's okay. Smile, he is here because he is your friend."

Matt turned to look at me, "You are unbelievable. That is why she loves you."

I was a little embarrassed, but I just directed him in the right direction, "Just head that way; we're right behind you. Wait to put her down till someone helps, okay?"

He grinned, "I got it."

I went back to help Jake grab stuff. He huffed at me, "You know he is in love with your wife."

I turned to him, "Jake, he is her friend, be nice."

"How can you let him touch her?"

"It's for her not me, besides, brother, you were the only one she let into her heart."

I looked right at him, and he looked away from me, "James I didn't know ..."

I put my hand on his shoulder, "Jake, it is you I have the hardest time with, because you get to keep touching her."

He pleaded, "But, it's not like that anymore, I swear."

I knew he still loved her; I could see it in his eyes and his actions, but feeling his heart hurt for her was the hardest. I smiled a little and started to grab bags, "Sometimes we have to be okay with things we don't like, little brother; I still feel your heart." I had to lighten the conversation, "And shit, why did we want him to bring girls? This is ridiculous. Sarah is never this bad."

He started to laugh, "It was your idea." But then he stopped and looked at me shocked, "That is why. You wanted to preoccupy all the guys here with other girls."

I tried to stifle my grin, but I couldn't help it. I knew each and every one of these guys wanted to talk to her alone, to see if she was happy with me. Deep down I knew I had nothing to worry about, because I felt it in her heart, but a little assurance was always good.

"Almost all her friends are guys, so yes I wanted to distract them. Wouldn't you?"

"No, I wouldn't have allowed them to come here."

"I said it is for her, not me."

We started to head down to the tents with all the bags. Jake lead the pack, and I stayed behind to watch carefully over my Sarah. I was thankful Matt stayed close to me. He kept looking at me to make sure I was still okay until we got down to the tents.

Sarah was directing him to the boy's tent. I didn't want her going in with him, so I tried to get him to stop, "Hang on, I will be right with you." I didn't want her alone with him in the tent, as just a precaution, "I will help her; give me a second."

I went in and dumped all the bags on one bed, "Well, you guys can figure things out." They were slowly moving bags to different cots. I went to catch up with Matt and my sweet beautiful wife. He walked in carrying her, but I followed quickly with his bag. Brian was in there and jumped up when they walked in. He was looking very upset. I butted in, "Matt this is Brian, Brian-Matt. Oh, and this is Blaire."

They all shook hands. I grabbed my Sarah under her arms, "Come here, baby."

She gave me a look, so I set her down. She knew I was getting a little possessive, so I had to get her mind off of it, "I think they are getting the Jet skis down if anyone wants to go play, and the floating dock is out."

Brian moved forward to us, "Is Sarah going?"

I tucked her behind me, 'Nope, she's still healing, but the rest of you can go. It's all fun and games this weekend. Food will be here about 10:00 pm." I pulled her out with me.

"James, I haven't talked to Matt yet."

I pulled her along with me, "I know, baby, but you will hurt Brian's feelings. You have all weekend to talk to all of them, and you will have to remember, that this is going to be hard for me."

She turned on me grabbing my shirt, "Than why, James? You know I would rather be here alone with you."

God, I needed her to say that. I kissed her forehead, "You need to see your friends too." I was really trying to be supportive. I wrapped my arms around her and walked back to where everyone else was sitting. Danelle was on a bench by herself. I guided Sarah to her. She let go of me and went to Danelle. I liked that best of all. Kylie moved to the other side of her and took her hand. This was really weird. It was going to take time to get used to.

Jason walked over to me, "Hey, she isn't' saying a whole lot. Is she okay?"

I turned to walk away and he followed. We got to the gate, and I gestured for him to walk through. He stopped on the other side of the gate, "James, why is she like that?"

I really didn't want to get into the details of it, "Jason, I understand why you wanted to wait for her to grow up. Some things have happened, and she wasn't ready to deal with them, and she is having a really tough time right now. I wanted this weekend for her to forget about some of the stuff that happened and for her to have fun. So, number one, she is going to talk to each of these guys on their own, and we have to be okay with it. They are her friends..."

"James that's just not right. How can you...?"

"Please, Jason. Second, you have to keep your thoughts about how she looks to yourself, unless it is good. Anything you would think that isn't good, keep it out of your head."

He looked at me with animosity, "Why?"

"Jason, she feels things in people's minds, and she is easily upset. Please don't think anything negative."

"What happened, James? It can't be just the appendix that did this?"

I could hardly look at him, "If I tell you she will know you know, and you will feel bad, and she can't go through any sadness this weekend, so I will tell you but not till you are leaving. I am trying to keep her on the happy side, okay?"

He wasn't okay with my explanation, but didn't want to do anything that would hurt her, "Is she upset about the scar?"

I shook my head, as my face grew hot with embarrassment, "No, we used an old Indian remedy, and you can hardly see it."

"James will you just tell me, and what the hell do you mean she will feel what I am thinking?"

"Let's just say, we're married and things happen."

"So, she got some of your talents because you're married?"

I was so relieved he came up with that. It was an easy out, "Yes, something like that. Please do not think anything bad."

He was more comfortable with this, "Of course not."

We headed back down to the group of people.

She was sitting there smiling. Dad, Sam and Jake were helping Wilson. I noticed there were more than two Jet Skis now, so I walked down to help out.

"Wilson, Sarah's best friend had a birthday yesterday, and we didn't know about it, could we…?"

"You don't have to say another word. I have been waiting for a birthday. I have something very special. Sarah and her friend will love it."

"Wilson, when is Josie coming. I would like to help her with her stuff."

He pulled out his phone, "She is here now."

I took off to the back and went to help her. Jake was behind me but past me quickly moving to her. He hugged his mom and I grabbed her stuff. She looked a little nervous. Jake was trying to make her more comfortable, and I couldn't help myself, "Sarah feels very strongly about Wilson; you know he helped us when I had to leave before. Sarah asked for you to be here."

That did ease the atmosphere somewhat, "He said you were polite."

It was more than that, "I'm not being polite. We just want Wilson to be happy too, and he is very happy when you are here."

That made her glow with happiness. Jake mouthed a thank you to me. I nodded his way as we walked her stuff up to Sam's room, "Oh, we shouldn't take his room."

Reassuring her I explained, "He kind of likes the idea of being in a tent close to the girls. I think you could say he is thankful."

She laughed, and Jake was embarrassed, "Jake, are you staying in the tents too?"

He looked at her not know what to say, "I would like to, but I have all my stuff in the room next to Sarah and James's room, so if they need me I am close. I'm just trying to keep Sarah safe, mom."

She scowled at this.

She was right. He should be with the rest of them having fun, not working and helping me with Sara, but I needed him, "You know that we need Jake here. He has saved my Sarah, and he helps me more than I could ever hope for. We are really lucky you and Wilson are willing to let him help us."

I could tell she was leery about what I was saying. Was I laying it on too thick? Jake was nodding behind her. Oops. I will lay off a little, "I think Wilson is in the kitchen if you would like to see him. He is coming to my rescue again with a birthday cake."

"Whose birthday is it?"

"Sarah's best friend, Danelle."

"Really, how old is she?"

"She just turned 15."

"She is younger than Sarah?"

"Yes, but she acts like she is 30. You will meet her when you come down. Please make yourself comfortable. I am sure Clarissa would want you to."

Bringing up Clarissa was a comforting thing to do. I went out to let Jake deal with his mother alone. I also wanted to get back to my sweet

Sarah. I ran outside and down to the beach to find her. Sarah had made her way back down to the dock. Danelle sat with her on the bench watching everyone playing in the lake. I held back to kept my distance. This might be the right time for her to talk to one of them alone.

Jason gestured to me, "Did you want me to go down there?"

I grinned and finally took my eyes off of her, "No, she is doing fine." But I couldn't keep my eyes off of her. My heartfelt warm and I was pleased that she was down there on her own.

"James. Is Josie here?"

I knew that was Clarissa's voice, but I really didn't want anyone to talk to me right now, "Yeah. I helped Jake get her settled into Sam's room." I really wasn't paying attention to her. I just wanted to watch Sarah.

"James! Sit… she is fine."

Clarissa got my attention enough for me to notice that she wasn't the only one looking at me. Jason and Kylie were watching me too. I took a chair but didn't relax. I sat on the edge watching her. Matt was getting out of the water. He was taking her hand; Danelle was getting up and took her other hand. Shit… what are they doing? She is going to get hurt. I stood up to go help.

"James, sit. She is fine. Concentrate on the feeling and don't watch. You can stay more focused that way."

I glanced at Clarissa again. That was the first time anyone had told me what to do. I sat down and focused on the ground. I channeled everything to her. I felt a sharp pain and with the shock of it, I looked up at her. They were helping her sit at the end of dock. They had rolled up the bottom of her pants, and she was going to put her feet in the water. I sighed with relief and turned to Clarissa, "You will have to help me with that."

She sighed, "This is a good weekend to learn, James. There are a lot of people here to help her. Practice shutting her out too, will you please?"

I shook my head no, "I can't do that."

"But if you learn how, you will be able to do it when you have to."

I knew she was talking about the desire that builds in me for her.

I couldn't help but watch. Matt and Blaire were getting along with Sam and Brian. I was happy about that. Jason and Kylie were sitting with me trying to make small talk. I was trying to be polite, but Sarah is my everything. Finally, Jason and Kylie got bored with me and moved down to change to go out on the Jet Skies. Clarissa motioned for me to come to her, "Josie is on her way, but let's try something. What is she feeling now?"

"Not much, maybe a little uneasiness."

"Why would she feel that way?"

"She doesn't really get along very well with the girls from school."

Clarissa was disappointed, "Why is that?"

"Hang-ups… she doesn't realize how great she is."

She shook her head, "That is why she is perfect for you; she needs you."

She was right. That is exactly why Sarah was perfect to me, "Yeah, which is a huge part of it."

"Okay, block it. Concentrate on her friend; tell me what she is thinking."

I directed my eyes to Danelle.

"No, James, eyes on me and focus on her friend."

I corrected her, "Danelle."

"Yes, look at me. What is Danelle thinking?"

"She is thinking something is wrong that she doesn't know about."

Clarissa was pleased with this, "Do you feel Sarah when you do that?"

I didn't like the point she was making, "No."

"Okay, what about Danelle's brother, Brian?"

"Yeah, it's Brian." I searched for him. It helps if I can see where he is.

She pulled my face up, "You're focusing on where he is and not his brain. Feel for it. You don't need to see him."

Letting my eyes fall to the ground I replied, "He's happy he is here. He likes that Matt brought girls, but he is worried about Sarah and that she isn't talking much." I felt tears come to my eyes as they burned.

"Does that bother you?"

I shook my head, "No, not really, at least not about the part that he is worried about her. I know she loves me. I always feel that from her. Even when Jake..." I stopped. I froze and stared at her. I didn't want her to feel bad about anything with him. I was happy to have him here, and that he helped me in so many ways.

"James, Sarah told me. I know you are happy he is here, and yes, her love for you is radiant. I sometimes can't block it myself."

I was pleased to hear that Sarah's aura radiated to more than just me.

Clarissa was pleased with me and spoke softly, "We will work on this more later. Josie is... Hello, dear, I am glad you came." Clarissa was getting up to hug her. I moved over, so she could have my seat. I went back to the chair, because I heard Sarah say my name in her thoughts with a little panic in her plea. I got up and walked down to the dock. When her eyes met mine they were full of relief.

"I will take you." She had to go to the bathroom, quit literary, now.

Jake must have been behind me, because he showed up, "Danelle, do you want to go jet skiing?"

"I've never been on one, and I didn't bring a suit."

## 46. Exciting

### Sarah:

"**D**anelle, you can use one of mine."
That did not make her happy at all.
I whispered, "James got me a one piece if you are interested."
Then she smiled at me, "Really?"
Jake was really excited that she agreed to go on it with him. He said she could do all the driving. James was giving me a piggy back up to the apartment. I gave Danelle my one piece, and she went to the bathroom. She locked the door to get dressed, which was a good idea around here with Jake and his walking in on me all the time. I knocked probing her to come out of the bathroom.
She wasn't happy, "Sarah, I look like a dorky kid."
I held back my laughter, "Would you rather have a bikini?"
"No, then I would really look like a little girl. Why did they have to invite all those other girls?"
She emerged from the bathroom, "See!"
"You look fine." I tried to reassure her, but maybe distracting would be better, "I think James was trying to distract Brian and Matt from me. He knew they were my friends, but he didn't want them to spend time alone with me."
"Well, you shouldn't. You're married to him now."
"Danelle, Brian and I are really good friends too."
"What are you saying?"

"We sometimes talk about stuff."

"What kind of stuff?"

"Sex, I asked a lot of questions, and he was very honest with me. Also I was helping him to slow down, so he would learn how to treat a girl special and not like a piece of ass."

Of course that made her laughed, "He is not happy you got married."

"He will find someone better. He just needs time to grow up."

"So you are talking more."

I shrugged and that feeling swept over me. I didn't want to feel this way.

"Do you want to tell me the whole truth and nothing but the truth so help me... da.da.da.da.da."

"Nope, not now... maybe later."

She glanced at me suspiciously, "James seems really sweet. How is it going here?"

She was making me feel again and those uncertainties were moving in, but James has been nothing but good to me, "He has been very good to me."

"Sarah, I don't want to hear crap like that."

She made me laugh with that, "Danelle, I mean he is very patient. We can't even touch without pain shooting through my inners. Last night when we were sleeping, he put a pillow between us so that he wouldn't be... you know... tempted."

"I think I like him more and more."

"Good, he is a very good man."

"So what about Jake? You had feelings for him?"

"Danelle, he is in my heart. He helped me when James was gone, but I am in love with James and Jake will find someone better for him than me."

I could feel her hopefulness, but her words didn't match what she was feeling, "Like one of the girls out there?"

I laughed a little, "Nope, he was mostly irritated."

"How do you know that?"

"I just know. Watch him and you will see it too. It will have to be someone that is not going to put up with shit, and someone who doesn't drool all over him. He doesn't like that."

She wrinkled her nose, "He is only 18 and he is a doctor?"

I grinned really big, "Do you want to see his handy work?"

Her expression went to quizzical. I unzipped my pants and pulled down my underwear a little.

She traced her hand along it, "He cut you open twice, right?"

"Yep."

"Once only a week ago?"

"Yep"

"Shit, Sarah, this is really, really amazing."

I was grinning from ear to ear, "Oh, James did have an old Indian remedy he put on it too."

She pulled her hand away from me, "Sarah, it hardly looks like you had anything done."

"I didn't look at it yet. So, it's not too bad?"

"You could wear a bikini and no one would even notice." She was impressed with Jake's work.

I handed her a tank top to wear over the suit, "Are you ready?"

Slipping the tank top over her head she shrugged her shoulders.

We walked out where James and Jake were waiting for us. James came to me right away, and Jake stood up mesmerized by Danelle. He was adorable in his swimming trunks and a t-shirt.

I was surprised that he was still thinking about us while he was looking at Danelle's eyes but he still asked, "Are you two coming down?"

I wanted some alone time with James, "I could use about 15 minutes."

Out of the corner of my eye, I could see James's face lighten up as he replied, "Jake, we'll be down in 17 minutes, if you want to time us."

Danelle pulled Jake's arm in front of her to look at his watch, "You have 16 minutes, or I will be back."

Jake wrapped his arm around her neck, "By the way, I am keeping this one."

Neither of us said a word, as they walked away.

James turned to me as soon as we stepped back into the apartment and closed the door, "How are you doing?"

My heart was so filled with loving him, "Do you know that you are the best person in this world."

He walked slowly to me stopping only when he was in front of me. He traced his hands on my cheeks, as I stared into his eyes. He leaned in a little, so he could trace his lips on mine, "I am so in love with you, Sarah."

My heart was pounding so hard my chest was heaving. I pressed my lips to his desperately.

Jake and Danelle walked back in, "See, I told you; we can't leave them alone."

"Jake, out, please." James had his eyes closed as he said this.

Danelle spoke up, "James, you promised me... none of this crap...out, the both of you."

"I am so going to enjoy having you here. He doesn't get mad at you like he does with me."

Staring at James I slowly licked my lips, and said, "Okay, were coming." We started to walk to the door. Jake and Danelle walked out first, so James closed the door, locked it, and turned to me, "Quick, come here. I just need a little more, so I can be strong the rest of the night."

I almost ran into his arms. The kiss was deep, hard, and intense. He held my head to his with his hand gently behind my neck. It was so good I was getting dizzy and the tingling was starting. I wanted to feel him next to me, "James, tingling."

He stopped and kissed my forehead, "Then I am good; how about you?"

Not wanting it to be over, and yet not wanting to get carried away, I slowly nodded. He unlocked the door and they practically fell in when he opened it.

I started to laugh, "See, we just needed a minute."

Danelle grabbed his ear and pulled him from the apartment leading him away, "You promised me, and that was wrong, James."

Jake was laughing, "I really like her."

I shook my head no, "Danelle, not so rough with him; please be nice. It was my fault."

Jake grabbed my arm, "You are not stopping her. I like this."

"Jake, please, don't encourage her. She is very strict without any encouragement."

We followed as quick as I could go, "Jake help me."

He picked me up almost as easily as James did. I was trying to get him to go faster, but he wouldn't budge. Clarissa made Danelle let him go. I was trying to get down, so I could make sure James was okay.

"Sarah, stop you'll hurt yourself. Let James help you. We will be there shortly."

James helped me off of Jake's back. Quickly turning to him, "I am so sorry."

He grinned at me, "I guess there'll be no kissing this weekend."

I chuckled a little and so did he.

Jake picked Danelle up, and threw her over his shoulder, "We can go now."

He was taking her to the lake.

James wrapped his arms around me, "So what do you think?"

"Jake knows what I think, so I am staying neutral; he has to figure it out on his own."

"Oh, you are good at this matchmaker thing."

"But I don't want to do that. She is 15, James. She is too young for anything."

He pushed me away and turned me to look at him, "You feel you are too young for me."

"No, but I was definitely too young to be pregnant."

He smiled at me, but carefully glanced around to make sure no one heard me, "Okay, do you want to go sit?"

We sat with Kylie and Jason. Some of the girls were changing and coming up to sit by the fire. James and I tried to introduce them all to Josie and Clarissa. Wilson came down, "James, I could use your help."

He scooted me to the end of the chair. Carl was putting things away for the evening. Brian was still sitting on the dock waiting for Danelle to come back.

James whispered in my ear, "You should go keep Brian company; he is worried about Danelle."

I smiled, "I know that, but James?"

"It's okay, Sarah, I have to help Wilson."

He jumped out of his seat and ran up to the house. I tried to get up and a little pain shot through me, so I sat back down. Kylie noticed that I could use some help, so she got up to come help me. Jason stood up with her; he was being more respectful to her and I liked it. Jason moved to one side and Kylie to the other. I pushed up again, only needing a little help.

"Where are you trying to go?"

"I need to talk to Brian; he is worried about Danelle." They walked with me so I asked, "So things are going good with the two of you?"

They looked at each other and smiled, but I waited for a reply from Kylie.

"I am very happy. He is a very good man." She hugged me, "Sarah, I wanted to thank you. It was your boldness and strength that made me want to do better."

Jason squeezed my hand.

"How is Tony doing? Are you still helping him? I feel so bad that I have stolen all his helpers."

He got a great big grin. "Well, he is continuing to have dances; they are not as good as it was when you were there, but Kylie is working there with me till they can come back."

I gave her a hug, "You are helping me again. You just get better and better."

She gripped my hand, "Sarah, are you doing okay?"

"It's still a little painful." I didn't want to tell her, that it was some things that people said that made me sad. I was glad they didn't know. We got to the dock, and I went to Brian by myself sitting down by him.

"Hey, you married old lady."

I didn't say anything. I scanned the lake searching for Jake and Danelle.

"So…" He turned to me, "How are you really?"

Not wanting to give him the wrong idea I shrugged, "Most of the time okay. The pain has been miserable, and some of the stuff I have been through I wouldn't wish it upon anyone. It hurts to sit, and it hurts when I try to stand. I have to keep these needles in and get hooked up every day, and I don't have any time alone. James is afraid to leave my side, so if he does Jake is there."

"Shit, Sarah, that wasn't what I was expecting."

I smiled, "Otherwise, I am good."

He laughed, "You are just full of goodness, aren't you."

"Do you want to play basketball? I think I could dribble."

He laughed, "You should be up there with your husband." He cringed with saying this.

"James actually suggested I talk to you."

He was surprised by this, "Why?

"The same reason he invited you here. You are my friend."

He sat quietly. I took his hand in mine, "Brian, why did you come?"

He took a deep breath, "I wanted to know if you were happy. I mean you got married on your death bed; is this really what you wanted? After all, you are only 16." He just had to throw in the little reminder of my age.

With the thought of having James the rest of my life, my lip quivered as I tried to reply, "Did I want to get married at 16? No. Do I want to spend the rest of my life with James? Yes."

His attention went back to the lake, "There is something else."

Confused I asked, "What?"

"Sarah..." He swallowed hard. He was having a hard time saying what he wanted to say. He turned to me taking my other hand in his, "I miss you."

I just stared at him with understanding, because I missed him too. Shit, this made me feel awful; he could see the darkness was moving in, because the tears were welling up in my eyes.

"Sarah, no I miss everything. The friendship, the talks, the games, your scolding me so I am a better person, and most of all I miss your smile. I am miserable without you in my life. Even if it is just friendship, I have gotten so I need you."

Oops the tears were leaking out and tracing down my face; I tried to wipe them, as he stood up, "Shit Sarah, James is going to kill me. I made you cry. Do you want me to go get him?"

"Sit down; he knows I'm okay." I took a deep breath.

"Why do you think he invited you here?"

Brian sat back down staring at me. He was speechless.

"Brian, he is allowing me to keep you as a friend."

He got very defensive about my comment, "He allows you?"

"Brian don't you see it's not like that; he invited you because he knows I care about you too. Think about it, how hard it is for him to stand in that window up there watching me talk to you and not tell me we can't be friends. I know that is what I would be doing. Instead he invites you here and lets me spend a little time with a friend and doesn't complain at all."

"He doesn't get jealous?"

"Yes, he does, but he deals with it. Very well, I might add. I wouldn't be able to handle it.

"He feels everything from you?"

"Yes, he is learning to feel others too. Why? You're not going to purposely test him again?"

Brian looked at James in the window.

"Brian, please behave."

"No Sarah, I was just..."

"What?"

"Nothing." He turned forward looking at the lake. We were still holding hands.

"I don't see them." I was getting worried. It was starting to get dark, and they were nowhere to be seen. Brian leaned a little to me and pointed out, so I could follow his finger.

"Oh, what are they doing?"

"How come you let her go with him?"

"He is just trying to entertain her. She feels weird with all the other girls here."

"Hey, I wanted to talk to you. Who is this Matt? I don't like that he thinks you have something together."

I laughed, "Matt is my friend too, Brian. He was the one I played volleyball with, and he took me to the airport to try to get James to stay with me instead of leaving again."

"Leaving again?"

"He came home for one day in the middle of his time away, just to spend it with me. Matt rushed me to the airport, so I could beg him not to leave again. He is also special to me, so please be nice."

"I don't like it. I was on the list before him."

"Brian, there is no more list. There is only James."

His face sagged in defeated.

"Hey, besides, he brought all these girls to play with for you."

"What... why?"

"He knows I wanted you to be happy too, and Brian you are a player."

Embarrassed, he avoided my eyes, "He does have good taste. I would say 8 out of the 10 are really cute. Are they your friends?"

"Not really. I am a dork at school, and they actually make fun of me."

"So this must feel pretty good, kind of rubbing it in their faces."

"No, Brian, not at all. In fact, I really don't want them to treat me any differently, because it would be fake. I don't need friends like that, when I have friends like you and Matt." This made him smile.

I could feel the warmth of James's love filling me so I knew he was on his way down the dock. He walked to my side and sat down by me.

"Brian, do you think we should go get them? Danelle is getting frustrated, and Jake can't quit laughing, because she keeps killing the motor."

Brian laughed, "You can feel them too?"

James explained, "I'm learning how to channel my thoughts to other people, so Sarah doesn't drive me crazy by holding hands with another man." James squeezed me.

Brian laughed, "Yeah, I don't know. Are they okay?"

"Yes, they are. In fact, she just got the hang of it, and Jake flipped off the back. Oh, she stopped again."

"I suppose we could give them a little more time."

I turned to James with a start; I have to go to the bathroom again.

He looked at me, "Now?"

I nodded.

"You will have to excuse us for a minute."

Brian looked up at us like we were running off to be together. James leaned down a little to Brain, "Bathroom break."

"James, please don't announce those things." I pushed him and felt the pain. I grabbed my stomach.

Fear came in Brian's tone, "Sarah!"

Assuring him the best I could, saying, "I am fine."

As good as my James was he asked Brian, "Do you want to help her up?"

He lifted me to James's back. James could have done it on his own, but he was being nice to Brian.

"I think I will stay here till they get back."

James glanced over the lake, "They are on their way now. You should come up. We did something special for Danelle's birthday."

He came up with us, and a couple of girls made room for him. I could see it in his eyes that he was seeking my approval so I smiled and nodded, "Just be safe, please. Your mom would kill me if you got into trouble here."

He laughed.

James was taking me to the house.

Carl spoke up, "Hey you two, you have friends here."

James turned to reply to his father. He had a look, "She has to go to the bathroom."

Carl gave us a disapproving look. I nuzzled into James neck, and he turned to take me to the apartment. He walked me all the way to the bathroom, "I suppose you can do this alone."

"James, you know I can... out."

He did what I asked, and when I finished I came out. He wasn't waiting for me by the door. I went out to the living room, and he was sitting in a chair by the table. I walked over to him, "That was hard for you, wasn't it?"

He smiled and pulled me to sit on his lap, "You know when he looked up at me?"

I smiled, "Yeah, I'm sorry if he was testing you. I told him to behave."

"He was behaving; he said thank you to me."

I was pleased with this. I moved closer to him, and traced my hands along his face to coax him to look up at me. His hands moved to my waist, but under my shirt to touch my skin. I traced my lips over his while gazing into those warm brown eyes, "Do you know how much I love you?" I kissed his top lip, his bottom lip, but when he returned my kiss his grip tightened.

"James, be careful."

It lessened, but his kiss turned seductive. His hands moved up to my back and traced there. My body melted into his while my temperature rose in my veins. I could feel his excitement, as it pressed into me. I gasped for air out of the sheer pleasure of this. Agony filled James, while he let the desire take control. The warmth of his arms cradled me to him, his mouth trailed my neckline speaking against my skin, "Sarah, we shouldn't be doing this; you're going to get hurt."

I was enjoying him so much, and my head wasn't clear. I moved my mouth back to his not wanting to think about the consequences until I felt the tingling rising from my toes. If it made it to my inners I was going to pay for this seduction. Not wanting to stop I still had to warn James, "James. Tingling... wait..." If he was having the same need as me, it was going to be very hard to stop.

Though he stopped kissing me, we still embraced full of emotion. James whispered, "Did we stop in time?"

I was trembling, but my stomach didn't contract. I sat there trying to calm my heart. I laughed easily to not make it hurt.

"Sarah, did we stop in time?"

I looked down at him wanting more, but the pain would be next. I smiled at him, "I think so, James."

"You are such a bad girl."

"I thought I was good, and that is why you love me."

He smiled, "Well, if I go back out there, everyone is going to know what you do to me."

I grinned, "Do you feel me?"

He closed his eyes, "Yes, and it sucks," He kissed me one long kiss. Danelle and Jake walked in.

"You have got to be kidding me. We can't leave you two for a minute, and you run back in here. Have you two been in here the whole time? Damn it, Sarah, did you forget about the pain?"

Feeling a little guilty after seeing the disgust on their faces I didn't know what to say. I went to get up, but James held me tightly not letting me move away from him. Confused about his determination to keep me there I gave a wondering expression. He raised his eyebrows shaking his head no.

Trying to stall I asked Danelle, "Are you going to get changed?"

She eyed me not trusting what my thought was, "Yeah."

"Okay, I will wait for you."

In a scolding tone she directed us, "You should stop doing that."

I smiled, "I will... just go. I will wait here."

She pleaded, "James, please, you promised."

Giving Jake a suggestive glance, I wanted to let him know she needed to leave the room, which *did not* make him happy, "Shit, you guys are horrible. Danelle, come on." He led her to the bedroom.

Our eyes locked as soon as they were gone. Seeing a grin grow on James's face, it made me grin with him. It was short-lived because he scolded, "Sarah, I have to take a shower now; thanks a lot."

I kissed him again so deep, and he was returning it. Oh how I loved to kiss him. He gasped words in between each kiss, "Sarah..., no..., shower..., now..." He pushed me away, helping me up, but as soon as our lips parted he went in Jake's room quickly. He peaked around the corner at me, "I will be down shortly."

I smiled and hurried to him and kissed him by the door. I thought the lecture was over when Jake walked back out to the living area, because I had already moved away from James.

But I was wrong. "Are you really that stupid, Sarah?"

"No, but you are making it more exciting."

He glared at me, "What?"

"You are making us sneak to be together; it's more fun that way."

He looked at me, "You have got to be kidding me."

I grinned at him, "Besides, James is getting really good at stopping before I feel the pain."

Now he was pissed at me, "Do you realize that he has to take a shower, because you like to turn him on?"

I walked away from him feeling horrible. I went out the door but stopped, "Tell Danelle I am waiting out here." I went and stood by the gate.

James came running out; his hair was still wet. I didn't like that he felt everything from me on top of what I do to him, "I'm sorry, James, I shouldn't have tempted you like that."

"Don't feel this way, baby. I love when you do that to me. I will take anything you will give me. I just wish I had better control over my emotions for you." He pulled me into him hugging me tightly.

Jake and Danelle walked out.

Danelle was a little nicer, "Can you please try harder to not get mushy."

Still in our embrace we turned to them replying at the same time, "We'll try harder."

I kissed James on the cheek, and he squatted so I could get a piggy back. We headed down to the fire pit. When Jake helped me down I noticed that everyone was by the fire now. I walked over to Clarissa and hugged her, "Thank you so much."

She seemed pleased with an approving grin.

I glanced at Josie, and then turned to her more excited, "You are here. Thank you for coming."

She actually stood up and hugged me, "Thanks for inviting me."

I was pleased that she was being much more personable. James had already gotten ready to hold me in a chair. Danelle took my spot, "Nope, you two can't be together."

The girls from school laughed. Carl put out his arms to sit with him, so I went to him. The girls quit laughing. There was now a table set up with everything ready for food.

"The pizza should be here any minute," Clarissa announced. She directed her attention to Jake who was standing by James, "Hey, should we set up the volleyball net?"

Matt was all over that. He jumped up and followed Jake like a puppy dog, and so did Blaire. Wilson came down to help. I watched him, "Wilson, why don't you let the boys do that? Come and sit down."

Clarissa looked at me, and Carl pulled me into him whispering in my ear, "Hey, Clarissa is the boss."

I didn't want to do anything that she might not like, so I leaned forward so that I could see her expression, "Is that okay?"

She reassured me, "Sarah, of course it is."

She took Josie's hand, "He is part of this family." Then she turned to Josie, "and so are you."

Josie got all teary eyed.

I leaned into Carl and whispered, "You are her man, aren't you the boss too?"

He lifted my chin, "I am just happy she still wants me, Sarah."

I closed my eyes and nuzzled in. He was so much like my James. They were deciding teams for volleyball, but most of girls just wanted to watch. I sat there in Carl's arms while James had Danelle in his. He was picking on her and she was getting irritated. We heard another car arrive, and Jake and James both jumped up. They were play fighting, as they walked up to get pizzas. They came down and had five each. I shook my head in disbelief. They put them on the tables and everyone went to eat.

As people got done eating, they went back to making up teams for volleyball. Carl and Wilson were going to play. Danelle stayed with me. She didn't want to make a fool of herself in front of the girls from my school. Jake wasn't going to let her get by with not playing, so he grabbed her and pulled her with him. She actually was pretty good when we played at her house. James, of course, came to take his dad's place. Danelle kept her eyes on us, but there wasn't much to see, since we were on our best behavior.

Matt yelled, "We get Sarah."

James laughed, "Sorry, Matt... Sarah can't play yet."

"Come on, James; she is the best player here."

He pushed me out to look at me, so I shrugged my shoulders. He was questioning me with his eyes, "You are going to have to play for me when you are better. I have never heard a guy say a girl was better than him."

Matt laughed, "Oh, I did not say that."

We all laughed. Some of the girls from school moved closer to us. I watched Danelle and Jake. He didn't direct her to make her better, but he didn't have to, because she was pretty good.

Matt even noticed, "Where are you from?" I heard him ask her.

Jake grabbed her, "Matt, don't even think about it. Her brother is here, and she is too young for you."

"Hey, I was looking for a partner till Sarah can get better."

Jake smiled really big, "Nope, she lives up north." He was very protective and Brian noticed.

When they were switching out teams, Brian ran to us, "Hey, does he have something for my sister? He is too old for her."

Reassuring him I explained, "Nope, he is just protecting her for me…that's all."

Carl and Wilson gave up after the first game complaining about being too old, and too tired. Wilson came to sit really close to us, "Sarah, your friend…did you want to make a big deal or keep it private?"

Explaining it to James, "If she is like me she would want it private, especially since she doesn't know everyone."

"We'll keep it private. We'll grab it when we go back in."

Wilson was giddy, "I hope she likes my creation."

Jake took everyone up to the house for bathroom breaks. There was a working facility out by the pool that I never noticed before, so they wouldn't have to disturb us or walk through Clarissa's home. I was happy about that, however, the girls were not. As they gathered around some of them started to ask questions, but I wasn't ready for questions.

# 47. Readings

**F**irst of all they wanted to understand how everyone knew everyone. Alissa knew me, so she was more outspoken. I didn't know if she was either trying to destroy me for Matt hitting on me or trying to embarrass me. I wasn't quite sure yet.

"So, Jason and Kylie... are they a couple?"

James held me tight, "Yes."

"And how do you know them?"

I grinned at them pleased to answer this one, "They are James and my best couple's friends."

Kylie reached for my hand and squeezed it. I noticed Clarissa giving me a look of encouragement, so I tried to feel where Alissa was going with this. I tried but got nothing.

"How about Brian?"

Still feeling somewhat comfortable I replied, "He is a close friend of mine from my Cabin and Danelle, his sister, is my best friend."

A couple of the girls looked at me weird. Having someone that was younger than me as a best friend just didn't sit right with them. "So... Brian is just a friend?"

Oh, I got it now; they were looking to see who was free. That's cool; at least they're asking.

Alissa asked James, "And you don't mind Sarah having guy friends?"

He held me tighter, "Nope, I trust her, and I know she loves me." He kissed my cheek making me feel warmth spreading through my body.

Brianna spoke up next, "And is it Will... he is with Katherine?"

"Yes, Will is my brother-in-law, and they are engaged." Katherine looked at me with surprise on her face, but smiled.

Sam came running over, "And I am the youngest brother, and yes I am available."

"Sam, you are terrible."

He was boasting his charm.

Alissa stepped in again, "And Carl and Clarissa?"

"Mom and Dad to James and his brothers."

"Wow, you have a beautiful home." They both smiled, and Clarissa responded, "Why thank you."

Brianna had to get her input again, while all the other girls were there now listening, "Wilson is it and Josie?"

"They are..." Clarissa stopped me by butting in, "Carl and my best friends. Just like Family."

I was waiting for the big question, '*Jake*'. One of the other girls couldn't contain herself. I think it was Chloe, "And how does Jake fit in?"

I knew he was the one they were all wondering about, "He is my..." oh shit Josie is here, "...my doctor."

They all dropped their mouths open, "Oh, he is Wilson's and Josie's son, so he is here as a favor to Carl and Clarissa."

He came running up to hear it. He was a little embarrassed that we were talking about him, and he also felt what they were thinking. He came over and took my hand, as he confirmed, "And Sarah is very special to me."

I glanced up at him. He leaned down to James and me, "I don't like what they are thinking. It is creeping me out."

I laughed, as James hugged me more and kissed my cheek again.

Things calmed down after that, and people just started to talk on their own.

Carl, Clarissa, Wilson, and Josie all went up to the house. Brian, Matt, and Sam were trying to coax girls to play volleyball some more. Only a few would play. Jake refused sitting in a chair next to James and I. Danelle came and sat in front of him on the same chair. Not cuddling but keeping a close eye on James and me. I noticed the girls from school were watching James and I a lot. Jason and Kylie retired about midnight, and Will and Katherine were quick to follow. James was very attentive, kissing my hand, my cheek, and my neck. Danelle wasn't pleased, but Jake explained he was making me feel good in front of the girls from school. After that, she was more lenient about it. I was getting really tired and started to dose off in James's arms.

The next thing I knew Jake was picking me up. I peeked at him through very droopy eyes, "James?"

"Yes, Sarah, I was just letting him get up."

I hugged him more and whispered into his neck, "Thank you." And I lightly kissed him where I was, his neck.

"James, here, quick take her."

I was confused by his quick need to get rid of me. James took me, and I curled into his arms, "Something wrong?"

"No, baby, It's okay. I've got you." I closed my eyes and nuzzled into him. "James, why do you love me?"

"Because you let me." He kissed my forehead.

"What does that mean?"

"I will show you when you are awake." I opened my eyes trying to keep them open, "I would wake up enough to find out, please."

He chuckled, "You are so sleepy; just close your eyes."

"Is Danelle coming?"

"I am sure she won't be far behind us."

He set me down in the room. I started to take my pants off. He grabbed the door, "Sarah, you have to be more careful. There are a lot of people around."

I pulled off my sweatshirt and started to undo my bra. I was so tired. I just wanted to crawl in bed. I pulled it off under my tank top and stumbled.

"Sarah, what are you doing?"

"Getting changed. Grab me a pair of shorts, please." I was stepping on my jeans to pull them off the rest of the way, and I was stumbling more and almost fell.

"Hey, Sarah, let me help you. You are going to fall and get hurt."

"James… just so tired." I didn't wait for the shorts; I headed to the bed stumbling but crawled in.

He came over with some shorts. "Sarah, we shouldn't let you stay up so late, and you have to put shorts on. Danelle is sleeping in here."

"Okay, James, anything you say."

"I like you like this; you let me win."

"Yep, you win; it's bed time." I could hardly keep my eyes open.

## James:

She was so cute being this tired. I was trying to put shorts on her, but she wasn't helping my case, "Sarah, can you help me here?"

"Yep, James, anything you want."

I think I spent more time putting clothes on her then ever trying to take them off. I was laughing to myself. I had to lift her butt to pull them under her. I stopped to trace the scar.

"Um, James, that feels so good."

Okay, maybe I shouldn't have done that, but she liked it, so I traced it more. I love her noises when she likes something. I pulled down the front a little more and leaned over to trace my mouth over the scar. She wrapped her fingers in my hair and moaned with pleasure.

"Sarah, you shouldn't make noises like that."

"It feels soo good, James. You're making me dreamy."

This wasn't hurting her, and I loved that she was letting me touch her. Kissing her with a smile on my face, I watched her melt into my touch. I loved her like this, and it tempted me more, so I glided my hand over her stomach.

"Oh, James, I miss this."

I moved up to her face, "Darling, I am afraid to touch you. What about the pain?"

With an adorable little smirk on her face she enticed me more, "No tingling, yet."

She was coaxing me to keep going; I was so happy with this. When she opened those beautiful piercing green eyes, they locked with mine. They didn't seem to be filled with desire; it was more like complete happiness.

"Do you want more?"

She closed her eyes and made a small growling noise of, "*um hun.*"

"Sarah, you're not even awake. I don't want to hurt you."

"I'm just very relaxed, James."

I traced my hand across her waist and kissed her shoulder, which made her purr like a kitten. I pulled her tank top up enough to trace my mouth over her belly. Her fingers entangled with my hair kneading with satisfaction. She was enjoying this so much. My heart was racing, and I was totally turned on by the sounds of satisfaction coming from her. I slid her top off and moved over her, pulling the covers over our heads.

She giggled, "We are being very bad, James."

I moved to her face, "Sarah, you need to tell me right away if you start to feel the desire."

"It's coming, James, I will let you..."

That is when I planted a kiss on her neck. She couldn't finish her sentence, but she did moan lightly. Knowing my time was limited I quickly pulled off my shirt and lowered my chest to rub against hers, "Sarah, how are you doing?" My body was tense, as I felt her against me, and I was shaking with excitement.

She traced her hands down my back as far as she could reach, "James, I am so hot."

"I know, baby." I closed my eyes. Her body was calling to me, and I was struggling with my desire to push to her, and the joy of making her happy. I pulled away from her not letting myself get carried away.

"James!"

"It's okay, just relax." She wasn't in pain yet, and her body was begging me. I traced my chest against hers again. She tilted her head back groaning with delight.

Even though she was enjoying this, I knew the pain would come to her soon, "Baby, how is the tingling?"

"Not coming yet." If I didn't stop this soon, I would be coming.

I leaned down to her, "Sarah, I can't do this."

She opened her eyes, "I'm sorry, James, it's okay. I understand."

She was breaking my heart, but I liked that this felt good for her. I moved to her side and pulled her to me to hold her, "Sarah, can we try something?"

Raising her eyebrows she was eager to try anything, "Whatever you want."

I took her face in my hands, "Sarah, look at me."

She opened her eyes; they were still relaxed. I had to try. I used my mind and pushed into her. Her eyes went soft and almost sad; she opened her mouth to breathe and her chest was panting.

I was worried this was too much for her, "Hey, how does it feel?"

"For real or in my mind?"

Pleased that this felt real to her I confessed, "Mind."

"We're not supposed to do that."

Keeping her eyes locked to mine, "I will suffer if it makes you happy."

Sadness crept into her eyes; she didn't want me to suffer. I used my mind to push to her again, really slowly.

"Oh, James. You shouldn't do…"

She didn't finish what she was going to say. Instead she gasped and her eyes melted into mine glazing over.

This worried me, "Are you in any pain at all?"

She bit her lip and shook her head no. I felt my body trembling with need. I concentrated on doing that again.

"Ooh, James."

I panicked, "Good or bad, tingling yet?"

"No, not yet. It just feels so amazing; I want more."

With her naïve surrender, her noises, and those eyes mesmerizing me, I knew we were not going to make it to her 18th birthday. I went really slow with my mind, but watched the pleasure on her face. I wanted to rip her clothes off and push to her so hard. It was taking everything I had to not attack her right now. I used my mind to move around in her.

"Wait, wait, James. Don't move. My stomach is tightening."

It was easy to stop my mind; it was my body that wanted more. I felt her warmth around me. My heart was still racing, but I pulled her close to me, "Hey, are you okay?" Her whole body was trembling, "Sarah, are you in pain?"

"Stomach is really tight, and I'm afraid to move."

I pulled her tight to my body to help her with her trembling. I traced my hand over her face, "You are pleased?"

She gave me a slight smile but then it saddened, "You're not?"

I was making love to my wife, and I made her feel good, "I am, more than you know."

That must have satisfied her enough, because she closed her eyes and went to sleep almost immediately. I eased away from her, and she didn't move. I went and took another cold shower. I took a lot longer than I planned on. I had to make sure I would not have the desire to go back to her. I leaned against the wall, closed my eyes, and tried to breathe slower. When I could breathe again, I pulled myself from the shower. I got dressed again, not wanting to, just wanting to go back to her so I could hold her, kiss her, feel her in my arms. This is all I wanted, to be with her. I walked out and crossed over to the bed and sat down to look at her. She was so beautiful, and she didn't even know it. I traced back the hair from her face with my fingers and touched the smile lines along the side of her mouth. She stirred, her lips gently lifting.

She pushed to my hand, "James?"

"Yeah, baby?"

"What are you doing?"

"I should go check on Danelle; are you okay?"

"Better than okay, but James...? She was grabbing my shirt to come closer.

I leaned over her, "Yeah."

"We're not supposed to do that. It's bad for you."

"It doesn't matter."

She smiled at me. I took her hand in mine and pulled it to my lips kissing her palm.

"James."

"Yeah?" I couldn't help to grin at her. She was all mine, and I was the one she wanted to be with.

"Why do you love me?"

"Sarah, why are you asking me that?"

"Because this, all of this. Your life has been turned upside down because of me."

"Oh, baby, don't you understand that you are my soul mate. You are everything I could dream of."

"Don't play with me. I really want to know."

I traced my fingers through her hair till she dosed off. I got up and walked out to check on Danelle. Some of the girls, along with Matt, Brian, and Sam were all still playing volleyball, while others gathered by the Fire. I think it was Alissa who looked at me, as I walked back down. Jake was back in the chair where he was before. Danelle moved to the chair were I was holding Sarah. Alissa spoke to me, "Hey, is Sarah okay?"

I grinned with embarrassment thinking of what we just did, "Yep, she will be. She's just been through a lot in the last month."

Danelle disapproved of my look, and she was shaking her head no.

I leaned down to Jake, "Hey, are you okay?"

He looked up at me, stood up, and gestured for me to follow him. We didn't go far before he stopped and turned around, "James, I am sorry."

I didn't know what to say, so I just watched his motions. He avoided my stare. "James when I... she... I couldn't... James, I am sorry."

I smiled at him, "I know, brother, but you didn't, and that is all that matters."

He glanced up at me, "Really?"

What could I say? He felt bad that he had mixed feelings when she kissed his neck. I knew she wasn't in love with him. She does care for him, but it was more like a thank you than anything else. I grinned at him, "Why is Danelle still out here? She should be heading in."

"She is kind of keeping an eye on her brother."

I smiled, "Sarah used to do that. It helped him not to be stupid."

"What?"

"He is in love with her too; did you know that?"

Jake shook his head, "I thought so. Doesn't this bother you that all these people are in love with your wife?"

"Yeah, wouldn't it you?"

He laughed at me, "Then why would you invite them all here?"

"Because I want her to love me more. What better way to show her I trust her."

"Damn, I wouldn't be able to do this."

I put my arm around his neck, "If I didn't trust anyone it would be you. Her heart hurt when she let you go."

"You knew when she let me go?"

I smiled, "It was in the hospital. I felt her pain, and I held her while she cried."

"James, I am so sorry. I would have never… if I knew what I know now."

"I know and that is why I trust you the most. I can trust that if I need help with her, it's you who loves her enough to help me."

He smiled at me with understanding. We both went back to Danelle. I put my hand on her head, "Hey, are you tired yet?"

She was very determined, "Nope."

I could tell by the way she looked that she was tired. I noticed Brian having fun, and I was pleased that he was more interested in playing with the girls that Matt brought along, "You know he's a big boy."

"Where is Sarah? She wouldn't let him act stupid like this."

I laughed, "Yes, she would have. She just would have lectured him later."

She glared at me but laughed, "I guess you're right, but he is acting stupid."

Jake laughed, "That's normal, isn't it?"

Danelle turned on him very angrily, "Then why aren't you over there flirting?"

"You must not have noticed. I'm far from normal."

That made her happy, but she turned on me, "So, how would Sarah feel about you being out here?"

"Hey, don't get mad at me. I'm not over there with the girls. You know Sarah is the one I love."

"She would still want you in there with her."

"I know; she is sleeping and I…" I grabbed her and pulled her to me to sit in front of me facing the fire, then I wrapped my arms around her neck, "I am checking on you, and she would want me to do that, too."

She pushed me away from hugging her, "Stop that, James, you are not going to soften me. I am not like Sarah."

I leaned forward, "Oh yes you are, maybe even more direct."

Jake sat down paying attention to what I was doing with Danelle. She pushed me away harder turning to me, "Why, because I see through you and don't put up with your shit."

I laughed and so did Jake, because he even liked that one, "Maybe, so which one is Brian after tonight?"

She evaluated both Jake and me but huffed a little and turned back to watch Brian, "Okay, you see the one in the white shirt there?"

I leaned forward, and Jake moved his chair closer to hear.

"She wants him…just watch her. She is really working it, but she is not good enough."

We both laughed, and I encouraged her to go on.

"And see that one over there on the blanket? She has been eyeing him. She is encouraging him to come on the blanket with her. Now watch, he will look at her, but..."

"But what?" I was finding this intriguing. She didn't have feelings, and she was hitting it on the nose.

"Well, that is his reserves. Now watch. The one he wants is that one in the bright tank top who is not giving him the time of day." She turned to look at me, "You feel things, right?" I laughed. I could see Jake out of the corner of my eye nodding.

"So how am I doing?"

I grinned, "Well so far, you are correct all the way around. She is too good for him, and she knows it."

Danelle turned to Jake, "The only one that she thinks is good enough is you or James. James is taken, so she has her mind set on you."

"Oh... hell... no! She is scary." He was laughing.

"Look at that player. That's Blaire, right?"

I nodded.

"Both of those girls want him bad enough that they are willing to share. He has been kissing both. James, this is like and orgy."

I just about choked, "It's not supposed to be like that."

She turned on me, "Well, you made it awfully easy for all of them."

"Do you want me to put a stop to it? I can, you know."

She grinned, "Oh, I don't know about that. You would have to be up all night."

I found her hilarious and started to laugh. Jake joined in with the laughter.

"No, I find it funny, and if Brian holds out for the one he wants, nothing is going to happen today. Sarah at least taught him that." She turned to me again, "James, I'm sorry. You probably don't want to know that."

I tried to hold back my smile, "Danelle, I already know."

"Then you know he is in love with her, too."

"Yep, knew that."

She shook her head, "Do you think she will love you more if you invite them to be around her?"

I was impressed yet again, "I swear you are so much like her and even more honest."

Jake was enjoying this as much as I was. I wanted to push it further. I found it very interesting that she could pick this all up with body language, "So Matt, what is he thinking?"

"You tell me."

I squinted my eyes, "This is easy for me; I can feel them. He likes them all, but he wants something more. He is still a virgin, and he wants someone special. He wants someone like Sarah."

She looked at me, "You are good."

I turned her so I could see her face, "I cheated; I listened to him."

She didn't approve but laughed as she asked, "Jake, do you feel things?"

He put his head down, "I don't think I am as good as you or James."

"Give it a try. Tell us why he wants someone special like Sarah?"

He looked at him. I had to help him like Clarissa helped me, "Hey, Jake, I had to look at them before, but Clarissa says to not look at them and concentrate on feeling them."

His eyes dropped, "Well he is definitely in love with Sarah, but it's different. He doesn't want to be with her; he understands the desire you two have to be together, but he wants what you have with her."

He looked up at me waiting for me to agree or disagree. I smiled and nodded letting him know that he was right.

Danelle turned on me again, "He loves her though, so don't let your guard down. He would wait till she was unhappy with you."

I had to laugh, "And how does Sarah feel about that?"

"She is clouded by you. She doesn't see any of it, but she knows and she loves the attention. So, James, you really need to give her a lot of attention, or you are going to be miserable, but if you do… Well let's just say she is going to make you a very happy man."

I chuckled to myself, "She already does, Danelle."

"Hey, I didn't mean sexually. You are a horny dog."

I laughed even more, "I didn't mean it that way either. Where is your head?"

She gave me a very disapproving look, "You're the one that set this all up. I have been watching it for hours."

"So why don't you go to bed?"

"And miss this stupidity… are you kidding? I am having fun with it."

I loved her attitude and outlook on this evening and laughed again. I tried to see what Jake was thinking, but he was pretty open-minded right now.

"You know what the best part is?"

Jake turned to her, "What is that?"

"When they try to snub Sarah, or myself, I have ammo."

I felt Jakes heart skip a beat. There was something going on here. I glanced between them and concluded, "I like the way you think, but I am not staying out here any longer."

"Yeah, I guess I could go in."

Jake spoke up, "I will stay with you if you want to stay out here longer."

She smiled but glanced at me for approval, and I was stern with Jake, "You will take care of her and keep Sam from her."

She turned to question me.

"Sam has a slight crush on you, but, Danelle, he would not be good for you, because he is destined for Amelia."

I didn't surprise her with that, while she turned to Jake, "You'll stay with me, and not chase the girls?'

"No, not interested at all."

She agreed explaining herself, "I would like to make sure he doesn't give in."

I got up kissing the top of her head."

She pushed me to stop, "James, stop that."

"Danelle, you're like a little sister to Sarah, sorry."

I went back to the apartment and crawled in bed to hold Sarah. She nuzzled into me making me feel more loved than I could ever imagine.

## 48. Sparks

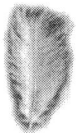

**Jake:**

I was sitting next to Danelle watching everyone playing around. I sat back to get comfortable to stay with her. I didn't mind she was a little funny, "So what are you thinking?"

"I'm tired, but he will be stupid."

"He is allowed; he's old enough to make those decisions."

"But he was doing a lot better. Sarah makes him want to be a better person."

"Yeah, she does that to people. Do you have a hard time watching his stupidity?

"I see a lot of stupidity, including James and Sarah's."

"What?"

"She is too young to get married, and it is going to be a lot of work for him."

"Why do you say that?'

"She is 16, so she still is a child. She may be very honest, but she will need a lot of attention, and he will have to balance it very carefully. She is depressed already. I see it."

Surprised that she knew this already, but I couldn't say anything. It was up to Sarah to tell her why she was depressed, "Well, maybe there is more to it than that. Don't be so quick to judge. I think James is doing a really good job."

She glared as her glance came back to me, "You really believe that?"

"I believe he loves her enough to deal with anything."

"What do you mean?"

I laughed, "No, this is something I am not comfortable with."

"Why?"

"Because, it's their business."

"But you know something? That makes you believe they can do this."

"You know what... we need to change the subject. So, you play volleyball pretty well."

She glared at me and shook her head, "You're not very good at changing the subject."

I couldn't help but laugh at her.

"So did you fall in love with Sarah?"

*Very blunt.* I didn't know how to answer her. She was a silly little girl; I didn't have to hide anything.

"I do care about her, but we're not getting on that subject. We've talked enough about them."

"We weren't talking about them. I was talking about you. That is why no one here is good enough."

I just about choked, "What?"

"When he was away, you were with her."

"Not the way you're thinking."

"I know that. I mean you spent time with her. You know how she is. You are in love with her."

"No, not anymore."

She laughed, "I knew it. You were...in love with her?"

"No, that's not what I meant."

"Now you are squirming." She started to laugh, "Oh my god. You are so in love with her."

"No, and you are not funny." I was trying to get her to stop talking about it. She wasn't listening to me. James was hearing everything, and this would hurt him more. I went to her, put my hand over her mouth, and looked her in the eyes, "Danelle, please, James can focus on more than just Sarah. Drop the subject please. He is my brother, and I am not allowed to have any feeling toward her. I squelch them, so please STOP!"

She stopped giggling, "Oh, I'm sorry. Sorry, James."

"You say that like he can hear you."

"Well if he can feel me, then he can hear me too, right?"

I rolled my eyes, "Yes, you're probably right."

"One more question."

I swallowed.

"Did you kiss her?"

"Nope, oh shit, I did, but it was a really a quick peck on the lips. I don't even know how to kiss someone properly."

She wasn't smiling anymore, and I just confessed something I wasn't proud of. God, this was embarrassing.

"What?"

"It was just a quick kiss; I was trying to keep her from going to him."

"Not that part, the other part."

Shit she did catch that. Great... 18 and never really kissed anyone. Why am I telling this to her? After all, she was still a little girl. It wouldn't matter to her anyway.

"What part?" I was trying to avoid the subject.

"You have never really kissed anyone?"

"Have you?"

"NO, but I am 15."

"Well, I have been a little busy."

"That sounds snobby, and you are so good looking, that I thought they would be worshiping the ground you walk on."

"Oh, like those girls here. They make me sick, with the thoughts they have. I don't need stupid games like that. I have my work, and I am happy to have that."

"Until Sarah."

I had wanted to kiss her so badly at her house. I shook my head disapprovingly, "Are we back to that subject again? I told you I didn't want to talk about her... them... like that anymore. Do you want to go play video games or something? I really don't want to do this anymore."

She stood up and put out her hand, "Yes, I will drop the subject. How much do you want to bet that James is in bed with her?"

"I won't disagree with you there."

This little girl had my hand and was leading me back to the apartment. Why was I having butterflies? I shook my head trying to get rid of this feeling. We walked in and I let go of her hand and pulled out video games, "Anything in particular?"

"Nope." She was walking over to the bedroom door which was closed. "Do you think we should check on them?"

I laughed, "You can look, but if you see something you didn't want to see, don't blame me."

"I thought you said they couldn't be together"

"They shouldn't, but I won't say they don't try."

"Oh, well I guess it's the couch for me."

I laughed lightly, "I could take the couch, and you can have my room."

"Or we could stay up?"

"That works for me."

She started to wander around looking at everything, "This must be nice."

I stood up, "Hey, do you want to see the other room?"

"Your room?" She looked uncomfortable.

"No, silly, come here." I went and grabbed her hand leading her to the game room.

Her eyes brightened, "You guys have this all the time. That is so cool. I would rather play pool."

"Really?"

"Yeah, I suck at video games. "

I smiled, and we played pool for hours. We laughed and still talked about Sarah, how she always finds a way to get her way, her brother who was stupid, the resort her family owned, water skiing, and tubing. I think we hit every subject including my schooling. She was a little intimidated after that.

We finally got tired and moved to the couch, "Hey, you may think this is really mean and maybe a little gross, but do you want to play a trick on them?"

"What kind of trick?"

I filled her in on the whipped topping, the fake fight James and I had to pay her back, and then her disappearing on us.

"So what is your idea?"

"If you will play along, come in there with me, and I will ask James for a condom... of course... just joking with him. I bet they will both wake up and freak out."

"Isn't that a little mean?"

"Well yes, but I owe them both big time from the whipped topping."

"Yeah, let's do it."

I took her hand, and we went to the door. I was laughing, and she started to. We stopped there till we could stop giggling, and we slowly opened the door. I looked first to make sure nothing was going on. They were sleeping; James had put the bed pillow between them. I pulled her in, "See, he tries to stay away from her, because of her surgery; if they do it, it will hurt her and maybe tear the stitches."

"Okay, more than I wanted to know."

Her eyes locked on mine, and I realized she had really beautiful blue eyes. I looked at her for a minute and then went back to the task at hand. I let go of her hand at the top of the steps and moved down to the bed.

"Hey James...James..."

He moaned, "What do you want?"

"Do you have a rubber?" I was trying to hold in the laughter.

"Jake, who? Don't you want it to be special?" He opened his eyes and saw Danelle behind me.

"Jake, no. You are not doing it with Danelle."

Sarah sat up grabbing her stomach, "Jake, no, she's too young."

James was coming off the bed at me. I started to laugh and so did Danelle; she actually fell to the ground laughing. I couldn't stop it either and sat down holding my stomach laughing so hard, "Oh, Sarah, I'm sorry if that hurt you, but the look on your faces, was..." I was laughing so hard now. I lay back holding my stomach.

Danelle was almost crying, "Sorry guys, that was just too good."

Sarah was pissed. She lay back down and looked the other way. James wasn't happy either, now standing looking at us both, "Not funny you two...out. Sarah is in pain, thanks to the two of you.

"I'm sorry, Sarah." I was crawling to her side of the bed.

"Jake, you are not funny at all." She wouldn't even look at me.

"Here, I'll hook you back up, so you can have some pain meds. I'm sorry."

James was crawling back to bed, close to her, tracing his fingers over her face, "Sarah."

She rolled back to him. I could see her smile.

"Sarah, are you smiling?"

"No, Jake, I am pissed at you for even kidding like that. Yes, I need pain meds."

I tried to straighten up and do what I had to do. Danelle came over and sat on the bed next to Sarah, "That is what you two get for sneaking off together."

I was pleased that she wanted revenge too.

"So what are all these for?"

Sarah turned to us.

I pointed at one, "This one is vitamins and nutrition," I touched the next one, "And this one is for fluids and pain meds"

She was still curious, "So, why do you need all this?"

Sarah smiled, "They want me to gain weight."

I laughed, "Sarah, I don't just want you to gain weight, you *need* to gain weight."

Danelle looked at her, "You do need a little weight."

I looked over James, who had adjusted the pillow and moved behind Sarah to support her body. He kissed her shoulder.

I gestured to Danelle, "Guys, a child is in the room."

James got a big grin on his face. I looked down smiling. He kissed Sarah's cheek, "Hey, I should let Danelle sleep..." He was rolling out of bed.

I was going to say something, but Danelle said it, "Hey, James, it's okay. Jake said I could stay in his bed."

James and Sarah said at the exact same time, "No."

Danelle and I laughed, but I reassured them, "Hey, I will sleep on the couch."

James looked at us both, "Jake, can I see you in the living room?"

He was moving to the door so I followed. What was he worried about?

He turned on me when we got to the living room, "Jake, that wasn't funny; she is only 15."

"James, we were just kidding."

"So you want to let her use your bed?"

"James, I will sleep on the couch. It's not that big of deal."

"Jake, I don't know how to say this..."

"What, spit it out?"

"Do you like her?"

"She is a little girl... no, James. That is just wrong. Why would you even say something like that?"

He was looking guilty, "I fell in love with Sarah when she was 15. She turned 16 shortly after we figured it out, but I loved everything about her and she was only 15, and Jake, I was 19. Please, just be careful; if I could do it over again, I would have waited longer before kissing her."

I had to set him straight, "James, no, I was just spending time with her. She doesn't fit in with all of them. It's not like that."

He looked at me, and there was relief in his face. He wiped his hand over his face. I watched him walk around the couch and sat down, "It wasn't my fault though."

I didn't like that he felt that way, "Everyone has a choice, James."

He laughed, "Yeah, I use to feel that way till she came along."

"What do you mean it wasn't your fault?"

He glanced up at me, "Do you really want to hear this?"

I shrugged my shoulders but sat down.

He was going to tell me, "You know she was with Jason for a little while, right?"

"Well, I kind of guessed that."

"He was her first kiss, but he didn't stop there."

Now I was confused. This was hard for James to talk about.

"He didn't do that, have sex with her, but he made her...." He was cringing like he couldn't say it.

"Are you telling me he aroused her?"

He laughed, "Yeah, in technical terms, but because she was already.... How about I just say pleased, she was very eager and..." He looked up at me.

"She gets you going?"

Ashamed he continued, "Jake, even her kiss is so delicious; I tried to stay in control and keep it slow, but she wants to feel that with me, and I am stupid and give in, a lot."

I laughed, "So, she is a horn dog?"

"Only because we keep pushing the line."

"Well, at least you know she likes what you do for her."

He was shaking his head in disbelief that I put it that way, but I still had to remind him, "James, it is still a choice, and right now with her pain, it should be an easy choice."

"Yeah, that's what you think."

"I saw the pillow, nice touch."

He looked up smiling at me guiltily, "Jake, she makes noises when she sleeps, and it drives me crazy."

"I said you could bunk with me for a while. Especially since I know once you do that, it's more apt to want to do it again."

He looked at me and smiled, but he was shaking his head no. He didn't want to be away from her.

"Okay, I guess I am tired. I will let Danelle have my room. We'll figure something else for tomorrow."

He got up and walked back to the room. Danelle was sitting cross legged on the bed talking to Sarah, and she was sitting up now. The pain meds must have kicked in. I grabbed James's arm, "Hey, I just gave her pain meds; she is feeling pretty good right now, can you stay in control, because it would hurt her."

He looked at me and grinned, "Yeah, I am fine."

I didn't know if I could trust that, but I was trying to stay neutral, "Hey, Danelle, if you want to grab your bag, I will take you to your room."

She laughed, "I don't know, I don't think they should be left alone." She was being playful.

Sarah took her hand, "Hey, we'll be fine. I will see you in the morning."

She got up and I grabbed her bag and followed her out of the room. I stopped at the door looking back, "Both of you think pain, and I mean it."

Sarah laughed; James looked at me and smiled a calming smile. I knew he would be okay for the night. I walked into my room holding the door for her. She was uncomfortable with me in the room with her. I turned on the bathroom light, "Here is the bathroom, and…" I set her bag on the bed, "Here is the bed." I looked at her, "Well, I will see you in the morning." I went to walk out.

"Hey, wait."

I turned around, "Yes."

"What did you and James talk about?"

"He and Sarah… get some sleep. We have a lot to do tomorrow."

She smiled at me, "Are you sure you're okay with this?"

I gave her a patronizing grin, "I would make you sleep on the couch if I wasn't. I will be fine."

I closed the door looking back at her, "Are you okay?"

She smiled, "Yep."

I closed the door and walked to the couch and lay down. I took a deep breath. It hit me like a flash. Was Sarah talking about Danelle? She is too young, but she is so like Sarah; James even says that. They couldn't be thinking of her. She was still a baby. Is that why James came and talked to me? No, it couldn't be. Though, she didn't drool over me. She was very straight forward and… no. I can't even think about that. I would be a virgin until I was 21. What am I thinking? No…..NO….No? It can't be. James walked out of the room. I looked at him, "NO, James, no way."

He stood there and smiled, "I am glad you feel that way. Good night."

## Sarah:

I laid back down watching James come back to bed, "Did you check on Jake?"

"Yep."

He was crawling in bed with me to hold me. My heart was pounding, because he was holding me. He kissed my neck and my cheek, "I love you, Sarah."

I leaned back to him, "He knows?"

James smiled, "Yeah, but he doesn't want to believe it. It's a good thing. Time will be good; she needs to grow up more."

"I should have grown up more too, James. That is what you are saying, isn't it?"

He smiled at me, "Yes, Sarah, I feel like I am taking away your innocence."

I rolled over, as he moved to let me. I touched his face, "That was my doing; James, I want you."

"But you have had me since that first day you walked in and I was at the Table with your dad. It's those damn green eyes of yours, the way you had confidence and determination, and your abusive behavior."

"What?"

"You weren't very nice to me; do you remember that?"

"You were staring, and it made me uncomfortable."

"So, does this make you uncomfortable?" He picked up my hand and kissed it.

I smiled at him, "No, James, I love you."

He hovered, "I want to make love to you so bad, to make you scream my name from pleasure."

"James, pain."

He smiled, "I didn't mean today. I'm just planning ahead."

I kissed his lips lightly, "Do you have rubbers?"

He looked at me funny. He wasn't pleased, "Why would you ask that?"

"James, what if I heal and we're ready and I am not on the pill yet. I really don't want to do what we did already, and if we want to wait for a baby then we have to think about other means of protection, right?"

He was smiling but looking guilty. I squinted my eyes at him, "You have some?"

His grin got bigger, "Yeah, I picked some up, but there is no rush, Sarah. You really need to take your time with this. I don't want to cause you pain ever, for whatever reason."

I smiled at him, "Can I see one?"

"Why?"

"I don't know what they are, what they look like."

I could tell he was reluctant, "Sarah, see, this just isn't right."

Trying to make him feel more comfortable, "My doctor gave me a couple and some foam, but I didn't know how that works either."

He shook his head no.

"James, let me see one, please."

He pushed himself up and grabbed it out of the top drawer and handed it to me. I flipped it around. I looked at him. He was lying back down next to me, but not cuddling any more. I held it up and opened it.

"Sarah, you're wasting it."

I laughed, "How does it work?"

He laughed out loud.

"James, don't laugh at me. I really don't know."

He turned his face to mine, "I just never discussed condoms before, especially when I wasn't going to use it."

I lifted my eyebrows.

"No, Sarah, don't even think about it. It is not happening."

"Fine, show me how they work."

He took my hand and put up one finger and took the condom and put it on the tip of my finger and tried to roll it down.

"Well, it's supposed to just roll down around it. But your finger is too small." He laughed a little.

More determined I encouraged, "Then show me for real."

"No, It…" he was looking down at himself, "…will get the wrong idea."

I pushed myself to sit up; it was a little painful, but only when I tried to use the muscles. "James, show me."

"No, it would be too hard for me. Now, lie down and go to sleep."

I turned to him, "You really won't show me?"

"No, Sarah. If I put that on it will think it's going to get some, and darling you can't even sit up without pain. Now please lay back down, because we need to get some sleep."

I traced my hand across his chest.

"Sarah, stop and go to sleep."

I traced the top of his pants with my finger slightly under the edge. He closed his eyes, "Please, baby, no, not yet. Give yourself a few more weeks."

"James, you are sending me away in two weeks. I want to try before I go home, even if it hurts."

"No, not happening." He grabbed my hand and sat up enough to hold me to lay down with him. He kissed my hand and then my cheek.

"When we finally get to do this, Sarah, I want to make you feel so good you will scream my name begging me for more. So you have to be completely healed before we try. Sorry, Sarah, that is final."

I smiled. I did love him so much. The screaming thing I was doubtful, but it would be fun to let him try. At least I think so.

## 49. A New Day

    **I** woke with my arms around the pillow. I peeked over it, and James wasn't there. I was still hooked up to the IV so I rolled over to get up, and I stumbled to the bathroom. In the last week I had come a long way, I only needed to support myself a little, the bleeding was almost done, and the pain was bearable. The biggest struggle I had; was with the IV tube and getting dressed. I grabbed a sweatshirt and headed to the living room to find Jake. I wanted to be disconnected, but he wasn't in here either. I huffed as I pulled the tubes up and through the arm while heading down to the fire pit to find my men; that had to be where they were.

    They had a whole buffet set up with griddles and pancake batter ready to go. Wilson was showing James what to do with the bacon, but at the same time he was telling Jake what to do with the sausage. Wilson noticed me first and deserted James and Jake making his way to me. He wrapped me in his arm, kissed my head, and moved me to an oversized lawn chair. Alissa and Chloe were walking out of their tent and saw this. The look on their faces showed me that they didn't believe how these people all cared for me. It wasn't like school, where no one noticed me walking into a room. They walked over and sat on a couple of chairs by the fire, which was still going. Wilson propped a pillow behind me and tucked me in with a comforter, "Sarah, I will have yours ready in a minute."

    He moved away from me almost running into James, as he made his way to me. He sat on the arm and leaned down to kiss me lightly, "Good morning, baby. You should still be sleeping; it's too early."

    Not really knowing what time it was I asked, "What time is it?"

    He smiled and leaned over again, "We'll just say that you will need a nap later."

His attention was making me so happy, and I loved all the kisses. The girls from school were really put off that this gorgeous man loved me. I smiled as he kissed me again. I licked my lips, as he pulled away from me, but he came back and whispered in my ear. "Why do you lick your lips after I kiss you?"

I was completely embarrassed, "To savor the taste."

He smiled and laughed a little, "I am so in love with you."

My heart was filled, as he got up and moved back to help with the food. I noticed that he would look up at me and smiled while he was working on the food, but it was only because I found it hard to drag my eyes away from him.

Chloe decided to try and be more nosey, "Sarah, you're married to him, right?"

Boasting with pride and a little embarrassed, I glanced over at him. I was a little surprised by his questioning facial expression.

"Ah, yeah."

"Your mom and dad are okay with it?"

I cringed with that thought. I needed him here right now; I was really uneasy with all of these questions. All I could think was, *please James I need you*, but I replied to her, "We really didn't give them a chance to have an opinion."

"What do you mean by that?"

I felt panicked, *James please come here. This doesn't feel good.* I really wasn't comfortable answering questions, because I knew they would use it to hurt me later. I was somewhat comforted when I saw James nudge Jake. Jake got up, headed to me and squatted down in front of me. He was staring at my face, as he spoke for me, "James asked Sarah to marry him about two and half months ago, but their plan was to wait till she was 18. However..." He was messing with the IV lines working on disconnecting them, "Sarah, couldn't live without him and got really sick. She scared us, because she was going to die and in order to save her... James had to sign the papers as her husband. They were married in the hospital to save her life." But then he leaned to whisper to me, "And broke a lot of hearts in the process."

I watched him still working on disconnecting me, but my heart was filled with sadness. I never wanted to hurt him; it was just that I needed him so much at the time. I didn't feel like smiling anymore, "Jake." I was shaking my head no.

He wasn't angry or sad, but he was smiling, "There you're free. How do you feel this morning?"

"Jake, you know I didn't mean to."

He put his finger to his lips to hush me, "Sarah, it's okay."

I needed to make things okay for Jake, and I didn't know how to. I wanted James to make everything better, so I glanced over to him. I felt horrible until I saw his smile. He put his hand on his chest and mouthed to me, "You picked me." I could see that this made him the happiest person here. The weight lifted in my chest knowing that I loved him with every part of my heart.

Jake was tucking me back in when Alissa and Chloe caught my attention. They were both observing everything going on; all the secret motions, eye contacts, everything that was private to us.

I don't think Chloe had good intentions, because she wouldn't let it go, "So do you even have a ring?"

I smiled sinfully and held up my ring finger.

"Holly shit, how big is it?"

I shrugged my shoulders but I heard James, "Not big enough."

I looked over at him shaking my head with disbelief. I felt it was way too big.

"Did you pick it out yourself?"

I grinned, "Nope, I didn't know he was going to do this."

She came over and looked at it closely, "Is it real?"

Jake was very upset with her question, "Yes, it is."

I really didn't ever question whether or not it was real. It didn't matter to me, because I loved James.

Some of the other girls were adventuring out. Wilson was encouraging everyone to come in and eat.

James yelled to me, "Sarah, you want to go get the rest of them up?" I tried to get up and almost made it, but of course the pain gave me a quick sharp jilt. James came running, "Sorry, sweetie, but I forget because you just look so healthy to me." He helped me up slowly, kissing me on the cheek, as he directed me down to the tents.

I walked down to the boy's tent and walked in. I woke up Brian first, and got a really big hug good morning. He walked out. I woke Matt next. He pulled me to him, "How are you doing?"

Pleased that he was very comfortable here, I tried to reassure him, "Okay."

"How is it going, being married and all that?"

Well, that wasn't a question I wanted to answer, so I just smiled. He wrapped his arms around my waist, "Oh, that good, huh. Well at least I know how much he loves you, or I wouldn't be happy about this."

I messed up his hair.

"Hey, are the girls being nice?"

I shrugged my shoulders.

I could see the sadness sweep over his face but he was determined, "I will watch more carefully. After this, they will all want to be your best friend."

"No, Matt, it will be faked. I don't want them to treat me any differently than the way they always do. Honestly, I don't mind not being seen."

"Sarah, you just don't get it. You are amazing. I think a lot of it is jealousy."

I shook my head no, "I really don't like to be noticed."

He traced his hand on my face, "But, Sarah, if people knew the real you, not the one who hides, they would know how great you are."

I shook my head no, "Matt, please. I like it that way. They will be meaner if they know me, like stabbing me in the back. I don't know if it was a good idea to even invite them here."

"Sorry, James asked and said it was for you."

"I know, just don't push, okay?"

"Yeah."

"Time to eat."

"OH," He got up and woke Blaire. I walked to the girl's tent. There were four still sleeping. I woke each of them. One was the really pretty girl. She was the best looking one in the whole school. It was Allison, and she didn't look pleased that I woke her let alone touched her, but she tried to be unpleasantly friendly.

"So, Jake is your doctor?"

I didn't look at her, "Yep."

"How come he doesn't have interest in any of the girls here?"

I tried to hold back my grin, "He is just picky."

She seemed to be evaluating me, "If you weren't married, I think he would have feelings for you."

I couldn't tell if that was a statement or a question. I avoided looking at her, but went on to explain, "He is just doing a favor to Clarissa and Carl, and that is it."

I could tell she didn't trust me. I couldn't look at her and avoided her eyes. I was very self-conscious now, fidgeting, as I woke the others.

"You know, if you did your hair and wore makeup, you could be pretty."

My eyes flashed back to her to see a smile on her face. I didn't know how to take her. I still didn't trust her.

"I think you should let me help you."

I shook my head no, "But thank you."

She looked at me and lifted my chin, "Sarah, I can have any guy I want; I can help you, really."

I smiled, but went to wake the others, "Hey, food is ready."

I walked out and into the next tent which was Will and Katherine's. I unzipped the tent but announced that I was coming in.

"Sarah, privacy."

I had my hand over my eyes, "James said the food was ready. You guys have to come now or miss out."

"Sarah, out. We'll skip breakfast."

I backed out without looking. I went to Jason's and Kylie's tent. I didn't want to go through that again, so I didn't go in. I just announced breakfast, but I heard Kylie, "Hey, Sarah, you can come in."

I unzipped the tent and walked in. Jason was smiling, but he avoided looking at me. Kylie reached for my hand. They were still lying in bed, but fully dressed. She pulled me to the bed in between them. They were both propped up on their sides looking at me. I felt really stupid. Kylie was comforting, "So, James is taking care of you, right?"

I grinned, "Yeah, but it has been really weird."

Jason wiped the hair from my face, "Sarah, I wanted to thank you."

I felt really weird being between them, but I glanced at his face.

"Yeah, Kylie and I are getting married."

Kylie spoke next, "And I was wondering if you would be my Matron of Honor?"

I was completely relieved after they explained what this was about, "I am so happy for the both of you." I hugged Kylie first then Jason, "When is the wedding?"

"This time next year. We needed time to plan it out."

Jason whispered, "We didn't want to do it in a rush like two other people we know."

I bite my lip, uncomfortable with the conversation.

"Sarah, you are too young to be married. I thought you were going to give him the ring back and wait awhile."

I looked at Kylie for reassurance; it was okay to talk to Jason. She nodded to me like she was okay. I looked at Jason again, "Jason, I wanted to, but under the circumstances things changed, but he wants to make it as normal as possible for me. I have to move home for the school year."

"What?" I could tell he didn't like this idea, not any more than I did.

"Yeah, he thinks I should have a normal teenage life."

"That is just stupid. You'll get sick again if you're not together. I watched you deteriorate without him."

I grimaced, "I feel that way too; can you talk to him and tell him that? I don't want to go home. I want to stay with James, forever."

He laughed a little, "Well, he is pigheaded... I will see what I can do."

They both kissed me on the cheek and helped me up. We all walked up to the fire pit together. James came running over, and whispered in my ear, "I don't want you to leave either, but having people gang up on me is not fair."

I glared at him, as he scolded. He was going to get it from me now, "You know I hate when you listen to my conversations."

He laughed, kissed me softly, and went back to helping get food for everyone.

Clarissa and Carl came down with Josie, but they were very cuddly. Carl had his arms wrapped around Clarissa and was very attentive to her; touching her lightly on the small of her back, tracing his hands down her arms, kissing her neck and her cheek. They had a steamy night, and I knew this... why? Because that is how James is with me when we get hot together. I was feeling the desire to play with James. He looked at me at the very second I thought it, and he chuckled to himself. Jake noticed and asked him what that was about. James shook his head trying to shake off what I was wanting. Sam went over to the guys to help them. James showed him what he was doing and then came to me. I could feel the girls from school watching. He had my plate in his hand and helped me to scoot up, so he could crawl in behind me. He put a blanket over me, and I scooted back into him. I started to eat, as he lightly traced his hands over my stomach under that blanket.

"James..." I leaned back to look at him disapprovingly, "Stop that."

I went back to eating. He leaned to whisper in my ear, "You're hot right now."

I leaned back and gave him another disapproving look, "James?"

"You were calling to me." He laughed.

"James, no, there are people around."

His grin was sinful, as he kissed my cheek, and he continued to softly trace my stomach.

I leaned back and whispered with a pleading tone, "I will get hotter."

Trying to be nonchalant about it, he mouthed to my ear, "That's the idea."

I tried to eat faster, so we could sneak off together. When I finished eating he said really loud, "Are you ready to go change?"

I was trying to refrain from giggling, but I was over ready, "Yeah, I am ready." He helped me up and picked me up to carry me. I looked at him and wrapped my arms around his neck.

Jake yelled out, "I will be there in about 10 minutes to get changed myself."

We both laughed. James turned around to look at him, "Don't come in; she will be changing."

James was taking me to the apartment. We got to the door and Danelle was coming out. James set me down. He messed up her hair, "How did you sleep?"

She got a huge grin on her face. I could tell she liked it, "I didn't want to get up."

Jake came running, "Hey, you two are behaving."

James directed him buying us some time alone, "Hey, will you take Danelle down to get food?"

"I can take myself." She was looking uneasy about going down there.

Jake picked her up over his shoulder, "I will be back; you two have 10 minutes."

"Jake, put me down; I can walk." This came from Danelle.

"No, I have you." He was twirling her and making her scream. We both laughed and walked in. I went straight for the bathroom, changed female stuff and came out. He had clothes picked out for me.

"You picked out my clothes?"

His eyebrows rose suggestively, "Do you remember the picture you sent me?"

I looked at him confused, "No."

He held up the bikini, "This is the suit you were wearing under the wet suit; I could just see a glimpse of it, and I wanted to see it fully."

He held up a tank top and white shirt, "This was what you had on at Tony's, and the picture was very sexy; I have to see it for real."

Then he held up a skirt, "This, well I just want to look at your legs."

"You are torturing yourself, and the bikini... it will show my stomach."

"Not if you wear a tank top over it."

"I could wear shorts, and you would still see my legs."

He smiled, "But this will sway to your movements. Please?"

How could I say no to a face like that, "Anything for you, but I am putting the bottoms on myself. I am still gross."

"You were going to let me help you?"

I wanted him to touch me, "I love when you touch me."

He bit his bottom lip, handing me the bottoms, and gestured to the bathroom. I went in and changed the bottoms. When I came out I still had the tank top on, but he was in swimming trunks that hung so low you could see every ripple of his abs, and they lay nicely along his butt. Oh, today was going to be hard. He was going to put on a muscle shirt but stopped, as I walked out. James locked the door, "Holly shit, girl."

I scolded, "Hey, settle down. Jake is going to be here in 10 minutes."

He grinned, "But I locked the door."

I was full of mischief too, "You are going to make me hotter?"

His grin gave me the answer I didn't want. He held up the bikini top and smiled, "This next?"

I nodded. He tied a knot in the straps that would go around my neck and looked at me as if to see into my soul, and it was making me nervous. I didn't know how much I could handle without pain. He stood in front of me and looked me in the eyes, "Can you handle this?"

I shook my head no, but he reassured me with a grin, "I swear I put clothes on you more than I try to take them off." As he lightened the mood I laughed.

We heard Jake, "Hey, I'm back; are you two almost ready?"

We both smiled, gazing into each other's eyes, but James answered, "Nope."

"Fine, I will get dressed, but then you have to be done."

James grinned at me, "Well, I guess we should hurry it along then."

I nodded while he moved closer to me pulling my tank top off over my head. He pressed his chest to mine, wrapping his arms around me, and running his fingers down my back. He slowly let go and walked around to the back of me putting the strap over my head and reaching to the front to cup my breast into the top. He breathed in my ear, "You are so soft, and smell so sweet." He pulled the straps to the back and tied them. He took the tank top and moved around me to the front of me putting it over my head. He helped me putting one arm at a time through each of the straps and slowly traced his hands down my sides, as he lowered the top. I smiled at him and giggled a little, as his hands tickled my sides. A grin appeared on his face, as he whispered, "Ticklish?"

He grabbed the skirt and squatted down for me to step into it. He traced the back of my legs, as he brought the skirt up to my waist, moving to his knees to have his mouth next to my stomach. He traced his hand along the scar, "Sarah, you can hardly tell it's here; have you looked?"

I glanced down at him, gasping, because I could hardly breathe, "Not really." I ran my fingers through his hair; my chest was heaving quickly with anticipation. He came to kiss and suck on my stomach. I closed my eyes; I was getting dizzy and light headed, "OH JAMES." He wrapped his hand around to the low part of my back to pull me closer to him.

He was making me hotter, "Sarah, how are you doing?"

I tried to get it out through my deep breathing, "Hot, very hot."

He was more aggressive taunting me, "The heat coming from you, Sarah... I am so..."

Knowing this was torture for him I had to make him stop, "James, stop."

He moved up to me, "You don't want me to..."

"No, the pain will come, and you will be miserable."

He swept me to him, holding me and kissing me so deeply, that the air was knocked out of me. All this cupping and licking was not helping me at all. He traced his hand down my sides to lift my leg up to his waist.

"James, it's starting."

He mouthed to me with a grin, "The tingling or the pain?" as he kissed me more.

Gasping with my reply, "Tingling."

He slowed as his hand lowered my leg slowly. He brought his hands to my face and lightly traced his lips over my face. I took a deep breath to try to calm down, and we heard a knock at the door, "Hey, are you two ready?"

James pulled his face away from mine and grinned, "So, are you ready?"

I shook my head no.

He smiled, "Look, darling, I made it through without having to take a cold shower." His grin was wonderful and melted my heart. I reached to touch his chest. He pulled away, "Nope, you can't do that, because it wouldn't take much, Sarah."

I was confused how that worked. He could touch me, but I couldn't touch him.

"I told you before if you let me be the one in control I can handle it better, but if you touch me... that is when I lose control, so..." He took my hands put them together and kissed them, "We'll save that for later."

I sighed with disappointment. I wanted to touch him. He held up the shirt to help me put it on. He replied to Jake, "Jake, we're almost ready."

He tried the door, "James, you locked the door."

"Yep, you tend to walk in even when we're not ready."

I turned around; he tied the front of the shirt, and helped me roll up the sleeves. He grabbed his tank top and opened the door. Jake almost fell in, "You two, no more today."

We both smiled, but James started to laugh, "She will have to get changed later, Jake."

"Not with you. I will have to help her to keep you two apart."

I was determined, "Sorry, Jake, James will have to help me."

James grinned with my answer to Jake. He pulled me closer, as we headed out the door. They let me lead the way down to the lake.

I felt extremely good when I heard Jake say, "Why are you letting her wear that?"

"I picked it out; why?"

Jake was seriously not happy about this, "There are too many guys here who like her, so you shouldn't let her prance around tempting them."

"Jake, yes, but it's to rub it into the girls from school, too."

James caught up to me, so I crawled on his back for a piggyback ride whispering in his ear, "You are the best."

## 50. The Love Story

The day started off okay. Some were playing volleyball, and some were swimming off the floating dock. Sam and Brian were getting the Jet Skies down and in the water. I walked to Danelle to see how she was doing. She was fine, and excited for the day. She hurried up to the apartment to get dressed.

Jake came over, "Hey, where did your friend go?"

"To get dressed." I glanced up at him with a huge grin on my face.

He shook his head, "What?"

I got a really serious look, "What?"

"You're looking at me funny."

"And there is something wrong with that?"

He was embarrassed, "Oh, would you just look at your husband."

I did turn to admire James, but there was something sparking between Jake and Danelle.

Jake was getting frustrated with me, "Sarah, no. Stop thinking that way."

"I wasn't thinking anything, why what do you think I was thinking?"

He walked away from me, so I was busting my gut laughing. "Jake, don't be mad."

He didn't even turn around.

I watched as everyone stayed busy. Danelle wanted to go down and play in the water, but of course I couldn't. She decided to go anyway. Sam got to her first, but Jake objected to the attention he was giving her. Jake did a good job keeping her company. Jealousy filled me to the core; I wanted to be able to play in the water.

James noticed I was just sitting here pouting, and decided to do something about t it, "Do you want to try the Jet Ski? We could go slowly"

Hope filled me with excitement, "Really?"

"Sure, whatever you want."

I stood up just a little too quickly and felt the pain. He helped me with his shirt that I was wearing and then the skirt. He took my hand in his and we walked down together.

Jake came to stop us, "James, hitting the waves will hurt. What are you thinking?"

"We'll go really slowly. No hitting waves." James helped me on and got on behind me.

"James, no!"

"If you don't trust me, then come with us."

He jumped on another machine.

Danelle yelled after him, "If you are watching them, I am coming with you."

Jake grabbed her arm and pulled her on with one swipe. James kissed my shoulder and started to go really slow, "Any pain, darling, please tell me."

I leaned back into him closing my eyes, "I am in heaven."

He swayed slowly back and forth giving the effects of a light wave. This was almost as good as riding the bike with him. He did go slow, avoiding the waves, while Jake and Danelle hung back. I traced his arms with my hands and completely relaxed. I didn't know how long we were gone, but I was almost falling asleep in his arms. The engine cut.

I opened my eyes, "No, James, I was enjoying this."

He kissed the back of my head, "You were sleeping. You need a nap. I told you, you were up too early."

"No, James, I was napping already. More please."

"Sarah, you will take a nap, and I will take you again later."

I was bummed out. I loved being held in his arms with the strength of his body supporting me.

Jake and Danelle jumped off their wave runners, "What's wrong?"

James held out his arm to stop them from overreacting, "She was falling asleep."

Jake held my back, while James got off, and then he pulled me down helping James until he could take me in his arms.

"James, you're treating me like a baby."

A smirky little grin came to his face, "You are my baby; I love you, and you're tired. Please let me?"

I smiled and curled into him while closing my eyes. I heard a lot of people asking if I was okay, but I was just tired. He took me to bed.

Jake and Danelle were not far behind.

James laid me down and Jake quickly moved in to hook me back up to the IV bag again.

"No, Jake, not during the day. You said..."

Danelle sat down next to me, "Hey, maybe you need this."

I didn't want it. It made me feel week and vulnerable. Plus, she would be out there alone with the mean girls from school, "But you will be alone."

Jake spoke up, "We will entertain her. Come on, Sarah, behave. You'll be hooked up just while you're sleeping."

I rolled over and closed my eyes again. It didn't take long.

When I woke, James was sitting up next to me. I closed my eyes and grinned, as I traced my hand along his waist, "You didn't have to stay with me."

"Yes, I did. I only want to be with you."

I reached for him and closed my eyes again. He ran his fingers through my hair, "You didn't have any pain with that, right? I mean, you fell asleep so it didn't hurt, right?"

"Not at all, James, thank you. I needed that."

"Hey, you have to eat. You missed lunch."

"What time is it?"

"It's already 5pm."

"What... I slept really long."

"Yes you did, but you will be able to stay up later now, and I won't worry so much."

We went out to join the rest. It seemed that everyone was worried about me, but only until James got me to the chair. The grill was going, so after he got me settled he went to help Wilson.

They were making some potatoes on the grill along with the steaks. I went and sat between Carl and Clarissa, "This is too much, Clarissa."

She hugged me tightly, and Carl kissed my head. I curled up in between them while James continued to help Wilson.

When everyone else finished eating, they started to play again. Jake and James put speakers in the windows, so we could have music. When he came out he walked me down to the dock. He wrapped his arms around my waist and danced slowly with me, as we looked at each other in the sunset. My heart was full of love, as I gazed into his beautiful, warm, deep brown eyes.

## Jake:

As I sat down where Sarah usually sits, I watched her and James on the dock. I was feeling a little irritated. I know James loves her; I know he is my brother; he seems to be a good man, but I could be a good man too. I wanted to be the one down there with her. No, I don't, but the way she looks at him. I looked up to see Danelle moving to sit on the foot of the lawn chair I was sitting on, so I moved my feet to make room. That's when I observed the other girls moving in closer, my mom and dad cuddling with smiles on their faces, and the approval of Clarissa's smile at what I was noticing. I wanted my mother to be happy and she was enjoying the thought of all these girls wanting to get to know me, but they really didn't do it for me. My attention was on the two down on the dock. I wanted what they had. I was happy that I wasn't the only one concentrating on them; Danelle was captivated by them also, and she was leaning with her chin in her hands watching them too.

Some of the girls started to ask questions, probably to distract me from watching James and Sarah on the dock.

"So, Jake, what kind of doctor are you?"

Okay with the interruption, I glanced over to the girl that asked the question. I think it was Brianna. Trying to be polite I answered her, "Emergency Room." I still couldn't keep my mind off of those two down on the dock.

Someone else asked, "Where do you work?"

That was a good distraction, because the realization hit me that I wasn't working for anyone now. Shit, I have to do something about that, now that Sarah is getting better. "Umm, I am temporarily just Sarah's doctor. I will try to go back to the hospital in two weeks."

My mom was full of anticipation, "You are thinking about staying in the cities?"

Of course, her excitement caught my attention. Her smile was a mile wide. I was a little embarrassed with her reaction. Everyone was going to think I was a mama's boy with the way she was smiling, "Yeah, I am going to try and get my old job back."

She melted into dad even more with the satisfaction of me being around more. I felt good about wanting to stay, and I would get to see them more. Not being able to stay distracted for long, I found myself glancing back down to the dock where James and Sarah were so captivated with each other. Something new was happening, which I have never felt before; my heart actually hurt. I wasn't supposed to feel this way, and I knew it. I shook it off in time for the next question.

"What hospital are you talking about and where is it?"

This time it was Chloe asking the question.

"Edina." Why couldn't I keep my eyes from drifting back to the dock?

The really pretty girl, according to Danelle, asked me, "Are they like this all the time?"

I had to chuckle to myself and let it slip out, "No, usually worse."

Clarissa disciplined me, "Jake, it's not that bad."

Clarissa, my real mom, and I exchanged smiles with complete understanding of each other.

The pretty girl asked again, "What do you mean?"

Matt walked up at the perfect time letting me off the hook on explaining, "Well, if it is like it was at the airport, I understand that." He was chuckling to himself, as if he had a secret that none of us would understand.

They were all interested in his story, including myself. I moved towards the end of the chair more, trying to encourage him to continue, but he was distracted by the pretty girl's legs. I coughed to mask my laugh and to get his attention back, so he could continue with the story. He squeezed in-between her and Chloe, "Well, James was gone for a while, but while he was gone he came back for one day to be with her."

Did anyone else know about this? I glanced around finding that there was confusion on almost everyone's face until my eyes fell on Danelle. She didn't even bother to be distracted by the story, her attention stayed with James and Sara. Brian walked up in time to hear the story. Jason moved forward in his seat, but was still holding Kylie's hand, and I could see the interest in his movements. The only one that seemed very pleased with this story was my dad. He already knew about this; I could tell by the guilty grin on his face.

You could tell that Matt liked being the center of attention. As he explained, he seemed to juice it up for the rest of us. I took one more glimpse at them on the dock, but quickly gave Matt my attention. I couldn't really tell if Danelle knew about this, but she did turn to listen also.

He was going to make it really juicy, "Sarah called me from her cell phone and asked me to do her a favor. She picked me up and it was like 10:30 pm, and I had to sneak out. I thought for one brief moment..." He stopped, I knew what he felt. He thought she was coming to be with him.

He shook his head; I think to rid himself of the thought and then continued, "Well, anyway, when she got to my house she was a mess, she gave me her car keys and I didn't know what she was thinking. When we got in the car she was upset asking me to take her to the airport."

This time he laughed with the memory, "I thought she was running away to be with him, but she looked so sad I had to take her. When we got there she was out of the car before I could put it in park. I got out and ran after her, but of course she was looking for him. Once we figured out the general idea of where he was we took off running." He stopped to see if everyone was still listening. When he was satisfied that everyone's attention was still on him he went on, "I saw James before she did. I knew it was him because of his misery." He asked my Dad who was also smiling, "Do you remember their Misery?"

My dad nodded and then looked down. I was confused now. Why was my dad there?

"To tell you the truth he was worse than her. When she ran to him I couldn't believe how miserable they were to be apart, for the little time they were going to be separated. When it was time for James to leave...I was miserable just watching them." His eyes focused on my Dad again, "Wilson was trying to pull James to the boarding runway, and they wouldn't let go of each other. I was frozen; I didn't know what to do. I was ready to beg him to stay myself."

Dad spoke up, "If it wasn't for Matt's help, I wouldn't have been able to get them apart and when she yelled to him, I thought he would never leave."

Matt laughed, "I wouldn't have left."

I knew her better than the rest of them. I spoke with determination, "She made him leave!"

All the attention moved to me. I should have kept my mouth shut. Thank god Jason spoke up to explain, "She told him if he didn't finish, they wouldn't be together."

I had heard the same conversation. My eyes drifted back to them; feeling better about her being with him, but only a little.

"Jake, why would she do something like that?" This was coming from Alissa; she had gotten up and moved to sit in front of Matt.

He was tracing his hands down her back. I gave him a disapproving glance, but he was unaffected by glare; with a great big smile on his face.

Jason took over telling the story, "That's funny in itself. She felt if he couldn't finish his commitment to complete the course he was taking, then he wouldn't be able to commit to her for the rest of his life."

Alisson, the pretty one, according to everyone here, looked directly at me, "So, did he finish?"

Everyone that knew about it laughed.

I was going to answer Alisson, but Danelle turned to me laying those little blue eyes dreamily on me. Okay, forget about the little girl; she's way too young. "He did, but while he was away she got sicker and sicker. She was fighting to make it until he got back, thanks to Carl."

He spoke up as soon as I said it, "Don't bring me into this. I just told her it would wait till he came back."

It was Carl's declaration, that it would wait for James to come home, that kept her fighting for as long as she did, "You kept her fighting till he could make it back, but she shouldn't have waited. She wouldn't have gotten so bad if she didn't push to wait for him to come home."

"Jake, she made it through."

I was still angry about this whole marriage thing on her death bed. I tried to smile, but it may have come out as a smirk of disgust.

I got up, but Danelle stopped me, "Jake, sit down. Give them more time. They are behaving."

I couldn't take anymore, "Just going to change." I managed a wry smile the best I could and walked away. I felt like I was finally letting her go. I didn't want to, but I knew they would be happier without me here to remind him, besides I couldn't go far, because he was my brother. I took a lot of deep breaths as I changed, but that wasn't enough. I walked to the couch, sat down, and put my head in my hands; I had to never look at her that way again. I was doing pretty well until tonight. What the hell was my problem?

I heard a voice, "Hey, are you okay?"

I wasn't happy to see the girl standing there in the door way. It was the pretty girl, but I didn't want anything to do with her. I pushed myself up, walked to the door where she was standing, and decided that this is not what I wanted. I didn't stop when I got to her; I continued out the door, but as I passed her she grabbed my arm to stop me, and she said to me, "Hey, I could help you. I am good at making people feel better."

Yes, I bet she was good in more ways than I wanted to know. I tried to be polite, "Thanks but no, I am fine." I turned and kept walking. I didn't want anything to do with that one. I went back to the lawn chair I was in before and sat down. Danelle hadn't moved.

She turned to me, "That didn't take long."

"What?"

Danelle leaned more to me, "That didn't take long."

I didn't get what she was talking about, "I just went to get changed."

She gave me the most unbelievable look, "I saw her follow you. She would have taken your mind off what you are thinking."

Her eyes were so blue, the color of... the Caribbean Sea. *Stop it, Jake,* is what I had to think in order to answer her, "I wasn't thinking anything, and she is..." I leaned to Danelle whispering, "Easy. She probably has a disease or something." I grabbed my shirt, "I just changed...changed...and that's all."

Her eyes sparkled like the sun reflecting off the water. *I have to ignore those eyes. Sarah is wrong about this, because she is too young. Just look at her mouth. See, that is much better, comforting, sweet, and perfect in a way. Perfectly colored without anything on them and the way she smiled... oh, she has dimples. Jake, knock it off!* I couldn't help myself, "What are you smiling about?"

Her cheeks turned a slight touch of pink. Was she embarrassed? Those eyes came back to meet mine, this time full of surprise. Which made sense when she replied, "You're not a jerk."

That was it; she turned away from me to look at the dock. My attention followed where hers went and we were watching James and Sarah again. They were happy together the way they were talking, swaying, and looking at each other.

I leaned to Danelle wanting to comment on the two of them together, maybe a little too close, because my chest rubbed against her shoulder; she jumped involuntarily, as she glanced over her shoulder at me.

I was as surprised as she was, because it was like an electrical shock, "Sorry, I was just going to say they do look good together."

She grinned, "Auh, yeah. Did you just give me a shock?"

I laughed, "Yes, I guess I did."

"It hurt, you know."

I rubbed the spot, "I didn't mean to; we should go break them up. I mean all these people are here to spend time with her, right?"

"I still think she is sad, it shows in her face. Look at the smile, it's ..."

"We shouldn't be watching them, because it's private."

"So, if the pretty girl isn't good enough for you, which one of these girls sparks your interest?"

I had nothing to hide; she was a little girl asking me an honest question. Shit, there is the honesty that James talks about. Shit, just... be honest, "None of them. Silly girl games don't do it for me."

"Really?" She leaned into me, and I got a shock this time, but it wasn't electrical. This was an invasion of her privacy, because it was what she was thinking. I actually heard her thoughts, which surprised me, but yet... relieving that it was innocent and honest. She was thinking I was so cute, which made her wonder why I wasn't interested in any of the girls here. I really did feel like I was violating her in some way, but the thought of what James was talking about... the honesty and innocence of her was refreshing. I put a little distance between us, knowing what she was thinking was weird for me. Her eyes squinted, hiding those blue eyes from me. I offended her by putting some space between us. So much that she move further away from me. I wanted to comfort her, let her know that it was me not her, but she was a little girl, so I let it go. Thinking that I was making her uncomfortable, I decided it was time. I got up and put out may hand, "Come on, let's go gather them up."

The sparkle in those blue eyes was back, and she took my hand. I pulled her to her feet, but let go of her hand. As we got close they kissed, "Okay, you two. Enough is enough; people are talking."

James bent down and picked her up, hugging her and twirled her around, setting her back down, and then he kissed her forehead, "I am so in love with you, little girl."

Her arms wrapped around his waist.

Danelle scolded them, "You're not supposed to be mushy around me please. There are virgin eyes and ears here."

We all started to laugh. James let go of Sarah and wrapped his arm around Danelle's neck, "So, is my brother entertaining you enough, or do I need to pick on you?"

She pushed him away, "You are so playing volleyball, even if Sarah can't."

"So you are going to be nice to me?"

She shrugged her shoulders giving him the shove off, "Well, you're not as big of a jerk as I thought you were."

"NO, I'm still a jerk. I am a guy."

She laughed and pulled him to the volleyball court. I walked with Sarah to get her settled. As we walked to the fire pit she hip checked me, "Are you okay?"

I wanted to be fine, but I didn't know how I felt right now, so I lied, "Yep, just fine."

"Jake, I wasn't the only one feeling you."

"Fuck, I wasn't trying to. It's just... I am really trying. I don't want to feel this way, and he is my brother. It's just...."

Her eyes were green, a vicious green. Piercing, stabbing into my heart, but yet they were caring in an engulfing way; her eyes searched my face, and she finished my sentence, "Not easy. I know. Can I just say one thing?" She stopped and stepped in front of me. I glanced over to James, and he was watching.

"Fine, hurry up, please."

"I'm sorry. I wasn't fair to you."

Shit, I did not want to do this. I avoided her gaze; I didn't want to look into her face, "I knew it was wrong too, Sarah. It wasn't entirely your fault, but it's done and he's here, and you just need to drop the subject. I will be fine."

She turned to walk up continuing to talk, "He felt it and pointed it out to me. Jake he wants to make sure I get what I want without being selfish."

"Yeah, how is that going for you?"

"If I wasn't sure, I would have kissed you at my house."

My heart dropped out of my chest. She was sure she loved him. I closed my eyes to endure the sadness.

"Jake, I don't want you to feel this way. What can I do to help?"

"Not talk about it, okay?" I was short with her, but I needed to think about something else. I glanced over at James; he knew I was hurt, and I could see it in his face.  He was going to come over, and I put up my hand to stop him.  I helped her sit.

"Jake, you don't have to…"

In the coldest possible way I was forceful, "Stop, I am fine.  Just let me do what I have to.  Okay, Sarah!"

She looked up at me, as I tucked a blanket around her.  I took her arm examining the IV port "There, you are fine."

I stood back up, but she grabbed my arm, "Jake?"

I didn't wait to see what she wanted, "Sarah, I am going to go play volleyball."  I leaned down to her talking quietly, "Please let me."  I would have stayed with her if she would have asked.

That actually seemed to make her happy, "No, you go.  I want you to have fun.  It's good for you."

I shook my head no and walked away.  That's what she did for me; she just wanted me to be happy and have fun…not be uptight and serious all the time.

## 51. Old Tale

### Sarah:

**B**rian saw that I was alone and he came over, "My turn."

Feeling James in my heart, I glanced over to make sure he was okay with this. To my surprise he seemed to support it with a nod and a grin, however, Jake was not happy. Brian crawled in behind me on the huge lawn chair, and we talked about me going home for school, what James's plans were, and how this whole thing was going to work out. I wasn't sure how everything was going to work out. We still needed to talk more about it, but I broke down every time we discussed me going home for the school year. I needed to stop doing that. Wilson brought me out a sandwich, so I could keep up my energy after missing lunch. As everyone gathered by the fire, Carl started with the story of how they descended. James came back and kicked Brian out, so we could cuddle for the story.

*Back long ago, we were named by our future. There was a young man destined to be the great chief, but he was to be part of the land. His name was Sugmuk, which meant earth. He could feel the earth beneath his feet, winds at his face, and the change of weather. Then there was a young maiden, Mapiya, which means heavenly. She was destined to be married to young Sugmuk. As were most young maidens, they were promised to the men they were supposed to marry. Mapiya, did not want to marry Sugmuk so badly, that she looked for a way out of the arrangement. She could only think of one way, and that was to end her life. She set out to the mountains to beg for them to take her from* her life and to serve the Spirits. When she got to the top of the largest mountain she could find, she laid there and waited for days without food or water. Sugmuk was devastated; he understood the importance of their union and what it would mean to the future of our tribe. He sent out search parties, unsuccessfully, until he begged the ancestors for help to find her. That night he spent in the woods in turmoil, but was given a gift. As the night went on, he had animal visitors that he was able to converse with in his mind. As the young maiden, Mapiya, laid their waiting, she was also given a gift. The ancestors gave her a gift of moving the wind. As the rain moved in, she was able to push it away. As the wind picked up, she was able direct it away. As she noticed this, she was happier to be alive, when a very large eagle came to visit her. She fed him some crumbs she had left in her pocket. To her surprise, she felt him tell her she would be okay and her Sugmuk would come to save her. If she allowed him to, he would marry her. She tried to explain she was scared and too young, and that she needed more time. He gave her words of wisdom to say, and he left a feather for her, let him bless her with the feather and say the words, and you will be forever happy with Sugmuk. Next she encountered a stag. He directed her to get up and follow him. As they moved down the side of the mountain, she realized she would not find her way home. The stag told her the story of her destined husband and his need for her to be complete.

 James pulled me in tighter; his mouth was at my ear, and I could feel him breathing. Carl felt the torment between James and I, and his attention came to us with a scolding glare. My love for James was so deep, and James was obsessed with me. We were doing the wrong thing and we both knew it, but yet we couldn't help ourselves. Carl went back to telling the fable, without much notice from anyone else that he was teaching us with this story.

 As they moved slowly down the mountain, Sugmuk was letting a mustang take him wherever he felt necessary to find his love. He lay back on this mustang and closed his eyes to ask the ancestors to help him find his destiny. He wandered for days and she walked for days. At last there was hope when they saw and then ran to each other. Sugmuk was running to his future, and Mapiya was running to the safety of his arms. She did want to be with him, but she wanted more time. He was content with this and they waited. As they waited they spent every minute of time they could together. She explained what happened on the mountain, and he explained his time in the woods. As time whet on, they agreed to be married. On their wedding night she gave him the gift of the eagle's feather. She was nervous and chanted in her head the saying the eagle had given her. It took them to a magical place where they were happy to share with each other the gift of oneness. These are the great, great, great grandparents to me, and to my sons.

 We all watched as he pulled Clarissa closer to him.
 Wondering how he could preach to James and me about the things we were doing wrong, when all this time Clarissa and he had done the

wrong thing also. Everyone was quiet for a little while, and nobody seemed to want to move. I heard my James whisper to my ear, "Sarah, you are reading into it too much; it's just a story." He kissed my ear.

His reaction made me think about it even more. It explained the feelings, how they feel what people are thinking. It explains the waiting, but he would be better if he was with..." He whispered in my ear, "Don't even think about it; you are my soul mate and you know it. It is just a story. If my dad really felt that way... would he be with Clarissa?" I wrapped my hands around his arms to tell him I was okay. It was very late, and the fire was dying down. I closed my eyes to enjoy being in his arms.

"I think I should take you to bed."

I was tired, but I didn't want this time being in James's arms to end.

Danelle stood up, "Yeah, I am tired too."

Wilson stood up abruptly. "Sarah, James... remember... something special."

James pushed me forward, "Sarah, we have something for Danelle."

Excitement ran through my veins. We were going to celebrate Danelle's birthday. James helped me to my feet, and I grabbed Danelle's arm that was in the cast. I didn't pay attention to what everyone else was doing, because I had one thing on my mind. I, however, did not let Jake off the hook, "Jake, come help us please."

He followed but he seemed to be pouting.

When we got to the patio, James went with Wilson up to the main house. I walked in and directed her to sit in a chair next to the table.

"Sarah, I just want to go to sleep. Jake, I will take the couch tonight."

"No, I am fine on the couch. I will watch a movie or something."

I didn't like that he was totally bummed out. It was bothering me that he was moping.

James walked in with the cake smiling, "Happy Birthday, Danelle."

Jake livened up a little with the sight of the cake.

Danelle was embarrassed, "You guys didn't have to do this."

We all smiled at her. There were candles on the cake, so we lit all 16 of them. We didn't sing happy birthday; she was happy about that. She did make a wish. She closed her eyes and we all got her wish. *Just wait for me.* What she wished for surprised me. I turned to James with a flicker of wonder. He was pleased with the thought of what it was for. Neither of us could look at Jake, but she blew the candles out, not leaving one burning.

We cut the cake, and it was the dreamiest cake I had ever tasted. It was a light fluffy cake like angle food, but had chocolate toffee melted into it and covered with cool whip. When I tasted it my eyes went wide with surprise, and so did Danelle's. I giggled a little trying to explain about the Cool Whip, "Wilson thinks we have a thing about whipped cream."

She didn't seem surprised, "I heard, and there are two cans of Redi Whip in your fridge."

We all laughed again, even Jake this time.

When we were done having cake, James walked over to Danelle and put his hands on her shoulders, "Do you want to stay with Sarah tonight? I could sleep on the couch."

She tipped her head back to see him, "I think you will be worse tomorrow if you don't sleep with her. Something about being apart and desperately needing to be together makes me think that you should stay with her."

He hugged her around her neck.

Jake spoke up again, but this time putting his foot down, "Her things are in my room; I will sleep on the couch again."

"You don't have to; I will sleep on the couch," Danelle didn't want to put him out at all.

He sounded so depressed, that it bothered all of us.

"I'll watch a movie or something; really, it's okay." He got up and moved to the couch and laid down turning on the TV.

We all watched as he walked away and then exchanged glances of confusion. I wish he wouldn't act this way; it was making me feel even worse about our time together. Danelle shrugged her shoulders, but then stood up moving to the bedroom. I cut her off for a hug. Next I took James's hand in mine to lead him to our room.

We entered the room together. James's hand pulled me to a stop by the dresser. He was going to help me pick out something to sleep in. I knew he liked the sexy stuff, so I waited with a grin on my face. He pulled out a regular pair of shorts and t-shirt. This was not like him, so I frowned at him.

"Sarah, please. I'm behaving here."

I huffed with disappointment and grabbed the clothes. I went to the bathroom to get changed, but James blurted out, "You can get dressed out here."

He was the one wanting to behave, so I stopped just short of the bathroom; I gave him my most flirty smile, eyes that would beg him to seduce me, and contradict all of it as I replied, "Still gross, James."

He was struggling with the thought of coming to me. He shook his head incredulously, so I entered the bathroom and closed the door.

When I came out, James was in the living room talking with Jake. I crawled into bed, covered up, and curled up on my side, with my arm out for Jake to hook everything back up.

When Jake walked in he looked very angry. I wondered what James had said to him to make him angry. He was already down in the dumps. I will have to scold James if he hurt Jake. As he move toward me his look softened, "No arguing tonight?"

"Nope, you're the boss."

James stayed back and watched from the dresser pulling out sleeping pants and a muscle shirt.

Jake was taking his time hooking me back up to the IV. I could see the hesitation as he asked, "Did you step on the scale today?"

Not really wanting to discuss my weight, of course, I avoided the scale, "Nope, I don't want to know. I don't feel any fatter."

He laughed at me and James chuckled from afar.

"Fine, but we are checking tomorrow night."

I nodded as he got up and made his way to the door, "James pain, remember the pain."

"I heard you."

"You could bunk with me on the couch. We could play video games."

I saw James smile, "Sorry, Jake, I am tired. Aren't you?"

He nodded but didn't push the issue. He walked out not even giving a glance back at me.

I rolled to my side curling up facing James by the door. He turned around taking off his t-shirt; oh my god the muscles in his back were amazing. My hands craved the feel of them. He reached up to put the muscle shirt on, and his shoulder blades flexed and moved. The heat was building from my gut with desire to touch him, run my hands over his body, and feel him next to me. I don't know if it was because we were trying to behave, or because we were newlyweds, but I wanted him with every inch of my body. I didn't want to think about the pain, but of course that was always a factor in what we allowed ourselves.

"Sarah, no." It was like he was yelling at me.

I didn't want him to be mad at me, "Sorry, I couldn't help myself."

He peeked at me over his shoulder, smiling, with the adorable dimple showing in his cheek. Trying to stay in control of my emotions I forced the grin away from my face. That was only until I saw him undoing his pants. My eyebrows went up as far as they could go, while I anticipated what was next in his undressing. As he slowly pushed his pants down he continued to lecture me, "Sarah, you *can* help it. Please think about the pain."

Yeah, because that was going to work; he pushed the pants down over his butt, pulling down the boxers so low his gluteus maximums was hinting at revealing itself. My eyes widen for the possible chance of seeing that perfect ass... but no, he was able to push the pants further down without revealing any more. Now... to those thighs. I sucked in a breath to prevent drooling over this perfectly sculpted body. How could he be attracted to me being only skin and bones now? Finally, some relief, as he pulled on sleeping trousers. He came and crawled into bed curling up facing me. He was as excited as me to be lying here together.

Being careful about not touching him I pleaded, "If you won't let me touch you with my mind, let me touch you for real."

"No, I will get excited; I will push you, and you will have pain. I will be all worked up, and then miserable for having desires, when I know they are wrong because it hurts you."

"Boy, I was just asking to rub your back, but if you feel that way... good night."

I rolled away from him. I felt his breath on my neck; I reached to touch his face, and he wasn't there. He was using his mind to comfort me. I rolled over to him, "You can't do that if I can't."

Full of mischief he flirted, "I just wanted to get your attention."

He did it for me in so many ways. I melted into putty from that little grin that emerged on his face, and the smoldering look in his eyes that he was laying on me. I took a deep breath to calm my heart and let it out, "You always have my attention. Don't you feel that?"

He entangled our fingers and sucked me into him further with his charm. Even though I was so taken with him after we laid there for a while staring at each other I became irritated, "Okay, Mr., roll over." He wasn't going to trust me. I shoved him and pushed him to roll away from me, "Not that, just do it."

He rolled over. I moved my hand under his shirt and started to rub his back. The muscles were so tight. As I focused on different muscles he slowly relaxed. I heard him mumble, "I am supposed to be taking care of you."

"You are; you just don't understand how this takes care of me."

At least he laughed lightly, as he closed his eyes to enjoy the back rub. When I started he was very tense, but without pushing anything he relaxed right into slumber. The heavy breath and the soft snore gave it away. I lightened my touch not wanting to wake him, but continued on as I stared at this perfect being next to me. He was everything I could ask for and more. I curled into him more, draped my leg over his, and rested my head on the back of his shoulder. I continued to trace his back with my hand, as I started to drift off. I would wake a little and rub and dose off. I loved to feel his muscles in his body, because in some deep place in my head it made me feel very safe, even though his arms were not wrapped around me.

The dream came swiftly. It had been a long time since I dreamt of the house. We were walking in and the candles were lit. I walked slowly around the room, as he stopped in the doorway to watch me move through the room. He was tense, and I was dreamy. He directed me to the table where a box was and a couple of papers that were lying there. I looked at the papers and tears came to my eyes. These were not tears of sadness, on the contrary, whatever these papers were it filled me with complete happiness. He moved quickly to me to wipe the tears before they could spill. My heart was racing and the feeling was so deep so pleasing to me. He opened the box watching me to see my reaction. He pulled a night gown from the box holding it up for me to see. It was white silk with a low drop v neck line, slim fitting, and floor length. No sequins, no lace, nothing too elaborate, but it was elegant  He helped me get changed very slowly, seducing me with every movement but slipped the gown over me as I watched him. The light touch of his hand traced my body with every movement caressing my body with tingles. It surprised me when he kissed my nose and walked out. How could he leave me standing here alone full of want? I sat and looked at the papers not being able to see them in the dream, but it was creating a warmth building up from my toes moving all the way through my body to my fingertips. Whatever was on these papers seemed to be something that I would have wanted. I found myself taking a pen in my hand and signing them even though my hands were trembling. When he came back in the room, he had a robe on. He slowly made his way to me, taking my hands in his, leading me to the fireplace. His face was so serious it made me nervous. He untied his robe, sitting down on the white fluffy rug, pulling me to stand straddled over him. He ran his hands up my thighs, pushing the gown up, as I lowered myself to him. He traced my face with his hands and kissed my neck all the while rubbing against me. It wasn't long before he filled me with the warmth of him. His lips were desperate to suck me in, as we move together as one. The agony of desire was apparent when our eyes met. The movements were slow and drawn out to last as long as possible. I found myself digging my fingers into his back pulling myself closer to him. I wanted to be in his skin, be part of him, and make him happy he was with me. Something from within me was building and building; something was happening to me. I pulled tighter to him; I knew what was happening, but as amazing as this felt, it also filled me with fear. I was afraid of being completely vulnerable, but James's strong arms pulled me in holding me tighter. His lips came to my ear, "It's okay, baby." I pushed to see his face. I needed to see that he was feeling the same way I was feeling. His eyes were confusing to me. Mostly, he looked determined, and on the other side of it he looked lost in the pleasure of it. He gasped, "Let it happen, Sarah. I love you." I let myself fall into every part of him. I was his completely, and I would allow him anything and everything, because he was my world now.

"Sarah, you have to wake up, baby. I can't do this. Sarah, baby, please wake up."

The dream was gone, but he remained. I was happy that he was still here with me, but I didn't want the dream to end, "Sorry, I just miss feeling you."

"Sarah, we can't really do that right now, and you are driving me crazy."

"James, it's so weird. I feel like we have been together for a long time. I know it's just a dream, but I miss how you feel."

He moved up a little and pulled me in, underneath him, "Sarah, I want to share something with you, but I am afraid how you are going to take it."

I opened my eyes lovingly, "Is it going to ruin this really good feeling I am having right now?"

"I'm not sure."

I was hesitant if I wanted to know or not, "Will it end our relationship?"

"I am almost 99.9% sure it won't, but you might be a little mad."

"I don't want to know then. I am kind of in heaven right now." If it wasn't going to ruin our relationship, I really didn't care. I closed my eyes to submerse myself in the memory of the dream.

He rolled away from me with a low huff.

I grabbed for his hand; I didn't want him to move away from me, "Wait, is it that important?"

I tried to judge his mood; he wasn't mad, but maybe a little flirty, "Nope, you just got me a little hot. I need a shower."

I rolled back over and curled up to fall asleep feeling satisfied. For some reason the dream didn't cause the normal pain that came with getting hot over James in real life. My body felt like jello, as I sunk into the bed in bliss.

I heard the door open behind me; I was worried that James needed help with Sarah. They do shit they shouldn't be doing all the time, "Is Sarah okay?"

"Um, it's not about Sarah."

I heard Danelle's voice. I sat up and pulled the blanket over me more. Whatever I do, I cannot look into those eyes of hers. She might think I am a total weirdo with how taken I get when I look in them, "Couldn't you sleep?" I was wiping the tiredness from my eyes to help avoid hers.

"No, do you mind?"

I moved over on the couch to give her room to sit, "Did you want me to put a movie in?"

"I don't care. I just never had a room to myself before, so it's weird. I can't sleep."

"You don't have your own room?"

"No."

"You share with Brian?"

"Yep. He sleeps on a mattress, and I get a very old couch. It's nothing like this."

"Then you should be sleeping like a baby in a regular bed. That is an amazing bed. Mine wasn't even that good." I picked up the remote and started to look for something better on TV.

The quietness was okay, and then I found an old movie, "Is this okay?"

"Yes."

I noticed that she was curled up on the other end of the couch. I made myself more comfortable too. It was quiet for so long that I thought she was sleeping but she spoke softly, "It's not the bed; it's being alone. It seems lonely to me without hearing someone snoring."

"Your brother, he is a player? No?"

Oops, I almost looked at her. Take a deep breath and just wait until she says something.

It took a while but she finally asked, "What do you mean?"

"Well, what do you do when girls are over?"

"I usually try to fall asleep really quickly."

That absolutely shocked me, so I finally turned to her, "You're kidding?"

She shook her head no, so I quickly turned back to face the TV. She continued to explain, "I would have been perfectly fine staying on the lounge in their room. It would have felt more like home."

"Oh, that's kind of disgusting."

To that she didn't reply. She pulled the blanket over her a little and shut her eyes. Thank god she closed those eyes. I flipped through the movie channels trying to avoid adult content movies, which at this time was more difficult than I thought. I forced myself up and grabbed a movie and threw it in. She curled up putting her head down on the arm rest.

"Are you tired?"

"Yes, just not used to being alone."

I moved back to find a spot at the other end of the couch. I fluffed out the blanket to cover both of us. I watched her, as she pulled it up around her face. She looked at me and the staggering blue hit me. They were not very characteristic for a dark brunette haired girl. I must have stared at her for too long, because she closed her eyes once again. She is really going to think I am catatonic.

Silence had taken control again. It was peaceful, and I could see why it was more comforting to have someone in the room with you. You can hear them breathing; for me, I could hear her breathing, as it grew slow and peaceful.

"Jake, thank you for today. I had fun, most of the time."

I had thought she was sleeping, so when she spoke again I must have jumped a little. I tried to recover right away, so that she wouldn't notice, "You're welcome." I closed my eyes relaxing into slumber.

I must have dosed off, because I woke to her putting her head in my lap. I didn't move with fear that I would scare her. This felt warm, inviting, and oddly enough, comfortable…all accept that little twinge in my gut. How stupid was I being? She was a little girl. No matter, if she was a little girl or not, I liked it, I liked it a lot. I found myself scooting down more and closed my eyes again.

I woke again after a while, and I was lying with her almost on top of me. Shit, what was I doing? I slowly moved out from under her trying to not wake her. She curled into me more. Fuck, this is not good. People would get the wrong idea, and she was only 16. It took me an hour to get out from underneath her without waking her. I went to my room and grabbed a pillow and blanket and made a bed on the floor. I turned it back to TV and found a decent movie and closed my eyes to sleep on the floor. How I went from a bed, to the couch, to the floor I had no idea. I closed my eyes and felt her hand drop to my chest, like she was checking to see if I was there, but in her sleep. When I looked up at her, she was still sleeping, to my relief. That is when I was able to close my eyes again.

## 52. New Feelings

### Sarah:

**I** knew as I woke up this was the last day of summer for James and I. He was going back to school tomorrow, and I was starting my college classes, even though I had already started. I tried to peek at him, but the pillow was between us. He was very serious about not getting carried away, so he wouldn't hurt me. I moved the pillow and curled into him. He traced his hand along my back. We were so in tune with each other, that it didn't surprise me that he was awake also.

It was like my whole body was excited to hear him. My heart pounded harder and harder when he turned to me wrapping his arms around me. When his eyes opened they were full of glimmer, as if he was also excited to see me. I felt like the nurses looking at Jake when a giggle inadvertently escaped me. He shook his head disapprovingly, "You can't keep your hands off me, little girl; what am I going to do with you?"

Even though he was teasing I found myself flirting with him, "I can think of a few things."

That was all it took for him to please me more by tracing his lips on mine. Words came with his touch, "Well, good morning to you too." He pressed his warm full lips to mine lightly. When he released me he continued, "Your dream was really nice. It has been a while since you dreamt of us together. Glad to see you still dream of me."

I could have stayed in bed all day with his kisses. They weren't taunting, hot, or sexy, but they were home for me, and they were all mine.

"So, is there something you want to do on the last day of summer for us?"

"James, I don't like that you do that. I have no privacy." He had been listening to my feelings again.

"Yes, but I also am better because of it."

"What do you mean?"

"I know what you want when you want it. It's kind of like cheating, but I am able to make you happier because of it. If I wasn't able to know what you are thinking, I would be lost and do things wrong with you."

"I don't think so. You are so good to me."

He raised his eyebrows and grinned. His hand moved to my waist, "Like right now, you want me to touch you. It makes you feel loved." His hand traced under my shirt along my waist.

How could I argue with that, "Okay, you have a point."

The look in his eyes filled with excitement, his mouth turned up with a grin, and he started to tickle me, "Wait no, James, I didn't ask for that." He was pulling me more underneath him. I was giggling and struggling to push him away. He used his body to hold me down more. He was driving me crazy while the tickling persisted.

"James, no, I didn't ask for this."

"Oh yes you did. You wanted to be playful."

I got really serious trying to not let the tickling work, "Stop, James, right now or..." the tickling was too much causing me to giggle with protest, "Please, James, no."

The door swung opened, as Jake stormed in, "You guys have to quiet down or you're going to wake Danelle."

Even though James had a pleasant tone he scolded, "Jake, do you ever knock?"

We could tell he wanted to laugh, but he was going to be strict with us, "Well at least you're not doing what I thought you were doing, and no, I will not knock. If I am always expected to barge in, it will help you two behave. Sarah, think 13 weeks and remember the pain. James you're not being strict enough."

James huffed but stopped tickling me. He gazed into my eyes for the briefest moment. Only long enough to make my heart thud and my stomach to do a half turn. He moved to kiss my forehead and pushed himself away from me getting up.

In protest I scolded, "Hey, we weren't finished discussing things."

He chuckled as he continued to move away from me, "Yes we were, and Jake is here to disconnect you. I am going to the bathroom." He stopped outside the bathroom door glancing back at me, "Is that okay, darling?" I knew he was playing with the silly grin still on his face.

I rolled my eyes and huffed, "Do I have a choice?"

After James went into the bathroom, I held out my arm for Jake. I wanted these out so bad, that I could pull them out completely myself.

Jake walk over to me, "Are you ready to get on the scale?"

I was still feeling good and didn't want to spoil my mood, "Nope."

Thinking back to last night, I gave Jake the once over. He seemed a little better today; the sadness had gone away. It seems like he does better when it is just the three of us together. He actually had a smile on his face, while he was disconnecting the IV.

There was one thing that I thought of that I didn't like, "Can you hear us from your room?" The puzzled look on his face told me he didn't get where I was going with this, so I continued, "You said we would wake up Danelle?"

He avoided my stare while continuing to undo my IV lines, and his face was blank, "No, she slept in the living room on the couch. She's not used to having a room to herself."

I completely understood this, because I was surprised to see that myself. "So where did you sleep?"

I wondered if they had spent the night together on the couch. I wondered how that went.

I must have had a look of surprise or something, because when he looked up at me he scolded, "Sarah, stop that. She is only 16."

I tried to contain my excitement, "I didn't say a word, but you like her eyes."

"You are not funny, and stay out of my head."

"You were the one just thinking about it."

His face stayed serious, but I could see the hint of a grin, "Did you really start liking James when you were 15?"

Still trying to contain my smile I replied, "Yes."

As he worked on my arm I had to try, "Jake, can we just take them out? I am so tired of them."

"We'll see... you need to get on the scale."

"NO, I just don't want them anymore, and I am eating."

"But you're not gaining the weight like you should be."

James was walking back to the bed. He lay down sideways with his face close to me, "Jake, she just doesn't want it to get in the way of attacking me. We should leave them in longer so she behaves. Sarah, remember pain?"

As much as Jake didn't like me in his head, I didn't like that James was in mine. I was full of embarrassment now.

"James is out of the bathroom; let's go, light weight."

I was not happy about the scale, "Fine, but if you don't do it soon, I will do it myself."

Jake didn't have patience like my James, "That isn't funny, Sarah; get your butt in the bathroom."

Jake only put out his arm for me to support myself, as I got up. I was happy he didn't help me; however, he raised his eyebrows to James as if to ask how much pain I felt.

James elaborated, "You are doing better, with very little pain that time."

I huffed, "This mind reading is going to get to me."

I wanted to do this alone, but they both followed me to the bathroom. Holding up my hand to stop them from joining me at the scale, I went in. I stepped on the scale and pouted. This was going to be a long wait, "Shit."

They both peaked around the corner at me.

Reading the scale, I already knew my answer, "Shut up, Jake, or I will take them out myself."

"I will just have to put them back in, but it might be a good idea to change them today after everyone leaves. How much did you weigh?"

I lied, "Almost there."

James knew better, "You are a terrible liar. How much, Sarah?"

They both walked in and pointed for me to get on again. I only stepped on the scale again, because I couldn't get myself to say it. I had lost the weight I had gained; it was back down to 106 pounds. Jake and James were as confused as I was flustered over the whole thing.

What hurt the most was when James walked out without a word.

I pleaded with Jake, "What am I doing wrong?"

He tried to comfort me with a slight grin, "Nothing, were going to up your intake."

"But I can hardly eat the four cups."

"How about four times a day at least until you have to go home? I know once you're there your eating habits will go back down to almost nothing. You need a good base before you go."

One: I wanted to put the weight on, and two: I didn't want to go home. Unwelcomed tears filled my eyes. Everything was not okay if I had to spend one day without James.

"Hey, you're upset. Sarah, don't do that."

Danelle must have walked into the bedroom, because I heard her ask, "What's going on?"

Jake took my face in his hands, and wiped the tears from my cheeks that had spilled over; all the while he tried to make me feel better, "Sarah, it will be okay." He turned me, and we walked out of the bathroom together. James was leaning on the wall outside the bathroom looking miserable. Danelle was evaluating things trying to figure out what was wrong.

I stood in front of James, "I am trying. I don't know what I am doing wrong."

He took my face in his hands just looking at me, "It's okay; I am not taking good enough care of you."

I shook my head no. It wasn't true.

Danelle asked again, "What is going on?"

Jake answered her, "Sarah is supposed to be gaining weight and she did a very little, but she lost what she gained. James, don't be stupid; that is not your fault. Quit your pouting. Her body has been on a loss kick for how long, and you expect it to change in one week; come on and get over yourself. I bet in a month of eating like this she will gain weight."

James took my hand in his. His eyes were full of sadness.

I gave him a disapproving smile, "We should go down and see about breakfast. I am sure Wilson has something planned."

The sadness did not go away, but James tried to smile. Jake took Danelle by the shoulders, ran his hands down her arms, and directed her out of the room, "You can go get dressed while we wait for them."

James wrapped his arms around me pulling me to him. I traced my hands down the front of him. He was happier before I stepped on the scale, "We could go back to playing."

"No, you need.... God, Sarah, stop! You are going to drive me crazy, and you need to be totally healthy before we do anything like that."

I turned away from him and dug in the drawers. I grabbed out another bikini top and tied a knot in the strap. I pulled my shirt off and slowly put the top over my head. I pulled the straps around the back, dangling them, so he would tie them. He huffed and came to tie them, but did it without touching me even a little. I pushed down the shorts to step out of them. He traced his hands down my back. The reaction I was looking for. I grabbed new bottoms and turned to him, "Bathroom."

He grinned but stood there stunned. I smiled and walked around him to the bathroom. I was only spotting a little. That was a good sign. I came out, and he was digging for something.

"What are you looking for?"

He stopped, but he didn't say anything.

"James, what are you looking for?"

"I'm just trying to get my mind off of you." He went back to digging pulling out shorts and stood up. I walked up behind him and traced my hands around the openings of the muscle shirt. He grabbed the top of the dresser with his hands. He wasn't looking at me, "We are setting ground rules, Sarah. You have to gain so much weight... you have to be able to do things... before we even consider being together. After everyone leaves we are sitting down and making a list."

I wrapped my arms around him and kissed his back, "Baby, I will do whatever you want."

"Good..." He turned around and lifted me to him, "Right after I attack you, you are driving me crazy." He headed towards the bed. I was giddy with happiness that I could still get this reaction even after he was disappointed in me. He lowered me to the bed supporting my weight the whole time. The kissing came intensely, while his hands embraced me. I wrapped my legs around him to hold him there. I liked this but Jake wasn't going to be happy, "We can't do this; Jake is going to come through that door any second..."

In walked Jake, turning his head with his hand over his face, "Shit, you two, do you ever stop thinking about doing it?"

I laughed, "Jake, we have rules now. So we're not doing that."

James pushed away from me pulling me to my feet. We walked to the dresser and James pulled out a cover up for me and put it over my head. I slipped into it and laughed some more. I kissed him on the cheek and walked over to Jake and turned him to the door, "Jake, you are unbelievable." I was pushing him from the room, so James could change. As I was directing him towards the door of the apartment, Danelle walked out of Jake's room. She had on a bikini top and shorts. I stopped, "Danelle?"

She smiled and pulled my arm to follow her. I let go of Jake and followed her to the bedroom.

Jake stood there mesmerized.

"Do I look ridiculous?"
"No, Danelle, you look amazing. Why?
"I don't like looking like a little girl."
"I know the feeling."
"Do you have a tank top or something I can put over the top?"
I smiled, "Yeah, I'll be right back."

I almost ran from the room. Jake inquisitively lifted his eyebrows, as I went by. I could see he was having the same reaction that I did, "She looks really good, doesn't she?"

He didn't say a word but nodded. His nonverbal response made me grin. I continued my way to the room knocking as I walked in. James was standing there in boxers. I loved the way they sat so low around his hips, and that this hunk was all mine.

"No, Sarah."

I walked up to him and traced my fingers along the front of them, "You are so sleeping like that tonight. No arguing about it either, but I have to get something for Danelle." I walked away from him and started to dig in the closet. I found what I was looking for, a tank top with a slight slit in the front with a tie. I rushed toward the door to head back to Danelle.

James was concerned, "What are you doing?"

I stopped and turned to him closing the door a little, "Danelle is wearing a bikini, and I am getting her a tank top, but James..." I hesitated, "Don't make a big deal about it; she is really nervous about how she looks."

He was surprised and inquisitive, "How does she look?"

I giggled and moved to him to talk really quiet, "She walked out in shorts and the top, and I think Jake is standing there speechless." I put my hand over my mouth, giggling. He laughed and pushed me back out the door.

Jake was still standing there stunned. I pointed at him, "She is very nervous about this, so be nice and shut your mouth for heaven's sake. Jake! Jake! Hey. I mean it. Please, don't make a big deal about this."

He shook his head no.

I went in the room and gave her the tank top. She put it on and complained, "Didn't you have any normal ones?"

I liked that she looked this good, "This one will look better with the shorts. Sorry."

She was hesitant.

"You look just fine."

She got an uneasy expression, "Do I look older?"

"Danelle, sometimes it's okay to be yourself. You know where looking older got me. Just take everything really slow, please."

"Sarah, what are you talking about?"

I wanted to tell her the whole truth about everything. I didn't know if I could tell her where it really got me without having a total nervous breakdown. I was dumbfounded on what to say to her.

Taking a deep breath I was going to try to explain, "You like Jake, right?"

"No," But a guilty as charged grin came to her face.

"I know he is adorable..." I was scrambling to make her surer of her feelings, "Just do me a favor, and be yourself... just be you. We are a lot alike, and he likes honesty and no girlish stupidity. If you are yourself, he will figure it out someday."

Knowing she didn't want to confess her feeling she still asked, "You think so?"

I nodded, "But don't push the issue. Don't change; you are great the way you are."

I knew he liked it that I was very honest and the youth part is where that was the advantage. We weren't afraid to say what we were thinking.

We walked out to find James and Jake waiting. I stood in front of her, "Guys, let's go."

She stayed behind me trying to walk down to the fire pit. Jake stopped and grabbed her around the waist putting her over his shoulder and took off running. James waited for me, "I think we are going to have problems with those two."

He was right about those two, but maybe not for a while. He helped me to get on his back for the long walk. Jake took her all the way to the water. He was trying to dump her in without success, because she was clinging to him. That brought back a memory of a snow bank. I giggled. Brian was walking out looking at me and James, "What are they doing?"

Nonchalantly, I shrugged it off, "Jake's just dumping her in the lake to wake her up."

That didn't help him with the uneasiness of seeing them together. Because I was okay with it, he tried to be too, by ignoring it, "Are you hungry? I am starving."

He made me laugh lightly to myself. As we made our way to the table I noticed that Wilson had outdone himself again. Something else I noticed was that he was cuddling with Josie behind the table. They were engulfed in each other sharing whispers. I nudged James and gestured to the tables. James took my hand but only until we reached them. James moved behind the table pushing them both away, "Wilson, it's our turn. Go sit with your wife." James came back to me, and I was already preparing two plates. James was pleased, "We think the same thing."

I handed him a plate, and we finished getting them ready. I gave him my plate, and he walked them to Wilson and Josie.

"The deal is, Wilson, you need time with your wife. We will take care of everything, and you can relax."

I liked when James wanted to do something nice for Wilson. He was such a good man.

Brian walked up to me, "Are you doing better today?"

I knew he was missing our time together, "I miss you, too."

Wanting James to be a part of this I directed my question to him, "Sweetheart, when can we go to the lake?"

Satisfied that I included him he grinned with his reply, "Whenever you are ready. Tony would like to see you too."

I reassured Brian, "Next weekend unless something else really bad happens."

That was what he needed to hear. I helped serve him food.

Carl and Clarissa were coming down wrapped in blankets. My mind didn't have to wander to know how their night went. Clarissa was smug, but the hint of a smile was directed at me. James moved close to me and nudged me to make sure I was noticing them. Almost getting lost in their connection with each other, James had to remind me that we were serving food. We started to make plates for them, and I wasn't the only one that couldn't wipe the smile from my face. It was as if it was a private joke between the four of us. Clarissa leaned to us a little, "Yes, quit your grinning... you two."

We both started to giggle.

"Yes, it is the passion, but you two still have to be careful."

We were both embarrassed after she scolded us. I couldn't force my eyes back to her even if I wanted to. She was irritated that we were avoiding her stare, "Sarah, I told you..."

Fear filled me that I was still doing what was bad for us. I love James, and I just couldn't... not show it. To my relief, when I peeked up at her, she nodded to the lake with the most approving smile I have ever seen.

Knowing exactly what she was talking about now; I was surer about them then I have ever been. James glanced at me inquisitively.

"By the way, I am serious about you two being careful. Now that you have been through so much, please take the precautions to not get pregnant."

She had both our attention again, but she was smiling and Carl was chuckling quietly. I think he was enjoying that she was scolding us.

"Now, Clarissa, be nice to the children. You know how we were."

I think that was the first time I heard him stand up to her.

She was instantly irritated, "That is exactly why they need to be careful."

Were they going to have an argument right here in front of us? No, they couldn't do that. They are so perfect together. I didn't want them to argue over James and me.

"Clarissa." His voice was very direct and disciplinary. He wrapped his arms around her and whispered in her ear. We could see her melt into him, as he continued to speak privately to her.

A grin of embarrassment came to her face, "We'll be taking this to our room."

We gave them the plates, and they started to walk away from us. Carl looked back and winked. We both started to laugh.

James walked up behind me and whispered in my ear, "That makes me really hot for you."

I was agreeing with him, "Me too."

We smiled at each other, as long as we could, before being interrupted by some of the others wanting to eat.

They were serving themselves, thankfully, because I didn't want to take my attention away from James. Reluctantly, we released each other gawks to serve everyone their food. James was really clingy, holding my hand and kissing it, as we helped to serve the food. The girls watched my James with adoring eyes. I was getting uncomfortable, but he made sure I knew I was the only one for him. Everyone seemed pretty nice this morning. Jake and Danelle came back up and Jake was mad that I was helping. I liked helping, so I tried to let him know I was okay. He took me and pushed me to a chair, "James, please. She needs to gain weight and not burn calories."

"So what am I supposed to do…nothing but lay around?"

He grunted, "Yeah, pretty much."

He went to help James. They were fun to watch as they joked and messed around. Sam didn't want to be left out, so he went over to play with them, but they ganged up on Sam. He was very happy about the attention. Something I already knew was very apparent as I watched them; they were all so good looking. Sam looking like a thin James, but Jake was really handsome in his own distinctive way.

Danelle came over with two plates and handed me one, "Jake is making you eat."

I took the plate from her, nibbling while scrutinizing her, "So how did it go?"

"How did what go?"

"With Jake at the lake…"

"I don't know what you mean?"

I gave her a disapproving look. I knew she knew what I was talking about.

"What?"

"Danelle, your wish!"

"What wish?"

"Last night before blowing out the candles."

Her eyes got huge, "You know what I wished?"

I smiled, "Since I married James, yes, I feel things sometimes."

She was horrified, "You get those, because you married him?"

"He has gifts and he… Yeah, I felt your thoughts." I couldn't tell her why.

She covered her face, "So, James knows too."

I swallowed, "Danelle, you didn't say a name. It's okay. They don't really know it was about him."

"They?"

"Oh, um… yeah, Jake has the same level as me. Carl just started to work with me, and Clarissa has a little bit, too. I think it happened when we got married." I was leaving out the part about the baby.

She covered her face, "He knows?"

"Danelle, I don't think so. I read into it. You didn't say a name. Come on, just be yourself."

"I am mortified."

"Oh, don't be and besides your 16. You should just let time take its course."

"He's like a kid, my age. I forget he's a doctor when we're just hanging out."

I reassured her, "Danelle, he is still very innocent. He hasn't even really kissed anyone, so it means something to him."

"He kissed you."

"It was a quick peck to try and keep me from going to James. It wasn't like when I kiss...." I hesitated as I glanced over to James. He took my breath away, as our eyes met.

"You are really in love with him?"

My eyes dropped to my food. I was a little embarrassed that I was caught looking at him again, "Yep."

"What ever happened to the big brother thing you assured me at one time."

Shrugging my shoulders with not being able to deny it, "Yep, I didn't realize it, not till I was in way too deep to get rid of the feelings."

She looked over at Jake, "Do you think he would wait for me?"

"Yeah, actually, I do. James is still waiting for me."

"What, you still haven't?"

My eyes flashed to her. I wanted to tell her, but I couldn't right now. I would have a nervous breakdown, "Kind of..."

"Now how can you say that? I think it's pretty obvious if you have or haven't."

"Then technically, yes."

"How was it?"

I had to look away, but then I peeked back up at her, "You'll get grossed out." I was embarrassed.

"I sleep in the same room as my brother, and sometimes I am not completely asleep, Sarah. It couldn't be any worse than that."

I searched her face to really see if she could handle this, "Okay, but you are going to get grossed out."

I was trying to evaluate her, but she was really good at holding back her facial expressions.

"Okay, we were playing, and he was already done, and I pushed him in. It only lasted a few seconds because he was getting aroused and it hurt from the surgery so he didn't stay there." I looked at her, and her face did not change. I waited longer, and she still wasn't saying anything.

Finally, she broke, "Yep, that is gross, and you did this since your surgery; are you stupid? And you could get pregnant that way." Her whisper got a little louder. "Sarah, you are supposed to discuss big decisions like that with me."

I didn't realize this was going to go in this direction. The black cloud was moving in, and my heart was hollowing out. Air was escaping my lungs without refilling. It must have shown on my face. I was getting fearful with what was happening. I set down my plate.

"Sarah, what is going on?"

I was holding the arms of the chair.

"Sarah, are you okay? It's really not that bad. I was just…"

James grabbed me out of the chair and started to walk away holding me, "What happened, baby? You have been doing so well. I can hardly breathe, Sarah…Why?"

I buried my face to his body. I was gasping for air, "Shit." Was all I could get out.

He half heartily laughed, "What happened?"

I just shook my head. Back to the not talking, it was so much easier to try to breathe if I didn't talk when I felt like this. If I talked the air would be sucked from my lungs, and I wouldn't be able to breathe at all. I grabbed his shirt to a fist in my hand and closed my eyes to try and breathe. Panic was there as I tried to get the air back into my lungs.

## 53. The Passion

### James:

**I** was having a hard time breathing. Her emptiness was engulfing me. I needed Jake and hoped he was behind me. I didn't know if I could make it to the apartment. I was trying to breathe and kept asking, "Sarah, why?"

She wouldn't even look at me. She was letting it overwhelm her with instant depression. Thankfully, Jake was running up behind me. I turned to him and tried to hand her to him, but she wasn't letting go. Danelle came running after us. Not knowing how to ask for Jake's help again, I kept going. He grabbed a hold of me and supported me as much as he could while I tried to carry her. I was gasping for air, "Sarah, I can't make it. Your feelings are killing me."

Jake grabbed the gate, as I went through it stumbling. I was just thinking... if I could get to the door.

"What is going on?" Danelle was extremely worried, but Jake tried to keep her back to give me room. I fell to the couch holding her, wiping the tears from her face, and I pulled her into my body so I could rock with her. I glanced over at Danelle, and she seemed devastated.

"Did I say something wrong?"

Jake noticed that I was looking at her with speculation. Jake stepped in and pulled her to sit at the table holding her hands in his, "What were you talking about?"

"She and James... that was all."

Sarah's eyes finally found mine. Those green eyes were so hurt and sad. I pulled her closer to me to hold her tighter, "Hey, what is wrong?"

Her grip got tighter. She was gasping for air. I thought I was going to pass out from the pain of complete sadness from her.

"James, you know what we were talking about. Sarah says you can tell what people were talking about, and Jake, you too."

Jake looked at me for the answer, and I shrugged my shoulders, "I wasn't focused on her; we were goofing around, Jake; how about you?"

"No… nothing, I didn't think we had to. She was so good."

Danelle was so freaked out, but I needed to understand, "Danelle, exactly what were you talking about?"

She didn't want to explain; she was shaking her head no.

"Danelle, it doesn't matter. I can't help her if I don't know why she's feeling this way; please, tell me."

Danelle was devastated. I could tell she felt it was her fault as she explained, "I was yelling at her, in a whisper, but I was scolding her."

"What were you scolding her about?"

She didn't want to say.

"Danelle, that's what I love… the honesty. Get it out, please."

"Fine, but you're going to be mad at me."

"No, I won't."

"I was mad at her for having sex with you so soon after her surgery. James, you should have known better, and she could have gotten pregnant, and she is too young and you know it."

I felt the hole in Sarah's heart opening more to the guilt. I was getting light headed, "Jake, tell her but outside please, that made it worse." I was getting dizzy from the oxygen not being able to get to my lungs.

Danelle was very angry with me, "She's pregnant, James?"

"Jake, take her out, please."

I pulled Sarah to me and leaned back, "Baby, it wasn't a choice that could be changed. We had to do it."

I felt it stop engulfing her. It wasn't getting worse. I took a deep breath, "I had to make you do it, Sarah." It worked again. If I took the blame from her, the pain eased. I pulled with all my strength to take more of the sadness from her. I pulled her face up, so she had to see me, "I had to make you do it, or I would have lost you." The tears were streaming down her face, but she gasped a huge breath, and I could breathe again. I traced my lips over her face where the tears were falling and whispered to her, "I was selfish; I really wasn't ready to die, and if you can remember this, I cannot live without you."

She gave me a slight smile, and I felt the relief immediately. She tried to talk to me, "Does pain ever go away?"

I sighed with relief, "I hope so." I tucked her back into my body. Danelle came back in and had tears in her eyes. She came to sit on the arm of the couch looking at us. She shook her head. I put my fingers to my lips to hush her. I didn't want the sadness to come back. She scooted down beside me and wrapped her arm around Sarah, and put her head on my shoulder. She said really quietly, "Sorry."

I shook my head. Talking about it did not make it better. Not yet.

Jake leaned on the back of the couch, "James, how are you doing?"

Sarah looked up at me with very sorry eyes.

I smiled at her and spoke to Jake, "I am okay now."

She put her head back down on me.

"Do you need me to get you anything?"

What would I do without Jake? "Nope, I've got what I need right here, Thanks."

Her grip got tighter again.

"Why don't you two head back down and let everyone think it was maybe something with the IV, so people don't ask questions."

Jake went in the other room and came out with some stuff, "We were going to change them anyway. It will fit better if I do this." He tried to pull her arm, but she wasn't letting go of me.

"Sarah, let me take the IV port out."

She glanced up again and put her arm out, but turned her face to me again burrowing it into my chest. Jake put pressure on the first one and took off the tape then pulled it out. Her body tightened, as he pulled it out. He tapped the cotton over the top of it. He removed the tape on the second one, pulling it out the same way, and taping it up again. "There, Sarah, you win today. I will have to put new ones in later, okay?"

She agreed not being able to dispute putting it back in later. Jake put out his hand for Danelle. She glanced up at him and shook her head no.

I reassured her, "Hey, she will be okay. We will be down when she is ready."

She shook her head again.

I knew she felt bad but I reassured her, "Really, Danelle, you didn't know, and it would be better to not talk about it, so please go. She will be okay."

Jake put out his hand again. She took it this time and got up to go with him.

## Jake:

I took Danelle out closing the door behind us. She stopped and turned on me, "I feel awful; I had no idea."

I gave her a quaint smile.

"NO, it's not okay. Every time someone mentions a baby, is she going to do that?"

I avoided her eyes, "It will get better with time."

"How many people know?"

"Just our family and now you."

"Her mom and dad don't know. What if they start to lecture her about birth control or not having children yet, because she needs to finish school or she is too young. Who is going to pick up the pieces when you two aren't around?"

Shit, I didn't think about that. If she was going to live at home, we might have to tell them. They are married, so they would have to expect that they are having sex. I didn't know what to say, so I just stared.

"No comment!!!"

"No, I was just thinking about what you said, sorry. We didn't think about that at all. I guess I will talk to James."

"Yeah, I think you better. I thought she was having a heart attack. Shit, Jake. You and James are both old enough to know better. God, I can't believe you didn't tell me."

"It wasn't my call on who to tell and who not to tell. It's her choice."

She was really angry at me. I argued my point, "I didn't do anything wrong."

She did lighten a little as she continued, "Shit, she was supposed to talk to me before any big decisions. Damn her. I would have told her straight up... no. Don't do it yet, especially after surgery. I thought you were interrupting them, because you wanted to keep them apart."

She was still raving a little. I had a hard time following her, but I heard the last part.

"No, she will hurt something if they are together again. I know they will be together now, but not that way for awhile; they need to make sure she is healed before doing that again."

She cracked a smile, "I am still mad at you."

I was so confused, "What did I do?"

"It's what you didn't do. You could have told me, when I said she still looked sad. I knew there was something wrong and you blew me off."

"Like I said, it's up to Sarah. I couldn't... doctor's confidence."

"Yeah, but if you care about her, you just should have told me."

I didn't know what to say. I turned to walk away from her.

"Hey, why won't you talk to me?"

I turned back to her, "You're mad at me. I thought I should give you some space."

"I'm not really mad at you; I just feel bad. If I would have known I could have controlled my comments."

I had to laugh. I didn't know if I believed her about her watching what she would say. She was so brutally honest. Shit. No, not her! She is too young.

"Well, if you aren't mad at me and you can hold your tongue..." I glanced at her to see how that went over but finished my sentence, as I was reading her, "You can help me do damage control."

I was relieved when I held my hand out for her, and she took it. I didn't mean to offer her my hand it just came so naturally, like we were together on protecting James and Sarah from each other. We let go as soon as we got so people could see us. I didn't know if she let go for me or her, but she did let go.

We reassured everyone that Sarah was fine, and when people started to ask questions I could see Danelle's comfort level go down. I got up and started walking to the lake, gesturing for her to follow me.

"What?" She was irritated with me.

I was trying to get out of a situation, "Let's go for a ride, and then we don't have to answer any more questions."

She was happy with this, "Good idea. I didn't like having to do that. My brother is going to be so bummed."

"You can't tell him."

She was surprised, "Why not? He cares about her."

"Yeah, but it has to be her decision."

"So, I can't tell him about this?"

"No, it wouldn't be fair to her. Let her do it in her own time."

I got on the Wave Runner and pulled her up. She wrapped her little arms around my waist, and I took off. We got to the other side of the lake, and I shut it off. She was totally hanging on to me with her head resting on my back, but my stomach was doing some kind of flips, and I needed to not feel this way. She is a little girl. "Hey, do you want to try and drive again?"

"No, I suck at it."

I laughed, "Come up here; you do just fine."

She was standing and walking on the edge to move to the front. I started it again, she started off, I slid all the way back, and she killed it. I laughed, "Okay, again."

She tried again, and this time I held around her waist and one hand reached forward to hold the handles with her. She was going. I let go of her hand, but kept one arm around her. We went on a wild ride. It helped wash away the bad feelings from dealing with Sarah. She slowed but was still driving, "How do you do it?"

I leaned forward, "What do you mean?"

"Deal with having to take care of her while she loves someone else?"

"It's not so bad; James loves her and he is my brother. I see how he takes care of her."

"So, he is good to her?"

"Yes."

"That's good."

"Yeah, sometimes he is not strict enough, but I am working on it."

"What do you mean?"

"She is 16, and she had two surgeries. He shouldn't give into her with the sex thing."

"What?"

"She wants to make him happy, and she thinks *that* will make him happy, but he loves her so *that* really doesn't matter to him."

"It does matter. They are married."

"No, it's more like a benefit." I hope that came out right.

She turned to me a little letting the machine die, "What do you mean? That is what married people do!"

"I think that it's both yes and no. There is a lot more to a marriage than sex. They need to be friends, too."

"You don't think they are?"

"Yeah, actually I do, but they are so obsessive. You let the machine die."

She made a funny face, "Yeah, I'm done. You can drive."

She stood back up and started to move behind me.

"Did you want to go in?"

"No, I'm just done driving. Thanks."

I started it up and took off again. I did some wild driving, and she held tighter. I liked it, so I kept it up.

## Sarah:

I took a deep breath. I loved when he held me. I was in heaven even though it was the sadness that brought us to this point again. He traced his finger along my face and let me stay here. Nothing else mattered. I felt better in his arms.

"Baby, how are you doing?"

I raised my face to him, but I couldn't talk yet, so I just stared into his eyes.

He grinned playfully, "Do you want to make out?"

He knew how to make me feel better.

"I do have a question for you, and I know you can't answer me right now, so it will have to wait till later."

I shook my head no.

"Are you sure you want to hear my question?"

I nodded. He was trying to make me feel better, and it was working.

"Do you discuss everything with Danelle?"

I shrugged my shoulder and nodded a little.

"No, I mean everything."

I gave him my most innocent pouty look I could muster; considering how I was feeling, I think it was a really pitiful one. I tried to get it out with one breath, "Some."

"So you have talked about how I look naked?"

I shook my head no with disgust.

"She knows we have had sex in our dreams?"

I shook my head no.

"So what do you discuss with her?"

I shrugged my shoulders.

He lifted my chin to study my eyes with appreciation, "Do you know you have the sexiest eyes I have ever seen?"

He was so confusing. He raised his eyebrows, "You do, and I find you so irresistible, when you look at me like that."

I gave him a half smile. He cupped my face in his hands and he started to kiss me so lightly, tracing his lips on mine. He knew how to fill my heart with happiness. He pressed his lips against my top lip as I pressed my lips around his bottom lip and then again. My heart was pounding with a passionate fire. He laid me down on the couch, lying down next to me, propping his head up on his hand. He traced his fingers over my face lightly, as I closed my eyes to enjoy his touch. He came in for another kiss and moved to trace his hand on my stomach ever so lightly. He was kissing me lovingly, deeply, and softly. I was getting so lost in him. He stopped slowly and mouthed to me, "Are you ready to go down?"

I shook my head no.

Feeling his smile on my lips he pushed further, 'You know you have to be."

I shook my head no, but I was getting closer with his persuasions.

"Oh, you want to play?"

I did want more; more soft touches, more sweet kisses, and more of him, so I nodded.

"Later, we have to go down. People are going to leave today and I will play with you till you hurt, and I have to take a shower."

I shook my head no, "Kissing is good."

He raised his eyebrows, "You want more kissing?"

I nodded profusely.

"Okay, but later. Everyone is going to think we're doing it."

I was happy about that, "You're hot."

He laughed, "Oh, you want them to think we're doing it because I am hot."

I nodded.

He shook his head no, "You, little girl, are very bad."

"I try."

He laughed again, "Okay, we are going down, but you have to try and control yourself."

I shook my head no, "Need more kissing first."

"No, we need to get down there, and you know it."

I grinned and moved my hands under his shirt tracing up to his chest, looking deep in his eyes, "Please, it helps."

He melted and kissed me so good; it was like we were apart for a month. I loved the way he kissed me. It was so much deeper than kissing; it was telling me he wanted me forever. He stopped with our lips together but mouthed to me, "You know I could stay here forever."

That is what did it for me, and I was very happy now. I needed to hear him say something as wonderful as that. He growled a little, "Come on; we have to go back down." He was pushing himself up, and I shook my head no, desperately. I didn't want this to end. A flash of knowledge appeared on his face, "Do you know what the best part of you not talking is?" He raised his eyebrows, as I waited to find out. He chuckled, "I win."

I shook my head no and crossed my arms in protest. He pulled me up, "I love when you pout, but we're going."

I shook my head no. He picked me up facing him and started to kiss me. I wrapped my arms around his neck, while his arms were holding my legs. I thought I was going to win, and we would go to the bedroom. I was smiling with the kiss. He walked out of the apartment holding me. I stopped kissing him to show him I wasn't happy. He kissed me quickly, and his eyes lingered on mine. Next he pleaded, "Come on, Sarah, you can't stay mad at me. Matt and Brian would be so bummed if they didn't get to see you before they left."

I shrugged my shoulders like I didn't care.

"You do care, now behave."

I teasingly gave him an evil grin.

"No, don't do it."

I pulled closer to him and whispered in his ear, "I just want you." I could tell he was smiling. I kissed his ear breathing a deep breath into it.

"Oh shit, don't do that. It is not..." I licked his earlobe to entice him. "N o t  F a i r, shit."

He pulled me tighter, the kissing resumed, and I was enjoying every minute of this. When we got closer, he stopped and pulled his face away from mine, so that his eyes could meet mine again, "You are going to drive me crazy."

"Not if you give me what I want."

"So now you can talk? What are you telling me that you want? Because if you are telling me what I think you are it would be painful, so I know you're not talking about *that.*"

I was happy about my answer, "You."

Even though he was being forceful, he was happy about me wanting only him, "You already have me."

I kissed his nose before he set me down. We were almost to the fire pit, and he took my hand kissing it, as we walked the rest of the way holding hands. Brian stayed back, but Matt came running. He glanced at me, but moved to the other side of James. I heard him ask James in a low voice, "Is she okay?"

I peeked around James, "Yes."

James held my hand tighter, "Matt, she is okay." He nudged Matt, "We just needed some alone time."

Matt turned in front of us pleased with that answer, "Sarah, you could have gone about that a different way. You're married now." He grabbed my arm, "You don't have the IV in; can you play now?"

I shook my head no.

James pulled me in front of him, "Matt, you'll have to give her a couple of months before she can play."

What pleased me the most was that James kissed my neck lightly.

Matt was persistent, "But if you guys can do that, she should be able to play."

I giggled as James scolded Matt, "We didn't do that."

"If you're sneaking off to be alone, what did you do?"

He definitely had my attention now, and I couldn't wait to hear James explain this one. James couldn't believe that Matt would even ask such a question. James took the easy way out by saying, "You should just think about that question awhile."

Matt stopped in front of us making us halt. He was confused. He tilted his head, "I still don't get it."

We both started to laugh. James put his hand on his shoulder, "Matt, you're thinking too hard. Let's go play."

"You're going to play?"

James wanted to make sure I was still okay. He waited for me to let him know. I was fine now that he made me feel better, so I gave him a little smile and a nod.

"Yes, let me get Sarah to a chair."

"James, no. Go... I will be fine."

"Jason, come on. You're playing."

Kylie, Danelle, Jake, Will, Katherine, Sam, Matt and Blaire were playing. It was almost all guys playing. I watched my James. The girls from school were trying to soak up as much sun as they could. Brian was out with the girls, trying to get them to play in the water with him. Wilson walked Josie to her car; she needed to get some things done before the week started. I went to sit with Carl and Clarissa. I sat between them.

"So, Sarah, have you tried to feel anything else this weekend?"

I really didn't want to know what they were all thinking. I had tried once but didn't feel anything, "Not really."

Carl pulled me close, "Do you want to try?"

Of course, I wanted to try if it was my James. My eyes floated instinctively to him.

"Not his, you already do that enough." Carl scolded.

Okay, so I was guilty of that. What can I say... I love him.

"How about your friend Matt? He seems innocent enough."

If I was going to read his mind I had to look at him, but Clarissa turned my face to her, "It works better if you are not looking at them. Just use your mind."

I closed my eyes, but spoke what I was feeling, "He likes James and Jake. He likes that they are taking care of me. He wonders about Wilson. He can't believe Jake's his son." I took my focus off of him.

"See how easy it is?"

I didn't think it was easy. I felt like I was trespassing.

"Now, try one of the girls from school."

I shook my head, "I don't want to know what they are thinking."

Clarissa took my hand, "Sometimes knowing things, helps you handle things differently."

Carl spoke to her, "Clarissa, if she doesn't want to know, that is okay too."

Clarissa reassured me, "How about the one with the red bikini on; the one that is talking to Brian?"

I glanced up to see that it was Alissa. She was kind of seeing Matt. I looked at Matt, but he didn't notice and wasn't paying attention at all to her. I dropped my eyes to the ground to concentrate, "Why does he have to like her?" I said this as I felt it. I looked up at Alissa. I was angry that she was interested in Brian, "I have to tell Matt, she is a..."

Clarissa put her hand on my shoulder, "Just because you feel what people think doesn't mean you have to handle everyone's problems, Sarah. Pick and choose. It might work out without doing anything, so just store the info."

I glanced back at her, but I was still angry.

"Okay, Sarah, how about the pretty one, Alison. See if you can figure out why she thinks so highly of herself."

I took my eyes off of everything and focused my eyes on the ground while my mind concentrated on Alison's thoughts. She was thinking about my James. That he could do so much better than me. I already knew that. It was still hard to hear, but I could handle that. She was hoping to get to talk to him without me around, since Jake turned her down. I was floored. I didn't know if I wanted to cry or kill her.

Clarissa pulled me tighter to her, "Yes, which is why sometimes it comes in handy. You have nothing to worry about."

My body was shaking with anger, as the tears welled up in my eyes, "How could anyone be so cruel; she was invited here and that is...."

Clarissa smiled at me and Carl kissed my cheek, "Sarah?"

I didn't know how I was feeling, and my eyes fell on James. He knew instantly as soon as I felt it. He was already walking to me. Everyone was yelling at him for walking away from the game.

Clarissa tired to sound nice, but she was scolding me again, "Sarah, we are going to have to work on blocking feelings too. It's not good for James to feel everything."

I tried to ease the moment, "Earlier he didn't. When I was upset, he didn't know."

She smiled, "That was because he wasn't focusing on you, but Sarah, he focuses on you about 98% of the time."

Carl put his arm around me, "More like 99% of the time. Sarah, you will have to learn to block him. It's not healthy for James to be that tuned into you."

I wanted to learn, "I could use some privacy. I will try; what do I need to do?"

James got to us, "You two shouldn't have.... she didn't need to know that." He took my hand pulling me to him. I stared at him confused, "You knew?"

His eyes were soft and sweet, as they stared into mine, "Sarah, I knew as soon as they got here, but it doesn't matter." He led me to the chair. He sat down pulling me to sit with him. He wrapped his arms around me. He kissed my shoulder and whispered in my ear, "You, Sarah, are so much more to me. You just do it for me every way possible. You, my sweet, are the whole package." He kissed my ear.

I nuzzled into him, "Has anyone ever told you, you are crazy?"

He smiled and whispered, "About you."

I reached back to touch his face. He leaned into it and kissed my palm. He was turning me on, and we were just sitting here. He whispered again, "Your body is calling for me."

"James, shhhh."

I really hated that so many could feel our thoughts. I was reminded when Clarissa scolded us, "James, have some control."

His focus released me, moving to her, as he chuckled. Carl was chuckling too, as he stood up, "When people are gone, let me know, and I will help clean things up. Clarissa, I think I know how James feels. You need to come to the house with me."

We both looked up at them. She was giddy and stood quickly to go with him. They were playful, as they started to walk away. Clarissa looked back at us, or at me, "Told you the passion is..." She took a deep breath and they hurried out of sight. I leaned sideways, so I could see James. He looked very serious, and I touched his face, "That would be us if we could do that right now."

He got a great big grin, "I can wait for that. I won't be able to control myself at all. I think we'll have to plan on three days of being completely alone once it happens."

I looked at him confused, "I thought it didn't take that long?"

He smiled at me, "You don't know what I want to do to you, and besides it's all the playing we are going to do."

"James, I'm getting hotter."

"Oh Baby, I know. Your body is almost screaming at me to give you things that we just can't do."

"So, what kind of playing? Are you talking about the feather?"

"Nope."

"Why not?"

"We won't need it. We're married, and we just won't need it."

I didn't get why we wouldn't need it. I had heard the story; I knew what was supposed to happen; obviously, I pushed it too far once already, but if we were to really do this, I thought we had to use the feather. He smiled guiltily and entangled our fingers bringing one hand to his mouth. He sucked on one of my fingers.

"James, Danelle. We have to behave for her, please."

He whispered in my ear, "Even if I do this." I felt a kiss on my stomach.

"James, stop that."

He was taunting me more with his mind.

"James, if you're not careful, we will end up in the apartment."

"No, Baby. Just relax and close your eyes and take a nap. I will hold you."

"I won't be sleeping with you doing that."

"Close your eyes."

I leaned into him more. I felt his mouth trace over my neck and his hands trace my waist.

I gripped his fingers tighter. I thought about tracing my hands over his abs.

His breath came to my ear, "No, no, no. Sarah, you can't do that. I will lose control."

I laughed, "Then you have to stop."

He laughed, "Okay, I get it."

We stopped the mind games; we stopped the playing, but it was going to happen, and soon, if I had anything to say about it.

## 54. Saying Goodbye

Jason and Kylie walked back up, "So, did Sarah tell you?"

I shook my head no, "I left that to you guys. It's your good news."

James was confused as he squeezed me tighter.

Jason sat down next to us, "James, how would you like to be my best man?"

He pushed me forward so fast I got a jolt of pain.

Kylie grabbed me, "James, be careful."

He was getting up to hug Jason, "I am so happy for you."

He moved to Kylie and hugged her picking her up, "And you little lady. I don't know how to explain the difference in you. You helped my Sarah." He kissed her cheek.

"Yes, anything for you two."

Kylie took James hands in hers, "It was your help to let me see that it wasn't Sarah's fault, but it wasn't all Jason's fault either. I am learning and we are going to be great."

James kissed her cheek again, "Wow, so when is the date?"

"A year from now, so we have all summer to get things done."

He hugged Jason again.

"Hey we were thinking about taking off, but I think Danelle and Brain were going to ride back up with us. How mad do you think they would be?"

"I will go get Brian; he will be bummed but he'll get over it."

James said he would go get Danelle. I walked down to the lake. Brian sat up right away so I only had to yell a little, "Hey are you riding with Jason and Kylie?"

"Shit, WHY?"

"They are thinking about leaving."

I was getting a bad vibe from Alison, the pretty one. She was actually enjoying talking to Brain now. I grimaced with a smile directing it at her. She was taken aback from me. He dove in, swam to the dock, and was climbing the ladder to get out so quickly that it surprised me. I handed him a towel and he wiped himself a little and wrapped his arms around me, hugging me, "I had so much fun, Sarah, I can't believe you are going to live like this."

I wasn't smiling now, "I'm not; I am moving home in two weeks."

"Oh, he is really making you do that?"

I grimaced, "Yep, but I don't want to talk about it. I might get upset."

He pulled me to sit on the bench with him. He held my hands, "Sarah, are you still coming up north?"

"Of course. I was thinking about asking James about next weekend, but I won't let it go longer than two weeks."

He seemed to be in another world as his attention wandered out to the floating dock, "Do you think James would want to have another get together? I would like to see her again."

Disgusted with that thought I glanced where he was looking. I could read her mind, and she wasn't a nice person. I bit my tongue about her but agreed to ask James, "I will ask, but this was kind of a lot."

He huffed a heavy breath before replying, "I should go get my stuff."

I hugged him, "Brian..."

He pushed me away to see my face, "What?"

"I still need you as a friend. I hope that is okay?"

He grinned, "As long as your husband doesn't mind."

"He won't as long as you behave."

He grinned and chuckled a little, "Well, I guess that won't be a problem with you being married."

We both laughed together. He helped me up, and I walked with him to the tent, "Brian, I've got to go talk to Danelle before you guys go. I will meet you at the car."

He leaned in and kissed my cheek, "I wouldn't be able to do that with James around."

I smiled slightly, "No, I guess not."

I walked slowly back to the apartment. I walked in, and Jake was standing in the door way to his room and James was sitting on a chair at the table. Something was wrong, and I didn't understand why they both looked uneasy. I was a little confused.

James stood up, "You want to talk alone?"

I nodded. Jake turned to me.

"That means you too, Jake."

His mouth attempted a smile before turning to walk out. He stopped at the door, "Sarah, I did tell her, but you should have earlier. That wouldn't have happened."

He was right. I should have told her right away so that I didn't have a total meltdown that she was blaming herself for. I walked in as she was putting her stuff together, "So you are riding with Jason and Kylie?"

She didn't look at me, "Yep, I feel better about it now that I know they don't do that crap anymore."

I chuckled a little. She turned around eyes filled tears. She came running to me and wrapped her arms around me, "Sarah, I am so sorry. I wouldn't have said those things if I knew and you just should have told me."

I hugged her back, "Danelle, you are going to make me cry."

"No, no. I am sorry."

"Danelle, I didn't tell you because I can't talk about it yet. So when I can you will be the first person I run too, okay?"

She nodded, "Are you okay?"

The tears welled up in my eyes, "See, let's wait till next time."

She nodded, "When will you be up?"

"Not sure, depends on the husband and the warden."

"Jake is not a warden. He cares enough about you to not want to see you get hurt."

"I know, Danelle, I was just teasing. I wouldn't have gotten through all this without his help. James knows it too."

"Yeah, we had a nice discussion after you went to bed last night."

"Really, so it went okay?"

"James is in love with you; that much I am sure of, but Sarah…"

I was confused by her hesitation, "What?"

"Marriage is a choice. Now that you made that choice it's a commitment, and it needs to be worked at. Don't always expect him to take care of you. He might need to be taken care of sometimes."

I already knew that, but it wasn't going to be a problem. I loved him more than anything. "I will work on it every day. I promise."

"Don't promise me. He is the one you need to commit to."

I hugged her.

We heard the door. We smiled at each other. James walked in. He took Danelle's bag and walked out with us following. Jake stood up as we walked out the door. He put his arm around her shoulder reaching to me, "Did you have a nice talk?"

I glared at him over her, "I think maybe you already know the answer to that one."

He laughed and James turned around walking backwards, "And so do I."

"James, I told you I need a little privacy. Can you stay out of my head some of the time?"

He came back to grab me, "But I can make you happier if I know what you are thinking." He picked me up and twirled me, "See, you just get better and better. I am so in love with you, little girl." He kissed me so deep.

"James!!!" Danelle complained, "I haven't even left yet. Can you please control yourself a little?"

We were going out the gate. Kylie, Jason, and Brian were all standing there waiting. James set me down as soon as he saw them all. He was embarrassed by his obsession with me. He took my hand, and we walked to them giving hugs and kisses, however when James got to Brian he put out his hand, "Just wanted to thank you."

Brian didn't understand, "For what?"

"You had a hand in taking care of her… just wanted to say thank you."

Brian put out his arm to shake James's hand, but moved into hug him, "Take care of her, or I will hear about it."

I scolded this time, "Brian, you said you would behave."

He confirmed his statement, "Danelle will tell me."

I hit him in the arm, but not very hard.

James grabbed my hand, "You don't want to do that. Remember the last time you hit him?"

I couldn't hold it in. I started to laugh so hard that James came to around the back of me holding my stomach; of course he was laughing too.

Brian was curious, "What happened when she hit me that day? Oh James, Sorry about that. I just had this gut feeling you two were…well, together. Oh my god I was right."

James tried to explain while laughing, "We thought she broke her hand. It swelled so bad even with ice, that she went to the doctor."

Danelle was laughing, "Brian iced for three days. It was huge; black and blue."

Even though we were all laughing they got in the car slowly. Jake stood back, but I pulled him forward. I saw Danelle look at him with a smile, and a small wave. He turned a little red and waved a small wave back. James squeezed my hand, too. They drove off. The three of us walked back down to where everything was.

Matt came running, "Sarah, the girls are bummed that Brian left and Jake won't give them any attention, so they want to go. I hope that is okay."

I nodded, and James let go of my hand, "You guys can talk for a couple of minutes. Jake and I have to start to clean up."

Matt took my hand and we sat down on a bench, "So, I will get to see you in two weeks, right?"

I nodded.

"Sarah?" Something was on his mind. He squinted his eyes as he spoke, "Something is wrong, but I bet you don't want to talk about it."

It wasn't that I didn't want to tell him; it was that I couldn't tell him. I shook my head no.

"Can you tell me one thing?"

I waited to see what he wanted to know.

"Does it have to do with how it is going here…with James, because if you're not happy I will take you out of here right now even if I have to take on the whole lot of them."

Matt's friendship was true and I was thankful. He didn't have to take on everyone. I was happy here, and I never wanted to leave. I shook my head no.

He leaned back in the seat and pulled me back putting his arm around my shoulder, "Do you ever think you will tell me, because I don't think I could handle running you to the airport again."

I giggled, "You won't have to do anything like that again. He is home to stay."

"You do love him?"

"Yes, I do."

"You would have to be completely in love with him in order to turn this body away."

"Oh, yes, the male god."

"You know it."

"So, what is going on with Alissa?"

"I think she likes that Brian guy."

"How do you feel about that?"

He was okay with it. I could see it and feel it before he explained, "Sarah, she doesn't fit my standards anymore. I want something better than that."

"Like Alison?"

"Hell no. She is fake and creepy. I caught her looking at James and I wanted to deck her, but I can't hit girls so I told her I would ruin her life if she did anything unethical."

"Why thank you, Matt. That was very...I don't think there is a word for it."

"You don't seem surprised?"

I wanted to explain this, "You know how I said James feels things?"

He turned to me, "He didn't feel it, did he?"

Being careful so he would understand, "Yes, and so did I."

"Sarah, I am so sorry. I should have known better than to invite someone so shallow."

"It's okay. No damage done." I leaned into him to hug him.

He backed away, "Um, no you're married and I am not doing anything that will upset him, unless you need me to."

I shook my head no, "Thanks, Matt."

He stood up looking at the girls exiting their tent with bags in hand, "I guess that means I have to get going. Call me Monday before school. I will meet you before class, so you don't have to deal with them."

I nodded and watched as he took off. I slowly moved to follow until I got to James. He pulled me in close, "Doing okay?"

I grinned at him and nodded. Jake and James went to help grab bags. Wilson came down, "Should I bring in the dock?"

James and Jake were walking everyone out, but James grabbed my waist to walk with me up to the cars to say goodbye. I hugged Matt and thanked everyone for coming. Alison couldn't even look at me. I didn't feel inferior anymore. James shook Matt's hand, "I can't say enough about how you helped us."

Matt grinned.

"I will be calling you next week to talk to you about Sarah and going to school."

"Really?"

"Yeah, I will need your help more, if you don't mind. I don't know how good she will be by then."

"James, I will be fine."

"Sarah, Matt will help you for a little bit."

"James, we haven't discussed this."

"Sarah, no we haven't, but we will. Matt, I will call you."

He laughed. I wasn't thinking this was funny. They got in and drove away. I turned on James, "You don't think I am going to be okay by then?"

James was being playful, "Just taking care of my baby." He picked me up and started to walk back in.

Jake yelled after us, "Hey, James, we're cleaning things up."

"I will be right there. Get Sam to help, and I will be just a couple of minutes."

"James, think pain."

"I am, Jake, 10 min at most."

"If you're not down in 10, I am coming to get you."

"Be my guest."

We were through the gate and he was smiling, "Are you still hot for my body?"

"I am always hot for you." I kissed under his chin and traced up his jaw.

We barely made it in the apartment before the passion kicked in. He sat down in a chair and had me sit facing him on the chair. I cringed a little.

"See, remember the pain, Sarah."

"Yeah, James, remember the pain."

I kissed his lips. His hands moved to my waist and gripped firmly and he kissed my neck and moved down as he squeezed my hips tighter. I leaned my head to his with desire. He moved his up to mine as our faces touched with agony knowing we couldn't go any further.

"Sarah?"

I closed my eyes. I wanted to be with him so bad, "Yes James," as my chest heaved to breath.

"There is food in the fridge. There are three plates measured out for you. Shit." He kissed my cheek searching for my lips trying to refuse his desire. I wrapped my hands in his hair pulling him back far enough to engulf in kissing him. He scooted down on the chair and pulled me up a little. I could feel his desire, and my heart jumped into over drive. His hands wandered in places that made fire grow within me. My body reacted to his touch, wanting so much more. His hands gripped my hips pulling me against his erection. As if we could not live if we were apart we entangled our mouths to mirror our bodies.

James groaned, "Sarah, you need to eat." He pressed his lips against mine but nibbled and sucked. I was a goner. I was completely his. He could do anything he wanted because I wanted him so bad, but he spoke softly, "I need to help."

Knowing he should go, but not wanting him to, "Yes, you do."

He traced the back of his hand against me, "The heat from you is unbearable."

I closed my eyes and quit kissing him biting my bottom lip. He turned his hand over and traced it again.

"James, my heart hurts because I want you so bad right here and now."

He leaned his head to mine and moved his hand away from me wrapping his arms around me. He sat up more so our bodies could touch and he was kissing me so aggressively, rubbing against me, "Oh, Sarah.

What am I suppose to do? I absolutely need you right here, right now. You have no idea."

We heard the door handle. James pulled me closer and hugged me. I wrapped myself around him putting my head on his shoulder facing away from the door.

Jake walked in, "James, that's 10 minutes. She needs to eat; did you tell her about the food in the…James."

He lifted his head from me. Jake walked out and closed the door. I pulled away from him, and he had tears in his eyes. I grabbed his face, "James?"

He pulled me close and held me there. I tried to move away from him, but he held tighter, "Sarah, please don't move an inch."

I stayed there and wrapped my arms around him. We stayed there till the breathing was almost normal; my heart was still racing.

"Shit, Jake is going to be pissed at me."

"James, we didn't do anything."

He pulled back a little to look into my eyes, "Sarah, you don't understand. If he wouldn't have… I wouldn't have been able to stop."

"You would have, James. I know you, and if there was pain you would have stopped."

"No Sarah…" He had tears dripping down, "I don't think I could have. It's because of doing the mind thing. It drives the desire in me for you, and I just wouldn't have been able to stop. I am so sorry."

I grabbed his face, "James, I wanted you just as bad. This is not all you."

"Sarah, we have to agree to not use the mind anymore; I am getting weak and I never want to hurt you.'

"I promise to not use the mind anymore, and James you will not hurt me. I trust you."

"I don't trust myself, because the things I want to do to you… It just wouldn't be good."

He pushed me up very carefully, as he stood with me. He still had his arms wrapped around me, but walked me to the kitchen. He let go of me and opened the fridge, "Sarah, please eat. I have to wait till you weigh 120 lbs; I promised Jake."

"You did what? What if I don't want to weight that much? I was thinking 115 lbs tops."

He was irritated, "I can't touch you again till you are 120 lbs, and I need for you to hurry and get there, because I am going crazy here."

I smiled and took out a plate, "I will work really hard at it. I want to be with you too."

He smiled, "I have to go help."

He kissed my forehead and walked out. I stood there in shock. That was torture for him, and it hurt him. I warmed up the plate and sat down at the table to eat wondering how I could ever make this right if I really don't want to gain that much weight.

# 55. End Of Sadness

**I** ate the whole plateful of food. I wanted to walk down and check on James, because I was so worried. I put in a movie realizing that it wouldn't be a good idea to go to James. I pulled out my computer and sat down. I went through one section of the second class I hadn't been through. I huffed when I was done. I put my computer down and lay down, curling up on the couch. I didn't see much of the movie, because I fell asleep.

I woke to James lifting me to take me to the room, "James, no I'm okay. I can get up."

His mouth came to my ear, "Sarah, I am okay now, shhhh."

He laid me down sitting on the side of the bed putting a blanket over me. He traced his hand along my cheek, "What you do to me, just..."

"James, don't. I will want you again."

He pulled his hand from me. I grabbed his hand pulling it to me and kissed it.

"Nope, you can't do that either." He tried to smile even though I saw the sadness, "Well, this is going to be hard. We can't even touch each other."

This was not helping how I felt.

He giggled a little, "Yep, that look does it too." He stood up and leaned over me and kissed my forehead, "I will wake you for dinner."

I didn't want him to leave, but I gave in and closed my eyes.

He pulled out the big pillow and moved it in front of me, so I could curl up to it.

"It's not the same, James."

He laughed with a sigh.

When I got up I realized that I still didn't have the IV in. I went to the bathroom, brushed my teeth and washed my face, to wake up more. Completely rejuvenated I stepped on the scale. 108 lbs. That was weird. I fluctuate through the day. I walked out to the living room to find Jake and James both sitting on the couch, one on each end. I walked around in front of them. James sat up grabbing my hand. "Sarah, you're up."

I turned and sat down in-between them.

"Jake, should my weight fluctuate throughout the day?"

"Yes, could be as much as 5 lbs, why?"

"Because I gained 2 lbs."

He laughed, "It will be gone in the morning. Are you hungry?"

"Nope, just wondering."

I leaned into James, and he wrapped his arm around me. We didn't say a word. The night dragged on and on. James finally pushed me up a little and got up. He went and got another plate out and heated it up, "Time to eat." I wasn't happy, but I gave him a half grin when he handed me the plate, "Please eat."

I didn't say anything as I ate. I was almost finished when I got up and went to the kitchen. James was standing behind me, "It's not all gone."

I just stood there, and I couldn't say anything. He would think I wasn't trying. He traced his hands along my arms, "Please, Sarah."

I turned to him and leaned to his ear, "James, if I eat anymore it's not going to stay down." I looked at him with tears in my eyes.

"Okay, Baby." He took my hand and led me back to the couch.

We sat back down and Jake looked at me, "You okay?"

I didn't want to explain why I couldn't eat anymore. Feeling like I was disappointing James was bad enough. I curled up next to James again letting Jake know I was okay. The night seemed to drag on, and my stomach was settling. When I didn't feel sick anymore I found it annoying that it was too quiet. I nuzzled James more and poked him in the ribs. He didn't move. I looked at Jake, and he was too quiet. I got up again with James pushing me up, so I didn't feel pain. I walked to the kitchen.

"You're hungry again?"

"Nope." I grabbed both cans of whipped topping and turned around.

James stood up and started to back up, "Sarah, don't even think about it."

I felt mischievous and wanted to have some fun, "It's too quiet in here."

"We can find something to do, just not that, Sarah."

Jake didn't move, "She won't do it. Sit down."

I walked over and squirted some on his hand.

He licked it off, "Sarah you need to stop. You are going to get hurt."

I squirted a huge lump on his hand again and moved towards James, smiling.

He pointed at me with a serious expression, "Sarah, stop it right now."

I grinned and moved closer moving around Jake. Jake grabbed me by the waist. I squirted over my head at him, "You did not just do that." He grabbed my arms to stop me. James came and grabbed me. Jake pulled the cans from my hands. James picked me up and carried me to the couch and sat down, "You are not funny."

Jake walked back to the fridge and put them away, "James, remind me these need to go upstairs."

He came and sat back down. When James let loose I picked up my computer and opened it. I did the third assignment and sent it in. I closed the computer.

James stretched and looked at the clock, "Shit, I have to go to bed. I have to be up at 6 am."

I turned to stare at him full of panic.

"No, don't do that. It's going to be fine. Jake will stay with you during the day. You won't be alone."

"Yeah, Sarah, I will make phone calls to work on getting my old job back."

I couldn't say anything. I was going to be away from James.

"We need to put the IV lines back in, Sarah." Jake grabbed my hand and led me to the bedroom. I sat on the edge of the bed and held up my arm.

"No. We're doing the other arm now."

I held out the other arm. He put one in and I cringed. He was surprised that I cringed, "Is that okay?"

I nodded, but my thoughts went back to James in the other room. He was going to leave me tomorrow. How was I going to handle that?

Jake put the other one in.

"Ouch, Jake. That did hurt."

He grimaced, "Sorry."

I needed James. I found myself watching the door waiting for him to come in. I needed to see him as much as I could before tomorrow. Finally James walked in, but he didn't come to me. He grabbed sleeping pants, a muscle shirt, and went in the bathroom. Jake pulled my face to him, "We have doctor time while he is getting dressed. Do you need to talk to me about anything?"

I shook my head no. He tried to preoccupy himself by examining the IV but asked, "How's the bleeding?"

"Almost gone."

His face brightened as his eyes met mine, "Really?"

"It's not supposed to be?"

"Well, it's possible, but it has only been a little over a week. How about bowl movements?"

"You're talking about pooping again, and yes I am doing that."

He evaluated my face to see if I was telling the truth. With skepticism he continued, "Every day?"

I was horrified, "Every day?"

"Yeah, that would be normal with all the eating your doing."

"Not every day, maybe every other day."

I could see a hint of concern in his face.

"No, Jake, no more problems. I can't handle anymore."

"I will talk to Wilson, and we will put more fiber in your diet to see if that helps. If it's not better by Thursday, we'll do another scan."

"NO, I am fine. I need to be with James; you know that."

This worried him more than I thought was any of his business, "No, you need to be okay first."

"This is going to be a pain in the ass."

"Sarah, try harder to think how hard this is on him."

I held up my arm, "Sleeping. How am I going to sleep with it in this arm?"

He laughed, "Hey, lay down. I want to check your stomach."

I laid down with the tubes laying over me. This was going to irritate me beyond words. He pushed on my stomach on the good side. There was discomfort, but the extreme pain was gone. He moved to the middle. It was tender in a few spots, so I was cringing. He watched my face but moved to the other side. His movements were in a circular motion.

"Okay, yeah, Jake, it still hurts there." I pushed his hands away.

He shrugged to show me he didn't care if I liked it or not, "I didn't feel anything, so that's a good thing."

James walked out of the bathroom, but avoided giving us any attention. Why was he not looking at me? Jake stood up and walked toward him, "James, you can bunk with me. It would only be for a little while."

He cannot leave me alone! Why would Jake even say something like that? To my relief he told Jake he was okay and finished with, "She needs me."

Thank god that my husband knew I needed him. My heart filled with warmth knowing he was going to come to bed with me. Jake walked out and closed the door. James came to crawl in with me wrapping himself around me. I had to lie away from him because of the IV lines.

"James?"

"Yes, Sarah."

"Can we switch sides tomorrow? These are going to bug me."

He laughed out loud. He kissed my neck and lay with his body next to mine wrapping his arms around my waist. He moved his legs to intertwine with mine.

"James, isn't this too hard for you?"

"Yes and no, but I can't stay away from you, so please let me."

My heart was beating hard again. He kissed my neck and then my ear, "Sarah, can we lay naked together?"

I tilted my head back to him, "It will be harder for you."

"No, baby. I need to feel you."

I nodded to him. He lifted my shirt over my head; it draped on the cords for the IV. He sat up taking his shirt off quickly and scooted out of his pants and boxers. He slowly pushed mine down; he laid back down pulling me next to him, wrapped his arms around me, and he whispered in my ear, "This is what I needed. How are you doing?"

"James."

"Yep."

"Do you want to try? The pain was better."

"Nope, just want to hold you like this."

I pulled his hand to my lips and kissed it. Both our hearts were racing, but we didn't do anything to entice those feelings. I was enjoying his touch too much to want it to end.

In a way I felt like this was the end of our childish games, and this is where I got to be a married woman. How do you decide when you are ready to make the change? I wasn't ready for the change, really. I was only 16 years old. I should still be worried about what dress I was going to wear to the next dance, and if I would have a date. Now I have a date for the rest of my life, and I tell myself I don't want any of those things… but did I? I love everything about my James, but how was I going to keep him happy for the rest of our lives if it was just him and I? Tomorrow would be the first day of our plan for the future of our lives together.
I felt his breath at my ear, "Everything will be fine, Sarah. I am in love with you and we will be happy for the rest of our lives."
I held his arms tight around me, as I thought about how we have spent the beginning of our marriage and how I felt that it was full of growing tears, but now that would end and we would be on our way to a new beginning.

# Characters

Sarah Sullivan/Swanson
Paula Sullivan — Mom
Tucker Sullivan — Dad

James Swanson — Sarah's Boyfriend/Husband
Carl Swanson — James Dad
Clarissa Swanson — James Mom
Will Swanson — James Brother 2nd oldest
Sam Swanson — James Brother 3rd
Tamara — James Sister youngest
Katherine — James Betrothed/Will's Girlfriend
Amelia — Sam's Betrothed

Jake Phallen — Doctor/Brother
Wilson Phallen — Clarissa's Houseman
Josie Phallen — Wilson's Wife/ Jake's Mom

Danelle Turner — Sarah's Best Friend
Laura Turner — Danelle's Mom
Paul Turner — Danelle's Dad
Brian Turner — Danelle's Older Brother

Jason Gasser — Tucker's 2nd Employee
Kylie — Jason's Girlfriend
Tony — Tavern Owner
Sandi & Kate — Sarah's Dance Helpers
Dr. Justin — Sarah's First female Doctor
Mykala — Brian's Girlfriend
Matt Erickson — Friend of Sarah's
Tommy — Brian's Friend

# Upcoming Sequel – *A New Beginning*

## 1. *A little doctoring*

**I**t was the first day of our new future; when I woke up, he was gone. I sat up panicking, searching for a clock. It was 8 am, so I pushed myself up quickly. I wanted to be disconnected from the IV that restricted me from any quick movements. I called out to Jake, who was my doctor and James's Brother, "Jake. JAKE!"

I got no response, so I pushed myself out of bed and grabbed the IVs and walked out to the living room. I didn't know where Jake was, but I knew James was already at school. I went to the kitchen and grabbed a bowl and some cereal. I leaned over to get the milk out.

Jake walked in with a tray, "Hey, what are you doing? I have food for you." He set the tray down and came to rescue me. He poured the cereal back in the box and pointed to the table.

I grabbed the IV and started to make my way to the table, complaining the whole way, "Jake how long do we have to keep the IVs in this arm. I use my right arm and this sucks."

He laughed at me, "A while, so quit complaining. I will disconnect you; give me a minute."

I sat down noticing how much food was on the tray, so I asked, "Are you eating with me?"

"No. I ate with my dad. That is all for you."

"Jake, I can't eat all this."

They were trying to fatten me up after being sick for so long.

He gave me a disapproving glare, "Try."

He pulled up a chair, but it was hard to eat when he was working on disconnecting me from the IV, "Are you going to eat?"

"As soon as I have my arm back."

He laughed, "Okay, you are feisty today."

"No, I was hungry. Now you're making me wait."

He laughed again. I sat patiently; well, maybe not. He got done and confirmed, "You're good to go."

I ate the pancake first with the 2-sausage links. Then I ate the cottage cheese with the fruit. I was able to get it all down. I tried to not pay attention to Jake in his room, pacing, but he was on the phone and it seemed to be a heated conversation. Contemplating if I should try to distract Jake, or just get up and do my own thing I noticed a deliveryman was at the door. When I opened it he asked for Dr. Phallen. Now I had a good reason to distract him. I walked to his door knocking cautiously, "Jake, there is a delivery guy at the door."

He made his way to the door continuing his conversation on the phone, "Fine, he's here, but I am not promising anything." He hung up the phone with a lot of attitude and took the package that was being delivered. The scowl on his face made me want to avoid him the rest of the day. After accepting the package and closing the door in the delivery guy's face, which seemed rude to me, he pulled out papers and spread them out over the table. I grabbed the tray to make more room for him and headed to the kitchen.

Jake was irritated, "Sarah, I can get that."

"No, Jake, it fine." I washed up the dishes and stacked them for going back upstairs. Glancing at Jake I noticed that he was scrambling through the papers. Deciding that it wouldn't be good to distract him I took the tray and headed for the door.

"Sarah, I said I would take care of it!"

"You're busy and I have nothing else to do. Sit, I am fine." I walked the tray upstairs. Wilson was there busy with making something, so I sat on a stool.

"Jakes is irritable today." I was trying to get info.

"It's another special case like yours, Sarah, where the illness is not explainable."

"So he is good at that, figuring out what the problem is."

Wilson was cautious, "He doesn't want to get attached to another patient. That was hard for him. Distance is good for him."

I smiled, but didn't feel any better, "I'm glad he wasn't distant with me. I wouldn't have been able to trust him."

"Sarah, you are the exception to the rule. He really does care."

Feeling like I should explain, "Wilson, I was unfair to him. He will always be special to me, but I do love James."

"I know he cares about you more than he should, but he knew that you were taken when he took the job."

Still feeling bad I replied, "I'm sorry."

"No, no Sarah. He had a choice just like everyone else. He knew and was warned to not fall in love with you, but…" He face grew to the biggest grin, "You are just so darn adorable."

I heard Carl from the living room, "Yes, you are, and that is why we all love you."

"I don't want to be adorable; I just want to be normal."

Shaking his head he leaned in to kiss my forehead. Then he confirmed, "And that is exactly why you are adorable. Hey, shouldn't you be working on school stuff? Today was the first day."

Being a little proud of myself I filled him in, "I checked last week and they hadn't posted any new assignments. I already did the first two in one class, and three in the other. I should be about a week ahead."

He laughed. "Is it hard at all?"

Carl walked into the kitchen and poured himself a glass of orange juice, but I knew he was paying attention to our conversation. I gestured to both of them with my reply, "Nope, I am hoping it gets more challenging."

"Why don't you go discuss Jake's case with him? Sometimes asking questions triggers answers."

I was seeking Carl's support when I pleaded, "I am scared of him right now. He's really tense and irritable."

Wilson was more determined, "Yes, but you have a way to ease things. Do you remember how much you softened him when he was searching your files? I do." I didn't like that he brought that up in front of Carl.

I already felt bad enough, but with his wink and grin I did feel better about wanting to help Jake. "Fine, but I'm not bugging him if he doesn't want me to be nosy."

Carl walked me down the stairs, hugged me, kissed my forehead, and then gave me a little shove to go back inside. I eased my way in without sparking any interest from Jake. He was now sitting, but one hand clutched his hair while the other skimmed a document. There was room on the other side of the table, so I grabbed my computer and book and plopped down. I was trying to make it look like I had stuff to do. I started to read my book highlighting important stuff, but I still wasn't distracting Jake at all; he was still engulfed in the documents. I grabbed one of his pieces of papers, pulled it in front of me, and started searching the symptoms online. There were an endless number of things that could be wrong with this person from the symptoms I was reading. I grabbed another piece of paper, scanning it for more information. Finally, something that I could bring up, a word I didn't understand, "What is this word?" It was like old times when he took it from me hastily, "What are you doing grabbing my papers?"

I ignored his animosity and persisted, "What is that word?"

Finally, a break in the seriousness on his face; he shook his head and huffed a chuckle but said the word out loud and explained what it was.

I knew I was breaking him. I searched the word and started to read about it, but asked, "So what is wrong with her?"

Back to being huffy he replied, "You tell me; you're doing the searching."

That was an invitation to me, so I moved to a chair closer to him and searched a few more things. That is when I started to ask questions. Everything I picked up and every document that I read, there were a lot of things I didn't understand. After about 20 minutes he was getting irritated with me. I stayed quiet for a little bit, but I remembered that he told me that if there was a fever that it was bacterial. I had to make sure, "Jake, didn't you say that if I had a fever it was bacterial. She doesn't have a fever."

It was like seeing the answer flash into his eyes as they locked with mine. Slowly, that smile that I completely enjoyed grew on his face. He stood up and pulled out his phone hitting a button, shook his head, and made his way to the room, but as he moved passed me he placed his hand on my shoulder and gave me a quick squeeze. I felt good, real good, that I did something that made him smile once more. I stopped and listened, but continued to look at more papers. He came out smiling, "Well, they are going to do the test. I will know in two hours."

"What?"

He just stood there smiling, saying to me, "You're good."

"I didn't do anything."

He grinned, "You asked the right question. That is what medicine does. You look for the right and wrong questions. You, however, will find out if you are right in two hours."

I shook my head.

"Do you have more school work? I could help you."

I shook my head no.

He confirmed, "You're caught up?"

"I am ahead of the game. I have to wait till they post more assignments."

He laughed, "So what are we going to do today?"

I shrugged my shoulders.

"Pool, movie, what are you up for?"

His phone rang saving me from having to decide what we were going to do. He walked into his room. I sat back down and started to read through the files. I wrote down more questions. I left them on the pile and walked over, curled up on the couch, and started to flip through the channels.

He came out excited. "I will be starting work on Thursday."

"Really, so I will be alone?"

He smiled, "No, I am working 5 pm to 5 am, in the ER. It's the hospital close to your mom and dad's, so I can pick you up from school and hang out until James can get there."

"Oh, you guys have this planned out?"

He looked up at me, "Well, yes we do."

"Great."

"What?"

"I was still hoping he would change his mind."

Jake smiled, "Normal life."

"But, Jake, my life is no longer normal."

"Is that your strategy for the argument?"

"Yeah, do you have one better?"

"No, but I'm not the one trying to talk him into letting you stay here. You are going to have to do a lot better than that."

He sat back down at the table, "What is this?"

"More questions." I went back to watching TV. He was shuffling through the papers. I lay down and closed my eyes

Jake was waking me up. He helped me sit up, "It's time to eat." He had a tray and put it in front of me on the couch. I started to eat. I didn't care what I was eating anymore; I just ate so I could be with James. I shoved it all down, but wondered how much they were stuffing me with, "So how much food is this?"

"It's four cups. But you are going to try and eat 4 times a day. Next meal at 4 pm and the last will be a smaller snack like 3 cups of food at 7."

"Great."

"Sarah, behave. James is going to lose it if you are not improving. So, since he is not here, I get to be the bad guy and be strict with you." He laughed.

I glared at him, "You will soften with time."

He laughed even more, "I don't think so, but you can go ahead and try."

I huffed and finished my food. I tried to get up myself and he moved to grab the tray, "You don't have to push yourself that way, you know."

I smiled and still got up, "Bathroom"

He smiled and let me go by. He went back to the table.

I came out and sat down on the couch and looked over at him. He was going through the papers.

When he noticed that I was there he asked, "How do you know what questions to ask?"

"I don't, but I didn't understand most of it, so those are questions that I didn't understand."

He smiled and got up calling on his phone walking to his room again. I lay back down.

He came out grinning from ear to ear, "Sarah, I would not have been able to come up with that on my own. It was too simple and I was looking too deep." He came over and was lifting me to stand. He hugged me and twirled me, "Sarah, you might want to think about being a doctor. You're pretty good at this."

"Jake, you would have figured it out eventually...like you did with me. You were looking too hard."

He smiled and let go of me and walked away, "I just wanted to say thank you."

I lay back down and nonchalantly asked, "What time is James supposed to be here?"

He chuckled, "Between 3 and 4 pm. Why? Is it that bad to spend time with me?"

I smiled, "No, you need me now, so we will be fine. I'm just board."

"You get board easily."

I closed my eyes, "Yep."

I dozed for a while, but was really awake by 3 pm. I walked to the door and back to the couch. I walked around the couch and back to the door. Jake was reading through the case more.

For some reason it was irritating me, "I thought you had it right now."

"There is still one symptom that doesn't fit, so we ran more tests, and now we are waiting for the results to come back."

I looked down at him, "So I wasn't right?"

"Well kind of, but I need to get more test results to be sure. What are you doing?"

"Nothing." I paced back to the couch, picked up the remote and flashed through a couple of channels, set it down and walked around the couch back to the door.

"Do you want to eat early, because you won't want to eat when he gets here?"

I grinned, "Sure."

I sat at the table close to the door. Jake got the tray of food and brought it to the table. I ate but watched out the door, "Jake, what time is it?"

He laughed. "It's going to seem longer if you are anxious."

I glared at him to show I was not happy with that reply.

"Fine, it's 3:35 pm."

I took a deep breath and hurried to finish. I looked out the door. I picked up the tray and walked it to the kitchen. I was washing up the dishes quickly.

Jake scolded, "Sarah, you don't have to do that."

I retorted, "I'm passing time, Jake."

When I was finished I turned around to check the time, which was 4:05 pm. I walked to the door and looked out. No James. I walked back to the couch, flipped through channels again. I walked around the couch and turned to the door.

James was walking through it with his eyes only on me. He dropped his bag and I met him half way.

"Sarah, I am so proud of you." One hand wrapped around my waist to pull me in close and his other came to my face, "You didn't torture me with your thoughts."

I threw myself around him as he lifted me. We were already on the way to our room.

Jake scolded, "Hey, none of that you two. Come on. It sucks sitting here while…"

Jake's voice faded as James breathing became more apparent.

| | |
|---|---|
| Forever Yours | Book 1 |
| Wasting Away | Book 2 |
| Growing Tears | Book 3 ☺ |
| A New Beginning | Book 4 |

Melissa M. Marlow
www.mmmarlow.com
mmmarlow@comcast.net

Made in the USA
Charleston, SC
14 November 2012